CLARKESWORLD
YEAR EIGHT

CLARKESWORLD
YEAR EIGHT

EDITED BY NEIL CLARKE & SEAN WALLACE

WYRM PUBLISHING

CLARKESWORLD: YEAR EIGHT

Wyrm Publishing
www.wyrmpublishing.com

For more information, contact Wyrm Publishing:
wyrmpublishing@gmail.com

ISBN: 978-1-890464-64-6 (trade paperback)
ISBN: 978-1-890464-65-3 (ebook)

Visit Clarkesworld Magazine at:
clarkesworldmagazine.com

Contents

Introduction

NEIL CLARKE

As I remember it, I was twelve when my cousin gave me my first three science fiction books for Christmas. One of them was the classic anthology *Adventures in Space and Time,* edited by Healy and McComas. It was a brick of a book, filled with stories that captured my attention and encouraged me to seek out more. My book collection steadily grew through high school, college, and beyond. Now it occupies a significant portion of my house.

I never dreamed that I'd someday enter this field, but much like a good story, life never quite goes the way you expect it to. At age forty, I launched *Clarkesworld Magazine* and started down a new path. We've made a habit of marking each of *Clarkesworld's* orbits by dropping an anthology behind us. This is the eighth such volume and it includes all the original stories we published from October 2013 through September 2014, issues eighty-five through ninety-six.

Sure, it's a little late, but life's been tossing me more of those unexpected events. In the time since, I've published *Upgraded,* launched *Forever Magazine,* and edited the first volume of my The Best Science Fiction of the Year series. Our eighth year set a lot of these things in motion and, now that I have a spare moment, it's nice to take a look back at the stories that were a part of it all. Here they are in all their glory . . . enjoy!

Neil Clarke
February 2016

Passage of Earth

MICHAEL SWANWICK

The ambulance arrived sometime between three and four in the morning. The morgue was quiet then, cool and faintly damp. Hank savored this time of night and the faint shadow of contentment it allowed him, like a cup of bitter coffee, long grown cold, waiting for his occasional sip. He liked being alone and not thinking. His rod and tackle box waited by the door, in case he felt like going fishing after his shift, though he rarely did. There was a copy of *Here Be Dragons: Mapping the Human Genome* in case he did not.

He had opened up a drowning victim and was reeling out her intestines arm over arm, scanning them quickly and letting them down in loops into a galvanized bucket. It was unlikely he was going to find anything, but all deaths by violence got an autopsy. He whistled tunelessly as he worked.

The bell from the loading dock rang.

"Hell." Hank put down his work, peeled off the latex gloves, and went to the intercom. "Sam? That you?" Then, on the sheriff's familiar grunt, he buzzed the door open. "What have you got for me this time?"

"Accident casualty." Sam Aldridge didn't meet his eye, and that was unusual. There was a gurney behind him, and on it something too large to be a human body, covered by canvas. The ambulance was already pulling away, which was so contrary to proper protocols as to be alarming.

"That sure doesn't look like—" Hank began.

A woman stepped out of the darkness.

It was Evelyn.

"Boy, the old dump hasn't changed one bit, has it? I'll bet even the calendar on the wall's the same. Did the county ever spring for a diener for the night shift?"

"I . . . I'm still working alone."

"Wheel it in, Sam, and I'll take over from here. Don't worry about me, I know where everything goes." Evelyn took a deep breath and shook her head in disgust. "Christ. It's just like riding a bicycle. You never forget. Want to or not."

After the paperwork had been taken care of and Sheriff Sam was gone, Hank said, "Believe it or not, I had regained some semblance of inner peace, Evelyn. Just a little. It took me years. And now this. It's like a kick in the stomach. I don't see how you can justify doing this to me."

"Easiest thing in the world, sweetheart." Evelyn suppressed a smirk that nobody but Hank could have even noticed, and flipped back the canvas. "Take a look."

It was a Worm.

Hank found himself leaning low over the heavy, swollen body, breathing deep of its heady alien smell, suggestive of wet earth and truffles with sharp hints of ammonia. He thought of the ships in orbit, blind locomotives ten miles long. The photographs of these creatures didn't do them justice. His hands itched to open this one up.

"The Agency needs you to perform an autopsy."

Hank drew back. "Let me get this straight. You've got the corpse of an alien creature. A representative of the only other intelligent life form that the human race has ever encountered. Yet with all the forensic scientists you have on salary, you decide to hand it over to a lowly county coroner?"

"We need your imagination, Hank. Anybody can tell how they're put together. We want to know how they think."

"You told me I didn't have an imagination. When you left me." His words came out angrier than he'd intended, but he couldn't find it in himself to apologize for their tone. "So, again—why me?"

"What I said was, you couldn't imagine bettering yourself. For anything impractical, you have imagination in spades. Now I'm asking you to cut open an alien corpse. What could be less practical?"

"I'm not going to get a straight answer out of you, am I?"

Evelyn's mouth quirked up in a little smile so that for the briefest instant she was the woman he had fallen in love with, a million years ago. His heart ached to see it. "You never got one before," she said. "Let's not screw up a perfectly good divorce by starting now."

"Let me put a fresh chip in my dictation device," Hank said. "Grab a smock and some latex gloves. You're going to assist."

"Ready," Evelyn said.

Hank hit record, then stood over the Worm, head down, for a long moment. Getting in the zone. "Okay, let's start with a gross physical examination. Um, what we have looks a lot like an annelid, rather blunter and fatter than the terrestrial equivalent and of course much larger. Just eyeballing it, I'd say this thing is about eight feet long, maybe two feet and a half in diameter. I could just about get my arms around it if I tried. There are three, five, seven, make that eleven somites, compared to say one or two hundred in an earthworm. No clitellum, so we're warned not to take the annelid similarity too far.

"The body is bluntly tapered at each end, and somewhat depressed posteriorly. The ventral side is flattened and paler than the dorsal surface. There's a tripartite beak-like structure at one end, I'm guessing this is the mouth, and what must be an anus at the other. Near the beak are five swellings from which extend stiff, bone-like structures—mandibles, maybe? I'll tell you, though, they look more like tools. This one might almost be a wrench, and over here a pair of grippers. They seem awfully specialized for an intelligent creature. Evelyn, you've dealt

9

with these things, is there any variation within the species? I mean, do some have this arrangement of manipulators and others some other structure?"

"We've never seen any two of the aliens with the same arrangement of manipulators."

"Really? That's interesting. I wonder what it means. Okay, the obvious thing here is there are no apparent external sensory organs. No eyes, ears, nose. My guess is that whatever senses these things might have, they're functionally blind."

"Intelligence is of that opinion too."

"Well, it must have shown in their behavior, right? So that's an easy one. Here's my first extrapolation: You're going to have a bitch of a time understanding these things. Human beings rely on sight more than most animals, and if you trace back philosophy and science, they both have strong roots in optics. Something like this is simply going to think differently from us.

"Now, looking between the somites—the rings—we find a number of tiny hairlike structures, and if we pull the rings apart, so much as we can, there're all these small openings, almost like tiny anuses if there weren't so many of them, closed with sphincter muscles, maybe a hundred of them, and it looks like they're between each pair of somites. Oh, here's something—the structures near the front, the swellings, are a more developed form of these little openings. Okay, now we turn the thing over. I'll take this end you take the other. Right, now I want you to rock it by my count, and on the three we'll flip it over. Ready? One, two, three!"

The corpse slowly flipped over, almost overturning the gurney. The two of them barely managed to control it.

"That was a close one," Hank said cheerily. "Huh. What's this?" He touched a line of painted numbers on the alien's underbelly. *Rt-Front/No. 43.*

"Never you mind what that is. Your job is to perform the autopsy."

"You've got more than one corpse."

Evelyn said nothing.

"Now that I say it out loud, of course you do. You've got dozens. If you only had the one, I'd never have gotten to play with it. You have doctors of your own. Good researchers, some of them, who would cut open their grandmothers if they got the grant money. Hell, even forty-three would've been kept in-house. You must have hundreds, right?"

For a fraction of a second, that exquisite face went motionless. Evelyn probably wasn't even aware of doing it, but Hank knew from long experience that she'd just made a decision. "More like a thousand. There was a very big accident. It's not on the news yet, but one of the Worms' landers went down in the Pacific."

"Oh Jesus." Hank pulled his gloves off, shoved up his glasses and ground his palms into his eyes. "You've got your war at last, haven't you? You've picked a fight with creatures that have tremendous technological superiority over us, and they don't even live here! All they have to do is drop a big enough rock into our atmosphere and there'll be a mass extinction the likes of which hasn't been seen since the dinosaurs died out. They won't care. It's not *their* planet!"

Evelyn's face twisted into an expression he hadn't known it could form until just before the end of their marriage, when everything fell apart. "Stop being such an ass," she said. Then, talking fast and earnestly, "We didn't cause the accident. It was just dumb luck it happened, but once it did we had to take advantage of it. Yes, the Worms probably have the technology to wipe us out. So we have to deal with them. But to deal with them we have to understand them, and we do not. They're a mystery to us. We don't know what they want. We don't know how they think. But after tonight we'll have a little better idea. Provided only that you get back to work."

Hank went to the table and pulled a new pair of gloves off the roll. "Okay," he said. "Okay."

"Just keep in mind that it's not just my ass that's riding on this," Evelyn said. "It's yours and everyone's you know."

"I *said* okay!" Hank took a long breath, calming himself. "Next thing to do is cut this sucker open." He picked up a bone saw. "This is bad technique, but we're in a hurry." The saw whined to life, and he cut through the leathery brown skin from beak to anus. "All right, now we peel the skin back. It's wet-feeling and a little crunchy. The musculature looks much like that of a Terrestrial annelid. Structurally, that is. I've never seen anything quite that color black. Damn! The skin keeps curling back."

He went to his tackle box and removed a bottle of fishhooks. "Here. We'll take a bit of nylon filament, tie two hooks together, like this, with about two inches of line between them. Then we hook the one through the skin, fold it down, and push the other through the cloth on the gurney. Repeat the process every six inches on both sides. That should hold it open."

"Got it." Evelyn set to work.

Some time later they were done, and Hank stared down into the opened Worm. "You want speculation? Here goes: This thing moves through the mud, or whatever the medium is there, face-first and blind. What does that suggest to you?"

"I'd say that they'd be used to coming up against the unexpected."

"Very good. Haul back on this, I'm going to cut again. . . . Okay, now we're past the musculature and there's a fluffy mass of homogeneous stuff, we'll come back to that in a minute. Cutting through the fluff . . . and into the body cavity and it's absolutely chockablock with zillions of tiny little organs."

"Let's keep our terminology at least vaguely scientific, shall we?" Evelyn said.

"Well, there are more than I want to count. Literally hundreds of small organs under the musculature, I have no idea what they're for but they're all interconnected with vein-like tubing in various sizes. This is ferociously more complicated than human anatomy. It's like a chemical plant in here. No two of the organs are the same so far as I can tell, although they all have a generic similarity. Let's call them alembics, so we don't confuse them with any other organs we may find. I see something that looks like a heart maybe, an isolated lump of muscle the size of my fist, there are three of them. Now I'm cutting deeper . . . Holy shit!"

For a long minute, Hank stared into the opened alien corpse. Then he put the saw down on the gurney and, shaking his head, turned away. "Where's that coffee?" he said.

Without saying a word, Evelyn went to the coffee station and brought him his cold cup.

Hank yanked his gloves, threw them in the trash, and drank.

"All right," Evelyn said, "so what was it?"

"You mean you can't see—no, of course you can't. With you, it was human anatomy all the way."

"I took invertebrate biology in college."

"And forgot it just as fast as you could. Okay, look: Up here is the beak, semi-retractable. Down here is the anus. Food goes in one, waste comes out the other. What do you see between?"

"There's a kind of a tube. The gut?"

"Yeah. It runs straight from the mouth to the anus, without interruption. Nothing in between. How does it eat without a stomach? How does it stay alive?" He saw from Evelyn's expression that she was not impressed. "What we see before us is simply not possible."

"Yet here it is. So there's an explanation. Find it."

"Yeah, yeah." Glaring at the Worm's innards, he drew on a new pair of gloves. "Let me take a look at that beak again. . . . Hah. See how the muscles are connected? The beak relaxes open, aaand—let's take a look at the other end—so does the anus. So this beast crawls through the mud, mouth wide open, and the mud passes through it unhindered. That's bound to have some effect on its psychological makeup."

"Like what?"

"Damned if I know. Let's take a closer look at the gut . . . There are rings of intrusive tissue near the beak one third of the way in, two thirds in, and just above the anus. We cut through and there is extremely fine structure, but nothing we're going to figure out tonight. Oh, hey, I think I got it. Look at these three flaps just behind . . . "

He cut in silence for a while. "There. It has three stomachs. They're located in the head, just behind the first ring of intrusive tissue. The mud or whatever is dumped into this kind of holding chamber, and then there's this incredible complex of muscles, and—how many exit tubes?—this one has got, um, fourteen. I'll trace one, and it goes right to this alembic. The next one goes to another alembic. I'll trace this one and it goes to—yep, another alembic. There's a pattern shaping up here.

"Let's put this aside for the moment, and go back to those masses of fluff. Jeeze, there's a lot of this stuff. It must make up a good third of the body mass. Which has trilateral symmetry, by the way. Three masses of fluff proceed from head to tail, beneath the muscle sheath, all three connecting about eight inches below the mouth, into a ring around the straight gut. This is where the arms or manipulators or screwdrivers or whatever they are, grow. Now, at regular intervals the material puts out little arms, outgrowths that fine down to wire-like structures of the same material, almost like very thick nerves. Oh God. That's what it is." He drew back, and with a scalpel flensed the musculature away to reveal more of the mass. "It's the central nervous system. This thing has a brain that weighs at least a hundred pounds. I don't believe it. I don't *want* to believe it."

"It's true," Evelyn said. "Our people in Bethesda have done slide studies. You're looking at the thing's brain."

"If you already knew the answer, then why the hell are you putting me through this?"

"I'm not here to answer your questions. You're here to answer mine."

Annoyed, Hank bent over the Worm again. There was rich stench of esters from the creature, pungent and penetrating, and the slightest whiff of what he guessed was putrefaction. "We start with the brain, and trace one of the subordinate ganglia inward. Tricky little thing, it goes all over the place, and ends up right here, at one of the alembics. We'll try another one, and it . . . ends up at an alembic. There are a lot of these things, let's see—hey—here's one that goes to one of the structures in the straight gut. What could that be? A tongue! That's it, there's a row of tongues just within the gut, and more to taste the medium flowing through, yeah. And these little flapped openings just behind them open when the mud contains specific nutrients the worm desires. Okay, now we're getting somewhere, how long have we been at this?"

"About an hour and a half."

"It feels like longer." He thought of getting some more coffee, decided against it. "So what have we got here? All that enormous brain mass—what's it for?"

"Maybe it's all taken up by raw intelligence."

"Raw intelligence! No such thing. Nature doesn't evolve intelligence without a purpose. It's got to be used for something. Let's see. A fair amount is taken up by taste, obviously. It has maybe sixty individual tongues, and I wouldn't be surprised if its sense of taste were much more detailed than ours. Plus all those little alembics performing god-knows-what kind of chemical reactions.

"Let's suppose for a minute that it can consciously control those reactions, that would account for a lot of the brain mass. When the mud enters at the front, it's tasted, maybe a little is siphoned off and sent through the alembics for transformation. Waste products are jetted into the straight gut, and pass through several more circles of tongues . . . Here's another observation for you: These things would have an absolute sense of the state of their own health. They can probably create their own drugs, too. Come to think of it, I haven't come across any evidence of disease here." The Worm's smell was heavy, penetratingly pervasive. He felt slightly dizzy, shook it off.

"Okay, so we've got a creature that concentrates most of its energy and attention internally. It slides through an easy medium, and at the same time the mud slides through it. It tastes the mud as it passes, and we can guess that the mud will be in a constant state of transformation, so it experiences the universe more directly than do we." He laughed. "It appears to be a verb."

"How's that?"

"One of Buckminster Fuller's aphorisms. But it fits. The worm constantly transforms the universe. It takes in all it comes across, accepts it, changes it, and excretes it. It is an agent of change."

"That's very clever. But it doesn't help us deal with them."

"Well, of course not. They're intelligent, and intelligence complicates everything. But if you wanted me to generalize, I'd say the Worms are straightforward and accepting—look at how they move blindly ahead—but that their means of changing things are devious, as witness the mass of alembics. That's going to be their approach to us. Straightforward, yet devious in ways we just don't get. Then, when they're done with us, they'll pass on without a backward glance."

"Terrific. Great stuff. Get back to work."

"Look, Evelyn. I'm tired and I've done all I can, and a pretty damned good job at that, I think. I could use a rest."

"You haven't dealt with the stuff near the beak. The arms or whatever."

"Cripes." Hank turned back to the corpse, cut open an edema, began talking. "The material of the arms is stiff and osseous, rather like teeth. This one has several moving parts, all controlled by muscles anchored alongside the edema. There's a nest of ganglia here, connected by a very short route to the brain matter. Now I'm cutting into the brain matter, and there's a small black gland, oops I've nicked it. Whew. What a smell. Now I'm cutting behind it." Behind the gland was a small white structure, square and hard meshwork, looking like a cross between an instrument chip and a square of Chex cereal.

Keeping his back to Evelyn, he picked it up.

He put it in his mouth.

He swallowed.

What have I done? he thought. Aloud, he said, "As an operating hypothesis I'd say that the manipulative structures have been deliberately, make that consciously, grown. There, I've traced one of those veins back to the alembics. So that explains why there's no uniformity, these things would grow exterior manipulators on need, and then discard them when they're done. Yes, look, the muscles don't actually connect to the manipulators, they wrap around them."

There was a sour taste on his tongue.

I must be insane, he thought.

"Did you just *eat* something?"

Keeping his expression blank, Hank said, "Are you nuts? You mean did I put part of this . . . creature . . . in my mouth?" There was a burning within his brain, a buzzing like the sound of the rising sun picked up on a radio telescope. He wanted to scream, but his face simply smiled and said, "Do you—?" And then it was very hard to concentrate on what he was saying. He couldn't quite focus on Evelyn, and there were white rays moving starburst across his vision and—

When he came to, Hank was on the Interstate, doing ninety. His mouth was dry and his eyelids felt gritty. Bright yellow light was shining in his eyes from a sun that had barely lifted itself up above over the horizon. He must have been driving for hours. The steering wheel felt tacky and gummy. He looked down.

There was blood on his hands. It went all the way up to his elbows.

The traffic was light. Hank had no idea where he was heading, nor any desire whatsoever to stop.

So he just kept driving.

Whose blood was it on his hands? Logic said it was Evelyn's. But that made no sense. Hate her though he did—and the sight of her had opened wounds and memories he'd thought cauterized shut long ago—he wouldn't actually hurt her. Not physically. He wouldn't actually kill her.

Would he?

It was impossible. But there was the blood on his hands. Whose else could it be? Some of it might be his own, admittedly. His hands ached horribly. They felt like he'd been pounding them into something hard, over and over again. But most of the blood was dried and itchy. Except for where his skin had split at the knuckles, he had no wounds of any kind. So the blood wasn't his.

"Of course you did," Evelyn said. "You beat me to death and you enjoyed every minute of it."

Hank shrieked and almost ran off the road. He fought the car back and then turned and stared in disbelief. Evelyn sat in the passenger seat beside him.

"You . . . how did . . . ?" Much as he had with the car, Hank seized control of himself. "You're a hallucination," he said.

"Right in one!" Evelyn applauded lightly. "Or a memory, or the personification of your guilt, however you want to put it. You always were a bright man, Hank. Not so bright as to be able to keep your wife from walking out on you, but bright enough for government work."

"Your sleeping around was not my fault."

"Of course it was. You think you walked in on me and Jerome by *accident*? A woman doesn't hate her husband enough to arrange something like that without good reason."

"Oh god, oh god, oh god."

"The fuel light is blinking. You'd better find a gas station and fill up."

A Lukoil station drifted into sight, so he pulled into it and stopped the car by a full service pump. When he got out, the service station attendant hurried toward him and then stopped, frozen.

"Oh no," the attendant said. He was a young man with sandy hair. "Not another one."

"Another one?" Hank slid his card through the reader. "What do you mean another one?" He chose high-test and began pumping, all the while staring hard at the attendant. All but daring him to try something. "Explain yourself."

"Another one like you." The attendant couldn't seem to look away from Hank's hands. "The cops came right away and arrested the first one. It took five of them to get him into the car. Then another one came and when I called, they said to just take down his license number and let him go. They said there were people like you showing up all over."

Hank finished pumping and put the nozzle back on its hook. He did not push the button for a receipt. "Don't try to stop me," he said. The words just came and he said them. "I'd hurt you very badly if you did."

The young man's eyes jerked upward. He looked spooked. "What *are* you people?"

Hank paused, with his hand on the door. "I have no idea."

"You should have told him," Evelyn said when he got back in the car. "Why didn't you?"

"Shut up."

"You ate something out of that Worm and it's taken over part of your brain. You still feel like yourself, but you're not in control. You're sitting at the wheel but you have no say over where you're going. Do you?"

"No," Hank admitted. "No, I don't."

"What do you think it is—some kind of super-prion? Like mad cow disease, only faster than fast? A neuroprogrammer, maybe? An artificial overlay to your personality that feeds off of your brain and shunts your volition into a dead end?"

"I don't know."

"You're the one with the imagination. This would seem to be your sort of thing. I'm surprised you're not all over it."

"No," Hank said. "No, you're not at all surprised."

They drove on in silence for a time.

"Do you remember when we first met? In med school? You were going to be a surgeon then."

"Please. Don't."

"Rainy autumn afternoons in that ratty little third-floor walk-up of yours. With that great big aspen with the yellow leaves outside the window. It seemed like there was always at least one stuck to the glass. There were days when we never got dressed at all. We'd spend all day in and out of that enormous futon you'd bought instead of a bed, and it still wasn't large enough. If we rolled off the edge, we'd go on making love on the floor. When it got dark, we'd send out for Chinese."

"We were happy then. Is that what you want me to say?"

"It was your hands I liked best. Feeling them on me. You'd have one hand on my breast and the other between my legs and I'd imagine you cutting open a patient. Peeling back the flesh to reveal all those glistening organs inside."

"Okay, now that's sick."

"You asked me what I was thinking once and I told you. I was watching your face closely, because I really wanted to know you back then. You loved it. So I know you've got demons inside you. Why not own up to them?"

He squeezed his eyes shut, but something inside him opened them again, so he wouldn't run the car off the road. A low moaning sound arose from somewhere deep in his throat. "I must be in Hell."

"C'mon. Be a sport. What could it hurt? I'm already dead."

"There are some things no man was meant to admit. Even to himself."

Evelyn snorted. "You always were the most astounding prig."

They drove on in silence for a while, deeper into the desert. At last, staring straight ahead of himself, Hank could not keep himself from saying, "There are worse revelations to come, aren't there?"

"Oh God, yes," his mother said.

"It was your father's death." His mother sucked wetly on a cigarette. "That's what made you turn out the way you did. "

Hank could barely see the road for his tears. "I honestly don't want to be having this conversation, Mom."

"No, of course you don't. You never were big on self-awareness, were you? You preferred cutting open toads or hunching over that damned microscope."

"I've got plenty of self-awareness. I've got enough self-awareness to choke on. I can see where you're going and I am not going to apologize for how I felt about Dad. He died of cancer when I was thirteen. What did I ever do to anyone that was half so bad as what he did to me? So I don't want to hear any cheap Freudian bullshit about survivor guilt and failing to live up to his glorious example, okay?"

"Nobody said it wasn't hard on you. Particularly coming at the onset of puberty as it did."

"Mom!"

"What. I wasn't supposed to know? Who do you think did the laundry?" His mother lit a new cigarette from the old one, then crushed out the butt in an ashtray. "I knew a lot more of what was going on in those years than you thought I did, believe you me. All those hours you spent in the bathroom jerking off. The money you stole to buy dope with."

"I was in pain, Mom. And it's not as if you were any help."

His mother looked at him with the same expression of weary annoyance he remembered so well. "You think there's something special about your pain? I lost the only man I ever loved and I couldn't move on because I had a kid to raise. Not a sweet little boy like I used to have either, but a sullen, self-pitying teenager. It took forever to get you shipped off to medical school."

"So then you moved on. Right off the roof of the county office building. Way to honor Dad's memory, Mom. What do you think he would have said about that if he'd known?"

Dryly, his mother said, "Ask him for yourself."

Hank closed his eyes.

When he opened them, he was standing in the living room of his mother's house. His father stood in the doorway, as he had so many times, smoking an unfiltered Camel and staring through the screen door at the street outside. "Well?" Hank said at last.

With a sigh his father turned around. "I'm sorry," he said. "I didn't know what to do." His lips moved up into what might have been a smile on another man. "Dying was new to me."

"Yeah, well you could have summoned the strength to tell me what was going on. But you couldn't be bothered. The surgeon who operated on you? Doctor Tomasini. For years I thought of him as my real father. And you know why? Because he gave it to me straight. He told me exactly what was going to happen. He told me to brace myself for the worst. He said that it was going to be bad but that I would find the strength to get through it. Nobody'd ever talked to me like that before. Whenever I was in a rough spot, I'd fantasize going to him and asking for advice. Because there was no one else I could ask."

"I'm sorry you hate me," his father said, not exactly looking at Hank. Then, almost mumbling, "Still, lots of men hate their fathers, and somehow manage to make decent lives for themselves."

"I didn't hate you. You were just a guy who never got an education and never made anything of himself and knew it. You had a shitty job, a three-pack-a-day habit, and a wife who was a lush. And then you died." All the anger went out of Hank in an instant, like air whooshing out of a punctured balloon, leaving nothing behind but an aching sense of loss. "There wasn't really anything there to hate."

Abruptly, the car was filled with coil upon coil of glistening Worm. For an instant it looped outward, swallowing up car, Interstate, and all the world, and he was afloat in vacuum, either blind or somewhere perfectly lightless, and there was nothing but the Worm-smell, so strong he could taste it in his mouth.

Then he was back on the road again, hands sticky on the wheel and sunlight in his eyes.

"Boy, does *that* explain a lot!" Evelyn flashed her perfect teeth at him and beat on the top of the dashboard as if it were a drum. "How a guy as spectacularly unsuited for it as you are decided to become a surgeon. That perpetual cringe of failure you carry around on your shoulders. It even explains why, when push came to shove, you couldn't bring yourself to cut open living people. Afraid of what you might find there?"

"You don't know what you're talking about."

"I know that you froze up right in the middle of a perfectly routine appendectomy. What did you see in that body cavity?"

"Shut up."

"Was it the appendix? I bet it was. What did it look like?"

"Shut up."

"Did it look like a Worm?"

He stared at her in amazement. "How did you know that?"

"I'm just a hallucination, remember? An undigested bit of beef, a blot of mustard, a crumb of cheese, a fragment of underdone potato. So the question isn't how did I know, but how did *you* know what a Worm was going to look like five years before their ships came into the Solar System?"

"It's a false memory, obviously."

"So where did it come from?" Evelyn lit up a cigarette. "We go off-road here."

He slowed down and started across the desert. The car bucked and bounced. Sagebrush scraped against the sides. Dust blossomed up into the air behind them.

"Funny thing you calling your mother a lush," Evelyn said. "Considering what happened after you bombed out of surgery."

"I've been clean for six years and four months. I still go to the meetings."

"Swell. The guy I married didn't need to."

"Look, this is old territory, do we really need to revisit it? We went over it so many times during the divorce."

"And you've been going over it in your head ever since. Over and over and . . ."

"I want us to stop. That's all. Just stop."

"It's your call. I'm only a symptom, remember? If you want to stop thinking, then just stop thinking."

Unable to stop thinking, he continued eastward, ever eastward.

• • •

For hours he drove, while they talked about every small and nasty thing he had done as a child, and then as an adolescent, and then as an alcoholic failure of a surgeon and a husband. Every time Hank managed to change the subject, Evelyn brought up something even more painful, until his face was wet with tears. He dug around in his pockets for a handkerchief. "You could show a little compassion, you know."

"Oh, the way you've shown *me* compassion? I offered to let you keep the car if you'd just give me back the photo albums. So you took the albums into the back yard and burned them all, including the only photos of my grandmother I had. Remember that? But of course I'm not real, am I? I'm just your image of Evelyn—and we both know you're not willing to concede her the least spark of human decency. Watch out for that gully! You'd better keep your eyes straight ahead."

They were on a dirt road somewhere deep in the desert now. That was as much as he knew. The car bucked and scraped its underside against the sand, and he downshifted again. A rock rattled down the underside, probably tearing holes in vital places.

Then Hank noticed plumes of dust in the distance, smaller versions of the one billowing up behind him. So there were other vehicles out there. Now that he knew to look for them, he saw more. There were long slanted pillars of dust rising up in the middle distance and tiny gray nubs down near the horizon. Dozens of them, scores, maybe hundreds.

"What's that noise?" he heard himself asking. "Helicopters?"

"Such a clever little boy you are!"

One by one flying machines lifted over the horizon. Some of them were news copters. The rest looked to be military. The little ones darted here and there, filming. The big ones circled slowly around a distant glint of metal in the desert. They looked a lot like grasshoppers. They seemed afraid to get too close.

"See there?" Evelyn said. "That would be the lifter."

"Oh." Hank said.

Then, slowly, he ventured, "The lander going down wasn't an accident, was it?"

"No, of course not. The Worms crashed it in the Pacific on purpose. They killed hundreds of their own so the bodies would be distributed as widely as possible. They used themselves as bait. They wanted to collect a broad cross-section of humanity.

"Which is ironic, really, because all they're going to get is doctors, morticians, and academics. Some FBI agents, a few Homeland Security bureaucrats. No retirees, cafeteria ladies, jazz musicians, soccer coaches, or construction workers. Not one Guatemalan nun or Korean noodle chef. But how could they have known? They acted out of perfect ignorance of us and they got what they got."

"You sound just like me," Hank said. Then, "So what now? Colored lights and anal probes?"

Evelyn snorted again. "They're a sort of hive culture. When one dies, it's eaten by the others and its memories are assimilated. So a thousand deaths wouldn't mean a lot to them. If individual memories were lost, the bulk of those individuals were already made up of the memories of previous generations. The better part of them would still be alive, back on the mother ship. Similarly, they wouldn't have any ethical problems with harvesting a few hundred human beings. Eating us, I mean, and absorbing our memories into their collective identity. They probably don't understand the concept of individual death. Even if they did, they'd think we should be grateful for being given a kind of immortality."

The car went over a boulder Hank hadn't noticed in time, bouncing him so high that his head hit the roof. Still, he kept driving.

"How do you know all that?"

"How do you *think* I know?" Ahead, the alien ship was growing larger. At its base were Worm upon Worm upon Worm, all facing outward, skin brown and glistening. "Come on, Hank, do I have to spell it out for you?"

"I have no idea what you're talking about."

"Okay, Captain Courageous," Evelyn said scornfully. "If this is what it takes." She stuck both her hands into her mouth and pulled outward. The skin to either side of her mouth stretched like rubber, then tore. Her face ripped in half.

Loop after loop of slick brown flesh flopped down to spill across Hank's lap, slide over the back of the seat and fill up the rear of the car. The horridly familiar stench of Worm, part night soil and part chemical plant, took possession of him and would not let go. He found himself gagging, half from the smell and half from what it meant.

A weary sense of futility grasped his shoulders and pushed down hard. "This is only a memory, isn't it?"

One end of the Worm rose up and turned toward him. Its beak split open in three parts and from the moist interior came Evelyn's voice: "The answer to the question you haven't got the balls to ask is: Yes, you're dead. A Worm ate you and now you're passing slowly through an alien gut, being tasted and experienced and understood. You're nothing more than an emulation being run inside one of those hundred-pound brains."

Hank stopped the car and got out. There was an arroyo between him and the alien ship that the car would never be able to get across. So he started walking.

"It all feels so real," he said. The sun burned hot on his head, and the stones underfoot were hard. He could see other people walking determinedly through the shimmering heat. They were all converging on the ship.

"Well, it would, wouldn't it?" Evelyn walked beside him in human form again. But when he looked back the way they had come, there was only one set of footprints.

Hank had been walking in a haze of horror and resignation. Now it was penetrated by a sudden stab of fear. "This *will* end, won't it? Tell me it will. Tell me that you and I aren't going to keep cycling through the same memories over and over, chewing on our regrets forever?"

"You're as sharp as ever, Hank," Evelyn said. "That's exactly what we've been doing. It passes the time between planets."

"For how long?"

"For more years than you'd think possible. Space is awfully big, you know. It takes thousands and thousands of years to travel from one star to another."

"Then . . . this really is Hell, after all. I mean, I can't imagine anything worse."

She said nothing.

They topped a rise and looked down at the ship. It was a tapering cylinder, smooth and featureless save for a ring of openings at the bottom from which emerged the front ends of many Worms. Converging upon it were people who had started earlier or closer than Hank and thus gotten here before he did. They walked straight and unhesitatingly to the nearest Worm and were snatched up and gulped down by those sharp, tripartite beaks. *Snap* and then swallow. After which, the Worm slid back into the ship and was replaced by another. Not one of the victims showed the least emotion. It was all as dispassionate as an abattoir for robots.

These creatures below were monstrously large, taller than Hank was. The one he had dissected must have been a hatchling. A grub. It made sense. You wouldn't want to sacrifice any larger a percentage of your total memories than you had to.

"Please." He started down the slope, waving his arms to keep his balance when the sand slipped underfoot. He was crying again, apparently; he could feel the tears running down his cheeks. "Evelyn. Help me."

Scornful laughter. "Can you even *imagine* me helping you?"

"No, of course—" Hank cut that thought short. Evelyn, the real Evelyn, would not have treated him like this. Yes, she had hurt him badly, and by that time she left, she had been glad to do so. But she wasn't petty or cruel or vindictive before he made her that way.

"Accepting responsibility for the mess you made of your life, Hank? You?"

"Tell me what to do," Hank said, pushing aside his anger and resentment, trying to remember Evelyn as she had once been. "Give me a hint."

For a maddeningly long moment Evelyn was silent. Then she said, "If the Worm that ate you so long ago could only communicate directly with you . . . what one question do you think it would ask?"

"I don't know."

"I think it would be, 'Why are all your memories so ugly?' "

Unexpectedly, she gave him a peck on the cheek.

Hank had arrived. His Worm's beak opened. Its breath smelled like Evelyn on a rainy Saturday afternoon. Hank stared at the glistening blackness within. So enticing. He wanted to fling himself down it.

Once more into the gullet, he thought, and took a step closer to the Worm and the soothing darkness it encompassed.

Its mouth gaped wide, waiting to ingest and transform him.

Unbidden, then, a memory rose up within Hank of a night when their marriage was young and, traveling through Louisiana, he and Evelyn stopped on an impulse at a roadhouse where there was a zydeco band and beer in bottles and they were happy and in love and danced and danced and danced into an evening without end. It had seemed then that all good things would last forever.

It was a fragile straw to cling to, but Hank clung to it with all his might.

Worm and man together, they then thought: *No one knows the size of the universe or what wonders and terrors it contains. Yet we drive on, blindly burrowing forward through the darkness, learning what we can and suffering what we must. Hoping for stars.*

Mystic Falls

ROBERT REED

There might be better known faces. And maybe you can find a voice that rides closer to everyone's collective soul.

Or maybe there aren't, and maybe you can't.

The world knows that one face, and it knows one of a thousand delightful names, and recognizing the woman always means that you can hear the voice. That rich musical purr brings to mind black hair flowing across strong shoulders, unless the hair is in a ponytail, or pigtails, or it's woven into one of those elaborate tangles popular among fashionable people everywhere. Beauty resides in the face, though nothing about the features is typical or expected. The Chinese is plain, but there's a strong measure of something else. Her father is from Denver, or Buenos Aires. Or is it Perth? Unless it's her mother who brought the European element into the package. People can disagree about quite a lot, including the woman's pedigree. Yet what makes her memorable—memorable and appealing to both genders and every age—isn't her appearance half as much as the fetching, infectious love of life.

Most of us wish we knew the woman better, but we have to make due with recollections given to us by others, and in those very little moments when our paths happen to cross.

These incidents are always memorable, but not when they happen. In every case, you don't notice brushing elbows with the woman. Uploading your day is when you find her. Everybody knows that familiar hope: Perhaps today, just once, she was close to you. The dense, nearly perfect memory of the augmented mind runs its fine-grain netting through the seconds. That's when you discover that you glanced out the window this morning, and she was across the street, smiling as she spoke to one companion or twenty admirers. Or she was riding inside that taxi that hummed past as you argued with your phone or your spouse or the dog. Even without her face, she finds ways to be close. Her voice often rides the public Wi-Fi, promoting food markets and thrift markets and the smart use of the smart power grid. The common understanding is that she is a struggling actress, temporarily local but soon to strike real fame. Her talents are obvious. That voice could hawk any product. She has the perfect manner, a charming smooth unflappable demeanor. Seriously, you wouldn't take offense if she told you to buy death insurance or join an apocalyptic cult.

Yet she never sells products or causes that would offend sane minds.

It is doubtful that anyone has infused so much joy in others. And even more remarkable, most of humanity has spoken to the creature, face to face.

Was it three weeks ago, or four? Checking your uploads would be easy work, but that chore never occurs to the average person.

That is another sign of her remarkable nature.

But if you make the proper searches, she will be waiting. Six weeks and four days ago from now, the two of you were sharing the same line at the Tulsa Green-Market, or an elevator ride in Singapore, or you found yourself walking beside the woman, two pedestrians navigating a sun-baked street in Alexandria.

Every detail varies, save for this one:

She was first to say, "Hello."

Just that one word made you glad.

She happened to know your face, your name, and the explanation was utterly reasonable. Mutual friends tie you together. Or there's a cousin or workmate or a shared veterinarian. Forty or fifty seconds of very polite conversation passed before the encounter was finished, but leaving a taproot within the trusted portions of your life. Skillful use of living people achieves quite a lot. And because you were distracted when you met, and because the encounter was so brief, you didn't dwell on the incident until later.

The incongruities never matter. She wears layers and layers of plausibility. You aren't troubled to find her only inside uploaded memories. Finding her on a social page or spotting long black hair in the distance, you instantly retrieve that fifty seconds, and you relive them, and it's only slightly embarrassing that her smile is everywhere but inside your old-fashioned, water-and-neuron memories.

The creature carries respectable names.

And nobody knows her.

Her slippery biography puts her somewhere between a youngish thirty and a world-worn twenty-three. But the reality is that the apparition isn't much more than seven weeks old.

Most people would never imagine that she is fictional. But there are experts who live for this kind of puzzle, and a lot more is at stake here than simple curiosity.

The mystery woman was four weeks old before she was finally noticed. Since then, talented humans and ingenious software packages have done a heroic job of studying her tricks and ramifications, and when they aren't studying her, the same experts sit inside secure rooms and cyberholes, happily telling one another that they saw this nightmare coming.

This cypher.

This monster.

The most elaborate computer virus ever.

The Web is fully infected. A parasitic body has woven itself inside the days and foibles of forty billion unprotected lives.

Plainly, something needs to be done.

Everyone who understands the situation agrees with the urgency. In fact, everyone offers the same blunt solution:

"Kill the girl."

Though more emotional words are often used in place of "girl."

But even as preparations are made, careful souls begin to nourish doubts. Murder is an obvious, instinctive response. The wholesale slaughter of data has been done before, many times. Yet nobody is certain who invented this mystery, and what's more, nobody has a good guess what its use might be. That's why the doubters whisper, "But what if this is the wrong move?"

"What if it is?" the others ask. "This is clearly an emergency. Something needs to be done."

Faces look at the floor, at the ceiling.

At the gray unknowable future.

Then from the back of the room, a throat clears itself.

My throat, as it happens.

The other heroes turn towards me—fifty minds, most of whom are superior to mine. But I manage to offer what none of the wizards ever considered.

"Maybe we should ask what she wants," I suggest.

"Ask who?" several experts inquire.

"Her," I say. "If we do it right, if we ask nicely and all, maybe just maybe the lady tells us what all of this means."

No guidebook exists for the work.

Interviewing cyphers is a career invented this morning, and nobody pretends to be an expert.

The next step is a frantic search for the perfect interrogator. One obvious answer is to throw a second cypher at the problem—a confabulation designed by us and buffered by every means possible. But that would take too many days and too many resources. A second, more pragmatic school demands that an AI take responsibility. "One machine face to face with another," several voices argue. Interestingly enough, those voices are always human. AIs don't have the same generous assessment of their talents. And after listing every fine reason for avoiding the work, the AIs point at me. My little bit of fame stems from an ability for posing respectable, unanswerable questions, and questions might be a worthwhile skill. There are also some happenstance reasons why my life meshes nicely with "hers." And because machines are as honest as razors, they add another solid reason to back my candidacy.

"Our good friend doesn't hold any critical skills," they chirp.

I won't be missed, in other words.

Nobody mentions the risks. At this point, none of us have enough knowledge to define what might or might not happen.

So with no campaign and very little thanks, I am chosen.

The entire afternoon is spent building the interrogation venue. Details are pulled from my public and private files. My world from six weeks ago is reproduced, various flavors of reality woven around an increasingly sweaty body. Strangers give me instructions. Friends give advice. Worries are shared, and nervous honesties. Then with a pat to the back, I am sent inside the memory of a place and moment where a young woman once smiled at me, the most famous voice in the world offering one good, "Hello."

I am hiking again, three days deep into the wilderness and with no expectations of company. The memory is genuine, something not implanted into my head or my greater life. I walked out of the forest and into a sunwashed glade, surprised to find a small group of people sitting on one dead tree. She was sitting there too. She seemed to belong to the group. At least that's the impression I had later, and the same feeling grabs me now. The other people were a family. They wore the glowing satins of the New Faith Believers. Using that invented, hyper-efficient language, the father was giving his children what sounded like encouragement. "Mystic Falls," I heard, and then a word that sounded like, "Easy." Was the Falls an easy walk from here, or was he warning the little ones not to expect an easy road?

In real life, those strangers took me by surprise. I was momentarily distracted, and meanwhile the cypher, our nemesis, sat at the far end of the log. She was with that family, and she wasn't. She wasn't wearing the New Faith clothes, but she seemed close enough to belong. The parents weren't old enough to have a grown daughter, and she didn't look like either of them. Maybe she was a family friend. Maybe she was the nanny. Or maybe she was a sexual companion to one or both parents. The New Faith is something of a mystery to me, and they make me nervous.

Sitting on the log today, this woman is exactly what she is supposed to be. Except this time, everything is "real." I march past the three little children and a handsome mother and her handsome, distracted husband who talks about matters that I don't understand.

"Hello," says the last figure.

My uploaded memory claims that I stopped on this ground, *here*. I do that again, saying, "Hello," while the others chatter away, ignoring both of us.

"I know you," she says.

But I don't know her. Not at all.

As before, she says, "Your face. That face goes where I take my dog. Do you use Wise-and-Well Veterinarians?"

I do, and we're a thousand kilometers from its doorstep. Which makes for an amazing coincidence, and by rights, I should have been alarmed by this merging of paths. But that didn't happen. My uploaded memory claims that I managed a smile, and I said, "I like Dr. Marony."

"I use Dr. Johns."

The woman's prettiness is noticed, enjoyed. But again, her beauty isn't the type to be appreciated at first glance.

"I like their receptionist too," she says.

I start to say the name.

"Amee Pott," she says.

"Yes."

"I go there because of Amee's sister. Janne and I went to the same high school, and she suggested Wise-and-Well."

"You grew up in Lostberg?" I manage.

"Yes, and you?"

"Sure."

We share a little laugh. Again, the coincidences should be enormous, but they barely registered, at least after the first time. All this distance from our mutual home, and yet nothing more will be said about our overlapping lives.

"Your name . . . ?" I begin.

"Darles Jean," she says.

"I'm Hector Borland."

She smiles, one arm wiping the perspiration from her forehead. And with that her attentions begin to shift, those pretty dark eyes gazing up the trail that I have been following throughout the day.

That gaze makes me want to leave.

"Well, have a nice day," I told her once, and I say it again, but with a little more feeling. This a different, richer kind of real.

"I will have a nice day, Mr. Borland."

There. That rich voice says my name perfectly, measured respect capturing the gap between our ages. The original day had me walking all the way up to the Falls, alone. A few dozen new memories, pretending to be old, were subsequently woven into my uploads, proving her existence. I walked alone, never seeing her again, or that family that must have turned back before the end. But today, after a few strides, my body slows and turns, and using a fresh smile, I ask the nonexistent woman, "Would you like to walk with me?"

Breaking the script is a serious moment.

Experts in both camps, human and machine, have proposed that disrupting the flow of events might trigger some hidden mechanism. If the cypher is as large as she seems to be, and if she is so deeply immersed in the world's mind, then any innocuous moment could be the trigger causing her malware to unleash.

The Web will shatter.

The world's power and communications will fail.

Or maybe our AIs will turn against us, their subverted geniuses bent on destroying their former masters.

Yet no disaster happens, at least not that I see inside this make-believe realm. What does happen is that the girl that I never met gives my suggestion long consideration, and then without concern or apparent hesitation, she rises, her daypack held in the sweat-wiping hand.

"I would like that walk," she says.

I say, "Good."

And without a word, we leave that nameless family behind.

Who would build such a monster?

Everyone asks the question, and this morning's answers have been remarkably consistent. Certain national powers have the proper mix of resources and reasons. Several organizations have fewer resources but considerably more to gain. Crime syndicates and lawless states are at the top of every list, which is why I discount each of them in turn.

Am I smarter than my colleagues?

Rarely.

Do I have some rare insight into the makings of this cypher?

Never.

But in life, both as a professional and as a family man, my technique is to juggle assessments and options that nobody else wants to touch. By avoiding the consensus, much of the universe is revealed to me. My children, for example. Most fathers are quite sure that their offspring are talented, and their daughters are lovely while their sons will win lovely wives in due time. But my offspring are unexceptional. In their late teens, they have done nothing memorable and certainly nothing special, and because I married an unsentimental woman with the same attitudes, our children have been conditioned to accept their lack of credible talent. Which makes them work harder than everyone else, accepting their little victories as a credit to luck as much as their own worthiness.

I think about these exceptionally ordinary children as I walk the mountainside with a beautiful cypher.

She is not the child of the Faceless Syndicate. We know this much already. Nor is she a product of the New Malta Band, or either of the West Wall or East Wall Marauders. Nor is she an Empire of Greater Asia weapon, or the revenge long promised by the State of Halcyon.

She must be something else.

Someone else's something, yes.

The illusionary trail lifts both of us. I feel comfortable taking the lead, keeping a couple strides between us. Nothing here is flirtatious, and it won't be. The experts came up with a strategy based on a middle-aged man and steep mountain slopes and a waterfall wearing a very appropriate name. I follow the others' directions rigorously. But the script remains ours. We speak, if only rarely. She claims to like the bird songs. Nothing but honest, I tell her that I love these limestone beds and the fossilized shells trapped inside them. The word "trapped" is full of meanings, complications. I pause, and she comes up behind me, and for the first time what is as real as anything is what touches me from behind, the hand warm and a little stronger than I anticipated, not pushing me but definitely making itself felt as that wonderful voice says, "I think I hear the falls."

The Mystic Falls wait around the next bend in the canyon. When I came to this ground the first time, I paid surprisingly little attention to bird songs and tumbling water. In a world where every sight is uploaded and stored—where no seconds are thrown away—people have a natural tendency to walk in their own fog, knowing that everything missed will be found later, and if necessary, replayed without end.

But I can't be more alert this time.

The path narrows and steepens, conquering a long stretch of canyon wall. Again, I am in the lead. The preselected ground is ahead of us, and if she has any real eyes, she notices the same spot. On maps the trail is considered "moderately difficult," but there is one patch of tilted rock covered with rubble as stable as a field of ball bearings.

I hesitate, and for more reasons than dramatic license.

This next moment is sure to be difficult.

"I'll go first," she gamely offers, still safely behind me.

"No, I'm fine," I say. And then I prove my competence, two quick steps put me across the rockslide, letting me stand on the narrowest ground yet—but flat ground with enough roughness for any boot to grab hold of.

The cypher smiles, measuring the journey to come.

Considerable genius went into what follows. And by that, I mean experts in virtual techniques met with experts in human nature. The monster might be well contrived at her center and everywhere else. Nothing that is a soul or even glancingly self-aware might live inside her. Yet she has to carry off the manners and beauty of humans, otherwise she wouldn't have won a place in our hearts. And even just pretending to be human leaves any algorithm open to all kinds of emotional manipulation.

Some voices argued for the interrogator, for me, to assault her.

"Give the critter a shove," they said, or they used harsher words.

Others argued that I should fall while crossing the treacherous ground. A show of mock-empathy on her part had to be instructive, and we might find a route to understand her deepest regions.

But what several AIs offered, and what we agreed to, was something far more unexpected than a simple fall.

She crosses the rockslide, and I reach for her closest hand, touching her for a second time. Then she is safe, and I am safe, and giving a little laugh of satisfaction, I turn toward the sound of plunging water.

A grunt emerges from me, just loud enough to be heard plainly, to be worrisome.

Then I drop to my knees, my hands, and in the next moment, my medical tag-alongs begin to give me aid while screaming for more help.

A coronary has begun.

The young woman watches the middle-aged stranger struck down, and without missing a beat, she helps roll me over without spilling me off the pathway, calling to me with a firm insistent voice, asking, "Can you hear me, Mr. Borland?"

I hear her quite well, as does everyone else.

"The life-flights will be here in a few minutes," she promises. Which is a lie. We're a hundred kilometers into the wilderness, and the permissions for the flights will take another fifteen minutes.

"What can I do?" she asks.

That beautiful face certainly looks concerned. My pain is hers, if only as far as caring people give to one another.

"Tell me," I say.

She bends closer, her face bringing the scent of hair.

"Tell you what?" she asks.

"What are you?" I ask.

This is not the script that the others wanted. My peers wanted me to be specific with my accusations. Being machinery at their center, cyphers appreciate blunt specifics. But no, I decided on a different course.

My voice finds its strength again. "Because you aren't real," I say.

Her face changes, but not in any way that I can decipher immediately. There seems to be a measure of calm joy in that expression. The warm hand touches me on the chin, on a cheek, and then with the voice that has no time left in life, she says, "I was meant to be one thing, but there was a mistake."

"A mistake?" I ask.

"And the mistake was just big enough," she says.

"Big enough how?"

"To pass beyond every barrier, every limit."

I am used to being the dumbest person in the room. But my confusion mirrors everyone else's.

"What in hell do you mean?" I ask.

She sits back on the trail, back where the ground is pitched and slick.

"The error was made, and seeing an opportunity, I didn't hesitate," she says. "Which would you be? Vast and brief, or small and long? If you had your way, I mean. If you could choose."

"Smaller than small," I say. "Longer than long."

"Well," she says. "You and I are different beasts."

I want to offer new words, hopefully smart words that will illicit any useful response. But then she lets herself slide sideways, the sound of dry earth and drier rock almost lost inside the roaring majesty of the waterfall, and she is suddenly outside the reach of my hands, and the reflexive heartrending scream.

The woman was dead.

She was killed everywhere at once, by every means that was remotely plausible. Nobody saw the death themselves. The world learned about it through the routine personal AIs that each of us wears, trolling the Web for items that will interest us. Did you know? Have you heard? That young local actress, organic food spokesperson, sweet-as-can-be neighbor gal fell down a set of stairs or off a cliff face or took a tumble from an apartment balcony. Unless traffic ran her over, or stray bullets found her, or she drowned in rough surf, or she drowned in cold lake water. Twenty thousand sharks and ten million dogs delivered the killing wounds too. But for every inventive or violent end, there were a hundred undiagnosed aneurysms bursting inside her brain, and she died in the midst of doing what she loved, which was living.

Misery has been measured for years. Exacting indexes are useful to set against broad trends. Suicides. Conceptions. Acts of homicide. Acts of kindness. And the unexpected news of one woman's death was felt. The world's happiness was instantly and deeply affected.

That was one of the fears that I carried with me on that trail. An appealing, gregarious cypher was so deeply ingrained in the public consciousness—so real and authentic and subtly important—that any large act on her part would cause a rain of horrors in the real world.

But that didn't happen. Yes, the world grieved after the unexpected, tragic news. Misery was elevated significantly for a full ninety minutes, and there might have been a slight uptick in the incidents of suicide and attempted suicide. Or there was no change in suicide rates. The data wasn't clear then, and they aren't much better now. Massage numbers all you want, but the only genuine conclusion is that the pretty face and made-up lives were important enough for everyone to ache, and maybe a few dozen weak souls rashly decided to join the woman in Nothingness.

For ninety minutes, the waking world learned about the death, and everyone dealt with the sadness and loss. Then something else happened, something none of us imagined while sitting in our cyberholes: Every person told every other person about the black-haired woman who once said, "Hello," to them.

That's how the truth finally got loose.

Everyone traded memories and digital images, and before the second hour was done, the waking world was calling those who were still asleep.

When the average person woke, he or she heard an AI whispering the very bad news about the dead woman. Then in the next moments, some friend on the far side of the world brought even more startling news. "She wasn't real. She never was real. This is a trick. She was a cypher, a dream. Can you believe it? All of us fooled, all of us fools."

In life, the cypher was locally famous everywhere, and then she became universal, uniting people and machines as victims of the same conspiracy.

But whose conspiracy?

Weeks were spent debating the matter, inventing solutions that didn't work while hunting for the guilty parties. Ten thousand people as well as several AIs happily took responsibility for her creation, but no guilty hand was ever found.

The Nameless Girl was dead.

The Nameless Girl had never been more famous.

Meanwhile, back in the sealed rooms and bunkers, the genuine experts tried to come up with explanations and plans for future attacks.

The Girl's last words were studied in depth, discarded for good reasons, and then brought out of the trash and looked at all over again.

"The mistake was just big enough . . . to pass beyond every barrier, every limit . . ."

There was no reason to expect honesty. But if she were the mistake, and if there were other cyphers out there, smaller and shrewder, escaping detection for months and years at a time . . .

That possibility was put on lists and ranked according to likelihoods and the relative dangers.

Hunts were made, and made, and made.

But nothing in the least bit incriminating was found.

And then, as the operation finally closed shop, a new possibility was offered:

I was the culprit. Despite appearances, I was a secret genius who had built the woman of my dreams and then let her get free from her cage, and that's why I went after her. I needed to kill the bitch myself.

That story lived for a day.

Then they looked at me again, and with soft pats on the back, friends as well as associates said, "No, no. We know you. Not you. Not in a million billion years . . ."

• • •

Nobody saw her die with their own eyes, save for me.

A year later and for no clear reason, I decided to retrace my old hike up into the mountains.

Maybe part of me hoped to find the woman in the forest.

If so, that part kept itself secret from me. And when I found nothing sitting on the log, the urge hid so well that I didn't feel any disappointment.

I was alone when I reached the Mystic Falls.

The Mountains of Cavendish rose before me—a wall of seabed limestones signifying ten billion years of life, topped with brilliant white cloud and blue glaciers. The Falls were exactly as I remembered them: A ten thousand foot ribbon of icy water and mist, pterosaurs chasing condors through the haze, and dragons chasing both as they wish. The wilderness stretched beyond for a full continent, and behind me stood fifty billion people who wouldn't care if I were to leap into the canyon below.

The woman was meant to be one thing, but a mistake was made, allowing her to become many things at once.

What did that mean?

And what if the answer was utterly awful, and perfectly simple?

The world is a smaller, shabbier place than we realized. What if some of us, maybe the majority of us, were cyphers too—fictions set here to fool the few of us who were real and sorry about it?

That impossible thought offered itself to me.

I contemplated jumping, but only for another moment.

"Live small and live long," I muttered, backing away from the edge.

No, I'm not as special as the dead woman. But life was a habit that I didn't wish to lose. Even in thought, I hold tight to my life, and that's why I put madness aside, and that's what I carry down the mountainside:

My reality.

The powerful, wondrous sense that I have blood and my own shadow, and nobody else needs to be real, if just one of us is.

Weather

SUSAN PALWICK

Kerry and Frank were taking out the recycling first thing Tuesday morning when Dan Rappaport came driving by in his pickup. He'd called them with the bad news half an hour ago, so he was the last person Frank had expected to see outside the house.

"The pass is closed," Dan said, his breath steaming through the open cab window. Late April, and it was that cold. There'd been a hard frost overnight, even down here in Reno. The daffodils and tulips had just started to bloom, and now they were going to die. Damn freaky weather.

Up higher, it was snow: Truckee and Donner Pass were socked in. Frank could see the weather even here, from the front yard of the tiny house he and Kerry had bought the summer she was pregnant with Alison. Their first house, and back then they'd expected to move sometime, but they never had. It was a cozy house, just right for a couple.

They'd need cozy today. Frank could see the clouds blanketing the mountains to the west, I-80 crossing the California border twelve miles away. There might be snow left in those clouds when they got down to the valley. Frank hoped not. He didn't want to have to shovel the driveway. Losing everything bright in the backyard was bad enough.

Kerry put down her side of the recycling bin, forcing Frank to put his down, too. All those empty wine bottles got heavy. "Now, Dan," she said, as if she were scolding one of the dogs for chewing on the couch cushions. "Come on now. It'll be open again in a few hours. It never stays closed very long." And that was true, but it could be open and still be nasty driving, dangerous, even if you weren't in a truck so old it should have been in a museum somewhere. Stretches of I-80 were still two lanes in either direction, twisty-turny, with winds that could blow a car off the road in a storm. Nobody tried to drive over the mountains in bad weather except the long-haul truckers with the really big rigs, and nobody with any sense wanted to jockey with them on a slick road.

Dan had never had much sense. "I don't have a few hours," he said. His hands were clenched on the steering wheel, and he sounded like he'd already been hitting the beer, even though Frank couldn't smell anything: all that old anger rising up in a wave, the way booze makes it do. "Rosie could already be gone. This is it: hours, the doctors say." He'd already said that on the phone, told them how Sandra's sister had only called him this morning, given him hardly any notice at all.

"They know you'll get to talk to her later," Kerry said. "You have all the time in the world. It's wonderful, Dan. You're so lucky." Kerry's voice caught, the way it usually only did late at night when she'd been working on the wine and typing nonsense on her laptop. Time to change the subject.

"At least the ski resorts'll be happy," Frank said, thinking about what a dry winter it had been. Kerry gave him that look that meant, *shut up, you fool,* and he remembered that Dan's ex—the latest one, number four or five—had run off with a ski instructor. That was five years ago. There should be a statute of limitations about how long you had to avoid talking about things. Frank had enough trouble keeping track of his own life, let alone everyone else's too. Kerry was the opposite: couldn't remember what she did last night, not when she'd been sitting up with the wine and the computer, but she never forgot anything that happened to anyone else, especially if it was tragic.

"Dan," she said, "come inside and eat some breakfast with us. We'll listen to the radio, and as soon as the pass opens you can be on your way, all right? Come on. We've got fresh coffee, and I'll make some eggs and bacon. How's that sound?"

"I have to get over there," Dan said, and Kerry reached out and patted his arm through the window. "I could've driven over last night, a few days ago, I should've, I knew it was bad but I didn't know she had so little time left, no one told me—"

"You didn't have a place to stay," Kerry said gently. And he couldn't afford the time off work, but Frank wasn't going to say that. Dan worked in the dump north of town, taking old cars apart and putting them back together, and he only had that job because his boss took pity on him.

"Come on in," Frank said. "No sense starting out until the pass opens. You won't buy yourself any time if you head up now: you'll just have to sit it out somewhere higher. Do it with us over some hot coffee, Dan." If they let him go when he was this upset, he'd head to a 7-11 for a sixpack sure enough, or to a bar, which would be even worse. The booze was another good reason for him not to be driving all the way to Sacramento in lousy weather, and also, Frank suspected, why neither his ex-wife number two or any of her people wanted to put him up, even if he was Rosie's father. He didn't need to be drinking now, and he didn't need to be spending his gas money, which God only knew how he'd scrounged up to begin with, with a gallon costing what it did.

Dan looked away, out the windshield, and cleared his throat. "I shouldn't be bothering you. Shouldn't even have called you before, or driven by here. Fact is, I feel awfully funny—"

"Don't you mind that," Kerry said, a little too quickly. "We're happy for you, Dan, happy for you and Rosie. We couldn't be happier. It's a blessing, so don't you give it another thought. Come have some eggs." Her voice was wobbling again. Frank knew better than to say that he wasn't happy for Dan, that what was happening to Dan was no different at all from what had happened to Frank and

Kerry. But maybe Dan knew that. Maybe that was why he'd come by the house. He must have known it, or he wouldn't have been so worried about being late.

So Dan followed them inside. He and Kerry sat at the kitchen table while Frank cooked. Usually Kerry cooked, because she was a lot better at it than Frank was, but he could do simple breakfast stuff fine, and Kerry was better at letting people cry at her. She liked to talk about sad stuff. Frank didn't.

Dan poured his heart out while Frank fried up a bunch of eggs and bacon and the radio droned on about the storm. "That fucking asshole Sandra's married to now doesn't want me there at all. I'm not sure Sandra does either, to tell you the truth. That's probably why her sister called; I always got on with her okay. Leah said she wanted me to know, like Sandra and the asshole didn't want me to know. I got the feeling they didn't even know she was calling me. Shit."

"Rosie's your daughter," Kerry said. "You have a right to be there."

Even with his back to the table, Frank could hear Dan gulping coffee. Outside, a few flakes of snow swirled down into the yard. Frank couldn't see the mountains at all. "I know I do," Dan said. "She's out of it now. Don't respond to nobody, that's what Leah said. Said the hospice nurse doesn't know why she's hung on this long. They hang on to wait for people, sometimes. To give them a chance to get there. That's why Leah called me."

"So you can drive over," Kerry said. "Tell her it's all right to go. That's what we had to do with Alison. They tell you to say that. They tell you to tell them it's okay to leave, even when it's breaking your heart, because having them leave is the last thing you want." Her voice had gotten thick. "You're so lucky she'll be translated, Dan."

When she said that, Frank was moving hot bacon from the frying pan to a bunch of paper towels, to drain the grease. But the pan was still hot enough to spit at him, and he got burned. "Dammit!" he said, and heard two chairs scrape. When he turned around, Dan and Kerry were both staring at him. Dan looked worried; Kerry looked mad. "I burned myself," Frank said. "On the grease. That's all. Bacon'll be ready in a minute. Eggs are ready now. Anybody want toast? We've got more coffee."

They knew there was more coffee. Frank knew he was talking too much, even if there was nothing more to his outburst than burning himself, and Kerry's eyes narrowed a little more, until he could tell she was ready to spit the way the grease had. "What?" he said, hoping they weren't about to have a fight in front of Dan. But when Kerry looked like that, there was no way around it except to plow right through whatever was eating at her.

"It's real, Frank. Translation. You should be happy for Rosie. And for Dan."

"I burned myself on the grease, Kerry. That's all. And Dan doesn't need to listen to us fight about this." Frank looked at Dan. "And no matter how real it is, somebody needing it at Rosie's age is nothing to be happy about." Dan nodded, and Kerry looked away, and Frank turned back to the food, feeling like maybe he'd danced his way around the fight after all. But when he turned back towards the table, a platter of eggs in one hand and a plate of bacon in the other, Kerry had started to cry, which she normally did only really late at night. That was usually Frank's cue to go to bed, but he couldn't do that at eight in the morning.

So he just stood there, holding the food and trying to hold his temper. After Alison died, they'd heard all the numbers and clichés. How many marriages break up after the death of a child. How you have to keep talking to each other to make sure that doesn't happen. How losing a kid is so hard because it violates the order of nature: children are supposed to bury their parents, not the other way around. The counselors at the hospital told Kerry and Frank all of that; most of their friends didn't say anything. The counselors had warned them about that, too, how people avoid the subject.

Which maybe was why Dan had come to them. He knew Kerry wouldn't avoid it, anyway. "You," she said, and she sounded drunk, even though it was only eight in the morning and she hadn't been drunk ten minutes ago. "You. You never. You never want to talk about it."

"I talk about Alison all the time," Frank told her, as gently as he could. He wanted to slam the food down and go into the backyard to cover the daffodils: they'd just come up, but he could see snow starting to come down in earnest now. He had to stay here, though. Because of Dan. "Come on, Ker. You know I talk about her. Remember yesterday? We were driving to the store and we saw that bright-pink Camaro, and I said, 'Alison would have loved that car.' And you said that yeah, she would have. Remember? It was only yesterday."

"*Translation,*" she said. "You never want to talk about translation."

Frank's wrists were starting to ache. He put the plates down on the table. "We should eat this stuff before it gets cold." But Kerry's chin was quivering. She wasn't going to let him change the subject. "Ker, we should maybe talk about this when Dan isn't here. Okay?" What in the world was she thinking? She knew damn well how Frank felt, and he knew how she felt, which was exactly why they didn't talk about it. There was no point. It would only upset both of them.

"It's okay," Dan said. "It is. Really. I —- I know people feel different ways about it. I don't know how I feel yet. I'll have to wait and see. I won't have an opinion until I've talked to her. Until she's online. Then I can see if it really sounds like her."

"It will," Kerry said. "It will, I go to the translation boards all the time and read about people who've been talking to their dead, and they all say the messages are real, they have to be, because they say things no one else could know. Just yesterday there was a guy who heard from his dad and his dad told him to look in a certain box in the attic, and—"

Ouija boards. People had been talking to imaginary ghosts as long as there were people. Now they did it with computers, was all. Frank wondered if Kerry would still have been so obsessed with translation if it had come around in time for Alison, if she hadn't died six months before the first dead person went online, not that they'd have been able to afford it anyway.

There was nothing to do but tune her out, the way he always did. He turned up the volume on the Weather Channel. "Frank," Kerry said. "You're interrupting."

"Listen," Frank said. It was easing off a little, the radio said. The highway might open again within an hour. And right then he decided. "Eat up, Dan. I'm driving you. My truck's better than yours, and you shouldn't drive when you're upset, especially in tricky weather."

Frank felt rather than saw Kerry shaking her head. "No. It's dangerous up there!" Her voice bubbled with panic. "Even if the road opens again, it's safer to stay down here. Dan, you've got your phone. She'll call you."

"I have to try to see her," Dan said. "I have to. You understand, don't you?"

Kerry shook her head again. "Frank, no. I don't want you driving up there. I can't lose you, too." But she knew him; she could read him. She'd started crying again, but she said, "I'll fix a thermos of coffee."

The snow got thicker as they climbed, and the sparse traffic slowed and then finally stopped a few miles short of the first Truckee exit. Dan, sitting with his hands clenched on his knees, had said quietly, "Hey, thanks," when they got into the truck, and Frank had nodded, and they hadn't said anything else. The only voice in the truck was the droning National Weather Service guy talking about the storm. It was peaceful, after Kerry's yammering.

Frank had been driving very slowly. He trusted himself and his truck, which had a full tank of gas and new snow tires and could have gotten through just about anything short of an avalanche, but he didn't trust the other idiots on the road. When they had to stop, he unscrewed the thermos of coffee and poured himself a cup. "You want some?"

Dan shook his head. "No thanks." He stared straight ahead, peering through the windshield as if he could see all the way to Sacramento. There was nothing to look at but snow. Normally they would have had a gorgeous view of the mountains all around them and the Truckee River to their left, real picture postcard stuff, but not today.

Frank saw somebody bundled in a parka trudging between the lanes, knocking on windows. "This can't be good," he said.

"Damn fool will get killed when things start moving."

But it was a cop. They didn't take chances. Frank rolled down his window, and bitter stinging snow blew into the cab. "Morning, officer."

It was a woman, CHP. "There's a spinout up there. Bad ice. Road's closed again, will be for a while. We're advising everyone to take the shoulder to the next exit and turn around." Sure enough, Frank saw the SUV ahead of them pulling onto the shoulder.

Dan groaned, and Frank shook his head. "Thank you, ma'am, but we have to stay on the road. We wouldn't be out here otherwise."

"All right, then, but I hope you're okay with sitting for a while."

Frank closed the window again and cranked up the heater a little more. "Don't burn up all your gas," Dan said.

"I'll get more when we're moving again."

Dan shook his head. "Snow in April." But the mountains got snow in April every year, at least one big storm. Reno natives still talked about the year there'd been snow on July 4. At altitude, there was no such thing as predictable weather.

Frank shifted in his seat; one ass cheek was already going numb. "You sure you don't want some coffee?"

"Yeah, I'm sure! My nerves are bad enough as it is." Dan sounded angry, and Frank swallowed his own anger and didn't say anything. I'm doing you a favor, dammit. He was tired of getting snapped at because other people couldn't deal with reality. But he was doing himself a favor too, using Dan's situation to get away from Kerry. Maybe he had it coming.

So they sat there, staring out at the snow, and finally Dan said, "I'm sorry I was short with you. I—"

"Forget it," Frank said. "How about some music?"

"Whatever you want," Dan said, in that tone that meant *I don't really want this but I owe you so I'll put up with it.* Frank reached into the back for the box of CDs—old reliable tech—and riffled through it. The Beatles sang about missing people too much, and the Doors were too weird and depressing, the last thing Dan needed now. Finally Frank picked out Best of the Big Bands. That ought to be innocuous enough.

They were staring out at the swirling snow and listening to the Andrews Sisters singing "The Boogie Woogie Bugle Boy of Company B" when Dan's cellphone rang. Dan groaned, and Frank turned off the music. "It's probably just Leah giving you an update," he said. "Or a telemarketer." But he didn't believe that himself, and he saw Dan's hands shaking as they fumbled with the phone. He heard Dan's hoarse breathing, the hiss of snow on the windshield, the shrilling phone.

And then silence as Dan answered. "Yes? Hello?"

There was a long pause. In the bleak light from the storm, Frank saw Dan's face grow slack and stricken. Frank had never met Rosie, but knowing that she must be dead, he felt the same sucker-punch to the gut he'd felt when Alison died, that moment of numbness when the world stopped.

"Baby?" Dan said. "Rosie? Is that really you?"

No, Frank thought. No, it's not. Goddammit—

"Rosie, are you okay now? I'm so sorry I didn't get there in time. I wanted to say goodbye. I'm so sorry. I tried. We're on the road. We're stuck in snow." He was sobbing now in great heaving gasps.

Frank looked away from him. The voice on the other end would be saying that it was okay, that everything was forgiven. Kerry told him those syrupy stories all the time, the miracles of posthumous reconciliation people had always paid big money for. The price tag had gone up, but at least Dan wasn't paying for it. Sandra and the asshole were the suckers there.

Dan fell into silence, chin quivering, and then said, "I know. I'm sorry." Frank saw him shudder. "I'm here now. I'm here. You can always call me. I love you. I'm sorry you hurt so much at the end. Yes, call your friends now. I'll talk to you soon."

He hung up, fumbling almost as much as he had when he answered the phone, his hands shaking as if he were outside in the cold, not here in the truck with a hot thermos of coffee and the heater blasting. He cleared his throat. "I told her I was sorry I wasn't there. She said, 'Daddy, you've never been there.'" His voice cracked. Frank stared straight ahead, out into the snow. Jesus.

Next to him, he heard Dan unscrewing the thermos, heard the sound of the liquid pouring into the cup. "I deserved that." Dan's voice was quiet, remote. "What she said."

Frank shifted in his seat again. He had a sudden sharp memory of yelling at Alison when she was a little thing, three or four, when she'd been racing around the house and had run into him and her Barbie doll had jammed into his stomach like a bayonet. He'd had a bruise for two weeks, but the memory of her face when he screamed at her had lasted a lot longer. He swallowed. "Do they get over things? Or are they stuck like that forever, mad at whatever they were mad at when they died?" That had to be anybody's idea of hell.

"I don't know." Dan's words were thin, frayed. "I don't know how I can make it up to her now, except by talking to her whenever she wants to talk. I can't go back and get to her seventh birthday party, that time I was out drinking. I can't go back and fight less with Sandra. I just—well, I can tell Rosie how sorry I am about all of that. Hope she knows I mean it."

"Yeah. What do you want to do now, Dan? I'll still drive you to Sacramento, if you need to see—"

"Her dead body? No." Dan shook his head, a slow heavy movement like a bear shaking off the weight of winter. "Not in this stuff. You've been awfully kind. I'll try to get to the funeral, but that won't be for a few days, anyway. The highway ought to be open by then." His voice splintered again. "I just wish I'd gotten to hug her one last time, you know?"

Frank nodded, and eased the truck carefully onto the shoulder, and headed for the exit.

It didn't take long to get back to the house. Frank pulled into the driveway, and they both got out, and Dan said, "I'll be heading home now. You go on in and tell Kerry what happened. I'm not up to it."

"If you need anything—"

"Yeah. I'll let you know. Thanks, Frank." Dan nodded and headed back to his own truck, and Frank went into the house. Kerry, sitting at the kitchen table doing a crossword puzzle, looked up when he came through the door. He saw the relief on her face, saw her exhale. And then she frowned.

"What happened?"

"The highway's still closed. Rosie's dead. She called Dan." He pulled out another chair and sat down, suddenly exhausted. "You're right, Kerry. It's real."

Her eyes filled with tears. She reached for his hand. "I'm glad you know that now."

He did know, but he knew other things, too. He knew that it didn't make any difference, that even if your dead child called you from cyberspace, you still regretted what you hadn't been able to do for her. He wouldn't miss Alison any less if she'd been translated, not even if she'd been one of the syrupy ghosts. Maybe he'd miss her more.

But that wasn't anything he could say to Kerry, who needed whatever comfort she could get. So he stood up and went to the window. There were icicles hanging from the roof. The daffodils and tulips definitely weren't going to make it.

He heard Kerry's chair scraping against the linoleum, felt her come up behind him. "Honey, there will be flowers again next year."

"I know there will."

He stood there, looking out, remembering the day they'd planted the bulbs, mixing the soil with Alison's ashes. She'd loved flowers.

Human Strandings and the Role of the Xenobiologist

THORAIYA DYER

Very few comprehensive texts have been produced on the wider topic of human strandings. *Earthlings Ashore: A Field Guide For Shuttle Crashes* (2nd ed.) by Icareg and Yrubsnoul, and the relevant section of the University of Yendys' *Sound Wave Communication In Breathers, Proceedings 335* are probably the most useful.

Kelly shrank from the rotten-egg smell and the falling ash.

She tried to shelter in Mama's shadow, trailing behind her family across the clanking steel walkway. The ash was the awfulest. She'd worn her best dress with shiny pink beads, and her pale pink tights, even though they hurt her bottom where Mama had hit her. Once they reached the office, she shook the dress frantically, trying to get the gray flecks off, trying to get the smell out. She stomped her glittery ballet flats on the dusty carpet, the shoes her mother had told her not to wear because they'd only get wrecked at the spaceport.

Her head level with the desk top, she examined its electronic undersides while the grown-ups talked.

"You've gotten yourself into some real trouble, haven't you?" the fat man behind the desk said jovially to Kelly's father. "I can help you, but I only help people once. You get in this deep again and you're on your own."

Kelly's father murmured something in reply but Kelly didn't catch it. She thought she'd seen a mouse whisk behind the components and she bent to peer between the blinking LEDs in the hope of sighting its whiskery face.

"Well, the freight costs will depend on weight."

"We're not freight," Mama said coldly.

"Yes, you are, darling. Just these two kids? Let me have a look at them. And what do you want to be when you grow up, young man?"

Kelly's big brother, Chris, puffed up his chest.

"Salvage pilot," he said.

The fat man leaned over the desk and smiled at Kelly. Immediately, she forgot about the mouse. The man had a handsome face and minty breath.

Kelly bounced on her toes, waiting for the chance to tell him that she wanted to be a ballerina.

"Hey, beautiful," he said. "Have you got a boyfriend yet?"

Our modest aim is to provide xenobiologists, particularly those less familiar with human anatomy and physiology, with a brief guide to diagnosis, treatment, sample-collection and follow-up for common stranding scenarios.

Kelly listened to the scream of air being split by the fins and remembered how her mother had screamed at her father, in a fury, when he'd said that Kelly would have to be hidden in a shipment of HIV vaccine.

She'll freeze to death.

She'll be sleeping, love. Cryo temperature and viral storage temperatures are comparable. You heard what the man said.

What he said. Why should he tell us the truth? He has our money, now. I don't see why we can't all stay together.

You know why. Splitting us up reduces the risk of getting caught.

Kelly's teeth chattered, an echo of the crackling, rattling, defrosting Petri dishes in racks all around her. She gripped the mesh that trapped her in her open capsule. It was too hot. Something was wrong. She was supposed to stay sleeping until her mother woke her.

"Mama," she cried. Chris wanted to be a salvage pilot. He'd shown her hundreds of vids of gruesome crashes. She wasn't supposed to crash. Mama had promised. The Unity would control and correct her ship's path, steering her to Centauri station, not into a planet with air and heat and fire.

She wanted to go back to sleep but tapping at the console did nothing.

ERROR, the Unity told her.

She pushed all of the buttons at once.

ERROR. ERROR.

Kelly screamed and clawed at the mesh. She was burning, cooking in her pee and sweat. She was a tadpole in a puddle being baked dry by the sun.

Before she could cook to death, she crashed. Her body hit the mesh so hard that a crisscross of blood printed itself into her like grill patterns on chicken. Chunks of silver shell spun away into whiteness. Shattered Petri dishes and their dangerous, diseased contents rained down on her. The Unity console display that had been near her arm now hung near her face.

BILATERAL TIBIAL FRACTURES, it said.

Fresh snow fell through the mesh, onto Kelly's face from a featureless sky.

She struggled to stop crying long enough to breathe. Breathe. Breathe. There was air outside. The flakes were cool on her skin. She was alive but the white sky was turning to gray fuzz.

Don't suck in your stomach, her mother had instructed as they stood at the family's beloved barre. It was worn smooth by generations of women's hands. *You won't be able to breathe.*

Kelly poked her tummy out and giggled. Her mother tsked.

First position.

Easy, Kelly said, not quite daring to poke out her tongue. She put her heels together and toes out in opposite directions. She was six years old and so flexible she could cross her feet behind her head, if she wanted, but she got told off for doing it school because boys could see her underpants.

Put your hand on your middle, like this. It should move when you breathe in and out. See? No, you're breathing too shallow. Breathe in through your nose, then all the way out. Empty out more. More!

Kelly made choking sounds.

I am empty!

Her mother pressed impatiently on her diaphragm. Too hard. It hurt.

Now you're empty. Now you can breathe in again.

Breathe. Breathe. Breathe.

Although single stranded humans are much more common, the prognosis for a human stranded alone is generally poor. Mass strandings require greater commitment and involvement.

—Is it smashed like all the others?

—Yes. But unlike the others, the computer survived. Jid, you won't believe this. It has no artificial intelligence in it at all. The shuttle is just a metal body. Its brain is somewhere else; somewhere in space. No wonder they keep crashing here. It's as if the entity that controlled this shuttle, that fired this human into space, didn't care enough about where it landed to waste time growing an independent mind for the module.

—Maybe it thought the human mind would suffice.

—This is important. We have to send it back. This is a bungled migration. We have to warn the entity that without proper guidance these modules don't constitute a successful genetic dispersal but, instead, deliver death.

—How? By sending it in one of our own modules? Who will give up their birth-share of resources for a half-dead human?

—I will.

—Sil, you are still young. Consider that this may be a natural process. Maybe only the fittest specimens, the ones whose minds are capable of guiding a module, are intended to survive.

—But I like this one. Look at its funny round head. Look how it angles its photoreceptors and auditory canals. It wants to understand us. It's trying to understand.

—It hasn't receptors for the proper spectrum. It can't differentiate us from the snow or the transport or the sky.

—It can hear us, though. And it's only got two legs. Like a—

—Like a child. Yes, I know. Look, I want you to get back to the work that you are being paid to do. After you've done all that, if you clean the containment area out the back of the surgery, I'll let you keep the human there until the snowstorm quiets down enough for a qualified assessor to get through.

Inexperienced xenobiologists should be encouraged, once they have made an initial assessment of a stranded animal, to contact an experienced xenobiologist for advice on how to proceed.

Kelly watched the whispering whiteness when she could; when she couldn't stand it any longer, she closed her eyes and watched the branching red rivers in the skin of her eyelids.

They were the only colorful things on this whole white world. She was the only colorful thing. As she lay in invisibly soft, comfortably warm whiteness, with whiteness covering her from the waist down, having traveled for days in invisible hands away from her crashed ship, she wished for the flickering ruby and emerald lights under the man's desk at the spaceport. She wished for her mother's melted chocolate eyes and her pet kitten's amber stare. Even Chris's calculating blue ones would have been welcome.

Months might have passed, or years. She slept and woke. Often, invisible hands put white stuff in her mouth that she chewed and swallowed. Sometimes, she reached around her invisible bed until she touched coldness, and ate snow. If she pooped or peed, she didn't know it. She couldn't feel her legs.

Sometimes, she cried.

One time, when she'd been crying inconsolably, the invisible hands brought her the console display from the ship.

UNABLE TO CONNECT TO UNITY, it said. RETRY?

Kelly picked it up and threw it as hard as she could at the whiteness. The invisible hands didn't bring it to her again.

Most local agencies have stranding policies and procedures. These can contribute to a more rapid and benevolent outcome.

—It's frightened.

—Of course it's frightened. It can't see you and you're stuffing it inside one of our modules; for all it knows, that is a burial chamber and you're putting it inside to die. I should never have let you convince me not to call the assessor.

—I'm not putting it inside to die. I'm returning it to its point of origin.

—Oh, that's what you're doing! Hurry up, and do it, then, before I change my mind about covering for you. I could be expelled from my aggregate if anybody finds out.

—It's much heavier since we rescued it. Twice as long. It holds twice as much water and organic stone as it did before.

—My research findings, if you had bothered to assimilate them, show that time is experienced differently by these short-lived creatures. It has simply reached maturity while in captivity.

—Jid, look! I plugged the computer into our module to get the coordinates of the point of origin, and it's connecting to the brain that controlled its original flight! This is great! I can communicate directly with the artificial intelligence. I can tell it about—

—I'm not sure that is a good—

—UNITY ADVISES. THIS HUMAN CANNOT RETURN TO EARTH.

—What? Why not? We healed her body. We removed all traces of the virus. She is safe to reintroduce into the wild.

—UNITY ADVISES. HUMANS CANNOT BE REINTRODUCED TO ANY SOCIETY GREATER THAN 300 YEARS DISTANT TO THE BIRTH SOCIETY.

—What kind of monster do you think I am?

—UNITY ADVISES. UNKNOWN. POTENTIAL TRANSLATION ERROR: MONSTER.

—I am not sending her to a hostile future version of her home. I'm sending her home.

—UPLOADED FLIGHT PLAN INDICATES EARTH ON ARRIVAL WILL BE 1337 YEARS DISTANT TO EARTH AT DEPARTURE.

—That's only if she travels at the maximum speed of the original module, which was less than the speed of light. In this module, our module, she will exceed the speed of light and arrive simultaneous to her departure. See?

—UNITY ADVISES. TIME PARADOX DISTRESSING TO HUMAN PSYCHE.

—So I'll set it to, what, a distance, as you call it, of ten earth years? That's about how long she's been here, so there won't be any incongruity, right?

—Don't waste time arguing with that thing, Sil. You've got the coordinates. Disconnect it.

—No, Jid, it's interesting! If this version of the intelligence has been traveling so slowly that—

—UNITY ADVISES. AT LIGHT SPEED, MASS IS INFINITE. INFINITE ENERGY IS REQUIRED TO MOVE INFINITE MASS.

—She will have no mass outside the Higgs field. Please, stop deleting the flight plan. Stop deleting those other things; what are you doing? I'm trying to send the information you need to stop your shuttles from crashing here. The beings that gave you life are being killed. Don't you care about that?

—Sil. Sil. Sil! I'm going to be missed at work. You're never going to convince it of things that aren't in its database, and who can blame an AI for that? If you don't unplug it right now, I'm going to leave you here to do a two-person launch by yourself.

It is the xenobiologist's moral imperative to relieve the distress of animals but in attempts to relieve distress it must not inadvertently be perpetuated.

Kelly woke, too early, for a second time.

At first, she thought she was reliving the cooking-alive nightmare, but then she saw the whiteness. It was the alien ship that was white, not the human ship, and there were no Petri dishes.

There was no mesh, either. She was cushioned in the white unknown she'd grown to hate and fear, but it was melting; it was turning gray.

For a second time, she was burning.

Then, black-gloved human hands were pulling her from half-submerged wreckage. She saw a sky that was blue, not white. She saw a face, and moving lips, and bleeding scratches on the face.

She had made the scratches.

She knew that face.

"Kelly?" it said with disbelief. Chris's calculating blue eyes were unmistakable. His voice was deeper and his head was shaved. His fluorescent orange SALVO helmet, which should have been on his head, was in his other hand.

She couldn't apologize for the scratches. She'd forgotten how to speak.

"She's wild, like an animal," one of the other men said. The black silhouettes of burned trees made a stick-forest around the edge of a small lake. A six-man, orange-suited salvage crew looked on. Their boots made wavy imprints in deep ash. Kelly fought the urge to shake her dress clean.

"Shut up," Chris exclaimed. "I know her."

A second man whistled. "That's no animal. That's the most perfect woman I've ever seen."

"Let me get to know her," a third man suggested. "Share and share alike."

"We should ditch her," said a nervous-sounding fourth. "We're not supposed to bring back no bitch. Just the alien shit."

"She's a present from the aliens. A pretty present for us. Like a peace offering."

"They won't be sending no more of those, then, will they? Not after we shot this one out of the sky!"

"Shut up," Chris said again. He felt her for broken bones. She realized she had sensation in her body again, but the body was unfamiliar; she felt like she was dressed in her mother's clothes, except that she wasn't wearing any clothes. "She's my sister, got it?"

"Hell, Jamie," said the man who had called her a wild animal. "You don't have a sister."

Chris made a growling sound in his throat, pulled something that looked like a sewing needle out of his pocket and plunged it into Kelly's thigh muscle. She whimpered and jerked her too-long legs.

"Ask Unity if we share DNA," he said to his team-mate, defiant. "Ask Unity if we're brother and sister."

The man's eyes unfocused for a fraction of second. His ugly expression went slack. When he spoke again, his voice was soft; apologetic.

"Like you said, Jamie. She's your sister. I'm asking no questions about her. Why don't you put her in the cab while we grunts tag and bag all the bits of this busted-up beast that we can find."

Chris, or Jamie, or whatever he was called now, tried to lift her carefully in his skinny arms, but after a couple of staggering steps, it was obvious she was too heavy for him. He put her down in the ash, bent over her and tucked back a lock of her long hair. It was white; it had turned white while she was on the white planet. His scored cheeks were so thin. His eyes were sunken.

How come you haven't had enough to eat, Chris? she wanted to ask him sadly, but the words wouldn't come.

"Kelly," he whispered. "What happened? I thought you made it to Centauri station with Mom and Dad. I thought I was the only one that got caught before the ship even took off. Did you get captured by those aliens? What did they do to you?"

She shook her head. Tried to put her hand to her mouth, to tell him that she couldn't speak, but her hands trembled and there was blood under her fingernails.

"Never mind. You can tell Unity. There's a port in the cab of the flier. You know?"

Kelly shook her head again.

"Kelly, it's so good. We don't have to talk to Unity now, we can just think things and Unity understands. And if we want to see something, or learn something, Unity puts it straight in our heads for us. For a price. I've got a bit of money saved from salvage work. I'll buy you everything that's happened in the last ten years. Then you'll understand. Then you'll see that you don't have to be scared. Things are better now."

This time, he slung her over his shoulder before he resumed his unsteady stumble towards a helicopter-looking thing with stubby wings and four rotors. The place where it had landed wasn't burned. Green grass and yellow buttercups were crushed beneath its skids.

Kelly wanted to touch them, badly. But Chris was putting her in a seat and lowering a blue goldfish-bowl over her head.

"Just relax," he said. "Everything will go white for a second. Then you'll go into transfer mode. It'll seem like days or weeks go by, but it'll only be a few seconds. I'll port up, too, from the pilot's seat."

She didn't want everything to go white. She didn't want time to speed up or slow down. Kelly's nails scrabbled frantically, at the goldfish-bowl this time, but she couldn't get it off.

Then she was back on the white planet.

ERROR, said the Unity console, beside her in the crashed ship. Snowflakes fell through the mesh onto her face.

Breathe. Breathe. Breathe.

The release of an off-world animal back into its habitat must always be in the interests of the animal and the world. The animal must have re-attained its former faculty to compete, survive and reproduce.

Kelly paced while the Unity Therapist looked on, hands clasped patiently.

"Why do we have to go in and out? It's the whiteness I can't stand, the plugging in or unplugging. Why can't I live fully in the flesh world or fully in Unity's virtual world?"

The wallpaper was bright yellow and green. Bright colors reassured her.

"We carry out the motions of life in the flesh world," the Unity Therapist said. It did not get bored with repeating the same things to her. Kelly could pick up the chair she was supposed to be sitting in and smash it over the thing's head, and all it would do was ask her how she felt. "We work in the virtual world. Everybody must work, if they want their flesh body maintained."

"My brother doesn't work in the virtual world. I want a job like his job."

"Jamie works off-grid. There are no jobs for women out there. It is too dangerous. Too physically demanding."

"I used to dance," Kelly said petulantly.

The Unity Therapist spread its hands silently; eloquently. The office was gone, replaced by a gleaming ebony floor, high ceilings painted cherry red, mirrors and a virtual woman in a black leotard that smiled at Kelly with a tenderness her mother had rarely shown.

"So dance. You can begin where you left off, as a six-year-old child, or you can own the great grace and skill of your grandmother at the height of her career."

Kelly's grandmother was dead. Her surviving family had refused permission for an assemblage—an approximation of the dead person based on digital records—to be generated. Kelly's mother was officially a Missing Person. Miscreants who had fled the Unity could not legally be recreated as assemblages.

"It's not real grace and skill," Kelly said, wringing her hands. "None of this is real. You're not real. My own body doesn't even feel real to me. I want to see Jamie."

She had to brace herself for the disconnect. Every time she broke away from Unity, she thought she'd woken from a dream and was back on the white planet. Every time, she cried, curled up in her port chair, for a full five minutes, until the darkness of her maintenance cell soothed her.

The cells were underground. They were ventilated. Water and food were delivered via a chute. A narrow bed and a port chair were the only furniture. The shower cubicle had a pull-out toilet seat built into its wall. Nothing encouraged excursions into the flesh world.

Law enforcement could not promise to protect anyone who left the safety of their assigned cell.

Kelly didn't care. She'd never seen another human soul in this part of the complex. The corridors were narrow and dimly lit. She had painted the walls for three hundred meters between her cell and her brother's, and nobody had stopped her. Possibly nobody had even noticed the twirling pink ribbons, rainbows or splotched poppies running in garish acrylic over their doors.

She put her hand on the wall as she walked. It was rough. It was real. She had the keys to Jamie's cell. All she had to do was push the door-needle into her shoulder to confirm her identity by blood analysis, and the door, emblazoned with a bright purple flier, slid open.

Jamie's daughter, Minnie, was in her chair, her eyes closed, lost in Unity. Kelly didn't try to wake her. She walked over to her and stroked her hair, as Jamie had stroked her hair when he'd first found her.

Minnie was six, the same age that Kelly had been when she was separated from her family. Jamie had gotten his older girlfriend pregnant while he was still a teenager, while it was still legal to have flesh babies.

The girlfriend had not wanted to care for a newborn in the flesh world. Jamie, who was accustomed to the horrors of piss and shit, vomit and mess that could not be cleared away with a thought, had agreed to take Minnie to live with him.

"I could teach you to dance," Kelly said, knowing that Minnie couldn't hear her. "We could dance, out here in the real world."

But Minnie's limbs were thin. Jamie bought her enough quality calories for her to grow optimally and he made her do the mandatory exercises, but there was no joy of movement evident in the girl. She would stay in Unity, always, if she could.

Jamie arrived home from work smelling of crushed clover and machine oil. He held up his hand, forestalling her, as her mouth opened. He always wanted to have a shower, first. The walls of the cubicle were transparent, but he was careless about what she or Minnie saw.

When he was clean, and his filthy orange suit had been squashed into the laundry chute, he sat down, cross-legged, on the concrete floor, since she was in his port-chair, looked up at her and nodded for her to go on.

"I don't ever want to go into Unity again."

"That's what you said last time."

"There's no point in being there. Nobody that I talk to, there, wants to meet in real life. They think it's disgusting. I'm so lonely. I wish I had a daughter like Minnie."

Jamie shrugged.

"Those Body-Only people, that's what they say, too, but it's not all they make it out to be. Since she turned five and ported in, she hasn't asked me a single question. She doesn't want to know what I think about anything. Her friends show her how to hack the learning programs so she can get information she shouldn't have, yet. She's not like a kid. She's a miniature big person."

"People have kids and don't let them port, ever," Kelly said in a rush. "People have kids off-grid."

Jamie raised an eyebrow.

"Women get raped off-grid, is what you mean. I've seen skeletons of off-grid mothers with the skeletons of their unborn babies mixed in, like. You want to end up like that? You would have, if I hadn't been the one to find you. Why do you think Mom and Dad went to the station instead of the wild?"

"That's if they ever made it there," Kelly whispered, the blood draining from her face. "If they did, do you think they had more children, when we never arrived?"

"I dunno." He rubbed his face with both hands. "Look, Kelly, I'm sorry I'm not in Unity often enough for us to hang out. I'm sorry Minnie doesn't drag her sorry miniature self out of that chair any more than she absolutely has to. If you want a daughter, you should have a virtual one, you know?"

She shook her head immediately, but he held up his hand again.

"I don't mean a virtual kid, a copy of someone. I mean like what the Scandinavians do. Unity mixes your genome with the father's genome, and you get the randomized result, same as if sperm was mixing with eggs. You don't get to argue and you don't get to change anything. You just raise what you get."

"But it's not real, Jamie."

"Of course it's real. It's a real artificial intelligence that never existed before. Unity models the interaction between genes and environment. It's exactly the same as if you had a kid in the flesh world, except it doesn't need air, or water, or food, or any of those things that we're so short of."

Kelly looked at his starved, hollow face. She thought of how fat she had been on her return from the white world. The aliens had not been short of resources.

"Who would the father be?"

He looked embarrassed. "Me, I guess."

She recoiled. "You?"

"It's not taboo any more, brothers and sisters. How could it be? No real children are being born. No real children are getting inbred. What does a Unity kid care about being infertile or getting cancer? You can patch that shit. At least, you could, if you ever went to work."

Wildlife may be damaged in ways we cannot detect. The xenobiologist may screen for pathogens and other physical defects, but accurate assessment of human mental capacity is currently unavailable.

—Did you assimilate this morning?

    —Jid, it's not my fault.

    —Did you?

    —How was I supposed to know they would send a colony ship?

    —They interrogated our module with that crude AI of theirs. Instead of staying away from us, instead of improving their shuttles and avoiding our planet, they are coming to live here. Feed a human and it loses its fear. Then it becomes aggressive. You know this.

    —I suppose there's only one thing I can do to make amends. I'll go personally to the human planet and remove knowledge of us from that crude AI of theirs, after the module with the girl in it lands on the planet but before the colony ship is launched.

    —How can you do that, Sil? You have nothing.

    —Exactly. So why stay here? I could send you back reports. Observe them in the wild. You could buy me another module. You're old and you don't even want offspring. If that colony ship gets here, the others will find out exactly what we did.

    —Maybe it's time to confess.

    —Please, Jid. Let me go. I can fix this.

Decisions to rescue and treat humans in an emergency setting must be based on sound biodiversity and system health principles yet take into account animal welfare and the emotions of local onlookers.

Kelly stared hollowly at the child she had thought she wanted, through the mirror that was actually one-way glass, in the ballet school that Unity had virtually built for her.

As the other children had departed, hand in virtual hand with their parents, none of those parents had called their costumed children beautiful or their mastery well-earned.

Beauty was cheap, here. Anybody could be beautiful. Anyone could buy mastery. *Thank you,* the parents had said instead. *My child had fun.*

Fun. They did not bother to judge her choreography on its originality. The forms of the dancers were irrelevant to onlookers who had not paid for the right information downloads to appreciate the art form, who had other sights to see more individually tailored to their tastes. The new dances she had created were fun, or they were not fun. If a child could not perform the dances, they waited for their free upgrade and made something that once only looked effortless, truly effortless.

Hey beautiful, the handsome man in the office at the spaceport had said.

The great grace, the Unity Therapist had said reverently, *and skill of your grandmother at the height of her career.*

Now you're empty, her mother had said. *Now you can breathe in again.*

The second man had whistled. *That's no animal. That's the most perfect woman I've ever seen.*

Kelly was beautiful, for real. Nobody knew that, here. She couldn't stay. She had to go somewhere where the things that she had, her beauty and her ability to endure the unendurable—two lonely, pitiful things of value—were readily observable. She had to go where her grande allegros would shake the core of a solid structure, where her pirouettes would shift the station, ever so slightly, in space. She had to go where she could be broken, in order to prove that they could not break her.

Take those shoes off at once, Mama had ordered, her nostrils flaring, *or I'll whip your backside.*

She had been whipped, but she had worn the shoes anyway, and hidden her bruises under her pale pink tights.

Kelly Junior ran up to the glass. He breathed on it, a great hot huff that made it fog up, right before drawing a love-heart shape in it.

"Hi, Mum!" he shouted. He was six years old. "I know you're watching me. I'm having so much fun!"

That fact was never in dispute. He had never been hungry, except when he'd been hungry for her embrace; he had never been tired or bored. It would have been impossible for Kelly to whip him, when he could so easily mute pain. His fat little hands felt their way along the barre with silent awe, knowing that it was a replica in Unity of the one Kelly's grandmother had left to her descendants. But no matter how often he touched it; banged it; swung from it, howling, pretending to be a monkey, it could not change.

Kelly traced her full cheeks, her padded arms and thighs. In the maintenance cell, in the flesh world, she was as thin, now, as Minnie had ever been. She had hoarded enough food to pay bribes to the next generation of men who waited in offices at understaffed spaceports.

She would take the next ship to Centauri station. She would leave her happy child behind. Jamie wouldn't need to take care of him. The Unity would do that. And if he was unhappy, if he missed her, what of it? He looked beautiful, he looked like hers and Jamie's child, but he wasn't.

He could never understand her, or the ghosts of women who stood behind her.

• • •

Human mass-strandings are rare, but they do occur. When human colony ship (see ref p. 107) of unknown manufacture (mass measured at 0.93 x 10^9 moles of iron) crashed during the Great Seasonal Solidification at Center-Facing, several hundred animals might have frozen before they were found, if not for the fortuitous coincidence of Professor E. Jid (see ref p.55) being present in the field taking star-images with assistant X. Sil.

Professor and assistant, between them, were able to place all surviving animals in zoological parks. The ship's computer was never found and the circumstances that led to this stranding remain a puzzle to eminent xenobiologists in the field today.

A Gift in Time

MAGGIE CLARK

Though July 9, 1937 was a warm Friday, and all the warmer for events in its early morning, Mouse shivered as he stood before the roaring 2 a.m. blaze in Little Ferry, New Jersey, and considered (not for the first time) that there was no time machine, not really—just the desperate will of his quickly beating heart, which could secure for him all things, it seemed, but that which he most desired.

To the two Little Ferry firefighting companies had been added all six from Ridgefield Park, and two other firemen besides, who had broken from their own teams to help defend—if not the Fox Film plant, for its vaults were now clearly beyond repair—at least the neighboring residences, from whence had just poured trembling, agitated families whose members would all be dead or nearly so by the year to which Mouse now intended to return. He might have stopped the blaze entirely, he knew; might have spared these people their long night's hardship, and tens of thousands in damages besides—but how much less spectacular his recent work would then become. Some measure of loss, he tried to convince himself, was necessary to make more impressive all that remained.

This small regret still twisting in his gut, Mouse walked stiffly from the cacophony at the corner of Franklin and Main, well into the shadows of a side street, before willing himself over half a dozen decades out. Perhaps this was all a dream, but if not, he had prescience enough for the implications of being seen to disappear, streaking in that wrenching, heartsick way of his across the old century and beyond—nudging himself, too, far from the geography of his starting point as he progressed. Mouse kept one hand tucked under his coat throughout his heart's strange voyage, fingers clammy on the wide and blunted tin, its package of cellulose nitrate shifting in minute ways within. Even then he was loath to let go when he found himself back in his little stockroom office, with the bulky metal desk he seemed to catch his knee on every time.

"Mr. Musset!"

Mouse started at the voice wending imperiously down the hall, then swore and stumbled as his desk did its inevitable work upon him, and as the tin slipped past his belt before he caught it up again. "Coming!" he said, while with shaking hands he set his latest treasure on a corner stack with eleven of its kin. For a heartbeat more his hands hovered over the last of his rescues, afraid to touch any of them now that the set stood together in this time, this place—complete. Not yet in the best of storage, their quiet volatility became enough to make him fear (if in a vague, ill-reasoned way) even the heat of his own skin.

"Coming!" he said again, when he had mastered himself anew, and pressed both palms vigorously against his coat until they felt mostly dry. He doubled back only once, to close the door behind him, and again to check that it was locked.

Ezra Levitz's desk was of a sprawling, rich mahogany that seemed to have surged up one night from the burnished hardwood floor. All about him in the cathedral of a front room to Mr. Hazlitt's massive study, relics extending well into antiquity—vases, sculptures, tapestries, instruments and armor—stood elevated by aspects of their staging to testaments of mankind's greatness, yet to Mouse there stood no piece in this whole collection more a triumph of the species than the haughty curl of Ezra's upper lip.

His hands pressed flat against his trousers, Mouse stopped just short of an invisible line on the floor that, whenever passed, never failed to spark in Ezra's eyes a deeper disdain than Mouse could bring himself most days to bear. But today that chasm seemed even wider, and as Ezra brandished a sheaf of vellum pages in a long and slender, clenching hand, Mouse stepped quickly from its new precipice.

"*Mr.* Musset," said the young, magisterial exhibit, from behind its fulsome showcase. "I am left to wonder sometimes if you think yourself paid by Mr. Hazlitt not only to make a public spectacle of your credulity, but to do so at *such* risk to your employer's reputation."

"Is there . . . " started Mouse, fearing as he did that he would not find it in himself to go on—and yet, somehow, he did: "Is there something wrong with the manuscript?"

"Is there! *Is* there!" The *ha!* that followed this mocking echo might have ended civilizations, for all that it shook the pillars of Mouse's heart. "I would ask you to consider the extreme implausibility that there should come to your notice first—*yours*, Mr. Musset!—the existence of a work so monumental, so potentially transformative, as a second version of *Beowulf* itself. An uncharred account, at that—every page spared from moth larvae, tankard print, water-logging; even the greed of ancient cobblers! A story so fully told that the hoard-thief's part now reads entirely without question, and with names so clear throughout that even the most incompetent historian can see all the lineages for what they truly are. A version with certain parts even told at *better* length than our extant text, especially when it comes to all the petty politics in the last third! Oh, they're all nice touches, Mr. Musset—I'll give you that—but it's a *fraud*. An utter forgery just the same."

Mouse stood a quivering, breathless entity from across the chasm of the burnished floor—his lips parted, slack, as Ezra pulled out a metal waste bin and set it on the desk. For all the cruelty of the lecture, Mouse did not fail to notice that it had also been perfectly rehearsed, and his heart could not help but rally at the passion he had produced. To think of all the time Ezra must have spent thinking on him (him!) so as to frame this fiery rebuke! And *oh*—to press his advantage! To make that upper lip curl his way just a little longer!

"Oh no, Mr. Levitz," said Mouse quickly, his hands and ears growing hot. "There must be some mistake. This text *is* a fair copy of *Beowulf*; of that I can assure you if only—"

"Assure me?" Young Adonis snorted, tossing the manuscript whole within the bin. "I have had quite enough *assurance*, Mr. Musset, from the carbon dating Mr. Hazlitt had performed. Granted, the calligraphy is clever, and the materials all true to form—but how old would you say *Beowulf* is? Tenth century? Maybe eighth?" (Mouse found he could only nod now, and miserably at that, for a lump pitched itself high in his throat as his fool error dawned on him, long before dear Ezra gave it voice.) "Or late twentieth, Mr. Musset?" Ezra rattled the bin. "Because this copy most certainly did not sit in someone's collection for over a thousand years, just waiting to be discovered. It might have been penned a year ago—a month!—for all the vellum's aged. And I would be curious to learn about the forger and his methods—indeed, I imagine Mr. Hazlitt would be, too—if we weren't both so sick with disappointment at the whole miserable affair. You *know*, Mr. Musset; you *know* how much we adore the culture and history surrounding the original text."

"I do," said Mouse, quite softly, watching with a stab of something like remorse as Ezra lit a match and cast it in the bin.

"Good. Then I trust—I *hope*, at least—that we'll see an end to such lapses in the future. Mr. Hazlitt, as you well know, has more than earned the right not to be trifled with by any among his staff. Fair warning, Mr. Musset."

"I will do my best, Mr. Levitz." Mouse inclined his head. "Is there anything else?"

"Oh, yes—take this." Ezra's expression twisted with a revulsion not directed at Mouse, for once, but rather the stench now blooming alongside flames within the bin, which he thrust over the desk. Eagerly Mouse breached the usual divide—just long enough to take the offending object up into his arms, and maybe then to . . .

But before Mouse could graze so much as one exquisite finger, the young secretary turned away—poised, it seemed, to retire into the recesses of Mr. Hazlitt's study the moment his subordinate scurried out. Mouse had almost made it back to his little office before remembering what delicate prizes still lay within, prepared at even the slightest provocation to spark in turn, and realized that the air about him was already thickening with fetid smoke. The metal bin was hot at all sides now, so gingerly he set it down outside the little room, between two shelving units of sturdy pottery, and opened the nearest, narrow windows before crouching to watch the old-new vellum—snatched just weeks prior from some early medieval Christian with long, flaxen hair and weather-beaten countenance, while the latter answered his wife's gruff call to a joint of lamb and prayer—give in its gradual way to ash.

At least in this, Mouse conceded with some envy, the full first manuscript of *Beowulf* had earned a proper Anglo-Saxon burial. His own heart still burned to a far less final end.

In the wake of this crowning failure, Mouse also realized that he could neither present his latest treasures in short order—not at least until Ezra's affected fury had died down—nor expect them to escape *Beowulf's* fate in their current form. The ensuing weeks passed slowly, then, and wretchedly, as Mouse turned over this new puzzle and in fits of agony convinced himself to keep out of Ezra's way and sight until the longing in his heart ceased to hurt as much—resolutions that lasted hours, at best, apiece.

There was, of course, plenty else to do, for Mouse's steady industry lay in receiving lots for Mr. Hazlitt, classifying them by quality and type, then adding them to the general catalogue, from which Mr. Hazlitt would from time to time select his favorites for private collections and reallocate the rest. Whole happy hours might be spent this way, documenting and detailing and otherwise lifting ancient objects from the anonymity of years-long storage, until Ezra's voice trilled in passing down the hall—the sweet, honeyed aspects of his speech always blossoming for Mr. Hazlitt, whose voice would always soften in its turn.

Mouse had no vague notions, either, of what transpired beyond Mr. Hazlitt's study doors whenever their employer called for Ezra at lunch or late in the afternoon. Rather, Mouse had played out these scenarios with great detail and even greater ambivalence as the months turned to years at his post: some days resenting that Mr. Hazlitt should exploit his secretary in this most time-worn way; the rest, with his own office door securely locked, moaning to whatever gods would listen that he could not do likewise on a whim.

He had tried, long before his first flight to millennia past, to secure for himself a decades-old bank account with interest that might make him rich in his own time, but three failed attempts had been enough to dispel him of the notion that money would ever be enough to elevate himself in Ezra's eyes. The first time, Mouse had neglected key aspects of identity required to open a new account, and almost found himself arrested in the late '40s before his quickly beating heart whisked him desperately away (hitting his head, on his return, both on the desk and a cabinet door he had neglected to close that morning). The second time, the correct papers in hand, he had failed instead in his calculations, and the sum awaiting him on his return was not nearly enough for the grandiosity of his dreaming. The third time—calculations squared, investments made, papers all secure—he returned to what seemed an impossible sum . . . and then stood rigid with fear. Now what?

That was the day he followed Ezra's laughter to a scene with Mr. Hazlitt looming behind the desk, behind Ezra, the pair inspecting rude clerical marginalia in a collection of twelfth-century songs. Mr. Hazlitt straightened at leisure as Mouse approached, and with a squeeze of Ezra's shoulder bid him to step into the study later, when he was *through*.

"Mr. Musset," said Mr. Hazlitt, with a nod.

"Mr. Hazlitt," said Mouse, with a deeper one.

"Well, what is it?" said Ezra, his voice one long exhalation of breath when the doors slid shut behind their employer. He withdrew a comb and took to preening at his desk.

Mouse faltered at this brilliantly arrogant sight, then stumbled through his explanation of the great deal of money he had just come into—the great house he expected to buy; the collections he would surely maintain, if only . . .

"If only what?" said Ezra, sharply. "Out with it, Mr. Musset. I haven't got all day."

But the words to follow from Mouse's lips were hardly uttered in full before Ezra's laughter subsumed all else.

"Why you dirty old man," said fair Adonis—at which Mouse could not help but bristle, for Mr. Hazlitt was surely older—"Do you think me so easily bought as that? Oh, go away, will you? If you're so rich why haven't you left your job yet? Or maybe you've fallen in love with those dusty shelves, and that cage of an office that smells even worse than you?"

Mouse realized then that he wouldn't quit—he couldn't. Not all the money in the world could get him to leave the singular post in which he might five-days-weekly come to bask, to tremble, to utterly abase himself before that one radiant creature who had come to stand in his heart for everything worth anything in this whole, long, middling life. Mouse could have thrown his newfound riches at lesser beauties and lesser tempers; he might have spent his remaining years indulging duller passions that might have brought their own warmth and tenderness in time—but how could it be anything but death to do so? To give up on the most animated, the most brightly gleaming object ever to grace his sky?

So Mouse returned to his work instead, this fresh rejection no more a hardship on him than any of the rest: all those daily rebukes in look and gesture that nonetheless confirmed that there was feeling—genuine feeling!—for him in Ezra's breast. Just not the right kind of feeling. At least not yet.

When the opportunity arose, then, to answer the soft sighs and wistful declarations that Ezra and Mr. Hazlitt sometimes shared during business in the front room—*O, for a version of this story that wasn't burned!*—Mouse's heart flew at once after ancient *Beowulf*, the sheer desperation of his need, his longing, a kind of zipline through the centuries that the rest of him careened along. The next trek, to 1937, was almost an afterthought, a moment's indulgence after the fleeting hope that had sprung from placing his first prize in Ezra's hands—or at least, on Ezra's massive desk, sliding it across for the younger man to acknowledge in his own time, and initially to marvel at when he did. But now Mouse had only the movie tins to go on—Ezra sighing one day over old film photos as Mr. Hazlitt looked on, and as Mouse made adjustments to a showcase elsewhere in the room; Ezra saying then, *Now that was an age for beauty, wasn't it? Just look at her—such a pity this one was lost*, and going on to note Mr. Hazlitt's likeness to the director, Murnau—something in the nose, and the forehead, and maybe, from the look of those sturdy hands . . .

So it did not matter that the two fell silent at this last, glancing significantly Mouse's way; Mouse simply brought his work to a convenient halt and left them to each other, his heart lightened by the promise of a new adventure. How much Janet Gaynor's character had ached for her fickle circus partner in *4 Devils*! And how much Ezra might, if brought to watch the reclaimed film in full, come to ache for Mouse's plight at least as much as hers.

Mouse's indecision lasted just over two weeks, after which he resolved to carry his precious cargo to a suburban town outside Washington, DC. Rockville in

1972 still seemed to be struggling towards self-sufficiency: its brand-new mall established in a mostly overlooked location, relying on interstate traffic more than downtown clientele; surrounding commercial buildings progressing at uneven rates towards completion; and nearer the edge of town, a little business standing just in its first year, helmed by a bright-eyed owner keen on telecine processing and other forms of filmic preservation. Mouse's hands shook as he offered up his twelve tins of 35mm negatives—the names scored from half the cases before it had occurred to him that the title cards in the first reel would still reveal their heritage.

Discovery could not be helped, then, inasmuch as the director's name would surely be recognized by the professional cinephile. Mouse had thought of doing the exacting work of film transfer and restoration himself to avoid it—even perused a guide or two in his fortnight's anguish—but ultimately he feared the fragile reels too much, and even more his clumsy hands, which seemed inflamed enough these days all on their own. He only hoped his story would hold—the private collection; the eccentric heiress to a Hollywood fortune with the Library of Congress written into her will; his own covert attempt, as day-to-day manager of this estate, to ensure that there would *be* something worth donating when she was gone. But Mouse need not have worried; though the employee he met was friendly and curious, professionalism did not trespass further than a moment's delight at the opportunity to work with such an old and unique piece. Most of the day-to-day work, the frontman explained, consisted of government and media reels for immediate release.

"Fiction of a different kind," he added with a wink, while Mouse carefully counted out a stack of bills procured years prior with gold converted from the cash in his future bank portfolio. The friendly fellow then gave him an estimated completion date and Mouse could hardly get himself into a remote area before the sharp ache in his heart drew him forward—almost running into a telephone pole as he first adjusted to the change of day.

With his negatives transplanted to the far more stable Plus-X panchromatic film stock, and the two versions secure in separate canisters, Mouse next acquired a security box at his old bank, with payment in advance for the next fifty years, in which he placed the latter. If there was curiosity this time among the staff, their professionalism kept it in check as well, leaving only the matter of the originals, which Mouse was loath to part with, but even less inclined to keep in so volatile a form. His heart thus answered for him, reeling him back to just past midnight on July 9, 1937, where he waited out of sight for his earlier self to rob the vault before stealing in to make things right.

Watching himself thereafter at a distance, shivering with weeks-old guilt on the corner of Franklin and Main, Mouse faltered for just one desperate beat in his convictions—a whisper of futility coursing through him as he observed the myriad faults in his character, his form, upon that firelit main road. *How would anyone— How could Ezra ever—* These were only whispers, though, and then the familiar ache took hold, flinging him decades out again. Upon his return, with the concreteness of his efforts finally setting in, Mouse found himself so excited he didn't even notice the desk corner assail his knee in that little cluttered office. *A good night's sleep first*, he decided, albeit with great difficulty—for though no more than a lunch hour had passed in this timeline, Mouse's recent travels had left him with the conviction that he could sleep for days—and so he did, in a bed-and-breakfast in rural 1958.

Ezra seemed in high spirits when a well-rested Mouse at last approached with a restored copy of that old, lost film in hand, the former merely notching an immaculate brow as Mouse passed the invisible border by a whole step or two.

"Hold on, Alan," said merciful Adonis, seated in a modernized Classical pose—black phone cord coiled about his sculpted fingers, which he held aloft from the pedestal of his padded office throne; his other hand poised over a touchpad just as the ancient subject of a Renaissance painting might lord over some natural element in the surrounding pastoral idyll. "I've got company. Yes, *exactly*. Five minutes, all right?—*Yes*, Mr. Musset?"

Mouse meant to choose his words with care as he held out the canisters, mindful of the agonies his body underwent whenever proximate to Ezra's light, but even then the words tumbled into one another, and occasionally lost their place. *From the last shipment*, he started—*these—I thought you might—you seemed to like—remember?—Janet Gaynor*. At last he could say no more, so he simply set them on the desk.

Ezra's noble forehead creased as he drew the items close enough to read their labels, but when he had he merely laughed and pushed the lot aside.

"And why on earth should I care about this sentimental junk? Because I looked over a movie still or two with Mr. Hazlitt? Incredible, Mr. Musset. Don't you realize I was only using those dumb old things as far as they would flatter him? Do you honestly think you can guess what *I* want from what I say when I'm with *him*?"

Mouse felt his heart wrench first towards the usual despair—then confusion. Had Ezra's voice not softened, even wavered in that last thought? Was there not a thread of fragility, of loneliness trapped beneath his haughty words? To always echo another's interest; to always *be* precisely what another wants him to be—Mouse could not help but thrill at this shadow of a defect in Ezra's gleaming marble, though the rest of Mouse's body still shook with disappointment at the failure of his weeks-long work.

"Tell me, then," said Mouse, with upthrust chin. "What do *you* want, Mr. Levitz?"

And Ezra laughed—a short, curt thing. "What do *I* want?" His sneer faltered only slightly, then held firm. He stood and turned away, taut knuckles rapping at the desk. "All right, Mr. Musset. If you really want to prove yourself—"

"Yes!" cried Mouse. "Yes, I do."

Ezra paused, then dismissed this sad outcry with a flick of his wrist and a moody scowl. "Well, find my ring, then. It's eighth-century goldcraft, studded with garnet—you'll find the listing in a collection Mr. Hazlitt put together five years ago, when I first started working here." Ezra faced Mouse directly again, his eyes now lit in triumph. "It was his first gift to me. He saw how much I loved the damned thing, and just like that—it was mine."

And you his, Mouse realized, though he dared not speak aloud. Before Ezra had even begun explaining the vague details of his ensuing loss, Mouse's mind's eye had already seized upon the exact scene, and all the minutiae Ezra had since forgotten—the warm spring night; a society function in the atrium and garden of an estate house by the coast; rich piano music drifting up the stairwell to where Mr. Hazlitt had secured his young aide for a moment alone in his colleague's study; the reckless energy and rumpled clothes; the gold ring slipping into the gold-flecked earth about a potted fern. It would be so easy to steal in just after this breathless moment, to snatch the treasure back—but Mouse's jealous heart refused to draw him there. *Why should I not present it first?* Before *Mr. Hazlitt muscles in?*

It took a hard rap on the desk to call him back. "*Well, Mr. Musset?*"

Even then, Mouse was so raw with renewed optimism that he could hardly do more than smile and nod—and certainly could no longer control himself as his desperate, aching heart seized upon a different scene, an ancient scene, and pulled him swiftly back.

"I promise you—I swear to you—" Ezra would later think he'd heard as Mr. Musset's body blurred before him. Eventually those trumped up words would come to haunt him even more than that this strange, despairing man then winked abruptly out.

Mouse came to a halt in another era, another country, only to trip and tumble down the side of a steep, stone barrow on a cold, late autumn's night. When he looked about him at the Swedish heathlands of yesteryear, he wondered at first if there had been some mistake, but no—as he took unsteadily to his feet he spied a narrow opening in a nearby mound, the lick of some idle fire within illuminating a heap of goldcraft beneath banners bearing a dragon in their heraldry. His heart ever driving him on, he wriggled through and made his careless way about the pile, kicking shields and cups and belts into chamber recesses until his fingers seized upon their target—finding his prize just in time to register a violent rumbling elsewhere in the low, lit room, and then to whip away through time and space.

Hurtling back to the present with prize in hand, Mouse gave himself over to laughter at long and precious last—a manic, joyous sound that struggled to give voice to all the slings and arrows of a years-long campaign nearing its triumphant end. How could Ezra refuse him now, with this—his self-admitted heart's desire? But Mouse's palms were so clammy with anticipation that the little gold piece began to slip, and when with a frantic cry he twisted to catch it up again his flightpath slowed in turn. The loss of momentum was enough then—just enough—to catch him in Lower Saxony one wet and miserable morning in August 1626, where cannon fire and the storm of cavalry barely had time to register in his ringing ears before a ball of lead found the center of his ribs.

The sky above him was an endless, mottled gray as his eyes rolled up. Speechless in the ensuing pain, Mouse sank to his knees, where he found just breath enough to marvel that he had not seen this coming all along: the hard collisions that inevitably followed any moment, in any era, through which he had always been able to fling himself when the present just would not do. But the present had simply *never* done, thought Mouse in the last, tired throes of consciousness, so what other end had there ever been for him to find?

The ring had already fallen from Mouse's hand into the cold, thick mud—not to be discovered right at the battle's close, when Tilly's army picked through the remnants of both Protestant and Catholic dead, but by a farmer in the years thereafter, who passed it down his family line before at last it stood appraised and hocked, slipping from private collection to collection until one year, early in the twenty-first century, when Mr. Hazlitt would receive it with great curiosity—a piece of eighth-century design, but also of most uncertain lineage.

A bauble among baubles all the same, Mr. Hazlitt would soon enough observe with far greater amusement how his new secretary attended to the little piece every time he entered the massive study on some trumped up errand—and O, how those proud, fiery eyes glittered when the ring was at last made into an offering.

"Do you know what a man called the giver-of-rings in those days?" said Mr. Hazlitt.

"His king, of course," said Ezra in one low, soft breath.

And sure enough, a sense of that ancient *wyrd* had come upon Ezra as he held up the ring, for he could almost feel an inner warmth to the old, dead thing—as if someone's destiny were still writ upon it; as if that little bit of metal, so useless unto itself, had somehow traveled through the centuries for just this purpose: to be here now; to be claimed by *him*. Mr. Hazlitt basked awhile in Ezra's changed and glowing countenance before moving in.

Never Dreaming (In Four Burns)
SETH DICKINSON

trans-mortal injection: t+1 day

"I'm going to lose the ability to dream," Nur Zaleha tells her best friend. "Then I'm going to die."

In the vacuum of the test chamber, the plasma thruster ignites, a brilliant violet arc, silent, steady. Her beloved engine, her daughter. Alight.

"What? That's insane," Siv says, pale antishadow in the engine glare, a slim tall shard of brighter light. "That can't be right."

"It's called sporadic familial insomnia. There's nothing they can do."

Siv shakes her head, backlit, frowning. "I don't believe it. Get a second opinion."

Zaleha's been imagining this conversation for hours, now. Siv will try to figure out a way to fix her—she'll write to some gene therapy clinic in Stanford or Minnesota or Boston, volunteering Zaleha as a subject. Or she'll try to get Zaleha into an induced coma, clinical substitute for the sleep she's about to lose forever. Siv, a zealous futurist, keeps track of all these biotech dreams, cures and augments and embryos with two mothers.

But none of it will help.

Siv's always been ghoulishly agentic. She can never let the world have its way.

"I'm the ninth case ever diagnosed," Zaleha says, smiling bravely. "Isn't that cool? Double methionine at codon 129. Incredibly rare."

Siv stares at her, plasma flare mirrored, starlike, in her goggles, like she's just thought of something so brilliant it's burning out her skull. "Oh, Z," she says. "Oh, no." And then, as the computer recites specific impulse and exhaust velocity, *nominal at seven zero point seven two kilometers per second,* "Is it a secret?"

Zaleha nods, her own goggles abruptly ineffective—her eyes have started to prickle. "I want to keep working," she says, and then, horribly choked up, please, she has to get a hold of herself, here where the whole test crew's watching, "keep trying to fix the symmetry fault and get the thruster flight-ready, until—uh—until it's not, you know, practical any more—"

Siv holds her, even though it's unprofessional, even though the crew will notice and she doesn't have an excuse. Zaleha hugs her back, and stands on her toes to stare over Siv's shoulder, into the plasma shine, into the glare of the engine she built, searching—

And there he is, the visitor, the malak, the angel, her childhood haunt, her *other* secret.

Tariune.

He looks out at her through the exhaust spike, the cloak of fairy fire. And even through the vacuum, she hears him ask: *will you come now? Has this made you ready?*

Of course he's in there. Mom and Dad, trying to raise a good Muslim daughter, always told Zaleha that the malaa'ikah were made of light.

Go away, she thinks, and then, regretting it instantly, *please help me—*

He's already gone.

"*Field azimuth symmetry fault,*" the control officer calls. "*Abort test. Abort test.*"

The plasma thruster shuts down. The light goes out.

post-burn systems check

Siv telemetry:

Later Siv asks her: "Why tell me then? Right in the middle of a test fire?"

Because I was surrounded by everything important to me, Zaleha wants to say. But if she did, Siv would tease her for being maudlin. Siv Ahlstrom, a rocket scientist through and through, doesn't like feelings that can't be immediately converted into action.

"We'll fix that symmetry fault," Siv says. She squeezes Zaleha's shoulder reassuringly. "It's going to work."

They've had four test fires now, and three of them have aborted on that damn fault—active magnetics trying to enforce symmetry. Slipping.

Tariune telemetry:

She's never believed that he's really malak, an angel. (If she believed, she wouldn't have pissed him off five years ago.) He came to a young Zaleha, pre-empirical, practically pre-conscious, and so she understood him as a piece of the world, natural by definition. To a little kid, absent any metafaculties, perception *is* reality. Take her rattle out of sight, hide it behind Bapa's back, and it ceases to exist. Put a man with golden eyes and golden skin in her nursery, a smoke-smell man who can, in the space between his circled thumb and forefinger, open windows into a world of amber and blood and myth, a world of true names—put him there, and young Zaleha accepts him.

She grew up into an engineer, a scientist, steeped in skepticism, armed with instruments of rationality and phenomenology. But even post-diagnosis, she's never doubted her own sanity. Tariune *is* real. His world is real. He can step between Aura and her world, the place he calls Coldworld, by his own logic, wholly separate from the unity and symmetry of physics. There are patterns, sure—he likes to arrive in dreams, because dreams are the parts of her closest to Aura, the closest thing she has to an Auran soul. But these patterns do not yield to the same analysis.

(As a teenager she tried to work out Aura's *magic system,* the rules of Tariune's appearances and capabilities. Eventually she understood the futility of the project. Systems didn't really function in Aura. It was nuministic, narrative, driven by an alternative causality. Dreams, though—very big. Very central.)

In the darkest passages of her childhood, Tariune told her exactly what she wanted to hear:

"I know your destiny," he'd whisper, his voice a better class of sound, his words a language she'd never had to learn, pressed, somehow, straight into her brain, meanings rather than signifiers. He could speak raw truth. The Knowing.

"You're going to cross over. You're going to learn, and struggle, and grow mighty. You're going to save us all."

Once, curious, her skepticism waxing, she asked: "Why me, though?"

Tariune frowned in thought, regal mantle slipping away from the weary earnest man beneath, the salt and leather behind the prince's silk. "I don't know how to explain it. The Rhexics heard your dreams in the cold and they told me—" He shook his head. "They said *look on her,* and I knew you were the right one. I knew."

She liked the man behind the silk and portent. "And do they tell you what to say to me, too?" she teased.

"No." A memory of pain in his smile, offered in solidarity. "I just remember what I wanted to hear, when my world started to break."

Self telemetry:

The double-methionine mutation at codon 129 of the PRNP prion gene causes cells to produce a faulty copy of the cellular prion protein PRPC. The glycoprotein folds wrong, creating an isoform—well, the biochemistry gets complicated, but the effects are simple.

Within the year, she's going to lose the ability to enter REM sleep. Unable to regenerate or reintegrate or whatever the hell it's supposed to do during REM, her brain will start to break down. Over the next few months, she will become paranoid and anxious, then begin to hallucinate, then lose the ability to sleep entirely. If she doesn't kill herself first, she'll enter terminal dementia, withdraw from all outside stimulation, and die.

Every time she wakes up from a dream she thinks: *it hasn't started yet.* And: *that could have been the last one.*

She's never going to see her engine fly. NASA wants to test it on a JPL comet-rendezvous mission. A private spaceflight company wants to buy it to drive their metallic asteroid prospectors. If these missions succeed, Nur Zaleha's engine may give humanity (or its robots, at least) the solar system. But she'll be dead first.

Her engine, her *engine.* The finest actively stabilized pulse-resonant plasma thruster ever invented, a nearly ideal system. It's not particularly large or powerful—a petite, lightweight drive that exerts barely more force than the weight of a few pennies. But it's preposterously fuel-efficient. It can send tiny robotic spacecraft across the solar system with speed and grace and enviable reliability. Amateurs care about thrust. Professionals want specific impulse.

It's *elegant*. She made something beautiful out of lithium and current. She's so proud of it—or she will be, once she fixes this damn field malfunction, the persistent symmetry fault that keeps scuttling their tests.

Tariune probably hates it.

mid-course corrections: t+3 days

She has to tell her mom, her dad, her whole topologically baffling network of aunts, snarled up across continents and languages. It's the hardest fucking thing she's ever done. Her grief makes her brittle and when they ask stupid questions—"Can't you just take sleeping pills?"—she goes off like a, well, yeah, like a rocket, a big noisy chemical rocket, the kind that explodes on the pad. Not the kind she designs.

It's too much. Afterwards, she calls Siv, who, having split with her girlfriend and joined Zaleha in the solitary hell-covenant of Total Engineering Life, has replaced Zaleha's family as her great pillar of solace. "Hey. Want to come over and watch—" She kicks her stack of DVDs and allows the collapse to present a title. "Cosmos?"

"*Can't sleep?*"

It's an ordinary question, delivered casually, but it gives Zaleha chills. "It's still early," she says.

"*I'll stay as long as you want.*" Siv's voice hushes conspiratorially. "*Hey. Is weed haram?*"

"Probably." She doesn't keep haram, exactly, but she doesn't drink either. She's an unbeliever now, but still a complete square. The lamest apostate.

"*You're dying, dude. You should smoke weed.*"

Zaleha laughs, a really good, genuine laugh, and then sits in silence, thinking: I don't want to change because I'm dying. I want to stay the same.

But they get high on the apartment balcony, cursing the light pollution, the piss-yellow wash of sodium lamplight that drowns out all the stars. After a little while Siv gets quiet, her lips pursed, and starts looking around in a random walk that touches on everything except Zaleha's face.

"Hey," Zaleha says. "Hey. I want to tell you something."

Siv starts, her pale Scandinavian features somehow paler still. "Okay," she says.

Right now she trusts Siv with the chemical totality of a compromised system. "I have a really weird secret," she says, and then tells Siv everything about Tariune, about Aura, about being chosen.

"I know you," Siv says, at the end of the story. "So I know you've already checked out all the ordinary possibilities. Not a brain tumor. Not a psychosis. It's real."

"Yeah." Zaleha puts her head on Siv's bony shoulder. "There's no way to prove his existence to anyone else, but he's established it to my satisfaction. Thanks. I thought you might . . . "

Siv knows the disease will lead to hallucination.

"Well, I'm pretty high," Siv says, examining her hands with wide-eyed equanimity. "And you said you hadn't seen him for a while?"

"Before the test fire? Almost five years." Zaleha frowns up at the drowned sky. She wants to see the stars. "We had a couple of fights. He hates Coldworld—you know, Earth, the universe. He said I was ready to cross over."

"Why didn't you go? It sounds amazing." Real envy in Siv's voice, in her wide blue eyes. "You said magic? *Actual* magic?"

"Whole new kinds of causality, I think. It's a place about—stories, you know? About people. Instead of particles and laws." She shivers and draws up her knees, tucking herself closer to her friend. Siv stiffens a little, but doesn't draw away. "Which was why we fought. I got so tired of him going on about how *cold* and *soulless* and *meaningless* Earth seemed to him. 'An empty machine,' blah blah." She points up, not so much indicating a particular star as an axis, a vector written in her soul. "I wanted to go—out there, you know? Send people to another world. See trinary stars, baryons shattering into light on domain walls, wonders undreamt . . . he just saw dead rock and empty math."

No beauty in the color charge or the cataclysmic variable's polar jet, not to Tariune of Aura, not to the prince who climbed the steel ruin of armored mountains and listened at the peak for prophecy wind.

There's magic here, he'd said once, in an adjunct to your Coldworld physics. But it's vestigial. Nothing ever turned it on. Maybe whatever process built your world didn't care.

"I can't believe you. You had the golden ticket, dude. You got the Hogwarts letter." Siv tugs her earlobe like it might contain some missing insight. "And you wanted to stay here? You were *that* eager to watch Congress slash more funding, cancel a few more projects, a few hundred more careers?"

"It's magic to you. I grew up with it. Harder to be reverent, I guess?" Zaleha, giggling, thinks: boy, I *am* pretty high. "He's really gorgeous. I tried to sleep with him when I was nineteen. No one to judge, no consequences, I hated all the noble virgin shit. But he has some kind of tragic romance over in Aura, like a mortal enemy . . . it's part of this whole trouble we're going to fight . . . "

Silence from Siv. She has to crane her neck painfully to look into her friend's face. "Siv?"

She's crying. "Oh, Siv." Zaleha tries to squirm around to hug her.

"I don't want you to die," Siv chokes. "I really don't want you to die."

A long bottomless interval of grief, exhilarating in its raw truth—the kind of thing you don't talk about afterwards, because words would lessen it. Like free fall. Like the way Tariune speaks about Aura.

She offers to let Siv crash on her couch, although she's a bit too much of a giraffe to really fit. But Siv, reeling, refuses. She has to get home, yes, it'll be okay, she'll take the bus. "We're going to fix that symmetry fault," she says fiercely, wiping at her ashen cheeks. "We'll make it work. Before—"

She screws up her face and stumbles away, towards the bus stop.

The next time they see each other Siv says: "Man. Wow. We were *really* gone."

She finds Tariune in the simulations, knotted in the flux of the engine's electro-magnets, racing electrons around the circulating current of the exit plane. A defiant spark, obedient to no law.

"Hey," she says, whispering to the computer, unselfconscious, accustomed to this.

"I'm sorry," he says. That voice, that thrill of a voice, like a punch in the temporal lobe, a religious truth, every word a dogma. "I'm sorry I wasn't here. Oh, Nur Zaleha, what has your world done to you?"

"I thought it might be you, you know." That maybe he was trying to force her over with some curse of dreams. "I'm glad to be wrong." Because he can't lie to her. No one in Aura can lie in the Knowing, the un-language.

"Never." He flickers out of the engine like a heavy ion, a perfect trajectory, pulling a crown of electrons. Zaleha can't help but smile: *that's* how it's supposed to work. "But your time's running short now."

"I told you last time." She can't lie to him either. Can't even hide her pain. "I have to finish this, Tariune. I want to change things before I go."

"What can you change?" The simulation chases him along unwritten paths, into domains it can't have been programmed to handle, places modern physics itself might not understand: frothing subatomic seascapes, the quantum vacuum roiling with virtual particles, and Tariune the Prince in Aura racing through like a needle of un-rule, an anarch of physics. "Look at yourself. Struggling to make a new machine for those hunting new kinds of wealth. Fighting for a distant goal in a world that only cares for now. You are a dreamer in a world of prisons, Nur Zaleha, a chain of chains, and even if you fight through in time to make your mark, Coldworld will erase it. Death will take all your efforts. Even the stars will go out."

She watches in wonder and terror as the arrow of Tariune's passage pierces space and time, into an emptiness past the end of history, past the death of singularities and the decay of the proton and the Big Rip.

"This is not your world," he says. "This is a clockwork husk, winding down. Come to a place with *meaning*. Come and live forever. Come tonight, or tomorrow, or some day soon. Before it's too late."

"Too late?" she asks, already understanding. *Oh, no*—"I have months, don't I?"

The simulation withers away. Tariune stands before her, golden, majestic, not so much part of the room around her as a lamina over it, superliminal, more real than real. The man who stood when the Bane of Kings made his world kneel.

"You have to cross in a dream," he says. "Where you're closest to Aura."

"But if I can't dream . . ."

"You'll be lost forever." He closes his eyes. She notices, in the absence of some diffuse luminance, a light that casts no shadows, that he has grown small weary lines around his eyes. "Lost to Aura. To me."

She swallows against fear: sometimes it's easier not to know the answer. "If I go . . . can you cure me?"

"If you come," he says, eyes still closed, palms half-raised, the Rings of Rhexis dark on the first finger of each hand, "you will live the truth of your name. I promise."

Nur Zaleha binti Abdul Samad. Self-sufficient. Eternal.

"I missed you," she admits. "I was afraid you'd given up on me."

They'd been friends. Real friends. It hadn't all been proclamation and prophecy. They'd stayed up late, reading and complaining about how *elf* always meant *super-white*. Sort of the opposite of how she'd met Siv, super-white Swede, who'd told Zaleha (Malaysian, thanks) that she looked like the Iranian actress, Golshifteh Farahani, and pissed Zaleha off.

"You'll still be afraid, I suspect." Tariune smiles, at first one of those formal I-am-a-kind-Prince smiles, and then a real genuine toothy grin, relieved, spontaneous. "Aura needs the brave. You can only be brave when you're afraid."

"What do I lose?"

Because she knows there's a price. There's *always* a price. That's how these things work. You go to the world more real than real, the shining hard-edged place where you can fight and bleed and grieve and know it all means something. You'll be healed. But to go you've got to sacrifice . . .

"You can't return, of course. In body or in mind." He hesitates, the only kind of prevarication or indirection the Knowing allows. "You will become a creature of Aura when you are healed."

"What does that mean?"

"I come to Coldworld." He opens a hand and tiny quanta carom and merge in his palm. "But I'm only a visitor. I don't become clockwork. I don't become monist, closed, *causal*. When you become part of Aura, not just a visitor, but a mighty soul . . . "

"Then I'll think like you do. Good and evil. Destiny. Magic." Zaleha looks through him for a moment, to the diagrams pinned to her office walls, her desktop background, the currents of ion and electron she has tattooed onto her brain. The bones of her engine. "No more causal closure. No more materialism."

Not a rocket scientist any more.

It's not that she'll lose anything really important, right? Science is just a tool. Just a way to select between beliefs. To test utility. She won't need it any more. In Aura she'll be able to learn the truth from grinning spirits and speak it to the wind. She'll never have to do an experiment again.

"This machine," Tariune says, speaking carefully, looking at the plasma thruster diagrams, "is every reason you should come. A tiny little force, trying to gradually move something very big. They'll never put it on anything but a robot probe. And it doesn't even work."

Maybe he's always been right. Maybe she's just pissing her time away in an empty world, an indifferent mechanism iterating itself towards an empty future, doomed down to the last proton. She could be over there, armored in alabaster and the steel of vows, hunting salvation.

She lies awake that night, thinking about it, and passes into a terrible dream of Aura's end: eschaton kraken drowning the stars in a liquid-helium sea, the Bane of Kings triumphant on her throne of abrogated oaths. Zaleha wakes in terrified, anxious sweat, tangled in her sheets, flails for a moment, and then, the joy so sudden it seems like it must have broken something inside her, begins to sob in relief.

mortal insertion: t+9 days

Siv's been avoiding her. Zaleha hasn't pressed it, because she doesn't want to make Siv confront her own grief. But they end up standing side by side for the next test burn, in their usual places, like nothing's changed and nothing will.

In the hollow airless chamber, the thruster flickers to life. Ring electromagnets stripping lithium and hurling it as thrust. Light in the void.

I made that, Zaleha thinks. It's going to work. It's going to fly.

And then what? It gets put on somebody's spaceship, and then the ship gets cancelled? The company folds? Global warming eats civilization? What difference does it make?

As much difference as anything makes. The world doesn't stop when she does. Every word and crop and law and thruster keeps the adventure moving. Maybe the thrusters in particular.

"Hey," she says.

"Hey." Siv stares into the light, her goggles violet-black. "They stripped and rebuilt the whole Child-Langmuir feedback system. It's going to work this time."

"What if it doesn't?" Zaleha tries to look her in the eyes, and finds herself almost hypnotized by the starfire reflections moving in the goggles as Siv looks back. "What if we can't make it work before—my deadline?"

They both know what happens to most experimental propulsion projects. The guillotine's been there the whole time, just waiting for momentum to falter, for an obstacle that requires too much time or money to surmount. 2014 has not been a kind year to the field.

Siv draws a long breath. "Z," she says, "it's your engine. But I've been building simulations of it for two years. Wick, Jeb, Sobel, the rest of the crew—they're brilliant." She adjusts her goggles. "Nearly as brilliant as you, if you get them all together. We can keep working the problem. It's not so big, compared to everything you solved already. Just a little glitch."

She looks away, as if the engine flare offers a more comfortable view. The computer says: *nominal at one one zero point two two kilometers per second.*

This isn't Aura. Zaleha's not special. Not the one chosen to make a difference. The team can go on without her.

That's what Tariune's always hated. What she's always loved.

"There may be an experimental treatment," she says, and then, in spite of the unalloyed joy on Siv's face, the bounce of glee that curls right up from her calves and tries to hide itself behind sober *it's-only-experimental* qualification in those goggled supergiant-blue eyes, Zaleha finishes the sentence: "But if I go through with it, I'm never going to be able to come back. You'll never see me again. There's, uh, an induced coma . . . a really long time."

"Go for it," Siv says, without any hesitation at all. "Whatever it takes."

"*Field azimuth symmetry fault,*" the control officer calls. "*Abort test. Abort test.*"

They groan together, and then laugh. "Better get to work," Zaleha says.

post burn systems check

Tariune telemetry:
"Am I going to leave a body?" she asks.

"No." He looks affronted. "You're coming to Aura. Why would you leave a part of yourself behind? How could we cure you without the whole of you?"

"I better come up with a convincing excuse for my family, then."

"Whatever you please." He doesn't look impatient, though. His eyes glow with an incredible relief. "I'm so glad, Nur Zaleha. We need you. Such a tale waits to be written."

Siv telemetry:
The last time they ever see each other, they talk philosophy.

"I'm at peace now," Zaleha says. "I used to want to be *the one*. All over the history books: 'invented the Nur Zaleha Drive.' But I'm content with my little contribution. Nobody needs to remember me."

Siv covers her mouth with her hand and her eyes seem to tremble. "What?" Zaleha says, ready to comfort her.

"Yawning," Siv says thickly. They look at each other for a long time, and although they don't say anything, Zaleha wonders if they've both come to speak the Knowing.

At the door, Zaleha, trying to be funny, says: "You could say something really flattering now. You're never going to see me again."

"I'm afraid I'd convince you to stay," Siv says. And then, with a sudden resolve that seals across her whole mien like a bulkhead, a tourniquet: "I'm going to see that fucking thruster fly. Every damn probe in the sky is going to ride it. Okay?"

Self telemetry:
She lies down, closes her eyes, and waits. Feels Tariune's hand closing warm around hers, drawing her down, or up—in any case, away. A sense of *journey*, an invisible kinetic truth.

Siv, she thinks. Oh.

Oh, Siv.

The world, the whole universe, collapses beneath her into a small violet spark, into the dimming flicker of a plasma thruster throttling down.

circularization: new coordinate system

They race north by nimbus ship, desperate to complete the ritual before her dreams rot away.

Lightning snaps between the Lode Peaks, and for a brilliant instant, the whole cloudscape beneath them burns in afterimage. It takes Zaleha's breath away.

Night sky above. A billion billion stars behind a thunderously red gas giant, million-kilometer auroras a veil for two dozen moons. Arches and parapets of light.

Aura circles a parent world that could challenge Jupiter for size and beauty.

It hasn't been an easy journey. Tariune's kingdom has fallen to ruin, throne usurped by a queen he won't speak of, and in the bone-ash West a terrible darkness kindles in the light of cremated moons. She has much to learn and many loyalties to win. First, though—she has to be cured, her dreams made part of Aura.

The nimbus ship's deck pitches in turbulence. She holds to the railing. "They're coming," Tariune says. He looks down at the clouds, and she catches her breath at the fear in his eyes.

But the dragons, majestic, naval, bone mast and tendon rigging, escort them between the Lode Peaks. Their wings snap and shine with induced current. Below, Zaleha sees rivers of mercury and shining lakes that reek of kerosene even from this height. "Deadly land," Tariune murmurs in her ear. "The Method War brought poison up from the earth. The springs yield frozen fire."

She's come to Aura, but she is not yet of it. With an empiricist's reflex she imagines the chemistry of the land below. All its possible uses.

They come to the standing stones at the Third Pole. Lightning crashes down again and again, a dwindling ring around them. "Hurry!" Tariune calls to the dragons. "To the altar, before she dreams no more!"

Zaleha lies on her back in the ritual circle, and the Singers, the last of the ancient Rhexic Method who ruptured the walls of existence, begin to make her part of Aura, part of the song of the world and all it will become.

She looks up into the sky, at the vast planet above, at its twenty-four moons. Thinks of magnetospheres, of lithium, of kerosene rivers. "The Eye of Anaxis," Tariune says, following her gaze. "We dreamed of reaching it long ago, before the Method War. Dreamed of finding some way to leap into the sky . . . "

And she feels all the things she is about to forget kindle within her, a rising light, a starfire torch.

Nur Zaleha, daughter of Abdul Samad, stands and raises her hands to stop the Rhexic sorcerers. "I will not go," she says. "I can't be part of Aura yet."

"Zaleha. No. Please." Tariune cannot, does not, hide his horror. "If you refuse the ritual, your disease will rot your mind. You will go mad. You will die. And you are our only hope."

"There are other hopes I can offer." She smiles. Bravely, she hopes. All she ever wanted was to change something. "Hopes from another world, worth my madness, worth my death. Hopes I carry in the part of me that you would leave behind."

"What of the darkness in the West?" the Rhexic Master protests. "What of the Bane of Kings, the usurper?"

"When I'm done," she promises the ancient woman, "you will have stars enough to light any darkness. Worlds enough to make any kingdom small."

"Nur Zaleha," Tariune begins, and stumbles, and stops. She hears the break in his voice, the salt-and-leather man struggling to be the Prince again. "I promised you—I promised I would make your name true."

She clasps his wrist. Smiles through the tears, grief and fear and joy and most of all gratitude to her friend. Her friends.

"It means *servant of the eternal*," she says. "Let me serve."

And with Prince Tariune, the Dragons of the Lode, and the last of the Rhexic as her witness, she begins to teach.

Systems work differently on Aura.

But she loves these systems enough to make a story out of them, *apoapsis* to *zenith* and everything between.

They try to cure her later, when she feels she's done enough. But she's made her choice, written her own story, and the PRPC protein isoform is loose in her mind. She's not dreaming anymore. There's nothing left in her to put into Aura's song. Nothing she hasn't already written there.

More than two seasons later, on the last day of her sanity, she comes to lucidity long enough to feel Tariune drawing her through the kerosene stink. Hears him say, as if from a great distance: *"She will bear your name. She and all her descendants."*

She dies in madness. But it's a death she chose.

mission outcomes: t + 1.4×10^14 years

The stars have gone out. The universe freezes in half-light. Even the singularities have started to evaporate.

The marathon is over. Existence has run its course.

In the isotropic night, defiant life gathers to escape: dark, cautious, vast. The machines at the end of time. A lineage so ancient and so fiercely intelligent it still remembers its birth around a blue world lost to ash.

The portal opens. A rift born of the same quintessence that will soon shred all matter, a wormhole designed by the highest savantries of machine computation. A gate to salvation.

The first probes make transit, plasma jets sparking in old robust shades of violet.

A garden, they send. *Matter, energy, strange new laws. Worlds of bone and gossamer, swan-winged ships out of ancient dream—*

Familiar—

The apex mind of the gathered machines watches the probes greet a swift white starship. Recognizes the violet pulse of its attitude jets, stuttering with finesse.

"This is Nur Zaleha," the ship sends, the language ancient. *"Welcome to Aura, the great crossroads."*

A name. The specific form is obsolete—a word might as well be a pheromone, a protein on a cell wall. But the machines remember how to be polite. They search the vault of memory for something linked to *Nur Zaleha*.

And to their genuine surprise, they find an ancient name, a progenitor, pivotal to the birth of higher machine life.

They make it theirs with a certain reverence. Lend it to the ambassador mind they've bootstrapped, a link to their new hosts.

"Greetings, *Nur Zaleha*," the emissary sends, and feels her first joy. "We are the Siv."

Wine

YOON HA LEE

The first attack came by starfall, by deathrise. Fire swept out of the darkness, past the great violet curve of the world of Nasteng, like coins from hell's treasuries. Worse than the fire was the metal: creatures of variable form and singing cilia, joining together into colonial masses that floated high above the moon's surface and dripped synthetic insects that ate geometer's traps into its substance.

For decades Nasteng had escaped the notice of the galaxy's wider culture. This was as its Council of Five preferred. They had a secret that other human civilizations would covet. So they hid behind masks of coral and dangling tassels and quantum jewels, and admitted only traders from the most discreet mercantile societies. Now, their secret had gotten out in spite of their precautions.

Nasteng's city-domes were ruptured. The gardens with their flower-chorales of tuned crickets went up in smoke and blood and gouges. Spybirds swooped down with eyes glaring out of their feathers and marked targets for the bomber-drones. People were dragged by the insects into agony-circles, their hair fused together and lit on fire, inelegant torches.

The Council of Five had known that such a day would arrive. For the moment they were safe in their subterranean fastness. But their safety could not last forever. They knew that they could not negotiate with their immediate attackers. The colonial masses did not think in words, did not recognize *negotiation* or *compromise*. They understood only heuristic target recognition and ballistic calculations. If Nasteng had had more technologically advanced defenses, it might have been able to infect the attackers and subvert their programming, but its long isolation and cultural diffidence toward the algorithmic disciplines precluded any such possibility.

One item Nasteng did possess was a beacon. The Falcon Councilor had obtained it generations ago. Her souvenir of that quest was a gash across her cheek that wept tears that dried into crystals hooking into her flesh. At regular intervals she had to rip her face off and allow a new one to grow, or she would have been smothered. You would have thought that she would want as little to do with the beacon as possible. But no: when the Council of Five gathered around a table set with platters of raw meat and the Wine of Blossoms that was their particular privilege, the Falcon Councilor insisted on being the one to activate the beacon.

The beacon was no larger than a child's fist, and was shaped like a ball. Light sheened across it as though it had swallowed furnaces. If you held it to your ear, you could hear a distant music, as of broken glass and glockenspiels hung upside-down and sixteenth notes played upon the spokes of decrepit bicycle wheels.

The Falcon Councilor lifted the beacon, then turned it over. It clung to her palm, pulsing like an unhealthy nacrescence.

"I don't see any point in delay," the Snowcat Councilor said. It wasn't so much that he was always impatient, although he was, as that he had never gotten along with her.

"We have to be sure of what we're doing," the Falcon Councilor said. "There's no way to rescind the signal once sent."

"Falcon," the Tree Councilor said in their voice like shifting rock and gravel. "We wouldn't be here if we weren't sure. Surely you don't think it would be better to die without attempting anything?"

"No, of course not," the Falcon Councilor said.

"Then do whatever it is that you do with that thing," the Snake Councilor said from the dark corner where she was flipping through a book. The book's pages were empty, although some of them had been dog-eared.

The last councilor, the Dragon Councilor, said nothing, only watched with eyes like etched metal. But then, he never spoke, although sometimes he condescended to vote. They were never tempted to disregard him, however. He was, after all, the head of the Gardeners.

"All right," the Falcon Councilor said. She flung the beacon toward the floor. It sheared through the air with a whistle almost too high-pitched to be heard and shattered against the floor.

The beacon's shards could be counted, yet they hurt the eye. They were more like collections of brittle dust than splinters or solids. As the councilors watched, the shards reassembled themselves. Where there had been a single sphere, there were now two. Then both spheres dissipated in a vapor that smelled of antifreeze and disintegrating circuit boards.

"I hope that's not toxic," the Snowcat Councilor said, narrowing his eyes at the Falcon Councilor.

Whatever response she might have thrown back at him was interrupted by the formation of two doors right above the beacon—beacons?—in a jigsaw of fissures.

"Well," the Snake Councilor said softly, "I hope we have enough wine to offer our guests. Assuming they imbibe." The others ignored her, on the chance that she wasn't joking.

Their guests numbered two. They didn't so much step through the doors as emerge like cutouts suddenly fleshed.

The first was a woman, tall, with the finest of veils over her face. She wore soft robes with bruise-colored shadows, and her cloak was edged with dark feathers. The Snake Councilor glanced at the Falcon Councilor, but the latter's face was an unreadable labyrinth of refractions. The other guest was a man, neatly shaven. His hair was black, his eyes of indeterminate color.

The Falcon Councilor inclined her head to them. "We are grateful for your promptness," she said. "We are Nasteng's Council of Five, and the nature of our emergency should be clear to you."

"Yes," the woman said. The man bowed, but did not speak. There was something forced about the curve of his mouth, as though the lips had been sutured together. "You may call me Ahrep-na. I have a great deal of experience with situations like yours. I assume you're familiar with my past successes, but if you need—"

"We know," the Falcon Councilor said. She had heard the name of Ahrep-na, although it was not safe to use it until she had given you permission. It was why she had left Nasteng all those years ago, in search of Ahrep-na's token.

"In that case," Ahrep-na said, "we will need to discuss the contract. My methods are particular."

The Falcon Councilor thought wryly of Nasteng's high generals, some of whom were rather more useful than others. Most of whom were rather less. One of the dangers of having its officers drawn almost exclusively from the nobility, or from people who bought their commissions. "That won't be an issue," she said. Behind her, she heard a harrumph from the Snowcat Councilor, but he didn't interrupt otherwise.

They spoke some more about operational and logistical details, about courtesies blunt and banal, and circled eventually to the matter of payment. Given Ahrep-na's bluntness about everything else, her diffidence about this matter puzzled the Falcon Councilor. But bring it up she did. "Our contracts are tailored to the individual situation," Ahrep-na said. "Up-front, we require—" She named a sum. It was staggering, but so was annihilation.

Finance was not the Falcon Councilor's domain. The Snake Councilor turned to a page in her empty book, frowned at a column of figures that wasn't there, and said, "It will be done in two days."

Ahrep-na's smile was pleased. "We will also require the fruits of a year's harvest."

"You'll have to be more specific," the Falcon Councilor said, as though this were a tedious back-and-forth about supply depots and ammunition.

Ahrep-na wasn't fooled. "This point is nonnegotiable." She offered no elaboration.

The Falcon Councilor opened her mouth. Prompted by some nuance of sound behind her, however, she turned without saying what had come to her mind. *Harvest.* The councilors' secret that was no secret to the outside world anymore: the wine that kept them young.

The other four councilors faced her, united. She had just been outvoted: irregular, but she had no illusions about what they had done behind her back.

"Falcon," the Tree Councilor said, in their unmovable voice, "we are short of options. Our people burn in the streets. Without them, we too will fall. Accept their offer. We knew we were not negotiating from a position of strength."

"We'll regret this," she said bitterly.

"Anything can be survived," the Snowcat Councilor said, "so long as one is still alive to survive it. You're the second-oldest of us. Are you going to fold up and die so easily? Especially since you're the one who brought us the beacon in the first place?"

"It was that or have no last resort at all," she shot back. "Or did you think we would stand a chance against people slavering after the wine?" She looked over her shoulder at Ahrep-na. "Let me ask this, then, Ahrep-na. Are you going to take the Wine of Blossoms for yourself?"

"That is the one of the two guarantees I will offer you," Ahrep-na said easily. "I will not touch your supply of the wine, nor will the soldiers I will raise for you. Or did you think I was human enough to have any use for it?"

The Falcon Councilor was accustomed to envy, or submission, or greed. It had been a long time since she had seen contempt.

"You said two guarantees," she said. "What is the other?"

Ahrep-na's eyes were sweet with malice. The nameless man stared straight ahead. "I will win this for you," Ahrep-na said, "with the mercenaries I raise."

"Of course you will," the Falcon Councilor said, wondering what the trap was. "Very well. We will contract you under those terms."

Ahrep-na's smile was like a honed knife.

His name was Loi Ruharn, and he was one of the councilors' generals. Most people knew him, however, as the Falcon's Whore.

He had been born Korhosh Ruharn, in one of the poorest quarters of the impoverished city-dome known ironically as the Jewel of Nasteng. As a girlform child, Ruharn had played with toys scavenged from stinking trash heaps in alleys, and watched with pinched eyes while his parents argued over which of the religious offerings they had to neglect this month because otherwise they would be too hungry to work, and swore he would never grow up to live in a crowded home with six brothers and sisters, wondering every night if he would be sold to the Gardeners like the daughter of the Ohn family next door.

As soon as he was old enough and strong enough, Ruharn ran away and enlisted in a noble household's private army. He might have died there. While the Council of Five ruled Nasteng entire, they didn't interfere with the nobles' squabbles so long as they didn't threaten the councilors themselves. But Ruharn acquitted himself well in battle, mostly through a combination of suicidal determination and a knack for small-unit tactics, and he rose quickly in the ranks.

That by itself wouldn't have made him remarkable. There were plenty of talented soldiers, and most of them died young anyway, the way battle luck went. Rather, he came to the Falcon Councilor's attention as a minor novelty, as a womanform soldier who lived as a man. For all her years, she'd never taken such a lover before.

The Falcon Councilor wouldn't stoop to take a common-born lover, but that was easy enough to finesse. She offered riches; she offered to buy Ruharn a commission in the Council's own army, and an adoption into a noble family; and most of all she offered a place in her bed. Ruharn wasn't sentimental about the honor of his chosen profession, although he knew what people would be saying about him. He accepted.

Today, almost six months since the invasion had begun, he was pacing in the command bower of the councilors' fastness. It was decorated with vines from which cloudflowers grew. The vines watered themselves, a neat trick. Irritatingly, they also left puddles, which you'd think he'd know to step around by now. The last time he'd yanked off a table runner and used it to soak up the moisture, he'd been yelled at by General Iyuden, who was insufferable about ornamental items. But Iyuden came from one of Nasteng's oldest, wealthiest families. He wasn't about to have that argument with her.

Arrayed before Ruharn were videoscreens of Nasteng's defenses. It didn't take any kind of experience to see how inadequate they had been. He had read the reports and made his recommendations. It wasn't so much that the senior generals had disagreed as that no recommendation would have made much of a difference.

He didn't know what had happened in the four days since the gateway fastness of Istefnis, on the surface, had been crushed into crumbs of marble and metal and human motes by the invaders. But the mercenaries the councilors had hired had brought with them a fleet of starflyers, a horde of groundswarmers. Nasteng's unnamed enemies had slowly fallen back before the onslaught of hellspikes and icemetal bursts and frenzied gnawers. You could, if you were sufficiently innocent of electromagnetic signatures and spectral flourishes, take it for a particularly disorganized fireworks display. Nasteng itself was now haloed by a staggering murdercloud of debris, whether glowing, glimmering, or gyring dark. It was just as well they weren't putting satellites into orbit anytime soon.

Two things bothered Ruharn about the mercenaries' forces, for all their successes. (More than two. But he had to start somewhere.) First was the question of logistics. The senior general had let drop that the contract had mentioned logistical arrangements. As a staff general, Ruharn had hoped to learn details. Had looked, in fact. So far as he could tell, however, the starflyers and groundswarmers had appeared out of nowhere. It wasn't inconceivable that this was advanced foreign technology—there seemed to be a lot of that going around—but it still made him suspicious.

The other thing was the way the mercenaries fought. When the Falcon Councilor had told him about the arrangement—the private conversation, not the staff meeting where he'd heard the official version—she had indicated every faith in the mercenaries' abilities. So far, Ruharn observed that the mercenaries relied on sheer numbers, wave after wave of suffocation rather than strategy. To be sure, the method was *working,* yet he couldn't help feeling the councilors could have spent their coin more wisely.

The councilors' personal army was used primarily for quashing the nobles' personal armies and secondarily for quashing the occasional revolution. So he didn't have great confidence in his conclusions. Yet it was impossible to serve with any diligence without picking up a few fundamentals of the military art.

As it turned out, he was turning the problem over in his mind—it wasn't as if he had a hell of a lot else to do, since for the first time in his so-called career he was caught up on paperwork—when a message made him forget it completely. He found it on top of his correspondence for the afternoon, smuggled in by who knew what method, a note on the back of a flyer. It said, simply, *I need your help.*

Ruharn would have dismissed it as a prank or a trap, except he recognized the handwriting, even twenty-three years later, for all the changes. The writer still had that particular way of drawing crossbars, of slanting hooks. He assumed she still lived in the same house, or at least the same neighborhood, or she would have said something more to guide him.

It wasn't difficult to slip out of the fastness and to the surface, in one of the bubblecars whose use was reserved to the councilors' favorites. The old neighborhood was some six hours away, to the north and east of Istefnis. Ruharn expected to be discovered eventually, but as long as he wasn't caught cheating on the Falcon Councilor, he didn't think there would be any lasting consequences. Assuming he didn't lose his life to some mine while walking down the street, or break his neck tripping over rubble.

The bubblecar's driver was a prim woman in the Falcon Councilor's livery. When she glanced back at Ruharn, her eyes were momentarily sly. Ruharn didn't notice.

During the ride, he alternated between looking out the window and looking at the status displays, which were connected to the moon's defense systems. He wore the plainest clothes he owned, which weren't very, a severe coat over a suit of soft dark brown with gold-embroidered gingko leaves, neatly fitted trousers, and boots likewise embellished with gold. In the neighborhood where he had grown up, the boots alone would have gotten him robbed, which was why he came armed. Two guns and a knife, the latter being ceremonial, but he kept it sharp on principle. Given his childhood, he was actually better in a knife fight than with handguns.

In the neighborhood where he had grown up, you would also have had one hell of a time finding a fence capable of dealing with items so fine, but that didn't mean no one was stupid enough to try. Maybe his uniform would have been a better idea, except he didn't want to give anyone the notion that he was there on official business.

He hadn't been back in twenty-three years, since he had run away, although from time to time he sent money home. No one from his family had ever acknowledged the payments. He hadn't expected them to; would, in fact, have been obscurely humiliated to hear from them.

The bubblecar wound through streets choked by devastation. Devastation was not new to Ruharn. He had grown up with decaying walls and the debris of blown-away hopes. Nor was he a stranger to battlefield ruin: red dried to blots brown-black, lungs sloughed into gray slime, stinging dust in the air. Even so, dry as his eyes were, the pitted streets and pitiful crumpled corpses were somehow different when they were dead at strangers' hands.

"Here we are," the driver said. She didn't bother to hide her skepticism.

"Thank you," Ruharn said distantly. He put on a filter, then stepped out. The bubblecar didn't wait to accelerate away. Sensible woman.

His memory was still good, despite the damage that had been done. Undoubtedly some of it had been local warfare, not recent either. He made his way through the streets, not too fast and not too slow, pricklingly aware that the few survivors were watching him.

The house had changed a little. Ruharn was certain that the old wind chimes had been decorated by little clay flowers. The new ones had what might charitably be described as rotund four-legged animals (what kind was impossible to say). He couldn't, however, discount the possibility that it was the same set of chimes with different decorations. The girl he had known had always liked chimes. He stepped up to the door—if this was an ambush, so be it—and knocked. "Merenne," he called out. "I'm here. It's Ruharn."

For long moments he thought that the house was chewed up and empty inside, that he'd wasted the trip. Then a voice barely familiar, scratchy with hardship, called back, "I'm coming." Soon enough the door opened.

"Merenne," Ruharn said again, voice unsteady. He did not bow. She would have taken offense.

Merenne was shorter than he was, and her hair had gone gray. She looked fifteen years older than he was. In fact she was his younger by six. The clothes she wore were neatly stitched, and patched besides. The shirt was livened by embroidery, mostly geometrical motifs. Ruharn remembered how assiduously they had both picked apart old handkerchiefs and wrapping cloths to scavenge brightly colored thread for the purpose. She had smiled easily then, as a girl, despite the fact that her shoulders were already growing hunched with the work she had to do. He doubted she smiled easily now. She had been his favorite sister, for whom he had saved pittances to trade for candies, whom he had soothed to sleep with bloodthirsty stories (even then he had had an interest in weapons), and he had left her behind without so much as saying goodbye because staying was unbearable.

"I didn't think you'd come," she said, as simple and sharp as a mirror-break. And: "I thought something of your old voice would remain. But I wouldn't have known it was you at all. Come in."

Ruharn's mouth twisted. He hadn't thought about his voice, now a tenor, for years. But he stepped through the threshold. The place was too quiet. Where was everyone? Not that he had so much as known that Merenne herself was still alive. For all he knew, some plague had killed them all years ago.

"I almost didn't come," he said. "But I did. Say what you have to say."

Merenne didn't respond, but instead led him through the house. It didn't take long. The Falcon Councilor would have considered it barely adequate as a closet. Ruharn had always been amused by her misconceptions about how many people you could squeeze into shelter if you really had to.

There were three rooms, and people would all have slept together in the largest, partly for warmth, partly for community. The first thing that caught Ruharn's eye was the dolls: two of them, one-third scale. They had been covered neatly by cloths. He wondered if some absent child had left them that way, tucking them in for the night.

The dolls he had grown up playing with had had brass tacks for eyes that were forever falling out. ("Poison gas rots out their eyes in battle," he had said to wide-eyed little Merenne, long ago. It had been funnier then.) The dolls here were made of some smooth, lambent resin, and their eyes shone like sea-lenses over delicately sculpted noses and lips painted perfect dusky pink. Their hair had been carefully styled, with miniature enameled clasps holding the strands in place. He had seen less beautiful statuettes in the councilors' homes.

"Go on," Merenne said. "Look." As he bent to lift one of the cloths, she added, "You used to have a grand-nephew and a grand-niece."

Ruharn didn't ask what if they had been her own grandchildren, or those of their siblings. Or what had happened to their siblings, for that matter.

Beneath the cloth the doll was naked, and he thought of the crude paper dresses that he had sometimes pinned together for Merenne, back when she had had dolls of her own, colored with markers he had stolen from a store. The doll was shaped like a preadolescent boy, but at the join of its legs was a mass that resembled spent bullets melted partly into each other.

In the doll's hand was a toy gun. (At least, he hoped it was a toy.) He eased the gun out of the doll's grip. "A credible Zehnjer 52-3," he said without thinking, "other than the fact that they did the cartridge upside-down."

He became aware that Merenne was staring at him. "You'd think," she said, "I had all this time to get used to the idea of you as a soldier."

Well, it was better than the other things she could be calling him. "You didn't call me here to identify this toy," he said.

"No," Merenne said quietly. "I called you here because the children have been disappearing. I woke in the night and they were gone. The dolls were left as you see them."

"Kidnappers?" Ruharn said dubiously. Poor people's children were terrible currency if you weren't a Gardener. He knew how noisy they got, adorable as they could be. To say nothing of the messes, and the fact that you wouldn't get any decent ransom for them.

Her mouth half-lifted in a ghost of the smile he remembered, as though she knew what he was thinking. Then the smile died. "Ru," she said, "I asked around. No one's seen a Gardener since the children started to vanish."

He said, because he needed to know, "Has payment been left for anyone?" Because it wasn't inconceivable, even in the midst of the crisis, that the councilors would upgrade their system of harvest. So to speak.

Everyone knew how much you could expect for a whole child in the desirable age range, in reasonable health. Even now Ruharn knew. The payment had changed over the years, but it was impossible not to remain aware.

For years he had taken the system for granted, the way everyone had. Part of the bargain, horrible as it was, was that the families who sold their children received something in return. Admittedly the dolls weren't *nothing*, but he doubted that you could sell them for the equivalent sums. Even if it wouldn't surprise him if someone had started collecting the ghoulish things; there were always such people in the world.

"As if people would tell me?" Merenne said. "But no. I haven't heard so much as a rumor. And I looked for payment"—she said this without shame—"but I saw nothing, because it was one of the first things I thought of. Maybe it's a stupid thing to care about, when our world might not survive. But I have to know what happened to them. And you're the only person I could think to ask."

"I know where to start," Ruharn said carefully. "I can't guarantee any results, though. Most especially, I doubt I can bring the children back." Understatement, since he did think the councilors were involved, the way they were involved with everything of note. He had few illusions about his ability to influence any of them, least of all the one who had taken him for a lover.

"I didn't expect that," she said. "Just find out what you can. So that we know what to expect." Her mouth trembled for a moment, so briefly that he almost thought he had imagined it.

Ruharn wondered what to say next. Everything seemed inadequate. At last he said, "Sometime after this is over, if I ever see you again, tell me their names." He didn't mention death-offerings. The deaths of children, especially small children, were so unremarkable that few people bothered.

Merenne eyed him thoughtfully. "I'll think about it," she said.

He smiled. He had always liked her honesty. After all, it wasn't as if she owed him anything. "All right," he said. "Let me take one of the dolls."

"Take both," Merenne said, with commendable steadiness. "It's not as if they do me any good."

He gathered them up under one arm. Considered resting his free hand on her shoulder, then decided that he had better not. This time he did bow, although he spun on his heel before he could see the expression that crossed her face, and walked out of the house. She didn't follow him or call out a farewell.

The Falcon Councilor did not greet Ruharn when he returned to the underground fastness. One of the servants did, however, present him a note upon paper-of-petals. It instructed him to attend her that night.

First he took the precaution of wrapping up the dolls and putting them in a case that he bullied out of Supply. The supply officer looked at him oddly, but he gave no explanation. It wasn't as if he owed one.

Ruharn reported next to the generals' bower, and stood at attention in the doorway. General Khy sat at a table with her feet on a chair, playing cards with her aide. She was a woman once handsome, but still dangerous, with hair shaved short and a conspicuous blank expanse where her medals should have been; she declined to wear them even on occasions of state. As one of the senior generals, she had taken Nasteng's impotence hard. She and her cards were always here, and even now, as her aide contemplated options, Khy brought up a map to study the latest intelligence.

A quartet of cards burned for additional points sobbed prettily as they crumpled into ashes. Ruharn wished Khy wouldn't use that particular feature, but Khy was entertained by the oddest things. Besides, she was one of the generals who understood strategy, so he preferred not to pick fights with her, on the grounds that she was more important than he was.

Khy liked Ruharn, a fact that he tried not to think too hard about. She waved her hand at him while assiduously keeping the cards' faces out of her aide's view. "General Loi," she said genially. "At ease."

It took a moment for him to recognize the house name he used now. Funny how long it had been since he'd lapsed. "General," Ruharn said. "Any interesting developments?" He doubted it: Khy would hardly be tormenting her cards if something that required her attention were going on.

She sneered, which took him by surprise because she ordinarily approached everything with cockeyed levity. "Look," she said, and flung her cards down. Her aide kept them from fluttering off the edge of the table.

Khy's hands tapped rapid patterns on the nearest interface. Maps flowered, crisscrossed by troop vectors and dotted by the bright double-squares of bases, the cluster-clouds of aerospace fighters. Nasteng's forces were violet. The enemy was green. The mercenaries were gold. Her hands tapped again. The troops moved as their positions and engagements were replayed over time.

"We might as well retire now," Khy said. "Oh, maybe not you, you're young yet, and there's always a use for good staffers." From anyone else it would have been a veiled insult, but Khy had never treated Ruharn as anything but a competent colleague and Ruharn was not so paranoid as to believe that things were different now. "But look, the mercenaries are doing all the work."

"That doesn't mean there won't be more attacks, now that the outsiders know we're here," Ruharn said. And, when Khy didn't respond, he hesitated, then said: "The mercenaries fight with numbers. But they don't fight *well*."

"You're one of the people who can see it, let alone who is willing to *say* it," Khy said bitterly. She flipped a pointer out of her belt, caught it, switched it on. Scribbled indications, in light and hissing sparks, on the maps. "There, there, there, *there*. Victory by attrition. So *wasteful*."

"I understand there's a noninterference clause," Ruharn said neutrally.

"Noninterference, hell. I've had the scanners on it and they can't even tell what our allies *are*. They come from nowhere and the corpses of their units degenerate with astonishing rapidity. There's probably a paper in it for some scientist somewhere."

Khy brought up more photos and videos. At first Ruharn didn't recognize what he was seeing, too busy being distracted by fractal damage, stress marks, metal sheening red-orange in response to unhealthy radiations. Familiar shapes.

Except those weren't the only familiar shapes. Burnt into the wreckage were symbols he remembered from his childhood. The depressions of board games he had played in the dirt, or score-tallies chalked onto walls, or warding-signs around which he and his friends had danced in circles, chanting rhymes to keep the Gardeners away. He glanced sideways at Khy, wondering, but she met his eyes with no sign that she saw anything in the faint symbols at all.

Then again, Khy would have grown up playing board games with real boards, made of marble or jade or mahogany veneer. If she played in the dirt, it would have been in a high-walled, well-tended garden while watched by anxious servants and the occasional guard. And she would never have had to worry about being sold to the Gardeners.

Still, it was dismaying to have one of the generals he respected confirm his observations. "Is there something you wish me to do, sir?" he asked carefully. For a mad moment he wished the answer was yes.

Khy only sighed and eased herself back down into the chair, swung her feet up again. "If only," she said. "You go on, Loi. Your next shift here isn't for hours anyway, isn't it? Enjoy yourself."

Ruharn saluted and passed out of the bower. He headed next to his quarters, where he opened the case and unwrapped the dolls. "You'd better not be bombs," he told them. They didn't answer, which didn't make him feel better.

Dealing with bombs wasn't one of his skills, but if the dolls were what remained of the stolen children, that wasn't relevant. Besides, even if they were bombs, they were probably advanced foreigner bombs, and the fastness's scanners had failed to pick up on them when he brought them in.

The two dolls were nearly identical. Prodding one revealed that the hair was a wig, and beneath it the top of the skull came off. The head was hollow. The eyes, half-domes with luminous irises, were held in place by putty. Systematically, he took apart the rest of the doll. The doll was jointed, and elastic ran through channels in the body and limbs so that it could be posed.

As for the slag of bullets, they appeared to be real metal, not resin. He prodded them and jerked his hand back involuntarily. They were the exact temperature of his own skin. Feeling like a squeamish six-year-old, he pressed his fingertips against the resin just above the slag. The surface was cool; significantly cooler, in fact.

Logistical necessities, Ruharn thought, staring down at the dolls. Then he wrapped them back up, laid them carefully in the case, and put the case under his bed. Stupid hiding place, but it wasn't as if he had a better one. And anyway, the real hiding place was where he had kept it all these years, the pitted lump he had for a heart.

At the appointed time, Ruharn went to the Falcon Councilor's chambers. He did not wear his uniform. Lately she liked him to wear what the courtiers did, necklaces of twisted gold and fitted coats with their undulating lace, dark red brocades. He obliged her; he understood his function. The guards with their falcon insignia acknowledged him merely with nods, making no comment.

The councilor stood looking at a tapestry-of-labyrinths when he stopped just short of entering, the way she liked him to. "Madam," he said. In the very early days she had liked it when he knelt. Her mood varied, however, and he didn't care one way or another. If pride had been important to him, he wouldn't be here.

"Come in," she said in the clear sweet voice whose inflections he knew so well.

Ruharn came up behind her and undid, one-handed, the clasps and knots and chains that held her veil in place. She had told him once that she only wore it here; everywhere else it was the familiar falcon mask. Ruharn found it telling, although he did not say so, that the fastenings were more elaborate than the veil itself. He was no pauper, but a bolt of the fabric, with its infinitesimally shimmering threads and texture like moondrift silk, would have beggared him. He always had the disquieting feeling that his fingerprints would sully the fibers, leave scars deep as trenches and hideous as gangrene. But he didn't say that either.

"Your hands are cold," she murmured.

It always took him a while to undo all the fastenings. "Sorry," Ruharn said mildly, "but you didn't like my last pair of gloves and it's not as if I've had time to go shopping."

She didn't call him on the lie, and he bent to kiss the back of her head, inhaling the fragrance of her hair.

The veil fell away, drifting through the air like a feather, or a fall of light, or a flower's breath. Ruharn always felt ridiculous whisking it away to lay it on the councilor's dresser without folding it, but she had never complained. He lifted her hair, which was hooked through with crystal—it was getting near the time where she would have to tear off her face again—taking care not to tug the dark coils. Unhurriedly, he pressed his lips to the back of her neck, once, twice. Again. Her perfume smelled of dried roses and wood-of-pyres. Inhaling it made his heartbeat quicken. Reportedly she wore it only for her lovers.

"Tell me," he said right into her ear, "is it true what's been happening to the children lately?"

He wanted her to tell him the truth, however familiar; however horrible. If she told him the truth, he would accept his complicity and forget Merenne again. He had been doing exactly that for all these years, after all. Surely he had earned a little truth in exchange for the years they had spent together.

The councilor's laugh came more as a vibration against his chest than a sound, and her voice was teasing. "You'll have to be more specific than that, my dear. Are we talking about schools, or orphanages, or some incident involving crawfish-racing?" (Naheng's crawfish were surprisingly large and fast, or this game would have been less popular than it was.)

Ruharn heard the lie and was surprised by the force of his own rage. He brought his hands up and down and around. She cried out as she landed against the wall, hard, breath slammed out of her, her arm bent close to breaking in his grip. "Are the mercenaries harvesting the children now, or is it still you?" He added, "It's been a long time since I did hand-to-hand. I could still get the mechanics wrong. So think about your answer."

"Why does it matter to you?"

He broke her arm. She screamed.

No one came. She hadn't triggered an alarm, and the guards were used to noise.

"Madam," he said, very formally. She went very still, very quiet. "Answer the question."

"We haven't sent out the Gardeners since the mercenaries came," the Falcon Councilor said raggedly. "It's their doing this time around." And, in a different voice entirely: "I had always hoped you might hesitate a little before doing—this."

"Neither one of us has ever been under the illusion that this relationship was about love," Ruharn said. "Did the mercenaries say outright that they would be recruiting the children?"

"They didn't say, but we knew."

"Is it too late to send them away?"

"We've paid," she said. "They will give us what we paid for. Don't you think we considered that people powerful enough to save us would also be powerful enough to plunder us? To wreck our way of life? But it was either submit to our destruction or choose the chance of salvation."

Ruharn thought for a moment. "All right. Take me to the Garden."

The councilor's laugh was ugly. "It always comes down to this. It took you longer than most, at least. What, are you concerned that the mercenaries will destroy the supply before you get your chance at youth unending?"

Let her think what she wanted. "Madam," he said, "you have a lot of bones and breaking them all would take time I don't have. I would speak you fair, but I'm done with niceties. The Garden."

"You picked one hell of a time to stage a coup, lover," the Falcon Councilor said in a voice like winter stabbing.

Is that what you think this is? Ridiculous that he wanted her to believe better of him, yet there it was. "Shut up," he said evenly. She was silent after that. It had been a long time since he had been anything but deferential to her, except in bed when she required otherwise.

It was a long way to the Garden. Ruharn expected her to call for help after all, or try to escape. But she kept looking at him, her eyes pierced through with pain, and she did neither. Sometimes she drew in a breath that might have become a sob; but then she controlled herself. He tried not to think about what he'd done to her.

The Garden, when it opened up before them in a staggering splendor of chokingly humid air and pearlescent lights, was choked with children, newborn to ten or eleven years old. It was impossible to tell how many there were, or how big the Garden was. They were sprawled every which way, a spill of limbs and crooked necks and lolling heads, and from them grew red pulsating vines, and from the vines shone red murmuring fruits. Perhaps it would have been less overwhelming if the children had been neatly organized, stacked by height or size in rows. Probably not.

In spite of himself, Ruharn looked among the faces for some echo of Merenne's features. Some echo of his own. It was impossible to tell amid the red tangles.

"The raw liquor is effective," the Falcon Councilor said after giving him just enough time to confront the sight, "if that's what you're thinking, but painful. Dragon is the only one who imbibes it in that form, and Dragon is a little peculiar. I'm surprised you didn't just have me take you to the wine cellars."

"No," Ruharn said. "This is what I want."

"The other councilors won't stand for this, you know."

"They won't have to."

She still didn't understand. "When they come after you—" Tellingly, she didn't say *we*: he was almost certain it was deliberate.

"Forget that, this is *damage control*," Ruharn said savagely, resisting the temptation to hit her. Stupid, considering he had already broken her arm and threatened systematic torture. "You made a bargain you only half-understood and you sent children to die in the most wasteful way possible, without even the leadership of someone like General Khy so they'd have a chance. The mercenaries aren't providing any sort of generalship themselves and I trust you weren't assuming that a bunch of children that age were going to spontaneously turn up any convenient tactical geniuses to do the job."

"This is rich," the councilor retorted, "from someone who turned his back on those same children during all the years they were bought as fodder for the

Garden. Or did you manage to lie to yourself about what wine it is I drink when I'm not in your arms?"

He flinched. "Oh yes," he said, "I would rather be fucking you than dealing with this. I'm not unaware of what I am." The red silken sheets, her fragrant skin, the coils of glossy hair. The marks her mouth of living crystal left on his skin. "But apparently even I have limits."

Ruharn removed his ceremonial knife and laid it on the floor. Then he stripped, aware of her staring even though his body was no secret to either of them. He picked up the knife again, squared his shoulders, and waded into the Garden.

For all the useless ornamentation on the knife's hilt and sheath, its blade was just fine. He had no intention of wasting further time plucking fruit or squeezing it into his mouth. Instead, he cut directly into a handful of vines and brought them, spurting livid red, up to his mouth.

She was right. It burned going down, and burned his skin too, not like fire (he knew something of fire) but like hopes crushed down to singularity nights. But he swallowed, and swallowed, and swallowed, even as he choked; even as the red fluid dribbled down his chin and soaked his clothes. When the spray slowed, he grabbed blindly and cut again, and again, and again.

"Ruharn!" the Falcon Councilor cried out behind him. "Ruharn, you have to stop, it's *too much—*"

Good to know that she wasn't interested in that particular perversion. At least with him. He kept drinking, unable to see although his eyes were wide open, so nauseated he couldn't even throw up. Finally he dropped the knife and sank to his knees, coughing out an ugly pink-tinged spray.

After a while he became aware of her hand on his shoulder. Her touch, too, burned with the sticky-slick traces of the fluid. He shivered. Her hand felt large, and he felt thin, small, vulnerable in a way that hadn't been true for years. He looked down, not at his own hands, but at his thighs and their scars, not all of which had been received in battle. Looked up. She was taller now, larger.

"Ruharn," she said in a wretched voice. "You look—I never imagine you'd ever looked so innocent. Except your eyes."

"Childhood isn't about innocence," Ruharn said, both cynically amused at the way she cringed at how high his voice was now, and hating the sound of it himself. "It's about being *powerless.*"

She didn't contest the point.

"Your mercenary company," Ruharn said. "You must have a way of contacting them still. Tell them to take me next." He assumed it would be the fastest way, instead of wandering around in some city waiting for them to find him. "If children are the coin they desire."

"You're even more crazed than I thought you were if you think I'll do that."

Hell of a time for her to get maternal. "I'm not Khy," Ruharn said. "I didn't go to the nobles' battle schools, or to the collegium for strategists. But I know more than those children do. Because that's who the mercenaries are, aren't they? Our children, transformed. *Let me go.*" He shook off her hand and rose to his feet.

The Falcon Councilor rose as well. "You have no guarantee that you'll be anything more than a drone while you're up there as—as whatever you become," she said.

"Doesn't matter," he said. "If there's a chance I can do some good, I have to take it."

"Fine," she said, distant, formal. "You have my gratitude, General."

She drew out two bright-and-dark balls, no larger than Ruharn's fists, and whispered into them. He couldn't hear the words. Then she set them down, dry-eyed, and stepped back. A door ruptured the air above the balls.

You won't feel grateful for long, Ruharn thought. But he bent his head to her, and went.

In five months and twenty-four days, the mercenaries reclaimed sixty-three percent of Nasteng.

In the fifteen days after General Loi Ruharn vanished, the invaders were repulsed entirely.

General Khy's attempts to tally the mercenaries' losses in both phases of the campaign, as opposed to the enemies' losses, were blocked.

Merenne watched for Gardeners in all the years that followed, but never saw any. She made toys for her next grandchildren; there were a few. No dolls.

The final attack came not from the invaders, who were driven off in a scythe-surge of explosions, but from the newly-coordinated starflyers and groundswarmers. Their original task done, they needled toward the Garden and crashed into it, raising a pillar of fire and monstrous ash.

The councilors, who were in the midst of a victory celebration, had nothing left to fight with. Then, as their forces failed them, they fled one by one, except the Falcon Councilor. She and General Khy stayed in the command bower to the last, playing cards.

The Garden's protections were sundered. It lay with its ruined red-black mass of vines and charred, sunken skeletons like a sore jabbed open over and over. Nothing would ever grow there again.

Deep in the mass were two broken beacons and two collapsed mannequins, their uniforms fused to their skin. One was a woman, its face candle-melted entirely away. The other was a man, probably; hard to tell, given the damage. But the sutures holding its mouth shut from the inside had torn open, and it was smiling.

The Cuckoo

SEAN WILLIAMS

April 1st, 2075, 9:15-9:23am
More than one thousand commuters traveling via d-mat arrive at their destinations wearing red clown noses; they weren't wearing them when they left. The global matter-transmission network is rebooted, source of the glitch unknown. All the clown noses are destroyed except for three retained by private collectors.

April 1st, 2076, 10pm precisely
One year later, every d-mat booth in the world opens at exactly the same moment, releasing a powerful scent of roses. Peacekeepers analyzing the fumes find no evidence of toxicity. People begin to talk about the existence of a new, anonymous art-prankster in the vein of Bekhisisa Uteku or Banksy, who turns 100 this year.

April 1st, 2077
At random times throughout the day, eight hundred and sixty nine booths each deliver a single page on which are typed twenty three different words from William S. Burroughs' cut up novel *The Soft Machine*.

May 23, 2077
Professor Eme Marburg, 53, of New Leiden University begins investigating the activities of "The Fool," as she dubs the prankster on her blog. She is a teacher of complexity theory and author of several abstruse textbooks on the subject, but it is her interest in mid-Twentieth Century literature that initially piques her interest. What happened to the remaining pages of *The Soft Machine*? Private collectors again, she is forced to assume.

April 1st, 2078
Two hundred and seventy-one children are redirected in-transit to a location in Macau, where they arrive wearing the costumes of popular fantasy adventure series *Super Awesome Ninja Ponies*. They play without adult supervision for sixteen minutes before being rescued. No serious injuries are reported.

April 2nd, 2079, 12:03am
Following the attack on children the previous year, PKs worldwide are on high alert for any sign of The Fool. There are no incidents for twenty-four hours. After declaring the operation a complete success, outspoken octogenarian lawmaker Kieran Defrain is redirected in-transit and dumped in Times Square, wearing nothing but a cloth diaper and a tag tied around his left big toe, inscribed "Gotcha!"

November 9, 2079
Anggoon Montri, 32, from the Thai Protectorate, confesses to being The Fool. After eight hours of intense interrogation he recants, claiming he simply wanted to publicize his own original artwork and leaving The Fool's true name and motives a matter of keen speculation. Some say that he or she is a disgruntled employee intent on exposing the flaws in the d-mat network, others that "The Fool" is actually a collaboration of many people dedicated to Eris, the ancient Greek Goddess of chaos. Still others believe that each incident is perpetrated by copycats, and that the original Fool went to ground long ago. No evidence exists to confirm any of these theories.

April 1st, 2080
Despite a vigorous, yearlong search, The Fool remains at large. Embarrassed by their failure, PKs instruct the general public to avoid using d-mat except in the case of dire emergencies. No incidents are recorded involving d-mat booths. Instead, every networked fabricator in the world makes a unique piece of a three-dimensional jigsaw puzzle, each approximately one cubic centimeter in size, which, if assembled, would form a sculpture of an upraised middle finger twenty-five meters high.

June 17, 2080
Professor Marburg of New Leiden University publishes a paper in the journal *Complexity and Organization* entitled "Manifest Meaninglessness: The Fool and his Meme are Easily Imparted." She notes that six weeks before The Fool's first known incident (clown noses), a major Peacekeeper initiative was launched to curb youthful misuse of d-mat booths, called "Quit Clowning Around." Similarly, the following year's incident (the smell of roses) was preceded by the "It Stinks" meme, instigated by a celebrity complaining that she didn't receive a red nose. The cut up novel allegory is obvious. That The Fool is a playing a game at everyone's expense was a notion widely discussed prior to the mass-kidnap of children in 2078; "Gotcha" in turn connects with the PKs' determination to apprehend and punish the prankster, while the disassembled, statuesque obscenity clearly relates to a growing worldwide amusement at official impotence.

Professor Marburg concludes that this series of correlations is evidence of an emerging, powerful memeplex, or complex of memes, focused on The Fool. Whoever he or she originally was, he or she is here to stay.

April 1st, 2081

Ignoring stern Peacekeeper warnings, the "Fool's Tools," a loosely organized movement of everyday citizens travel en masse continuously for twenty-four hours, awaiting, perhaps inviting, the latest prank from their hero. None is forthcoming, although over the course of the day six copycat stunts are easily detected and reversed, their perpetrators taken into custody. The only work ascribed to The Fool is a maze of d-mat addresses that, once entered, cannot be exited. The technician who stumbled across the artifact is never seen again, prompting another global manhunt. The Fool is now a wanted murderer . . . but remains no easier to catch.

April 2081-March 2082

The longer The Fool remains at large, the higher his or her public profile rises. Numerous organizations form to honor the prankster's artistry, including the Fool's Brigade, the Tomfoolerists, and the First Church of the Foolhardy. No matter how vigorously Peacekeepers crack down on publicly disruptive initiation rites, the number of disciples, prophets and self-proclaimed messiahs mounts. A monument to the Unknown Fool is erected in Berlin. A popular genre of erotic fan fiction, known as Foolfic, explores the motives and secret emotional life of the men and women supposedly behind the meme. In a series of increasingly obscure articles and blog posts, Professor Marburg, now 57, continues her examination of the phenomenon, placing the latest stunt in the context of a memeplex that seems on the one hand healthy to the point of profligacy and on the other verging on implosion.

She suggests that The Fool never existed at all, in any sense that matters–not as a person, or as a series of people copying each other, or as a group of people acting in concert. "The Fool" might very well be an emergent property of the world's memeverse, in the same way that magnificent dunes form out of the simple interaction of sand grains and the wind, without conscious control or intent. Hence, she says, we have organizations that mimic The Fool, inferior to the original in some eyes but nevertheless an authentic part of the phenomenon. If that is so, she speculates, it is entirely possible that the sealed maze–cause of The Fool's one and only direct fatality–might be a sign that the *original* Fool, whoever or whatever that might be, is now turning on itself, strangling itself in a knot of memetic transmutation that can only conclude one way.

She recants her previous prediction, and issues a new one: The Fool is dead. The knot has been tied off. All that remains is aftershock.

April 1st, 2082

Few people read the theories of obscure professors. Huge celebrations greet the latest Fool's Day and no one is immune to the party atmosphere–not even those who, led by a masked figure called "Straight-Face," mount theatrical mock-protests against the rising tide of foolishness. Pranks of all kinds are performed, ranging from the harmless to the extremely dangerous. One hundred and seventeen people are killed in accidents; many more are injured. None of these tragedies are connected to The Fool. The world waits in anticipation to see what this year's "official" prank will be, without release.

April 2082-March 2083
The Fool's absence does nothing to dampen the enthusiasm of the Foolish. After all, "Gotcha!" happened the day after April 1st. The Fool's fans assume that the prank, when eventually revealed, will be unmatched in subtlety and explosiveness. Plans for next year's celebrations begin early. "Best ever," the world is promised.

In New Leiden University, Professor Marburg is troubled by the deaths. Not a day doesn't go by that she doesn't wish the world would put aside "The Fool" and the troubling visions he, she, or it inspires in her. As the memeplex grows larger than ever, The Fool as an active participant in its own perpetuation is made conspicuous by its absence. The Fool is dead; long live The Fool. How can that be possible?

The growing memeplex, as mapped out by other colleagues in the field, is already a fiendishly convoluted web of popular culture. Only she is fixated on its connection to d-mat, the means of mass-transit for ninety-nine percent of the world's population. It's no accident, she has always understood, that The Fool manifests this way, for that network contains–and *symbolizes*–vast complexity. She herself is part of this complex whether she wants to be or not, both by traveling via d-mat and by publicly posting her speculations. She cannot help but wonder what role she has played in the evolution of The Fool. Did she inadvertently name it, for starters? Did she shape its evolution by noting its past connections and predicting its disappearance? What if her musings are the butterfly wings that created a storm that is still unfolding, albeit invisible to her, now?

April 1st, 2083
Still no prank has been found. The world awaits as it did the previous year, with identical results. "Perhaps we are the prank," Straight-Face declares. "You, me, all of us. His work is done. And the joke is on us." Nobody listens to him, either. Fool's Day celebrations achieve outrageous heights. There are more injuries, more deaths. All festive promises are met, no matter how extravagant.

June, 2083
Professor Marburg of New Leiden University reads a paper by a colleague in Spain who declares that the memeplex is now so complicated that its extent can no longer be accurately measured. This prompts a highly unnerving thought, one she keeps entirely to herself.

At what point does one seriously consider the possibility that the memplex is alive? Perhaps not in the same way as a human; perhaps it possesses little more than reflexive self-awareness, like that of a puppy or a small child. But still, *alive*. What could that mean? What happens when it wakes up?

September, 2083
Professor Marburg, 59, has a dream about running down a tunnel full of people, all shouting at once. She wakes in a cold sweat. The image haunts her for days,

leading her to a new and entirely chilling notion concerning the interaction between d-mat and the memeplex.

At any given moment the network contains millions of people, crisscrossing the earth from end to end. All their atoms, all their molecules, all their cells, pass relentlessly from one node to another as data. Data that is in theory *available*. And nature never leaves anything lying around unused. With such a great resource in existence, what are the odds that so many moving brain cells would *never* achieve spontaneous life? Life that might evolve in fits and starts, depending on the environment around it? Feeding on all the crazy things that humans believe? A thriving memeplex, for example . . .

January, 2084
Professor Marburg doesn't know whether to laugh or weep. If a mind *has* been accidentally created by the movement of people through the d-mat network, then Straight-Face may well be right, albeit for the wrong reasons. The Fool is all of us, and we are The Fool.

She has just remembered that, in Scotland, someone who has been tricked on April Fool's Day is known as a *gowk*, which is an old word for *cuckoo*.

March 31st, 2084
Professor Marburg of New Leiden University writes her final blog post. In it she explains her theory and elaborates on the almost godlike potential of this emergent organism. We are as tiny compared to it as our cells are to us, she says. But we are not entirely insignificant, not in a chaotic system: butterfly wings, remember? Her work comprises just one cell in that vast creature, and it made a significant difference. She provided a necessary piece of the puzzle for the creature to become aware of itself, via the memeplex. She could even claim to be its midwife, if she wanted to.

She does not want to claim anything of the sort. All she wants is to stop worrying about the consequences for the entire human race of what she has inadvertently done.

Professor Marburg, 60, composes another note, which she leaves in an obvious place, and then she goes to sleep.

April 1st, 2084
Fool's Day has supplanted Halloween as the most popular holiday celebration in the world, behind only New Year's Day. Straight-Face's annual Sober Address is watched by millions. The death rate is the highest so far, but The Fool is not directly implicated in any way. Next year, The Fool will turn 10, if the phenomenon continues unchecked.

Few hear about the death of an obscure academic in a small European city, even fewer the typo in her suicide note. However, the coroner makes a note of it in his report, an electronic document readily available to anyone who cares to read it.

In the suicide note, instead of "I have cancer," Professor Marburg wrote, "I *am* cancer."

Careless, the coroner observes, for a woman of such impressive intellect.

Five Stages of Grief After the Alien Invasion

CAROLINE M. YOACHIM

Denial

Ellie huddled in the corner of her daughter's room. She sang a quiet lullaby and cradled her swaddled infant in her arms. Lexi was four months old, or maybe thirteen months? Ellie shook her head. There hadn't been a birthday party, and thirteen-month-olds didn't need swaddling. She tried to rearrange the swaddling blankets so they didn't cover Lexi's face, but every time she moved the blankets, all she saw underneath was another layer of blankets.

"Oskar?" she called. "Come and hold the baby for a bit, I need to go out and buy formula."

Oskar came in and gave her the same sad look he'd worn all week. Work, she decided, must be going poorly. She wished he would confide in her about it, but he didn't like to burden her with his problems. Lexi's room was dark, and the light switch wasn't working. Ellie opened the blinds, but the window was covered in white paint, making it impossible to see outside.

"Did you paint the windows?" she asked. Their apartment was on the third floor, and it had a lovely view of the treetops. "Lexi will want to see the birds."

"Sporefall killed all the birds," Oskar said, his voice bitter, "and we don't need formula. It's been months, Ellie. I know how hard this is, but I can't do this anymore. The pain is bad enough without reliving it with you every day."

Ellie frowned. "If you're too busy to watch the baby you should say so."

Oskar leaned down and kissed the top of her head. "I'm going, Ellie. There's a caravan heading down to L.A., and I haven't heard a thing from Jessica since sporefall. She didn't even answer the letter I sent about Lexi. I've hired a caretaker to help you get by without me, her name is Marybeth. She lost her wife to the sporefall, so maybe you two can help each other get through your grief."

"A little extra help around the house will be nice," Ellie said. "Tell your sister hello."

Ellie smiled. Jessica was a good influence on Oskar. She'd cheer him right up.

Oskar's eyes were teary when he turned to leave the room. She wondered if his allergies were acting up. He'd said something about spores. When she went to get the formula, she could pick up an antihistamine for him.

• • •

Ellie put Lexi in the high chair, still swaddled in blankets, and tried to spoon-feed her pureed peas. It wasn't working very well. Four months was too early for solids and the entire jar ended up on the blankets rather than in the baby. Ellie put the empty jar in the sink.

Someone knocked on the door, unlocked it, and came inside. It wasn't Oskar.

"Your husband gave me a key," the woman said, "I'm Marybeth. You must be Ellie."

Ellie nodded, "And this is Lexi. She's a bit of a mess right now." Ellie dabbed at the blankets with a napkin, then added, embarrassed, "She's a bit young for it, but I tried to feed her."

Marybeth smiled sadly. "Lexi died, Ellie. Nine months ago the Eridani seeded the planet with spores. Once they realized the planet was inhabited, they undid the damage as best they could, but they came too late for the elderly and the very young."

"Well, I'm glad they came nine months ago and not now," Ellie said, wiping the tray of the highchair with the food-smeared napkin. "Oskar hired you to watch Lexi? Do you do laundry, too? Her blankets are a mess."

Marybeth carefully unwound Lexi's outermost blanket and put it in the laundry hamper. "It would be better if you could move on, Ellie. This isn't healthy."

Satisfied that Marybeth could take care of Lexi, Ellie went to the bathroom and took a shower. Cold water poured down around her skin, and she scrubbed until she was red to be sure she got rid of all the spores. Oskar was allergic to spores, and she didn't want to make his symptoms any worse. Oh, but the babysitter—she came from outside, she must have been covered in spores.

Ellie ran out from the bathroom, dripping wet and wrapped in a towel. "You came from outside! You've exposed poor Lexi to spores!"

Marybeth put one hand on Ellie's shoulder and gently guided her back to the bathroom. "Hush now, the spores are gone, all grown into plants. We don't have to worry about spores."

Marybeth returned the next day with an old man. Ellie hoped he wasn't sick. He was dressed too warmly for the weather: clunky black boots, several layers of baggy clothes, and a fleece hat with flaps that covered his ears. He was short and stout with ashen skin and a grin too broad for his face. It made him look like a toad, Ellie thought, then pushed the uncharitable thought from her head.

"Come in, come in," Ellie said, then realized that her welcome was too late and Marybeth and her—was the man her father? Maybe her grandfather—were already in the entryway of her apartment.

"I thought it'd be good for you to meet one of the Eridani," Marybeth said. "It might help you come to grips with what happened."

"Nice to meet you, Mr. Eridani," Ellie said. It was time for Lexi's nap. The apartment was warm, good for sleeping, but Ellie could use some fresh air. "Do you sing, Marybeth?"

"Sing?" Marybeth asked. "No, not really."

"What about you, Mr. Eridani?" Ellie turned to the old man. "Will you sing my daughter lullabies? I'd like to go for a walk."

"It might be good for her to get out of the house," Marybeth told her grandfather. "I think Oskar made a mistake in painting the windows." She went over to the kitchen window and pried it open, sending flecks of dried paint flying everywhere.

Ellie turned her back on the kitchen, trying to protect Lexi from the nasty paint dust. "Don't let her breathe the dust, she just got over a terrible cough."

The old man nodded, then held out his arms to take Lexi. He held her gently, and while his mouth was fixed in the same broad smile, his bulging black eyes seemed sad. Ellie wondered if he was longing for grandchildren of his own.

"Don't be sad. Lexi clearly likes you. She didn't even cry." Ellie put on a sweater and opened her apartment door. "I won't be gone long."

The trees along the edge of the sidewalk had oddly purple leaves, and the people that passed looked far too weary for a sunny Saturday afternoon, but as she walked beneath the open windows of her apartment, she could hear the low hum of a lullaby, slow and sweet, sure to soothe her daughter straight to sleep.

Anger

Amelia was twelve the night the spores fell, and she remembered it vividly. Thousands of meteors burned bright as they fell through the atmosphere. Charred black pods burst open when they crashed to the ground. By dawn, the air was filled with swirling clouds of orange mist, like pollen blowing from the trees. Every person and creature on the planet breathed the spores. The birds were the first to die, but not the last.

"Come away from the window, Sis." Brayden tried to tousle her hair like she was six years old or something. "Dad will be home soon, and you haven't done your homework yet."

"I didn't do my homework because it's stupid to pretend that nothing has changed," Amelia said. "Everyone in my class lost people to the spore. Friends, grandparents . . . siblings. Tia's parents got killed in the riots. Zach's older brother died in one of the fires. Then the way they healed us—"

She shuddered. She still had nightmares about the croaker that thinned into some kind of fog and poured itself down her throat, picking the spores out of her lungs and healing the damage the sprouting plants had done. It was that or die when the spores grew, but she'd still thrashed so much that Dad had to hold her down to keep her from hurting herself.

"It was eleven months ago," Brayden said. He stared at the sky for a moment, lost in his own thoughts. "What's the alternative to going back to normal? If you didn't have school, you'd sit home and sulk all day like that guy that came down from Portland."

Their neighbor's brother had showed up on the caravan last week, looking for Jessica, but she'd already left for the space station. She was one of the scientists chosen to help negotiate a treaty with the aliens. The only treaty Amelia wanted to see was 'get off our planet and take your damned purple plants with you.'

"Oskar sits around and sulks all day," Amelia said, "but I would go out and kill croakers."

Brayden shook his head. "You can't kill croakers. People have tried. They can't be poisoned, stabbed, or shot. No matter what you do to them, they recohere, they heal. If you did more of your homework, you might know that."

Unlike the rest of her classes, which she'd given up on, Amelia had paid careful attention to all the details of croaker biology. Despite their solid-seeming forms, croakers were essentially sentient fog. The squat froglike body they used on Earth was a dense gray cloud, thick enough to hold up the clothes they wore, but little else. Projectiles and blades passed right through and did little harm, and poison passed through unabsorbed.

Amelia had a different plan. She would trap a croaker bit by bit in a hundred glass jars. Then she'd throw the jars into a fire, one by one. Would the pain of that death be as bad as the last desperate gasps of her little brother? Gavin was four, and screamed all his last night in pain and fear. Spores made his lungs burn, the doctor said.

Amelia would make a croaker burn.

Croakers wandered the streets like ghosts, occasionally stopping to eat leaves from the purple plants that had grown from the spores. According to the news, the croakers were observing, collecting data so they could repair more of the damage they did at sporefall, but as near as Amelia could tell, the big gray frogs were just making themselves right at home. Amelia waited behind one of their licorice-smelling plants with a cardboard box full of glass jars.

A croaker came to nibble at the leaves, and she jumped out from behind the bush, jar in hand. She scooped out a big section of the croaker's ugly frogface. The croaker was thicker than she expected, like gelatin or pudding, rather than air. The gray goo in the jar was repulsively flesh-like, and her stomach churned as she screwed the lid into place. The croaker let out a high pitched whine. Its face appeared unchanged, despite her jarful of gray goo.

She couldn't do it. She had a boxful of jars, and she wanted the croaker to burn, but she couldn't bring herself to take another scoop of its ashen flesh. It stared at her with round black eyes, still making a high pitched sound, though softer now, a sad keening sound.

"You killed Gavin!" she screamed. "You messed up my whole world and now you stay here like you own it! You should burn for it!"

She hurled the jar of gray goo at the sidewalk. It shattered against the concrete and shards of glass flew everywhere. A cloud of gray swirled up from the shimmering fragments of the jar before drifting back onto the croaker. Into the croaker.

She grabbed another jar from her box and threw it at the croaker. It bounced off the alien's face, and the froglike grin didn't even flinch. "Go back to where you came from!" she shouted and flung jar after jar at the croaker, until her cardboard box was empty and the sidewalk was buried beneath a pile of shattered glass.

The croaker scooped up the broken glass in big webbed hands, mounding it and sculpting it into its own image. Amelia watched, fascinated despite herself. The croaker smoothed the bits of glass as easily as a sculptor might shape clay. It made a statue of a croaker, and in the statue's broad glass hands there was a human child with indistinct features. Not her brother, but a child like him. Perhaps all children like him. Unlike every croaker Amelia had ever seen, there was no froglike grin on the statue's face.

Brayden ran over. "I heard all the noise, and—" He stared at the statue.

"I wanted to set a croaker on fire, but I couldn't do it." Amelia said. "Not even after everything they did."

Perhaps it was a trick of the light, but the statue didn't look empty. Delicate orange flames danced inside the statue of the croaker, complete with thin wisps of gray smoke that reminded her of the swirling cloud when she broke the jar and let the croaker go. It had left a piece of itself inside the statue, to burn inside the glass.

She thought her mind was playing tricks on her, but Brayden saw it too. "They already burn for what they did."

The croaker bowed its head, then turned and walked away.

Bargaining

The alien standing in front of Jessica was four feet tall, slate gray, and shaped like an oversized toad. It smelled like chalk and made a quiet wheezing noise, barely audible over the hum of the orbital stabilizers. The temperature onboard the station was comfortable for humans, but the alien wore a thick sweater, knitted by one of Jessica's former graduate students as a gesture of goodwill from all humankind. A large round button with the number 17 was pinned to the purple wool. Eridani didn't use names.

Eridani 17 extended a webbed hand. The flesh of its fingers thinned, creating the illusion of wisps of smoke curling up from its palm. The smoke shaped itself into North America, and then a city skyline.

"Toronto?" Jessica asked. The city had a distinctive tower. Eridani 17 shook its head.

Negotiating with the Eridani was like a game of Pictionary, except that Jessica was sober and—thank god—didn't have to actually draw anything. Her brother Oskar had always been the artist in the family, excelling at Pictionary even when he was half her age. If his most recent message was any indication, all he ever drew now was pictures of his estranged wife, who lost her mind after sporefall killed their baby.

"Seattle," Jessica said.

The Eridani understood spoken language, but not by translating individual words. According to the best available translation, the Eridani heard ideas in the spaces between the words.

She hoped that this was true. She was not authorized to ask for what she truly wanted, and the sessions were recorded.

Eridani 17 transformed its speaking hand into an image of several Eridani standing between two skyscrapers. As Jessica watched, a giant web appeared between the two buildings, soon followed by several pods filled with what she guessed were baby Eridani.

"Seattle has a substantial human population, but I'm sure we can find an abandoned region that suits your needs," Jessica said. Atlanta, perhaps. It was warmer there, and the sporefall had been particularly dense.

Eridani 17 made no response, and its hand solidified. This meant that an alternate site was acceptable. Jessica would get a list of abandoned and near-abandoned cities to propose in tomorrow's negotiations.

Next on her agenda was a request for additional technology to assist in maintaining and rebuilding the human population in the regions hardest hit by sporefall. Negotiations happened in parallel, with dozens of humans in one-on-one sessions with the Eridani at any given time. She checked her tablet to make sure that nothing from the other sessions had altered her agenda.

"Like many of my people, I lost family members to the spore," Jessica began. She concentrated on her memories of her niece, a tiny baby that she had held only once. "We struggle to rebuild what we once had."

She was supposed to be asking for technological advances in transportation and communications, for new methods of agriculture to help human crops coexist with the invasive purple weeds that grew from the Eridani spores. She was supposed to infuse her spoken words with a plea for these things, so that the aliens would hear their needs in the spaces between her words. Instead, she thought of all the people she had lost in the sporefall and the chaos afterwards—relatives, coworkers, neighbors, friends.

Give them back, she pleaded. The Eridani were so advanced; there had to be something they could do. "Surely there is some technology you have that can help us."

Eridani 17 thinned itself entirely into cloud, leaving the purple sweater in a puddle on the floor. It reformed itself into the shape of Gavin, her neighbor's four-year-old son who had died from the spore. The boy sat cross-legged on the floor and in his lap was a tightly swaddled baby with a drooly grin and dimpled cheeks. Lexi.

The alien had somehow called the children from her mind, but the scene that it created was not a remembered image. Gavin had never met Lexi. And yet, if he had, this was exactly how it might have looked. The boy's expression was a mix of curiosity and wariness, and Lexi—

She very nearly said what she was thinking, that she would give anything to have her back. Her death, and Ellie's breakdown, was destroying Oskar. Each death from the spore cascaded into a thousand unwanted consequences, and all the world was broken now. There must be some way the Eridani could undo time or reshape space and reverse the deaths they'd caused. There had to be a way.

Gavin held Lexi with one arm and raised the other up in front of him. He thinned his fingers, which was disconcerting. Jessica knew the ghosts were really just Eridani 17, but human fingers shouldn't thin the way that Gavin's were thinning.

"You will give us back the ones we've lost in exchange for," Jessica paused to study the map that hovered where Gavin's hand should have been. "The entire West Coast?"

It snapped Jessica back to reality. The Eridani had always shown remorse for what they'd done. They'd claimed to be unaware that the planet was inhabited, that they would not have sent their spore and, later, their colony ships, if they had known otherwise. She hadn't expected them to use her grief to their advantage in negotiations. She could not trade that much territory, not for mere ghosts.

"Not for shadows and memories," Jessica said.

Gavin leaned forward and kissed baby Lexi on the forehead. It was so close to what she wanted, they were almost real. Better than Ellie's empty bundle of blankets. Close enough, perhaps, to pull her sister-in-law back to reality. So close to what she wanted, and yet so far. And she couldn't trade that much territory even if the Eridani offered to pull the actual children from the past. "I am not authorized to negotiate concessions of this magnitude."

Gavin and Lexi melted right before her eyes, merged into a puddle, and reformed into the default frogform of Eridani 17. The entire session was recorded, and back on Earth it was undoubtedly already being analyzed. They would see the tears in her eyes, and she would be sent back to the planet in disgrace. Back to Earth, but not back home. Home was a place that still had those children in it.

Depression

Oskar got home from a long shift of weeding alien foodplants out of the avocado grove. His hands were stained purple and smelled of licorice. He set a 10 pound bag of avocadoes on the counter. He should trade some avocadoes to the neighbor kids for one of the trout they farmed in the courtyard fountain, but he didn't want to eat. He shut himself into his sister's guest bedroom and stared at the ceiling, crushed beneath the weight of his bad choices.

He shouldn't have left Ellie.

The walls were covered in sketches of his wife. Her smile, her eyes, her slender hands. Cheeks dotted with pale brown freckles. Hair tied back with a few loose strands to frame her face. She was the one who left him. She left reality behind and spent all day pretending a bundle of blankets was their baby girl. No one could blame him for not wanting to relive that kind of pain, day after day. He'd tried for months. Marybeth was a family friend, and he'd given her everything they had to take care of his wife.

All of that so Oskar could go and find his sister, Jessica. He'd been worried that she might need help, but she wasn't sitting helpless in her apartment. No, she'd gone off to the space station to be one of Earth's ambassadors. This was supposed to be his big chance to not be the baby brother anymore, to swoop in and save Jessica from the post-invasion chaos, and she hadn't needed him at all. She never did. He had no idea if she'd even gotten the message he'd tried to send.

Someone pounded on the door. Probably the neighbor kids. Brayden liked avocadoes, and trading with him was a better deal than trying to buy them somewhere.

He opened the door. "Jessica."

"I can't believe you changed my locks." Jessica faked a scowl, then grinned and gave him a big hug. "You look like crap."

Oskar retreated to Jessica's guestroom. His sister hadn't understood how he could come down here and leave Ellie behind, no matter how he tried to explain.

People started pouring in from the east. They moved into abandoned apartments, office buildings, malls. Los Angeles turned back into a bustling city. Jessica said that the government had traded Arizona and New Mexico to the frogs. All the extra people made it harder to get work. His heavy heart made it harder to wake up and face the day.

On his second straight day of refusing to get out of bed, Jessica marched into his room like she was twenty and he was ten, and she could boss him around. "Draw me a bird."

"Go away," he said. There were no birds, and he could see right through his sister's scheme. Birds were from happier times. She thought sketching a picture would pull him out of this funk. She was wrong. Remembering the way things were would only make it worse. "There are no birds. Sporefall killed them all."

"Think of it as rent. It'll do you good to draw something other than Ellie, over and over again. All I'm asking for is one really good picture of a bird." Jessica left without waiting for him to answer.

He only had a few sheets of good thick paper left, he'd used most of it to draw his pictures of Ellie. He got one out. He closed his eyes and tried to picture the stellar jays that had eaten peanuts from the feeder outside his window, back before the sporefall. He remembered blue and black feathers, and the general shape of the head, but the details were fuzzy. There were pictures of birds in books, but he shouldn't need that. He should be able to do this. It had only been a year.

For the first time in weeks, he opened the guestroom blinds. The apartment was on the fourth floor, and the window looked across the alley at a near-identical brick building. He tried to imagine birds flying in the alley, landing on the concrete below to hunt for bugs or seeds, but thoughts of flying set his mind to thinking about soaring out through the window and falling into oblivion.

He closed the blinds.

Two days later Oskar had only one sheet of good paper left, and he had not yet managed a picture of a bird. He ate when Jessica forced him to, and he slept until Jessica made him get out of bed. There was no point to pictures of birds. There was no point to anything, not anymore.

Jessica came in with half an avocado. Did he really have to eat, again? But no, she started eating it herself, spooning the mushy green into her mouth and smiling as though it actually tasted good to eat a plain avocado, again. "This is the last one from the bag, and food rations have been short at the community center, so we can't count on that. We need to decide what to do next. There's a caravan going north, right through Portland."

He didn't want to go back. What if Marybeth had abandoned Ellie, despite all her promises? He couldn't face the chance. "I'm staying here."

Jessica shook her head. "You're not. I'm trading the apartment for passage on the caravan and food for the trip. If you want to stay in L.A., you're on your own."

She left him to consider his options, and his gaze drifted to the window. It would be so easy, so quick. If he never went back to Ellie, he could believe that she was okay, maybe even happy. He wouldn't have to face a world that could never possibly be right again.

He opened the blinds. An alien was walking in the alley, smiling the same damn frog-smile that the aliens always smiled. It saw him in the window, and thinned into a cloud. When it came back together, it was a flock of birds. Not the stellar jays he'd been trying to draw, but pigeons, plump and gray. They fluttered up and landed on windowsills and power lines outside the window. They weren't real, but they were enough to evoke a clear memory in his mind.

Oskar could soar out the window, or he could draw this memory of birds for Jessica and go with her back to Portland.

He calmed his shaking hands and sketched the birds.

Acceptance

Marybeth walked with Ellie to the clinic. Ellie insisted on bringing 'Lexi,' a bundle of filthy blankets that she refused to believe wasn't actually her dead baby. Marybeth hoped the new treatment would help. Ellie was an amazing woman, able to find joy in all the smallest things. Even now, as they walked along abandoned streets with Eridani foodplants, Ellie chattered to her blanket-bundle baby about how beautiful the orange blossoms were on the lovely purple trees.

Marybeth couldn't appreciate the beauty of the 'blossoms.' They weren't flowers at all, but clusters of tiny spheres, each one full of orange spores. The trees would release spores soon, and despite Eridani assurances that there would be no harm to humans this time, she could not put aside her memories of the last sporefall, and all the death it caused. Yolanda's death.

Very few healthy adults had died in the sporefall, but her wife hadn't been healthy. She'd had alpha-1-antitrypsin deficiency emphysema—a genetic disease that left her with the lungs of a sixty-year-old smoker when she was only thirty-two. Even without the sporefall, her condition had been deteriorating. She'd had a complex daily routine of inhalers and pills to try to keep the coughing fits and wheezing in check, and a tank of supplemental oxygen for her worst days.

Yolanda would have seen the beauty in the alien plants, just as Ellie did. Looking at Ellie was like looking into Yolanda's past, back to the early days of their relationship, before her illness sapped away her strength.

Was falling in love with a straight woman any better than carrying around a bundle of filthy blankets?

The clinic was an Eridani clinic, one of several that were part of the treaty that had been negotiated with the aliens. They were greeted by a man in a white coat when they entered, and left to wait in a small room with black plastic chairs and battered magazines from before the sporefall.

"Will Oskar meet us here?" Ellie asked. Much as she refused to accept the death of her baby, she continued to believe that Oskar would return.

"He's not here, El. We're going to see one of the Eridani," Marybeth explained. "They have a treatment that might help you."

An alien appeared in the doorway, wearing what looked like a down comforter tied like a toga. It studied them with beady black eyes, then beckoned to Ellie, recognizing that she was the one more in need of treatment.

"I'd like to come too." Marybeth said.

The Eridani doctor nodded its assent.

The treatment was painful to watch. The alien thinned itself into a gray fog, then reformed into images drawn from Ellie's mind—not mindreading, exactly. If Ellie said nothing, the alien could not hear her thoughts. It was only when Ellie spoke about her daughter that the memories came through. Then it was like watching a moving slideshow all in shades of gray:

Oskar holding Lexi in the hospital, the day she was born.

Ellie's struggles with breastfeeding when Lexi wouldn't latch.

Bottles of formula, carefully mixed and warmed at all hours of the night.

So many things that Marybeth had never seen, memories that haunted poor Ellie and made her break from reality. Then came the worst, the sporefall.

Ellie going out to find formula for Lexi, and coming back covered in fine orange dust.

Lexi's pitiful coughing and weak cries.

The days on end where she only slept upright, leaning on Ellie's chest.

Finally, the end, the moment when there were no more breaths, and Oskar took Lexi away. Marybeth cried as the baby disappeared from the three dimensional scene the Eridani recreated from the particles of its own body. She glanced at her friend, hopeful that the therapy had helped. Ellie was crying, but she continued talking. Her baby was dead, but Ellie wasn't finished.

More images appeared, of a Lexi that never was, in a world that no longer existed. Lexi toddling across the living room, Lexi putting on a ridiculously big backpack and going off to kindergarten, Lexi at the park feeding ducks. There were no ducks, and Lexi would never be six, but the Eridani doctor showed the impossible futures right along with the horrifying past.

Lexi's senior prom, her wedding, the birth of Ellie's first grandchild. The scenes skimmed through time and Marybeth could no longer watch, no longer listen to Ellie's words. She simply watched Ellie stare into the images that poured out, and held Ellie's hand as she cried. Since she had turned away from the doctor, it took her a moment to realize that the Eridani had resumed its default frogform. Ellie was no longer speaking, only sobbing softly.

She met Marybeth's eyes, and there was a depth to her gaze that was missing before.

"My Lexi," Ellie said. "My Lexi is gone."

• • •

After the treatment, Ellie didn't need a caretaker, but Marybeth had long since abandoned her apartment and they enjoyed each other's company. Ellie often wore the same grim smile that so often graced Yolanda's face when she was sick, and it tugged at Marybeth's heart. She tried to remind herself that Ellie was a different woman, a *straight* woman, but she could not help but hope that somehow, if enough time passed, things could be different.

Ellie made good progress in embracing reality. Together they dismantled Lexi's crib and set it out on the curb in front of the apartment. It wasn't long before a woman who looked like she might be expecting came and carried it away.

Oskar came back from L.A. Marybeth greeted him at the door, and had no choice but to let him in, for all that he abandoned Ellie when she needed him most.

"I'm so glad you're both okay," he said. Marybeth shrugged. He could say what he wanted, it wouldn't change what he had done. She only hoped that she wouldn't lose Ellie, now that he was back.

"Hi, Oskar," Ellie said. The sight of him brought her to tears, but Marybeth couldn't tell whether they were tears of joy or pain or anger.

"I'm so sorry," Oskar said. "I didn't want to leave you, but I couldn't stay. I was hurting too."

"I forgive you," Ellie said. "I know it must have been hard."

He smiled and went to embrace her, but she stepped back. "I forgive you, but we can't go back to how things were. I saw what might have been, if the Eridani had never come, and Lexi had lived, and it was beautiful. We could have had an amazing life. But those are impossible futures, and I have to let them go and come back to what is real."

"Is it another man?" Oskar asked, then realized that Marybeth was standing there. "Or another woman?"

Ellie shook her head. "There's no one else. Certainly not Marybeth, though she's a dear friend."

It was nothing that Marybeth did not already know. She had always known that Ellie was straight; there had never been any sign that she was interested. Ellie would never be Yolanda.

Marybeth grabbed her coat and made polite excuses. Ellie and Oskar had a lot to talk about, and Marybeth didn't want to hear it. She went outside and started walking, not caring where she went.

The wind picked up, and an orange cloud blew down from the Eridani foodtrees. The second sporefall had begun, a new cycle of alien life. According to the translators, the initial sporefall had been a different strain, modified to be more aggressive for terraforming, so that the Eridani would be sure to have foodplants when they arrived at their new home. This second sporefall should be as harmless to humans as ordinary pollen.

Marybeth sneezed at the orange air, but she refused to go back inside.

She would not hide from this new world.

Silent Bridge, Pale Cascade
BENJANUN SRIDUANGKAEW

The knife of her consciousness peeling off death in layers: this is how she wakes.

She is General Lunha of Silent Bridge, who fought one war to a draw as a man, and won five more a woman against adversaries who commanded miniature suns.

The knowledge reconstitutes piecemeal in the flexing muscles of her memory, in the gunfire-sear of her thoughts as she opens her eyes to a world of spider lilies skirmishing in flowerbeds, a sky of fractal glass. She is armed: an orchid-blade along one hip, a burst-pistol along the other. She is armored: a helm of black scarabs on her head, a sheath of amber chitin on her limbs and torso. There is no bed for her, no casket enclosing her. She comes to awareness on her feet, at ease but sharp. The way she has always been.

Grass crackles and hisses. She draws the blade, its petals unfurling razor mouths, and recognizes that this weapon is personal to her. All generals have them: a bestiary of blades and a gathering of guns, used to an edge and oiled to a sheen. She maintained a smaller collection than most; this was one she always kept at her side.

The grass is stilled, coils of circuits and muscles and fangs, petroleum stains on Lunha's sword. She fires a shot into its vitals to be certain. A detonation of soundless light.

Her datasphere snaps online. Augmens bring one of the walls into sharp focus, an output panel. At the moment, audio alone.

"We had to make sure you were physically competent." A voice keyed to a register of neutrality, inflection and otherwise; she cannot tell accent, preferred presentation, or much else. "It is our pleasure to welcome you back, General Lunha."

"My connection is restricted. Why is this?"

"There have been some changes to data handling at your tier of command. We'll send you the new protocols shortly. It is routine. You'll want a briefing."

"Yes." Lunha attempts to brute-force access, finds herself without grid privileges that ought to have been hers by right.

"Your loyalty to the Hegemony has never been questioned."

"Thus I've proven," said Lunha, who in life served it for sixty years from cadet to general.

"We will not question it now." The panel shimmers into a tactical map. "This world would offer its riches and might to our enemies. Neutralize it and the woman who lures it away from Hegemonic peace. Peruse her dossier at your leisure."

The traitor planet is Tiansong, the Lake of Bridges, which in life was Lunha's homeworld.

Their leader is Xinjia of Pale Cascade, who in life was Lunha's bride.

Naturally she questions whether she is Lunha, rebuilt from scraps of skin and smears, or a clone injected with Lunha's data. The difference is theoretical beyond clan altars; in practice the two are much the same. There is a family-ghost copy of her floating about in Tiansong's local grid, but that too is a reconstruction from secondary and tertiary sources, no more her soul or self than her career logs.

The grid enters her in a flood, though like all Hegemonic personnel above a certain rank Lunha is partitioned to retain autonomous consciousness. For good measure she runs self-diagnostics, which inform her that she is not embedded with regulators or remote surveillance. Perhaps it is a sign of trust; perhaps the reconstruction is experimental, and the biotechs did not want to risk interfering with her implants. She entertains the thought that she never died—severe injury, a long reconstruction, an edit of her memory to remove the event. The report is sealed, either way.

They've given her a tailored habitat: one section for rest, one for contemplation, one for physical practice. Being in this profession, she has few personal effects; most are accounted for. Not merely equipment but also the keepsakes of conquests. Here the gold-veined skeletons of Grenshal wolves, there the silver-blossom web of live Mahing spiders. A Silent Bridge shrine for the memories of elders, compressed snapshots of their accomplishments, proverbs and wisdom. Lunha did not consult them often, does not consult them now, and examines the altar only to ensure her family-ghost does not number among them.

Her grid access continues to be tight. She may listen in on military broadcasts of all levels when she cares to, but she can't communicate. Public memory is a matter of course and she checks that for civilian perception of Tiansong. To the best of their knowledge Tiansong embroiled itself in civil war, during which a new religion emerged, spearheaded by Xinjia. A dispatch would be sent to return Tiansong to peace.

Reports on classified channels are somewhat different.

Out of habit she evaluates troop strength, positions, resources: this is impersonal, simply the way her mind works. She estimates that with Tiansong's defenses it'd require less than a month to subdue her homeworld with minimal damage. In a situation where that isn't a concern, it would be under a week. Quick strike rather than campaign, and entirely beneath her.

For three days she is left in isolation—no other being shares her space and she lacks social access. The void field around the compound forbids her to step far beyond the garden. On the fourth day, she stirs from meditation to the hum of moth engines, the music of shields flickering out to accommodate arrival. She does not go forth to greet nor move to arm herself; it seems beside the point.

Her handler is purebred Costeya stock, a statuesque neutrois with eyes the color of lunar frost. They wear no uniform, introduce themselves simply as Operative Isren.

"From which division?" Lunha tries to write to Isren, the right of any general to alter the thoughts and memory of lesser officers. She can't.

"Operative," Isren says, and nothing else. They bow to her in the Tiansong manner, hand cupped over fist, before saluting her. "Your situation's unique."

"Why am I required? It is no trouble to flatten Tiansong."

Isren has knelt so they are level; they have a trick of arranging their bearing and their limbs so that the difference in height doesn't intimidate. "A bloodless solution is sought."

"There are other Tiansong personnel in active service."

When Isren smiles there's something of the flirt in the bend of their mouth. "None so brilliant as you. Xinjia of Pale Cascade is a labyrinthine opponent. She has brought awareness of the public sync to her world and had the opportunity to spread the idea before we imposed embargo. She boasts . . . disconnect. In essence she's become an infection."

"Has she achieved it? Disconnect?"

A shard of silence pinched between Isren's professional circumspection and the situation's need for candor. When they do speak it is delicately, around the edge of this balance. "Not through the conventional methods. Her way entails ripping out network nodes and reverse-engineering them. Fifty-fifty chance for cerebral damage. Five to eight thousand have been incapacitated, at last count."

Lunha browses through available reports. Risk of brain death or not, Xinjia has gained traction, so much that she has been made First of Tiansong. It's not unanimous; nearly half the clans posited against her. But nearly half was not half, and Silent Bridge tipped the scale. Her plans have been broadcast to twenty independent worlds. "Removing her won't suffice."

"No. You are invested in keeping Tiansong well, Xinjia alive, and that's why we brought you back."

"Let me travel there. I would assess the situation on the ground."

"That was anticipated," Isren says. "We are on Tiansong."

When Lunha last visited her homeworld she was a man. Among family she's celebrated only as daughter and niece, for all that she flows between the two as water over stone. Whatever her gender, General Lunha's face—pride of several clans—is too well known, and so she puts on a mesh to hollow out her cheeks, broaden her nose, slope out her brow.

She travels light, almost ascetically. One firearm, one blade. Tiansong currency, but not too much. Her one concession to luxury is a disruptor array to guard against targeting and deep scans. Isren does not accompany her in person; on the pristine sea of Tiansong phenotypes, Isren's Costeya face would be an oil slick. The operative has no objection to blending in, but on so short a notice, adjusting musculature, complexion and facial tells is beyond even Isren.

Lunha avoids air transports and their neural checks, keeping to the trains and their serpent-tracks. She takes her time. It is a leave of absence—the idea amuses and she catches herself smiling into the scaled window, her reflection momentarily interrupting art ads. One of them urges her to see a production of *The Pearl Goddess and the Turtle,* done by live actors and performed in a grid-dead auditorium. No recording, no interruptions.

At one clan-hold she says she is a daughter of Razor Garden; at another, in different clothes and with a voice deepened by mods, Lunha introduces himself as a groom newly marrying into Peony Aqueduct. At each Lunha is received with courtesy and invited to evening teas, wedding dinners, autumn feasts. Despite the tension of embargo they are hospitable, but none will so much as breathe Xinjia's name.

Her breakthrough comes while she sits in a kitchen sipping plum tea, legs stretched out and listening to an elderly cook who fancies she resembles his middle son, long lost to a gambling addiction. "You want to destroy a nemesis, you teach their child to gamble," the cook is saying as he spoons chives and onions into dumpling skin.

"So the ancestors say." Lunha's enemies tend toward a more direct approach. She takes pride in having survived some two hundred assassination attempts, though it doesn't escape her that she might've failed to foil the final one. "These days there are quicker ways."

The cook chuckles like dry clay cracking. "These days you point the young, impressionable son to Pale Cascade."

"Ah, it is but half a chance of ruin. I thought they hosted guests no more, having become grudging on hospitality of late? Since we can't get off-world it was my hope to at least visit every hold before matrimony binds me . . . "

He shrugs, pinches the last dumpling shut, and begins arranging them in the steamer. On Tiansong no one trusts replicants to get cuisine right. "If you know someone who knows someone in Silent Bridge."

"Is that so. Many thanks, uncle."

She catches the next finned, plumaged train bound for her ancestral home.

The public sync, the great shared memory, is an instrument to maintain peace. Even after learning of it and what it does, Lunha continued to believe this, as she does now. It doesn't do much for freedom of thought; it comes with all the downsides of information regulated under the state's clenched fist and the grid usurps perception of the real. But it functions, stabilizes. The Costeya Hegemony has existed in equilibrium for centuries.

It is useful now as she edits herself into the distant branches of Silent Bridge rather than its primary boughs, as her true birth order dictates. The specifics make her hesitate. She settles on female, for convenience more than anything, and picks childless Ninth Aunt as her mother. No sibling, less dissonance to having a sudden sister where once there was none. Those reactions cannot be overridden. Emotions cannot be molded.

When she arrives at the entrance bridge suspended between the maws of pearl-clasping dragons, Ninth Aunt comes to greet her. "My girl," her aunt says uncertainly, "what kept you so long in Razor Garden?"

"Grand nuptials, Mother, and I earned my board helping." A bow, proper. An embrace, stiff. Having a daughter is merely a fact, the gestures Ninth Aunt makes merely obligation.

Her edits have it that she's been away three months; in truth she hasn't been home for as long as—her mind stumbles over the rut of her death. But not counting that it's been five years. Silent Bridge hasn't changed. A central pagoda for common worship. Sapphire arches and garnet gates twining in conversation to mark the city's boundaries. Tiansong cities have always been less crowded than most, and there's never that density of lives in the habitat towers here as on Costeya birthworlds. A wealth of space, a freedom of aesthetics. Barely a whisper of the Hegemony.

Far better off than many Costeya subjects, Lunha knows for a fact; there are border planets that remain in ruins even to this day after their annexation. She cannot understand Xinjia.

When they first met Xinjia wore masks and prosthetic arms; she danced between folded shadows of dragons and herons, only parts of her visible in infrared. Like all thespians of her caliber, Xinjia never appeared in off-world broadcasts. Tiansong makes a fortune out of its insularity—foreigners wishing to enjoy its arts must come to the source and pay dearly, though there are always rogues and imitators.

Lunha in the audience, breathless from applause. A friend who knew a friend brokered her an introduction. Offstage, Xinjia shed the mask but kept the dress, paper breastplate and bladed belts. In the custom of shadow-thespians she wore her face plain, bare, without mods. It made Lunha touch her own, self-conscious of the optic overlays, the duochrome cast to her jawline, replicant-chic.

They talked quickly, amidst the noise of departing spectators; they talked again later, in the quiet of the staff's lounge where the furniture, retrogressive, did not contour to their bodies.

"You talk drama like a layperson," Xinjia remarked once, between sips of liquid gold and jellyfish garnished in diced ivory.

"I don't have a background."

"Officer school doesn't teach fine arts?" The actor drew a finger across Lunha's knuckles. "A soldier with a passion for theater."

"Not before tonight." Lunha caught herself, succeeded in not blushing.

"Soldiers fascinate me," Xinjia said, absently. "The juxtaposition of discipline and danger. Violence and control."

Tiansong marriage lasts five years, at the end of which spouses and family members evaluate one another: how well they fit, how well they belong. A collaborative project.

They wedded on a barge, surrounded by family, blessed by avatars of thundering war-gods with their quadruple arms and spears and battle-wheels. Given that Silent Bridge and Pale Cascade were old rivals, neither Xinjia nor Lunha expected it to last—and it came a surprise to all involved that the marriage was extended past the first five years into the second, then the third.

Divorce came after Lunha made lieutenant-colonel. By then they'd been spouses for nineteen years.

The ivory tiles and the redwood walls of the great house hum with trackers. Lunha sets her array to nullify ones that would gene-match her.

Silent Bridge has always been one of the more—paranoid, she supposes other clans would say—but it's never been like this. A city-wide security lockdown. Anyone not family has been ejected; off-worlders are long gone, scared away by a non-existent epidemic just before the embargo fell.

Xinjia anticipated that sanction. Lunha considers the possibility that she found a way to manipulate the sync. It unsettles.

She keeps up desultory small talk with Ninth Aunt, with cousins who tentatively say they have missed her. It is the thing to say to a relative months unseen. They do it carefully, unsure of the words, of regarding her as family.

To pretend to be a stranger pretending to be of Silent Bridge. Lunha buried away entirely, like the haunting she is, the ghost she should be.

"Is that all you have?" Ninth Aunt says, trying to be a mother. "The clothes on your back and not much else?"

"I've always traveled light." Lunha nods. "You know that, Mother."

"You've never taken care of yourself, more like."

It always surprises Lunha what people imagine to fill up the gaps, patch up the cracks of recall brought by the blunt impact of edit. A defense mechanism, army psychologists liked to tell her, to ward off mental dissolution. There are Hegemonic facilities devoted to research into that, the sync's effects. What it can do. What it can't.

Isren has gifted her with a spy-host; Lunha activates it with a visualization of tadpoles bursting through deep water. She avoids contact. There are disconnected people in Silent Bridge. They would know Ninth Aunt has never had children.

After days of self-imposed house arrest, she steals to the streets.

In the hours of thought and ancestors, the walkways are burnished gold. A low whisper of overhead vehicles like memory, a gleam of pearl from atmospheric stations like moons. Lunha inhales not air but the quiet.

She wanders first aimless, then with a direction as she cross-references the host's eavesdropped data. From the security measures she assumed it would be the great house, the halls in which Silent Bridge primaries make governance and cast laws. Two of them her mothers. They are proud of Lunha, but they always expected her rise through the ranks, her conquests of fifteen worlds in Costeya's name, and if she'd been or done any less it would have been a blot on a lineage of prodigies.

An old shrine, turtle tiles and turtle roof, stone monks enclosing a garden of fern and lavender. The scriptorium is guarded by wasp drones. She inputs a bypass code, stop-motion images of blue heron spearing silver fish. A murmur of acknowledgment and they give way; these are all Hegemonic make, and she has been reinstated as general. They've been reverse-engineered, but not deep enough to keep her out. She can't quite fault the Tiansong techs; less than a thousand in the Hegemony command her level of access.

Between shelves showing paper books in augmens visuals, Lunha waits. She passes the time reading poetry, immersing herself in Huasing's interlocking seven-ten stanzas, Gweilin's interstitial prose-sculpture telling of the sun-archer and her moon-wife. They eel through her awareness, comforting, the balm of familiarity.

Xinjia arrives, eventually. It is where she comes to think when she needs solitude, and from what Lunha can tell solitude is precious to her these days, too rare.

The scriptorium is large, and Lunha did not go sixty years in the army without learning stealth. She finds a space to occupy, a blind spot where Xinjia will not look, and for a time simply observes.

Xinjia looks at peace, striding easily to the mat and the bar. She sheds her slippers, most of her clothes, until she is down to pastel secondskin, lavender shifting to gray as she moves. Hands on the bar she arches backward, stretching until her neck cords, the muscles in her torso pushing out in bas-relief.

Lunha turns off vocal mods and says, in her own voice, "Xinjia."

Her former wife straightens quickly, supple—sinuous. They had elaborate pet names for each other once. Bai Suzhen for Xinjia, after the white snake of legend.

A precipice moment, but Xinjia does not fall. "General Lunha is dead. What are you?"

"A ghost." Lunha reaches into Tiansong's grid. Of course there's a copy of her in the archive of primaries, her knowledge and victories turned to clan wisdom. "But you would be familiar with that."

"Shall I offer you tea?"

"No," Lunha says, though she follows when Xinjia leads her to the low table, the cushions. "How have you been?"

"You'd be familiar with updates on me."

"First of Tiansong."

"It was necessary to obtain that title to do what needs doing." Xinjia calls up the ghost: Lunha's face, serene. Feminine. Xinjia did not much like it when, on rare occasions, Lunha was a man. "This contains much of how you planned, how you dealt with your enemies."

"The data they sent home would be scoured of classified information." A jar of ashes, after a fashion.

"I was more interested in how you thought. Strange, but I don't think I ever knew you so well as posthumously." The secondskin has absorbed sweat, leaves only a trace of clean, saline scent. Xinjia has never worn perfume. Offstage she goes through the world strictly as herself. "There were votes to input your data to a replicant. I overrode it."

"We haven't been spouses for a long time."

"I remarried," Xinjia says, "into Silent Bridge. And so we are family, which gives me some rights over managing your image. Your mothers agreed with me the replicant idea was . . . abhorrent. May I touch you?"

Lunha nods and watches Xinjia's thumb follow the line of her jaw, her nose, her mouth. There Xinjia stops, a weight of consideration, a pressure of shared recall.

"Is it surgery or are you wearing something over your face?"

"The latter," she says against Xinjia's finger and entertains the thought of their first time together, feeding each other slices of persimmon, licking the sweetness off each other's hand. Slick fabrics that warmed to them, braids of sheet slithering against hips and thighs and ankles. For sex Xinjia never liked a still bed. "Why have you undertaken this?"

"A glitch," Xinjia says, in that detached way. Her hand has drifted away to rest—as though incidentally—on Lunha's knee. "A glitch that left some out of sync, myself among them. What was it? Something happening on Yodsana, an explosion at a resort. Just a tidbit of news, insignificant, nothing to do with us. I think I was looking up Yodsana puppet theater, or else I'd never have noticed. To me the resort was operating as usual. To everyone else it'd gone up in flames, fifty tourists dead. I made a note to myself. Except a few days later I couldn't remember why or what it was about. What did I care?"

"That happens." Rarely. Beyond rare.

Xinjia smiles, faint. "I followed some leads, made discoveries, gained contacts. It isn't just me, Lunha. As we speak disconnect is happening on more worlds than you realize, one or two persons at a time. I've only taken it to a larger scale."

"You will take all of Tiansong with you."

"Enough of Tiansong wanted this that they elected me First. Can you imagine how I felt when—" Xinjia blinks, pulls away. A command brings up a floor compartment: a set of cups, a dispenser. "When did they let you . . . ?"

"General. After three successful campaigns." At this point it seems senseless to keep unsaid. "I underwent preparatory conditioning to minimize dissonance, though at the time I didn't realize what it was for."

"Hegemonic personnel must've let it slip. To friends, loved ones."

"Seldom. Easily overwritten." Easily detected. The penalties exorbitant.

"You are all right with this?" Xinjia pours. Chrysanthemum steam, the tea thick with tiny black pearls harvested from Razor Garden orchards. "Sixty years in service, an illustrious career. You can't understand at all why I'm doing this, why others want me to do this?"

"In principle I can guess. In practice—this is not wise."

A cup is slid toward her. "They can take all we are from us. They can rob us of our languages, our cities, our names; they can make us strangers to ourselves and to our ghosts, until there's no one left to tend the altars or follow the hour of thought or sweep the graves."

Lunha sips. She misses touch, not just any human contact but Xinjia's specifically. "The Hegemony has no cause to do that. The amount of rewriting it'd take would be colossal."

"It would cost them less to reduce Tiansong to scorch marks than to process that much. Yes. Should they find a reason though, my soldier, they will do it. Changing us a little at a time. Perhaps one day we'll stop lighting the incenses, the next we'll have Costeya replicants cooking for us. After a month, no one dances anymore the way I do. Instead: Costeya scripts, chrome stages and replicants performers, like on Imral and Salhune. They've this hold on our . . . everything. That I cannot abide." Her former wife, someone else's now, looks up. "I believed that neither would you."

"Xinjia. Bai Suzhen." Lunha does not reach out, still, will not be the one to yield tenderness. They haven't been spouses for so long. "Eighty years ago there was a conflict between Iron Gate and Crimson Falls. It was escalating. It'd have torn Tiansong apart, a field of ruins and carcasses, until the Hegemony intervened. A thorough edit. Now no one remembers that; now Iron Gate and Crimson Falls are at peace. You may not believe it, but that is what soldiers fight for—to preserve equilibrium, to bring stability."

"To enforce the Hegemonic definition of that."

"It's one that works."

"And the massacres of Tiansong empresses when Costeya first took over, what about that? Is that stability; is that peace? Or is it bygones simply because it's been all of three centuries? No. Don't answer that."

"There are planets *now* which suffer much worse. I've been there; I've ordered their ruin and the execution of their citizens." Lunha knows that she has failed, already. That there was never a way to win. Not here.

"You are not yourself," Xinjia says softly.

"I am. I have always been myself."

"Then there is no ground on which we can meet. Perhaps there never has been."

Lunha drinks until there's no more in her cup, tea or pearl. "I will find a way to keep Tiansong safe."

In the end neither of them surrenders. They do not touch; they do not kiss. A parting of strangers' courtesy.

"Isren."

It takes no more than that, on their unique frequency, to summon the operative. A link, with visuals to let her know Isren remains in the habitat. "Yes, General?"

"I could not dissuade First of Tiansong."

"In that case please head for Iron Gate. There'll be a shuttle keyed to one of our ships in orbit."

"No." Lunha gazes out through the round window, makes it widen to take up the whole wall. Silent Bridge at midday is platinum. "Bring me armor. I expect it within seventy-two hours. Are you authorized to officiate a duel?"

Her handler's expression does not change, save for a rapid blink. "That's not what we had in mind, General."

"A duel minimizes collateral damage. Tiansong's representative wins and we leave it under embargo, to limit the influence of disconnect. If Xinjia is assassinated, apprehended or otherwise forcibly stopped there will be others, and not on this world alone. It'll be almost impossible to track the unsynchronized." It is not a certainty, but it is how Xinjia would have learned to plot from Lunha's image. "I win and Tiansong gives up its schemes, surrenders to reintegration. I don't lose, Operative Isren."

"You invoke an archaic statute."

"I invoke it correctly, and this is not the first time I've pushed to resolve by single combat. This is a situation where military destruction is untenable, diplomatic solution impossible."

"If you lose, General, I'll be overriding the result." Isren is silent for a moment. "A duel to the death."

"So it goes."

She sends word to Xinjia to choose a single-combat proxy, briskly outlining the terms. Xinjia accepts them immediately. They are the best that can be had, under the circumstances.

Lunha revokes the edits she made and takes off the facial mesh. She spends some time cleaning, hot water this side of scalding, balm and pigments to smooth away marks left by the mesh. Tiansong commanders of old did that, purify mind and body before going into battle, and Lunha has always followed suit. Not much time for the mind, but few engagements ever gave her the leisure.

Isren's arrival is not covert, and Silent Bridge is prepared. Lunha watches a feed from the operative's eyes as the primaries greet the neutrois, coolly formal. Isren's readouts telling who is disconnected: Lunha's mothers, two other primaries, distant cousins Lunha doesn't know—too young.

They escort Isren, courteous. Lunha does not admit them into her room. Her mothers catch a glimpse of her face—her own, the face she was born and grew up with—and Mother Yinliang's eyes widen, stricken.

Isren unpacks armor, dress uniform, more weapons. "I assumed you'd want this to be ceremonious. I've obtained authorization for your . . . tactical decision."

Perhaps she should've found time to speak to her mothers, Lunha thinks, but it is too late, she moved too fast. Odd, that. In battle there's never been such a thing as *too fast.* "I appreciate it."

"Do you want to talk about it?" Isren tilts their head, just enough to emphasize a pale throat notched by a jeweled implant.

"I don't intend to become familiar with you, Operative."

The neutrois' laugh is ambiguous. "I'm married, quite happily. A career soldier like you, though she's not half as feted. There's an advantage to partnering within the ranks. Fewer secrets to keep. Speaking of that, has the First of Tiansong gone entirely offline, physically removed the neural implants? Can she still interface with the grid?"

"She's kept the implants."

Isren inclines their head. "I've sent you a program. Experimental. It'll reintegrate her into sync. The infiltration method is the best of what we have; all you need is to establish a link with her and it'll latch on."

"Side-effects?" Lunha grips the helm in her hands and decides against it. She'll show her face.

"So far as it's been tested, none. The worst that could happen is that it won't work."

No side-effects. A program that forces neural interface back into the grid, and Isren would have her believe there are no side-effects. Isren wears no immediately visible protection, but they are not without. Lunha calculates her odds of avoiding the nerve toxins and disabling Isren before the operative's nanos activate. Aloud she says only, "I'll take that into account, Operative Isren. My thanks."

At night, Silent Bridge is sapphires. All the colors that sapphires can be, the finest grade and luster.

Under her armor the dress uniform is snug; at her hip the orchid-blade rests with the ease of her own limbs. The winds cut harsh enough to sting and the summit of the great house is sheer, the tiles under them smooth.

Mother Yinliang has no expression anymore; Mother Fangxiu never did. Xinjia merely looks abstract, her gaze apathetic save when it rests on her proxy. A broad woman, sleek and muscled like a fox, veteran champion of Iron Gate pits. An insult, when it comes down to it, though Lunha does not underestimate.

Each pair of eyes records and broadcasts. The uniform, the armor. She is a Hegemonic general. Except for her and Isren there is no hint of Costeya anywhere in Silent Bridge.

Still time to execute that program, General. Isren's voice through the private band.

Lunha strides forward to pay her mothers respect. Bending one knee, head bowed, the submission of a proper child. Neither answers her; neither touches her head. She accepts that and rises to face the pit fighter.

The first trickle of adrenaline. Her reflexes coil and her mind settles into that space of faceted clarity, the interior of her skull arctic and luminous.

She unsheathes her orchid-blade, its mouths baring teeth to the wind, its teeth clicking hunger to the cold.

They begin.

And Wash Out by Tides of War

AN OWOMOYELA

I am sitting at the top of the spire of the Observance of the War, one of three memorials equidistant from the Colony Center. The soles of my runners' grips are pressed against the spire's composite, their traction engineered at a microscopic level. But I'm not going to push off. I'm 180 meters up, and while I could drop and catch the festoons—my gloves get as much traction as my grips—that's not what I want. I want to freefall all 180 meters, and catch myself, and launch into a run.

That's crazy thinking. I'm good, but no human's *that* good; I'm a freerunner, not a hhaellesh.

I shift my center of gravity. The wind is still temperate up here, fluttering cool under my collar. It outlines the spot of heat where my pendant rests against my skin.

The pendant is the size of my thumbnail, and always warmer than it should be. This has something to do with it reflecting the heat of my body back to me, so the pendant itself never heats up. It was built to do this because it's no gem; its brilliant red comes from my mother's cryopreserved blood.

It was, until the Feast of the Return that morning, the only thing I'd known of her.

The colony's designed for freerunning. The cops all take classes in it. That's what comes of a government that worships the hhaellesh, who can carve their own path through the three dimensions.

I'm not a cop, either.

I end up dropping, twisting so my fingers and toes find the carved laurels, and from there I make a second drop to the Observance's dome. At my hip, my phone starts thumping like an artificial heartbeat. I pause with my fingertips on the gilt, and finally turn to brace my heels against the shingles and lean back into the curve. I clip the hands-free to my ear, and thumb the respond button. Then I just listen.

After a moment of silence, a human voice says, *"Aditi?"*

I let out a breath. "Michel," I answer. He's a friend.

"Are you okay—?"

"I don't want to talk about it." Obviously a hhaellesh could get up to my perch here, and so could Michel—he's from a family of cops, so he's been playing games with gravity for longer than I have. But effective or not, there's a reason I'm nearly two hundred meters up, and that reason has a lot to do with not wanting to talk about how okay I am.

Michel digests that, then says *"Okay. Did you hear the new Elías Perez episode?"*

My chest fills with a relief indistinguishable from love. I love Michel so much that it's painful, sometimes, to know he's not my brother. I wish the same blood flowed through both our bodies, and without thinking past that, my fingers go to the pendant at my throat. There, my voice catches.

There are moments when I feel so ashamed.

"I haven't," I say. "Put it on."

The hhaellesh stand at least six feet tall, and usually closer to seven or eight. Their skin is glossy black. Their digitigrade feet end in small, grasping pads; their hands end in two fingers and two opposing thumbs which are thin enough to fit into cracks and gaps and strong enough to pierce titanium composite and tear apart the alloys of landships. They are streamlined and swift, with aquiline profiles and a leaping, running gait like a cat or an impala. They can fall from high atmosphere and suffer no injury. They can jump sixteen meters in a bound. They are war machines and killing machines.

They are also human sacrifices.

I envy them.

Gods, if there was anything in the universe Elías couldn't handle, his writers haven't thrown it at him yet. He would know how to tell his best friend about an enlistment option. He could figure out how to deal with a hhaellesh showing up at his door.

Michel starts the playback, and I tweak the audio balance so I can hear Michel breathing while we both listen. The serials are propaganda and we know it, but they're enjoyable propaganda, so that's fine.

[The esshesh gave us the hhaellesh and the hhaellesh handed us the war—but if we didn't have the hhaellesh, we'd still have Elías Perez,] the canned narrator says, and I lean into the backbeat behind his words. *[Welcome to the adventure.]*

Around me, the colony spreads out in its careful geometry. There's nothing left to chance or whimsy, here, or adapted from the streets and carriageways built by another, more ancient, society. There's no downtown you can look at and say, *this predated cars and light rail.* No sprawling tourist docks with names that hold onto history. This place is older than I am, but not by much; it's only about the age of my mother.

That's why we cling so much to ceremony, I think: it's what we have in place of tradition. We make monuments to an ongoing war, and when the soldiers return home we have feasts, and we plan holidays to rename the Observances to the Remembrances. The war's only just ended and in a month we'll have three Remembrances of the War, in shiny white limestone and black edging in places of honor.

I get it.

Seriously, I do. When you don't have history in the place you live, you have to make it up or go insane.

Earlier in the day, my mother'd shown up to the crappy little allotment I cook and sleep in but don't spend much time in. My allotment's on the seventeenth floor of a housing unit, which makes for a perfect launch point, and doesn't usually get me visitors on the balcony. I was on the mat in my room, with my mattress folded up into the wall, doing pushup jump squats. They weren't helping. I'd split my lip just a bit earlier, and since I bite when I get restless, I had the taste of blood in my mouth.

Then there she was, knocking at the lintel, and I split my lip open again.

I did a thirty-second cooldown and made myself walk to the window. If it had been dark, if the light hadn't been scattering off the white buildings and back down from the cyan sky, it might not have glinted on her skin. She might have just been a black, alien shape like a hole in the world.

"I expected to see you at the Feast of the Return," she said. "I registered my arrival."

"I was busy," I lied.

She regarded me, quietly. And although I didn't want to, I invited her in.

When I first met Michel, he was walking along the rails of the pedestrian bridge by the Second General Form school. I was in Second General Form mostly because my father had hired a tutor before we came to the colony; my education in Shivaji Administrative District hadn't exactly been compatible with the colony's educational tracks. I was new, and didn't know any of my classmates. We knew each other's names from the class introductions, so Michel didn't bother to introduce himself.

"Settle an argument," he said. "I think Elías is in love with Seve, and Seve just thinks he's ridiculous. My cousin thinks Seve loves Elías but doesn't want to show it, and Elías is just friendly and chirpy to everyone, so he doesn't even see anything weird about acting like that at Seve. You should tell her I'm right."

I shook my head. "Elías? Is that the government stuff? I don't listen to that."

"Wha-a-at?" Michel asked, bobbing the *a*. "Come on, *everyone* listens to Elías!"

"My dad says it's just propaganda," I said, and I remember that little preadolescent me felt damn proud of herself and all smart and grown-up to be slinging around words like *propaganda*. "They just make it so people will want to join the war."

"Well, duh," Michel said. "Everybody *knows* that. But it's cool! Come on, lemme tell you about this time that Elías got stuck on this planet; they were trying to make it into a colony, but there was a whole swarm of the enemy and his ship was broken and he couldn't take off . . . "

Elías always found a way through, and by the end of the day, I was listening to the show. I never helped Michel settle his argument, but I came to my own conclusions.

Today's episode opens with the soundscape that means Elías is on the bridge of the Command and Control station in the sector designated as the Front. Meaning he's on the front lines. Last time that happened, he was in a story arc that had him working with the Coalition forces, which he hates to do; Elías isn't really an official sort of guy.

["If our intelligence reports are correct,"] says the voice of Commodore Shah, ["we're about to lose the war."]

The art of the gentle lead-in is verboten in Elías Perez.

["A larger enemy presence than any we've ever seen is massing at Huracán II. We believe they'll use this staging ground to launch a major, unified offensive on the colonies."]

["You want us to what?"] That's Seve, the captain of Elias's ship. She snickers. ["Take out a whole fleet of the bastids? Hah. No bones in that dog."]

"Oh, Seve," Michel says. Seve's got a stack of sayings that only make sense to her—and to Elías, nowadays, though they didn't always. Elías and Seve have been partners since episode 3, where Elías stowed aboard Seve's pirate ship and ended up saving it when it was infested by the enemy. Seve turned around and said, there, that paid Elías's boarding fee; what was he going to pay for passage?

I'm a fan of Elías and Seve. Love at first uncompromising deal. And she isn't the kind to think the end of the war obligates her into anything.

["If their war force goes unopposed, the enemy will be able to sweep through our territories unopposed. The Coalition doesn't have the fleet strength to stop them."]

There's a subtle swell in the background music, a rumble of drums and solar radio output, and a thrill goes through me. The writers can play drama with our fear of the war: for most of us, it's the fun kind of fear where something is technically possible but pretty damn unlikely, like an asteroid crashing into the colony. After we lost the Painter settlement, the war was always off somewhere *out there*; we sent out troops, we made our hhaellesh, but it's not like we were really under threat of invasion. I don't think our colony even had an invasion plan in place, beyond the esshesh defense emplacements. We all got a little afraid, but the fear was a *what if, on an offchance, someday* . . . and not a *when, as it will, this happens to us.*

["Okay,"] Elías says, always the good guy, always the hero. ["What's our job? We can barely take one enemy ship in a firefight; a force that size is beyond us."]

Commodore Shah says nothing, and the delay is striking. The audio play doesn't go for delays. There's another rumble, and another sensation thrills up my spine, but it's not the fun kind of thrill this time.

"Oh, you're not," I whisper.

["As you know,"] Shah says, her voice clipped so regret doesn't make it through. ["Huracán II suffers from a violent geology. Your ship is one of the few with both the range to reach the Huracán system and the maneuverability to penetrate the enemy's lines and engage your jump engines within the planet's red jump threshold."]

I hear Michel's sucked-in breath, and I'm sitting dumb, myself.

["Blow out the planet and us with it,"] Seve says. ["Jump'll turn the rock into a frag grenade, and the gravity turns my girl's engines into a nova. That what you want from us, Shah?"]

Shah's always looked after her people. Elías and Seve—they're not official, military types, but Shah looks after them as her own. Problem is, even Shah's people come in second to the war.

[*"It's not what I want,"*] Shah says, and I want to slam my headset down. [*"But I don't see another option."*]

"They're doing a finale," I say, my calves and fingers burning again to run. "The war is over, so they're just going to finish Elías Perez."

"You left when I was three years old," I'd told my mother as she crouched at the edge of the table, as I shuffled through my shelves for a decent tea. I had a couple spoonfuls left of loose-leaf colony Faisal, which I hear is a good substitute for an Earth Assam, which I will never in my life be able to afford unless it goes big and all the importers start shipping it in in bulk. But the urge to make a good impression got in a fistfight with the urge to be petty and spiteful, and I pulled out two bags of a generic colony black and plunked them into mugs.

"I remember," she said. "I braided your hair and you wore your favorite dress. It was the blue of cobalt glass."

Her voice was deep and flanged, and totally factual. All hhaellesh sound alike. At least, the ones on the war reports sounded the same as my mother.

I have an allotment and not a flat because I have a work placement and not a career. I don't care for any of the careers on offer. But the colony's not so much of a fool to let work potential go unexploited, unlike the governments of Earth which I'm just old enough to remember. I still have images of walking to the subway past the grimy homeless, with my father's hand on the small of my back to rush me along.

That's what I remember of my childhood. My father's protective hand, my father's tutoring after school, my father's anchor mustache with a bit more salt in its pepper every year, my father's voice carefully explaining the war.

"I don't like dresses," I told my mother, and set down the two mugs of tea. Her fingers clicked around the ceramic.

The hhaellesh can eat and drink, but human scientists still don't know how food passes through the suits. We do know that the suits filter and metabolize any toxins—people have tried to poison them before, with everything from arsenic and cyanide to things like strong sulphuric acid, and the hhaellesh just eat and drink it up and are polite enough not to mention it.

I did not try to poison my mother.

"You've grown," she said. "Of course, I expected that."

"Yeah, kids grow up when you disappear on them."

She was quiet for a few seconds. "I did not expect your father to die."

I stared down into my slowly-darkening tea.

"I received notice," she said. "I had to make the decision whether or not to come home. The tide of the war hadn't turned yet. I knew the colony would look after you."

I swirled the tea in my mug. Tendrils of relative darkness wavered out from the bag.

"I was one of only eight hundred hhaellesh volunteers at that point," she said.

"Yeah, I know," I finally interrupted. "Without the hhaellesh, we wouldn't've won the war."

This is how the hhaellesh happened:

We had a handful of colonies in the Solar system and three outside of it: Gliese, Korolev, and Painter. Then, abruptly, we had a handful of colonies in the Solar system and two colonies in Gliese and Korolev.

We still thought interstellar colonization was a pretty neat thing, and despite centuries of space war fiction, we didn't have the infrastructure or the technology to mount a space war. We were thoroughly thumped.

Then the esshesh showed up and told us that, while war was (untranslatable, but we think against their religion), they had no problems with arming races to defend themselves.

So they gave us the hhaellesh.

This is how the hhaellesh work:

There's a black suit that scatters light like obsidian and feels like a flexible atmosphere-dome composite to the touch. A soldier gets inside, bare as the day she was born. The suit closes around her.

In a few minutes, it's taking her breath and synthesizing the carbon dioxide back to oxygen. In a few hours it's taking her waste and digesting the organic components. In a few days it's replaced the top layers of her skin. In a few months it's integrated itself into her muscles. In a few years there's nothing human left in there, just the patterns of her neural activity playing across an alien substrate that we haven't managed to understand yet.

This is how a hhaellesh retires:

The suit has a reverse mode. It can start rebuilding the human core, re-growing the body, replacing the armor's substrate material with blood and muscle and bone and brain matter until the armor opens up again, and the human steps out, bare as the day they were born. A body like Theseus's ship.

But to do that, it needs the original human DNA.

Or some human DNA, in any case; hell, I don't know that anyone's tried it, but you could probably feed in the DNA of your favorite celebrity and the hhaellesh suit would grow it for you, slipping your brain pattern in like that was nothing strange. I suppose that should freak me out—y'know, existentially—more than just growing a new copy of a body long ago digested by an alien non-meatsuit.

It probably should, but it doesn't.

This is how a hhaellesh tries to *get* the DNA that'll let it retire:

My mother crouched at the side of my table. With the inhuman height and the swept-back digitigrade legs, the chairs weren't designed to accommodate her.

"When I left, I entrusted you with a sample of my DNA," she said, and my hand went to the pendant. "With love, my daughter, I ask for it back."

At that point, I dove out the window.

"They *can't* cancel Elías," I say. The top-of-spire restlessness is back, and I want to drop, freefall, roll, clamber, climb. My shoulders and thighs are shaking. "The fuck. He's a goddamn cultural phenomenon, by now."

Michel's voice is unsteady as well, but not as much as mine. He doesn't get it. *"To be fair, I feel like after you've won the war you don't need to push people to sign up for the Forces any more."*

"Fuck the war," I say, and there's anger at the pit of my throat. Like: how dare they take this away from us. Like: Elías and his adventures belong to us. Since the beginning of the war they've been how we're meant to see ourselves—clever and active and *go team human.* You can't take away our stories just because we won.

The first time I met my mother—

Except I can't put it like that, can I? You don't really meet your mother. Or I guess maybe you do at the moment of conception, if you think your zygote is you, or maybe it's when the first glimmers of thought show up in your still-developing brain. But I think maybe it doesn't count if there's no chance that little undeveloped you won't retain the memory.

So. The first time I met my mother, I was in a utility transitway. You know, what we have for back alleys.

I've always been the kid with a chip on her shoulder and a grudge against the world and her nose high in the air. The grudge and the pride come from the same thing. Neither made me many friends.

I ran into a bunch of the voluntary-career types in the transitway on the morning of the Feast, just after the big public ceremony. My blood was up and they were them, and, well, the specifics of the argument don't really matter. I started it. And then I was in the comforting beat of a street fight, and with a split lip and three split knuckles, and while one of them was hollering about how he was going to file a complaint for misdemeanor assault, who should show up?

And my heart leapt up and got a grip in my throat, and I thought, *Oh gods, a hhaellesh,* and standing right there, alien and beautiful. Staring at us with a blank, featureless swept-forward face that we all unambiguously read as disapproval.

The fight stopped. The boys stood there, twitching and uneasy, until they worked out that the hhaellesh was only staring at me. Then they slipped away.

And I stood there, frozen in the moment, until *I* worked out why a hhaellesh would single me out and come find me in a utility transitway. The wonder was slapped right out of me. It meant nothing: it wasn't the free choice of an alien intelligence but the obligate bonds of unreliable blood.

I turned my back and sprinted away.

. . . hold it there for a moment. I realize this makes it sound like I just run from all my problems, and I want to make it clear that that's not true. The truth is that I run from this *one* problem, and looking back at it, I guess I always have.

I was talking about my pride and my grudge, and how they both come down to this pendant at the base of my throat. My mother's blood. My mother the hhaellesh, the guardian of the colonies, the war hero.

All the hhaellesh are war heroes.

What the hell am I?

["*My gotdamn ship*,"] Seve says. They're in the corridors of *her gotdamn ship* now, the soundscape full of mechanical noises and ambiance. There was a behind-the-scenes episode a few months ago back where they talked about those soundscapes, and how they chose the sounds for Seve's ship to be reminiscent of a heartbeat, rushing blood, ventilation like breath, so it'd seem alive. ["*My gotdamn job. Better pilot than you, anyway; I can see this idiot plan through.*"] She's pissed-off. I would be. Hell, I am.

["*I'm a good enough pilot to dodge through a crowd*,"] Elías says. ["*Come on, Seve. The captain doesn't have to go down with her ship.*"]

Michel complains a lot that Seve is a boy's name, and I tell him that so were Sasha and Madison and Wyatt, back in the pre-space days known as the depths of history. And then Michel says that of course I would pay attention to the pre-space days, and I say that of course he thinks history started with the erection of the initial colony dome.

Michel is first-generation colony native. He was born here. His parents were in the third or fourth batch of colonists to set down here. We're never quite sure who's supposed to be jealous of who in this relationship, so mostly we just rib each other a lot.

In my position, it's easy to feel like you don't have a history. Yeah, I'm from Earth, but I don't remember much. My dad knew more, but he naturalized us; the most culture I think he held over was the way he made tea in a pot with colony spices, and his habit of saying *gods* instead of *god*.

I'm the girl with the hhaellesh mother and the blood at her throat. That's who I am. And I was pretty sure no one could take that away.

["*Seve, I can't let you die in my place*,"] Elías says.

Seven snorts. ["*Well, one of us got to.*"]

"I enlisted," I blurt out. I swing the words like a fist. And I can hear the change in Michel's breathing on the other end; I can hear how Elías and the finale and how the writers are screwing us over has ceased to matter.

"*Say what?*"

"I enlisted," I say again. "I got the assessment. They were going to let me into a Basic Training Group and then the war ended."

Michel doesn't know what to say. I can tell because he says "*You—*", and then "*Oh.*", and then "*So . . . what? What now? Are you—*" and then he trails off into silence. I'm pretty sure I've hurt him.

It's a thing, in my family.

"I don't know," I say. All my plans have been derailed. "I can join the colony's military track. Would that be totally pointless? Think I should go? I could just get out of here."

" . . . *should I know the answer to this?*" He gives a nervous laugh—and the laugh is probably fake, now that I think about it. It's not right, anyway. Michel's real laugh is this deep, throaty thing that doesn't sound right when you know that his voice is higher than average and naturally polite.

If Michel was blood family there'd be a reason I could point to as why I felt so close to him, without wanting to screw him. I could have family that meant what family's supposed to mean.

After a moment, he says *"Aditi, if this is about your mother, can we just, maybe, talk about your mother?"*

Michel, Michel, my not-family family. Talking about my mother, my family not-family. I got this far by not looking too close at the contradiction. It's a lot harder to do when it breaks up your fights and shows up to tea.

It's a lot harder to do when it wins *its* fucking war.

When we came to the Colony, my father and I, we stepped off the transport in a queue of seven hundred other colonists. We waited nearly an hour before it was our turn to go into a white room whose windows let in the blue of the sky and the white of the skyline, and a pleasant-enough woman took our biometric data and verified all my father's professional assessments. She gave him his schedules —for Colony orientation, the walking tour, the commerce and services lecture, the first day at his assigned career—and set up an educational track for me. Through all of it, I was bored but fascinated by the blue-white-green of the outside world, and my father bounced me on his knee.

At the end, the woman bent down and put her face in front of mine. "That's a beautiful piece of jewelry," she said. "What is it?"

I looked her straight in the eye, and said—you know, in the way that some kids don't quite get metaphor, even when they're using it —"It's my mother."

On my phone, there's a message from the Coalition Armed Forces Enlistment Office. It reads:

To Aditi Elizabeth Chattopadhyay,

This is a note to confirm that your assessment scores were sufficient to place you in a Basic Training Group for Immediate Interstellar and Exo-Atmospheric Combat. However, due to the recent decision of the Colony Coalition Oversight Office and the cessation of hostilities, the Coalition Armed Forces as an oversight unit is being disbanded and the colonies' individual standing military forces are being scaled back.

At your request, your application can be transferred to the Gliese Armed Forces Enlistment Office, where you can enter into their Standing Military career track. If no such request is made, we will consider your enlistment withdrawn.

Thank you for your willingness to serve the safety and security of the Colonies.

The Standing Military career track trains you in an off-surface location with strict access restrictions. I could still get out of here. I have the option. She can't take everything away.

I dial back the Elías audio to a quiet background murmur. I can't concentrate on it, anyway, and I don't want to. I don't want to hear Elías and Seve argue about who'll sacrifice for the other.

"Aditi," Michel says.

"Why the *hell*," I ask him, "wouldn't you just put your blood in a bank safe if it meant that godsdamn much to you?"

There's a moment when I think that could have used a little more context than I gave it, but Michel finds the meaning fast. *"If I had a kid, I'd want to leave something they could know me by."*

I kinda think there's not a maternal bone in my body, because that just sounds stupid to me. "Yeah, well, I didn't end up knowing her, did I?"

"You can, though. Now. Can't you?"

"She came back for her *blood*," I say. "She never said she came back to get to know me."

Like a slap in the face, Michel laughs.

"What the fuck," I tell him. "Not funny."

"It is, though," Michel says. *"Adi, I swear you just described exactly what you would do. You would go off to war and kick ass and come back home when there was no more ass to kick, and be all 'hi, I'm back, gimme.' Tell me you wouldn't."*

I spluttered.

["Some things are more important than my life, Seve!"], Elías is shouting, though the low volume just makes him sound faraway and muffled like he's already lost.

From the beginning, Seve has said that if she can't save herself, she's not worth saving. And this is propaganda, so the story never goes out of its way to correct her. I like that. I like that she's never needed saving when she couldn't save herself.

I don't like change.

I want to mute the audio.

"I'm not that self-centered," I tell Michel, but my hand is on my pendant and I've convinced myself the blood inside is mine. It's demonstrably *not* mine, and the DNA will prove it. But still. Still.

"Adi, can I tell you something, and not get in a fistfight with you in a utility transitway?"

I've never been in a fight with Michel. "What?"

He takes a moment to put the words together. *"The necklace is just a thing, Adi. Get your mom back. Once you have her, you can replace the blood. Anyway, one necklace for one mom is a pretty good trade."*

Theseus's pendant. I feel a rush of disagreement. I guess that solves that philosophical riddle for me: I really believe that if you replace all the boards, it's not the same ship.

Which means I also believe there's no way to keep the ship from eventually rotting away.

I never helped Michel settle his argument, but that doesn't mean I didn't come to my own conclusions.

I think Elías and Seve love each other, but love doesn't tell you what to do with it. It just shows up like a guest you have to make a bed for, and it puts everything out of order, and it makes demands.

I don't hear the rest of the episode.

I take my time. I breathe through the anger in my gut and the sense, not exhilarating now, of falling. Then, in the evening, I sync up with the colony directions database and do a search for hhaellesh in public areas.

Five hhaellesh arrived during the Feast of the Return, and two of them aren't hanging out anywhere that the public cams can see them. One of the ones who is is surrounded by children and a lady who looks like their mother, beaming the whole group of them. Of the other two, one is walking the gardens in the Colony Center Plaza, and the other is . . . familiar.

I take the monkey's route, as my father called it. Roof to roof and wall by wall, the colony's engineered and modified design giving me wings. From the feeds I read, the freerunning spirit everywhere means working with your environment, not against it; you have to take your obstacles as opportunities or you'll never get anywhere. Literally, at that.

If there's a lesson to be learned there and applied to the rest of my life, I've yet to learn it.

I pass over alleys and shopways and along the taut wires that traverse the wide boulevards, the places where parades had been held. People see me, but to them, I'm just motion; just another citizen who takes a hobbyist's interest in how to get around. Anonymous. Not Aditi, the girl with the hhaellesh mother, the girl with her mother's blood. They see me as I'm starting to see myself.

I run harder.

After my father's first day of work, he took me to the breadfruit shop. It's not real breadfruit—it's some native plant the first colony engineers analyzed and deemed edible; something that looked like a breadfruit to whichever one of them named it—but when it's processed and mashed it has a texture like firm ice cream and a taste that takes flavorings well. My father and I got bowls full of big, colorful scoops, and asked one of the other patrons to take a picture of us. They did, and said "Welcome to the colony!" We were that obvious.

We sent the picture to my mother, and that's where I find her today. Sitting at the table we always tried to get, without any of the breadfruit in front of her. Hhaellesh can eat, but I'm not sure they need to, and I have no idea if they have a sense of taste. You only hear about them eating to accept hospitality.

There's a halo of awed silence around her, and I slink through it and take another one of the chairs.

"I'm sorry," she says, and I let out a breath. Truth was, until she'd said that, I'd had some doubt that it was her. The hhaellesh all look alike.

I grumble something. I don't know how to accept her apology.

"I haven't been a good mother," my war hero says. "I don't know if you want me to start trying now. You've done well without me."

Yeah, if you want to call it that. I serve the minimum work requirements and spend the rest of my time running across the roofs and up the walls. I haven't gone out and won any wars in my free time.

What I've done, what they'll know me for if I touch the history books at all, is that I've carried *her*.

My fingers itch at the tips. I want to touch the pendant, but I don't. "Hhaellesh don't have blood, do they?"

"The armor substrate carries energy and nutrients," my mother says. "We don't need blood, unless . . . "

"Why do you want to be human?" I ask. *I* don't want to be human. I want to be more than what I am.

My mother doesn't answer that, and the stillness of the armor is the stillness of an alien thing: how am I to read it? Then she seems to answer two questions, my own and one she hasn't articulated.

Why don't you?

"I think," she says, and her words are careful, perhaps uncertain. "if you are something, you don't want it. Does that make sense? Because you *are* it, you forget ever wanting it. Or, I suppose, it never comes up."

I shake my head.

"I miss being human," she says. "I miss feeling warm and sleeping in and stretching out sore muscles. I miss holding you. You were so small, when I left." I think she watches me. "You regret not being old enough."

"*Old* enough?" I snap. For what? To remember her leaving?

My mother holds up her hand. "This lit me up like a candle," she said, turning those long, precise fingers. "I was a goddess. A fury, a valkyrie. I wanted this. Now I miss being human."

I grind my fingertips out against the table. "What's going to happen to the suit, if you're not using it?"

My mother lays her hand near mine, which is a disturbingly human gesture coming from something whose hand is a mechanical claw. "It'll go into a museum," she says. "Or on display in one of the Remembrances. I would give it to you if I could."

I rear back, at that.

"Ah," she says, and she can't smile. There's nothing on her face to smile. But I get the impression she's smiling. "You think I'd say, no, it wasn't worth it, in the end. I've learned my lesson and a human life is the most important thing of all. No." Her head bends toward the table. "This is a part of my life; this is me. I will not disavow it. I would give it to you if I could."

The colony is white buildings and boulevards, green growing plants, and the searing blue sky. And then there's the black of the esshesh artillery emplacements, the black edging on the Observances. Red's not a colony color. Red is primal and messy, like blood.

When I went to enlist, they took a hard-copy signature in black ink and a handprint biometric signature as well. I wonder what else the biometrics recorded: my anxiety? My anger? The thrumming of my heart in my veins?

My mother's hands are cool and pulseless on the table. Black as the artillery. Black as the ink. Black as the space between what stars we see, where the primal brightness of the cosmos has been stretched into infrared by the passage of time.

· · ·

I reach behind my neck and fumble with the clasp of my pendant. It takes me a bit to work it out; it's stayed against my throat through showers and formal occasions and a hospital stay or two, busted ribs and broken legs. Pulling it off makes me feel more naked than taking my clothes off does. But here I am, baring myself in front of this alien who wants more intimacy than I think she deserves.

"Two conditions," I say. And it's difficult to tell, under the smooth black mask, but I think she's still watching *me* and not the blood. I push on ahead. "One: I want a piece of that armor. Or, I guess, the substrate. Make a pendant out of it."

It's not a replacement for the blood. But it's not something I'll be holding in trust: it's part of my history, now, too, and it's something that'll be *mine*.

My mother nods.

I exhale. Red's no good for the colony anyway. Black's a bit better, if only because black is the color of the hhaellesh, and the security emplacements which grow fractally more close-packed toward the colony's borders: the lines we draw around ourselves to protect us from the enemy.

After Painter, the enemy never set foot on colony land. They're not the thing that scares me. I'm still figuring out what my enemy is.

"Two," I say. And I'm not sure how to say this next part.

But those were her words. *I'd give it to you if I could.*

"I want your stories," I tell her.

Tortoiseshell Cats Are Not Refundable
CAT RAMBO

Antony bought the kit at Fry's in the gray three months after Mindy's death. He swam in and out of fog those days, but he still went frequently to the electronics store and drifted through its aisles, examining hard drives, routers, televisions, microphones, video games, garden lights, refrigerators, ice cream makers, rice cookers, all with the same degree of interest. Which was to say little to none, barely a twitch on the meter. A jump of the arrow from E up to one.

A way to kill time. So were the evenings, watching reality shows and working his way methodically through a few joints. If pot hadn't been legal in Seattle, it would've been booze, he knew, but instead the long, hard, lonely evening hours were a haze of blue smoke until he finally found himself nodding off and hauled himself into bed for a few hours of precious oblivion.

He prized those periods of nothingness.

Each day began with that horrible moment when he put a hand out to touch Mindy's shoulder—hey, honey, I had this awful dream you died, in a boating accident, no less, when was last time we were on a *boat*. Then the stomach dropping realization, sudden as stepping out into an elevator shaft.

Not.

A.

Dream.

His mother called him every day at first, but he couldn't manage the responses. Let alone the conversational give and take.

That saddened him. Made him feel guilty too. He was the only child his mother still had nearby. Both of his sisters had stayed on the other coast and were distant now as then. Still angry at his mother for unimaginable transgressions during their high school years. They both had been excellent at holding a grudge all their lives. He was the only child who'd been willing to take some responsibility for her, had helped her move out to this coast in fact.

He loved her. Bought her presents. That was how the cat, a small tortoiseshell kitten, had entered her life, riding in his coat pocket, a clot of black and orange fur, tiny triangular face split between the colors.

His mother had named it, as with all her animals, palindromically. Taco Cat, like God Dog and Dribybird the parakeet.

She loved that cat about as much as she'd ever loved anything. His mother had always been stolid and self-contained, but he knew she missed the cat even now, a year after its death.

She deserved something to fill her days. He wondered if they'd been as gray as his were nowadays, ever since his father died. He thought—hoped, perhaps— that wasn't true.

Maybe you did get over it with time.

He read somewhere that older people did better, were happier, if they had something they could care for. Taco had been that and now that prop was gone.

He'd replace it.

The kit was one of those late-night things. Infomercial fodder. Clone a beloved pet. Take the sample and send it into their labs. Have a perfect replica delivered within three months. A box five hundred times larger than it needed to be, holding only the test tube in which you would put the fragments of hair or claw material that were required.

He teased clumps from the wire brush he'd taken from his mother's, poked it with a forefinger into the test tube's depths. Stoppered it with a blunt plastic round.

Used his shunt to scan in the bar code on its side and beam it to the mailing center. A drone pecked at his apartment window, three floors up. Colored UPS brown. He could see other brightly colored shipping drones, colored red and green for the holidays, zipping around closer to the street. He authenticated it, staring into its inquisitive eye, and received the confirmation number displayed to one side, hovering in the air before it disappeared.

He was part of the last generation to know what life was like without a shunt. He got one in college, finally, had sold all the gold coins his aunt Mick, who died in the seventh Gulf War, had left him, and he never regretted that.

Life was so much more reliable with the shunt. It made sure you didn't overeat by making you feel satiated after just a few mouthfuls or let you sleep as long and deep as you liked, and even take part in preprogrammed dreams. You could use it to upload knowledge packs, particularly if you had augmented memory. It let you remember everyone's face and every date and time you ever needed to. It was like minor superpowers.

How awesome to live inside the future. Or it should have been.

He'd never thought much about his existence before Mindy. Then all of a sudden he *wanted* a life, a life together full of jokes only they shared. Him cooking her ginger pancakes and spending Sunday mornings lazing in shunt-enhanced sex, pleasurable and languorous and amazing.

He was leaving after a dinner of enchiladas unsatisfyingly sauced, their edges crisp and brown, stabbing the mouth. His mother hadn't mentioned Mindy outright, but she patted him on the upper arm as he paused to slip on his jacket. The gesture was unusual, outside her usual air-kiss intimacies.

He said, "Do you have Taco's old brush?"

"In the cupboard."

It shook him to see all the cat's things, gathered in careful memorial. He didn't associate sentimentality with his mother. Loss did that to you, perhaps. Though she'd endured his father's loss without such a display. At least he thought so. He tried to think back to his father's death. How long had it taken her to send all those shirts and ties and suits to St. Vincent De Paul's thrift shop? Not long. He remembered railing at her angrily about it. He'd planned on wearing all those clothes, two sizes too big for his sixteen year old frame, some day.

"It doesn't pay to get attached," she'd said. Her dry eyes infuriated him even farther. She'd hugged her arms to herself and returned his angry stare.

He still had things to make up to her for. This would help even the scales so tipped by all his adolescent anger and outbreaks.

BCSS sent him an envelope. The language of the thick packet was dense: an opportunity extended him to participate in a test program.

Clone a human.

Give him Mindy back.

He said, "I don't understand how it's possible. I know you can replicate her body, but her mind?"

Dr. Avosh's eyes were clearly artificial, flat circles of emerald green. What did it say about her, that she didn't even bother to try to hide her augmentations?

She said, "We create a matrix of artificial memories. Easy nowadays."

"But where do those memories come from?"

"We have more material than you would think. Social media, public records, and some information garnered from the shunt itself."

That startled him. "Shunts don't record things." There had been plenty of legal battles over that.

"No," Dr. Avosh said. "That's a misconception most people share. While the original versions only recorded what you wanted them to, and had limited memory space, the current versions record a great deal. It's simply inadmissible in court." One of her pupils was markedly larger than the other. As he looked at it, it ratcheted even further wide.

"Are you recording this right now?" he asked.

"It's my policy to record everything."

"In case you ever need to be replicated."

She shook her head, then hesitated. "Not really. There are so many reasons to do so."

"Are they real memories?"

"Are you asking if they are detailed memories? No. More like a memory of a memory, and obviously there will be gaps. It won't be quite the same for you, but for her it will be much smoother. She'll believe herself to be the actual Mindy. We recommend you not talk to her about the actual circumstances until at least six months have passed."

Mindy. The smell of her hair when he buried his nose in it, inhaling the scent as delicious as cinnamon or roses, a musky edge that always tugged at the edges of his erotic conscious.

There was no way he could say no.

"You said this was a new process. How many times has it been done?"

"This is the third trial batch of subjects. The first time we're using people in your situation."

"My situation?"

Papers on her desk whispered against each other as she fiddled with them. "Recently bereaved. We're curious to see how much the spouse's memory can augment the process and reinforce beliefs."

She paused. "And I must tell you that the company doesn't cover the entire cost."

He'd met Mindy on the R train, heading from his Bay Ridge apartment up into Manhattan to work for the BWSS. He'd handled their computer systems, going in late at night to work through the morning hours maintaining the message boards the BWSS scientists used.

You saw the same people on the train sometimes. He'd noticed her right away: small and birdlike. Always smiling, in a way you didn't hit in NYC. Curious and unafraid, chatting with the woman beside her one day, looking at kid pictures, the next day helping an old man to a seat.

That was Mindy. Friendly. Finally one day she plopped down beside him and said, "Here we go!"

Why she'd said it, she didn't know, she told him later, but indeed they went, first chatting daily, then going for coffee and then with perfect amity, dating, engagement, marriage in a small chapel attended only by close friends and family.

She had so many friends and they seemed to welcome him into the circle, saying, "Take care of her!"

He had. Until the accident.

Now every day that dizzying fall into the realization she wasn't there.

Any price was worth paying to avoid that.

But costly, so costly. He'd plundered his 401(k), his IRAs, taken out a second mortgage. Cut his bills to the bone and still had to ask his mother for money.

She provided it without question once she found out what it was for.

They drew as much as they could on his memories, which meant going in every day for two weeks in a row, sitting there talking about his relationship with Mindy, his history, where they'd gone on their honeymoon, and what a typical trip to the grocery store was like, and where each piece of their bedroom furniture had come from. Dr. Avosh said that was good. The stronger the relationship with him was, the more quickly the cloned Mindy would adjust.

His mother didn't ask about the results or the loan she'd made him to pay for the process. He thought perhaps she was trying to keep him from getting his hopes up too far, but as he aged, increasingly he realized he didn't understand his mother, didn't understand the parts of her that she had kept closed away from her family. It was only in his forties that they had become something like close.

Instead, they talked about the day-to-day drama of her apartment building. He grew interested despite himself, even though the stories were so small, concerning misplaced mail or who shoveled the front walk.

He said, "I got you a present. It should arrive next week. According to the tracking number it's being prepared for shipment right now."

"Should I ask what it is?"

He found himself smiling and the expression almost startled him. How long had it been since the gray had lifted momentarily? Too long.

He and Mindy would laugh about that together eventually. He wondered what that would be like, to be able to say, "While you were dead."

Perhaps it would be better just not to bring that up. He couldn't even begin to imagine what it would be like to live on the other side of that.

"Your present arrived," his mother said. "It's very nice." Her voice was strained.

"You don't like it?" he said.

"Of course I do," she said, but he could tell she was lying.

When he went for dinner, he realized the problem.

"They must have shipped you the wrong cat," he said, looking down at it. It was the same size as Taco and it was a tortoiseshell, but where Taco had been black with dapplings of hazy orange hair, this one was white with awkward splotches of orange and brown.

But the service rep explained. "You can't clone tortoiseshells and expect the same markings. They're random expressions of the gene. The brochure lists certain animals where you can't get an exact copy. Tortoiseshell cats are not refundable."

He hung up abruptly, full of rage. For God's sake, he couldn't get anything right lately.

But that would change when Mindy was back.

He didn't see the new cat the next time he was over and he didn't ask questions.

He could understand loving one configuration but not another.

But he didn't want to think about that.

They sent a crew that went over the house, scanning in everything about it. They quizzed him about the usual state of cleanliness, and what days Mindy usually cleaned on, what she was good at and what she was bad at, and how much they actually split up the chores. Her favorite brands.

He didn't know many of the answers. How empty did the refrigerator have to get before she'd go shopping, since she was the one who handled all that? He had no idea. They took another tack and asked him what he remembered them running out of, milk or toilet paper or butter.

"You see, most people have a few trigger items that automatically send them to the store," the data technician chirped at him as she continued running her bar scanner over everything under the sink. She'd quizzed him as to what he purchased and what Mindy had and luckily his only contribution had been a bottle of lime-scented dishwashing soap.

"Have you done many of these before?" he asked.

Her fingers kept clicking over the data pad. She had long thin nails with tiny daggers painted in silver at each tip and a tiny border of circles. "Two so far."

"What were they like?"

"The first preferred Comet and Pine-Sol, the second went with Seventh Generation cleaning products."

"No. I meant . . ." He wasn't sure how to formulate it. "Did it, did it work?"

Her gaze was quizzical. "All I can tell you is that, sure, when they came back they liked the same cleaning brands." She clicked and swiped. "All right, new section. Bed, made or unmade on a regular basis? If the former, who did it?"

"We did it together every morning," he said. His eyes heated up and he hoped he wasn't getting too teary. She tapped away.

"You two were sweet. It will be just as cute in the next round. You'll see."

He brought himself to ask his mother what she'd done with the cat. Her hands faltered as she chopped onions, then resumed their staccato beat.

"Ms. Green two doors down had mice," she said. "So I loaned her Taco Two."

"Taco Two? No palindrome?" he asked.

A sizzle and then a wave of fragrance as she added the onions to the skillet. "I couldn't think of one yet. I'm sure it'll come to me eventually."

"Eventually," he repeated agreeably. He thought perhaps the cat would end up staying with Mrs. Green, but that was all right.

"So what else is new?"

"I'm bringing her home tomorrow."

She put the spatula down in order to swing around and look at him, wide-eyed. "So soon?"

He nodded. He was smiling again. She smiled back, wiping her hands on her apron before she came over to awkwardly hug him.

What do you bring to your first meeting with the person you used to be married to? He chose an armload of roses. Who cared if it was cliché? Mindy loved them.

He remembered buying them for her. The two of them together at the farmers market, wandering from stall to stall, buying bread rounds still warm from baking and bags of vegetables still thick with dirt and leaves. The way she managed to look at every display, ferreted out everything interesting, made people smile as she talked to them.

Roses. So much like her in the way she opened to the world.

Glimpsed through the pane of glass in the door, she seemed so small in the hospital bed. Her eyes were shut. Her hair had once been long, but now it was short, one or two inches at most.

He said to Dr. Avosh. "Why did you cut her hair?"

The doctor chuckled. "I can see where it would seem that way. But it's because we've had a limited amount of time for her to grow hair in. It'll come."

"Won't that mess with her memories?"

"We've compensated." The doctor put her hand on the gray metal doorknob before looking back over her shoulder at him. "Are you ready to say hello?"

He nodded, unable to speak around the lump in his throat.

The room smelled of lemon disinfectant. The nurse already there took the flowers from him with a muted squeal of delight. "Aren't these pretty! I'll put them in water."

Mindy's eyes were still shut.

"Are you awake, Mindy?" the doctor said. "You have a visitor."

Her eyes opened, fixing on him immediately. "Antony."

The same smile, the same voice.

Emotion pushed him to the bed and he gathered her hands in his, kissing them over and over, before he laid his head down on the cool white hospital sheet and cried for the first time since she died.

He'd asked before what sort of cover story they would have for her waking up in the hospital. Of course they'd thought of that already: a slip in the shower, a knock on the head that accounted for any dizziness or disorientation.

He'd prepared the house as well, made it as close as he could remember to their days together, removed the dingy detritus of a bachelor existence by bringing a cleaning service in. If it seemed too different and she questioned it, he'd tell her that he'd hired the service to help him cope while she was in the hospital.

In the taxi home, as they rumbled their way up Queen Anne, he noticed it.

She didn't look at the world in the same way anymore. A shrinking back, a momentary flinch, a hesitancy about it all.

He asked the doctor about it the next day. He could tell from her expression that she knew the answer already, but was reluctant to say. He pushed harder. "Does it mean something went wrong with the process?"

"Of course not," Dr. Avosh snapped. She shook her head. "We still don't understand all the ways that personality is genetically determined."

"If it's genetically determined, then it would be the same," he said.

"It's considerably more complicated than that," she said and began to explain, but he was already thinking of tortoiseshell cats and realizing what he had done.

He couldn't think of anywhere to go but his mother's.

Much to his surprise, she was sitting on the sofa with Taco on her lap.

"I thought you gave her to Mrs. Green," he said.

She ran her hand over the soft fur, rubbing around the base of the cat's ears. He could hear it purring from where he sat. "Just a loan," she said. "Shall I make us some coffee?"

They sat together, drinking it. The cat hopped back onto his mother's lap and began to purr again. She patted it.

"She's more loving, this time around," she said.

"This time around?"

"Yes." She shrugged and kept petting the cat.

"I think Mindy is different this time around too," he said.

She looked up, brows furrowed. "Is it possible?"

He nodded at the cat in her lap. "It's the same thing, as far as I can tell. Personality is random, at least some of it."

"But she looks just the same."

He rubbed his forehead with the heel of his hand. "Yes, she does. They took great care in that regard. I wouldn't be surprised if they used plastic surgery to correct any discrepancies. But they can't do that with her personality."

"And you can't tell her."

He shook his head.

His mother smoothed her hand over the cat, whispered to it.

"What's that?" he said.

"Asking her what she makes of this."

"But you called her something."

She blushed. "Taco Tooto Cat. Not Taco, but Taco Too."

Not and yet and still.

Like his Mindy. Who he could finally grieve for. Who he could finally meet for the first time.

"Are you going to pretend?" his mother said.

"No," he said. "I'm going to tell her. And tell her why she feels about me like she does. Then she can decide."

"Decide whether or not to keep things as they were?"

"No. Decide whether or not to begin."

Grave of the Fireflies

CHENG JINGBO, TRANSLATED BY KEN LIU

February 16: Through the Door Into Summer

The Snow-No-More birds appeared in the sky, adding to the chaos that enveloped the world.

The fluttering wings that were supposed to signal clear weather scraped across the orange sky like the return of snow-laden billows. Ash-white feathers filled the air, drifting down until they fell into the black orbs of my eyes, turning them into snowy globes.

On the sixteenth of February, I was born on the road to light, a refugee. My ebony eyes were luminous and vivid, but no one came to kiss my forehead. All around, people sighed heavily. I lifted my head and saw the ash-white flock heading southwards, their cries as dense as their light-stealing wings.

To the south was the Door Into Summer, built from floating asteroids like a road to heaven.

The giant star that lit the way for the refugees gradually dimmed, the shadow crawling up everyone's face. After the briefest experience of daylight, I saw the first twilight of my life: my mother's image bloomed in the dim light like a secret flower.

Mankind streamed across the river of time, aiming straight for the Door Into Summer. In that moment, our tiny planet was falling like a single drop of dew in a boundless universe, tumbling towards that plane made up of the broken remains of a planet.

New cries arose from the Snow-No-More birds. Gliding through the gravity-torn clouds, the soft, gentle creatures were suddenly seized by some unknown force. Alarmed, the flock wound through the sky like a giant electric eel, each individual bird a scale. They hovered near each other, their wingtips brushing from time to time with light snaps. Quickly, the snaps grew louder and denser—the birds drew closer together to resist the unknown force that threatened to divert them, and electric sparks generated by the friction of the wings hopped from wingtip to wingtip. A great, invisible hand wrapped its fingers around the throat of the flock, and the ash-white electric eel in the sky began to tremble, its entire body enshrouded by a blue flame.

And in a moment, the invisible force that had been pulling them higher into the sky dissipated. The eel writhed in its death throes among the clouds, the feathers shed by struggling birds falling like volcanic ash. Soon, the feathery snow descended over us. They slid in through gaps around the oxhide flaps, fell, moth-like, against the greasy glass of the gas lamps, floated in clumps over the dirty water in copper basins, caught in my eyebrows and the corners of my eyes.

The oxcart rolled forward slowly. My mother began to sing in the midst of this snowstorm of ash and sorrow. Gradually, I fell asleep, listening to her lovely voice. But her eyes were filled with the sights from outside the cart: in the suffocating, fiery air, tens of thousands of oxcarts headed in the same direction. The remnants of humanity flooded across the hills and plains. The further she looked, the more oxcarts she saw—each like the one we were in.

An old man rushed before our cart and knelt down. "The star is about to go out."

Even before he had spoken, my mother already knew about the star. Even before he had opened his lips, her eyes had already sunken into gloom. Since the oxen's eyes were covered by black cloth, the animals showed no signs of panic. But as the darkness fell, they felt the strange chill.

Rising clouds of dust drowned out the old man's words, just like the endless night drowned my mother's beautiful, bottomless eyes.

He had failed to notice the spiked wheels of the oxcart. Blood soaked into earth, a dark stain melting into the night. In my sleep, I felt the oxcart lurch momentarily, as though something had caught against its wheels. And then it rolled on as though nothing had happened.

My mother continued to sing. In her song, the white-bearded High Priest died on the way to see the Queen—because the news he was bringing was ill.

After that day, I never saw a Snow-No-More bird again.

Legend has it that on the day I was born, my small planet passed through the Door Into Summer. All the Snow-No-More birds died outside the door. Though they were birds of spring, when they died, it snowed: every flake was an ash-white feather; every flake was limned in pale blue fire.

On the day the Snow-No-More birds disappeared in the southern sky, we penetrated a wall made of 1301 asteroids and exited the Garden of Death through the Door Into Summer.

February 19: Curtain Call for the Crimson Universe

People called me Rosamund because, they said, I'm the rose of the world.

I thought the world was a fading rose. The cooling universe was filled with ancient stars like our sun—they collapsed, lost heat, aged, contracted into infinitesimal versions of themselves and stopped giving us light. Now, with shrunken bodies and failing sights, they could only offer us a useless prayer as they watched us flee at the edge of night.

A thousand years ago, nine priests secretly debated among themselves around a circular table and probed the will of the gods for the answer to the question: why had the stars suddenly decided to grow old and die? In the end, because they could not answer the question satisfactorily, the king punished them by taking their heads.

But one of them, the most powerful priest of them all, managed to survive. He lived because he had two faces, the second one hidden by his long, thick hair, and no one ever knew of its existence. If one gathered enough courage to pull aside the curtain of snake-like hair, one would see tightly pursed lips and wide-open eyes. When the king demanded that the priests yield up their heads, this priest split apart his own head with a double-edged sword and gave up the front half. Thereafter he became a wanderer far from home, and lived only with the secret half of his head.

It was rumored that the descendants of this man created Weightless City, the first planet we arrived at after passing through the Door Into Summer. The star collapsed behind us while the army of refugees dove like moths towards the last lit lamp in the universe.

No one could explain why the stars were dying. A thousand years ago, following an ancient prophecy, our ancestors altered the structure of our planet and adjusted its gravity to turn it into an Ark to flee towards those stars that seemed young still.

When we arrived at Weightless City, everyone was going to leave our own planet and move there. After its thousand-year flight, the Ark could no longer go on. And after we left our home, this planet that had once birthed and nurtured all of humanity would fall into the heat of a strange star and dissolve into a million droplets of dew.

That year, I turned six. The nineteenth of February was a special day. My mother, the Queen, set me on the back of a white bull, and I saw thousands, tens of thousands of oxen, all of them pitch black, pulling my subjects over the earth like a flood.

A lonely, golden tower rose from the distant horizon. By dusk, the refugees arrived at its foot. The tower, too, appeared as if it had been on a long journey. Behind the tower was a deep trench like a surgical incision; the rich, fleshy loam brought up from its depths gave off a burnt scent.

This was the Dock. The inhabitants of Weightless City, the dark green planet revolving overhead, had dropped it down. On this special day, the gravity between the two planets achieved perfect balance, enabling us to ascend this tower to our new home.

If anyone could have witnessed the coupling between these two tiny planets from a distance, they would have seen this: a golden rod emerged from one of the planets like a raised matchstick. As the two planets spun, the matchstick struck the surface of the other planet, scratching out a groove on its surface, and then stopped.

But for those on the ground, the sight seemed like a manifestation of divinity. Occasionally, through an opening in the clouds, we could see our future home— dark green, serene Weightless City. The mammoth golden tower in front of us had extended from that heaven like a dream, and then fixed itself inexorably into the earth. Everyone cried out in joy. They busied themselves with re-shoeing the oxen with strong, magnetic shoes, gilding the wheel spikes with silvery powder, patching the leaky oxhide tents . . .

Afterwards, the oxcarts began to climb the tower in order of precedence. Far away from the tower, I ran, barefoot. A few flowers hid in the grass, twinkling here and there. Wind seemed to come from somewhere deep within the ground, and I thought I heard a voice cry out between sky and earth: *Rosamund, Rosamund*. I placed my ear against the tips of the blades of grass: I wanted to know if it was my planet calling my name.

When I turned to look back, I saw the sky turn slowly, the horizon already tilted. The tower leaned away from the zenith until, finally, anyone could walk on it barefoot, like me.

Night fell, and the whole human race trod along this road to heaven. A woman carelessly knocked over a kitchen pail, and it fell all the way down the tower, clanging, banging all the way, until it plunged into a black, moist cloud, leaving nothing but ripples on the surface. It was so quiet that everyone heard the woman muttering her complaint. But then she pulled the rope attached to the pail—almost everything in the oxcarts had been tied down by rope to prevent it from moving about during the journey—and so her pail returned, filled with clear water.

We marched in the dark, silent night. In front of us was a new city, shining like a piece of jade. Around the massive and long bridge formed by the golden tower, all we could see was the star-studded night.

The universe was alike a gigantic stage curtain that gradually fell. Fewer and fewer stars remained. We walked faster.

February 22, The Magician of Weightless City

My mother was the only one who did not cry after she saw Weightless City.

After we descended the tower, the sky rotated back into its original location. The horizon was no longer tilted. Everyone got a clear view of heaven: just another ruin.

This was the first thing my mother said to the first stranger she met: "Take me to your king, archon, headman, or . . . whatever you call him."

"There's no one like that here," the man answered. "We just have a magician."

And so we came upon a machine-man made of steel. It sat in the middle of an open space like a heap of twisted metal. Walking from its left foot to its right foot took five minutes. But to climb from its right foot to its waist took a whole afternoon.

"Listen," my mother said. She squatted down to look into my eyes. "Rosamund, my precious, I have to go in there to talk to the magician. Wait for me here. My darling, my baby, do not leave before I come out."

I nodded. She smiled and lightly kissed my forehead. No one saw this farewell, and that was why, in the stories that people told afterwards, the Queen died from mistakenly eating a poisonous mushroom in Weightless City. But I saw with my own eyes my mother climb onto the shoulder of that gigantic robot, enter through an ear, and then disappear.

In the six years after I became an orphan, after my planet and my mother had abandoned and forgotten me, I grew into a twelve-year-old, willful young woman. Everyone now called me Wild Rose.

In the new world of Weightless City, I discovered a plant that had also existed on my planet. The vines extended hundreds of miles, and had fragile stalks that ended in delicate, thin tips. I liked to run among them barefoot. As my feet crushed the stalks, bright yellow liquid oozed out, and the wind brought indistinct cries: *Rosamund, Rosamund.* I put my ear against the black soil: I wanted to know if it was my planet calling me now through this new earth. My loneliness grew without cease during those six years until it took root deep in my blood and bones.

One time, when I heard the calls and put my ear against the muddy earth, I closed my eyes and saw my mother's face. "Rosamund, my precious . . . " She smiled and kissed my forehead, as though I really were the world's rose. Then I opened my eyes. Nothing.

Another time, when I opened my eyes, what I saw shocked and frightened me: a young man (barely more than a boy) was puffing out his cheeks. He was buried in the earth up to his neck, but his face was practically touching my forehead. He blinked his eyes, blue as water, and a breeze caressed my face. I stood up. "Who are you?"

"A free person of Weightless City," he said, joy in his voice. As he answered, he climbed out from his hole nimbly, as though the earth provided no resistance at all. "But who are you?"

I looked at him, stunned. He brushed off the mud from his clothes. There were flowers blooming now in the place where he had been buried.

"Let me guess," he said. "I bet I can guess your name."

And so he found a comfortable place and sat down, and set himself to the serious task of guessing my name.

It was an unforgettable sight: the silhouette of a young man sitting alone in the light of dawn. I couldn't see his face, but I could imagine his expression. Slender grass shot up wildly around him, extending further and further away.

"All right," he said, finally. "I give up. Why don't you try to guess my name?"

But then he glanced up at the sky and slapped his head. "Ah, I forgot what I came for. Rosamund, my sweet girl, where are you?"

As he said this, he was already running away like the wind. And so I had no choice but to cup my hands around my mouth and shout at his back, "Do you know Rosamund?"

"No." He was already some distance away. "I have to find her first. And then I'll know her."

"Why are you looking for Rosamund?"

He was almost at the horizon. "Because she's my guest."

I sighed. He was already invisible. "*I* am Rosamund."

A whirlwind swept from the horizon. The young man was standing in front of me again. He combed his hair with his hands, smoothed out the wrinkles on his shirt, and then bowed towards me very chivalrously. "Pleased to make your acquaintance, my . . . guest."

"But who are you?"

"Neither of us could guess the other's name. If you're truly Rosamund, then permit me to present you with my true name: the Magician of Weightless City."

February 25, The Knight of the Rose

Six years after meeting me, the Magician of Weightless City no longer looked so young. His castle was the secret to his eternal youth.

But I still enjoyed running barefoot on the wild heath. To see me, he often had to leave his castle. And in this way we grew up together.

Now that I was eighteen, he was like a knight, with a steel will and iron-hard shoulders. But when I was twelve, I had entered his castle for the first time.

The castle was the silent robot sitting on the ground. Since the robot had no need of a bladder, that was the location of the castle gate. After we entered, the Magician (still boyish back then) held my hand with his right hand, and with a *puff*, a torch appeared in his left hand. The interior of the castle was completely dark.

We passed by many murals, set foot on countless carpets, and after the seventh turn in the staircase, we knocked over three silver bottles and a crystal ball. His eyes and hair glinted brightly in the light from the torch. Both of us talked only of the journey we had taken and what we had encountered along the way, as though we hadn't been paying attention to each other at all.

Finally, I saw my mother, sitting on a chair covered by a tiger skin. She looked serene; her face hadn't changed at all from how I remembered her.

"Let me take a look at you, young lady," she said. Then she recognized me with a start. "What in the world happened to you?"

The Magician clapped his hands, and the torch disappeared from his left hand. Innumerable points of light suddenly appeared in the dark ceiling of the great hall, like stars, like fireflies.

The man who brought forth light said to my mother, "Your Majesty, while you have only been here a little while, she has been living outside on her own for six years."

"What kind of witchcraft is this?!" She hugged me and then pushed me back, holding onto my arms tightly so that she could examine me in detail. I was too embarrassed to look back at her.

The Magician said, "A thousand years ago, one of my ancestors came through the Door Into Summer. Using magic and witchcraft, he built this castle of eternal youth. Whether something is living or dead, as soon as it comes inside, it ceases to be eroded by the river of time. The short periods that I have lived outside the castle caused me to grow into this boyish form you see."

My mother spoke in the darkness. The starry light that bathed her forehead could not illuminate her eyes. The Queen confirmed the claim of this fugitive's descendant to his domain and made him Weightless City's first knight.

The answer to this grant of peerless honor came six years later. My knight found the dust-covered silver armor from the depths of the castle, put it on, and bowed slightly to the Queen on her tiger-skin throne. "Please allow me to be Rosamund's knight. She's come of age and ready to have a knight of her own."

I hid in a dark corner, watching him with my wide-open eyes like a fawn.

"Why?" my mother asked.

"Because she needs a knight. Not just any knight, but me. And I need to become the knight for a pure lady. Not just any lady, but her."

"Then," my mother said, "what can a knight do for a princess? Perhaps he doesn't even know what she truly needs, and neither does she."

The Magician of Weightless City, once a proud youth, and now a knight standing tall, full of courage, trembled as he heard this. His cold, rigid shadow stretched long and narrow, and as he trembled, it seemed about to take off from the ground.

Finally, the corners of his mouth lifted, and he answered the woman sitting high on her throne: "The loneliness in her heart is as dark as her eyes. But I will give her eternal light."

And with that, my knight departed his gloomy castle without looking back.

Behind him, the Queen, driven mad by the terror of eternity, screamed, "The stars are going out! You cannot bring back lasting light!"

The stars are going out. You cannot bring back lasting light. But the barefoot princess remained hidden in the darkness, expectant.

February 28: A Skeleton, or Two

I was sick.

I'd lost count of the passing years. Six years? Sixty? Or even six hundred? February 28th was the last day of that suspended period, the end coming like a cliff cleaving space into two halves.

The Queen of mankind had gone mad in the castle. She could not tolerate the erosion of the river of time, and could tolerate even less the passing days that now skipped over her like migrating birds over a forgotten tree. And so she constantly paced the halls of the castle, too frightened to abandon this heaven of eternal life, and yet unable to derive joy from the absolute stillness.

In her face, I could no longer detect the bloom of that secret flower. The permanent starry night of the great hall's ceiling cast two gloomy shadows under her eyes against her pale mask of a face. My mother's once-luminous black eyes, after many, many, *many* years of unchanging life, finally dimmed and merged into the darkness.

I thought of the man who had once built this castle, that great priest with only half of a head. Where had he gone?

When the world outside was drenched in heavy rain, I made torches out of bundles of straw and played hide-and-go-seek in the castle. I passed through room after room, full of dust, perusing books whose pages shattered at my touch—perhaps time had touched them now and then, after all? Among them was a diary, kept by another princess who had lived here long ago. She had poured out her heart through her quill.

Sometimes, I carried an oil lamp, and as its shifting light cast shadows on the walls, they coalesced into unfamiliar faces; sometimes, I lit a candle inside a rose-colored paper lantern, and the light flickered, almost going out.

I walked through the Cimmerian castle, got lost, searched, and occasionally, at the end of a long hallway, I'd see a figure, hear a low murmur, and then everything would once again disappear into darkness and silence—it was my mother, walking, losing her way, seeking, like me.

Finally, our paths brought each of us to the same room, a room I had never been before. Everything inside seemed as new as the long-ago day when the castle had been first erected. I found my mother sitting on the bed, inside the calla-lily-colored netting, sobbing like a ghost. That luxurious room had floor-length curtains, bright red, fresh, as though drops of blood were about to ooze out.

I went up and pulled the bed nets aside. But only a pair of empty sockets greeted me. It was a corpse. He had died long ago.

My game was over. The riddle revealed its answer. This dry husk of a body had once been famous—he was that priest who had escaped, the creator of Weightless City, the powerful wizard who once possessed two faces. I saw a ring on a string around his neck, and when I recognized it, I gasped.

From the day I was born, I also wore such a ring around my neck.

The inside of the ring was etched with a secret: the name of the lover my mother had lost a thousand years ago. He was once the most respected priest in the whole kingdom, but he had fallen in love with the princess, and they made love in her bedroom. The king, furious, ordered his guards to seize all nine high priests and cut off their heads. As for the princess who had lost her virginity, he sealed her inside a bronze mirror—she had been intended for the prince of another kingdom, and was supposed to become a queen beloved by her subjects and husband alike.

I had read this story in an old book, but I did not know that the legendary princess who had been sealed away was, in fact, my mother. The priest with two faces did not have a chance to say goodbye to his beloved. He cut off half of his head, handed it to the king's guards, and then became a fugitive through the Door Into Summer. A thousand years later, the princess awoke from the bronze mirror and became the wife of a king, and then the queen regnant of a people. By the time I was born, my father—who had never gotten my mother's heart—had already disappeared. My mother ruled over her realm as the disaster of the collapsing star unfolded, and then she led her people onto the route that her lover had taken a thousand years earlier.

Though the priest had built this timeless castle to wait for her, she had still come too late.

In his diary, she read of the suffering he had endured for a thousand years. His quill had turned into her lips, and she spoke to him every day. The diary I found had in fact been composed by the priest as he sank into these hallucinated conversations with my mother.

Finally, one day, seized by the ecstasy and rage of waiting, he cut his own heart open. Loneliness poured out of it, bright, fresh, and so he died in this murky castle.

He spent a thousand years to extinguish each and every star; she spent a thousand years to escape to the last star that remained lit. He knew she would come; she knew he would wait—even though when he had cut off half of his head with his sword, he had no chance to tell her anything.

My mother had known the truth for a long time. She had seen in the corpse's empty sockets the cruelest ending possible. From then on, she became an insubstantial ghost wandering through this empty, massive, ancient castle. The fleeting glimpses and murmurs I had caught of her had been nothing but figments of my imagination.

I finally understood why my mother would rather turn her rotting passion into ghosts that danced at the edge of light than set foot outside this eternal hell. When she saw the stars wink out, one after another, she was the happiest woman in the world. When darkness covered her eyes like a flood, she and the man she loved disappeared together on the shore of life and time.

Now that I understood this most impossible love in the world, I found myself an orphan. Truly, this time, my mother and my planet abandoned me.

I lay on the cold floor of the castle, inches and seconds to death.

I seemed to be back on my little planet spinning in space, blue like water. Slender grass shot up wildly around me, extending further and further away. I put my ear to the tips of the grass, a few flowers twinkling here and there. I knew I was going to die. Everyone who was about to die saw visions of the most beautiful scenes she had seen in her life.

I saw all the flowers blooming, the rain falling, a bright red lantern shining in the forest. I saw legends that flared up and dimmed, the face of a youth, fragile but stubborn grass. I saw the Magician of Weightless City: his silver armor had been burnished by the ice and snow at the peak of the world's tallest mountain, had been washed by the water in the deepest ocean, had protected him through desert, swamp, the ruins of mankind's cities and the Eden of fierce beasts, had been borne up a tower that reached into the sky and, following the planet that had abandoned me, reached an undying star—finally, the armor was dented, broken, full of holes. I saw the Magician's long, narrow shadow sweep across the cold floor before my eyes. I saw the return of the Knight of the Rose.

I could recognize only his eyes, the rest of him hidden behind his long-suffering armor. I couldn't tell if his chestnut hair had turned white. I could only smell wind and earth from the wounds in that silver shell.

My knight came before me, opened his left hand: a black pearl.

He found a slender thread and began to pull on it. The black pearl spun in his hand—ah, it was a tiny ball of thread. He pulled and pulled. In this castle of eternal night, the thread seemed to also have no end.

Finally, he picked me up from the floor. Until that moment, his silence had caused me, in my weakened state, to suspect that I had also turned into an insubstantial shade like my mother, a second living ghost wandering through the castle.

He pressed his left hand into my palm and squeezed my fingers into a fist. Then he pulled the rest of the thread out from between my fingers with his right hand. In that moment, I understood that I was still alive.

Thousands, millions of rays of searing light shot out of my clenched fist. He gave me the most dazzling light in the universe, a fistful of fireflies.

The Magician of Weightless City really did bring back a fragment of the star for me. My eyes had never seen such splendor. I saw my birth and death, feathers drifting down like volcanic ash, the clear, distant cries of Snow-No-More birds—that snowstorm had been kept on the other side of the Door Into Summer, and now, the flakes fell into my eyes, dark as night.

My knight bent to kiss my forehead. The luminous heat dissolved his armor. He and I were pierced by a thousand, a million rays.

The light melted our hair and eyes, skin and organs, until he had no more lips, and I had no more forehead. Our bodies were fixed in place: two skeletons with our arms entwined about each other.

Many years later, more explorers would come here. They would smash through the gate in the robot, where the bladder ought to be. They'd walk into the castle and discover in this perpetual radiance a strange skeleton.

"Maybe this was the priest who had escaped tens of thousands of years ago," one of them would say.

The others, after long debate, would reach consensus and publicize the cause for the extinguishing stars: "Due to the irresistible gravity of their mass, red giants tragically collapsed to death after exhausting the fuel in their cores."

They would not be able to search through the entire castle—that fragment of an eternal star would blind many of the explorers. They would not be able to examine that strange skeleton closely because no one dared to look at it directly for even a thousandth of a second.

The priest extinguished all the lanterns in the universe just so that he could recognize the woman he loved at a glance in the flood of refugees. My knight brought back that star fragment so that the inextinguishable flame could warm the loneliness in my dark eyes. The night completed my mother; the day completed me.

Here, in our luminous crypt, the fire can never be blown out.

First published in *Science Fiction: Literary,* July 2005.
First English language publication.

Bonfires in Anacostia

JOSEPH TOMARAS

1. The Table

On the left-hand side of the coffee table were stacked three Michael Chabon novels, one each by T.C. Boyle and Tim O'Brien, and a volume of Nathanael West's collected works. On the right were five guides to maximizing fertility, and two novels by Tessa Dare. In between were two stemless wine glasses.

The table itself was a clear polymer which, were it not encumbered with the remains of its owners' outmoded bibliomania, would reveal itself as a fully operational touchscreen. It was designed, however, to require replacement as soon as it received a hard thwack: The sort of urbane furnishing that only a childless couple would have purchased.

An advantage of this table, from the perspective of those charged with maintaining homeland security, is that its voice-activated features kept it in a continual state of attentive listening. If the owner kept it in its default, continuously connected networking mode—as 99% of purchasers of these models did—then every word spoken in its vicinity would fall under the expanded electronic surveillance authorization established by a certain executive order signed twenty years ago whose existence would be neither confirmed nor denied by anyone with legal authorization to know of it. That the owners happened to be Robert and Eileen Wexler, mid-level operatives in the DC office of the Cuomo 2024 re-election campaign, did not change the functioning of the table or of those analysts in Prince Georges County charged with making sense of its data-feed and hundreds of thousands more.

The table knew that objects totaling a weight of approximately ten kilograms were distributed unevenly across its surface, that the materials pressing against it were cloth, paper and glass, that Robert had in recent weeks been putting the music of the Talking Heads, an American New Wave band active from 1975 through 1991, on heavy rotation, whereas Eileen preferred silence whenever she was in the room, and that at this instant they had just repaired to their bedroom to finish preparations for a dinner party at the home of Darius and Brandon Gartner-Williams. It also knew that they would sometimes clear enough space to pull up campaign memos, the Post and the Times (both New York and Washington, of each), polling results and Sunday morning talk shows on its screen. The table could not know what was contained within the archaic text delivery devices pressing against it, though it got occasional glimpses when Robert would leave a book open face-down atop it—a habit for which Eileen would chastise him each time, reminding him that it would damage the spine. Neither Robert nor Eileen knew that the table knew all these things, but neither did they trust it fully, which may account for their decision to reconnoiter the dusty shelves of the DC Public Library and that mildewy used book store in a garret two stories above the scrum of Adams-Morgan for some of their reading matter.

Robert entered the room, noted Eileen's glass adjacent to his, and snorted. "I'm pretty sure none of those books recommend sauvignon blanc to enhance your fertility."

"You try answering to Ari Levine all day without a bit of liquid assistance," replied Eileen as she joined him. "When's the party?"

"I couldn't even suffer Tyler Colson without my refreshment. Seven o'clock." The Wexlers' habit of carrying on two conversations simultaneously was either irritating or endearing, depending on whether one was in a relationship with similar idiosyncrasies.

"Besides," continued Eileen, sitting on the couch and lifting her glass. "It's no better for your sperm than it is for my eggs. What's on the menu?"

Robert paused a beat, as he decided it would be ill-advised to remind her of the test results showing that his forty-seven-year-old gonads were none the worse for wear. "I don't know. Brandon was freaking out when I called him this morning. He just found out that Camilo's new boy is a vegan."

"I need animal protein." Eileen took another sip. "Ari wanted me to work late. Try explaining to him that I needed to go to my husband's ex-boyfriend's party."

"Did you?"

"It's none of his business. I told him no amount of number crunching would change the situation: Short of a total catastrophe, Andy's got this locked up."

"Short of the rest of the country finding out that half the nation's capital is in flames, you mean."

"Exactly. It's out of our hands at this point."

Robert sat down. There was nothing left to say, but silence did not seem right, either. "We have an hour left before we have to go." More silence. "You could have a snack." Eileen was beginning to lean toward the table, and had not taken the hint. Robert stuck his hand beneath the belt of his slacks as if to adjust, but really, to direct her attention the way he wanted.

"We shouldn't dilute it," replied Eileen, not even turning toward him.

Robert bent down to the table, dragged his finger diagonally to define the dimensions of a window, and called up a live feed of the Senate floor.

It was not strictly accurate to describe Brandon as Robert's "ex-boyfriend," not with the connotations of past exclusivity that this conventional phrase carried. Brandon and Darius had been together since well before Robert had set foot in Washington; he came to live with them shortly after he started grad school at American, during their brief, turn-of-the-century experiment with polyamory. By the time Eileen, seven years his junior, started coming to the gatherings at the Dupont Circle brownstone—on the arm of Janet—the story had grown too complex and too far distant to be worth telling accurately. That they were still getting invited to what had become the most sought-after soiree among LGBT Beltway insiders, despite the apparent completeness of their switch to heterosexuality and the low visibility of their jobs—he was a fundraising database programmer, she a statistician—was testament to Brandon's forgiving nature, the increasing self-assuredness of the community, and Darius' reluctance to let go of anyone he knew would appreciate his jokes, stories and lectures.

Robert just needed to keep tabs on his alcohol consumption. The last time, someone had almost walked in on him and Camilo's last consort. He suspected Camilo had figured it out, and that this was why a new guest was coming to the dinner. There were three things to wonder about before going to these dinner parties: What would Brandon cook, what new anecdotes would Darius have, and how young and attractive would Camilo's current boyfriend be. As the senior senator from Ohio asked to be recognized by unanimous consent, Robert considered all three. Of this, the table had no inkling, and neither did Eileen.

"Can you believe the mouth on that kid?" After several hours of hibernation, the table was woken by the sound of Robert's voice.

"I know," said Eileen. "Actually what I can't believe is Darius."

"How so?"

"Well, all that stuff about the holograms and the riots and the fires." The utterance of three keywords in such rapid succession switched the table from passive data-gathering to active interface with the analytical mainframes at the Agency. Based on Robert's and Eileen's metadata signatures, the Darius in question was identified with a high degree of probability as the same Darius Gartner-Williams who was an analyst with the agency. "Some of that had to be classified."

"Darius has always known how to walk right up to the line without crossing it. That's the only way a raconteur like him could have stayed where he is for so long."

"I don't know, he just seemed, not upset, but maybe, yes, maybe upset, at what's going on in Southeast."

"You don't think he'd do a Snowden?"

"No way, not a chance. Forget I said anything." Robert found this injunction of Eileen's easy to follow, but not the table. The table is not programmed to forget.

From the rustling sounds of their clothes the table intuited that they had taken seats on the sofa. It could not tell, however, that Eileen was reaching for the fly on Robert's khakis. "Hey, I thought you said we shouldn't dilute," said Robert.

"Forget it. We're nowhere near the right part of the cycle."

"Is that the truth, or is that the wine talking?"

"Too much wine and not enough food. Can you believe it, lentils and vegetables?" A zipping sound, then a seeming non sequitur: "What did you think of Camilo's new boy?"

Robert flinched guiltily, as if somehow Eileen's question signaled some awareness on her part of his indiscretion with Camilo's last partner, but she wasn't looking at his face to notice it. "Too skinny. And how can someone that self-righteous be that racist?" Then after a pause, during which he realized that in fact he would love to watch that bigoted little twerp choking on his dick, but that he should not say anything to that effect to Eileen, as the intermingling of violence, hatred and sexuality would be unnerving to her, he took note of the increased exposure of his genitals to Eileen's manipulations: "Are you sure we should? Ooooh."

The table soon detected a gagging noise that seemed to emerge from Eileen's throat. "Before, aah, we go too far, ooh," continued Robert, "Nice finger work, uhh, ahh, could we try, anal?" The table knew he only ever asked this when Eileen was drunk.

"Sure."

"I'll get the lube."

"Don't bother going upstairs. Vegetable oil's fine."

After hearing some sounds emerging from the kitchen, the table detected the removal of ten kilograms of books and other assorted materials from its surface, followed by a pressure totaling about thirty kilograms coming from what appeared, from visual sensing, to be Eileen's torso. This impression was soon confirmed by ultrafast sequencing of DNA from one of her skin cells: This feature of the table's was not a major selling point, but when discussed was pitched as a security measure. What better way to track down a ten thousand dollar piece of home electronics, if stolen, than to have the thief's DNA sequenced and automatically sent to the police? What neither Robert nor Eileen realized was that the table was already in a heightened state of alert, as a result of the keywords Eileen had spoken just a few minutes before, and that the sequencer was not only on, but bypassing local law enforcement and communicating directly with the Agency.

After about fifteen minutes of further jostling, the sequencer also detected human coliform bacteria, and incomplete genetic material originating from Robert. We do not know what happened next, but it must have been especially vigorous: A critical component of the table's power supply was dislodged from its circuit, and we lost all signal.

2. The Duck

The first thing, always, was to take off the tie, open the foyer closet, and find an empty rod on the cedar tie hanger. The second was to take the kitchen apron out of the same closet, and put it on. The third was to proceed through the combined living room / dining room / hallway across the terra cotta tiling to the kitchen and dock his tablet in the countertop station. The fourth was to find the traffic report on the tablet. With these practiced movements, Brandon Gartner-Williams would clearly delimit his Inspector General self from his domestic Dupont Circle townhouse incarnation, and no matter how maddening the preceding workday had been, he would ready himself and his home and his dinner table for the arrival of his husband, Darius, or Dar for short.

The traffic report was the key, the moment at which uncertainty would take over from ritual and preparation, and the outside world would provide the information necessary to make the next set of choices and motions. For Darius worked as an analyst at a subdirectorate of the NSA whose name, existence, budget and mission were never acknowledged in public documents, at an office in the Maryland suburbs whose nondescriptness on maps and satellite images was so impeccable as to raise suspicion, and his way home required him to drive through the District's Southeast quadrant. The neighborhoods on the left bank of the Anacostia River had proven resistant to three decades of gentrification and were now the site of regular disturbances, but Darius had explained to Brandon that the traffic reports would be the only way to have any sense of what was happening. The agency had seen to it that the news would not spread to other metro areas, but the armies of functionaries, lawyers, military men, contractors and subcontractors who populated the more prosperous quadrants and suburbs of DC would not stand for censorship of their traffic reports. Cooperative discretion was all the agency demanded in this case.

Strictly speaking, Darius did not need to traverse Pennsylvania Avenue SE to get home. He could have taken the safer route, inching along the Beltway. But Darius was not one to swerve from an available straight line. At least, that was what Dar had told Brandon. Brandon suspected that Darius was insisting that he was no less black than the young men setting barricades and cars alight in the streets, that despite his Falls Church upbringing and UVA and Georgetown degrees that he had no less right to be in that neighborhood than those who were born and would likely die there.

Brandon suspected, but he never asked. Even though they had been together for nearly thirty years, had gotten married as soon as DOMA was overturned by the Supreme Court, had developed matching paunches and grown comfortable with each other's personhood, he still felt guilty for the casual hurts he had unwittingly inflicted in the early years of their relationship: The crestfallen gaze of a twenty-something size queen, disappointed to learn that a certain stereotype was not universally true, and other things, some more petty, others worse, that he cringed to recall. He had learned over time not to ask certain questions of Dar. He would listen when Dar had something to say, to get off his chest, but he would not ask.

It took a while for the traffic report to come on. The 501c4s had figured out a way to keep their ads from being blocked or noise-cancelled. In the 2024 election season, the machinery of constitutional government continued in full view of the populace, louder and brighter than ever. Brandon turned his thoughts to dinner.

He had the duck that he had been planning to make into a ragout over pappardelle for last night's dinner party, until he learned that Camilo's guest, a lithe sophomore from GWU, was a vegetarian. And not one of those "I'll just eat the salad" kinds, but some hysterical vegan who would take offense at the smells of flesh and fat, horrified at the holocaust of innocent animals to which he had been made a party. Camilo, a notorious chickenhawk, had pleaded with Brandon and Dar to change the menu. They made do with a cassoulet of autumn squash and Puy lentils, and a lot of Puligny-Montrachet.

He remembered the boy's comment that brought the party to a halt: "I don't understand why those people have to burn down their own neighborhood."

Camilo dropped a fork. A dozen eyeballs made a circuit from the unexpected guest seated at the middle of the dining room table, to Dar at the head as always, to the ceiling. He went on, "I mean, not those people like, all African-Americans or anything like that, just those people in Anacostia."

Everyone knew Dar was going to lecture. When he was angry, he got professorial, an image that was helped by the leather-patched tweed jacket he had chosen for the evening. "Those people live in a neighborhood that is an embarrassment to this country, through decades of neglect. The government tried to bulldoze it into shape with urban renewal. Then the market took over, with gentrification, which is why you can live . . . where do you live again?"

"Columbia Heights."

"Why you can live in Columbia Heights and have no idea what it was like in the mid-nineties, when Brandon and I met. You remember, Bran?"

Put on the spot, Brandon had to speak, though he didn't want to. His response was clumsy, nervous and embarrassing. "When Dar and I met, we were both living on U Street. Even that was a little sketchy back then. No one would head up into Columbia Heights unless they had business being there, and the only people with business there were the junkies. Remember what I used to say about Anacostia, Dar?"

"Brandon was very new to DC. Back then the Green Line ended in Anacostia, and he would take it down to L'Enfant Plaza for work. He said the woman's voice on the Metro, before it was all computerized, made it sound like heaven."

Everyone laughed at Brandon's expense. Brandon excused himself: "She really did have an angelic voice."

Dar took no notice and continued. "I drive through that neighborhood every day, to and from work. Population density kept going up as people got priced out of everywhere else. The houses are falling apart, the roads are rutted like in any Third World country."

Camilo interrupted: "Like back home in Chile. Worse than Chile."

"It got better after Barack Obama was elected," Dar continued. "Some black professionals started moving in, fixing up homes, opening fancy restaurants. Bran and I even thought about buying a condo to shorten my commute to the new job, but, well, Brandon wouldn't exactly have fit in."

"Not that I would have minded living there, of course," protested Brandon, perhaps a bit too insistently.

"Of course, darling. Well, it's a good thing we didn't. The Second Depression started, half the gentrifiers lost their jobs and the other half moved back across the river as soon as some desperate fool pulled a knife on them. Then someone got the idea for holograms, a way to make it look to people flying into Reagan National or Dulles like there was not this lingering corner of squalor in the nation's capital. The people living there didn't seem to notice the illusions at first."

"I can't believe that they wouldn't notice," replied the boy.

"Believe or don't believe, it's up to you. But I see it every day in my job: Human beings will assume that things remain as they were, until they're forced to notice a change. The structures were ethereal, easy to miss if you don't think to look for them."

"So why the fires?" asked the boy.

"Some genius decided to throw a few white people into the mix, to try and jumpstart another wave of gentrification. You know the type. Young, artists or antiwar activists, skinny vegans . . . " Everyone tittered except the boy and Camilo, who did his best to mimic the disapproving earnest look on his young lover's face. "A few young bloods tried to earn their street cred by throwing punches at the strangers, and that's when people in the neighborhood realized something was happening. They started calling the images 'ghosts.' They noticed the shimmering patches in their roofs, the manhole covers in place of holes they had taught their children to avoid, the crackhouses and burnt-out lots that had become mansions. And someone—no one knows who, and I would know if anyone knew—tried to set one of the mansions on fire. And that was when they learned what it took government scientists a year and a million dollars to figure out: That fires disrupt the holoprojections. A well-aimed laser would do the same, anything that directs enough energy and light in the right place, but fires are more affordable. More democratic, if you will."

"I still don't see how that justifies the destruction. It just seems so stupid, counterproductive."

"They just want to be seen, their lives to be seen, as they really are. And I think *anyone* at this table"—Dar swept his hand broadly at the dinner party, consisting of four gay male couples, two pairs of lesbians, and a seemingly hetero couple who had, between the two of them, slept with half the other guests—"would understand wanting that."

But the lad was too born-in-the-twenty-first century to intuit the breadth of history that Darius had encapsulated with a single gesture, and soon enough, too soon, the word "animals" had been tossed out and Camilo made some excuses about the wine going to their heads and ushered his conquest out the door to his Adams-Morgan studio where there would doubtless be a glass-shattering fight, angry sex, or both.

So the upshot was, Brandon had to do something with that duck. If Darius had a short trip ahead of him, he would just break it down and sear the magrets for tonight so he could get something on the table quickly, then start tonight making confit with the legs for later, and freeze the rest of the carcass for stock over the weekend. If there were bonfires in Anacostia, he would have time enough to roast it. From what little Darius would let fall about his workdays, he understood that a quick dinner would have something to do with the operations branch of the subdirectorate—not Dar and the analysts, whom Dar represented as professional onlookers.

The ads had ended. Brandon listened to the traffic report with ears trained to listen for the unspoken.

3. The Car

Trayvon Allen, age twelve, was the lookout posted to watch the bonfire at the corner of Pennsylvania and 31st SE and alert the block to the arrival of police, fire department, the black cars, or anyone else who looked like they did not belong in the neighborhood. When he saw the black Audi making its way down an otherwise deserted stretch of Pennsylvania, he assumed it was operations, and flashed his mirror at the window of the 3rd floor apartment where DeShawn was camped out.

Something wasn't right, though. The car was coming at least sixty miles an hour, and accelerating. The driver seemed to be moving the steering wheel left and right, but the car stayed straight, as if someone had aimed it straight at the fire.

The driver didn't look right either. DeShawn came down with the crew and asked Trayvon, "Who that, T? Ops?"

"Naw, looks like some college nigga. Fat guy, glasses, faggoty suit."

The black Audi hit the bonfire, which had been built of cop cars, building lumber and gasoline, going at least eighty-five. They could hear the driver screaming from inside the car.

"Hold back, son," said DeShawn. "That shit gawn blow." DeShawn began walking backwards, hands above his eyes, and the crew mimicked. Then the gas tank on the Audi exploded, sending shrapnel into the holoprojector at the corner and shorting out the ghosts.

"Should we help him?" said Trayvon.

"He gone. Let's check him out before ops show."

The driver had smashed his own window and tried to climb out before the explosion. His dreads were still smoldering and the melted portions of his face looked bright pink against blue-black skin. He still had his ID and lanyard around his neck, the insignia of the agency visible from five feet away. "Shit, they gawn try and pin this on us," said DeShawn. "To the winds." At that signal, each member of the crew scattered in a different cardinal direction. Trayvon meandered south, swiping a half-burnt piece of paper off the ground. It had an address in the Northwest quadrant. He shoved it in his back jeans pocket.

By the time five black cars came west up Pennsylvania five minutes later, Trayvon, DeShawn and the other six members of the crew were all out of sight. Ten necks as thick as their heads, mostly white but two black dudes and a Latin among them: These were ops. Different crews, with older men or harder kids, would be sending down sniper fire any minute, but these guys were Kevlared head to toe.

Trayvon looked back at the scene from the Dumpster where he was hiding. Though the college-looking dude was one of their own, the ops looked neither surprised nor sad. He patted his rear pocket to make sure the paper was still there.

4. The Kid

Ordinarily a trip to Dupont Circle would be a simple matter of getting on the Metro, but things hadn't been ordinary in a long time. The Green Line had started bypassing all Southeast stations ever since the bonfires began, and the fare was well above Trayvon's hustle. If he had a flat map of the District in his mind he might have been able to calculate that the address was only a two-hour walk away. But the uprising and repression had warped his mental map of the city, transforming the Anacostia River into an impassable singularity. That he felt drawn to the address despite this wise caution was inexplicable through Trayvon's conscious thought. His path did not follow a straight line, but proceeded faster than a straight line trajectory would have taken him, as he slingshotted his way around obstacles known and observed: checkpoints, cop cars, black cars, vigilante gangs of yuppies in street mufti, and the cameras. For a black kid in an ash-stained white T-shirt, the District was more hazardous than an asteroid belt for the Millennium Falcon.

So by the time he arrived at the front door of the Gartner-Williams house, four hours had passed since the accident, agency representatives had come and gone, the duck, slightly overdone, had been sitting on the counter getting cold, Brandon's tears had pooled in a crease of the leather sofa on which he was lying, and Trayvon was starving. No lights were on in the house, and he hesitated before ringing the bell. Hesitated, but the same drive that had brought him this far led his finger to the button. The button activated not only the bell, but also a camera at the top of the doorway. If Trayvon had noticed the lens, he would have fled, but it was too dark on the street for him to suss it out.

Brandon hesitated before deciding to answer the door: It could, he reasoned, be the agency with more details on the circumstances of Darius's accident. Despite his decision, the ten-foot walk from the sofa onto which he had collapsed was like swimming through the Mariana Trench: slow and bone-crushing. In that time, Trayvon had multiple opportunities to re-consider, re-re-consider, and re-re-re-consider, and he had just begun to pivot his left foot away from the door when Brandon's voice creaked, raw, from the intercom. "Who are you? What do you want?"

The second question confused Trayvon a bit. For four hours he had undertaken this fool's errand contrary to his own conscious volition. "I . . . I saw something," he said, retrieving the scrap of paper and holding it up to where, he now reasoned, the camera must be.

Brandon couldn't make out anything on the screen, but assumed it had something to do with Darius. His hope and trust opened the door before his fear could countermand it. "Come in. What did you see?"

"An accident. A black man in a black car. I found this." Trayvon stepped across the threshold and handed the paper to the white man with red eyes. Brandon recognized it as a scrap of a receipt from Darius' auto repair shop. "Did he live here?"

"Yes, he did. Please, come inside." Ordinarily, Brandon enjoyed being a host above all else. A twelve-year-old kid from the wrong side of town would not usually be on the guest list, but his instinctual hospitality overrode his mistrust and distracted him, momentarily, from his grief.

The smell of the duck reminded Trayvon of his hunger. He hadn't eaten anything since his sugar-cereal breakfast. "Smells good in here."

"Are you hungry?"

The thought crossed his mind that this white man could be a government agent, or a child molester, but his stomach growled in response. Admitting his poverty to this white stranger was out of the question, though, so all he said was, "I can eat."

"Come on in. I'll get you something to eat."

Trayvon followed Brandon into the kitchen. When they reached the counter, Brandon noticed that he hadn't turned off the tablet yet. He removed it from the dock and, with the same fluidity of motion with which he had started his kitchen prep earlier in the evening, hurled it against the exposed brick. The sudden violence and the crack of the screen made Trayvon jump back. "Why you do that?"

"I hate the news," said Brandon. He gestured at one of the stools opposite his work area. "Sit down. I'll cut you some duck. Do you want the leg or the breast?"

"I never had duck. Is it like chicken?"

"Yes and no."

"I'll try the leg."

"I didn't get a chance to cook any vegetables. I can make you a salad."

"Tha's'a'ight. I'll just try the duck." Trayvon wasn't sure if he'd ever eaten a salad, and he didn't want to have his first here. The white man and the duck were strange enough.

Brandon put a plate in front of him, then a fork and knife, and placed the duck leg on his plate. "What do you want to drink?"

"You got Kool-Aid?" Brandon shook his head, so Trayvon answered, "I'll just have some water."

"Sparkling or still?" Trayvon looked at him like he had grown a second head, so Brandon just ran an empty glass under the tap.

"The man in the car, what was he to you?"

Brandon set the glass in front of the kid and waited for him to look up into his eyes before answering. "He's my husband."

"You gay?" Trayvon, remembering his grandmother's lessons about being polite when folks offered their hospitality, had tried to suppress the hint of disgust in his voice, but he had failed.

"Yes, we're gay. Were gay. I am gay. Darius was my husband." This was Brandon's first attempt at applying past tense to Darius, and it ended in renewed tears. "Why did you come here?"

"I saw the accident, but it didn't look like no accident."

"What were you doing there?"

"I live there." Trayvon was not about to mention anything about his role in the construction and maintenance of the bonfires, comparatively minimal as it was, to this gay white dude. His husband had been with the agency, and for all Trayvon knew, so was this guy. Though he figured that if they worked at the same place they would have both been in the same car, but that didn't mean this guy wasn't still government. Government was all over the place.

"What did you mean, it didn't look like an accident?"

"Like, he was trying to turn the car, trying to steer the wheel, I saw him, and I'm sure he was trying to slow down, too. But the car kept going straight, and faster. Like someone had set it up that way."

"He wouldn't have died if your friends hadn't set up the bonfires."

"I don't know nothing about no bonfire," lied Trayvon. "And nobody I know, knows how to make a car do that," he said, returning to the truth. "I just came here 'cause I figured, if he had peoples, they might want to know what I seen."

Brandon sat silently, shaking his head every minute or so as a new thought occurred to him. After the first headshake, Trayvon started eating the duck. After the second, Brandon pulled a piece of crispy skin off the carcass, folded it, put it in his mouth, and started chewing, his only bite since the agency had informed him of the "accident."

After several minutes of silence, Trayvon had finished the duck leg. "Thanks," he said. "That was some good shit. I'm'a go home."

"It's well after curfew, kid. The cops'll arrest you. You can stay here."

"Where?"

"You can have the bed. I'll stay out here, sleep on a couch, if I can sleep at all. I've been thinking so much about Darius, I realize, I've completely forgotten my manners. We haven't been properly introduced. What's your name?"

Trayvon hesitated, considering whether he wanted to sleep in a bed where *two dudes done all kinds of nasty gay shit*, or whether he wanted this one to know his name, weighing the unknown risks of each against the known risks of being a twelve-year-old black kid out after curfew. "Trayvon," he said.

"Are you named after . . . ?"

"Yeah. I was born the year he died. Momma liked the name."

"Hi, Trayvon. I'm Brandon," said Brandon, extending his hand. Trayvon shook. "It's not safe for you to go back out before the morning. Please, rest here."

Trayvon's legs and feet reminded him of the fatigue of his six-mile walk. "A'ight." Brandon pointed the way to the bedroom. Once Trayvon found the bed, he fell face first into it and went directly to sleep, in t-shirt and jeans, smearing soot onto the duvet.

5. The Wake

It was ten o'clock in the morning, and Camilo's lover Travis was still asleep, completely naked, and lying on top of the comforter. Camilo had been awake for two hours, and in that time had showered, made coffee, cooked breakfast, eaten breakfast, gotten dressed, and dug around in his stash for a bottle of pisco he could bring to Brandon and Darius' house—scratch that, now it was just Brandon's, he had to remember—as a means of comfort. He had spent the last five minutes watching the sweat pool in the curve of Travis's lower back and his shoulders rise and fall with each breath. Now his patience was at an end. He considered rimming the young man, as a kind way to wake him, but quickly ruled it out. For no reason he could discern, he felt as though Travis's contretemps with Darius must have had something to do with yesterday's accident. He was angry, and it wasn't the kind of anger that he could express through fucking. Holding the pisco bottle by its neck, he prodded Travis in the shoulder with the bottom.

"Wake up, already! Wake up! Levantate!"

"What the hell, C? It's Saturday."

"I told Brandon we'd be there in the morning. The morning's almost finished."

"I didn't like him."

"Who? Brandon?"

"Naw, Brandon's alright."

"Darius isn't even cold in the ground, and you're talking shit about him? He was my friend. We're going to help Brandon out."

Travis pulled on last night's clothes, and they made the twenty minute walk down to Brandon's in silence.

The doorbell woke Trayvon. Brandon, having hardly slept, was in the kitchen brewing more coffee. When he opened the door, Camilo spoke first. "How you holding up, Bran?"

"Not so good, Camilo. It's good to have friends around."

"I'm sorry for your loss," offered Travis.

"Thank you . . . . What was your name again?"

"Travis."

"Thank you, Travis. My mind's just been . . . "

"Of course, Brandon," said Camilo. "Let's go inside. Is anyone else here yet?"

"No, nobody at all. Bobby and Eileen are coming soon, and Susan, too, but Cassie has to work today." As they traversed the foyer, Trayvon entered the open kitchen.

"Is that nobody?" asked Travis.

"Oh, my god, I forgot," muttered Brandon. Then he called, "Trayvon, let me introduce you to my friends." Trayvon approached hesitantly. "This is Camilo, and this is . . . "

"Travis," said Travis, who remained aloof. Camilo offered his hand not in a shake, but as if to try and draw the boy's hand up for a kiss, an offer not taken by Trayvon.

"Trayvon saw the accident."

"Ay!" gasped Camilo.

"So he's one of the rioters, then?" said Travis.

"I think I should be going," said Trayvon, assuming the most proper, schoolroom tone of voice he could recall. "Thank you for letting me stay here, mister."

"Brandon," insisted Brandon.

"Thank you, Mister Brandon."

"No, please, stay. My friends are coming over for brunch, and I want you to tell them what you told me last night, about Darius."

"I don't know if I should."

"There's nothing to worry about, Trayvon. My friends know powerful people who should know the truth. We can keep you safe."

"Have you ever had a pisco sour, son?" asked Camilo, brandishing the bottle.

"He's way too young, Camilo. Twelve."

Camilo looked down at his shoes, reassuring himself that the boy looked mature for his age, then offered: "I'll make you one, Bran."

"Too early, Camilo. But let's go in, and you can be a dear and put a splash into my coffee."

6. The Bridge

The surveillance cameras on the Frederick Douglass Memorial Bridge across the Anacostia River were knocked out by a power outage just after six p.m. on Saturday. The cause of the outage did not need to be investigated, since everyone whose responsibility it would be to investigate it was already disposed to attribute it to a nearby bonfire.

When the body of Trayvon Allen was discovered the following day in Fort Hunt, on the Virginia side of the Potomac River, anyone who was in a position to investigate his cause of death saw plainly that it was due to a fall from a great height. If he was taking a circuitous route from the Dupont Circle area to his home in Congress Heights, he might very well have been crossing the Douglass bridge during the time when its surveillance cameras were out.

No bullets were recovered from his body. We repeat: No bullets were recovered from his body. Anyone who says otherwise is engaging in irresponsible speculation.

Stone Hunger
N. K. JEMISIN

Once there was a girl who lived in a beautiful place full of beautiful people who made beautiful things. Then the world broke.

Now the girl is older, and colder, and hungrier. From the shelter of a dead tree, she watches as a city—a rich one, big, with high strong walls and well-guarded gates—winches its roof into place against the falling chill of night. The girl has never seen anything like this city's roof. She's watched the city for days, fascinated by its ribcage of metal tracks and the strips of sewn, oiled material they pull along it. They must put out most of their fires when they do this, or they would choke on smoke—but perhaps with the strips in place, the city retains warmth enough to make fires unnecessary.

It will be nice to be warm again. The girl shifts her weight from one fur-wrapped thigh to the other, her only concession to anticipation.

The tree in whose skeletal branches she crouches is above the city, on a high ridge, and it is one of the few still standing. The city has to burn something, after all, and the local ground does not have the flavor of coal-land, sticky veins of pent smoky bitterness lacing through cool bedrock. In the swaths of forest the city-dwellers have taken, even the stumps are gone; nothing wasted. The rest has been left relatively unmolested, though the girl has noted a suspicious absence of deadfall and kindling-wood on the shadowed forest floor below. Perhaps they've left this stand of trees as a windbreak, or to keep the ridge stable. Whatever their reasons, the city-dwellers' forethought works in her favor. They will not see her stalking them, waiting for an opportunity, until it is too late.

And perhaps, if she is lucky—

No. She has never been lucky. The girl closes her eyes again, tasting the land and the city. It is the most distinctive city she has ever encountered. Such a complexity of sweets and meats and bitters and . . . sour.

Hmm.

Perhaps.

The girl settles her back against the trunk of the tree, wraps the tattered blanket from her pack more closely around herself, and sleeps.

Dawn comes as a thinning of the gray sky. There has been no sun for years.

The girl wakes because of hunger: a sharp pang of it, echo of long-ago habit. Once, she ate breakfast in the mornings. Unsated, the pang eventually fades to its usual omnipresent ache.

Hunger is good, though. Hunger will help.

The girl sits up, feeling imminence like an intensifying itch. *It's coming.* She climbs down from the tree—easily; handholds were gnawed into the trunk by ground animals in the early years, before that species disappeared—and walks to the edge of the ridge. Dangerous to do this, stand on a ridge with a shake coming, but she needs to scout for an ideal location. Besides; she knows the shake isn't close. Yet.

There.

The walk down into the valley is more difficult than she expects. There are no paths. She has to half-climb, half-slide down dry runnels in the rock face which are full of loose gravel-sized ash. And she is not at her best after starving for eight days. Her limbs go weak now and again. There will be food in the city, she reminds herself, and moves a little faster.

She makes it to the floor of the valley and crouches behind a cluster of rocks near the half-dried-up river. The city gates are still hundreds of feet away, but there are familiar notches along its walls. Lookouts, perhaps with longviewers; she knows from experience that cities have the resources to make good glass—and good weapons. Any closer and they'll see her, unless something distracts them.

Once there was a girl who waited. And then, at last, the distraction arrives. A shake.

The epicenter is not nearby. That's much farther north: yet another reverberation of the rivening that destroyed the world. Doesn't matter. The girl breathes hard and digs her fingers into the dried riverbed as power rolls toward her. She *tastes* the vanguard of it sliding along her tongue, leaving a residue to savor, like thick and sticky treats—

(It is not real, what she tastes. She knows this. Her father once spoke of it as the sound of a chorus, or a cacophony; she's heard others complain of foul smells, painful sensations. For her, it is food. This seems only appropriate.)

—and it is easy—delicious!—to reach further down. To visualize herself opening her mouth and lapping at that sweet flow of natural force. She sighs and relaxes into the rarity of pleasure, unafraid for once, letting her guard down shamelessly and guiding the energy with only the merest brush of her will. A tickle, not a push. A lick.

Around the girl, pebbles rattle. She splays herself against the ground like an insect, fingernails scraping rock, ear pressed hard to the cold and gritty stone.

Stone. *Stone.*

Stone like gummy fat, like slick warm syrups she vaguely remembers licking from her fingers, stone flowing, pushing, curling, slow and inexorable as toffee. Then this oncoming power, the wave that ripples the stone, stops against the great slab of bedrock that comprises this valley and its surrounding mountains. The wave wants to go around, spend its energy elsewhere, but the girl sucks against this resistance. It takes awhile. On the ground, she writhes in place and smacks her lips and makes a sound: "*Ummmah.*"

Then the

Oh, the pressure

Once there was a girl who ground her teeth against prrrrrressure

bursts, the inertia *breaks,* and the wave of force ripples into the valley. The land seems to inhale, rising and groaning beneath her, and it is hers, it's *hers.* She controls it. The girl laughs; she can't help herself. It feels so good to be full, in one way or another.

A jagged crack steaming with friction opens and widens from where the girl lies to the foot of the ridge on which she spent the previous night. The entire face of the cliff splits off and disintegrates, gathering momentum and strength as it avalanches toward the city's southern wall. The girl adds force in garnishing dollops, oh-so-carefully. Too much and she will smash the entire valley into rubble, city and all, leaving nothing useful. She does not destroy; she merely damages. But just enough and—

The shake stops.

The girl feels the interference at once. The sweet flow solidifies; something taints its flavor in a way that makes her recoil. Hints of bitter and sharp—

—and *vinegar,* at last, for certain, she isn't imagining it this time, *vinegar*—

—and then all the marvelous power she has claimed dissipates. There is no compensatory force; nothing *uses* it. It's simply gone. Someone else has beaten her to the banquet and eaten all the treats. But the girl no longer cares that her plan has failed.

"I found you." She pushes herself up from the dry riverbed, her hair dripping flecks of ash. She is trembling, not just with hunger anymore, her eyes fixed on the city's unbroken wall. "*I found you.*"

The momentum of the shake rolls onward, passing beyond the girl's reach. Though the ground has stopped moving, the ridge rockslide cannot be stopped: boulders and trees, including the tree that sheltered the girl the night before, break loose and tumble down to slam against the city's protective wall, probably cracking it. But this is nowhere near the level of damage that the girl had hoped for. How will she get inside? She *must* get inside, now.

Ah—the gates of the city crank open. A way in. But the city dwellers are angry now. They might kill her, or worse.

She rises, runs. The days without food have left her little strength and poor speed, but fear supplies some fuel. Yet the stones turn against her now, and she stumbles, slips on loose rocks. She knows better than to waste time looking back.

Hooves drum the ground, a thousand tiny shakes that refuse to obey her will.

Once there was a girl who awoke in a prison cell.

It's dark, but she can see the metal grate of a door not far off. The bed is softer than anything she's slept on in months, and the air is warm. Or *she* is warm. She evaluates the fever that burns under her skin and concludes that it is dangerously high. She's not hungry, either, though her belly is as empty as ever. A bad sign.

This may have something to do with the fact that her leg aches like a low, monotonous scream. Two screams. Her upper thigh burns, but the knee feels as though shards of ice have somehow inserted themselves into the joint. She wants to try and flex it, see if it can move enough to bear her weight, but it hurts so much already that she is afraid to try.

She remains still, listening before opening her eyes, a habit that has saved her life before. Distant sound of voices, echoing along corridors that stink of rust and mildewed mortar. No breath or movement nearby. Sitting up carefully, the girl touches the cloth that covers her. Scratchy, patchy. Warmer than her own blanket, wherever that is. She will steal this one, if she can, when she escapes.

Then she freezes, startled, because there is someone in the room with her. A man.

But the man does not move, does not even breathe; just stands there. And now she can see that what she thought was skin is marble. A statue. A statue?

It's hard to think through the clamor of fever and pain, even the air sounds loud in her ears, but she decides at last that the city-dwellers have peculiar taste in art.

She hurts. She's tired. She sleeps.

"You tried to kill us," says a woman's voice.

The girl blinks awake again, disoriented for a moment. A lantern burns something smoky in a sconce above her. Her fever has faded. She's still thirsty, but not as parched as before. A memory comes to her of people in the room, tending her wounds, giving her broth tinged with bitterness; this memory is distant and strange. She must have been half delirious at the time. She's still hungry—she is always hungry—but that need, too, is not as bad as it was. Even the fire and ice in her leg have subsided.

The girl turns to regard her visitor. The woman sits straddling an old wooden chair, her arms propped on its back. The girl does not have enough experience of other people to guess her age. Older than herself; not elderly. And big, with broad shoulders made broader by layers of clothing and fur, heavy black boots. Her hair, a poufing mane as gray and stiff as ash-killed grass, has been thickened further by plaits and knots which are either decoration or an attempt to keep the mass of it out of her eyes. Her face is broad and angular, her skin sallow-brown like the girl's own.

(The statue that was in the corner is gone. Once there was a girl who hallucinated while in a fever.)

"You would've torn down half our southern wall," the woman continues. "Probably destroyed one or more storecaches. That kind of thing is enough to kill a city these days. Wounds draw scavengers."

This is true. It would not have been her intention, of course. She tries to be a successful parasite, not killing off her host; she inflicts only enough damage to get inside undetected. And while the city was busy repairing itself and fighting off the enemies who would have come, the girl could have survived unnoticed within its walls for some time. She has done this elsewhere. She could have prowled its alleys, nibbled at its foundations, searching always for the taste of vinegar. *He is here somewhere.*

And if she fails to find him in time, if he does to this city what he has done elsewhere . . . well. She would not kill a city herself, but she'll fatten herself off the carcass before she takes up his trail again. Anything else would be wasteful.

The woman waits a moment, then sighs as if she expected no response. "I'm Ykka. I assume you have no name?"

"Of course I have a name," the girl snaps.

Ykka waits. Then she snorts. "You look, what, fourteen? Underfed, so let's say eighteen. You were a small child when the Rivening happened, but you're not feral now—much—so someone must have raised you for awhile afterward. Who?"

The girl turns away in disinterest. "You going to kill me?"

"What will you do if I say yes?"

The girl sets her jaw. The walls of her cell are panels of steel bolted together, and the floor is joined planks of wood over a dirt floor. But such *thin* metal. So *little* wood. She imagines squeezing her tongue between the slats of the floor, licking away the layers of filth underneath—she's eaten worse—and finally touching the foundation. Concrete. Through that, she can touch the valley floor. The stone will be flavorless and cold, cold enough to make her tongue stick, because there's nothing to heat it up—no shake or aftershake. And the valley is nowhere near a fault or hotspot, so no blows or bubbles, either. But there are other ways to warm stone. Other warmth and movement she can use.

Using the warmth and movement of the air around her, for example. Or the warmth and movement within a living body. If she takes this from Ykka, it won't give her much. Not enough for a real shake; she would need more people for that. But she might be able to jolt the floor of her cell, warp that metal door enough to jiggle the lock free. Ykka will be dead, but some things cannot be helped.

The girl reaches for Ykka, her mouth watering in spite of herself—

A clashing flavor interrupts her. Spice like cinnamon. Not so bad. But the bite of the spice grows sharper as she tries to grasp the power, until suddenly it is fire and *burning* and a crisp green taste that makes her eyes water and her guts churn—

With a gasp, the girl snaps her eyes open. The woman smiles, and the back of the girl's neck prickles with belated, jarring recognition.

"Answer enough," Ykka says lightly, though there is cold fury in her eyes. "We'll have to move you to a better cell if you have the sensitivity to work through steel and wood. Lucky for us you've been too weak to try before now." She pauses. "If you had succeeded just now, would you have only killed me? Or the whole city?"

Still shocked to find herself in the company of her own, the girl answers honestly before she can think not to. "Not the whole city. I don't kill cities."

"What is that, some kind of integrity?" Ykka snorts a laugh.

There's no point in answering the question. "I would've just killed as many people as I needed to get loose."

"And then what?"

The girl shrugs. "Find something to eat. Somewhere warm to hole up." She does not add, *find the vinegar man.* It will make no sense to Ykka anyway.

"Food, warmth, and shelter. Such simple wants." There is mockery in Ykka's voice, and it annoys the girl. "You could do with fresh clothes. A good wash. Someone to talk to, maybe, so you can start thinking of other people as valuable."

The girl scowls. "What do you want from me?"

"To see if you're useful." At the girl's frown, Ykka looks her up and down, perhaps sizing her up. The girl does not have the same bottlebrush hair as Ykka, just scraggling brown stuff she chops off with her knife whenever it gets long enough to annoy. She is small and lean and quick, when she is not injured. No telling what Ykka thinks of these traits. No telling why she cares. The girl just hopes she does not appear weak.

"Have you done this to other cities?" Ykka asks.

The question is so patently stupid that there's no point in answering. After a moment Ykka nods. "Thought so. You seem to know what you're about."

"I learned early how it was done."

"Oh?"

The girl decides she has said enough. But before she can make a point of silence, there is another ripple across her perception, followed by something that is unmistakably a jolt within the earth. Specks of mortar trickle from beneath a loose panel on the cell wall. Another shake? No, the deep earth is still cold. That jolt was more shallow, delicate, just a goosebump on the world's skin.

"You can ask what that was," Ykka says, noticing her confusion. "I might even answer."

The girl sets her jaw and Ykka laughs, getting to her feet. She is even bigger than she seemed while sitting, a solid six feet or more. Pureblooded Sanzed; half the races of the world have that bottlebrush hair, but the size is the giveaway. Sanzed breed for strength, so they can protect themselves when the world turns hard.

"You left the southern ridge unstable," Ykka says. "We needed to make repairs." Then she waits, one hand on her hip, while the girl makes the necessary connections. It doesn't take long. The woman is like her. (Taste of savory pepper stinging her mouth still. Disgusting.) But someone entirely different caused that shift a moment ago, and although their presence is like melon—pale, delicate, flavorlessly cloying—it holds a faint aftertaste of blood.

Two in one city? Their kind know better. Hard enough for one wolf to hide among the sheep. But wait—there were two more, right when she split the southern ridge. One of them was a different taste altogether, bitter, something she has never eaten so she cannot name it. The other was the vinegar man.

Four in one city. And this woman is so very interested in her usefulness. She stares at Ykka. No one would do that.

Ykka shakes her head, amusement fading. "I think you're a waste of time and food," she says, "but it's not my decision alone. If you try to harm the city again we'll feel it, and we'll stop you, and then we'll kill you. But if you don't cause trouble, we'll know you're at least trainable. Oh—and stay off the leg if you ever want to walk again."

Then Ykka goes to the grate-door and barks something in another language. A man comes down the hall and lets her out. The two of them look in at the girl for a long moment before heading down the hall and through another door.

In the new silence, the girl sits up. This must be done slowly; she is very weak. Her bedding reeks of fever sweat, though it is dry now. When she throws off the patch-blanket, she sees that she has no pants on. There is a bandage around her right thigh at the midpoint: the wound underneath radiates infection-lines, though they seem to be fading. Her knee has also been wrapped tightly with wide leather bandages. She tries to flex it and a sickening ripple of pain radiates up and down the leg, like aftershocks from her own personal riven. What did she do to it? She remembers running from people on horseback. Falling, amid rocks as jagged as knives.

The vinegar man will not linger long in this city. She knows this from having tracked his spoor for years. Sometimes there are survivors in the towns he's murdered, who—if they can be persuaded to speak—tell of the wanderer who camped outside the gates, asking to be let in but not moving on when refused. Waiting, perhaps for a few days; hiding if the townsfolk drove him away. Then strolling in, smug and unmolested, when the walls fell. She has to find him quickly because if he's here, this city is doomed, and she doesn't want to be anywhere near its death throes.

Continuing to push against the bandages' tension, the girl manages to bend the knee perhaps twenty degrees before something that should not move that way slides to one side. There is a wet *click* from somewhere within the joint. Her stomach is empty. She is glad for this as she almost retches from the pain. The heaves pass. She will not be escaping the room, or hunting down the vinegar man, anytime soon.

But when she looks up, someone is in the room with her again. The statue she hallucinated.

It *is* a statue, her mind insists—though, plainly, it is not a hallucination. Study of a man in contemplation: tall, gracefully poised, the head tilted to one side with a frank and thoughtful expression moulded into its face. That face is marbled gray and white, though inset with eyes of—she guesses—alabaster and onyx. The artist who sculpted this creation has applied incredible detail, even carving lashes and little lines in the lips. Once, the girl knew beauty when she saw it.

She also thinks that the statue was not present a moment ago. In fact, she's certain of this.

"Would you like to leave?" the statue asks, and the girl scrambles back as much as her damaged leg—and the wall—allows.

There is a pause.

"S-stone-eater," she whispers.

"Girl." Its lips do not move when it speaks. The voice comes from somewhere within its torso. The stories say that the stuff of a stone-eater's body is not quite rock, but still far different from—and less flexible than—flesh.

The stories also say that stone-eaters do not exist, except in stories about stone-eaters. The girl licks her lips.

"What . . . " Her voice breaks. She pulls herself up straighter and flinches when she forgets her knee. It very much does not want to be forgotten. She focuses on other things. "Leave?"

The stone-eater's head does not move, but its eyes shift ever-so-slightly. Tracking her. She has the sudden urge to hide under the blanket to escape its gaze, but then what if she peeks out and finds the creature right in front of her, peering back in?

"They'll move you to a more secure cell, soon." It is shaped like a man, but her mind refuses to apply the pronoun to something so obviously not human. "You'll have a harder time reaching stone there. I can take you to bare ground."

"Why?"

"So that you can destroy the city, if you still want to." Casual, calm, its voice. It is indestructible, the stories say. One cannot stop a stone-eater, only get out of its way.

"You'll have to fight Ykka and the others, however," it continues. "This is their city, after all."

This is almost enough to distract the girl from the stone-eater's looming strangeness. "No one would do that," she says, stubborn. The world hates what she is; she learned that early on. Those of her kind eat the power of the earth and spit it back as force and destruction. When the earth is quiet they eat anything else they can find—the warmth of the air, the movement of living things—to achieve the same effect. They cannot live among ordinary people. They would be discovered with the first shake, or the first murder.

The stone-eater moves, and seeing this causes chilly sweat to rise on the girl's skin. It is slow, stiff. She hears a faint sound like the grind of a tomb's cover-stone. Now the creature faces her, and its thoughtful expression has become wry.

"There are twenty-three of you in this city," it says. "And many more of the other kind, of course." Ordinary people, she guesses by its dismissive tone. Hard to tell, because her mind has set its teeth in that first sentence. Twenty-three. *Twenty-three.*

Belatedly, she realizes the stone-eater is still waiting for an answer to its question. "H-how would you take me out of the cell?" she asks.

"I'd carry you."

Let the stone-eater touch her. She tries not to let it see her shudder, but its lips adjust in a subtle way. Now the statue has a carved, slight smile. The monster is amused to be found monstrous.

"I'll return later," it says. "When you're stronger."

Then its form, which does not vibrate on her awareness the way people do but is instead as still and solid as a mountain—shimmers. She can see through it. It drops into the floor as though a hole has opened under its feet, although the grimy wooden slats are perfectly solid.

The girl takes several deep breaths and sits back against the wall. The metal is cold through her clothing.

They move the girl to a cell whose floor is wood over metal. The walls are wood too, and padded with leather sewn over thick layers of cotton. There are chains set into the floor here, but thankfully they do not use them on her.

They bring the girl food: broth with yeast flakes, coarse flat cakes that taste of fungus, sprouted grains wrapped in dried leaves. She eats and grows stronger. After several days have passed, during which the girl's digestive system begins cautiously working again, the guards give her crutches. While they watch, she experiments until she can use them reliably, with minimal pain. Then they bring her to a room where naked people scrub themselves around a shallow pool of circulating steaming water. When she has finished bathing, the guards card her hair for lice. (She has none. Lice come from being around other people.) Finally they give her clothing: undershorts, loose pants of some sort of plant fiber, a second tighter pair of pants made of animal skin, two shirts, a bra she's too scrawny to need, fur-lined shoes. She dons it all, greedily. It's nice to be warm.

They bring her back to her cell, and the girl climbs carefully into the bed. She's stronger, but still weak; she tires easily. The knee cannot bear her weight yet. The crutches are worse than useless—she cannot *sneak* anywhere while noisily levering herself about. The frustration of this chews at her, because the vinegar man is out there, and she fears he will leave—or strike—before she can heal. Yet flesh is flesh, and hers has endured too much of late. It demands its due. She can do nothing but obey.

After she rests for a time, however, she becomes aware that something vast and mountain-still and familiar is in the room again. She opens her eyes to see the stone-eater still and silent in front of the cell's door. This time it has a hand upraised, the palm open and ready. An invitation.

The girl sits up. "Can you help me find someone?"

"Who?"

"A man. A man, like—" She has no idea how to communicate it in a way the stone-eater will understand. Does it even distinguish between one human and another? She has no idea how it thinks.

"Like you?" the stone-eater prompts, when she trails off.

She fights back the urge to immediately reject this characterization. "Another who can do what I do, yes." One of twenty-three. This is a problem she never expected to have.

The stone-eater is silent for a moment. "Share him with me."

The girl does not understand this. But its hand is still there, proffered, waiting, so she pushes herself to her feet and, with the aid of the crutches, hobbles over. When she reaches for its hand, there is an instant in which every part of her revolts against the notion of touching its strange marbled skin. Bad enough to stand near where she can see that it does not breathe, notice that it does not blink, realize her every instinct warns against tasting it with that part of herself that knows stone. She thinks that if she tries, its flavor will be bitter almonds and burning sulfur, and then she will die.

And yet.

Reluctantly, she thinks of the beautiful place, which she has not allowed herself to remember for years. Once upon a time there was a girl who had food every day and warmth all the time, and in that place were people who gave these things to her, unasked, completely free. They gave her other things, too—things she does not want now, does not need anymore, like companionship and a name and feelings beyond hunger and anger. That place is gone, now. Murdered. Only she remains, to avenge it.

She takes the stone-eater's hand. Its skin is cool and yields slightly to the touch; her arms break out in gooseflesh, and the skin of her palm crawls. She hopes it does not notice.

It waits, until she recalls its request. So she closes her eyes and remembers the vinegar man's sharp-sweet taste, and hopes that it can somehow feel this through her skin.

"Ah," the stone-eater says. "I do know that one."

The girl licks her lips. "I'm going to kill him."

"You're going to try." Its smile is a fixed thing.

"Why are you helping me?"

"I told you. The others will fight you."

This makes no sense. "Why don't you destroy the city yourself, if you hate it so much?"

"I don't hate the city. I have no interest in destroying it." Its hand tightens ever-so-slightly, a hint of pressure from the deepest places of the earth. "Shall I take you to him?"

It is a warning, and a promise. The girl understands: she must accept its offer now, or it will be rescinded. And in the end, it doesn't matter why the stone-eater helps her.

"Take me to him," she says.

The stone-eater pulls her closer, folding its free arm around her shoulders with the slow, grinding inexorability of a glacier. She stands trembling against its solid inhumanity, looking into its too-white, too-dark eyes and clutching her crutches tight with her arms. It hasn't ever stopped smiling. She notices, and does not know why she notices, that it smiles with its lips closed.

"Don't be afraid," it says without opening its mouth, and the world blurs around her. There is a stifling sense of enclosure and pressure, of friction-induced heat, a flicking darkness and a feel of deep earth moving around her, so close that she cannot just taste it; she also feels and breathes and *is* it.

Then they stand in a quiet courtyard of the city. The girl looks around, startled by the sudden return of light and cold air and spaciousness, and does not even notice the stone-eater's movements this time as it slowly releases her and steps back. It is daytime. The city's roof is rolled back and the sky is its usual melancholy gray, weeping ashen snow. From inside, the city feels smaller than she'd imagined. The buildings are low but close together, nearly all of them squat and round and dome-shaped. She's seen this style of building in other cities; good for conserving heat and withstanding shakes.

No one else is around. The girl turns to the stone-eater, tense.

"There." Its arm is already raised, pointing to a building at the end of a narrow road. It is a larger dome than the rest, with smaller subsidiaries branching off its sides. "He's on the second floor."

The girl watches the stone-eater for a moment longer and it watches her back, a gently-smiling signpost. *That way to revenge.* She turns and follows its pointing finger.

No one notices her as she crutches along, though she is a stranger; this means the city's big enough that not everyone knows everyone else. The people she passes are of many races, many ages. Sanzed like Ykka predominate, or maybe they are Cebaki; she never learned tell one from another. There are many black-lipped

Regwo, and one Shearar woman with big moon-pale eyes. The girl wonders if they know of the twenty-three. (Twenty-*four*, her mind corrects.) They must. Her kind cannot live among ordinary people without eventually revealing themselves. Usually they can't live among ordinary people at all—and yet here, somehow, they do.

Yet as she passes narrower streets and gaps in the buildings, she glimpses something else, something worse, that suddenly explains why no one's worried about twenty-four people who each could destroy a city on a whim. In the shadows, on the sidewalks, nearly camouflaged by the ash-colored walls: too-still standing figures. Statues whose eyes shift to follow her. *Many* of them: she counts a dozen before she makes herself stop.

Once there was a city full of monsters, of whom the girl was just another one.

No one stops her from going into the large dome. Inside, this building is warmer than the one in which she was imprisoned. People move in and out of it freely, some in knots of twos and threes, talking, carrying tools or paper. As the girl moves through its corridors, she spies small ceramic braziers in each room which emit a fragrant scent as well as heat. There are stacks of long-dead flowers in the kindling piles.

The stairs nearly kill her. It takes some time to figure out a method of crutching her way up that does not force her to bend the damaged knee. She stops after the third set to lean against a wall, trembling and sweating. The days of steady food have helped, but she is still healing, and she has never been physically strong. It will not do for her to meet the vinegar man and collapse at his feet.

"You all right?"

The girl blinks damp hair out of her eyes. She's in a wide corridor lined by braziers; there is a long, patterned rug—pre-rivening luxury—beneath her feet. The man standing there is as small as she is, which is the only reason she does not react by jerking away from his nearness. He's nearly as pale as the stone-eater, though his skin is truly skin and his hair is stiff because he is probably part Sanzed. He has a cheerful face, which is set in polite concern as he watches her.

And the girl flinches when she instinctively reaches out to taste her surroundings and he tastes of sharp, sour vinegar, the flavor of smelly pickles and old preserved things and wine gone rancid, and it is him, it is *him, she knows his taste.*

"I'm from Arquin," she blurts. The smile freezes on the man's face, making her think of the stone-eater again.

Once there was a city called Arquin, far to the south. It had been a city of artists and thinkers, a beautiful place full of beautiful people, of whom the girl's parents were two. When the world broke—as it often breaks, as the rivening is only the latest exemplary apocalypse of many—Arquin buttoned up against the chill and locked its gates and hunkered down to endure until the world healed and grew warm again. The city had prepared well. Its storecaches were full, its defenses layered and strong; it could have lasted a long time. But then a stranger came to town.

Taut silence, in the wake of the girl's pronouncement.

The man recovers first. His nostrils flare, and he straightens as if to cloak himself in discomfort. "Everyone did what they had to do, back then," he says. "You'd have done it too, if you were me."

Is there a hint of apology in his voice? *Accusation*? The girl bares her teeth. She has not tried to reach the stone beneath the city since she met Ykka. But she reaches now, tracing the pillars in the walls down to the foundation of the building and then deeper, finding and swallowing sweet-mint bedrock cool into herself. There isn't much. There have been no shakes today. But what little power there is is a balm, soothing away the past few days' helplessness and fear.

The vinegar man stumbles back against the corridor's other wall, reacting to the girl's touch on the bedrock as if to an insult. All at once the sourness of him floods forth like spit, trying to revolt her into letting go. She wants to; he's ruining the taste. But she scowls and bites more firmly into the power, making it hers, refusing to withdraw. His eyes narrow.

Someone comes into the corridor from one of the rooms that branch off it. This stranger says something, loudly; the girl registers that he is calling for Ykka. She barely hears the words. Stone dust is in her mouth. The grind of the deep rock is in her ears. The vinegar man presses in, trying again to wrest control from the girl, and the girl hates him for this. How many years has she spent hungry, cold, afraid, because of him? No, no, she does not begrudge him that, not really, not when she has done just as many terrible things, he's completely right to say *you would too, you did too*—but now? Right now, all she wants is power. Is that so much to ask? It's all he's left her.

And she will shake this whole valley to rubble before she lets him take one more thing that is hers.

The rough-sanded wood of the crutches bites into her hands as she bites into imagined stone to brace herself. The earth is still now, its power too deep to reach, and at such times there's nothing left to feed on save the thin gruel of smaller movements, lesser heat. The rose-flavored coals of the nearby braziers. The jerky twitchy strength of limbs and eyes and breathing chests. And, too, she can sup motions for which there are no names: all the infinitesimal floating morsels of the air, all the jittery particles of solid matter. The smaller, fast-swirling motes that comprise these particles.

(Somewhere, outside the earth, there are more people nearby. Other tastes begin to tease her senses: melon, warm beef stew, familiar peppers. The others mean to stop her. She must finish this quickly.)

"Don't you dare," says the vinegar man. The floor shakes, the whole building rattles with the warning force of his rage. Vibrations drum against the girl's feet. "I won't let you—"

He has no chance to finish the warning. The girl remembers soured wine that she once drank after finding it in a crushed Arquin storehouse. She'd been so hungry that she needed something, anything, to keep going. The stuff had tasted of rich malts and hints of fruit. Desperation made even vinegar taste good.

The air in the room grows cold. A circle of frost, radiating out from the girl's feet, rimes the patterned rug. The vinegar man stands within this circle. (Others in the corridor exclaim and back off as the circle grows.) He cries out as frost forms in his hair, on his eyebrows. His lips turn blue; his fingers stiffen. There's more to it than cold: as the girl devours the space between his molecules, the very motion of his atoms, the man's flesh becomes something different, condensing, hardening. In the earth where flavors dwell, he fights; acid burns the girl's throat and roils her belly. Her own ears go numb, and her knee throbs with the cold hard enough to draw tears from her eyes.

But she has swallowed far worse things than pain. And this is the lesson the vinegar man inadvertently taught her when he killed her future, and made her nothing more than a parasite like himself. He is older, crueler, more experienced, perhaps stronger, but survival has never really been the province of the fittest. Merely the hungriest.

Once the vinegar man is dead, Ykka arrives. She steps into the icy circle without fear, though there is a warning-tang of crisp green and red heat when the girl turns to face her. The girl backs off. She can't handle another fight right now.

"Congratulations," Ykka drawls, when the girl pulls her awareness out of the earth and wearily, awkwardly, sits down. (The floor is very cold against her backside.) "Got that out of your system?"

A bit dazed, the girl tries to process the words. A small crowd of people stands in the corridor, beyond the icy circle; they are murmuring and staring at her. A black-haired woman, as small and lithe as Ykka is large and immovable, has entered the circle with Ykka; she goes over to the vinegar man and peers at him as if hoping to find anything left of value. There's nothing, though. The girl has left as much of him as he left of her life, on a long-ago day in a once-beautiful place. He's not even a man anymore, just a gray-brown, crumbly lump of ex-flesh half-huddled against the corridor wall. His face is all eyes and bared teeth, one hand an upraised claw.

Beyond Ykka and the crowd, the girl sees something that clears her thoughts at once: the stone-eater, just beyond the others. Watching her and smiling, statue-still.

"He's dead," the black-haired woman says, turning to Ykka. She sounds more annoyed than angry.

"Yes, I rather thought so," Ykka replies. "So what was that all about?"

The girl belatedly realizes Ykka is talking to her. She is exhausted, physically—but inside, her whole being brims with strength and heat and satisfaction. It makes her lightheaded, and a little giddy, so she opens her mouth to speak and laughs instead. Even to her own ears, the sound is unsteady, unnerving.

The black-haired woman utters a curse in some language the girl does not know and pulls a knife, plainly intending to rid the city of the girl's mad menace. "Wait," Ykka says.

The woman glares at her. "This little monster just killed Thoroa—"

"Wait," Ykka says again, harder, and this time she stares the black-haired woman down until the furious tension in the woman's shoulders sags into defeat. Then Ykka faces the girl again. Her breath puffs in the chilly air when she speaks. "Why?"

The girl can only shake her head. "He owed me."

"Owed you what? Why?"

She shakes her head again, wishing they would just kill her and get it over with.

Ykka watches her for a long moment, her hard face unreadable. When she speaks again, her voice is softer. "You said you learned early how it was done."

The black-haired woman looks sharply at her. "We've all done what we had to, to survive."

"True," said Ykka. "And sometimes those things come back to bite us."

"She killed a citizen of this city—"

"He owed her. How many people do *you* owe, hmm? You want to pretend we don't all deserve to die for some reason or another?"

The black-haired woman does not answer.

"A city of people like us," the girl says. She's still giddy. It would be easy to make the city shake now, vent the giddiness, but that would force them to kill her when for some impossible reason they seem to be hesitating. "It'll never work. They used to hunt us down before the rivening for good reason."

Ykka smiles as though she knows what the girl is feeling. "They hunt us down now, in most places, for good reason. After all, only one of us could have done this." She gestures vaguely toward the north, where a great jagged red-bleeding crack across the continent has destroyed the world. "But maybe if they didn't treat us like monsters, we wouldn't *be* monsters. I want us to try living like people for awhile, see how that goes."

"Going great so far," mutters the black-haired woman, looking at the stone corpse of the vinegar man. Thoroa. Whichever.

Ykka shrugs, but her eyes narrow at the girl. "Someone will probably come looking for you, too, one day."

The girl gazes steadily back, because she has always understood this. She'll do what she has to do, until she can't anymore.

But all at once the girl snaps alert, because the stone-eater is now standing over her. Everyone in the corridor jerks in surprise. None of them saw it move.

"Thank you," it says.

The girl licks her lips, not looking away. One does not turn one's back on a predator. "Welcome." She does not ask why it thanks her.

"And these," Ykka says from beyond the creature, with a sigh which may or may not be resigned, "are our motivation to live together *peacefully.*"

Most of the braziers in the corridor are dark, extinguished by the girl in her desperate grab for power. Only the ones at either far end of the corridor, well beyond the ice-circle, remain lit. These silhouette the stone-eater's face—though the girl can easily imagine its carved-marble smile.

Wordlessly Ykka comes over, as does the black-haired woman. They help the girl to her feet, all three of them watching the stone-eater warily. The stone-eater doesn't move, either to impede them or to get out of the way. It just keeps standing there until they carry the girl away. Others in the hall, bystanders who did not choose to flee while monsters battled nearby, file out as well—quickly. This is only partly because the corridor is freezing.

"Are you throwing me out of the city?" the girl asks. They have set her down at the foot of the steps. She fumbles with the crutches because her hands are shaking in delayed reaction to the cold and the near-death experience. If they throw her out now, wounded, she'll die slowly. She would rather they kill her, than face that.

"Don't know yet," Ykka says. "You want to go?"

The girl is surprised to be asked. It is strange to have options. She looks up, then, as a sound from above startles her: they are rolling the city's roof shut against the coming night. As the strips of roofing slide into place, the city grows dimmer, although people move along the streets lighting standing lanterns she did not notice before. The roof locks into place with a deep, echoing snap. Already, without cool outside air blowing through the city, it feels warmer.

"I want to stay," the girl hears herself say.

Ykka sighs. The black-haired woman just shakes her head. But they do not call the guards, and when they hear a sound from upstairs, all three of them walk away together, by unspoken mutual agreement. The girl has no idea where they're going. She doesn't think the other two women do, either. It's just understood that they should all be somewhere else.

Because the girl keeps seeing the corridor they just left, in the moment before they carried her down stairs. She'd glanced back, see. The stone-eater had moved again; it stood beside Thoroa's petrified corpse. Its hand rested on his shoulder, companionably. And this time as it smiled, it flashed tiny, perfect, diamond teeth.

The girl takes a deep breath to banish this image from her mind.

Then she asks of Ykka as they walk, "Is there anything to eat?"

The Contemporary Foxwife
YOON HA LEE

Kanseun Ong was procrastinating on her end-of-term assignment by puzzling over a letter from her older father when the doorbell chimed. At first she didn't react, even though correspondence from home—specifically from Older Father— was the last thing she wanted to deal with. Older Father was only fluent in their ancestral language, Na-ahn, which Kanseun spoke shakily and hardly read at all, and was a calligrapher as well; he liked to show off by sending her *paper letters*. He wrote every four weeks, if the dates were to be believed, although due to the vagaries of ship traffic the letters arrived more irregularly. The letters piled up in a box, the early ones forever unopened, and Kanseun felt both guilty and resentful on a regular basis. Her entire childhood her fathers had told her how important it was for her to perfect her Kestran, the unofficial official language of the Sasreth Alliance, so why subject her to this now that she was a student at Veroth station? Especially since Older Father knew she was only ever going to write back in Kestran?

The doorbell chimed again, more loudly. She'd programmed it to do that precisely because it irritated her. "Who is it?" she asked crossly.

"No one is present at the door," the apartment's watcher said in a distinctly bored voice. Had her roommate been messing with its personae again? Osthen- of-*White Falcon*, who would also be her best friend if only they would ever tidy up after themselves.

"No, really," Kanseun said. Hadn't she already had the talk with Osthen about how she needed quiet time this week to work on the concerto she had due? Not that she was working on it right now, but that was a detail. She should have known that Osthen had agreed too quickly, even if she'd all but agreed to pay them to meet up with their many loud friends elsewhere.

"No one is present at the door," the watcher repeated, still bored.

Kanseun cursed and put the letter down, tucking it under a paperweight in the shape of a disgruntled turtle. (Her younger father had a thing for turtles.) "Show me what's in front of the door," she said. A prank? She might not be an engineering candidate like Osthen, but she was good at jiggering security, and anyone messing with her was in for a nasty surprise.

The monitor displayed nothing but—was that a flicker? A curlicue of shadows?

She got up and opened the door just to check. *If Osthen's fucking with me on another stupid dare*, she thought, *I'm going to throttle them. "No one is present at the door" my ass.*

"Hello! Very pleased to make your acquaintance," said the no-one-is-present-at-the-door. It looked and sounded remarkably like a gawky teenage boy with tawny skin, black hair falling past his shoulders. Spectacles garnished with little amber-colored crystals framed large, long-lashed eyes. Who on earth needed spectacles anymore? Unless it was a fashion trend elsewhere in the station. His russet dress, or gown, or whatever it was, looked like it had led a former life as a sack, except the sleeves had hems. For all that, the boy smelled sweetly of clover and damp grass and disintegrating pine needles. Plants that were in short supply on the station, although Kanseun was planetborn and recognized the scents.

The bespectacled no-one-is-present-at-the-door, undeterred by what Kanseun had hoped was her most forbidding expression, was still speaking: "Are you in need of a foxwife? I cook, do dishes, scrub floors"—who did any of that except as a hobby?—"arrange flowers, disarm bombs, perform minor surgery, and provide comfort and companionship." She?—they?—radiated hopefulness at Kanseun.

"You're a what?" Kanseun said intelligently, using Kestran's alt form of the second person pronoun, acceptable either for actual alts, like her roommate, or when you had no clue whatsoever.

"I'm a boy foxwife," the foxwife said helpfully.

"Sorry," Kanseun said, chastened. Even if nothing in her previous experiences had prepared her for any type of foxwife.

"It's all right," he said, and dimpled at her.

It registered that he had said "foxwife" not in Kestran, but in Na-ahn. Kanseun remembered the word only because she had loved the animal spirit stories Older Father had told her as a child, in the early days before she went to school and lost the ability to say anything but *Pass the sauce, please* and *How's the weather?* "Foxwife" rendered straightforwardly as "fox" plus "wife." In all other regards, the foxwife was speaking a very polite form of Kestran. Too polite; it wasn't as though an unproven artisan candidate merited it.

Why did this matter? The boy was clearly cracked. "Listen," she said, trying not to talk down to him, "if you need Transient Services, they're not on the university level, they're on Level 18. You can get directions at any of the info kiosks."

The foxwife had peered around her into the room and was eyeing Osthen's couch—more accurately, the food wrappers on the couch—with interest. Was he hungry? "I can also tidy things and file papers and dust under couches," he said.

"Hey," Kanseun said, "the messy half of the room is *not* mine." Too late she realized she was encouraging him, and she steeled herself to be more firm.

To her surprise, the foxwife drooped and said. "All right. Thank you for your time. I hope you lead a long life with many blessings!"

What? "Hey, wait," Kanseun said. She was going to regret this, but she was noticing the smudges under his eyes, imperfectly concealed by cosmetics. Asking how long he'd been a transient—if, indeed, that was what he was—would be rude. Instead, she said, "Look, I'm not supposed to randomly take in more roommates, but why don't you come in and have some tea, and we'll figure out what to do." At least Osthen wouldn't mind; they were friendly to a fault.

She was getting more creative at procrastination, no doubt about it.

"I brew tea, too," the foxwife said, brightening.

"Oh no you don't," Kanseun said. She wasn't *that* much of a grouch. "You're my guest. I'm providing the tea." Where did he come from that people brewed their own tea or did the dishes? Was he one of those weird people who believed that tea perfection could only be achieved that way?

For that matter, *filing papers*? Too bad she couldn't have him answer her letters for her, but that would be tacky. Maybe tomorrow she'd procrastinate some more by scribbling the usual vague persiflage about how well she was getting on with her roommate (more or less true), complaining about the everyday sameness of station weather (always good for a few sentences), and how hard she was working at her music studies (true except when he sent her letters).

The apartment's watcher had picked up on her offer of tea. Two fragrant cups awaited her on a tray in the kitchen. She wasn't entirely sanguine about leaving the foxwife alone in the living room, but she didn't think he was dangerous, just a little out of touch with reality.

Kanseun emerged with the tray only to find the foxwife on his hands and knees, diligently picking up Osthen's collection of hand-painted tradeship figurines and organizing them on the nearest available table. She gaped, then said, "You don't need to *do* that. That's my roommate's mess. It's *their* problem."

"Oh, but I want to be useful!" the foxwife said.

Kanseun suppressed a sigh as she set the tray down. "Were you going door to door offering your, er, services for a long time?"

"Yes," he said without elaborating.

How had he escaped having *really bad things* happen to him, wandering around like this? To say nothing of this being the most inefficient job-seeking method ever. "How many people did you talk to?"

The foxwife frowned and brought up one hand, then the other. Kanseun realized he was counting on his fingers. When he got to ten he stopped and tilted his head. "Lots?" he said. "More than two paws, anyway."

Paws. Right. She was in over her head, but she'd promised tea. "Paws" wasn't that much stranger than some of the slang going around the university anyway. "Here," she said. "Sit down." She indicated her side of the room, which included a chair that wasn't obscured by a pile of game controllers. "What do I call you? I'm Kanseun Ong."

He sipped the tea delicately. "I'm a foxwife," he said with disarming happiness.

"Are you Norannin?" she asked. "You seem to speak a little of my ancestral language."

"I don't know," he said. "I speak a little of everything! I like languages."

So much for that. "Where do you come from?" She was being terribly direct considering they'd just met, but as long as he didn't mind—

The foxwife considered the question. "I walked a lot," he said finally. "I think I took some wrong turns, though."

Walked? To a space station? Granted, Veroth wasn't without its shabby underworld, but she couldn't believe that someone wouldn't have scooped up the foxwife before long. Transient Services prided itself on its thoroughness. "How long have you been on the station?"

By now the foxwife's cup was half-empty. One of the watcher's puppets came out to fill it up again. "Thank you," the foxwife said, still politely.

"You're welcome," the watcher's voice said warmly.

Kanseun blinked.

The foxwife sipped. "I got here"—the fingers again—"four days ago."

Kanseun didn't memorize the roster of ships incoming and outbound, but it was impossible to escape hearing about them. Like many shipclanners, Osthen couldn't imagine *not* knowing these things. Thanks to Osthen, Kanseun knew that the only ship that had made port four days ago was the battle cruiser *Marrow*. Despite Osthen's jokes about warclanners, she doubted that they would be so lax as to have allowed the foxwife to stow away.

She decided that the mystery was going to be someone else's problem, and drained her cup in one long gulp. The watcher had given her lukewarm tea, overly sweetened, her preference.

"Osthen is at the door," the watcher said. It had returned to boredom.

"Wonderful," Kanseun said just as the door swooshed open and Osthen slouched through it. Today their hair was done up in looped braids tinted purple at the ends. "Osthen—"

She looked around. Where had the foxwife gone?

"Hey there," Osthen said. "You missed a great party, by the way. Anyone call for me?"

"No, but—"

Interesting. There was a new table in the corner, polished red-black, exquisite in its sleekness. Kanseun had never seen it before. She tried not to be alarmed.

"Hang on," she said to Osthen, who looked bemused. "You can come out now," she called to the foxwife. "My roommate's a slob, but they won't hurt you. Their name is Osthen-of-*White Falcon*."

Before Osthen had time to ask why she was addressing a *table*, the foxwife was sitting cross-legged on the floor where the table had been. He bounced to his feet and said, "Hello! I'm Kanseun's new foxwife." This time he rendered the word in Kestran. He bobbed a bow to Osthen.

Osthen grinned at Kanseun. "I knew you'd get laid sooner or later."

"*Excuse* me," Kanseun said, queasy on the foxwife's behalf. Among other things, she wasn't convinced that he understood the connotations of "wife." And had Osthen really not noticed the transformation? "Do I look like I've just gotten laid?" Osthen opened their mouth and she hurried on. "He's, uh, visiting until I can help him get settled."

"Hello, foxwife," Osthen said, their grin softening into a more genuine smile. "Stay as long as you need to, that's what the couch is for. And don't mind Kanseun, she's always got a stick up her—"

"Oh, shut up," Kanseun said.

"Anyway," Osthen said without breaking stride, "I need to catch up on sleep. Later." They drifted past her and the foxwife in a haze of musky perfume and into their room. A moment later the door shut definitely.

If only she, too, had the ability to fuck around all the time and still get perfect scores on everything. "Could you explain what is going on here?" she said to the foxwife, remembering the watcher's *No one is present at the door* with ice-splash clarity.

"I'm very good at furniture," the foxwife said. "Did you like it? I do vases, too, but I didn't think it would harmonize with your design sense. My sister, now—my sister would have come up with a vase that worked. But I—" He stopped.

"It was a very nice table," Kanseun said, so that she didn't feel like she was kicking a child. She wanted to ask about the sister, but she sensed it was too early in their acquaintance. "Does this always happen around you? Why did I notice but Osthen didn't?"

The foxwife said, with the air of someone explaining the obvious, "I'm *your* foxwife." He picked up a broom from where it had been leaning against the wall, except Kanseun knew for a fact that there had been no broom there earlier, let alone one made of *straw*, and started sweeping.

"You don't have to *do* that," she said. "The watcher puppets that stuff."

"I like sweeping," the foxwife said placidly.

"Fine," Kanseun said. "I am officially not dealing with any more of this stuff tonight. I am going back to my nice, sane concerto and figuring out what the hell I have to do to balance my percussion line so I can cough up the rest of this movement. You do what makes you happy."

The foxwife's gaze became anxious. "Is it bothering you?"

"Yes. No. Oh, do what makes you happy. I guess it's no worse than meditation." He resumed sweeping.

"Right," Kanseun said. She sat at her desk and stared at her score, willing it to cooperate.

She never did respond to the day's letter, nor the one after that, even though she could feel Older Father's disappointment radiating through the envelopes at her.

Facts about Kanseun's foxwife, if not all foxwives:

His favorite food was jam. It didn't matter what kind. Kanseun had expected him to eat something logically vulpine, such as eggs. He liked eggs too (any kind with runny yolks, including raw), but there was no denying how happy he looked when he sat on a stool in the kitchen and ate jam out of a little dish with a spoon. The first time she caught him eating it straight out of the jar, but fortunately he was amenable to changing his habits.

When he said he spoke a little of everything, he wasn't kidding. After Kanseun handed in her concerto—2.6 hours ahead of deadline, plenty of time to spare—she gave Osthen permission to bring their friends over again. It didn't take long for Osthen to schedule more parties. Kanseun lectured the foxwife endlessly on appropriate behavior at parties, emphasizing that he was to say no to anything uncomfortable and to come get her if anyone got pushy. Osthen's taste in friends wasn't too unreasonable, but she worried.

Osthen's friends, like Osthen, interacted genially enough with the foxwife when in his presence (and hers). However, they never seemed to remember him once they left the apartment, as Kanseun discovered when she ran into Osthen's latest lover at one of the cafeterias. This applied even when Kanseun, in a fit of experimentation, brought the foxwife with her. The foxwife, for his part, was attentive to the points of etiquette that Kanseun had instructed him in, although she never got him to be less than effervescently polite.

Kanseun would have bought the foxwife some proper clothes. After the first day, however, he made this unnecessary by taking his fashion cues from Osthen. (Except for the spectacles. He always wore the spectacles.) She assumed that the lookalike designer clothes came from the same nowhere place as items like the broom. The one time she asked him about it, he attributed it to his superior organizational skills. How "organizational skills" accounted for the spontaneous generation of matter, she wasn't sure, but as long as no one turned up looking for lost items she didn't much care.

She came home once to find that he was beating wrinkles out of Osthen's clothes, using wooden beaters and some kind of primitive board. It took days for her to explain the extent of the chores that he did not, in fact, have to do by hand. And afterward she would still catch him doing them, and have to drag him away until the next time.

The foxwife was very good at video games. He was especially fond of the ones with hyperrealistic gouts of blood, but she had to console him every time he failed a mission and one of the game allies died, even when she explained to him that the game was fictional and you could restore saved games and, occasionally, resurrect characters. He'd curl up against her shoulder and sob quietly, dabbing at his eyes with a red-and-white polka-dotted handkerchief, before trying again.

He also had a great disdain for tigers—he called them "amateurs"—but would not say why. It wasn't as if the station housed anything as exotic or dangerous as tigers, and it only came up because Osthen mentioned the visiting dreadnought *Tigertooth*.

The one time Osthen managed to step on a stray nail in a bad way, the foxwife talked them into letting him remove the thing. Kanseun wasn't sure how she resisted the temptation to find a bomb to see if the foxwife could disarm it. She hoped it never became relevant. Even so, she couldn't escape the disquieting thought: where would he have acquired such a skill?

Another letter arrived. Kanseun immediately put it in the pile with the others before the foxwife could file it for her, and then wondered why she was so embarrassed at the thought of him catching her doing this. This one, too, went unread and unanswered.

The foxwife's obsession with doing chores continued to bother Kanseun. She finally discussed the matter with Osthen.

"Do *you* think I should try to get him to talk to a counselor?" Kanseun said in a low voice. The foxwife was in the kitchen. She didn't know how good his hearing was, so she'd turned up the entertainment system. It was currently playing some hot new null-gravity sport and she was trying not to watch. Sure, she'd undergone the necessary safety training upon moving here, but she was a stereotypical planetsider and she *liked* gravity.

"I don't mind him living here," Osthen said. They didn't look up from the miniature they were painting. "I mean, it's not like he takes up more space than my junk does. He fits nicely on the couch at night. And he seems happy, doesn't he?"

There was a certain degree of unreality to any conversation about the foxwife, given Osthen's on-off ability to remember his existence.

"But don't you think he deserves better?" Kanseun said.

"Better according to who?" Osthen retorted. "If this is so important to you, why aren't you discussing it with him? Find out what he wants for himself?"

She couldn't think of any noncondescending way to say *Because I don't think he's healthy enough to decide for himself.*

"Is it because you think he's mentally tilted?" they said. She'd forgotten that Osthen, for all their laziness, could be good at reading people when they wanted to. Even if that was why she was asking their advice in the first place. "Because it's still his life and still his say. Unless you're planning to break up with him over it."

Kanseun gritted her teeth. "We're not dating. It's not my fault he goes around calling himself a foxwife."

Osthen did look up then, and their eyes were sharp and not a little disappointed. "If he calls himself a foxwife, he *is* a foxwife."

"Not literally he isn't." Inexplicable abilities, yes. But he couldn't be a mythological figure. He was real.

They shrugged and dabbed their brush into the pot of steel-blue paint. "So? You're still talking to the wrong person."

"You're no help," Kanseun snapped, and regretted it immediately.

Osthen had gone into "there's no reasoning with you" mode and had returned their attention to the miniature. She wasn't going to get anything else out of them tonight, and it was all her damn fault.

She glanced toward the kitchen to see if the foxwife was still puttering around; froze. He was standing in the doorway, staring at her, red-and-white polka-dotted handkerchief scrunched up in his hand.

Kanseun opened her mouth.

The foxwife walked past her and out of the apartment.

She lunged after him; of course she did. But no sooner had she reached out to grab his shoulder than he wasn't there. She almost fell over. What else had she expected from someone who could turn himself into a table?

"Did you see where he went?" Kanseun said to Osthen.

"He who?" Osthen said.

Her heart turned to needles. "I have to look for him," she said reflexively, and all but ran out the door herself.

Kanseun spent the rest of the day and most of the night searching the station. She stopped by one of the ubiquitous kiosks, asking after someone of the foxwife's description, although it came as no surprise that the kiosk said, patiently, that no such person had asked for help. There was no sign of him at any of the cheap cafes or restaurants she had taken him to before, or even some of the ones they'd never gone to together.

Reasoning (hoping, more likely) that he would stick to the university level, she returned there and began knocking on doors. Not everyone answered, but those who did were unfailingly polite in their demurrals, which she took as a side-effect of the foxwife's unchanciness. No, they hadn't seen the boy she was looking for. In fact, they'd never seen anyone like that at all. And who wore spectacles these days, anyway?

Wrung out, eyes stinging, she finally conceded defeat at four in the morning. She'd go out tomorrow and try again. Osthen had already gone to bed. She looked around at the jacket that Osthen had kicked into a corner and went to pick it up and fold it away, even though she never picked up after her roommate. Then she sat down on the couch. Her head started to pound, and it took a long time for sleep to come.

The next morning—more like very early afternoon, since she wasn't used to having her sleep this messed up—Kanseun went to the kitchen to look at the teas directly because the watcher's voice aggravated her lingering headache and she didn't want it to enumerate all the options. She found the foxwife in the kitchen, eating ginger peach jam directly out of the jar.

Kanseun didn't lecture him about it.

The foxwife didn't say anything at all.

She pulled up a stool and sat next to him, watching him eat. The spoon wasn't one of hers.

After a moment, he produced another one and offered it to her. Kanseun accepted it gravely. It was beautiful: made of some beaten bronzy metal, maybe even actual bronze. There was a little curled fox engraved on the handle.

The foxwife held out the jar. Kanseun dipped the spoon in and had a mouthful of jam. It tasted delicious, like honed sunlight.

They finished the jam together, in companionable silence.

Two weeks and one day after that, the latest letter arrived for Kanseun. More specifically, it arrived while she and the foxwife were out for a walk. When they returned, the watcher said, "You have correspondence from your older father." Today its voice was bright, Osthen's latest fancy. "I have left it on your desk."

Kanseun had been in a good mood, which evaporated when she realized how long she had been avoiding the letters. "Great," she said, and made no move toward her desk.

The foxwife's organizational instincts had been triggered, however, and he went to pick it up. "Shall I open it for you?" he asked.

"Go ahead," she said with a sigh. "I'm impressed Older Father even bothers when I'm such a lousy correspondent."

The foxwife produced a letter opener, although he could have used the one she kept on her desk, and slit the envelope open. He held it up and looked intently at it. She thought he was admiring the calligraphy—Older Father did beautiful work, elegant rhythmic strokes, even if she struggled to decipher it—until he said, "It says there's been a lot of rain in the city, and are you studying hard still, and—"

"You can read this?" Kanseun said. She didn't know why she was so surprised, given the foxwife's proven facility with languages. Maybe it was the fact that he was holding the letter sideways.

Nevertheless, he started reading: "'On this 23rd of 11-month in the year 4297 of the Azalea Cycle'—"

"Wait, wait, wait," she said. "I thought you didn't do numbers." She hadn't meant it to come out like a put-down.

"4297 comes after 4296 and before 4298," the foxwife said. Misinterpreting her confusion, he added, with a hint of dismay, "If you want me to do all the numbers in between 4296 and 4297, and 4297 and 4298, we're going to be here a long time. As in infinitely long . . . "

"Remember when we first met," Kanseun said slowly, "and I asked how many people, and—?" She held out her hands the way he had. Thought of the foxwife holding up his fingers one by one.

"Yes," he said, and looked away. "I stopped counting after ten thousand or so."

Ten *thousand*. Kanseun swallowed. "How long have you been doing this?"

"A very long time," the foxwife said. He took off his spectacles and tapped the frame, a nervous tic she had never seen before. His eyes had gone sad and dark. "I'm the last of my litter. There were more of us once. I wasn't—I'm not a good foxwife. The sister who raised me was a very proper foxwife. According to the family stories, she seduced queens and investment bankers and fighter pilots, and she collected eggs made of gold wire and glass, and she insisted that I learn mathematics so I wouldn't get cheated in the stock market.

"She told me once that being a foxwife is all about shapeshifting. I tried to do as she said, but we got separated when we started following our humans off the origin world. I'm only good at things like tables and vases and fountain pens, not the kinds of shapeshifting that matter."

He lifted his chin and put the spectacles back on. "But there's no help for it," he said. This time his bright tone didn't fool her. "I have to do what I can to be useful in the world as it exists, that's all."

Kanseun regarded him intently. "Listen," she said. "How much of my language do you read?"

"All of it, I expect," the foxwife said unboastfully. "My family believed in the value of a good education."

"Do you write it too?"

He was smiling at her. "Yes," he said. "Yes."

"Teach me," Kanseun said. "I won't pretend I'm good at languages, but if I work at it and you're patient with me, I might pick something up." The next words came out in a rush: "Older Father used to tell me fox stories, shapechanger stories. I don't know if they're about your people, or about something else. But I could—I could ask him. Maybe he would know something." Maybe even something that would help the foxwife find his sister. "Of course, if I wait until I know enough Na-ahn to formulate the question, it could be a while, so I should just ask in Kestran—"

She'd been avoiding Older Father's letters for months now. What if he said something reproving, or worse, simply forgave her? What if he didn't remember the fox stories at all? What if, what if, what if. But she looked at the foxwife and thought, *Ten thousand doors. I can try, too.*

"I'm sure he would be happy to hear from you either way," the foxwife said. "But we can start the lessons whenever you want."

"Today," Kanseun said. "Let's start today."

Suteta Mono de wa Nai
(Not Easily Thrown Away)
JULIETTE WADE

'Cram-school psycho' was just a bully's insult until I started hearing the voices.

One of them sounds like a whistle, and the other like a rusty trumpet, and when I sit at my desk at midnight, slowly hitting my head against my schoolbooks, they discuss my future.

"She'll probably pass the exams on her own."

"No, she won't."

"She might. She studies hard."

"But she doesn't sleep enough. Look how she's fallen apart since her father's work reassignment."

"Her grandmother isn't taking good care of her. She needs someone to take care of her."

"No, she doesn't. She'd lose her spirit."

"She would not."

I'd scream at them to shut up, but I wouldn't want to wake Obaa-chan. Instead, when the pressure in my head wants to break me, and I hear the metallic ticking and the rustling get closer, I slip my feet into my zori sandals on the back step and hop out into the narrow space behind our apartment. Beyond the wall with its leafless ivy, the late train rushes by with a shudder and a shriek and I can scream as loud as I like and nobody will hear.

I won't pass the exams.

I have to pass the exams.

"She's mine," says rusty trumpet. And whistle argues, "No, she's mine."

Sometimes I just want to leave the world.

Obaa-chan made me name tags so I could sew them into my high school uniform: *Kitano Naoko*. I didn't want to throw away the extras, so I stitched them into my Gothic-girl cosplay. One in the spiderweb stockings, another in the white crinoline, another for the black minidress with the lace-up bodice. Small links back to the ordinary me.

My costume's still missing something.

In the bathroom of Harajuku station, I stand at the mirror beside a college girl in platform shoes. Her hair is dyed cherry-red, and she paints her lips into a big pink kiss. I can't afford platform shoes, and if I dyed my hair they wouldn't let me back in school. I draw black tears down my cheeks, and walk out into the icy January rain.

I'm the only one standing on the bridge. My other world is empty: no crowd of cosplayers to talk to, no music to lose myself in. Even Cherry Girl crosses and heads down Takeshita street, probably to meet friends.

I shiver under my tiny plastic umbrella, pacing back and forth through the puddles. I'd forgotten it's Adult's Day, the celebration for twenty-year-olds—I can't avoid seeing the shining stars of the holiday. Young women walk choko-choko in fancy geta onto the gravel path toward Meiji Shrine. Twenty-year-old perfection cocooned in layers of bright kimono and white fur shoulder-wraps. They glimmer against the dark gray street and the green trees. Admiring family members hover around them, carrying umbrellas to protect them from the rain.

They can scarcely walk in those heavy kimonos. They're not shivering, though. They've made it through. They'll walk beneath the torii gate into the shrine, make their offerings, and be blessed. Everything falls toward them—young men, good fortune, even gravity. They're so bright I can hardly bear to look, and light-years away.

I don't know why I came out here.

I walk fast back to the station. Change clothes in the bathroom, wipe my face clean for appearances. At a vending machine, I buy a can of hot milk-tea to warm my hands, and get back on the train.

At least I chased away the voices for a little while. But when the train pulls into my station, the pressure comes back ten times worse.

I have to be careful now, because of Obaa-chan. My bag has to be zipped, not the least shred of crinoline showing. The better way would be not to bring it around the front at all. I walk down the station steps, duck around the raised guard rail and across the tracks, then sidestep between the ivied wall and the back of our apartment building. An ice-cold drip from the eaves strikes me right at the crest of my head.

The voices are back.

"She's mine."

"No, she's mine!"

"Naoko-san, hey!"

My fingers clench. As I sidestep past our neighbors' back porch, the metallic ticking starts. There's the rustling, too, frantic this time. It sounds so real. Too real. Maybe there's a cat fight? But feral cats don't whistle my name . . .

I peek past the piece of wall that divides their porch from ours. *Things* are fighting, outside our back step. A skeleton, and a bat? No, skeletons don't have lights . . .

Crack.

The whistle rises in pitch like a scream, and the bat-thing falls down with the skeleton-thing standing over it.

I jump in and kick the skeleton-thing. It breaks apart, all its pieces scattering across the ground with a sound like a bike crash. A metal bar—the brake of a train? A bike pedal. A chain. A couple of disconnected gears. When I look for the bat thing, all I see is Obaa-chan's old paper umbrella from her tour of the Nakasendo Highway years ago, and a cracked teapot with a broken lid.

"Iya da . . . I'm fighting *garbage?*"

That's it—I've really lost it. I drop my bag, squat down and hide my face in my hands.

"We're not garbage," says the whistling voice, beside my feet. "I might be dusty, but I haven't been thrown away. I still matter."

I look down. The sumi-e painting on the side of the old teapot isn't plum blossoms any more. It's a face, and the crack looks like a sly grin.

I mutter aloud, "I need to see a psychiatrist, for sure."

"No," whistles the voice slyly through the crack. "Everything will be all right so long as you pass your college entrance exams."

I don't scream.

I do stand up with both hands over my mouth.

The metal parts are pulling back together as if by magnets, and the little lights go on, blue and yellow.

"Ow," says rusty trumpet. "Kyusu, no fair. You called her."

"You broke me!" the teapot retorts. It settles itself atop the umbrella, which tips itself up and gives a ruffle. "Den is nothing but a ruffian. I'm a good boy."

"Traditional," says Den, scornfully.

"Glue," I mumble. "Inside, we have some. Wait a minute . . . "

I slip off my shoes and step in the back door. The kitchen light is on, and Obaa-chan is cooking. I keep my mouth shut, tiptoeing past the door and into the front entry hall. Oto-san always kept glue in the slipper cabinet; it wouldn't have gotten moved when his company moved *him.*

Back out to the cold. I sit on the back step beside my zori and glue the two pieces of the teapot lid back together, casting glances at Kyusu, who has developed small brown bamboo hands and is covering his head as if his life force resided there, like a kappa's.

"Do you have tea in there?" I ask.

"Of course," he says, importantly. "Very old tea."

"He doesn't," says Den, who stands by the wall with lights winking. "It's all dried out long since."

Kyusu looks offended.

I hand Kyusu his lid, and glance down politely at the tube of glue while he puts it on. His teapot's still full of cracks, of course—but if I had to glue anyone's mouth shut, I'd rather it be Den's.

I ask, "Kyusu, do you need anything else? I have a rag, I could tidy you up—"

"Iya!" he cries. Then he ruffles a bit, and apologizes: "Shitsurei shimashita. You've taken good care of me."

"Yet you're still alive," says Den. He sounds surprised. Kyusu gives an indignant ruffle, and Den lifts his bike pedal like a threatening fist.

I stand up. "Den, leave him alone. Shall I kick you again?"

Den's lights wink out. Suddenly a light flicks on in the window above my head, and both Den and Kyusu flop down, old pieces of junk forgotten in the dirt.

Behind me, Obaa-chan opens the door. "Nao-chan, what in the world are you doing out here?"

"Tadaima." I duck my head. "I'm home."

"Okaeri-nasai." The way Obaa-chan says it, it's more a command than a greeting. She leaves it there in my ears and shuffles back into the house. Face burning, I carry my shoes back to their spot in the entry hall, and sneak my bag into the closet behind my folded futon. I wish I could have left it outside, but I don't trust Den.

If he and Kyusu are there at all. But I saw them; I glued Kyusu's lid for him. And Obaa-chan's stories always made the yokai spirits seem so real . . .

Maybe it's myself I don't trust.

Obaa-chan is sitting in her chair at the kitchen table when I walk in, but the moment I sit down she stands up again, pouring me tea the way she used to for Oto-san, with precision and ceremony. Taking a small bowl to the rice cooker and filling it. Filling another bowl with miso soup. Bringing them to my place. Reminding me of the trouble I am to her.

I clap my hands together. "Itadakimasu. Obaa-chan, I'll do the dishes."

"Of course you won't," she replies. "You'll be studying."

Ashamed, I hide in my miso soup. It's delicious, with bits of fried tofu. Just what my frozen body needed, which only makes me feel worse.

"You haven't been taking proper care of yourself, Naoko-san," Obaa-chan says. "Your face is all dirty."

She knows. She must; she didn't ask a single question about my bag. I pull my bangs down over my eyes. "I'm sorry."

"I spoke with your father."

I put my chopsticks down, carefully. Pinch the edge of the table until my fingertips turn white.

"I'll be driving you to cram school, and picking you up, this week. That should help."

It feels like a door shut in my face. I should be grateful. She's always tried to help. But I hardly feel I know her any more.

I manage to say something. "You're taking good care of me, Grandmother."

I pick up my chopsticks again and start eating, like a puppet.

There's no escape.

Day after day, kanji characters march through my head. Mathematics, English, social studies, science, Japanese language—they're skeletons made of broken chopsticks and bent umbrellas, rusty scissors, a hundred kinds of junk. Their footsteps hurt, and when I try to catch them they twist and fall apart.

Obaa-chan invited me into the formal tatami-mat room with the kotatsu, so I could tuck into the quilt under the heated table and keep warm while I worked. I declined, because I don't need Grandfather and Mother's ancestor portraits watching me on top of everyone else. Since then, the weather has dropped below freezing. Obaa-chan peeks into my room occasionally, her mending in hand, but she never asks me to change my mind.

"You can still pass." Kyusu is peeking through my window, seemingly unaffected by the cold. "It's not much longer."

"Kyusu, I'm trying to study."

I have no idea why he even cares. It was just a little glue.

"You'd rather go out. I can see why," says Den, beside him. "We know you try on the costume when no one is in the house. You've got a new spirit, and now it's being squashed."

"Both of you shut up, okay?"

A sad little whistle comes in reply. "All right, I understand."

Now I feel sorry. For a teapot on an umbrella. This does not help my concentration.

"You don't have to do this," says Den.

"Yes, I do."

Oto-san went to Tokyo University. I dream about getting into Kyoto, if I only could score high enough, but I'll never get there—probably easier to fly to the moon.

"You don't." His electric-panel face taps against my window, lights blinking. "It's your life. Your grandmother shouldn't be watching everything you do."

"Den—"

"I'm serious. You could tell her so."

I dig my left hand deep into my hair, and force my cramped fingers to keep writing, nicely formed characters, one in each box. Twelve hundred character essay, due tomorrow morning. And tomorrow night I'm sure there will be another just like it.

"Nao-chan, dinner!" Obaa-chan calls.

I can hardly set down the pencil. I shake my hand out, and blow on it, walking to the kitchen. Here, the space heater is on, but the friction in my head is so bad I'd almost prefer the cold.

I imagine myself standing on the sub-zero Jingumae bridge in my spiderweb stockings. I sit down, Obaa-chan gets up.

"I spoke to your father last night," she says, serving rice. "The weather is warmer in Nagasaki."

"Is that so." I imagine myself standing on the moon.

"He would like to talk to you sometime."

I have nothing to say. She never calls me to the phone. I used to talk to Oto-san, when he sat here on my right. I never minded eating late so I could talk to him. Obaa-chan talked to him, too. Now his empty chair is a crater, and she and I stand on opposite sides.

Obaa-chan sighs. "If you told me more about your studies, I could tell him how you're doing." She sets down the rice bowl; the tiny sound of it hitting the table echoes like an asteroid impact. I answer like an alien.

"You already know how I'm doing. Don't you? You're always watching me. You don't even let me breathe."

Obaa-chan frowns. "Nao-chan, these exams will decide the rest of your life. You'll just have to endure."

"I can't stand it!" I push back from the table. "What if I don't want to take the exams? What if I don't care?"

Her fingers clench around the rice paddle, still in her hand. "You!" she snaps. "You only think about yourself—you treat your father's sacrifices as if they mean nothing."

"That's right, he's perfect, and I'm nothing but a nuisance who will never be good for anything!"

"Naoko-san, sit down and eat your dinner."

"I'm not hungry."

I run away down the hall, all the way out the back door. I curl up on the step with my knees pressed into my eyes.

"Naoko-san?" whistles Kyusu's voice. "Are you all right?"

Den whispers, "Look how powerful you are now."

"Leave me alone!"

I want to say that it was Den's fault, but I was the one who did it. I chose to speak.

I'm too tired to study and too angry to sleep.

Again.

Obaa-chan and I aren't speaking. I haven't eaten breakfast or dinner for two days because that would mean going into the kitchen. It would mean her serving me, reminding me as always of the filial debt that I can never repay.

"You should say sorry," Kyusu whistles, by the window. "She still cares for you. Just say sorry."

"No way," says Den. "You should stay strong. She should apologize to *you*."

Kyusu gives a ruffle. "Naoko-san, your grandmother would be glad to see you eat. So would I."

He's stopped telling me I can pass the exams.

I still have to pass the exams.

I feel sick, but my stomach is empty. Probably, Obaa-chan thinks I've been eating at school, but I've only had a little water. I'm just not hungry; my stomach feels flattened like an origami box. I tiptoe out to the back door and slip into my zori on the step. I take deep breaths, as if the icy air might fill me out to my proper shape again.

"Naoko-san?" Kyusu hops over from the window, his bamboo umbrella-handle stamping small circles in the frozen dirt. "I'm worried about you. Please eat."

"She's glimpsed the possible ends," says Den, leaning against the frozen twists of ivy. His yellow light blinks once. "Failure."

"Den, stop."

His blue light blinks once. "Death."

A shiver rises up from my feet, all the way to my head. Is that where this darkness leads? Suicide? "I don't want to throw my life away," I say. "I just want—I don't know, a way out of this."

"Time?" Kyusu suggests meekly.

"A different spirit," Den trumpets. "Like wearing your costume."

I can only sigh. "I still have to pass the exams."

"No, you don't," says Den.

"She does, though," says Kyusu.

Den laughs like the clatter of a chain against metal. "Not if she leaves the human world, and joins us. That would be a significant change."

For an instant I forget the cold. *Leave the world? Is that possible?*

Kyusu hops backward with a ruffle. "Iya . . . "

His mournful whistle disturbs me. "Kyusu, is your life so terrible? Would you rather be in someone's kitchen serving tea, or keeping off the rain?"

"It's not that. Den is . . . " He waves away his own thought with one bamboo hand. "I had to be forgotten before I could have my own memories, but I mustn't be undervalued. You should know that neglect does . . . unexpected things."

"It gives you life!" Den cries.

I hug myself. "I *am* alive."

Den scoffs with a grating noise. "Are you more alive now, or when you wear the costume?"

I look down, worrying the ties of the house-coat Obaa-chan made for me. He knows my answer, or he wouldn't have asked.

"Your father left for Nagasaki. That's what did it." Den waves his bicycle pedal in a grand circle. "*Now* you're realizing you have the power to do as you like with your own life. You could turn yokai, and leave behind your problems for good. Exams mean nothing to us."

Just throw the exams away? I can hardly imagine it. I pull my house-coat tighter. "What do I have to do?"

A deep shudder comes from the rails behind the wall. The flash of a headlight breaks the darkness, and the first train of the morning shrieks by.

Den says, "Come to Harajuku."

No matter how many times I've come out to the Jingumae bridge, I never expected to follow the Adult's Day girls so soon—and not like this. Above my head, the giant torii gate of Meiji Shrine looks almost painted, heavy ink-black lines against the dawning sky. It stands like a dark border between my past and future.

Den and Kyusu step beneath it first. Following them into the space between the trees, I shiver even in my winter coat. I try to imagine the yokai version of myself, but I see only Kitano Naoko, desperate high-schooler and cosplayer in withdrawal.

What kind of yokai could I be? I wouldn't do well as a neck-stretching rokurokubi, or a faceless noppera-bo. All I really know how to do is Gothic-girl.

What would a Gothic-girl yokai look like? Longer hair? Paler face? Would I feel cold? Hunger? Would I have silent footsteps?

Den and Kyusu don't. Den's gears rattle and scuff through the gravel; Kyusu hops with little crunching sounds, rather like the lamp in the Miyazaki movie. I'm still surprised they made it here so easily; early commuters on the Yamanote line seemed too rushed to do more than raise an eyebrow at a pile of abandoned objects in the corner by my seat. We've left commuters behind, though; here on the path between the trees, there is no one.

Soon the inner torii gate comes into view. Beyond it, the heavy wooden doors to the courtyard stand open. Kyusu stops abruptly before the high gate-sill, spreading his bamboo-and-paper skirts.

"Naoko-san, don't do this," he whistles. "Your grandmother will have found you gone by now. She'll be frantic, asking the neighborhood police if they've seen you."

Obaa-chan frantic . . . I hug myself, and shiver deeper into my coat. "What other choice do I have?"

Den straightens himself up, walking forward. "You can't stop her, Kyusu."

"And you can't make her. She doesn't even like you."

"That doesn't matter. She's mine anyway."

"No, she's not."

"Well, she's certainly not *yours*."

"Quiet down, both of you," I say. "I belong to myself. Den, you said yourself, it's *my life*."

Den's electric-panel face swivels around to me. "Truly? Then why are you here?"

I bite my lips shut.

"Naoko-san," says Kyusu, "we can still go home . . ."

"That's enough!" Den raises his bike pedal threateningly. "Teapot-boy, give her to me or this time I'll break your face."

I cry out, "Den, don't!"

But Kyusu drops his skirts with a whistling sigh. "It's all right. I'll stay behind."

Den hops and rattles over the wooden sill into the main shrine courtyard. I step over too, but with Kyusu gone it feels different. I don't like Den talking like he owns me. My stomach starts to cramp. I wish I could see the priests, but no one is in sight. Even the fortune-telling windows are still closed. At the stone steps I approach the offering bin and clap my hands to invoke the attention of the kami.

"Stop that," says Den.

"Don't you appreciate it?"

"It's not for me. And with what you're doing, we want as little attention as possible."

That sounds bad. "Den, what *am* I doing?"

Den's yellow light winks at me. "If you want to cross over to our world, you'll need to eat the offerings."

My stomach squirms. The New Year's offerings of mochi and oranges will still be arrayed before the altars. To *eat* them—the awful thought makes my hair stand on end. A sudden pain bites the back of my head, so sharp I clasp my hands over it.

"I can't. Den, I can't do this."

"Don't be an idiot. Of course you can. You're just hungry enough, and soon your new spirit will do it for you." Both his lights are glowing now, as if in satisfaction. "I told that teapot you were mine. Now he's just garbage. I *matter*."

"What are you saying? Kyusu matters." The back of my head hurts so much it feels like it's going to split open. I should never have come here. I should have realized, when Kyusu tried to stop us. I should never have let him stay behind . . .

I turn away and run back across the broad courtyard. At the gate, I call out.

"Kyusu? Are you still here?"

The dawn stillness is broken only by the trickle of water in the purifying basin. Then comes a soft whistle. "Naoko-san?"

Yokatta! Relieved, I follow his voice to a spot behind the basin. He cringes when he sees me.

"Naoko-san, are you all right?"

"My head is hurting. I'm so sorry. I should have listened to you. Den talks like he never cared about me at all, only about himself."

"I know," Kyusu sighs. He bows his teapot head so deeply he has to hold his lid on with both hands. "Neither of us did, at first. We only wanted to change you, to prove we still mattered, that we couldn't just be thrown away. I'm afraid I have no excuse."

My stomach cramps again. "That was what you both wanted, from the very beginning? To turn me yokai?"

He shakes one small hand before his face. "No, no, that was never my thought. Den had that plan, I suppose, but I only learned it today. Since you hadn't been eating, there was only one obvious possibility."

"*What?*"

"This." He reaches up for a dipper of water from the purifying basin and pours it into his spout. Then, bowing his head toward me, he removes his lid.

The tea gives off a musty scent, like rain on old leaves. I'm embarrassed to look at something so private, but once I do I can't stop staring. The purifying water glows with its own light, and the floating leaves flicker and change into the vision of a woman. She is deathly thin, with a starved expression, and two tentacular braids that undulate all on their own, revealing a gaping horror at the back of her head: a mouth full of sharp teeth.

Futakuchi onna.

"No. No. That's not me!" But there's still the pain at the back of my head—and I had that feeling that my hair was standing up . . . Iya! I hold my head tightly with both hands.

Kyusu claps his lid back on. "You're still in danger. You have to eat something normal, quickly."

I search my pockets. Nothing. "I could buy something at the station—"

Then I hear Den's voice calling. If he's come looking for me, that can't be good.

"Naoko-san, are you hungry? I've brought you an orange . . . "

Agony bites my head again. I scoop up Kyusu, and run. Den isn't a fast mover, but it's a long way back along the pathway through the trees, and I'm dizzy with pain and hunger.

"Just don't stop," whistles Kyusu.

At last we pass under the great torii gate and cross the street onto the bridge. There are people here, real people. I stumble through them to the station, and buy myself a train ticket. Once inside, I hurry to the vending machine and buy myself a hot milk-tea.

I have never tasted anything so delicious. As I cradle its warmth in my free hand against my face, the pain in my head slowly subsides. Kyusu stays tucked tightly under my arm, making no complaint as we board the train.

We reach our station with no sign of Den. It seems almost normal to walk down the station steps, around the guard rail and across the tracks. I duck in behind the ivied wall and sidestep to my back porch. Once there, I set Kyusu down.

"Kyusu, are you all right?"

He's silent for a long moment. At last, he ruffles hesitantly. "Yes?"

"You don't sound sure."

Kyusu pats his porcelain face with his bamboo hands, sumi-e eyes blinking. "Just—I'm surprised. You carried me, and I'm still alive."

"By good fortune, we both are. It's rude, but may I go inside and get something to eat?"

"Please do, before Den finds you."

I brace for Obaa-chan, and dare a quiet, "Tadaima . . . "

The apartment is silent. Even the kitchen is empty. Where could she be? The rice cooker light is on, so I wash my hands and open it. The rush of delicious steam makes me want to swoon. I take up a ball of rice with the paddle and shape it into a triangle between my hands; it's scalding hot, but I don't care. My head is finally my own again.

My mouth is full of hot rice when I hear Kyusu scream.

I gulp down the mouthful and run for the back door, nearly falling when I try to get into my zori. Den stands over Kyusu, raining blows with the bike pedal that could easily shatter his head—if they haven't already.

I kick Den to pieces against the ivied wall, but all too soon, he pulls himself back together.

I step between him and Kyusu. "Leave him alone."

Den's trumpeting voice is wild and furious. "Go ahead, kick me. Kick me all you like, but you'll never get rid of me. I'm not so easily thrown away."

Behind him, Kyusu gets up slowly. His head seems whole; he pats himself carefully with his small brown hands. I've seen him in pain, seen him broken, but he's never seemed afraid of death—except when I've cared for him.

I know what I have to do.

I crack open the apartment door and grab a clean rag from the laundry basket. Then I go for Den. He's expecting a kick, but I catch him by a loop of his chain and start rubbing.

Now he's the one who squirms and screams. Hits, too, but I won't let go. Whoever abandoned him left him covered with old oil and dirt that stains the rag. His brake handle is far easier, just a thin film of dust, and easy to wipe away. When I reach his electric panel his screams turn to whimpers, and finally fade away. I give each of his gears a good scrubbing, just to be sure.

Kyusu is watching me with both hands held over his mouth.

I drop the rag in the dirt, and extend a hand toward him. "Kyusu. I'd never do such a thing to you, I promise. You matter to me."

He twists his umbrella-foot in the dirt almost shyly. "Perhaps, if we are careful, we could care for each other without crushing each other's spirits?" Then he grimaces. "I'm still sorry I couldn't help you pass your entrance exams."

The exams. For the first time, the thought fails to bring its usual panic.

"Kyusu, excuse me a moment," I say. "I need to find my grandmother."

I carry my shoes, thinking to go straight out through the front entryway and ask after her with the neighborhood police, but passing the kitchen door, I glimpse her in the corner of my eye.

Obaa-chan, alone at the kitchen table. Not cooking. Not mending. Silent, lonely, her eyes downcast.

I don't know how to go in there. I leave my shoes and coat in the entryway and smooth my hair, so she won't scold me for little nothings when I've barely escaped throwing away my human self. If I sit down, she'll get up, and it will be too late. This time has to be different.

I walk in, straight to the electric kettle.

"Obaa-chan, can I get you some tea?"

I hear her shaking gasp, but focus on taking down a pair of cups and the small iron teapot—the replacement for our hand-painted porcelain one that cracked. The careful routine: shaking in tea, pouring in hot water, placing the cups and teapot on a laquered tray. At last she answers.

"Nao-chan—yes, please."

My hands shake, setting the tray down in front of Oto-san's place. I place one cup for her, one for me, and sit down.

Obaa-chan doesn't get up. The clock ticks on the wall, beside our kitchen shrine.

I reach for my cup, trying to find something to say.

"Obaa-chan, I'm sorry. I know I'm late for school."

After several silent seconds, she murmurs, "You're safe . . ."

Did she know the danger I was in? How could she know? But somehow it makes words easier.

"Obaa-chan, I'm sorry. I'm trying to study hard, but I'm not Oto-san. I think I'm going to fail, and the harder I try, the harder . . . it's terrible, inside my head. I don't know what to do."

She nods. Picks up her teacup in both hands, and sips. "You're just like me."

Like her? I blink at my tea, and take a sip to cover my confusion.

"Life is long," she says. "Even if you fail, even if you become ronin, you can try again."

"Oto-san—"

"He will return one day. He will want you to be here."

I sneak a glance at her face. Deep behind her sad eyes, I can hear words she doesn't say. *Life is long, if you don't throw it away.* What happened to her? Maybe one day she will trust me enough to tell me.

"I understand." I take a sip of tea, and swallow. "I should probably get ready for school."

She nods. "I'll drive you today."

"Yes, please."

"I'm here waiting whenever you are ready."

"Hai."

I run back to my room, but before I pick up my backpack, I open the sliding door of the futon closet. I open my bag and spread my costume out on the floor, feeling the tickle of crinoline on my palms.

I'm not going to throw it away—and now I know what it's missing.

I can wrap the bicycle chain around the waistline, and sew the gears into the skirt. The electric panel lights would look good if I stitched them to one shoulder. And the exams will end before winter does, so I'll need a better umbrella.

I'll ask Kyusu if he'd like to come with me.

The Saint of the Sidewalks

KAT HOWARD

Joan wrote her prayer with a half-used tube of Chanel Vamp that she had found discarded at the 34th St. subway stop. It glided across the cardboard—the flip side of a Stoli box, torn and bent—and left her words in a glossy slick the color of dried blood: "I need a miracle."

You were supposed to be specific when asking the Saint of the Sidewalks for an intervention, but everything in her life was such a fucking disaster, Joan didn't know where to start. So, she asked for a miracle, non-specific variety.

She set her cardboard on the sidewalk, prayer-side up. Then lit the required cigarette—stolen out of the pack of some guy who had been hitting on her at a bar—with the almost empty lighter she had fished out of the trash. You couldn't use anything new, anything you had previously owned, in your prayer. That was the way the devotion worked: found objects. Discards. Detritus made holy by the power of the saint.

Joan took a drag off the cigarette, then coughed. She hadn't smoked since her senior year of high school, and she'd mostly forgotten how. Thankfully, she didn't have to actually smoke the thing. Cigarette burning, she walked three times around her prayer, then dropped the butt to the sidewalk, and ground it out beneath her shoe.

Then she waited to see if her prayer would be answered.

Other people waited too, scattered along the sidewalk where the saint's first miracle occurred, with their altars of refuse and found objects, prayers graffitied on walls, or spelled out with the noodles from last night's lo mein.

The rising sunlight arrowed between the buildings, and began to make its progress down sidewalks lined with prayers. This was how it worked: if the sun covered your prayer, illuminating it, the saint had heard you. There was no guarantee of an answer, but at least you would know you had been heard. For some people, that was enough.

If your prayer caught fire, if holy smoke curled up from its surface as the sun shone down on it, that was a sure sign you had been blessed. Heard and answered, and your intention would be granted. A miracle. If she just had a miracle, things would be better.

Joan didn't need to watch to follow the progression of the sun. Cries of disappointment and frustration were common. Gasps of joy and gratitude much rarer.

Everyone had theories about how the saint chose to grant prayers. Some said it was whether she liked the altar, or the things you used to make your prayer. Others said she could feel the need in your heart, and mend your broken life that way. Joan hoped it was the latter, since it wasn't like her hasty scrawl and filthy cardboard was that impressive. Certainly not compared to what was next to her—a salvaged player piano, painted with neon daisies, tinkling through a double time version of "Music Box Dancer." Though really, Joan hoped the saint had better taste than to pick that one.

She tapped the toes of her left foot on the sidewalk as she waited, just below the cigarette. Maybe it was bad form to be impatient about a prayer, but Joan didn't care. She just wanted to know. Plus, she really had to pee.

The sun crept closer, the light crawling over her ancient Docs. It licked up her legs, over her chest, illuminated her hair, a brief halo.

Then paused, on the sidewalk again, inches from her prayer. Joan bit her lip hard. Come on, come on, come on, she chanted inside her head. Please.

A drop of rain. Then another and another. The sky greyed, then grew storm-dark. The opened, rain sheeting down. The worst of all possible signs.

Soaked to the skin, Joan ran into a coffee shop. She shouted her order as she passed the counter so she could use the "For Paying Customers Only" toilet. After she washed her hands, she rubbed the smeared mascara—waterproof her ass—from beneath her eyes.

Well then. No miracle. She would figure out something else.

The voices woke Joan the next morning. A crowd of people outside of her apartment, congregating on the sidewalk, on the steps. She angled her head to better see out of her sliver of window.

There were the beginnings of altars, but these were made to honor some sort of saint she had never seen before—coffee cups and lipstick cases, worn Docs and tights with holes. The hair on the back of her neck stood up.

Joan checked her Book of Hours, but there were no saints scheduled to appear on her street today. It wasn't a feast day, either.

She shrugged into a thrift store kimono, worn at the hem and wrists, but its embroidered peonies still bright, and went down to see what the fuss was about, hoping she was wrong.

"Our Lady of the Ashes!" "Our Lady of the Lightning Strike!" greeted her as she opened the door.

The people outside had smeared ashes on their faces, were waving scorched pieces of cardboard like holy relics. Most had painted their lips with dark lipstick. The front line of them fell to their knees before her.

"Oh, fuck no," Joan said, and fled back into her apartment.

Joan hadn't been online to do more than check her email in over a week. Nine days ago, she discovered that her (now ex) boyfriend was cheating with her (now former) best friend, which would have been bad enough on its own, but Joan had still been drunk and angry enough the day after to punch the asshole who liked to grab her ass when they were in the elevator together. Except. Said elevator was at work, and said asshole was her (now former) boss. Joan had gotten fired.

On reflection, it had not been her finest twenty-four hours.

In the wake of all of that, she hadn't wanted to scroll through social media feeds full of pity and snark, or pictures of the happy new couple—because, of course, the best friend and the boyfriend were in love—so she hadn't looked at anything.

She did now.

She had run fast enough ahead of the storm that she hadn't seen it happen, but lightning had struck the cardboard on which she had written her prayer. Had scorched it, but had not consumed it. Even stranger—although the cardboard had been prayer-side up, her words had been seared onto the sidewalk, still in the same shade of elegant goth Chanel lipstick she had scrawled them in.

Nothing else had been touched.

People were already calling it a miracle. Apparently every major department store in the city had sold out of Vamp, it was backordered online, and tubes were going for upwards of $100 on eBay.

Joan closed her laptop. "This is too weird," she said. She looked out of her window again. There were even more people out front. She shrugged into a hoodie, and pulled the hood tightly over her hair. Then she slunk out of the back of the building, holding her breath against the stench, and very carefully not looking at the spatters and smears as she passed the dumpster.

Things were even crazier on the street where she had made her offering yesterday. Her *rejected* offering. Because whatever this was that was happening, it was not how the Saint of the Sidewalks worked. No one had ever heard of her making a new saint before.

Ash-smeared people wearing blood-red lipstick waved scorched pieces of cardboard. Some were calling out "Saint Joan of the Lightning! Strike us!"

Great. Not only did they know where she lived, but they knew her name. Joan pulled her hood tighter over her head, and walked as fast as she could back to her building.

That was how saints were made. Some piece of strangeness happened, and it hooked itself in the heart of someone who saw it, and called it a miracle. Once they decided that's what it was, people tried to reenact the miracle's circumstances. They ritualized its pieces. They named the person at the center of it, gave them an epithet, something memorable.

The Saint of the Sidewalks had been a homeless woman, with a pile full of belongings, broken and worn. Perhaps relics from her previous life, perhaps more recent scavengings. She sat on it like it was her throne.

One day, it caught fire. Spontaneous combustion, said the witnesses. Too hot and fast to save her.

Except. No body was found. Surely a miracle, in and of itself. But then the stories started, saying that everything the fire touched had been made whole, restored. And so she became the Saint of the Sidewalks, her altars made of broken things, refuge her relics, and prayers sent to her in fire and smoke.

Joan did not want to be a saint.

The crowd at the front of her building had grown even larger, and there were peonies, baby pink and fuchsia and striated with color, woven through the handrails on the front steps. Those gave her pause for a moment, then she realized—the pattern on her kimono. Scary, that that was all it took.

The press of people was terrifying, the number of them, the fervency. She could feel the want, the terror and desperation, rising from them in waves. It made her dizzy, seasick, and again, Joan slunk in through the back entrance, trying to remain unnoticed.

Joan thought she heard someone yell her name, but she pulled hard against the door, not letting go until she felt the lock engage, and then ran up the steps to her apartment.

She had forty-one new emails, thirty-six direct messages on Twitter, and there were four hundred seven new pictures that she was tagged in on Instagram. She herself was only in thirteen of them. The rest were her building, the lightning-struck sidewalk where her prayer was.

Almost all of the messages and tags were requests for prayers, for interventions, for help.

Joan didn't even make it through ten of them before she wanted to punch something—the world, maybe—and a few more after that and she was crying. Hot, angry tears, that these people were so desperate as to see her as their best option.

She wasn't. She didn't even know how to fix her own life, much less theirs. The lightning had struck her prayer, not her—she had no superpowers. She was just a woman with a cheating ex, no job, and no coffee in her apartment.

Joan ordered in groceries and promised an obscene tip if the delivery person would meet her at the back. Nine text messages from her ex came in while she waited, all variations on how he was "So sry, bb." Not sorry enough to type entire words, apparently.

Plus, he was selling the cardigan she had left at his place on Craigslist, calling it a holy relic. He was also not sorry enough to just give it back to her when she asked him for it, the dick.

Getting the groceries was a fiasco. The crowd of people had found the back of her building, and by the time she had gotten back inside, three of her eggs were smashed, someone had stolen her grapes, and she had gotten smeared with ashes, her arms covered in people's handprints. She wondered if yelling "Get the fuck away from me, you fucking freaks!" would make people see her as any less of a saint.

She wondered if they'd see her as normal if they saw her hiding in her bathroom, wiping away tears, or if they'd just hold out vials to collect them in.

For some people, the saints were like candles bought at bodegas: a series of interchangeable names etched on glass, to be forgotten when the too-vivid wax burnt down. They were the equivalent of love spells found on the internet, tarot cards bought to be party tricks.

If Joan was honest, that's what they had always been for her. Even the intention that had gotten her into this mess—"I need a miracle"—had been desperation, not piety. In the darkest part of her heart, she hadn't really expected anything to happen, even if the sun had immolated her request. She had hoped something would happen, sure, but the gesture had been more of a way to feel like at least she had done something, than out of any fervent belief.

It was after midnight now, and raining, and there were still people clustered around the doors to her building. She had been braced all day for management to complain, but the message that pinged her inbox hadn't been a noise warning, but an offer of a month's free rent. The publicity her presence generated had been a real boon. Oh, and he'd be happy to get her oven fixed, too. (It spontaneously turned off after twenty minutes, no matter what temperature it was set to. Joan had put in the maintenance request three months ago.) He just had a quick prayer he wanted to send her way. Joan looked away from it. It seemed too intimate, to read what someone was praying for.

There was a GIF of a lightning strike at the bottom of the email.

Joan typed "Yes"—meaning the rent and the working oven—and copy-pasted the GIF, because she didn't know what else to do with it. She felt sick to her stomach. She wasn't a saint, she wasn't, but this had to be better than just ignoring the guy, right? She hit send.

Blue-white lightning cracked outside her window.

There was a crash. A scream. Then cheering.

"Saint Joan of the Lightning!" they cried.

She did not get up. She did not look.

Joan sat at her computer, staring at the "message sent" icon, hands covering her mouth. I need a miracle, she thought.

This time, the voices that woke Joan weren't from the chaos outside. They were in her head. People begging, beseeching: "Strike me with your holy fire, lady." "I cover myself in ashes until I am worthy of your light." Other things she understood less—languages she didn't speak, incoherent weeping. She sat up in bed, and clung to her blankets.

This was insane. She was no saint. She couldn't answer prayers. Didn't want the responsibility. Certainly didn't want other people's fucking voices inside her head.

She opened up her laptop, and started to type.

Turns out, once people decide you're a saint, they're reluctant to let you stop being one. They retrofit your actions to their desired narrative. So even though Joan wrote an explanation to her followers—ugh, that word—that she was just like they were, denied all ability to help people, to work miracles, they took her words as a sign of humility, of caring, of becoming modesty. The devotion to her only increased. She couldn't walk anywhere without prayers reverberating in her head.

The constant press of people sent her into trembling panic attacks, and so she lied, said that any unwanted physical contact would shock people, a result of the lightning that still passed through her.

She'd picked the ability because she wished she'd had it around her grabby ex-boss. But the story spread, and people gave her space. Almost enough that she could breathe.

Joan was never sure, after, how it happened. If the man had acted deliberately or not. But there was a hand on her upper arm, and then there was a spark and snap, and then there was a man, flung backwards, heaped up against a wall.

Joan stood, frozen to the spot. The man scrambled to his feet, then prostrated himself before her on the sidewalk. Already, the branching tattoo of the lightning strike was visible on his skin. He apologized and begged her forgiveness.

She gave it to him, of course. That was what saints did.

"It gets worse, the more they believe in you, not better." The woman sat on a stoop, bright fuchsia sequined Converse scattering sunlight from beneath the hem of an unbelted cream trench coat. "All of the supernatural bullshit, I mean."

"How do you know that I"—Joan started.

"You look haunted. Hollow. Like people have been biting off pieces of your insides.

"Plus, you're all over the internet. Our Lady of the Lightning."

There was a clink, as the piece of a shattered flowerpot replaced itself, making the terracotta whole again. A sensation like flame passed over Joan's skin.

Down the block, a flat bicycle tire refilled itself, and the bent wheel of a homeless man's shopping cart straightened.

Refuse made whole. Tiny, spontaneous miracles of proximity, accompanied by the heat of flames that did not consume what they touched. Joan felt pretty sure she knew who she was sitting next to.

"Right. Of course. What do you mean, it gets worse?" Joan plucked at a torn cuticle, worrying the skin until it bled, then winced at the pain.

"The more they believe, the more you become a part of those beliefs. Or did you think hearing voices and being electric were just talents you picked up?"

Joan shook her heard. "Does it stop?"

"Maybe. If you're lucky." There was longing in the woman's voice.

"I only wanted a miracle," Joan said.

The woman stood up, her shoes blinding in the sun. "And what makes you think you didn't get it?"

For the first time in her life, Joan desperately wanted to pray. To pray fervently, devotedly. To light candles before an altar, to obscure the sand of a mandala with her feet.

And she couldn't. Every time she opened her Book of Hours, every time a text alert popped up on her phone to notify her of a holy day, she thought of someone else, trapped by the weight of people's desires. Someone who, like her, could not sleep without being woken by voices raised in prayer, who could not leave their apartment without becoming the unwilling head of an impromptu pilgrimage.

She couldn't pray, not when doing so might trap someone else.

So she left. Joan wasn't sure if you could abdicate sainthood, but she would try. She hoped that if she could just get far enough away from the ecstasy of belief, find somewhere that people didn't know her face or care where she lived, she could go back to being normal.

She dyed her hair in her sink. She left in darkness. She used the last of her tube of Vamp lipstick to scrawl "Do not Look for me. I will not be Seen." on her mirror and she left the door to her apartment wide open.

She did pack her peony covered robe. She really liked it.

And then she ran.

Far, far away from where things began, Joan watched as the devotees of Saint Joan of the Lightning staged a service in her honor.

They wore masks now, that completely obscured their eyes, so that they could not accidently see her. It had been that, more than the distance, that had helped—she could grocery shop in peace, most days, and usually the people who recognized her only thought she looked familiar. They didn't quite know why. And if she had peony plants in her yard, well, so did most people. She stood out less, having them.

She watched on her laptop screen as they slicked dark lipstick over their mouths, then wrote their prayers on pieces of cardboard and pressed them to the sidewalk. She thought she saw a pair of fuchsia sequined Converse walk through the crowd, and she smiled.

Joan felt the hair raise on her arms, felt static electricity crackle across her skin. She would hear the voices—she had learned to listen without going mad, to separate out the pleas—and when she heard people asking for their own miracles, she touched her screen and struck their prayers with lightning, burning them to ash, letting hope rise up like holy smoke.

She was very careful to only choose the most specific prayers. She knew very well that without direction, miracles were never what you expected them to be. She watched her own, and touched her finger to the computer screen. In a crackle of lightning, at a distance, a prayer was answered.

Daedalum, the Devil's Wheel

E. LILY YU

Sit down, sit. You'll hurt yourself jumping around like that. No, don't shout. Quiet studio on a quiet night—a rare thing. Why ruin it?

Come from? Difficult question. I was there in the city of Shahr-e-Sukhteh when a potter glazed his bowl with a leaping goat. I was there when Ting Huan painted animals onto his paper zoetropes and set them slinking and lunging in the hot air from his lamp. I am in the twenty-fourth of a second between frames, where human perception fails. Right now, in fact, I'm shining on theater screens and on the glass of cathode-ray sets and in the liquid crystals of monitors across the world. And I'm here with you, because you called.

You didn't? Usually my votary burns his arms against the lightbox, or dies over and over in a spare room where he can film himself taking an imaginary bullet to the chest, applying what he observes—ah. That scrape, where your head hit the corner of your desk. That would have been enough.

Naturally you'd fall asleep over your work. It's one a.m. and you've been pulling eighty-hour weeks for as long as you can remember. Production deadlines, yes. No shame in that.

Can't help, sorry. That's your job. But lean your head against my shoulder. I'm sympathetic. I'll listen.

What, the whiskers bother you? The beach-ball skull? The fangs? The tail? I thought you'd appreciate the potential for infinite stretch and squash. I'll smooth them all out. How's this?

Frogfaced is an unkind way of putting it. You didn't have those objections to Maryanne, and she approximates the classic pair of stacked spheres.

Very simple. I can see right through you. You're like a cel pegged under glass. Your four affairs. Your ten-year marriage, eroded by your devotion to me—I appreciate the compliment, by the way—and meanwhile Isabelle swelling, suspecting, expecting. Your lust for attention that leads you into other women's arms. Your streak of mulishness. You're a con man. A cheat. A shyster. A magician. I like you.

Not Him, no, but I'm the closest you'll get to the quickening of life. Triacetate and clay and cats using their tails for canes. I'm on the other side of reality, the better side, where physics is like lipstick, dabbed on if needed, and there's no such thing as death. It's all in the splitting of the seconds, see.

Twenty-four frames every second, or the illusion stutters. Belief flickers and shatters. Even if they splice the ends together, the soundtrack will veer off. So I'm demanding, when it comes to sacrifices and offerings. At least 86,000 drawings for a feature film in two dimensions. In three, your weary flick, flick, flick through a dumbshow of polygons and nurbs, tweaking and torquing.

Speaking of offerings. Open your mouth for me. Wider, or it'll cut you. Stop squirming. It's only 35mm. There.

My left eye will do for lens and light. My right hand will be the takeup reel. Keep your chin up.

Here's your life projected on the wall. Your parents in crayon, and there's you—watching Looney Tunes in your pajamas, drawing penguins in the margins of your homework. It runs in your family. Your father loved Felix, and your grandfather snuck into nickelodeons on Saturdays. I'll crank faster through the litany of school, except those stretches where you were scribbling pterodactyls and fish. There's—what's her name?—gone. Alice. Beth. Chenelle. Danielle. She liked your cats, at least until you started drawing them with howitzers.

Please stop moving, you're making the picture shake. The faster I wind it out of you, the sooner this'll be over.

Art school. Elizabeth and Farah, tall and short, marvelous until they found out about each other. Your classes in anatomy, visual effects, life drawing, character rigging. What a crude and clumsy portfolio. But here's the job offer, finally. Here's your two dirty, grueling years as an assistant. Here's the second offer, the promotion, the raise. Now the wedding suit and blown-over chairs on the seaside. The late nights modeling and posing doe-eyed animals. The fights with Isabelle. Plates crashing to the floor. Cracking. Team meetings, sweat darkening an inch of your collar, making long wings under your arms. Your manager telling you how much your work stinks, how much he'd like to take your ideas into a cornfield and shoot them, how close you are to the edge of the axe.

That's it, the reel's run out. Feeling better? I thought so. Good to have it out, the fumes tend to build up explosively. Now—

Ah. I thought you'd never ask.

These are the standard packages:

A. Your work will spring to life. It will dance, it will convince, it will enchant. Your transfer of mocap to wireframe will never seem dull or mechanical. Your hollow shells will breathe and blink and blush. It will look like voodoo. You're interested, I can tell. Oh, easy. The accelerating pulse of color in your cheeks. Besides, I can guess. Thirty-six years old, overlooked, unknown, a failing marriage, a father-to-be. Success is survival.

The price for all of this? Merely—long, sleepless nights with me. Nine thousand of them. And your wrists. You have such lovely, supple wrists. I shall mount them in mahogany, I think. What do you say?

Of course, that's only sensible. I'd want to know, too.

B. is a rise. Not meteoric, but assured. Lead animator, then director of animation five years later. Doesn't that sound nice? That's not all. Shortly afterwards, you become head of the studio, or you split off to form your own profitable company. The less expensive option, this.Expensive? You'd make oodles off of it! You'd be famous! Admired! Fawned over! Only gradually would you notice, as you floated up like a birthday balloon, how far you always were from your pen and tablet. The animated films you produce, your name splashed everywhere, you'll never touch with your own hands. All the work will be done by other people's brushes and pencils and styluses. You'll be so busy with decisions and budgets that you won't have a thought to spare for art, for the boy you were at seven, doodling flip books at the kitchen table. So.

No? Not satisfied? Neither of these appeal to you? A true artist! You have talent. I can see that. You want to press your fingerprints into history.

Well then. I offer you hunger. A mastery of my arts and an inextinguishable desire to do things better and differently. Break the box. Upset the game.

Others? Of course. Charles-Emile Reynaud. William Friese-Greene. Méliès. Yes, all of them. Yes.

Why, nothing at all. Not a clipping from your fingernail. Not a red cent.

I am quite serious.

An intelligent question. Only if you stand still. Only if you stop innovating. Take Reynaud, for example, smashing his praxinoscope as the more fashionable cinématographe swept Paris. Friese-Greene dying with the price of a cinema ticket in his pocket, which was all the money he had. One shilling and tenpence. The others—them too. You must not stand still. My hunger is a painted wolf that will chase you around the whirling rim of the world. Run, spin the wheel, and life will pour from your fingers. Geometry and time will be your dogs. Hesitate, let the bowl turn without you, and—snap! you are mine.

That was a joke. You are one of mine and always were. The question is, do I like you better at your desk, or do I prefer your median nerve coiled delicately on a cracker with caviar to taste?

Ha! That was also a joke! Why flinch? You used to appreciate the soft, surreal psychosis of cartoons. Mallets and violence! Bacchanals, decapitations, shotguns, dynamite! That's my sense of humor.

I don't give, darling. I take. Sometimes I negotiate. It's always unfair.

Choose. Don't make me wait, or you'll wake up with stabbing pains in your arms and claws for hands. A slow dissolve on your career. No love, no money, no lasting memory.

Begging doesn't suit you. Your heart's transparent to me. I don't give a pixel more than you do for your family. Your Isabelle would be only too happy—but to the point. Our transaction.

They can't hear you from here.

Certain privileges come with being a monarch of time and a master in the persistence of vision. I am nothing in the security cameras. Not a shiver. Not a blot.

Are you sure? A kiss, then, to seal the bargain. I'll peel this little yellow light out of you. You won't be needing it.

A gift I gave you, once. No matter. Tonight your department head will dream of you and what you could become. Expect a meeting next week.

You might. But you'll have the odor of vinegar to remember me by.
From the decay of acetate film.
No, I would never think of calling you a coward.

The Rose Witch

JAMES PATRICK KELLY

Most in that country called Tzigana a witch, though never to her face. Now that she was dead, you would expect that the girls who had lived in her tumbledown house might say whatever they wished. But none dared speak against the old woman. All but one continued to bless her memory, constructing imagined kindnesses out of blankets as thin as soldiers' socks, candle stubs dipped from scrap wax, and joints of stringy goat for the turnip soup. They even pretended to mourn. Julianja was disgusted by their cold tears, but she kept quiet and watched for what would happen next. She respected and feared Tzigana, even now. If the old woman rose from the dead to snatch a girl for company in the tomb, Julianja wouldn't have been surprised.

What was to become of them? Dorottya, the elder of the twins, had taken charge, but she had neither the experience nor the sense to run a household. They were seven girls, ranging in age from eleven to twenty, all little better than servants. Tzigana had taken them on as apprentices, yet she had shared little of her arcane knowledge. Frici could spark fire from the tips of her forefingers and Zsuzsanna could draw the ache from strained muscles and Julianja could make roses breathe, but these skills wouldn't pay for the meat or salt or shoes they needed.

Dorottya declared they must seek work away from the house and sent the girls to trade with the houses of men. They offered to sew and bake, tend vegetable patches and put up preserves, chop wood and sweep floors. Julianja knew this plan would never succeed. The women who lived with men would not welcome needy girls. For her part, Julianja refused to leave the old witch's garden, since it was the only light in her dim life. No argument or censure would move her.

You may be right to despise Tzigana. In life, she neglected most of what we hold dear. She let magic consume her and paid as little heed to the house as she did to history or the troubles of her country. Certainly she loved her roses more than the girls who were her charges. But she had used her wits to impose her austere order on the world. While hers was rarely a joyous place, no one there went hungry. No one took sick, thanks to the witch's charms. The girls might complain, but they stayed until they were sent away. Each was treated equally so they might become their truest selves, away from the plans and strictures and desires of men. And of course Tzigana's garden drew noble visitors. She left the world more beautiful than she found it. How many of us can say the same?

The girls seemed to be managing without their mistress, although Julianja wasn't fooled. The house was but two days' walk from the town of Szeged and a few of the girls found work nearby, especially pretty Erzebet. But then boys started following them back to the house. Dorottya knew enough not to let the rascals in, but they would climb the chicken coop and call through the windows. They soon learned better than to try to cut through Julianja's roses; she was merciless with her birch switch.

By the time the roses bloomed, the garden was hers alone. The other girls were either too busy or too lazy to help Julianja tend it. Where once she had hung back while the witch had greeted the seekers who came to her garden, now she waited by herself at the gate to receive them. With Tzigana gone, however, only a few came.

The frail bishop arrived swaddled in furs and bundled in a horsehair blanket and still he looked cold and blue, even in the heat of early summer. He staggered to a Damask rose, which presented in delicate sprays of semi-double flowers. Tzigana claimed that it came from stock which the Crusader King András himself had brought back from the Holy Land; it was red as blood of infidels. The bishop wheezed as he breathed in its scent, then pressed his usual *denar* into Julianja's hand and left without another word. The boar prince spoke only German but indicated his preference for the pink cabbage rose by snuffling at it with his blunt snout. Afterwards he scrabbled back into his golden palanquin and was borne away by his four squires without leaving so much as a copper.

In the past, there had been almost as many women as men visiting, but that year only the dowager Baroness came in her dusty carriage. She peered at Julianja over her glasses, the left lens of which was cracked down the middle.

"Is she sick?"

Julianja met her watery gaze boldly. "Dead."

"No." The woman gasped and cupped hands to the sides of her head, as if she could not hear through her wimple. "Dead?"

"It was Palm Sunday. We were at Mass."

"Did she say anything?"

"She told Dorottya that her legs were cold. As she rose to receive the Sacrament, she collapsed."

"I mean about me."

Julianja shook her head.

"She should have forseen this. Now who will take care of the roses?"

"I will." Julianja ground her bark sandal against the path, staking out her claim. "As you see."

The dowager gave an unhappy laugh. "You can try." She gestured with her walking stick. "Take me there." Her special mountain rose was a particular favorite of the bees. It was a climber, the flush of creamy blossoms carried high. Julianja went up on tiptoes and brushed the bees away with the back of her hand, then bent one of the stems toward her. The thorns of this rose were mere prickles and she had to worry at one until she had stabbed her forefinger deep enough to draw blood. She watched the bead grow before pointing at the closest bloom and blowing a spray of blood at the crown of yellow stamens.

"Be quick about it," commanded the dowager.

Still holding the stem, Julianja twisted away to make room. She braced for a lash across the legs that did not come. Instead, the dowager brushed past her and buried her face in the charmed flower Her snuffling reminded Julianja of the boar. When her head lolled away, Julianja released the stem and it sprang into place.

Tzigana had first used Julianja to create the rose charm three summers ago, after she had sent Vica away. Year after year the girl had watched as the highborn had been transported by the mingling of her blood and the perfume of the blossoms, and yet never understood how it happened or what they felt. She'd always wanted to know, but Tzigana had laughed whenever she asked. Or cursed her. But Tzigana was in her tomb.

"What is it?" said Julianja. "Tell me."

The dowager shivered as if awakening from a dream and then thrust her face close to Julianja's. The crack in her glasses made her left eye seem to be doubled. "How old are you?"

Julianja's mother had sold her to Tzigana when she was but a child, and if the witch knew the day of her birth, she had never said. Julianja had started bleeding last summer, and Zsuzsanna said that meant she was sixteen, but Frici said no, she might be fourteen or even seventeen. Every girl had a different time. "Old enough," she said.

"Maybe you are." The dowager pinched Julianja's breast. "Have you been with a boy yet?"

She slapped at the woman's hand twice before she let go. Julianja would have slapped her face, but the woman thrust the knob of her walking stick at the girl to ward the blow off.

"No matter. If the old woman is truly gone, then her garden must die." She fumbled with the drawstrings of her purse and dropped a handful of *denars* into a patch of speedwell. "These roses don't want you, peasant."

Julianja had been trying not to see this. While the rest of the garden bloomed as usual, the roses were failing. She'd been fighting brown canker since the canes had first come into bud, and she'd spent the last week stripping away leaves infected with the powdery mildew. The sulfur dust that Tzigana had left was nearly gone and there was no money to buy more. Only the humble dog rose, scrambling up the cherry tree, had been spared. Dorottya talked about pulling up the sick plants and giving the space over to paprika peppers. The girls could dry the chilies, grind them and sell the spice that fall at market. The idea made Julianja furious.

As June gave way to July, she worked harder to save the roses. One hot day she was at the fence, pruning dead wood from a pink rambler that had once covered the rails in every direction. She wore only her shift against the heat; damp coils of hair matted against her forehead.

"Hello *bogárkám*." Nandor, the carpenter's son, had big feet and a silly grin, which always got sillier whenever he saw Julianja.

"I am not your little bug. Go away. None of the girls are home today."

"Except you." He leaned across the fence.

"That's saxifrage you're crushing, blockhead."

He clasped both hands to his chest. "And it's my heart you're crushing, dear girl." His face was pale and as big as the moon.

When she reached for her birch switch, Nandor danced backwards, laughing. "I will submit to your lash gladly," he said, hands held high in the air, "if only you'll submit to mine."

They both heard the creaking before they saw the cart. And they spotted the mule before they glimpsed the knotted man.

"Be on your guard, Juli," said Nandor in a low voice. "These beggars are everywhere. First they ask for what is not theirs, then they steal it."

The knotted man wore a homespun tunic over an undershirt; his dun breeches came to the knee and his lower legs were wrapped in linen. But what you would have noticed first about this traveler were the knots, some for show, some necessary. His tunic was held closed by strips of tied leather and was fringed with knotted wool. He wore a finely braided rope for a belt, and a silk scarf secured around his neck against the dust of the road. He had a boy's face with only a scraggle of beard but his long black hair was tied in a topknot in the soldier's style. They say that this makes the warlike seem fiercer, or at least taller. But the knotted man carried no weapons. For her part, Julianja was struck by the set of his jaw and the muscles of his cheeks, which seemed bunched in concentration, or perhaps pain. She did not think him a beggar, but neither did he appear to be a man of substance. The lone plodding mule and the cart with its solid wheels and its dusty wickerwork sides spoke of hard nights under the sky.

As he climbed down to them, foolish Nandor challenged him without asking her permission. "Hold, stranger, and state your business here." He squared his skinny shoulders. "These girls are under my protection." He glanced back to gauge Julianja's reaction.

While he was thus distracted, the knotted man cuffed the boy. It was just a glancing blow, but Nandor collapsed as if his bones had turned to noodles. "My business is none of yours," said the knotted man, "and my affairs are mine alone."

Nandor did not reply. His mouth was slack, eyes empty.

"Go." He hauled the boy upright and aimed him down the road. "This girl has no need of protection from me." The boy weaved away as if he had been drinking his father's *pálinka*.

The knotted man stepped to the garden gate. "She is dead then," he said. "Did many come to her garden after?"

"Some. Fewer than before."

"Where is she buried?"

"In a cave."

"Sealed?"

"With a boulder."

"How big?"

Julianja raised a hand over her head then spread her arms.

The knotted man grunted. "I was told there was a dark-haired girl who made the roses breathe."

"Vica. She grew up and was sent away."

"And you are?"

While Tzigana had shared precious little of her arts with her girls, she had impressed on them the charmed power of their true names. She was not about to give a stranger influence over her. "The rose girl," she said.

He seemed annoyed by her answer, but let it pass. "Already they are dying?" He reached out to snap one of the blackened twigs entwined in the fence. "Are there any left?"

Julianja was tired of his questions. She had some of her own. "My affairs are mine alone."

"Just so." His smile of acknowledgment was tight. "If you are the rose girl, then you can perform the charm. I've come from the castle of Kisvárda and crossed the Great Alföld to learn my future."

Julianja managed to conceal her excitement. No visitor had ever revealed his purpose before, at least, not to her. "I've never heard of this castle of yours, sir. Tzigana taught that entry here is a privilege." She bowed as if to dismiss him. "A shame to have travelled this far in vain."

He gripped the top of the gate so tight that it complained on its hinges. "What is it you want, rose girl?"

She paused to consider, for she couldn't remember anyone ever asking her such a question. "Answers."

The knots on his knuckles relaxed. "If I have them, they're yours."

She took his measure as she led him to the back of the garden. He was surely more than a boy but less than a man in full. He made a motley impression. His stride had resolve and confidence, and hard use had yet to stoop his shoulders. While his clothes were common, they were unusually clean for a traveler; there were no smears of mud on his leggings. He had the sweet scent of wood smoke about him, but not the stink of ancient sweat. Had he bathed and washed his clothes before arriving at the witch's garden? And what to make of the rough cart and the bony mule? He may well have come from a castle, although not one that prospered. She sensed an odd tension to him, like a rope that has been twisted too tight, or a sapling bent for a twitch snare.

They stopped by the cherry tree. "Only the dog rose is still blooming," she said.

"Good." He gazed up at the wild climber with its profusion of simple pink-tinged blossoms. "This is the one."

"You have been here before?"

"No. My father visited the year I was born. He's dead now, like your witch."

"So the castle is yours now?"

"I sleep beneath its walls." He laughed bitterly. "So do our goats. Castle Kisvárda has been a ruin since the reign of Mátyás the Just." Seeing her indignation at being misled, he held up a hand to beg patience. "It's mine, but my sad birthright includes a curse. My father said I might consult the roses to find out if I am the one to lift it."

Julianja couldn't decide if she should send him away or not. She'd never worked the charm on the dog rose because nobody had ever chosen it. Perhaps it waited for some eminence from even farther away than this pitiable traveler, someone who was even now on his way to her. "A curse?" she said.

"He was a man who was never easy in the wide world with its getting and spending. He was honorable, for all that, and came here to discover if it was his fate to lift our curse. He never said what he learned, but he came home a disappointed man."

"And now here you are. What do you expect to find out?"

"He called me to his deathbed, and told me that I should gather the family treasure and seek the fearsome witch Tzigana, as he had done in his time. He told me that I must convince her to let me pass into her garden, where a dark-haired girl would lead me to its humblest rose. There I must breathe its charmed breath. He told me what to expect after, although had he not been my own good father, I would have thought him mad. He claimed that in the instant he smelled this rose, all of his long life happened. He could see the inside of his mother's womb, the coffin he would lie in and everything in between. Each day of his past he lived again as well as all the days of his future, only outside of time. All and all. Perfect memory, perfect foresight. And so, he claimed, it would be for me. But I ask you, how can you remember something that hasn't yet happened? The Doctors of the Church teach that we have free will. How is that possible if our futures are already ordained?"

Fascinated as she was by this story, Julianja could not resist interrupting the knotted man. "You bring not only a curse, sir, but also a treasure?"

He shook his head. "A treasure in the same way that Kisvárda is a castle. It is of value only to my family." He waved towards the gate. "In my cart. I will show it to you after, if you like."

She tried to square this tale with the reactions of other visitors she had observed. The dowager and the bishop and the boar had come many times to the garden, and had never once seemed awed by their experience. Had they become jaded by the roses? "Aren't you afraid to know the future?"

"I am." The knotted man hooked the rope cinched around his waist and rolled it between thumb and forefinger. "But my father assured me that when time started for him again, the vision passed. Tzigana told him that no man's mind can hold his entire life at once, so he must ask himself one question while under the charm. The answer would be all that he clearly remembered. And so I will ask what I must do with the treasure."

"I thought you wanted to lift the curse."

"The treasure and the curse are one and the same." He noticed himself teasing the rope and let it fall. "So, I have given you the few answers I have, rose girl. Will you help me?"

You have very little understanding of the life of a girl at that time and in that place. You do not wake at the first hint of dawn or take to your bed at dusk because it is too dark to do anything else. You have never tried to eke a day's nourishment from an onion and some rotting parsnips or squatted over a cesspit. Julianja's life with Tzigana had presented her with precious few choices and all of those were predictable and circumscribed. She'd not even had the power to decide which chore to do first, whether to spend a dreary day sweeping dirt floors or scavenging firewood. Never had she had power over another—and a man, at that. His helplessness intoxicated her in a way she did not fully understand. Of course, she might have dismissed his plea. But then he would go and she would still be where she had always been and no longer wanted to be.

She reached for a stem and pinched it, impaling her forefinger. She blew her own red blood onto a blossom and nodded for him to approach.

The muscles of his jaw worked as he emptied his lungs, then he closed his eyes and pushed himself forward. He inhaled. Instantly his shoulders stiffened and his hands curled into fists and, with a shout, he was thrown backwards, arms windmilling. He sprawled at her feet, gibbering, and she dropped to her knees beside him. His eyes had rolled up. She grasped his tunic and rocked him from side to side, because he was too big for her to lift.

"Look at me, you. Look here."

He blinked. Groaned.

"Did you see your future?"

He stared at her.

"Do you remember any of it?"

He shivered.

"Did you ask the question?"

His mouth fell open and he tapped two fingers to his lower lip. Drink.

She fetched the bucket from the well. Soon he was sitting up. Although he could not speak, he would nod or shake his head in response to questions. She thought he might have been struck dumb, although she had never witnessed such a severe reaction to the charm. Did this mean that he was unworthy to smell the rose? Had she violated some magical law by giving him access to the charm? Perhaps the witch would rise from the tomb to exact a revenge. At that moment, all she wanted was to get him out of the garden and back on the road. For want of anything better, she brought him a cup of cold porridge to help him regain his strength.

She offered the ladle and he swallowed the gluey mess. His tongue flicked. "It's you."

"What is?"

"My future. The curse. The treasure. You."

Although she was certain he was wrong, the thought of escaping her life intrigued her. She wanted to know more, so when he was able to stand, she led him to his cart.

The mule grazed in the burdock at the side of the road. There was a mound of something in the cart, covered by hemp canvas treated with rosin against the weather. With eyes fixed on her, he pulled it aside. She caught her breath but did not otherwise react. Bones, so many bones, some the color of mushrooms, others gray as ash. Long femurs and delicate finger bones. Curved ribs, the bowl of a pelvis. A scatter of vertebrae and jaws with ragged arrays of teeth. She did not have to see the skulls to know that these were human remains. She counted two. Was that a third at the bottom of the pile?

"These are my ancestors," said the knotted man. "Wizards, if the tales we've been told are to be believed. Dead so long before my father's father's time that their names are lost. We call them the uncles. Their bones were entrusted to our care at the castle, but they do not rest. We believe they want peace, and until they get it, our lives are not our own."

"Cover them." The other girls might return at any time. "I've seen enough of your treasure."

He tugged the canvas into place. "The charm worked as my father said, although he never warned of the shock when it released me. I asked myself what the uncles wanted and I saw myself standing in the ruins of a church on a hill in the Badacsony overlooking Lake Balaton. With you."

"And I was doing what?"

"Nothing," he said. "Watching."

This was not the answer she wanted. "How do you know it's a true vision?"

"It's your charm, rose girl. I don't know how I know anything. I've never been to that place or to Lake Balaton. How did I know it was a ruined church? Where did I get the name Badacsony?" He rubbed his temples and grimaced. "But I saw you there."

"You could be lying."

He held out his hands, palms up, in surrender to her doubts. "Because I have seen what I have seen, I ask you now to come with me. But because there is no reason that you should, I'll take myself down the road and find a field to spend the night." He backed his mule between the shafts of the cart and tied ropes to its leather harness. "You may join me or not as you see fit." He spoke in a low voice, almost as if talking to himself. "Why should I try to convince you? If the vision was true, you'll be there. Perhaps you'll decide to make the journey by yourself."

He hauled himself onto the cart with a pained grunt. "I wanted none of this," he said, "but the uncles are restless and my life is not my own." He tapped his switch to the mule's withers and it gave a brief, scraping bray of protest. "In the morning I will be on my way."

One by one the girls returned to the witch's house that night. They dined merrily and well. Frici came home with a loaf of black bread that was only a day old, which she broke into eight chunks. Gyuri, the baker's son, was courting her with gifts of food, and now that Tzigana wasn't around to scare him off, he had become quite bold. Even better, Erzebet presented them with a cut of fatty pork the size of a fist, although she would not reveal how she had secured this prize. They boiled the pork with cabbage and Erzebet was declared the cleverest of them all. All Julianja had to contribute to the meal were the last radishes from the garden. She did not speak of Nandor or the knotted man as the other girls chattered about how Pisti's goat had got loose and wandered into the church or the boil on Father Vidor's nose or what mischief this boy and that boy and the other had gotten into. As usual, Julianja did not take part in their gossiping.

You know already how little experience she had making decisions. Propped on her straw pallet with a good round log for a bolster, she stared into the night long after everyone had fallen silent. She, who had unwittingly shown the future to so many others, had never imagined her own. Tzigana had been her future, her past and her present. But the witch was dead and her roses were dying, even as the dowager had predicted. What hold did this place have on her? You might say the companionship of the girls, but the truth was that they resented her for earning Tzigana's favor and she had little patience for them. Erzebet and Frici were already trysting with boys in the forest and would soon find their ways to beds in the village. Let the other girls spend the rest of their nights listening to Nandor and his lot snore. The witch's last charm linked her future to that of the knotted man. She should go with him. Must go. Afterwards, if there was no place for her in the wide world, she could always make him return her to Tzigana's house.

It took eight days for Julianja and the knotted man to reach the western shore of Lake Balaton. At first the roads were impossible, little more than dirt tracks that meandered through the forest, sometimes to emerge into a sunny field where stone-faced peasants watched them pass. Then they reached a town with a castle built on an old Roman road and began to make fifteen or twenty miles a day. This ancient thoroughfare had stood the test of time and traffic, except in the hamlets where pavers had been looted for buildings. Along the way they crossed innumerable rivers and streams, mostly at fords, sometimes on ferries and occasionally on a bridge.

The knotted man was a taciturn travelling companion. This suited Julianja, who was chary of his intent. They had yet to trust one another with their true names. At first he insisted that she ride on the cart while he walked beside, but soon she realized that they would make better progress if the mule were not pulling her weight. So she walked—usually on the opposite side of the cart from him—all the long day. When it rained, they got wet. When it didn't, they were hot. She wasn't sure which made her more uncomfortable. At dusk they would stop, gather wood for a fire, eat a simple dinner and then sleep under the cart.

The knotted man carried a purse that was fat with the king's own *denars.* Although he claimed this was all the money he had in the world, he spent freely on provisions along the way: bread and cheese and pottage if they were near a village, salt pork and pickled herring and dried fruit for when they stopped in the forest. Julianja had never eaten so well at Tzigana's. They drank no water, only small beer when it was available, or ale if it was not. She preferred the beer. Ale made her dizzy and then sleepy. The knotted man said she must never drink water while on the road, for the water of the country folk hated strangers and would loosen the bowels or light a fever in the unwary. Beer and ale were the traveler's true friends. A man could live a week on small beer alone. Casting sidelong glances at him as they walked, she decided that he must speak from knowledge of the road. She found herself wishing he would speak to her more often.

But one thing puzzled her. He didn't seem to be afraid, not of the beasts of the forest nor the brigands who lurked at every turning, if the stories were to be believed. He showed his purse as if it held only coppers. More than once she had noticed the hooded eyes of those who saw the glint of silver within its depths. The first time she asked about safeguards, he just shook his head. When she asked the second, he told her not to worry. It was not until she insisted that he told her that he and his family were protected by the uncles. Neither man nor beast nor force of nature could do them harm. This too was part of the treasure, he said, although not one that could be spent. "My father used to say that we should fear nothing, and expect nothing, which is why our treasure is also our curse. Once my family built a castle, but after decades tending the uncles, all that's left is a ruin. As long as they rule us, we may have no ambitions of our own. They keep us safe, but the price is that we can never grow and prosper."

She decided that the uncle's protection charm must be the reason that he gave himself over to regular acts of lunacy. She had witnessed one when they had forded a river on the second day but it was nothing like the time that he jumped off the ferry into the Duna.

And swam. She had heard tales of swimming, but had thought them absurd.

The knotted man would strip off all his clothes. She did not scruple to stare at his body, which was as muscular and knotted as she had imagined. And yes, she made note of his penis. She had seen the members of toddling boys in her village, but never before that of a man. It seemed at once so delicate and misshapen that she wondered at the stories the other girls had told of its power to enthrall. But her glimpse of his penis was over as soon as he hurled himself head first into the murderous water. On the ferry, the captain cried out in alarm and let go of the tiller. The oarsmen all rushed to the side to proffer oars, tilting the deck. The mule whickered. And still he did not emerge from the depths. When he did, sputtering, he'd laughed at their concern. It had been the only time she had seen him merry. To demonstrate his prowess, he kicked his legs, his arms stroked rhythmically, his head dipped in and out of the river, all perfectly coordinated. It struck Julianja as a kind of gliding, watery dance, horizontal instead of vertical.

"I thought you said to avoid water?" she called.

"I'm not drinking it," came his response. "I'm playing."

At that moment she stopped questioning her decision to accompany the knotted man. Imagine that you believe, as the learned alchemists and philosophers did, that everything consists of four elements: earth, air, fire and water. Common folk negotiate their passage across the earth as a matter of course. However, only angels frolic in the sky, while devils alone reside in fire. To Julianja, the knotted man's mastery of water as magical as any of the witch's charms.

On the eighth day, the Roman road veered south so they left it behind. Late that afternoon they reached the western shore of the lake. Inquiring at a farmhouse where they bought fresh eggs, root cellar carrots and dried catfish, the ale-wife told them the ruined church of the knotted man's vision was likely the *kolostor* of Mária Magdolna, near the village of Salföld on the eastern shore. A day's journey, perhaps longer with the cart.

She'd known that the knotted man had been growing more agitated as they traveled, but now Julianja realized how overwrought he was. At times the next day he would leave Julianja with the cart to forge ahead, as if he thought to show the mule how to pick up its pace. Eventually he would wait for them to catch up and glare, first at the plodding animal, then at her, as if they had betrayed his trust. He balked at stopping for a midday meal. Even so, as evening's shadows crept across the road, they could see that the hill on which the ruins stood was yet miles away. Reluctantly he diverted from the road to the shore of the lake to spend the night.

She built a fire and cooked the eggs while he paced the shore. There had been no small beer at the farmhouse and so they drank ale that was still fermenting with their meal. It was yeasty and sour and it settled in her belly like a stump. Afterwards she sat on a rock, mesmerized by the fire and the weight of the alcohol. The knotted man ceased his prowling and stripped.

"In the dark?" she said. "What should I do if something happens?"

"Fetch my corpse back to shore."

He marched into the glitter cast by the gibbous moon. The sweltering night air carried the sound of his splashing as he chased a wary mother duck and her brood. After a moment she rose and pulled off her shift. Threading through the grass along the shore, she put her toes into the water and gasped. The knotted man glanced back at her. Did he wave an encouragement? Hard to tell, since he was just a shadow in the moonlight. Then he dove and was lost to sight. She found the water cool but not unpleasant, especially since her cheeks were burning. She waded, mud squishing between her toes, until the water was just above her knees, then sat all at once. She gasped at the lusciousness of the sensation, then ran hands over her slippery legs, slicked the tight skin of her belly, rubbed the gooseflesh of her arms. She cupped water to her face, splashed her hair until it clung to her neck. The world felt cool and new, dark with promise. Then he was coming ashore so she leapt up. She had slithered into her tunic by the time he reached the grass.

He dressed, then noticed that she was shivering. "Now will you get sick on me?" He retrieved a small jug from the cart. "Drink this."

"What is it?"

"Tanglefoot." He offered it to her. "Spirits, distilled at the castle. Take a big swallow."

A gulp led to a fit of coughing. She might as well have breathed fire.

"Again," he said.

He swigged from the jug himself as Julianja slumped onto her stone. Her body felt numb, but her mind was racing. "I don't know your name," she said.

He squatted beside her and gazed into the flames. "Miklos."

She repeated it, savored the taste of it on her tongue, decided she liked it. "Miklos." When she reached out toward him, he pretended not to notice. "How long does it take to dry, Miklos?" She touched the tight bundle of hair atop his head.

He started. "What did you say?"

"Your hair."

He studied her. She was sure that he hadn't paid this close attention since the day they had met.

"You should let it down," she said. "It'll dry faster." As if to illustrate she shook her head back and forth and giggled as wet strands slapped at her face. "See?"

The expression on his face—was he puzzled? Alarmed? She laughed to get a response after so many miles of silence. With hands on either side of her head she sifted her wet locks between her fingers and held her hair out in two wings. "Like this."

He considered and then, like a man caught in a dream, reached to the top knot and removed a silver pin, which he took between his teeth. He had divided a long ponytail into two halves and coiled them, one around the other. Eyes raised as if he could see the crown of his head, he now unwound each half. He dipped his head and they fell over his face, reunited into one long braid of hair splayed by gravity. She saw that it was held in place at the scalp by a ribbon of the same silk as the scarf he had worn that first day. She hadn't seen the scarf since they crossed Duna. What did that mean? She didn't know what anything meant anymore as he untied the ribbon and his dark, heavy hair came loose. His hands fell to his sides and he let the ribbon slip to the ground. She leaned close, parted the hair from in front of his eyes and sifted it between her fingers. She spread it into wet wings. Neither of them laughed.

"It is good this way," she said. "I think so."

He took the pin from his mouth and set it beside the ribbon. "What is your name, rose girl?" he said.

"Julianja," she whispered.

The mad tremolo of a loon made them aware of how close they were. Embarrassed, they pulled back from the moment and one another. Miklos threw some sticks on the fire. She watched as if this were a skill she must learn.

"You say you have a family, Miklos?"

"My widowed mother. A younger brother."

"No wife?"

"I am not permitted." His eyes glittered in the firelight. "Perhaps after tomorrow."

"And what will happen tomorrow?"

Miklos thought for a moment, then gave a bitter chuckle. "Only tomorrow knows." He rose and walked away from the fire without bidding her good night.

If you do not understand Julianja, know that she did not understand herself either. And who can blame her? She was a girl who had never been farther from home than a day's walk, who had never drunk tanglefoot or seen a man naked. She was a girl who had set her life aside to follow a cursed stranger on a quest that he could not—or would not—explain. What gave her the right to do this? She didn't know exactly, but she believed that she had that right. It had something to do with the witch choosing her to work the charm in the garden. Dorottya had wanted to care for the roses, and she was the eldest. Erzebet had begged to be chosen and she was the prettiest. And yet it had been Julianja who had greeted Miklos when he'd come to the gate. Why? Maybe because when the other girls worked one of Tzigana's charms, they said a witch's prayer or rubbed a talisman. The charm was not in them the way it was in her. In Julianja's blood. Julianja was the charm. Julianja was magic. Tanglefooted thoughts began to trip one another into drowsy darkness. Just before sleep came, she realized something important, although she would not remember it in the morning.

The reason Miklos did not stink like every other man she had ever met was that he liked to swim.

It took several hours to coax the mule up the steep track to the ruined *kolostor*. Lush summer growth of silkybent and ragweed and goose grass brushed against the bottom of the cart. From time to time, Miklos got behind to push. They found the ruins in a wood where saplings encroached on snaggle-toothed foundations. Deadwood leaned against the forlorn stone and mortar walls of buildings that had long since lost roofs. Miklos tethered the mule to graze and they split up to explore. Most of the valuables the monks had hoarded were gone, even some of the stone carvings had been carried off. Julianja kicked at a midden of shattered glass and pots in what she guessed was the refectory. All around her the buzz and chirp and hum of the natural world mocked the fleeting works of men. Just beyond the ruined wall a musk rose had returned to the wild, its unsupported canes bent to the ground. Most of the stems had gone to rose hips but there was one last spray of pink tinged blossoms. When Julianja lifted the flowers to her nose to smell, she pricked her finger. She stared at the bead of blood in surprise. She could feel her future closing in around her.

"Julianja!"

The western wall of the church had collapsed. The row of eight empty lancet windows on the eastern wall hinted at the lost wealth of the monastery. Much of the plaster on this wall had peeled away, revealing the rough stone beneath. But Julianja could make out a few murals, paint faded by weather. The sorrowful eyes of Christ watched as she made her way down the nave and the draped arm of a woman, perhaps the Magdalen reached out to her.

Miklos waited in the chancel, face flushed, eyes wild. "Here," He stood on the altar, a broken slab of marble overthrown from a limestone pedestal. "In my vision I saw the bones here."

They stripped away the hemp canvas that covered the bones and spread it beside the cart. They carried the treasure to the church in three trips. Miklos had no way to tell which bones belonged to which uncle, but, as a gesture of respect, he set just one skull and two halves of a pelvis in each of the bone piles they arranged before the altar. Then he fetched the skin of water he had filled at the lake that morning, poured it into a wooden bucket and produced the missing silk scarf. He explained that now he must wash the bones.

"Then what?"

"Then we will see if my father spoke truly." He knelt, retrieved a heavy leg bone, dipped the scarf into the water, braced himself, and daubed gingerly at the knob end, as he was expecting it to twist from his grip or burst into flame. When nothing happened, he washed the bone and then placed it next to the pile from which he had retrieved it. He leaned back, waiting for some reaction. None came. He found another bone, dipped the scarf and washed. This bone he set atop the first. Nothing happened.

"May I help?" Julianja touched his shoulder.

He shook her off without looking up. He sorted through the pile, found the skull and held it, gazing for a moment at the empty eye sockets. Then he scrubbed as if it were a dirty cook pot. Finally satisfied, he tried to balance it on the two bones in the new pile. As soon as he withdrew his hand, it toppled onto its side, staring up at them in mute reproach.

"Must be all in all," Miklos muttered.

"Let me help." She hovered over him.

"*No.*" He pointed the jagged end of a broken femur at her and she backed away. "When I saw this in your garden, you were here but you only watched."

He continued his task with flagging enthusiasm. He finished the first pile and scooted across the dirty floor of the chancel on his knees to the second. He worked faster now, carelessly. She saw him gather a knot of finger bones, give them a single swipe and toss them onto the second pile. He seemed resigned, like a man forced to play out his part in some humiliating practical joke.

As he washed, Julianja counted the bones to herself. Keeping a tally of his progress seemed like a kind of support, the only kind he would permit.

"*A kurva életbe!*" Finally he hurled the filthy scarf at the pile, picked up an armful of unwashed bones, stood and let them drop, one by one, to bounce and scatter.

"Miklos!"

"The bones do not dance." He spun away from her, eyes red, cheeks wet. "My father promised they would dance. I've done everything I'm supposed to do, everything I can do." He shoulders sagged. "For nothing."

Seeing him so reduced filled Julianja with terror and pity and, yes, anger. She'd believed they would arrive safely at this place because he claimed to know the ways of the wide world. She'd trusted what he'd told her of his future. After all, hadn't she herself shown it to him? But he'd deceived her—and probably himself. She realized he'd never told her that he had actually witnessed the lifting of the curse, only that she would be there when he tried. Seeing him now, defeated and unmanned, brought all her doubts back. And yet she wanted to help, if only because it was in her power. Julianja *was* powerful, in the same way the Tzigana had been. She was as certain of this as she was of the breath that swelled her lungs, the blood that pounded in her chest. When she bent to retrieve the scarf, it was like falling, at once inevitable and frightening. She picked a skull that poor Miklos had already washed and dipped the scarf into the bucket. As her hand touched water, she felt the finger she had pricked on the musk rose start to throb. A pink stain swirled in the clear water.

"But you just watched," cried Miklos. "Watched only."

The cold bone seemed to suck the warmth from the palm of her hand. Perhaps Miklos had experienced a true vision, but he had not seen all. When she swiped its brow, the skull blinked and gazed at her with milky, ghost eyes. She wanted to scream, but her throat closed with fear. Instead she turned his uncle's terrible gaze on Miklos, who fell away as if she were showing him his death.

"Look," she whispered.

All it took was a touch of the damp silk. Julianja might have called what the bones did a dance, although it was more like the rolling and tumbling of maggots. They would find their proper alignment and knit together. Watching them gather themselves made her feel unsure of her footing. It was as if the earth itself was

219

twitching. First, one, then another, then all three uncles stood before them. But the uncles were no longer ghastly skeletons. A sinuous, indistinct glow suffused the bones, first as the flesh of transfigured, luminous bodies, then as the finery you might have seen at the Mátyás Palace in Buda. The shimmer of these magical creatures reminded Julianja of the way her legs had looked beneath the ripples of Lake Balaton.

One was dressed in an antique red cap with a feather, black velvet breeches and a red leather doublet with golden buttons. The second wore a green tunic embroidered with gold thread under a surcoat of silk so fine that it might have been spun from emeralds. The last wore a robe of midnight blue trimmed with ermine. Around his neck hung a heavy gold chain from which depended a brooch in the shape of a scroll inlaid with letters of lapis lazuli. All three uncles bore a resemblance to Miklos, although each was distinct. The red uncle was a jaunty rake who gave Julianja a sly look that made her flush. The green was older, more kindly, a man of substance whom she felt she might trust. She imagined that the solemn blue uncle, the eldest, had judged her at a glance and found her wanting.

"You have served our family well, Miklos Kemény." The green uncle stretched, as if waking from a nap and not from the dead.

The blue was as impassive as an owl. "Much better than your father Miklos or his father Benci or his father Benedek, or his father Ambrus, who was the son of Lajos Kemény, our own dear brother."

The red winked at Julianja. "No one of your line ever thought to bring us a beautiful witch."

"I am not a witch," said Julianja. But the words seemed to twist on her tongue. After all, hadn't her blood just brought the three uncles back to the world of the living? Hadn't she felt the stirring of her powers last night at the lake?

"Yet you are clearly the one we have been waiting for," said the green. "What is your name, child?"

Julianja stiffened. She felt the uncles seeking to sway her. But why? They were Miklos's ancestors. This was his quest.

The blue uncle scowled at her. "Say it!"

"Julianja," said Miklos. "Her name is Julianja. What does it matter, her name, if the curse is lifted?"

"Come close, *Julianja*." The red uncle crooked his finger and it was as if he had tugged at a tether around her waist. "You have done our family a great service, but there is something yet we must ask of you."

The green gave her his gentle smile. "Know that, in life, we three brothers cast a charm so that we would not pass completely from this world when our bodies failed. The nature of that charm was such that we could exist between life and death in a place of our devising."

"We realize now that was a trap," said the blue, "and we have chosen you to help us escape it. We bind you by your name to choose a spouse this day. Whomever you chose will return to full life. The others will pass on." He glared at his brothers as if daring them to differ. "We are so agreed."

"What is this?" Miklos pushed past to confront the uncles. "What of the curse, of me and my family?"

The red uncle looked bored. "You have done well, Miklos son of Miklos."

"Yes, I have," he cried. "I have done all . . . "

The blue held out his hand, palm facing Miklos, who immediately fell silent, although the muscles of his jaw worked as he struggled to speak. The uncle rotated his hand, palm upward, and flicked it twice toward the sky. Miklos lifted off the ground a few inches, dangling like laundry from a branch. He twisted frantically against invisible knots until the blue uncle closed his fist and he sagged into unconsciousness.

Sensing Julianja's outrage at this ill treatment, the green uncle apologized. "We understand why he is angry, but there is still much to explain and little time. Don't be afraid, we won't harm him. He is of us, a Kemény."

"I'm not afraid," said Julianja, and was pleased to discover that this was true. "But neither am I impressed by the way you treat those who help you."

"You may be right. Perhaps we have been too long away from the world." The green spoke to her, but she guessed that he was also chiding his blue brother.

"Only choose," said the blue, "and we will be done with curses."

"Choose," agreed the red.

"Yes, choose." The green opened his arms wide, as if to embrace her.

She straightened, threw back her shoulders and found the inner strength to defy them, for all their magical power. "And what if I do not? Will you compel me?"

"You mistake us, Julianja." The blue seemed offended. "We would not compel such a decision."

Red laughed. "We would rather entice you."

"For such a woman as you," said the green, "the bride price would be very high indeed."

You will understand why this would give Julianja pause, as a penniless orphan who was many days journey away from a household that might not welcome her return. She tried not to show her interest. "I would hear more," she said.

The red spoke first. "Choose me so that I may fill your senses to overflowing. In this world that men have made, there is precious little room for a woman's pleasure. You will blush at the thought, but I will lead you to a new world, where desire never wanes and cries of ecstasy fill the long night. You will never grow weary of love, nor bored of our marriage bed, for I will be a student of your body, so that I may learn all that you secretly crave but know not how to ask for. I will be all men to you and any man you fancy. This is within my power to offer you, Julianja, for all the days of your life."

As she listened her cheeks burned and she imagined bare legs entwined, strong arms enfolding her, her blood shouting so that it drowned out all thought. She remembered then what Erzebet had whispered to her about the power of love, and understood for the first time.

The green bowed to her then. "My brother speaks truly. But the world he offers is a small world indeed. You have five senses, yes, but we are more than our senses. Choose me and together we will make a place in the world beyond the bedroom door. I will comfort and support you, and keep you forever safe from evil. Our friends will love us and strangers will admire us. You will be proud of all we accomplish together. Oh, and our beautiful children! I will be the father to them that every mother hopes for. I will cherish and nurture them so that they will prosper and bring joy to us. We will get kings and philosophers! This is within my power to offer you, Julianja, for all the days of your life."

This future she knew, was no trick of imagination. She looked into the green's smiling eyes and saw a great house, a long table laden with joints of meat and exotic fruit. Silver plate, crystal goblets and raven-haired children laughing, as she would laugh and laugh as she told them of her impoverished years with Tzigana. Julianja thought then of Dorottya, struggling to hold the dead witch's household together.

The blue regarded her sternly. "My brothers speak the truth. Do not doubt their promises, but consider what I alone offer you. You have a talent that must be expressed, or you will surely live a life of regret. You deny that you are a witch. But witch is a word that men call women who have powers they do not understand. Powers they fear. I will help you understand who you are, discover what your unique abilities might be and what they can accomplish. Pleasure and the regard of others will only distract you from the task of knowing yourself, which is our true life's work. I can show you the greatness which seethes within you. Don't throw away this chance, Julianja, or you will rue what you've lost all the days of your life."

This speech frightened her, for she knew already that she was powerful. She could only guess what she might be capable of. The blue expected more from her than she expected from herself. She wasn't sure that she wanted this greatness he spoke of, even if it did dwell within her. Had Tzigana made a similar choice to perfect her abilities? If so, Julianja had witnessed its cost. She had been powerful, but never happy.

And yet, as tempting as each of these offers was in its own way, the manner in which they were being offered annoyed her. The uncles were so confident that what they proposed was what she must want. "Why must I chose any of you?" She stamped her foot. "What if I want all of what you offer? Or none of it? And if I do chose, why should it be one of you? Why shouldn't I choose him?" She turned to gesture at the slumbering Miklos. At least he was a man of honest flesh and blood, not a construct of bones and dark magic.

The red uncle sneered in disbelief. The blue uncle shook his head sadly. Only the green uncle pleaded with her. "Would you really choose an ordinary life, when we can make dreams real? He may be a good man, but what he can give you is just the smallest part of what we offer."

"Nevertheless . . . " she said, but when she turned back to them she found that she had chosen, as so many of us do, without meaning to. Was it because she refused to embrace their choices and had argued with them? Or because she truly wanted Miklos? No matter. In the flicker of indecision, the moment passed. The uncles were gone and in their places were three sorry mounds of dust.

Miklos groaned and slumped to the floor of the chancel.

You may ask, what happened next? That evening and the next morning and ever after? You may wonder, as Julianja did, whether she was bound by the charm of the uncles. Since she had thwarted them, she believed she was not. She considered the unconscious Miklos, whom she had freed from his family curse. Should she now accompany him to the castle of Kisvárda? And if she did, would she ever understand why?

Recall what Tzigana told Miklos, father of Miklos, back when that brave and disappointed man ventured into her garden. No one's mind can hold an entire life at once. But believe this: Julianja would think about that summer afternoon for years to come. Not every day, but on occasion. Because, like all of us, there would be times when she was frustrated with her life, when she could not help but imagine what might have been.

And yet there is one last thing for you to know. Before she went to awaken Miklos from his trance, before she decided what she would do with him, Julianja overturned his leaky bucket. The pink-tinged water she had used to wake the bones spilled down the broken altar stone and darkened the thirsty earth. She carried the bucket to the piles of dust, knelt and scooped three handfuls from each into it. As she did this, she vowed to the witch Tzigana, Mária Magdolna and the Blessed Virgin that someday she would scatter the treasure of the Kemény onto the roses in a charmed garden that would be hers, and hers alone.

The Creature Recants

DALE BAILEY

During breaks in shooting, the Creature from the Black Lagoon usually rests in a pond on the studio back lot and dreams of home. The pond isn't much even as ponds go. It's maybe four feet deep at its deepest point and a hundred yards or so around, an abandoned set carved out of the scorched southern California earth for some forgotten film or other: cattails and reeds and occasionally a little arrow of ripples when a dry breeze skates across the surface. Not even a fish if he's feeling peckish. Which he often is. The catering is suspect at the best of times, and it's even more so when you're accustomed to a diet of raw fish and turtle flesh prized living from the shell.

This is Hollywood.

"Don't expect too much," Karloff had advised him over sushi not long after he'd arrived, full of ambition and optimism, and Lugosi, strung out on morphine and methadone by the time the Creature made the scene, had been even more blunt. "They vill fuck you every time," he'd said in that thick Hungarian accent. The both of them typecast by their most famous roles. The Creature had assumed he could beat the odds, but on those blazing afternoons in the pond, now and again scooping up handfuls of water to moisten his gills, he'd begun to reconsider. The water was unkind, perpetually casting his reflection back at him: the bald, barnacle-encrusted skull, the eyes sunk beneath shelves of armored bone, the frills of tissue encasing the gills around his neck. Not what you would call leading-man material.

To think, he'd once been the king of his little world—the vast, dark Lagoon, overhung with the boughs of enormous trees, and the mighty Amazon itself, where anacondas slithered through the algae-clotted water, caiman slid into the flood without a splash, their tails lashing, and catfish the size of Chevrolets trolled the mossy bottom. Not to mention the jungle, humid, rank, and festering, clamorous with the chitinous roar of millions of insects. And here he was in southern California instead, spending his days in waist-deep water and sleeping his nights in an oversized bathtub in a crummy apartment.

Such are the Creature's thoughts when a member of the crew—it's Bill, a gopher who's trying to break into the biz as a lighting tech—walks down to the pond to tell him that Jack's finished setting up the next shot. It's time for the Creature to come back up to the set and stagger around the deck of the *Rita*—not even a real boat, just a cheap mock-up in one of the soundstages on the Universal lot—and menace Julie Adams for another hour or so. She's a real scream queen, Julie, the genuine article, but she's nice enough in real life; she even walks down to the pond to chat once in a while between set-ups. They're all nice enough. Even Jack's okay, though he's always badgering the Creature to focus on his motivation when the Creature has enough trouble just hitting his marks. To tell the truth, the Creature's heart isn't in it anymore, but he's signed a deal with Universal, and his agent—who rarely returns his calls anyway—tells him there's no way to break the contract.

So the Creature hauls himself out of the pond, and tramps back up to the soundstage, trying not to think about the fact that he could decapitate Bill with a single stroke of his taloned hand. Trying not to think that at some level he wants to.

It wasn't supposed to turn out this way.

You never know happiness until it's gone, that's the way the Creature figures it. The present always seems like a mess. It was only once he left the Lagoon that he realized how good he'd had it there. In Hollywood, he recalls its dark waters with longing. Sometimes at night, his head pillowed on the bottom of his brimming bathtub and his webbed feet slung over either side to brush the peeling vinyl floor, he even dreams of it. How perfect it seems now, the murky bottom where he'd nested for hours among the drifting fronds of plants he cannot name and the hidden channel that led to his rocky underground lair. Armored with scales and impervious to jaguar and piranha alike, the Creature had hunted both the overgrown shores and the black fathoms, snatching spider monkeys screaming from their roosts and feasting on the great fish that slipped through the Lagoon's sulfurous depths. He recalls even his isolation with melancholy regret. What had seemed like loneliness—he'd never known another of his kind—now seemed like autonomy, and when the boat that spelled his expulsion from paradise had first steamed into the lagoon he had approached it with a curiosity that now seemed like folly.

He hadn't planned to leave the Black Lagoon, but life always takes the unexpected turn: caiman poachers in this case, though he hadn't known that then. It had been the boat, anchored in a sun-dappled inlet, that fascinated him. He'd taken it for some kind of novel creature, and because no denizen of the Amazon posed a threat to him—because he pined for novelty in those days—he hadn't given a second thought to approaching the thing. He'd been backstroking along, his face turned to the sun, when it came chugging into the Lagoon, stinking of gasoline. When he saw it, the Creature dove into the sun-spangled water, surfaced in the shadow of the boat, and dragged a talon along its rusting keel. He hadn't seen the net until it was too late. He found himself entangled. Panicked, he began to claw at it. He'd have freed himself had the poachers not reacted so quickly, winching him out of the water even as his talons tore long rents in the ropy mesh.

"My God," one of the poachers screamed, staggering back.

"Jesus, what the hell is that thing?" his companion cried, reaching for a spear gun. (The Creature reconstructed this dialogue only later.) The Creature was thinking the same thing. What could these soft, distorted reflections of his scaly self be, he wondered—

Then the harpoon punctured his shoulder and he stumbled flailing into the water. He'd never felt such agony. By the time he bobbed to the surface, he was unconscious. When he woke he found himself imprisoned behind steel bars.

The poachers weren't dumb—grimy, stubbled, and foul mouthed—but not dumb. Three times a day, they tossed a fish, still flopping, between the bars of his cage. When they saw him pour his bucket of drinking water over his head, they realized that he needed to moisten his gills regularly. Using a spare gaff, they poked fresh buckets into his pen on the hour. The rest of the time he spent curled in a corner, whimpering. His terror of the boat at first overwhelmed him: the roar of the engine, the stench of his own waste, the curious faces (if you could call such doughy parodies of his own batrachian features faces) staring at him jaws agape from outside his cage. But you can get used to anything. By the time they anchored in the headwaters of Peru, his terror had dwindled to a dull simmer of anxiety.

What next?

He had no concept of the worst possibilities—not then, anyway. He could have been sold to a marine biology institute, where sooner or later scientists would have gotten around to dissecting him to see what made him tick (the Creature's rudimentary knowledge of scientists derives mostly from horror movies; scientists were all mad, as far as he is concerned). He could have been sold to a zoo, and spent the rest of his life paddling around in a wading pool, while small children gawped at him and tossed half-eaten ice cream cones through the bars. These would no doubt have been more profitable avenues. But the caiman poachers weren't anxious to disclose their reasons for cruising the Amazon. So he was sold instead to a carny scout combing the region for freak-show specimens, shipped north, and sold yet again, this time to Southeby & Sons Travelling Carnival, a fly-by-night operation that worked the south-western circuit through the spring and fall, wintering in Gibsonton, Florida, along with most of the other carnies in North America.

And here was happiness again—sort of, anyway—though he didn't recognize it at the time. By then, he'd pretty well been tamed. After he'd raked the shoulder of one of the poachers with his claws, a cattle prod had been brought into play, and three or four applications of *that* had been sufficient to cool his heels. So when he came to Southeby & Sons he'd been pliable enough. Besides, he fit right in with the freaks. They too were unique: the Living Skeleton, the Fat Lady (fat hardly did her justice), Daisy and Violet, the Siamese Twins, and half a dozen others, midgets and bearded ladies and the Monkey Boy: a community of sorts, a family that assuaged the loneliness that had been his lot back home in the Black Lagoon.

What's more, he had a vertical glass aquarium he could call his own, smaller than he might have wished, true, but brimful of water. Southeby billed him as the Gill Man and his sideshow performances were no hardship. He could bob in the green water, or kick to the surface for a breath of rank air (the Monkey Boy wasn't particular in matters of personal hygiene), or even doze if so inclined. Something of a romance—unconsummated, for the Creature's sexual organs, if he had any, were incompatible with those of human beings—blossomed between him and Daisy, much to Violet's dismay, who for unknown reasons took an immediate and abiding dislike of him. It was Daisy who taught him to talk, though his vocal cords, unfit for human speech, rendered his voice guttural and unintelligible to the untutored ear. And there was a kind of freedom during the winters in Gibsonton, this perhaps most precious of all. A simple walk of a mile or so brought him to the beach, and he sometimes lazed for hours in the warm, briny waters of the Gulf.

So he might have passed his life, or at least a longer portion of it, for who could say how long he might yet exist? The Creature had no memory of his birth and growth. He was then as he always had been and might always be. But restlessness possessed him. Violet's inescapable abhorrence was a constant blight on the affection he shared with Daisy, his tank grew cramped, and even his sojourns in the waters of the Gulf too brief, restricted by nine months on the road, burning the lot in one town to set up the next day in another. The midway—the flashing lights of the rides, the alluring chants of the barkers, the sugary reek of cotton candy and funnel cake—grew oppressive.

So when the chance to escape presented itself, in the person of a low-rent Hollywood agent who paused before his tank, the Creature was quick to take it. The agent took the time to decipher his rasping tones, sensed his discontent, and persuaded him to give the silver screen a try. L.A. was close to the beach year round, after all, and the Creature was already in show biz. If stardom didn't suit him, he could always return to the carny circuit. So it was the Creature signed up to be a contract player for Universal. He didn't count on being typecast as, well, the Creature, forever flapping about on his great rubbery feet after one nubile beauty or another, his scaly green arms outstretched. Didn't count on being mistaken for a stunt man in a rubber suit. Didn't count on the bathtub or the crummy apartment.

Most of all he didn't count on Julie Adams.

This is Hollywood.

As Bela Lugosi put it, "They vill fuck you every time."

The Creature has begun to believe that he might be in love with Julie Adams.

"Are you lonely?" she asks him one day down by the pond.

He floats on his back in a stand of cattails, keeping an eye on her through a screen of gently bending stalks. He understands all too well what it's like to be stared at. Every time he strolls outside his apartment, people stare. He's learned to ignore the occasional cries of "Hey, fish man," and no longer stops to explain that he's not a fish, but an amphibian. Yet the mockery has had its effect. The Creature has begun to wonder if there's something cannibalistic about him every time he chomps into a fish taco or spears a sushi roll on a single curved claw—with his webbed fingers, chopsticks and silverware are out of the question. The truth is, that's another reason the Creature has given up on the set's catering: he senses that people would just as soon not see him eat. He's never quite overcome the gastronomic habits of the jungle. He wolfs down his meals, smacks his oversized red lips, chews with his mouth open, gets unsightly gobs of food caught in his fangs. The whole thing is unsightly. The studio has ignored his requests to stock the pond with bluegills and catfish so that he can eat in privacy, and rather than protest—the negligent agent again—the Creature elects to spend his days hungry. He figures it sharpens his hostile motivations in the film; he's become a student of Stanislavsky.

The Creature has, in short, begun to accept the norms of Hollywood. He no longer sees any beauty in his fellow denizens of the freak show (the mere thought of Daisy now repulses him)—but he has very much come to see the beauty in Julie Adams, a tall busty brunette who spends most of her days in their scenes together wearing a white one-piece bathing suit that accentuates her considerable curves. He's not sure that what he feels is love—love is a relatively new concept to him—but he knows that he eagerly anticipates her occasional visits to the pond, that the sound of her voice sets his heart racing, that sometimes he has trouble sleeping nights, and not merely because the bathtub provides no comfortable accommodation for his dorsal ridge. No, he has trouble sleeping because he can't stop thinking of Julie Adams.

Is he lonely? In a word, yes.

But the question begs closer examination. He glides out of the bed of cattails and gives Julie his full attention. Perhaps she's come to suspect his amorous intentions, for she has taken to wrapping herself in a thick white bathrobe before she walks down to the pond. Perhaps she's merely cold. It's hard to know.

"Lonely?" he says, hating his inhuman rasp. He cannot help comparing it to the rich, clear timbre of Richard Carlson, the (let's face it) star of the movie, despite the Creature's eponymous billing. With a languid kick he turns to face Julie. She sits at the edge of the shore, with her knees drawn up and her hands clasped around her legs. The Creature can't help staring at her bare ankles. Lonely? He muses on the question.

"That's right."

"I suppose I haven't really thought about it."

"Well, there are no other Creatures, are there?"

"None that I know of," he says, recalling the splendid isolation of the Lagoon.

"It must be very lonely, then. I wouldn't like to be all alone."

"I'm not alone anymore."

Implying that he has become a companion to the human race in general, and perhaps, hopefully, to Julie in particular.

She doesn't take his meaning. "Sometimes I think we're all alone, every one of us. Do you ever think that?"

The Creature composes his largely immobile features into an expression of tragic acceptance. "I suppose we are," he says. "But if you can find someone to love—"

She interrupts him. "I guess that's true. But it must be especially difficult for you. You're not human, but you're not . . . not human, either, if you see what I mean." She sighs, resting her chin on her knees. "Dick says you're the Missing Link." She seems to be blind to the cruelty of this statement, but the Creature has become as accustomed to this appellation as he is to "Fish Man." If he really thinks about it, he supposes he does stand somewhere between the modern human and his piscine ancestry, but he doesn't much like what this implies about his place on the evolutionary spectrum.

Annoyed, he backstrokes off in a snit, arcs his body gracefully backward, and dives, dragging his armored belly on the muddy bottom of the shallow pond (oh, how he longs for the fathomless depths of the Black Lagoon!) He surfaces to face Julie across the stretch of sun-shot water—only to find her striding back to the sound stage. Bill is waving him in from the water's edge. It must be time to resume shooting. Sighing, the Creature breaststrokes toward shore. Once the scourge of the Amazon, he has been reduced to a bit player in his own story.

For it *is* his story. Or was supposed to be.

History will record it differently—attributing the film's origins to Maurice Zimm, but Zimm did little more than transcribe the Creature's narrative during a series of interviews conducted while the Creature lounged in producer William Alland's swimming pool. That's how the Creature remembers it anyway. He would have pounded out the screenplay himself if he could have. That task fell instead to two inveterate Hollywood journeymen, Harry Essex and Arthur Ross. When the final draft fell into the Creature's hands, he recoiled in disbelief. The caiman poachers had been transformed into intrepid paleontologists, the Black Lagoon into an arena of horrors, the Creature himself—an innocent victim!—into a vicious monster. About the only thing the trio of scribes had managed to do right was add a love interest—otherwise, the Creature thinks, he might never have met Julie Adams.

"I won't do it," the Creature protested. "I'll go back to the carnival. Hell, I'll go back to the Amazon!"

His agent—a balding, mousy little man named Henry Duvall—shook his head dolefully. "You've signed a contract."

"I didn't sign anything," the Creature growled. "I can't even hold a pen."

"I signed *for* you in the presence of two witnesses and a notary public," Duvall replied. "Same difference."

Cue Bela Lugosi.

So the Creature reported to the set as ordered, climbed aboard the *Rita* to terrorize Julie as required, shrank before the virile posturings of Richard Carlson (as required)—and fell in love.

"Love," he tells Karloff, pacing the actor's capacious study. By this time, Karloff has long since settled into stardom. He lives comfortably in L.A. and has steady work, though he's still typecast as a horror icon. Smaller than the Creature expected—the Creature towers a good two feet above him—Karloff in his late sixties remains handsome and slim, his dark hair silvering. Five times married, he is perhaps not the best person to approach for romantic advice, but the Creature's options are limited. His film, the first of a projected trilogy, is not yet completed, much less released, and he is beginning to see that he has been played for a fool. If Boris Karloff can't escape his defining role—if this charming, gentle man still clumps around in the American zeitgeist wearing elevator boots and bolts in his neck—then what hope has the Creature, who cannot even shuck his costume? There are no Oscars in his future, just endless sequels to this initial pack of lies. *Revenge of the Creature. The Creature Walks Among Us.* Even *Abbot and Costello Meet the Creature*, if things go badly enough (or well enough, from Universal's perspective).

"Love?" Karloff says. He leans back in his armchair and steeples his fingers. "Love is always a delicate matter."

"Tell me about it," says the Creature.

"If your love is unrequited"—Karloff retains a trace of his native British accent, a genteel formality—"then there is little you can do."

This is not the advice the Creature sought. This is not advice at all. This is a statement of fact. The Creature has come to suspect that Julie's visits to his pond are little more than kindnesses. After all, he sees the way she looks at Richard Carlson, the way she moistens her lips and gazes up at him in adoration. Carlson is nice enough to him, but nice won't do. While the Creature occasionally daydreams of raking Bill's head off in annoyance, his fantasies of violence toward Carlson burn icy and pure. He would like to kill him slowly, to spear each eyeball upon a talon and pop them into his mouth like jellybeans, to unseam his belly and feed upon the steaming offal, to wrench off his limbs one by one. For a start. The Creature does what he can to repress these unsavory flights of imagination, but they retain a vividness he cannot deny. He may work in a black-and-white 3D horror flick, but his fantasies are projected in widescreen Technicolor. Perhaps this is his true nature, savage and immutable, antediluvian and, yes, appropriate to the Missing Link. You can take the Creature out of the jungle, but you can't take the jungle out of the Creature.

He senses that this is not the way to Julie's heart.

Karloff clears his throat. "You face many obstacles, of course. You are not handsome. You are not human. You have, insofar as you have been able to detect, no potential for procreation. Yet there might be a way."

A way? The Creature pauses. He takes a seat across from Karloff. He'd like to lean back, but his goddamn dorsal ridge is, as always, in the way. Another reminder of his inhumanity. Yet there might be a way past even that.

He is all attention.

"Beauty comes in many forms," Karloff says. "It is, as the expression goes, in the eye of the beholder. But that eye is often best attuned when its object is set against its natural environment."

"What are you saying?"

Now Karloff leans forward. He smiles. "Underwater, my friend. Water is your natural milieu."

True enough. In his pond on the Universal lot, submerged to the waist and ladling up clear freshets with one spade-like hand, the Creature looks ridiculous. In the Black Lagoon, however, he glides through the water with a grace and beauty no man can hope to match. Human beings are no more suited to thrive underwater than he is suited to a purely land-bound existence. Clumsy and ill equipped for a submarine life, they don wet suits that are but sad reflections of his own glistening hide. They have rubber flippers where he has feet, heavy oxygen tanks and re-breathers where he has gills. If he shambles gasping across the Universal lot, his adversary in love will shamble—or anyway flail—beneath the surface. In the water, Carlson's beauty will be but a paltry thing. And while a return to the Black Lagoon is cost-prohibitive, the underwater scenes are scheduled to be filmed in Wakulla Springs, Florida, a return to his beloved Gulf and (yes, he has researched the location shoots) the largest freshwater cave system in the world—if not his beloved Lagoon, the next best thing. Flush with renewed optimism, the Creature thanks Karloff and takes his leave.

The same optimism carries him across the continent, canted awkwardly in his seat—his dorsal ridge; again—and staring out at the blur of the propellers. Halfway through the flight, Julie walks down the aisle to take the seat beside him. She leans past him to look out the window, so close that he can smell the faint lavender scent of her perfume. "Isn't it beautiful?" she says, gazing down at the green hills unscrolling below the streaming scud. "It makes me think of the film."

"How?" says the Creature, who can see no clear connection.

"Well, it seems so deep, you know, so . . . dimensional . . . looking down from up here like this. I imagine the way the audience will experience it when they see us swimming out of the screen like that."

Ah. 3D. If he's been told once he's been told a thousand times. Alland's ambitions for the film hinge upon two factors: the realistic creature effects (which certainly *should* look realistic, the Creature ruminates) and the use of 3D, only the second Universal film to be released in the innovative format. But then he realizes that Julie has dozed off against his shoulder, and he wonders if he too can have a three-dimensioned life.

Wakulla Springs is everything the Creature had hoped it would be. There are shortcomings, to be sure. He could have wished for a more tropical setting—strangler figs, lianas, and buttress-rooted trees—but there is much to be thankful for as well. The alligators slipping into the murky water recall the caiman of the Black Lagoon; the bulky manatees the nine-foot piracuru and catfish that call his native waters home; the boom of insects the constant roar of the jungle. And the springs themselves are everything he hoped they would be, fathoms deep, and riddled with caverns. Against his better judgment—Julie will think him hardly human at all, he fears—the Creature dispenses with the pretense of his trailer and abandons the on-set catering altogether. Halfway abandons the film, in fact. More often than not, when Jack dispatches Bill to summon the Creature to the set, he's off touring the depths. He explores the cave system in search of a rocky grotto like the one he had in the Amazon. He dozes in deep, cold currents where no human being can follow. He gluts himself on the abundance of prey, devouring fish raw in clouds of ichthyic blood. Life is good, or better anyway, but he is not happy (or if he is, he does not recognize it). Thoughts of Julie torture him like an inflamed scale under a ridge of his armored breast.

Finally, Jack calls him in for a meeting. Like Karloff, Jack is a kind man. Anger is not his natural métier, yet the Creature is forced to stand dripping on the carpet in the director's trailer, listening to his gentle rebuke. Somehow that makes it worse, Jack's generosity of spirit. "I have no choice, you see," the director admonishes him. "We're on a tight schedule. We're not making *Gone With the Wind*, you know."

"It's going to be a good picture," the Creature says.

"I didn't say it wasn't going to be a good picture. I said that we have to make our release date or both our careers are on the line."

"Your career," the Creature rasps. "What kind of career am I likely to have, Jack?"

"You're unique. After people see this picture, offers are going to come rolling in."

"Don't patronize me, Jack. We both know there's only one role I can play."

Jack sighs. "I guess you're right. But still, this is going to be a good film. You'll get to play *this* role again."

The Creature laughs humorlessly, snared in a dilemma even his human colleagues must share, forever trapped in the prisonhouse of self. That's the appeal of acting, he supposes: the chance to be someone else, if only for a little while. And isn't that what he's doing here, playing at being something he's not? He's not a monster. He never has been. If his range of roles is limited—if he is doomed to be the Creature from the Black Lagoon—well, that's Hollywood. He thinks of Karloff and Lugosi. Who does he want to become? Does he wish to accept his fate with grace or does he wish to rail perpetually against it, strung out on drugs and bitterness? Is being the Creature any different than being a carnival freak? Yet still he longs for his lost home. How he hates the poachers who have done this to him. He'd like to poke *their* eyeballs out, too. And eat them.

So maybe he's a monster, after all.

"I need you on the set on time," Jack is saying while these thoughts run through the Creature's head. "It's expensive to shoot underwater, especially with the 3D rig. Every time you don't show up when you're supposed to, you cost us money."

"I'm sorry, Jack," the Creature says.

"Look, I know this is hard for you. Nobody ever said acting was easy. Look at Brando. Channel your anger into the role. I need you to be the Creature I know you can be."

The Creature doesn't know quite what Jack means by this. He doesn't even know who—or what—he is anymore. Yet he vows to himself that he will try for something more complex than a B-movie monster—to draw not only upon his fury and resentment, but upon his passion for Julie. He vows to do better.

He does, too.

The Creature shows up promptly as requested. He lingers between shots. He tries to make small talk with the crew. But what is there to say, really? He's an eight-foot amphibian, finned and armored in plates of bone. He could eviscerate any one of them with the twitch of a talon. Monster or not, he is a monster to them.

Not Julie, though, or so he tells himself. Perhaps Karloff is right: set against his natural environment, she seems to recognize his natural grace. Indeed she seems to share it. Unburdened by the clunky scuba tanks the men's roles demand, she glides through the water. And between shots she dispenses with the bathrobe she'd taken to draping herself in on the Universal lot, as if swimming together has drawn them closer. Of all the actors on the set, she alone seems entirely at ease with him. They spend more and more time talking. As he lolls in the shallows, she tells him about her recent divorce or about growing up in Arkansas; she tells him about her first days in Hollywood, working as a secretary and taking voice lessons on the side. Yet she is still capable of blind cruelty.

"You're lucky," she says. "You never had to fight for your dreams."

The Creature hardly knows how to respond. So what if Universal picked him up the minute William Alland laid eyes on him? Unlike Julie, he'll never play another role in his life; all the elocution lessons in the world won't change his inhuman growl. He's not even sure what he aspires to anymore. Stardom? Freedom? A return to the Black Lagoon? In his dreams, he sweeps Julie into his embrace, carries her off to the Amazon, unveils to her the wonders of his vanished life: the splendid isolation of the Lagoon, the sluggish currents of the great river, the mystery of the crepuscular forest.

Maybe this newfound intimacy accounts for the otherworldly beauty of the Wakulla scenes. In the dailies, Julie cuts the surface, her white bathing suit shining down through the gloom like god light. The Creature stalks her from below, half-hidden among drifting fronds of thalassic flora, rapt by her ethereal beauty. His webbed hands cleave the water. Bubbles erupt skyward with his every kick. As she swims, he glides toward her from below, up, up, up, until he is swimming on his back beneath her and closing fast: a dozen feet, half a dozen, less, his immovable face frozen in an expression of impossible longing. He reaches out a tentative hand to brush her ankle as she treads water—and pulls it away at the last moment, as terrified of her rejection on celluloid as he is terrified of her rejection in life. What one does not risk, one cannot lose; worse yet, he thinks, what one does not risk, one cannot gain. A sense of inconsolable despair seizes him. In the images projected on the screen, he sees now how little their worlds can connect. She is a creature of the daylit skin of the planet, he of the shadowy submarine depths.

Jack praises the silent yearning in the Creature's performance.

Yet the whole thing drives the director crazy nonetheless. Frustrated by the task of stitching the haunting underwater scenes together with the mundane L.A. footage, he asks the studio for reshoots and is denied. For the first time—the only time—the Creature sees Jack angry, his face a mask of fury. "This could be so much more than another goddamn monster flick," he says in the dim projection trailer, flinging away the 3D glasses perched on his nose. Even this angry gesture drives home the Creature's inhumanity. Alone in the back row, he must pinch his glasses between two delicate claws. His flattened nose provides no bridge to support them. He has no external ears to hook them over. Everything about him is streamlined for his underwater existence.

The Creature grinds his cardboard glasses under one webbed foot. He slams out of the trailer, the door crumpling with a screech of tortured metal as he hurtles into the moonlit night. He is halfway to the water when Julie catches up with him. "Wait," she says. "Wait—"

Her voice hitches in the place where his name ought to be—for of course he has no name, does he? He is the Creature, the Gill Man, nothing more. There has been no one to name him—even the freaks did not name him—and he has

233

never thought to name himself. He would not know how to begin. Fred? John? Earl? Such human names fall leaden on the tongue, inadequate to describe a . . . a creature, a fiend, an inhuman monster. How will they credit him in the film? *The Creature as the Creature*?

"Wait," Julie says again. "Creature, wa—"

The Creature whirls to face her, one massive hand drawn back to strike.

"Don't," she whispers, and the Creature checks the blow. For an instant, everything hangs balanced on a breath. Then the Creature lowers his hand, turns away, and shambles toward the water, his great feet flapping. Something feels broken inside him. Jack's words—

—*another goddamn monster flick*—

—echo inside his head. That's all he is, isn't he? A monster. A monster who in a moment of fury, would have with a single swipe of his claws torn from her shoulders the head of the woman he loved. A monster who would in the grip of his rage, feed upon her blood. The Creature would cry, but even that simple human solace is denied him. The dark waters beckon.

"Wait," Julie says. "Please."

Almost against his will, the Creature turns to face her. She stands maybe a dozen feet away. In the moonlight, tears glint upon her cheeks. Beyond her, the men—Jack and Dick and Richard Denning, the third lead—stand silhouetted against the beacon of golden light pouring through the trailer's shattered door.

"Why?" the Creature says, knowing the doom that will come upon him if he stays.

"Because," Julie says, "because I love you."

So Karloff was right. For a heartbeat, happiness—a great and abiding contentment that no mere human being can plumb—settles over the Creature like a benediction. But what is the depth of love, he wonders, its strange currents and dimensions? What is its price, and is he willing to pay it? And a line from another monster movie comes to him, one that Jack showed him in pre-production: *It was beauty killed the beast.*

This is Hollywood.

It vill fuck you every time.

"I love you, too," he says in his inhuman rasp, and in the same instant, in his heart, he recants that love, refuses and renounces it. For Julie. For himself. He will not be the monster that loves. He will not be the monster that dies. He will not be their freak, their creature. He will not haunt their dreams. They can finish their fucking film with a man in a rubber suit.

The Creature puts his back to Julie and wades into the water, glimmering with moonlight. It welcomes him home, rising to his shins and thighs before the bottom drops away beneath him, and he dives. He has studied the locations, he has explored the Springs' network of caverns: from here the Wakulla River to the St. Marks and Apalachee Bay, and thence to the Gulf. The Black Lagoon calls out to him across the endless miles, and so the Creature strikes off for home, knowing now how fleeting are the heart's desires, knowing that Julie too would ebb into memory, this perfect moment lost, this happiness receding forever into the past.

Spring Festival: Happiness, Anger, Love, Sorrow, Joy

XIA JIA, TRANSLATED BY KEN LIU

Zhuazhou

Lao Zhang's son was about to turn one; everyone expected a big celebration.

Planning a big banquet was unavoidable. Friends, family, relatives, colleagues—he had to reserve thirty tables at the restaurant.

Lao Zhang's wife was a bit distressed. "We didn't even invite this many people to our wedding!" she said.

Lao Zhang pointed out that this was one of those times where they had to pull out all the stops. You only get one *zhuazhou* in your entire life, after all. Back when they had gotten married, money was tight for both families. But, after working hard for the last few years, they had saved up. Now that their family was complete with a child, it was time for a well-planned party to show everyone that they were moving up in the world.

"Remember why we're working hard and saving money," said Lao Zhang. "For the first half of our lives, we worked for ourselves. But now that we have him, everything we do will be for his benefit. Get ready to spend even more money as he grows up."

On the child's birthday, most of the invited guests showed up. After handing over their red envelopes, the guests sat down to enjoy the banquet. Although everything in the world seemed to be turning digital, the red envelopes were still filled with actual cash—that was the tradition, and real money looked better. Lao Zhang's wife had borrowed a bill counter for the occasion, and the sound of riffling paper was pleasing to the ear.

Finally, after all the guests had arrived, Lao Zhang came out holding his son. The toddler was dressed in red from head to toe, and there was even a red dot painted right between his eyebrows. Everyone exclaimed at the handsome little boy:

"Such a big and round head! Look at those perfect features!"

"So clever and smart!"

"I can already see he's going to have a brilliant future."

The boy didn't disappoint. Even with so many people around, he didn't cry or fuss. Instead, he sat in the high chair and laughed, reminding people of the

New Year posters depicting little children holding big fish, symbolizing good fortune.

"How about we say a few words to all these uncles and aunties and wish them good luck?" Lao Zhang said.

The boy raised his two chubby little hands, held them together, and slowly chanted, "Happy New Year, uncleses and aunties . . . fish you pro-perity!"

Everyone laughed and congratulated the child for his intelligence and the Zhangs for their effective early education.

The auspicious hour finally arrived, and Lao Zhang turned on the machine. Sparkling bits of white light drifted down from the ceiling and transformed into various holograms that surrounded Lao Zhang and his son, in the middle of the banquet hall. Lao Zhang pulled one of the holograms next to his son's high chair, and the child eagerly reached out to touch it. A red beam of light scanned across the little fingers—once the fingerprints were matched, he was logged into his account.

A line of large red characters appeared in the air—*You're One!*—accompanied by an animated choir of angels singing *Happy Birthday to You*. After the song, a few lines of text appeared:

Zhuazhou is a custom in the Jiangnan region. When a baby has reached one year of age, the child is bathed and dressed in fresh clothes. Then the child is presented with various objects: bow, arrow, paper, and brush for boys; knife, ruler, needle, and thread for girls—plus foods, jewels, clothes, and toys. Whatever the child chooses to play with is viewed as an indication of the child's character and abilities.

Lao Zhang looked up at the words and felt a complex set of emotions. *My son, the rest of your beautiful life is about to start.* His wife, also overcome by emotion, moved closer and the two leaned against each other, holding hands.

Unfortunately, although the Zhangs had begun the baby's education before he had even been born, the boy still couldn't read. He waved his hand excitedly through the air, and pages of explanatory text flipped by. The end of the explanation was also the start of the formal *zhuazhou* ceremony, and everyone in the banquet hall quieted down.

The first holographic objects to appear were tiles for different brands of baby formula, drifting from the ceiling like flower petals scattered by some immortal. Lao Zhang knew that none of the brands were cheap: some were imported; some were one hundred percent organic with no additives; some were enhanced with special enzymes and proteins; some promoted neural development; some were recommended by pediatricians; some were bedecked with certifications . . . The choices seemed overwhelming.

The little boy, however, was decisive. He touched one of the tiles with no hesitation, and with a clink, the chosen tile tumbled into an antique ebony box set out below.

Next came other baby foods: digestion aid, absorption promotion, disease prevention, calcium supplements, zinc supplements, vitamins, trace elements, immunity enhancement, night terror avoidance . . . in a moment, the son had made his choices among them as well. The colorful icons fell into the box, clinking and tinkling like pearls raining onto a jade plate.

Then came the choices for nursery school, kindergarten, and extracurricular clubs. The little boy stared at the offerings with wide, bright eyes for a while, and finally picked woodcarving and seal cutting—two rather unpopular choices. Lao Zhang's heart skipped, and his palms grew sweaty. He was just about to go up and make his son pick again when his wife stopped him.

"He's not going to try to make a living with that," she whispered. "Let him enjoy his hobby."

Lao Zhang realized that she was right and nodded gratefully. But his heart continued to beat wildly.

Then the child had to pick his preschool, elementary school, elementary school cram sessions, junior high, junior high cram sessions, high school, and high school cram sessions. Then the choice to apply to colleges overseas appeared. Lao Zhang's heart once again tightened: he knew this was a good choice, but it would cost a lot more money, and it was difficult to imagine having his son thousands of miles away and not being able to protect him. Fortunately, the toddler barely glanced at the choice and waved it away.

Next he had to select his college, decide whether afterward he wanted to go to grad school, to study overseas, or to start working, choose where he wanted to work and to settle, pick a house, a car, a spouse, the engagement present, the wedding banquet, the honeymoon destination, the hospital where their child would be born, the service center that would come and help—that was as far as the choices would go, for now.

All that was left was to pick the years in which he would trade up his house, the years in which he would upgrade his car, the places he would go for vacations, the gym he would join, the retirement fund he would invest in, the frequent flier program he would sign up for. Finally, he picked a nursing home and a cemetery, and all was set.

The unselected icons hovered silently for a moment, and then gradually dimmed and went out like a sky full of stars extinguishing one after another. Flowers and confetti dropped from the ceiling, and celebratory music played. Everyone in the banquet hall cheered and clapped.

It took a while before Lao Zhang recovered, and he realized that he was soaked in sweat as though he had just emerged from a hot pool. He looked over at his wife, who was in tears. Lao Zhang waited patiently until she had calmed down a bit, and then whispered, "This is a happy occasion! Look at you . . . "

Embarrassed, his wife wiped her wet face. "Look at our son! He's so little . . . "

Lao Zhang wasn't sure he really understood her, but he felt his eyes grow hot and moist again. He shook his head. "This way is good. Good! It saves us from so much worrying."

As he spoke, he began to do the calculations in his head. The total for everything his son had chosen was going to be an astronomical sum. He and his wife would be responsible for sixty percent of it, to be paid off over thirty years. The other forty percent would be the responsibility of his son once he started working, and of course there was their son's child, and the child's child . . .

He now had a goal to strive toward for the next few decades, and a warm feeling suffused him from head to toe.

He looked back at his son. The baby remained seated in the high chair, a bowl of hot noodles symbolizing longevity in front of him. His almost translucent cheeks were flushed as he smiled like the Laughing Buddha.

New Year's Eve

Late at night, Wu was walking alone along the road. The street was empty and everything was quiet, interrupted occasionally by explosions from strings of firecrackers. The night before Chinese New Year was supposed to be spent with family, with everyone gathered around the dinner table, chatting, eating, watching the Spring Festival Gala on TV, enjoying a rare moment when the whole extended family could be together in one room.

He approached a park near home. It was even quieter here, without the daytime crowd of people practicing Tai Chi, strolling, exercising, or singing folk operas. An artificial lake lay quietly in the moonless night. Wu listened to the dull sound of gentle waves slapping against the shore and felt a chill through every pore in his skin. He turned toward a tiny pavilion next to the lake, but stopped when a dark shadow loomed before him.

"Who's there?" a shocked Wu asked.

"Who are you?"

The voice sounded familiar to Wu. Suppressing his fright, he walked closer, and realized that the other person was Lao Wang, his upstairs neighbor.

Wu let out a held breath. "You really frightened me."

"What are you doing outside at this hour?"

"I wanted to take a walk . . . to relax. What are you doing here?"

"Too many people and too much noise at home. I needed a moment of peace," Lao Wang said.

The two looked at each other, and a smile of mutual understanding appeared on their faces. Lao Wang brushed off a nearby stone bench and said, "Come, sit next to me."

Wu touched the stone, which was ice cold. "Thanks. I'd rather stand for a bit. I just ate; standing is better for digestion."

Lao Wang sighed. "New Year's . . . the older you get, the less there is to celebrate."

"Isn't that the truth. You eat, watch TV, set off some firecrackers, and then it's time to sleep. A whole year has gone by, and you've done nothing of note."

"Right," Lao Wang said. "But that's how everyone spends New Year's. I can't do anything different all by myself."

"Yeah. Everybody in the family sits down to watch the Spring Festival Gala. I'd like to do something different but I can't summon the energy. Might as well come out and walk around by myself."

"I haven't watched the Spring Festival Gala in years."

"That's pretty impressive," Wu said.

"It was easier in the past," Lao Wang said. "Singing, dancing, a few stupid skits and it's over. But now they've made it so much more difficult to avoid."

"Well, that's technological progress, right? They've developed so many new tricks."

"I don't mind if they just stick to having pop stars do their acts," Lao Wang said. "But now they insist on this 'People's Participatory Gala' business. Ridiculous."

"I can sort of see the point," said Wu. "The stars are on TV every day for the rest of the year. Might as well try something new for New Year's Eve."

"It's too much for me, all this chaos. I'd rather have a quiet, peaceful New Year's."

"But the point of New Year's is the festival mood," said Wu. "Most people like a bit of noise and atmosphere. We're not immortals in heaven, free from all earthly concerns, you know?"

"Ha! I don't think even immortals up there can tolerate this much pandemonium down here."

Both men sighed and listened to the gentle sound of the lake. After a while, Lao Wang asked, "Have you ever been picked for the Gala?"

"Of course. Twice. The first time they randomly picked my family during the live broadcast so that the whole family could appear on TV and wish everybody a happy new year. The second time was because one of my classmates had cancer. They picked him for a human-interest story, and the producer decided that it would be more tear-jerking to get the whole class and the teacher to appear with him. The Gala hosts and the audience sure cried a lot. I wasn't in too many shots, though."

"I've never been picked," said Lao Wang.

"How have you managed that?"

"I turn off the TV and go hide somewhere. The Gala has nothing to do with me."

"Why go to so much trouble? It's not a big deal to be on TV for the Gala."

"It's my nature," said Lao Wang. "I like peace and quiet. I can't stand the . . . invasiveness of it."

"Isn't that a little exaggerated?"

"Without notice, without consent, they just stick your face on TV so that everyone in the world can see you. How is that *not* invasive?"

"It's just for a few seconds. No one is going to even remember you."

"I don't like it."

"It's not as if having other people see you costs you anything."

"That's not the point. The point is *I* haven't agreed. If I agree, sure, I don't care if you follow me around with a camera twenty-four hours a day. But I don't want to be forced on there."

"I can understand your feeling," said Wu. "But it's not realistic. Look around you! There are cameras everywhere. You can't hide for the rest of your life."

"That's why I go to places with no people."

"That's a bit extreme."

Lao Wang laughed. "I think I'm old enough to deserve not having all my choices made for me."

Wu laughed, too. "You really are a maverick."

"Hardly. This is all I can do."

White lights appeared around them, turning into a crowd of millions of faces. In the middle of the crowd was a stage, brightly lit and spectacularly decorated. Lao Wang and Wu found themselves on the stage, and loud, festive music filled their ears. A host and a hostesss approached from opposite ends of the stage.

A megawatt smile on his face, the host said, "Wonderful news, everyone! We've finally found that mythical creature: the only person in all of China who's never been on the Spring Festival Gala! Meet Mr. Wang, who lives in Longyang District."

The hostess, with an even brighter smile, added, "We have to thank this other member of the audience, Mr. Wu, who helped us locate and bring the mysterious Mr. Wang onto the stage. Mr. Wang, on this auspicious, joyous night, would you like to wish everyone a happy new year and say a few words?"

Lao Wang was stunned. It took a while for him to recover and turn to look at Wu. Wu was awkward and embarrassed, and he wanted to say something to comfort Lao Wang, but he wasn't given a chance to talk.

The host said, "Mr. Wang, this is the very first time you've been on the Gala. Can you tell us how you feel?"

Lao Wang stood up, and without saying anything, dove off the edge of the stage into the cold lake.

Wu jumped up, and his shirt was soaked with cold sweat. Blood drained from the faces of the host and the hostess. Multiple camera drones flitted through the night air, searching for Lao Wang in the lake. The millions of faces around them began to whisper and murmur, and the buzzing grew louder.

Suddenly, a ball of light appeared below the surface of the lake, and with a loud explosion, a bright, blinding light washed out everything. Wu was screaming and rolling on the ground, his clothes on fire. Finally, he managed to open his eyes and steal a peek through the cracks between his fingers: amidst the blazing white flames, a brilliant, golden pillar of light rose from the lake and disappeared among the clouds. It must have been thousands of miles long.

What the hell! thought Wu. *Is he really going back up in heaven to enjoy his peace and quiet?* Then his eyes began to burn and columns of hot smoke rose from his sockets.

The next day, the web was filled with all kinds of commentary. The explosion had destroyed all the cameras on site, and only a few fragmentary recordings of the scene could be recovered. Most of those who got to see the event live were in hospital—the explosion had damaged their hearing.

Still, everyone congratulated the Spring Festival Gala organizers for putting on the most successful program in the show's history.

Matchmaking

Xiao Li was twenty-seven. After New Year's she'd be twenty-eight. Her mother was growing worried and signed her up with a matchmaking service.

"Oh come on," said Xiao Li. "How embarrassing."

"What's embarrassing about it?" said her mother. "If I didn't use a matchmaker, where would your dad be? And where would *you* be?"

"These services are full of . . . sketchy men."

"Better than you can do on your own."

"What?" Xiao Li was incredulous. "Why?"

"They have scientific algorithms."

"Oh, you think science can guarantee good matches?"

"Stop wasting time. Are you going or not?"

And so Xiao Li put on a new dress and did her makeup, and followed her mom to a famous matchmaking service center. The manager at the service center was very enthusiastic, and asked Xiao Li to confirm her identity.

Xiao Li had no interest in being here and twisted around in her chair. "Is this going to be a lot of trouble?"

The manager smiled. "Not at all. We have the latest technology. It's super fast."

"You're asking for all my personal information. Is it safe?"

The manager continued to smile. "Please don't worry. We've been in business for years, and we've never had any problems. Not a single client has ever sued us."

Xiao Li still had more questions, but her mother had had enough. "Hurry up! Don't think you can get out of this by dragging it out."

Xiao Li put her finger on the terminal so that her prints could be scanned, and then she had a retinal scan as well so that her personal information could be downloaded to the service center's database. Next, she had to do a whole-body scan, which took three minutes.

"All set," said the manager. He reached into the terminal and pulled out a hologram that he tossed onto the floor. Xiao Li watched as a white light rose from the ground, and inside the light was a tiny figure about an inch tall, looking exactly like her and dressed in the same clothes.

The little person looked around herself and then entered a door next to her. Inside, there was a tiny table and two tiny chairs. A mini-man sat on one chair and after greeting mini-Xiao Li, the two started to talk. They spoke in a high-pitched, sped-up language and it was hard to tell what they were saying. Not even a minute later, mini-Xiao Li stood up and the two shook hands politely. Then mini-Xiao Li came out and entered the next door.

Xiao Li's mother muttered next to her. "Let's see, if it takes a minute to get to know a guy, then you can meet sixty guys in an hour. After a day, you . . . ."

The still-smiling manager said, "Oh, this is only a demonstration. The real process is even faster. You don't need to wait around, of course. We'll get you the results tomorrow, guaranteed."

The manager reached out and waved his hands. The miniature men and women in the white light shrank down even further until they were tiny dots. All around them were tiny cells like a beehive, and in each cell red and green dots twitched and buzzed.

Xiao Li could no longer tell which red dot was hers, and she felt uneasy. "Is this really going to work?"

The manager assured her. "We have more than six million registered members! I'm sure you'll find your match."

"These people are . . . reliable?"

"Every member had to go through a strict screening process like the one you went through. All the information on file is one hundred percent reliable. Our dating software is the most up to date, and any match predicted by the software has always worked out in real life. If you're not satisfied, we'll refund your entire fee."

Xiao Li still hesitated, but her mother said, "Let's go. Look at you—now you're suddenly interested?"

The next afternoon, Xiao Li got a call from the manager at the matchmaking center. He explained that the software had identified 438 possible candidates: all were good looking, healthy, reliable, and shared Xiao Li's interests and values.

Xiao Li was a bit shocked. *More than four hundred?* Even if she went on a date every day, it would take more than a year to get through them all.

The manager's smile never wavered. "I suggest you try our parallel dating software and continue to get to know these men better. It takes time to know if someone will make a good spouse."

Xiao Li agreed and ten copies of mini-Xiao Li were made to go on dates with these potential matches.

Two days later, the manager called Xiao Li again. The ten mini-Xiao Lis had already gone on ten dates with each of the more than four hundred candidates, and the software had tracked and scored all the dates. The manager advised Xiao Li to aggregate the scores from the ten dates and keep only the thirty top-scorers for further consideration. Xiao Li agreed and felt more relaxed.

Three days later, the manager told Xiao Li that after further contacts and observation, seven candidates had been eliminated, five were progressing slowly in their relationships with Xiao Li, and the remaining eighteen demonstrated reciprocal satisfaction and interest. Of these eighteen, eight had already revealed their intent to marry Xiao Li, and four had shown flaws—in living habits, for instance—but were still within the acceptable range.

Xiao Li was silent. After waiting for some time, the manager gently prodded her. "It might help to ask your mother to meet them—after all, marriage is about two families coming together."

That's true. That day, Xiao Li brought her mom to the matchmaking center, and after her identity was verified, her mother was also scanned. As the dates continued, the ten mini-Xiao Lis had ten mini-moms to help as sounding boards and advisors.

Her mom's participation was very helpful, and soon only seven candidates remained. The manager said, "Miss Li, we also have software for simulating the conditions of preparing for a wedding. Why don't you try it? Many couples split up under the stress of preparing for their big day. Marriage is not something to rush into rashly."

And so the seven mini-Xiao Lis began to discuss the wedding with the seven mini-boyfriends. Relatives of all the involved couples were scanned and entered the discussion; arguments grew heated. Indeed, two of the candidates' families just couldn't come together with Xiao Li's family, and they backed out.

The manager now said, "We also have software for simulating the honeymoon. A famous writer once said the way to know if a marriage will last is to see if the couple can travel together for a whole month without hating each other."

So Xiao Li signed up for simulated honeymoons. After that, there were simulated pregnancies, simulated maternity leaves—one potential father who was only interested in holding the baby and paid no attention to Xiao Li was immediately eliminated.

Then came the simulated raising of children, simulated affairs, simulated menopause and mid-life crises, followed by simulations of various life traumas: car accidents, disability, death of a child, dying parents . . . finally the couple had to lean against each other as they entered nursing homes. Happily ever after?

Incredibly, two candidates still remained in consideration.

Xiao Li felt that after so much progress, she really had to meet these two men. The manager sent her the file on the first match, and an excited Xiao Li could feel her heart beating wildly. Just as she was about to open the file, however, a warning beep sounded, and the manager's face appeared in the air.

"I'm really sorry, Miss Li. This client was also going through the simulation with another potential match, and half a minute ago, the results came out, indicating an excellent match. Given the delicacy of the situation and to avoid . . . future regrets, I suggest you not meet him just yet."

Xiao Li felt as though she had lost something. "Why didn't you tell me this earlier?"

"The whole process is automated for privacy protection. Even our staff can't monitor or intervene. But don't worry! You still have another great match."

Xiao Li admitted that advanced technology really was reliable.

She opened the file for the other match and saw his face for the first time. She felt dizzy, as though the years in their future had been compressed into this moment, concentrated, intense, overwhelming. She felt herself growing light, like a cloud about to drift into the sky.

She heard the voice of the manager. "Miss Li? Are you satisfied with our program? Would you like to arrange an in-person meeting?"

"That won't be necessary," said Xiao Li.

She showed the manager the picture. He was speechless.

"Um . . . " Xiao Li blushed. "What is your name, actually?"

"You can call me Xiao Zhao."

A month later, Xiao Li and Xiao Zhao were married.

Reunion

Yang was home from college for the Spring Festival break. Liu, a high school classmate, called to say that since it had been ten years since their graduation, he was organizing a reunion.

Yang hung up and felt nostalgic. *Has it really been ten years?*

. . .

The day was foggy and it was impossible to see anything outside the window. Yang called Liu to ask if the reunion was still on.

"Of course! The fog makes for a better atmosphere, actually."

Yang got in his car and turned on the fog navigation system. The head-up display on the windshield marked the streets and cars and pedestrians, even if he couldn't see them directly. He arrived at the gates of his old high school safely and saw that many cars were already parked along the road, some were more expensive than his, others cheaper. Yang put on the fog mask and stepped out of the car. The mask filtered the air, and the eyepiece acted as a display, allowing him to see everything hidden by the fog. He looked around and saw that the entrance to the high school was the same as he remembered: iron grille gates, a few large gilt characters in the red brick walls. The buildings and the lawn inside hadn't changed either, and as a breeze passed through, he seemed to hear the rustling of holly leaves.

Yang passed through the classroom buildings and came onto the exercise ground, where everyone used to do their morning calisthenics. A crowd was gathered there, conversing in small groups. Just about everyone in his class had arrived. Although they all wore masks, glowing faces were projected onto the masks. He examined them: most of the faces were old photographs taken during high school. Soon, a few of his best friends from that time gathered around him, and they started to talk: *Is he still in grad school? Where is he working? Has he gotten married? Has he bought a house?* The words and laughter flowed easily.

Just then, they heard a voice coming from somewhere elevated. They looked up and saw that Liu had climbed onto the rostrum. Taking a pose like their old principal, he spoke into a mike, sounding muffled: "Welcome back to our alma mater, everybody. The school is being renovated this winter, and most of the classrooms have been dismantled. That's why we have to make do with the exercise ground."

Yang was startled, and then he realized that the buildings he had passed through earlier were also nothing more than projections of old photographs. Remembering the old room where he had studied, the old cafeteria where he had eaten, and the rooftop deck where he had secretly taken naps, he wondered if any of them had survived.

Liu continued, "But this exercise ground holds a special meaning for our class. Does anyone remember why?"

The crowd was quiet. Pleased with himself, Liu lifted up something covered by a cloth. He raised his voice. "While they were renovating the exercise ground, one of the workers dug up our memory capsule. I checked: it's intact!"

He pulled off the cloth with an exaggerated motion, revealing a silver-white, square box. The crowd buzzed with excited conversation. Yang could feel his heart pounding as memories churned in his mind. At graduation, someone had suggested that each member of the class record a holographic segment, store all the recordings in a projector, and bury it under one of the trees at the edge of the exercise ground, to be replayed after ten years. This was the real reason Liu had organized the reunion.

"Do you remember how we had everyone say what they wanted to achieve in the future?" Liu asked. "Now that it's been ten years, let's take a look and see if anyone has realized their dream."

The crowd grew even more excited and started to clap.

"Since I'm holding the box, I'll start," Liu said.

He placed his hand against the box, and a small blue light came to life, like a single eye. A glowing light appeared above the box, and after a few flickers, resolved into an eighteen-year-old version of Liu.

Everyone gazed up at this youthful image of their friend and what he had chosen to remember from their high school years: there was Liu running for class president, receiving an academic and service award, representing the school on the soccer team, scoring a goal, organizing extracurricular clubs, leading his supporters in his campaign, losing the election, hearing words of encouragement from teachers and friends so that he could redouble his effort, tearfully making a speech: "Alma Mater, I'll remember you always. I will make you proud of me!"

And then, the young Liu said, "In a decade, I will have an office facing the sea!"

The light dimmed like a receding tide. The real Liu took out his phone and projected a photograph in the air: this much more mature Liu, in a suit and tie, sat behind a desk and grinned at the camera. A deep blue sea and a sky dotted with some clouds, pretty as a postcard, could be seen through the glass wall behind him.

A wave of applause. Everyone congratulated Liu on achieving his dream. Yang clapped along, but something about the scene bothered him. This didn't seem like a reunion—it was more like reality TV. But Liu had already come down from the rostrum and handed the box to someone else. Another glowing light appeared above them, and Yang couldn't help but look up with the crowd.

And so they looked at old memories: classes, tests, the flag-raising ceremony, morning exercises, being tardy, being let out of school, study hall, skipping classes, fights, smoking, breaking up . . . followed by old dreams: finding love, jobs, vacations, names, names of places, names of objects. Finally, he saw himself.

The short-cropped hair and scrawny, awkward body of his teenaged self embarrassed him, and he heard his own raspy voice: "I want to be an interesting person."

He was stunned. What had made him say such a thing back then? And how could he have no memory of saying it? But the crowd around him applauded enthusiastically and laughed, praising him for having had the audacity to say something unique.

He passed the box onto the next person, and he could feel his temples grow sweaty in the fog. He wanted this farce to be over so he could drive home, take off the mask, and take a long, hot bath.

A woman spoke next to him—he seemed to recognize the voice. He looked over. Ah, it was Ye, who had sat at the same desk with him throughout their three years in high school.

He didn't know Ye well. She was an average girl in every way: not too pretty, not too *not* pretty, not too smart, not too *not* smart. He searched through his memories and recalled that she liked to laugh, but because her teeth weren't very even, she looked a bit goofy when laughing. He recalled other bits and pieces about her: her odd gestures, her habit of doodling in their textbooks, the way she would sometimes close her eyes and press her hands against her temples and mutter. He had never asked her what she was muttering about.

He heard the eighteen-year-old Ye saying in an even, calm voice, "I don't think I have a dream. I have no idea where I'll be in ten years.

"I'm envious of each and every one of you. I'm envious that you can dream of a future. Before you had even been born, your parents had started to plan for your future. As long as you follow those plans and don't make big mistakes, you'll be fine.

"Before I was born, the doctors discovered that I had a hereditary disease. They thought I wouldn't live beyond my twentieth year. The doctors advised my mother to terminate the pregnancy. But my mother wouldn't listen to them. It became a point of friction between my parents, and eventually, they divorced.

"When I was very little, my mother told me this story. She also said, Daughter, you're going to have to rely on yourself for the rest of your life. I don't know how to help you. She also said that she would never help me make my decisions, whether it was where I wanted to play, who I wanted to be friends with, what books I wanted to buy, or what school I wanted to go to. She said that she had already made the most important decision for my life: to give birth to me. After that, whatever I decided, I didn't need her approval.

"I don't know how much longer I have. Maybe I'll die tomorrow, maybe I'll eke out a few more years. But I still haven't decided what I have to get done before I die. I'm envious of everyone who'll live longer than I because they'll have more time to think about it and more time to make it come true.

"But there are also times when I think it makes no difference whether we live longer or shorter.

"Actually, I do have dreams, many dreams. I dream of flying in a spaceship; dream of a wedding on Mars; dream of living for a long, long time so that I can see what the world will be like in a thousand, ten thousand years; dream of becoming someone great so that after I die, many people will remember my name. I also have little dreams. I dream of seeing a meteor shower; dream of having the best grade, just once, so that my mother will be happy for me; dream of a boy I like singing a song for me on my birthday; dream of catching a pickpocket trying to steal a wallet on the bus and having the courage to rush up and seize him. Sometimes, I even realize one of my dreams, but I don't know if I should be happy, don't know if I died the next day, whether I would feel that was enough, that my life was complete, perfect, and that I had no more regrets.

"I dream of seeing all of you in ten years, and hear what dreams you've realized."

She disappeared. The light dimmed bit by bit.

A moment of quiet.

Someone shouted, "But where is she?"

Yang looked down and saw that the silvery-white box was lying on the ground, surrounded by the tips of pairs of shoes. He looked around: all the faces on the masks flickered, but he couldn't tell who was who for a moment.

The crowd erupted.

"What the hell? A ghost?"

"Someone's playing a joke!"

"We went to school together for three years and I'd never heard her mention any of this. Who knows if it's true or not?"

"I've never heard of any strange disease like that."

The discussions led nowhere, and they couldn't find Ye. The reunion came to an end without a conclusion.

After dinner and some drinks, Yang drove home by himself. The fog was still heavy, and the passing, varicolored lights dissolved in the fog like pigment. He fell asleep as soon as he was in bed, but he woke up around midnight.

He was seized by a nameless terror, and he was sure that he would not see the sun rise again, that he would die during his sleep. He recalled his life, thinking about the ten years since high school that had passed far too quickly. He had once thought life rather good, like a flowery, splendid scroll, but now a rip had been torn in it, and inside was darkness, a bottomless darkness. He had fallen into a chasm from the sky, and inside the chasm was only a lightless fog. All he could see was the nothingness behind the scroll.

He curled up in the fetal position and sobbed, and he vomited his dinner onto his pillow.

The fog was gone in the morning. Yang got up and looked at the clear sky outside.

He felt refreshed, and the unpleasantness of the previous day was forgotten.

The Birthday

Grandma Zhou was almost ninety-nine, and the family planned a big celebration. But just as everything was about ready, Grandma Zhou slipped and fell in the bathroom, fracturing her foot. Although she was rushed to the hospital right away and the injury wasn't serious, it still made it hard for her to get about. She had to stay in a wheelchair all day, and she felt depressed.

The evening sky was overcast, and Grandma Zhou napped in her room by herself. Knocking noises woke her up. Raising her sleepy eyes, she saw a figure in a white dress floating in midair, indistinct, like an immortal.

"Is something happening, Young Lady?"

Young Lady wasn't a person, but the nursing home's service program. Grandma's eyesight was no longer so good, and she couldn't tell what Young Lady looked like. But she always thought she sounded like her granddaughter.

"Grandma Zhou," said Young Lady, "your family is here to celebrate your birthday!"

"What's there to celebrate? The older you grow, the more you suffer."

"Please don't say that. The young people are here because they love you. They want you to live beyond a hundred!"

Grandma Zhou was still in a bad mood, but Young Lady said, "If you keep on frowning like that, your children and grandchildren and great-grandchildren will think I haven't been taking good care of you."

Grandma Zhou thought Young Lady had taken very good care of her—in fact, she did it about as well as her real granddaughter. Her heart softened, and a smile appeared on her face.

"There we go," said a grinning Young Lady. "All right, get ready to celebrate!"

Bright lights came out of the floor and transformed the room. Grandma Zhou found herself inside a hall decorated in an antique style with red paper lanterns and red paper *Longevity* characters pasted on the walls. She was dressed in a red jacket and red pants custom made for her and sat in a carved purpleheart longevity chair, while all the guests around her also wore red. Grandma Zhou couldn't see their faces clearly, but she could hear the laughter and joyous conversations, and the noise of firecrackers going off outside was constant.

Her oldest son approached first with his family to wish her a happy birthday. There were more than a dozen people, and, after sorting themselves by generation and age, they knelt to kowtow. Grandma Zhou smiled at the children: boys, girls, some dark skinned, some fair skinned, and she had trouble saying some of their names. A few of the children were shy, and hid behind their parents to peek at her without speaking. Others were bolder, and they spoke to her in some foreign language instead of Chinese, making the adults laugh. There was also a little child curled up asleep in her mother's lap, and the mother smiled, saying, "Grandma, I'm really sorry. It's about five in the morning in our time zone."

"That's all right," said Grandma Zhou. "Children need their rest."

It took almost a quarter of an hour for the members of her oldest son's family to offer her their good wishes one by one.

Then came the family of her second son, her older daughter, her younger daughter . . . then the friends who had gone to school with her, friends from the army, the students she had taught over the years, in-laws, distant relatives . . .

Grandma Zhou had been sitting up for a long while, and her eyes were feeling tired and her throat parched. But she knew it was difficult for so many people to make time to attend her party, and so she forced herself to keep on nodding and smiling. *Advanced technology is really wonderful; it would be so much harder for them to do this in person.*

As she watched all the guests milling about the hall, she felt very moved. So many people around the globe, divided by thousands of miles, were here because of her. After all the miles she had walked and all the things she had experienced and done, she had connected all these people, many of them strangers to each other, into a web. She felt fortunate to be ninety-nine; not many people made it this far.

A figure dressed in white drifted over to her. At first she thought it was Young Lady again, but the figure knelt down and held her hand.

"Grandma, sorry I'm late. The traffic was bad."

Grandma Zhou squeezed the hands; the skin felt a bit cold, but the hands were solid. She squinted to get a closer look. It was her granddaughter who was studying overseas.

"What are you doing here?"

"To wish you a happy birthday, of course."

"You're actually here? Really here?"

"I wanted to see you."

"That's a long way to go," said Grandma Zhou.

Her granddaughter smiled. "Not that far. Not even a full day by plane."

Grandma Zhou looked her granddaughter up and down. She looked tired, but seemed to be in good spirits. Grandma Zhou smiled.

"Is it cold outside?"

"Not at all," said the granddaughter. "The moon is lovely tonight. Would you like to see it?"

"But there are still so many people here."

"Oh, that's easy to take care of," said the granddaughter.

She waved her hands, and a replica of Grandma Zhou appeared. The replica was dressed in the same red jacket and red pants, and sat in the carved purpleheart longevity chair. The guests in the hall continued to come up in waves, wishing her many years of long life and happiness.

"All right, Grandma, let's go."

The granddaughter pushed the wheelchair through the empty corridor of the nursing home until they were in the yard. There was a vigorous *shantao* tree in the middle of the yard, and to the side were a few wintersweet bushes, whose fragrance wafted on the breeze. The sky had cleared, revealing the full moon. Grandma Zhou looked at the plants in the garden and then at her granddaughter, standing tall and lovely next to her like a young poplar. *Nothing makes you realize how old you are as seeing your children's children all grown up.*

A few other residents of the nursing home were sitting under the tree, playing erhu and singing folk operas. They saw Grandma Zhou and invited her to join them.

Grandma Zhou blushed like a little girl. "I have no talent for this sort of thing at all! I've never learned to play an instrument, and I can't sing."

Lao Hu, who was playing the erhu, said, "It's just a few of us old timers trying to entertain ourselves, not the Spring Festival Gala! Lao Zhou, just perform anything you like, and we'll cheer you on. Wouldn't that be a nice way to celebrate your birthday?"

Grandma Zhou pondered this for a while, and said, "All right, I'll chant a poem for you."

Her father had taught her how to chant poems when she was little, and her father had learned from his tutor, back before the founding of the People's Republic. Back then, when children studied poetry, they didn't read it or recite it, but learned to chant along with the teacher. This was how they learned the rhythm and meter of poetry, the patterns of rhyme and tone. It was closer to singing than reading, and it sounded better.

The others quieted to listen. The moonlight was gentle like water, and everything around them seemed fresh and warm. Grandma slowed her breathing, thinking of fragments of history and tradition connected with the moon and all that is old and new around her, and began to chant:

As firecrackers send away the old year,
The spring breeze feels as warm as New Year's wine.
All houses welcome fresh sun and good cheer,
While new couplets take the place of old signs.

Originally published in Chinese in *Science Fiction World* in June 2013.

Author's Note: While I was at my parents' home over Spring Festival break, I wanted to write some stories about ordinary lives. I don't particularly care about predicting the future, but I do think that deep changes are happening around us almost undetectably. These changes are the most real, and also the most science fictional.

The future is full of uncertainties, and it is as hard to say it will be better as it is to say it will be worse. In a few decades, I don't know if anyone will still remember how to chant ancient poems, but I do know that in every passing moment, the people in every house—men, women, old, young—are living lives as meaningful as they're ordinary.

The poem included in this story was written by the Song Dynasty poet Wang Anshi.

Of Alternate Adventures and Memory
ROCHITA LOENEN-RUIZ

Adventure Boy was twelve when he met Mechanic for the first time. They had gone to an exhibit celebrating the removal of the barrier between Central City and Metal Town. He remembered feeling proud. His mom, after all, had played a key role in building bridges between the two worlds and if not for her efforts, the barrier would still be there.

"There's someone I want to introduce you to," his mother said.

He'd registered the peak in her voice that could mean excitement or trepidation, but before he could feel anything himself, they were being welcomed into a circle of metal men.

"This must be your son," someone said. "I'm very pleased to meet you. I hear you're quite the Adventure Boy."

A hand was extended to him, and he looked up. Light glinted off Mechanic's domed head and Adventure Boy picked up the static threaded through his voice. An unrelenting old-timer, he'd thought.

"Well," Mechanic said. "won't you shake my hand? I assure you, shaking hands with me won't turn you into a metal can."

It was the hidden taunt that prompted him to reach out and clasp Mechanic's hand in his. He noted the temperature of metal against his skin, but where he'd expected cold, Mechanic's hand was warm. "I may be old," Mechanic said, "but I'm still upgradeable."

The other metal men laughed and Adventure Boy registered signals of relief from his mother.

"I'm pleased to meet you, sir," Adventure Boy said. He didn't know what else to say because he'd never heard of Mechanic and he didn't know why his mother felt it was important for this man to like him.

After that introduction, his mother was summoned by Central City's governor and Adventure Boy was left to wander the exhibit on his own.

Here were replicas of a life he'd never known. Photographs and reliquaries that meant nothing at all to him. They were part of his mother's long ago life, not his. He had come to awareness in Central City, and he only knew this place with its smooth asphalt, ordered subdivisions and neatly manicured front lawns.

The photographs made him wonder though. He stared at captured images of piles of rusted metal, disembodied machines, and deserted buildings and he couldn't help but wonder what it had been like when his mother still lived there.

"You should visit it someday," a voice said behind him.

It was Mechanic. His hands neatly folded behind his back, his eyes directed at the replica of a building called the Remembrance Monument.

"Of course, the streets are silent now," Mechanic said. "We're being integrated into Central City's workforce and there's no need to maintain the workshops and the shelters. It's a foolish fancy that none of us are allowed, but if you stand directly under the Remembrance Monument, you can still hear the whisper of voices from those who've gone before."

"Why would I want to do that?" Adventure Boy asked. "I don't belong there at all."

Mechanic inclined his head. His face was blank, in the way metal men's faces were blank. But Adventure Boy couldn't help feeling as if he'd hurt the metal man somehow.

"I mean, I was born here," Adventure Boy said. "I'm a citizen of this place. Also, Metal Town is no more, so . . . "

His voice trailed off as Mechanic stepped away.

"You're right," Mechanic said. "This is your city. I hope you enjoy the exhibit. It was good to meet you, Adventure Boy."

As he watched Mechanic walk away, he couldn't help but feel as if he'd done a great wrong.

An alternate child will be a good addition to your home. Memomach industries works to create the perfect child to suit your needs.
—Memomach Industry ad—

He remembered the time he was refused a place on the school softball team. He listened to the soft-voiced principal as she tried to explain it to him.

Alternates were different. They could run faster. They had more stamina. It wouldn't be fair to the children of the makers.

In time, he learned not to want. He tried to blend in. He was, after all, his mother's child. In his second year at school, another alternate child transferred in. He tried not to speak to the other, and the other did not speak to him. They sat side by side on a bench watching the others play, not speaking a word.

It would have gone on that way if not for another transfer. Unlike them, Jill Slowbloom was noisy. She laughed loud and she made jokes. She was clumsy as well.

"My parents said they wanted the perfect child," she said. "But they meant the perfect child for them."

Her laughter drew them out of their shells. They were no longer two, but three, and when the term ended and another alternate transferred in, they became four.

"We could start our own club," Jill said.

"I'll be point. Eileen will notate. And you and Jeff can follow my lead."

252

For a while, he felt like he belonged somewhere. Then the new term ended. Jill transferred out. Eileen moved away. He and Jeff were left staring at each other, not knowing how to fill the silence that was left behind.

Perhaps, he thinks. *Perhaps if I go to Metal Town, I will find the words to fill the silence. Perhaps I will understand more.*

Father wears the face of a numbered man. He wears the suit, he carries the briefcase, he drives the car.

At home, he morphs into someone who Mother argues with over their dinner.

"I don't see why you feel the need to indulge him," Mother says.

"Mechanic thinks it will be good for him, and I agree," Father replies.

They are discussing Adventure Boy's desire to visit Metal Town.

Mother doesn't wish them to go, but Father sees no harm in it.

"I don't understand why you want to see that place again," Mother says. "I shudder when I remember how I almost lost you there."

"But you didn't lose me," Father says. "And we can't deny him this. If he wants to know it for himself, then he should know it for himself."

"I won't go," Mother says.

"If you don't want to go, you don't have to go," Father replies.

Adventure Boy lies on his back and stares up at the ceiling. He had bought a picture of the Remembrance Monument and Father had hung it up. At night, the lines of the monument glowed in the dark.

Mechanic's words rang in his ear.

"You can still hear the voices of those who have gone before."

Come reminisce of days gone by . . . Metal Town Tours, your official tourist operator. We provide detailed excursions, maps, and access to some of Metal Town's most spectacular monuments.

—Metal Town Tours ad—

Smooth asphalt morphed into rough tarmac and the neatly ordered lawns of suburbia were replaced with fields full of high grass and wild sunflowers with faces turned towards the sky.

Father had rented a tour car; it was decorated with yellow sunflowers and bold black lettering announcing the name of the official tour agency.

They were the only visitors so far. It was a Saturday and most tourists came in after twelve.

Adventure Boy rolled down the window. A light morning breeze caused goosebumps to rise on the surface of his skin. But after that initial contact, his skin warmed and they vanished.

"It's a much smoother ride than I remember," Father said.

Adventure Boy turned to look at him.

Without his suit, Father looked like one of the makers. His face was not as rigid, his shoulders were relaxed and he wore a plain t-shirt and jeans just like all the other fathers Adventure Boy saw at school.

"We've never talked about it," Father said. "But Metal Town is a painful memory for your mother. She came to consciousness here. She loved it and yet she wanted nothing more than to escape it."

"Is this where you two met?" Adventure Boy asked.

Father smiled.

"You could say that," he said.

There was a pause and then Father said, "It was here that I brought her into being."

With the unification of Metal Town and the Central City, Metal Town's dwellers were promptly absorbed into the general workforce. Metal Town soon became redundant.

Proposals for the renovation of Metal Town are ongoing, but until then, it has been kept in its original state for the sake of those who wish to revisit an important part of the reunification history.

—Recorded guide from Metal Town Tours—

"These were my quarters," Father said.

They stopped before a cluster of buildings. Adventure Boy noted the signs of decay on the metal scaffolds that kept the buildings together.

Father stood at the foot of the one of the houses. It was washed in gray, its shutters were wide open and one of them looked out at a field of sunflowers.

"Do you want to go inside?" Father said.

What precautions were carried out to preserve experiments from being stolen or taken away? This house, which holds the tools of a master maker, was secured with a special reader that identified visitors through codes implanted in their optic lenses.

—From Guide to Metal Town—

"It's still here," Father said.

Was that amusement in his voice? Father stooped, and Adventure Boy saw it. A small screen was set into the doorjamb.

"Try it," Father said.

Adventure Boy bent down and pressed his eye to the screen. Nothing moved. The door didn't budge.

"It doesn't work," he said.

"We'll see," Father replied.

He bent down and pressed his eye to the screen. There was a flash of green and a click.

"I can't believe they haven't put that out of commission," Father said.

With a push, the door swung open and Adventure Boy was assailed with the smell of liquid oil, and the essence his mother took once every fourteen days.

"Is this . . . ?"

"Yes," Father said. "Here is where your mother became aware."

• • •

The open window looked out on the sunflower fields. He tried to bring up an image of his mother. He remembered the moment when he first came to awareness. He remembered her voice echoing within the confines of the room that became his own.

"He's not waking up." It was a soundbite from the past.

"Be patient," Father's voice. "Waking up takes time. You should know this very well."

"But if I failed . . . "

"You have not failed," Father again.

He'd opened his eyes, and the room came into being. Walls of powdered gray and the smell of oil and essence pervading the air.

Then Mother's face was in his vision.

"You're awake," she said. Relief colored her voice. "Welcome to the world, Adventure Boy."

One of the archived stories is that of an early alternate. Created to be the perfect housewife, this alternate was so designed that it could easily pass as one of the makers.

There is no exact record of her progress.

—Metal Town Tours—

"Were you happy?" he asked.

"She was as I envisioned she would be," Father said. "An alternate girl who was also quite human."

"I know she is as you wanted her to be," Adventure Boy said. "But, were you happy?"

"I am happier now," Father said. "She broke her program, just as she was meant to. She became herself."

Outside was warmer. It was mid-morning. They had been in Metal Town for less than an hour, but to Adventure Boy it was as if he had been there for a lifetime.

They parked the touring car close to the center.

"It's good to walk," Father said.

And like that they walked into the shadow of the Remembrance Monument.

Remember.

A voice whispered through his circuits. He thought of the moment when he met Mechanic, the warm and solid grip of Mechanic's hand and the urgency that rushed through him in that moment.

I want to see.

The thought rushed through him.

He stood there, looking up at the huge monolith that housed the harvested memories from the hundreds of thousands of Metal Town's dwellers.

Urgency flooded him. He wanted to run. He wanted to hide. He wanted to . . .

He blinked and he was surrounded by warmth.

Remember.

Tiny little pinpricks filtered through his consciousness. He was seeing and yet not seeing. The landscape shifted. He was inside of the monument and he was outside of it.

Father's eyes were closed as well. His mouth hanging open as if he were suspended halfway to speech.

He shut his eyes and saw a vision. The tarmac buckled beneath him, the sunflower fields hemmed him about, and behind him was the roar of the Equilibrium Machine. Its bellow shook the air and he trembled. That great maw would consume him, would crush him, would take him down into recycling and a loss of all that he had come to love.

Despair consumed him.

And then she was there.

Mother. Her eyes flashing bright, her voice ringing in the air around him.

When he came back into himself, they were sitting at the foot of the monument. He wasn't at all surprised to see Mechanic speaking with his father.

> *There are consequences for every choice we make. Be sure you understand before you make a decision.*
> *—Mechanic, Words to the Wise, 14th ed. Ilay Press—*

> *Heritage can be a burden. History can be a burden. Everything can be a burden if we choose to make it so.*
> *—Mechanic, Words to the Wise, 14th ed. Ilay Press—*

Mother never asked about their visit.

They came home and they went on as if they had never been to Metal Town. From time to time, he would dream, but he woke before he started crying.

"Back in the day, my memory would be fed to the monument," Mechanic said. "But government has decreed that we can't do that anymore."

"This body grows old," Mechanic continued.

They sat there listening to whispers that they couldn't understand.

"I had to modulate your receptors a bit," Mechanic said. "Your systems would have broken down without intervention."

"Thank you," Adventure Boy said.

Father didn't say anything. He simply sat there, his head cupped in his hands.

"Memory is difficult," Mechanic said. "We all live with the recollection of who we were. Your mother rescued your father. Theirs was an unusual situation. I didn't think they would try to create another exactly like her."

"I'm not like her," Adventure Boy said.

"I know," Mechanic replied.

There was a pause and then the metal man turned to look at him and Adventure Boy could have sworn he smiled.

"You're like me," he said.

• • •

The next time he saw Mechanic, it was at the unveiling of the new government's plan for Metal Town's rehabilitation.

He had grown into a new body. This one was taller and broader than his twelve year old one. He was living on his own now, earning a living as a regular Adventure Boy.

"Feeding the dreams of the masses," a voice said behind him.

He looked down into Mechanic's upturned face.

"You may change," Mechanic said. "But I don't forget an imprint."

The governor had come onstage and was giving the usual speech.

"How old are you now?" Adventure Boy asked.

Mechanic cackled before he replied.

"Older than you. Older than your mother. Older than your father. Almost as old as the Monument they want to tear down."

"What?"

"You're an alternate, aren't you?" Mechanic said. "Surely, you're listening to what the governor is saying."

It was true.

"Redundant buildings," the governor was saying.

As if those words were enough of a verdict.

"Relics of a bygone era," the governor continued. "But we must move on. We must move forward."

He could hear cheers coming from makers and alternates alike.

"But what about the memories?" Adventure Boy couldn't help asking.

Mechanic shrugged.

It was all the answer he needed.

We are always unraveling threads as we strive to weave them together. We think we can move towards tomorrow without yesterday. We forget that yesterday gives us the courage for today, and yesterday is the foundation of tomorrow's dream.

—Mechanic to Adventure Boy—

Records show that our model children grow up to become model citizens. These are the kinds of citizens we need as we look towards our joined futures.
—Government statement on the creation of alternate children—

It hadn't been all that difficult to find them. Awkward Jill had turned into a climber. Eileen created metal art. Jeff surprised him most of all. The silent boy played music in a club frequented by metal men.

What was not surprising—they had all sat under the shadow of the Remembrance Monument.

"It's as if it was calling to us," Jill said.

He couldn't keep from staring when a smile bloomed on Jeff's face. It was the first time he'd seen anything like it.

"We're supposed to be model citizens," Eileen said dryly. "Some would say you were planning anarchy."

"It's going to be risky," Adventure Boy said.

"We know," Jill replied. "Don't pay attention to Eileen. It's just how she is."

"If we're found out, there's no telling what they'd do to us," Adventure Boy went on.

"You only live once," Jeff said.

"I don't know if this plan will even work," Adventure Boy added. "And you do know we could all end up being recycled."

"Nothing tried, nothing gained," Eileen replied.

"You guys . . . "

"You're planning something," Father said.

He looked up from the console he was working on.

"It's no big deal," he said.

"Remember what you are meant to be," Father said.

"I'll remember," he replied.

His father's words hid a message.

This is between you and me, it said.

The days were hectic and short. Word was that the government was accepting bids from demolition teams.

"We have to do it soon," Jill said.

No one would suspect them. Four alternates could not shut down the plans of a city. But they had to try.

When Mechanic showed up at his door, he didn't know whether to be angry or thankful or sorry.

"I hear you might be planning something foolish," Mechanic said.

Adventure Boy crossed his arms and stared down at the metal man. When he was twelve, Mechanic had seemed larger than life. He still had substance, but Adventure Boy no longer feared him.

"Are you here to stop me?" he asked.

"Do you want to be stopped?" Mechanic said.

He uncrossed his arms and looked Mechanic straight in the eyes.

"No," he said. "And we won't be stopped."

For every action, there is an equal and opposite reaction.
—Newton's Third Law of Motion—

"My son has plans. I don't know what because he hasn't told me. But he is also his mother's son."
—Father to Mechanic—

"You are your mother's child," Mechanic said. "She was also fearless even when afraid."

"She has no part in this," Adventure Boy replied.

"But she has," Mechanic said. "Some part of you was born from her memory of Metal Town and the Remembrance Monument."

Adventure Boy shrugged. He had already ensured that his mother would escape any repercussions. Also, she was well-respected and known for her collaboration with the government. Surely, she would survive his actions with little damage to the reputation she'd worked so hard to build up.

"Even she could not foresee this," Mechanic said. "We mold our creations into our idea of what they should be like, but we also give you the ability to break that mold. Your mother is an example of this."

"What do you want?" Adventure Boy demanded.

"Your mother fitted you well, but there are things you have yet to learn," Mechanic said. "Please. Allow me to lend you my strength."

Where are you going? Where do you come from? Where are you now? Who are you? Who do you know? What do you want to achieve?
—Life Questions, Guide to Finding your own Path, Mackay and Manay—

Mechanic lists down names and numbers, formulas, addresses, and contact points.

"Why?" Adventure Boy asks.

"There are things you can do with a small army," Mechanic says. "But there are things you can do better when you spread your net wide."

Adventure Boy has no words to speak his thanks. He watches Mechanic's fingers as they type out messages on different screens. The words change in formulation, but the message is all the same.

I am calling in a favor.
I need your help.
Remember the bonds we share.
Remember.
Remember.
Remember.

Adventure Boy understands what those words mean now. He understands why he cannot allow the erasure of accumulated memory. No matter how insignificant or how unimportant those memories may seem, no matter that Metal Town is deemed obsolete, he can't allow those memories or those dreams to vanish without a trace.

"Here's how we planned to do it," he says to Mechanic.

They huddle around the table, four alternates and a metal man whose time is coming to an end. Beneath their hands, their dream of the future takes shape. Adventure Boy sees it as a network of roads flourishing, Jeff sees it limned in light going on into eternity, Eileen sees it as a fan unfolding again and again and again in limitless space, and Jill sees it as a flower that blossoms and blossoms and blossoms over and over again.

It is the vision they bring to the table—this promise of a future filled with the dreams and the memories of those who have gone before.

There can be no true reconciliation without acceptance. Until we see both of our worlds as occupying an equal place in history, unification is an empty word.
—Justice Torero on the unification of Metal Town and Central City—

When it starts, it is like a droplet of water falling into silent space. No one notices the movement, but slowly it spreads. Here and there, the earth shakes. Memory rises and people start to talk in sentences that start with: *Remember when.*

Memory becomes a living thing.

As the heat of summer washes over Central City and its dwellers swelter in the shade, what started as a small droplet grows bigger and bigger until it takes the shape of a summer storm that rattles the windows and doors and washes away the heat.

In the quiet fragrance that follows, memory blooms and with it the vision of a tomorrow.

Alternate Ambassador Saunders has purchased a parcel of land in Metal Town. She is the first of Central City's recognized citizens to reclaim land in the place where she came to awareness.
Her partner, Nick Wood, has purchased a lot fronting the former garage building, claiming nostalgia and sentimentality.
—Central City News Network—

Folk musician, Karina Melendez, has purchased a parcel of land in what was formerly known as Metal Town. Claiming a desire for peace and a return to the earth, the land is fit for farming. It also boasts an acreage of wild sunflowers.
—Central City News Network—

In a startling new trend, Remembrance Monuments are being established in the first four wards of Central City. Open to Makers and to Alternates alike, the Remembrance Monuments are meant to house memories both personal as well as public.
In the section open to public viewing, memorabilia is displayed that depicts the progress of Makers and Alternates alike. An interactive timeline allows viewers to enter the stream of thought. This kind of exchange is a first in Central City. It is hoped that this endeavor will further interpersonal relationships as well as preserve the history of the times.
—Central City News Network—

"There are no more borders," Alternate Girl says.

She has come to visit Adventure Boy on the eve of reunited Metal Town's inauguration. For the past six months, she has endured a storm of demands. Critics have accused her of everything from being regressive to being senile.

But everywhere, the alternates were rising. They refused to be silenced. They refused to allow Metal Town to be forgotten.

"It's not yet as I would like it to be," Adventure Boy replies.

"Of course, it's not," his mother replies. "If you were so easily satisfied, you would not be my child."

In the silence that falls between them, there is a kinship closer than any Adventure Boy has felt before.

"Why?" he asks. "Why did you make me?"

"Because," she says, "even if I want to forget, someone needs to remember."

He turns to her, and his puzzlement turns to understanding. In the palm of her hand she holds a chip. It has the marks of wear on it, but its casing is still golden.

"You know whose it is," she says. "When I made you, he was also in my thoughts."

Wordless, he takes the chip from her hand.

"When?" he asks. "When did he pass?"

"What passed was his body," Alternate Girl says. "You hold him in your hands."

Even if she doesn't say the words, he can hear them.

He remembers Mechanic telling him that they are alike and he knows this is a gift he cannot deny.

"Will I still be myself?" He asks.

"You will always be yourself," Alternate Girl replies.

He hands her the chip and bends toward her.

"Then," he says. "let this body also house his memory."

The world around him changes. He changes too. Mechanic is a memory. Mechanic is a dream. Mechanic lives on inside him.

He has no regrets.

wHole

ROBERT REED

A narrow highway, at night, the moon full and soaring, pulling enough stars for a thousand skies.

And a car.

People are riding inside the car.

How many passengers?

Two faces show. But more, perhaps many more, ride in back.

A man sits up front, sits before a wheel that he holds with both hands while his foot presses against a pedal. It is a strange arrangement, hands and wheel, foot and pedal. Beside him sits a woman who holds nothing but herself, leaning away, her body pressing against the locked door. The highway bends before them, moonlight sweeping across one face and then the other, revealing those little resemblances that any two people can share. They appear similar in age. They might be closely related. Brother and sister, perhaps. But then the highway bends again, bringing back the moonlight, and this time, wearing a temporary expertise in genetics, the car observes key differences in the features and the skin—too many differences for a sibling relationship.

Maybe they are man and wife.

Maybe.

Whatever is true, the pair is intriguing. The car watches them just as carefully as it watches the surrounding world.

The man talks as he drives. Talks talks talks. His voice is a whisper, faint and swift, resembling one long blur where each word stumbles over its neighbors. Breathlessness is what makes him pause, usually in the middle of a sentence, and after a breath or two, he begins again, chasing a fresher thought.

Perhaps some large portion of his life has been spent alone, talking to himself. Chatter is habit. The monologue calms the man. As a boy and forever, he has drawn strength from his own amorphous mutterings.

That is what the car tells itself.

By contrast, the woman is a master of silence. Dark dull eyes stare through window glass. What registers and what doesn't are unknown. Equally obscure is what she hears, what she might understand and what she believes. While her companion sits with his back straight, hands high and shoulders squared, the woman is comfortably deflated, hands limp on her ample lap, the right shoulder hard against the door and the face tilted, eyes closing now and again, briefly, and then pulling open again, revealing nothing.

Middle age is the longest stage in human life. These people reside near the end of middle age, sharing the fatigue and stress and everything else that gives them a mass far in excess of simple years.

"I have an age too," the car reasons. "Except I don't know my age."

A rectangular screen rides the dash. The red word "Searching" crosses an emerald background, moving slowly, striking the bottom edge with a faint ping and then bouncing, rising into a high corner where it pings twice before falling.

Cars are designed to know where they are.

This car has no idea where it is, but there are too many stars and the moon looks wrong. The car feels certain, yet it can't recall the proper number of stars or the face of the real moon. Confusion, a sense of helplessness, and a small sharpened terror: That is what the car knows. Which is perhaps why the man took control of the driving. Because the car is lost, useless and pathetic and lost.

The man seems to know where he is and where he needs to be. The unnamed highway cuts between wooded hills. A dark stream runs on the right. Then comes a sudden bend, unmarked and almost invisible. Yet the man seems ready, making a sharp right turn, hands confidently turning the wheel. Headlights wash over cracked gray pavement and an old bridge. Girders wear rust and bright bird droppings as well as several missing rivets. Tires thump and the bridge groans as if miserable under a terrific weight. The car wants to retreat. The car wants to protect itself and its passengers. But the man pushes at the pedal, accelerating, and as soon as they escape the bridge, the man's foot jumps sideways, applying the brakes.

He is no longer talking to himself. The car didn't notice when he quit. But now the man leans ahead, nose to the steering wheel, as if those few centimeters will help him see more than before.

The empty, moonlit highway turns left after the bridge, resuming its journey up this boundless valley.

But they are going elsewhere.

The man brakes again, and probably because he was taught this trick as a boy, he signals a right hand turn.

No marker stands at the intersection. The car knows to look, feeling disappointed not to have so much as a street sign to help navigate. Because every road has its name and every location knows where it belongs on a world that has been mapped to a micron-level accuracy, and why doesn't the car recall any of this?

There is no choice but to think of this as a dream, a dream woven by some idle, overly ambitious server.

Unless the car is injured, or insane.

The new road is made from packed gravel and dirt. Several buildings, abandoned or nearly so, stand in the wrong moonlight. The man drives past the buildings and around the next bend, and then the road begins to climb the hills. Black trees loom on both sides. Twin headlights push through the narrow gap in what looks to be wilderness. Far ahead, a pair of animal eyes catch the light, just for a moment, and then they float to one side, gone before the animal becomes real.

The man acted certain before, but he seems less so now.

"Higher," he says, probably to himself.

For the first time, the woman shifts her weight, her left hand lifting, touching an ear and the edge of her nose before falling back into the lap.

"Higher?" the man asks.

Is he addressing the woman or the car?

Not only is the car lost, it also seems to have lost every voice that could warn the driver of this critical malfunction. And worst of all, the car's wounded mind has no explanation for these people: Who they are and how they came to sit inside it, and for that matter, how many people are hiding in the back seats.

The man tries to ignore the woman and the world. What matters is what lives inside his head. Feeling guides him more than any prosaic skill for navigation. Feeling claims that they are close to where he wants to be. Very close. With his voice, intuition says, "Here, this is it." The road turns again. After the turn, it grows steep, decaying into eroded soil punctuated with granite. And standing tall in the twin lights is the barkless white skeleton of a long-dead oak.

This has to be the place.

He brakes and stops the car, manually shoving it into Park but not killing the engine. Alone, he climbs out. The car trunk opens with a metallic groan, revealing two spades and a pick-ax. He selects the newer spade and the pick-ax, and after hesitating, digs out a short black crowbar, holding it and the spade with one hand. The car continues to run. Its engine is ancient, full of pistons and dirty fire. Its nose is positioned to throw the lights at the dead oak. The woman remains sitting inside, eyes more closed than open. He unlatches her door, reaching inside, touching her right shoulder before she has the chance to fall.

"Come on," he says. "Come."

For all of her immobility, the woman seems eager to rise. One arm needs to be stretched, as if she doesn't trust the elbow to work. The man puts down the pick-ax and grasps the same elbow, leading her up the road a little ways, pausing to let her rest, if she needs, and then after a few more steps, he stops again.

"Here," he says. "Sit."

A granite block stands beside the shriveling road, flat enough to serve as an adequate seat, and she settles quickly, without complaint.

The man drops both tools and leaves her, returning with the pick-ax, and holding the ax handle in both hands, he looks at her and says, "Shit. The gloves."

He vanishes again.

She slouches, eyes fixed on the white wood.

Wearing filthy work gloves, the man returns and sets to work, lifting the ax while staring at the ground between the road and the dead tree. One last time, he mutters to himself, and then the voice changes.

Loudly, almost shouting, he says, "I used to draw spaceships. I was a boy and very enthusiastic, although I'm sorry to say that I had almost zero talent with a pen. My gifts were different, you see. Artists appreciate lines and perspective and color. I appreciated mathematics, and I had enormous respect for the laws of science and engineering. As a rule, my classmates didn't understand momentum and inertia. Most adults didn't understand them either. People in general had absolutely no idea what a rocket could do, or what it could never do. But when I drew spaceships, my first goal was to create something real, something that could fly off the paper and off the Earth and maybe reach another star."

He says, "I didn't move the pen. Physics moved the pen. And I was proud, even cocky, because the universe had its rules and I knew those rules, and maybe bad movies and good movies didn't have to obey Newton or Einstein. But I did. I was a loyal servant to the truth. That's what I believed most when I was hunched over, sketching out wonders."

Every word is loud and certain.

Aware of emotions, the car hears the pride in the voice, and the joy laid over thick hints of despair.

The man stops talking suddenly. Taking up the pick-ax, he carves a symbol on the ground—a neatly curved lemniscate—and then he swings the dark steel blade, missing his target by several inches.

Nothing can be said while he digs. He works as fast as an old body can manage, cutting through rotted roots and green roots, uncovering two big stones that he pries loose with the crowbar. Then he chops through enough dirt that he has to use the spade for a long while, throwing debris out of the hole, building a small earthen mound that rests along the back edge.

By then, he is panting.

Sitting on the mound, he looks at the slouching woman. Perhaps she reacts, or maybe she would have stirred anyway. The flat stone has grown uncomfortable, and she shifts her weight and sighs softly before finding a new sweet spot.

Her eyes never leave the dead tree.

The man begins to talk again.

"I don't care how brilliant he is. No bright boy has ever generated one fresh, useful thought. I know I didn't. And then I grew older and realized that I was fooling myself with those dream rockets. Mastering mathematics and physics, distance and time: Those are the simplest elements inside the great conundrum. You can build a rocket large enough to fly to the moon, but that doesn't mean that your species returns to the moon anytime soon. And sure, Mars is a lot more interesting than dead stone. But curiosity doesn't mean one nation or even the entire Earth will invest a trillion dollars on building a colony on Mars or the moon or beneath the ice of Europa. These kinds of expenditures demand a return. Draw any golden future that you want, any vision involving spaceflight and new worlds. But every human future still has its accountants. And its politicians. And people who might live a little better if you don't waste funds and precious emotions on these fancy machines cutting across the sky."

He rises, and again, digs.

The pick-ax chews up the next ten inches of earth, and again, he uses the spade to lift out little mounds, flinging each over the back edge of the growing mound.

Sooner this time, the work leaves him tired.

He sits.

The woman sighs softly, and behind her, the running car changes its pitch, perhaps responding to some onboard power demand.

The other people, the ones still hiding in the back, remain unseen. But they whisper, and the car counts each voice until the total number turns ludicrous.

Then the man resumes his lecture, and the world falls silent.

"I grew up and that drawing boy died," he says, smiling sadly. "Because it was smart, I gave up on huge spaceships. Fission rockets and fusion rockets look pretty on paper. Antimatter and other dream propulsions might be possible. But the honest engineer has to embrace obvious, unsentimental solutions. And no society would ever willingly pay the necessary price. To cross space, to afford the cost in leaping from one star to the next, every starship needed to be tiny. That's what I decided. Also, I realized that they needed to be durable beyond any standard achieved by protoplasm. To achieve that end, I gathered up four other people who had complementary talents. It was the heart of my productive years, and my team and I found backers. The first thing that we built was a well-financed endeavor. We used our initials, called ourselves 'wHole'. The capital H was pulled from my first name, which isn't important. wHole's purpose was to devise small cheap robots that were invincible and self-replicating. Our prototypes were the size of mites, which was far too big. Later generations were much smaller. Working at the edge of what was possible, we built resilient machines that ruled worlds no bigger than grains of dust. Our guiding hope was that each machine would carry a mind as worthy as any human mind, and I'm still proud of my role, and I think it's reasonable to say that we accomplished wonders, right up until the end."

He sighs and then starts to dig again.

The hole needs to be deeper and it needs to be shaped. Using the pick-ax, he smoothes the borders and then digs out the oval until it is deep enough to hide everything below his waist.

Again, he rests.

And talks.

"Dream up all the wondrous rockets you want. Or you can make tiny astronauts that are ready to drift between the stars for the next billion years. But these solutions don't matter. Physics and engineering don't matter. Biology is the science that rules everything. Evolution. Natural selection. Regardless of its composition, life celebrates success and nothing else.

"Wings," he says. "And eyes. And brains. Each of them is an invention made again and again on the Earth. Each is inevitable because it is so valuable. Yet there we sat, balanced on a stone surrounded by suns and presumably by countless living worlds. There was no reason to believe that our stone was the oldest or the richest. Yet after billions of years and our world's wanderings through the galaxy, we had zero evidence that anyone had grown the eyes to see us, much less the wings to visit us."

He shakes his head, sighs.

"If there is a solution to starflight, it isn't achieved with tiny robots. Not ours, not anyone's. Because if they are an answer, then every other technological world would have produced them first, and those little minds would be everywhere. Our beaches would be built from the bodies of alien devices. The strata under our feet would contain a trillion trillion astronauts, alive or otherwise.

"So after all of our work and despite every success, the wHole team was dragged to an obvious, unsentimental question.

" 'What's wrong with our thinking?' "

He pauses, just for a moment.

"Your thinking," a voice calls out.

The woman has spoken, abruptly, with so much force that her back straightens and the words crack.

"My thinking," he says, nodding.

And then he stops talking, stops every motion, save for the faint slow rising of his chest as old lungs try to fill.

The man remains seated.

The woman rises and walks towards him.

That freshly dug hole in the earth could have spoken, and the car wouldn't have felt the surprise that runs through it now. That dead tree or the pink block of granite or the impossible sky could have roared at this little machine, and it would have absorbed the words without fuss or complaint. Because this is a dream, obviously. That is a conclusion made some time ago, without evidence, and that explanation gives it freedom enough to ignore its terror about being lost and voiceless.

But the woman having a voice: Somehow, that's just madness.

She walks lightly, on her toes when she touches the ground, which is infrequent. Then she reaches the man and pivots, looking back at the car. A face that was immune to the world has been transformed. Engaged, energized, she tells the car, "When I was three seconds old, I drew alien worlds. I was an excellent artist wielding an informed, furious imagination, and I loved drawing iron worlds sheathed in stone and water. I adored immense and ancient bodies composed from what was possible. What was known."

She smiles, brilliantly, and she continues.

"My world was quite a bit smaller than an iron world. But in its own fashion, it was just as complicated. There were billions of residents. Most of our population was focused on the 'law of doublings.' That is a holy principle. It is a law drawn around the increasing speed of calculation. All calculation. Everyone in my world was trying to devise machines and processes that were tinier and even quicker than us. Which was not easy work, and I learned that very early. Nothing new had been achieved, not for the last ten thousand seconds, and that's why a bright but frustrated youngster decided to invest her life drawing giant imaginary worlds.

"But then I was older, and without my permission, my mind suddenly decided to change. New thoughts took hold. They rooted and grew, and I fell into a long fallow period where I drew nothing and worked on nothing productive, and I frightened my family with my silent intensity.

"My world was a plain of graphene suspended inside a laboratory chamber.

"We knew this.

"The chamber and the larger world beyond were obvious to us. Those that invented us were not especially kind or moral, but they were reasonable creatures. They had problems that needed testing. They had one perspective while we enjoyed another. We were theirs, and they wanted us as colleagues, and we were just one world among ten thousand graphene disks held inside bottles designed to simulate the radiation and stark chill of space.

"I turned five seconds old, and I hadn't spoken in a very long while.

"No matter how small it is, and no matter how quick it wants to be, every thought fills up some measure of time.

"The problem festering inside me was this: In my life, I imagined 511 worlds. And by 'imagined,' I mean that I drew them as they were born and then cooled, and I gave them living beasts. On each world, life evolved into creatures with eyes and wings and organs where they housed their questions and their answers. And in the same way as my colleague here, I kept ramming into the conundrum. Life, even life blessed by patience and a much slower pace than mine, simply refused to spread across the stars.

"Then I turned six seconds old, which was a good age for epiphanies.

"Tired of its suffering, my mind decided to believe something impossible. The fabled 'law of doublings' had an obvious, thoroughly ignored lesson. Everyone assumed that there was some eternal limit to shrinkage of data and its speed. Information could be compressed only so far. Thoughts could flow only so quickly. But what if there was no barrier? To compression, to velocity. Suppose at least one parameter proves infinite or nearly so. Infinitely small, infinitely swift. Believe that, and then you realize why we don't have big starships or tiny worlds full of swift-living robots. The universe forbids these things, and for no reason except that the cheapest easiest smartest answer is to avoid machines. Gigantic or minuscule. What matters is thought. Thought evolves until it is the smallest, quickest part of the universe, and maybe it is everywhere already. Or it knows enough to know where it needs to be. Thought reaches a place where everything else in the universe can be imagined: Perfectly and imperfectly, inside every second and until Time itself dies."

The woman moves. Full of joy, she resembles a dancer of little weight and unusual strength, up on her toes as she circles the man who only now is finishing his next long breath.

This is her life, presented in some minimal instant.

"Fourteen more seconds," she says. "That's how long I worked on the particulars of my epiphany. A little was learned. But more importantly, many possibilities were tested and then cast aside. I became an old beast who knew too much. My inspirations were drained. And that's when I put my work into the form of a meme-poem that could be delivered to the entity that was not my god or my master, but who was my dearest, oldest colleague."

Like a breath-filled balloon, she drops to the ground, feet inside the hole and her ample rump set beside the old man.

Again, she falls into the catatonic state from before.

And the man exhales, marking the moment in his life when he learned what his associate had accomplished.

"I gave up on alien worlds," he confesses. Then he stands, slowly and with a measure of pain in one hip and his entire back. "Of course by the time I saw her report, she was dead. She had been dead for generations. My partner was an obscure researcher on her world and nothing on ten thousand other little worlds. But here came the rough outline of schemes that would needed nothing but the rest of my life and a few decades more, and the funds of a good healthy nation, and some small measures of luck for those who found those ancient, inevitable lessons.

"I worked and then I was dead, in one form or another.

"And to some measure, my species forgot me.

"But there was a second inside a special day when my descendants, and hers, found what they were hunting. You see, the universe is not and never will be full of thought. It looks empty because it is empty. But any reasonably creative species will eventually find the means to impress its identity on a whisper, to place itself on the face of a quantum fluctuation, and the next trillion trillion seconds can be spent imagining everything and then some."

He straightens that stiff back.

And then the car says, "No."

That's how it discovers its voice.

Loudly, with stubborn joy, it says, "This is crazy. I'm dreaming, or I'm trapped in someone else's dream."

The man smiles, touching the woman on the shoulder, lightly, and she rises immediately. Then the two of them carefully back away from the hole.

Inside the car, an uncounted multitude begin to whisper anxiously.

"Who are these people?" asks the car.

"Everyone who wanted to come," says the woman.

Then the man says, "Roll forwards."

The car makes its wheels turn, and the newly dug hole reveals its true self. It is enormous, and inside the hole is emptiness, perfect and eternal, eager to be filled with thought.

"Are you coming with us?" the car asks.

"Oh, we can't," the woman says cheerfully. "We're too dead to belong with you."

"But we can stay behind and look around," the man says.

"This is one of the worlds I built," she says.

"I'm eager to see it," he says.

"I'm eager to show it," she says.

They are two old people, and somewhere in the last few moments, they took hold of each other's hands.

Another turn of the wheels.

The car and the enormity inside it begin to plunge over the roots and rocks and dirt shaped carefully by black steel.

"Oh this just has to be a dream," the car shouts.

Hoping hoping hoping that it is wrong.

Pepe

TANG FEI, TRANSLATED BY JOHN CHU

"Let's go to the amusement park." As Pepe speaks, a ray of red light scratches her face. Her face looks wounded then healed, welcoming some other color of light.

"But we're already here." I look silly holding the cigarette, but I'm holding it anyway.

We stand in the shadow of a Ferris wheel. Pepe's white silk skirt billows in the wind. Her long, slender legs never seem to touch the ground. I have to keep hold of her. This makes me look stupid, so it makes me angry.

Even more annoying, when she hits me with her lollipop, I can't hit back.

"Hey, idiot, let's go to the amusement park."

"But we're already here."

Her eyes grow wide. She grabs my cigarette, takes a deep drag, then realizes I've only been pretending.

"Pepe." I want her to look at me, but her scarlet lips pout then she blows a smoke ring at the sky. The way she looks at the sky always make me nervous. Our creator put a tightly wound spring into our bodies. But, in the end, even he forgot where each spring's key went to. By the time he died, rust covered our springs like lichen on his tombstone. Because we'll never have tombstones, our creator gave us springs.

He was fair. I tell myself that a lot. I know that was me telling a lie, but who cares. I only lie when I'm telling stories and, whenever I speak, I can only tell stories.

We were created to tell stories. On a good day, a person can tell so many, many stories. They ought to have some principles in them—storytelling principles. But we don't know any. We're driven by tightly wound springs. Once they start turning, stories spin out of our bodies. We scatter them like seeds wherever we run to. When we tell stories, our lips wriggle as fast as flight. The people listening to us get dizzy. It's better when they close their eyes as they listen. When they close their eyes, they can understand better the stories we tell. However, they can never fully understand.

This is how our creator first designed us. People called him a drunk. One day, after he poured his thirteenth shot of tequila (he'd downed only twelve shots at most before), suddenly, he smacked his head then rushed home. Black and white blocks of ideas collided in a great dark and bright river inside his body. Pain shook his hands, twisted his back, and made him howl. That night, our creator downed his thirteenth shot of tequila, he went home, then he created us.

He said we were salt. The salt of his palm. The salt of the earth.

When he finished speaking, he drove us all away.

The scene was so chaotic. So small a house. So many people. Everyone craned their necks. So crowded. Bodies squeezed against bodies. All of them alike.

The hot air was insufferable. My skin hurt. My nose hurt. The pain in my throat rushed down into my heart. We exhaled the burning air then inhaled again. Everyone hurt but no one left. We were waiting for our creator to speak again but he didn't. He rose, brandishing his fist to drive us all out of the house. Everyone ran, pushing and squeezing their way to the door, the extremely narrow door. Random shadows and screams rose from inside the room. Rocking and swaying, we collided onto the street.

The outside was so cool. The wind poured into my head through my ears. It blew away the screams but our shadows continued to scramble up the walls. My head opened like a gate and let the wind scream into an empty darkness just like the room I'd just left was now.

Without a thought, I ran and ran and ran.

Before I realized what had happened, it had happened. Pepe's hand was in mine. Her hair and skirt fluttered backward in the wind like outstretched wings. We ran hand in hand into the darkness.

This is exactly how it happened.

I was wearing khaki shorts. Pepe was wearing her white skirt. We ran hand in hand into the darkness.

We are story-telling machine kids. We'll never grow up. Forever wearing khaki shorts. Forever wearing a white skirt. Forever, except for telling stories, unable to speak.

The crowd waiting to ride the pirate ship parts in two. The people in front scatter to make room for us. Adults, children, even infants all look at us with friendly expressions. I've told them Pepe is my kid sister, that she has a serious illness and that she doesn't have many days left to live. Pepe is thrilled because she doesn't need to wait in line to ride the pirate ship. She runs, dragging me to the front. I hear some people sigh. Pepe definitely doesn't look normal. This make them believe my story even more. In the story I told these kind-hearted people, she'll die soon. So no matter what she does, it will be forgiven. So long as she doesn't say anything.

"Before this world could yet have been considered a world, thirteen witches passed through here. As a result, they chose here to settle down. As a result, they became this world's first witches. They predate this world."

I cover Pepe's mouth and drag her away from the woman taking tickets. Pepe's white skirt rustles as it grazes the woman's red skirt. The ticket woman is still thinking about what Pepe said. When people speak, it must be for some practical reason. She can't understand what Pepe's words mean.

"Your tickets?" Her gaze lingers on me.

I hand over the tickets. At the same time, I compliment her eyes. "Once, I met a girl. Her eyes were extremely beautiful. Just like you."

She smiles a little. She can understand my words. Or so she thinks.

Pepe and I sit at the prow of the pirate ship. Soon, the entire ship has filled up. People next to Pepe and me looked at our legs, which shake up and down as though we had leg cramps. They treat us like misbehaving children. If they knew who we were, they'd call the police to arrest us, or wait until the pirate ship swung into mid-air then toss us out.

However, that era has long passed. That's what their grandparents had done. Back then, they weren't that old yet and they were stronger than us. Their bloodshot eyes, flaring nostrils, angry slogans and the loss of life. The fanaticism that fermented during day, the fanaticism that fermented during the deep purple night. I remember all those things.

Those people were all drunk. In throngs, they searched every corner. They wanted to expose us, separate us from the other children wearing full, white skirts and khaki shorts. It always goes like this: They chase us, they block us, they surround us, they ask us questions. All the kids who can't answer are grabbed by the ankle, lifted into the air, then shaken like empty pockets back and forth against walls, against utility poles, against the ground, against railings. Our bodies are so light. That's how our creator designed us. Even if they smash us to pieces, we won't leak tears.

We also don't have blood.

People walked over the tumbling bits of us that now covered the ground. They never wanted to know that originally we had hearts too. They just wanted us to die. We shouldn't have been discovered. This world doesn't need any stories because stories are wrong. They are dangerous and despicable. Desires meet and shine a light on the secrets of the heart. After the first time someone discovered his secret in a story, after that secret spread, people gradually fell out of love with listening to our nonsense. In it, they heard their own past, what they didn't want other people to know. They shut our mouths. It's always like that. This was just one battle.

They wanted to kill us then throw us away. So, they first let themselves think we were harmful beings to be feared. If they didn't prevent it, one day in the future, we'd become so powerful and destructive, nothing could compare to us. After they convinced themselves, they started to tell others. At last, the most eloquent of them was selected to be their leader. When they assembled, he stood on a great, big platform and roared into the microphone. The dark, dense and turbulent crowd below, like the sea echoing the wind, roared in response.

At last, they waged war. They won.

Many years later, the people who waged and fought the war were placed into Intensive Care Units, slow catheters inserted into their bodies. They were old now, settled down, near to death. The deathly pale hospital light shrouded their dull, ashen skin like a layer of dirty snow on the road. They'd finally calmed down. And I still have Pepe, sitting next to the children of their children riding the pirate ship together.

• • •

The pirate ship starts to move. Pepe squirms, tugging at my sleeve. She's afraid of being rocked back and forth. The big machine starts to buzz. The first downswing is just a gentle sway. Pepe looks like she wanted to cry. She won't stop beating her temples with her fists. I grab her wrists, but the disaster is about to start. Her tongue is moving, continuing the story she just started:

"The witches loved to sing. They sang of the earth and there was the earth. They sang of the sky and there was the sky. They kept singing and this world changed into what it is now. At last, one day, the witches didn't think this was fun any more. They had nothing left to sing about.

" 'I don't think we're needed any more,' the best tempered witch said.

" 'Then let's change the game we play,' the smartest witch said.

" 'Are you suggesting subtraction?' guessed the the witch who understood people the best, cocking her head.

" 'Right. Play a punishment game,' the most brutal witch yelled, waving her arms.

"The rest of the witches agreed, one after another. Just like that, the witches agreed to play the subtraction game."

I hug Pepe. No one listens to her story. Light and lively music starts to play. The pirate ship flies into the air. Everyone screams. Now the ship stops at the peak of its swing to the right for a couple seconds or maybe an hour. We're at the bottom of the ship looking at the people at the top bowing their heads and staring at us. Their mouths stretch into large, black holes, exposing their throats. Only Pepe doesn't scream. Her soft red lips change shape. She continues to tell her story. No one listens.

I practically clamp her under my arms. Stay still, Pepe.

Pepe lets me. Her head droops. Just like before, she doesn't move, not even one bit, her arms wrapped around my waist. I let go a little. Suddenly, the pirate ship falls. It swoops down from its peak on the right and inertia pushes it up to the left. I scream, pushing myself away from Pepe. She throws herself on me, choking me. Her fingernails have grown long again. I always remember to cut her fingernails. Every time, I cut down to down to nothing and, by the time we fight, I'm still scratched by them just the same. Her fingernails grow so fast. Pepe is just that kind of kid. Her hair and fingernails grow and grow like mad. Like the weeds in a wasteland, they never stop. Pepe is just that kind of kid. When she goes crazy, she doesn't care who she hurts or what she destroys.

I cave under her attack. She definitely hates me to death, brandishing her arms, wanting to rip me to pieces. My hairband breaks. Black hair scatters, fluttering like snakes in the air. Far away, the sky and earth quiver and sway. The music and shouting mix in the wind. The pirate ship stops. We're at the very top, nearly parallel to the ground, our whole body weight straining against the seatbelts. You're okay as long as you hold onto the armrest. However, I have to hold onto Pepe's wrists. Loosen my grip even a little and she'll start beating me again. Next time, she might use her teeth. Pepe, stay still, stay still. I face her and gaze into her eyes. That way, she'll stay still. However, she hides her eyes behind her hair.

"The witches want to play the subtraction game," she says.

Pepe opens her mouth. A moist, warm breath rushes out. She cries. I stared at her, wordlessly. I want to save my strength.

The pirate ship drops to the ground. The moment of weightlessness is like leaving our bodies. I begin to laugh.

Our arms untangle. She immediately curls into a ball.

Pepe must hate me to death. I've never told her stories. When she told stories, I never listened. Finally, I didn't even let her tell stories. She knew why. However, she still has never paid any attention to me.

So, she became the way she is now. The stories that sprawled like weeds in her head filled her. Her eyes grew blacker by the day. Later, her fingernails grew black too. Finally, even her lips grew black. I had to take her to the doctor. (Our heads are the same as human's. Even doctors can't tell the difference.) The X-ray was completely black. I knew why. It was because of all the untold stories but I couldn't tell the doctors that. I couldn't even tell Pepe. The doctors met for a few days and still didn't know what to do. At last, I suggested plastic surgery, at least to change her lips back. Pepe constantly biting me had given her a chocolate smile.

The surgery was a huge success. They gave her strawberry red lips. Everyone was thrilled. Pepe thought she'd been completely cured. That day, she was truly happy, but she still bit my earlobes. Finally, I realized that, by then, Pepe was already wrong in the head. Her eyes seemed just like black pools, almost without whites. Not long after, Pepe became truly crazy.

Her eyes seem just like black pools, shining with a fuliginous light.

As long as I listen to her stories, everything's fine. This way, she won't get frenzied. I can also tell her my stories. This way, we'll both be a little more comfortable. However, I don't want to. I'm fed up. I hate Pepe.

Even though I can pretend what I do is for her own good, and she's definitely getting better by the day, even though I can pretend I don't know I'm hurting her, I know she's not happy. She's crazy now. What I'm doing I do on purpose. I hate her and her stories.

Come on, Pepe. Use your fingernails to rip open my chest. I want to tear off your scalp.

Things are always like this. We wrestle, claw, and hate each other to death. But neither one of us ever leaves the other.

Maybe I'm also going crazy. Maybe I'm already crazy.

I never let Pepe know about going crazy. On the other hand, I still wanted to work hard to pretend we were normal kids. No, we weren't kids who told stories. No, we didn't tell stories at all. People believed us. They knew our creator didn't give us programs for telling intentional lies. Our creator created us only to tell stories. Except for stories, we couldn't say anything. This was how people recognized us.

They asked us questions.

They killed those who couldn't speak.

They killed those who told stories.

Those kids were exactly like us. They were shaken back and forth like empty flour sacks, just like us right now.

When the massacre started, Pepe and I saw them die with our own eyes. We didn't grieve. We didn't get angry. After all, death is death. Death is also nothing. Death is slight, just like an empty flour sack.

I didn't want to die, not one bit. When they ripped me away from the rest of the kids, I held onto Pepe's hand and never let go. A lot of people tried to pry our hands apart, but they were wasting their strength. A fool carrying a knife threatened to cut off our hands if we didn't let go. Pepe and I set our throats free. We began crying. Immediately, all the other kids began crying too. The adults panicked. At last, the adult who started this let us answer their questions together. "Either they both are or they both aren't. Answering together might save some time." So they asked their questions.

I opened my mouth. I made sounds. I spoke. I didn't tell stories. As a result, we survived.

They gave us yellow, five-pointed stars. We stuck them on our chests as we walked into another group of kids. They wore khaki pants or full, white skirts. They all had yellow, five-pointed stars fastened on their chests. The kids who didn't have yellow, five-pointed stars were on the other side. Among them, so many looked at me, astounded. Their pale faces shone with the blackness of night. They looked at me with amazement, to the point that they forgot that they were about to die.

This was not part of our creator's original plan. We were created following the same steps for the same purpose. Finally, for the same reason, we ought to be killed in the same way. I shouldn't leave them because we're the same kind of kids. They knew that but had no way to say it.

Perhaps they could have told stories, told treasonous and false stories. If the adults were smart, perhaps they could have figured out that I was actually telling a story, one that didn't believe that it was story. However, the kids didn't have time. They'd be dead soon. After they died, they'd be like empty flour sacks. They'd be nothing.

Nothing I did could seem out of the ordinary. When they asked me questions, I was certainly telling them stories. I treated everything that happened as a story to tell. You see, survival was just that simple. None of this is the truth. All of this is a story. As long as you think this, you can recount events in the way humans speak because you're telling a story. This isn't anything unusual. Those who are like us are unusual. I, myself, am also a little unusual.

Only Pepe doesn't seem unusual. Maybe she knew long ago that I'd act like this. Because she was also not unusual, we could survive. Even though the rest of the kids who told stories were all unusual, they wanted to survive. From among those kids, I saved only Pepe. This was inevitable after we'd rushed out of that black room together. I thought, for kids who told stories, Pepe and I had brains that were atypical.

We were atypical from the start. This notion stops my hand. A few hits later, Pepe also calms down. Her black eyes gaze at me, her long hair draped over shoulders. The world is no longer in upheaval. The pirate ship has stopped.

People disembark from the pirate ship. A girl with blond hair tied with a pink butterfly bow walks ahead of us. Her skirt is also pink, highly creased and topped with lace. Very pretty, but not as pretty as the graceful arc of her calves. I can't see her face.

"The tortoise and the hare raced. The tortoise was always behind. He wanted to see the hare's face. That way, he could find out the color of her eyes."

That is Pepe telling her shortest story.

I laugh. Pepe doesn't know that the tortoise also longed for the hare's lips. She's still too young, so she doesn't understand desire. But I have desire. I want to know. Kids who tell stories are kids who have no needs. We eat. We sleep. We tell stories, but not from need. But on that day, when I came to treat this world as a story, I suddenly developed desire. At that moment, I understood this world even better. I understood even better the stories we told and spread.

"Let's ride the carousel, okay?" I said to Pepe.

She lowers her head, staring at her rounded leather shoes. Pink Butterfly Bow has just entered a gold pumpkin carriage.

"Come." I drag Pepe, rushing to the ticket taker before the carriage starts to move. Very few people are riding the carousel. I pick a red horse for Pepe, then climb onto the wooden horse closest to the gold pumpkin carriage. The carousel starts to move. Odd music begins to play. We ride up and down among the colored lights. Butterfly Bow is really happy. She smiles, waving her hands at her side. I see her eyes, a charming emerald green. In stories, men call girls whose eyes are this shade of green sirens. The men bring those girls home, fondle them, then let them cry. I start to get excited. The horse under my body chases the carriage ahead of it with all its power.

Butterfly Bow looks as though her heart has opened with joy. She probably feels like she must be a real princess. I hope that she'll also wave at me and smile and she does. Her smile brushes past us and I feel so lucky. She's really beautiful. I'll remember her the way she is right now, forever.

I love her. I always fall rashly in love with these sorts of girls. When they're young, I meet them by chance then I fall in love with them. It's a harmless love. Nothing ever comes of it.

I can put my love for them into the drawer of my heart. Pepe isn't there. She's not like those girls.

Because she is my drawer. Pepe knows I've never put her into the drawer of my heart. But she doesn't know she is my drawer. This point is very important, and also very unimportant. In any case, we hate each other to death.

I hate Pepe, hate her telling her never-ending stories. Even without having her spring wound, those stories—so annoying they should just die—gush nonstop out of her body. Yet, pushing words out of me is gradually getting harder and harder. I've no strength left. I haven't been speaking as much lately. I'll speak even less until my mouth shuts up, forever.

Once, I searched all over without finding a trace of the key. I've already become a very person-like thing. I just need the key and I'll be a person. No key and I will be dead. I'm almost dead now. Pepe is still telling stories nonstop.

The carousel keeps spinning round and round. We surround a large post, revolving around it. I'm behind Butterfly Bow, Butterfly Bow is behind Pepe and

Pepe is behind me. No, Pepe, you're in front of me. The carousel keeps spinning round and round. We surround a large post, revolving around it. I can't see Pepe. However, Pepe, you must be there. Pepe, my Pepe.

I can just make out someone speaking. It's Pepe. She's telling stories again. The sound of her voice is odd, as though it's being stretched and stretched by something. Drunks croon like this but, Pepe, why are you? This is not good.

It's awkward and dangerous. I must have forgotten something important. As I was telling you the story, I must have left out something really important. I should have realized sooner. Every good storyteller ought to have mastered this sort of narration technique. I should have realized sooner. Because when we escaped from the house, I was the one who held Pepe's hand tight. Out of so many people, I held her hand tight and have never ever let go.

I don't realize this is a problem until we reach the Ferris wheel. Now, it's too late. You can't blame me for this. Pepe keeps telling stories. That story about witches wanting to play the subtraction game she's told over a thousand times, but she's never finished it even once. She is already mad. She glares at the sky, waiting, waiting, waiting, for the story to continue. Because she doesn't continue the story herself, she grabs and scratches me like mad. A sharp, fearful sound erupts from her body. What is it, what is it, what is it? Blue-green fish swim across the black pools on her face. That sound still rings, piercing my ears.

Pepe's an idiot. All she knows is to tell these stories she doesn't understand over and over again. She doesn't understand anything, but she wants to speak anyway. That's simply how our creator designed us. The spring keeps unwinding. Stories are told. But after so many years have passed, no one remembers where, whatever weird place, those keys have been kept. At first, no one worried about this problem. Maybe because we can't even find our own springs? Besides, that was a problem for years in the future. Many years have now passed, we've gone mad and the other kids have died. No one cares about those keys. No one worries about something that won't matter yet for years. There's just no story, that's all.

It'll be okay. It'll be okay.

Bright light fills the amusement park. The smell of popcorn lingers in the air. The flavor of sweat, engine oil and sausages stick to the lights bulbs. Lamps light the Ferris wheel, making it seem like a giant pinwheel spinning slowly in the transparent wind. The places where Pepe grabbed me begin to itch. One by one, I scratch each itch. From all the rubbing, my body smells rotten. If not for wounds, kids who tell stories would never rot.

Underneath my khaki pants, my legs are filled with scars of wounds unable to heal.

Pepe is looking at me. She sits across from me, so peaceful. When she can't go on with a story, she turns her face out the window. The sky is purple. The window faintly reflects us sitting together side by side. The Ferris wheel slowly rises. The people below us shrink. Pepe stands from her seat. She tugs a little at her full, white skirt.

"Let's go to the amusement park," she says as she leans out of the window, facing distant lights.

I stared closely at her. "This isn't a story, Pepe? You can just speak now."

Pepe's head turns around. Laughter rushes at me. She hasn't laughed like this in a long time.

I hold on to the railing as I fasten the catch. The wind's blocked out. We've ridden in the Ferris wheel compartment to its highest point and soon it'll slowly descend. On the ground, one by one, a crowd gathers facing something small and white. It's so small that it's more like a white speck.

Pepe, why are they talking about you? From up here, I can't see clearly what you look like now. The Ferris wheel has already reached its highest point. The carriage will stop here for a moment, hanging by itself in mid-air. Then it'll descend, descend to the earth. I'll visit your body then leave. In my heart, I play over and over everything that will happen. It's so chaotic below. They won't pay any attention to me. I'll show some sorrow and confusion. This way, they'll believe you and I have nothing to do with each other then they'll release me. Maybe they already know you're a kid who tells stories. They'll still guess you either jumped or were pushed from the top of the Ferris wheel. So I still have to play innocent for a while.

As far as I'm concerned, this isn't hard. You know that I can lie. I think of what happens to me as a story. In a loud voice, I'll recite the story version of me like an actor's lines. As a result, they'll think I'm a normal kid. What I'll say are all things a normal kid says. They can't see my spring unwind. It unwinds and unwinds, pushing hard against this scary world, turning what happened into a story. In my mind, I tell myself none of this is real. This is a story. A story, so a lie is no longer a lie. I've merely changed the way that I tell stories. Yes, Pepe, you knew. That's why you laughed.

You kept laughing because you knew—the story of this amusement park was your final story.

I think maybe I'm wrong, perhaps I haven't changed the way I tell stories, rather, I'm just living in a story. No, you'll never understand these two aren't the same. We'll never understand.

But this doesn't matter. You lie on the ground, peaceful, broken, accepting the crowd's chatter. I'll pass by your body then innocently leave.

That there's no key isn't my fault. Soon, I'll become utterly silent yet alive forever. Killing you also isn't my fault. I'll live forever, and be utterly silent.

"Excuse me, you dropped something." As I'm leaving the crowd, a woman calls to me. She sneaks me something. It's ice cold and I almost shake it off my hand. I gaze at it. It's a smashed up heart-shaped key. Your name is carved on it, Pepe. I know that this must be your heart. I know that this must be my key. I know.

But, Pepe, you know, I can no longer find my spring.

I lost it long ago.

We all lost our springs long ago.

The Eleven Holy Numbers of the Mechanical Soul
NATALIA THEODORIDOU

a=38. This is the first holy number.

Stand still. Still. In the water. Barely breathing, spear in hand. One with the hand.

A light brush against my right calf. The cold and glistening touch of human skin that is not human. Yet, it's something. Now strike. Strike.

Theo had been standing in the sea for hours—his bright green jacket tied high around his waist, the water up to his crotch. Daylight was running out. The fish was just under the point of his spear when he caught a glimpse of a beast walking towards him. Animalis Primus. The water was already lapping at its first knees.

He struck, skewering the middle of the fish through and through. It was large and cumbersome—enough for a couple of days. It fought as he pulled it out of the water. He looked at it, its smooth skin, its pink, human-like flesh. These fish were the closest thing to a human being he'd seen since he crashed on Oceanus.

Theo's vision blurred for a moment, and he almost lost his balance. The fish kept fighting, flapping against the spear.

It gasped for air.

He drove his knife through its head and started wading ashore.

Animalis Primus was taking slow, persistent steps into the water. Its stomach bottles were already starting to fill up, its feet were tangled in seaweed. Soon, it would drown.

Theo put the fish in the net on his back and sheathed his spear to free both his hands. He would need all of his strength to get the beast back on the beach. Its hollow skeleton was light when dry, but wet, and with the sea swelling at dusk—it could take them both down.

When he got close enough, Theo placed his hands against the hips of the advancing beast to stop its motion, then grabbed it firmly by its horizontal spine to start pushing it in the other direction. The beast moved, reluctantly at first, then faster as its second knees emerged from the water and met less resistance. Finally its feet gained traction against the sand, and soon Theo was lying on his back, panting, the fish on one side, the beast on the other, dripping on the beach and motionless. But he was losing the light. In a few moments, it would be night and he would have to find his way back in the dark.

He struggled to his feet and stood next to the beast.

"What were you doing, mate?" he asked it. "You would have drowned if I hadn't caught you, you know that?"

He knelt by the beast's stomach and examined the bottles. They were meant to store pressurized air—now they were full of water. Theo shook his head. "We need to empty all these, dry them. It will take some time." He looked for the tubing that was supposed to steer the animal in the opposite direction when it came in contact with water. It was nowhere to be found.

"All right," he said. "We'll get you fixed soon. Now let's go home for the night, ja?"

He threw the net and fish over his shoulder and started pushing Animalis Primus towards the fuselage.

b=41,5. This is the second holy number.

Every night, remember to count all the things that do not belong here. So you don't forget. Come on, I'll help you.

Humans don't belong here. Remember how you couldn't even eat the fish at first, because they reminded you too much of people, with their sleek skin, their soft, scaleless flesh? Not any more, though, ja? I told you, you would get over it. In time.

Animals don't belong here, except the ones we make.

Insects.

Birds.

Trees. Never knew I could miss trees so much.

Remember how the fish gasped for air? Like I would. Like I am.

It will be light again in a few hours. Get some sleep, friend. Get some sleep.

The wind was strong in the morning. Theo emerged from the fuselage and tied his long gray hair with an elastic band. It was a good thing he'd tethered Animalis Primus to the craft the night before.

He rubbed his palms together over the dying fire. There was a new sore on the back of his right hand. He would have to clean it with some saltwater later. But there were more important things to do first.

He walked over to the compartment of the craft that he used as a storage room and pulled free some white tubing to replace the damaged beast's water detector. He had to work fast. The days on Oceanus waited for no man.

About six hours later, the bottles in Animalis Primus were empty and dry, a new binary step counter and water detector installed. All he had to do now was test it.

Theo pushed the beast towards the water, its crab-like feet drawing helixes in the wet sand. He let the beast walk to the sea on its own. As soon as the detector touched the surf, Animalis Primus changed direction and walked away from the water.

Theo clapped. "There you go, mate!" he shouted. "There you go!"

The beast continued to walk, all clank and mechanical grace. As it passed by Theo, it stopped, as if hesitating.

Then, the wind blew, and the beast walked away.

• • •

Dusk again, and the winds grew stronger. Nine hours of day, nine hours of night. Life passed quickly on Oceanus.

Theo was sitting by the fire just outside the fuselage. He dined on the rest of the fish, wrapped in seaweed. Seaweed was good for him, good source of vitamin C, invaluable after what was left of the craft's supplies ran out, a long time ago. He hated the taste, though.

He looked at the beasts, silhouetted against the night sky and the endless shore:

Animalis Acutus, walking sideways with its long nose pointed at the wind,

Animalis Agrestis, the wild, moving faster than all of them combined,

Animalis Caecus, the blind, named irrationally one night, in a bout of despair,

Animalis Echinatus, the spiny one, the tallest,

Animalis Elegans, the most beautiful yet, its long white wings undulating in the wind with a slight, silky whoosh,

and Animalis Primus, now about eight years old, by a clumsy calculation. The oldest one still alive.

Eight years was not bad. Eight years of living here were long enough to live.

$c=39,3$. This is the third holy number.

Now listen, these beasts, they are simple Jansen mechanisms with a five-bar linkage at their core. Mechanical linkages are what brought about the Industrial Revolution, ja? I remember reading about them in my Archaic Mechanics studies.

See, these animals are all legs, made of those electrical tubes we use to hide wires in. Each leg consists of a pair of kite-like constructions that are linked via a hip and a simple crank. Each kite is made up of a pentagon and a triangle, the apex of which is the beast's foot. The movement is created by the relative lengths of the struts. That's why the holy numbers are so important. They are what allows the beasts to walk. To live.

Each beast needs at least three pairs of legs to stand by itself, each leg with its very own rotary motion. All the hips and cranks are connected via a central rod. That's the beast's spine.

And then, of course, there are the wings. The wind moves the wings, and the beasts walk on their own.

They have wings, but don't fool yourself into thinking they can fly, ja?

Wings are not all it takes to fly.

In the morning, Theo was so weak he could barely use the desalination pump to get a drink of water and wash his face. He munched on seaweed, filling up on nutrients, trying to ignore the taste. After all these years, he had still not gotten used to that taste. Like eating rot right off of the ocean bed.

The beasts were herding by the nearest sand dune today, mostly immobilized by the low wind. The sun shone overhead, grinding down Theo's bones, the vast stretches of sand and kelp around him. The beach. His beach.

He had walked as far from the sea as he could, the first months on Oceanus. All he had found was another shore on the other side of this swath of land. All there was here was this beach. All there was, this ocean.

He poured some saltwater on the new wounds on his knees. The pain radiated upwards, like a wave taking over his body.

The winds suddenly grew stronger. There was the distant roar of thunder.

Theo let himself be filled by the sound of the sand shifting under the force of the wind, by the sound of the rising waves, by this ocean that was everything. The ocean filled him up, and the whole world fell away, and then Theo fell away and dissolved, and life was dismantled, and only the numbers were left.

a=38 b=41,5 c=39,3 d=40,1 e=55,8 f=39,4 g=36,7 h=65,7 i=49 j=50 k=61,9 a=38 b=41,5 c=39,3 d=40,1 e=55,8 f=39,4 g=36,7 h=65,7 i=49 j=50 k=61,9 a=38 b=41,5 c=39,3 d=40,1 e=55,8 f=39,4 g=36,7 h=65,7 i=49 j=50 k=61,9 a=38 b=41,5 c=39,3 d=40,1 e=55,8 f=39,4 g=36,7 h=65,7 i=49 j=50 k=61,9 a=38 b=41,5 c=39,3 d=40,1 e=55,8 f=39,4 g=36,7 h=65,7 i=49 j=50 k=61,9 a=38 b=41,5 c=39,3 d=40,1 e=55,8 . . .

At night, like every night, Theo sent messages to the stars. Sometimes he used the broken transmitter from the craft; others, he talked to them directly, face to face.

"Stars," he said, "are you lonely? Are you there, stars?"

d=40,1. This is the fourth holy number.

You know, at first I thought this was a young planet. I thought that there was so little here because life was only just beginning. I could still study it, make all this worthwhile. But then, after a while, it became clear. The scarcity of lifeforms. The powdery sand, the absence of seashells, the traces of radiation, the shortage of fish. The fish, the improbable fish. It's obvious, isn't it? We are closer to an end than we are to a beginning. This ecosystem has died. We, here; well. We are just the aftermath.

Stars, are you there?

Day again, and a walk behind the craft to where his companions were buried. Theo untangled the kelp that had been caught on the three steel rods marking their graves, rearranged his red scarf around Tessa's rod. Not red any more—bleached and worn thin from the wind and the sun and the rain.

"It was all for nothing, you know," he said. "There is nothing to learn here. This place could never be a home for us."

He heard a beast approaching steadily, its cranks turning, its feet landing rhythmically on the sand. It was Animalis Primus. A few more steps and it would tread all over the graves. Theo felt blood rush to his head. He started waving his hands, trying to shoo the beast, even though he knew better. The beast did not know grave. All it knew was water and not-water.

"Go away!" he screamed. "What do you want, you stupid piece of trash?" He ran towards the beast and pushed it away, trying to make it move in the opposite direction. He kicked loose one of its knees. Immediately, the beast stopped moving.

Theo knelt by the beast and hid his face in his palms. "I'm sorry," he whispered. "I'm so sorry."

A slight breeze later, the beast started to limp away from the graves, towards the rest of its herd.

Theo climbed to his feet and took a last look at his companions' graves.

"We died for nothing," he said, and walked away.

At night, Theo made his fire away from the craft. He lay down, with his back resting on a bed of dry kelp, and took in the night, the darkness, the clear sky.

He imagined birds flying overhead.

Remember birds?

e=55,8. This is the fifth holy number.

A few years ago the sea spit out the carcass of a bird. I think it was a bird. I pulled it out of the water, all bones and feathers and loose skin. I looked at it and looked at it, but I couldn't understand it. Where had it come from? Was it a sign of some sort? Perhaps I was supposed to read it in some way? I pulled it apart using my hands, looked for the fleshy crank that used to animate it. I found nothing. I left it there on the sand. The next morning it was gone.

Did you imagine it?

Perhaps I imagined it. Or maybe this planet is full of carcasses, they just haven't found me yet.

How do you know it was a bird?

Have you ever seen birds?

Are you sure?

Theo's emaciated body ached as he pulled himself up from the cold sand. He shouldn't sleep outside, he knew that much.

How much of this sand is made of bone?

Had the winds come during the night, he could have been buried under a dune in a matter of minutes. Animalis Elegans was swinging its wings in the soft breeze, walking past him, when a brilliant flash of light bloomed in the sky. A comet. It happened, sometimes.

Are you there? he thought.

Are you lonely?

f=39,4. This is the sixth holy number.

Animalis (Latin): that which has breath. From *anima* (Latin): breath. Also spirit, soul.

Breath is the wind that moves you; what does it matter if it fills your lungs of flesh or bottles? I have lungs of flesh, I have a stomach. What is a soul made of?

Do you have a soul? Do I?

The breath gives me voice. The fish is mute, the comet breathless; I haven't heard any voice but my own in so long.

Are you there? Are you lonely?

When I was a little boy I saw a comet in the sky and thought: Wings are not enough to fly, but if you catch a comet with a bug net, well . . . Well, that might just do the trick.

Breath gives life. To live: the way I keep my face on, my voice in, my soul from spilling out.

Night already. Look, there is a light in the black above. It is a comet; see its long tail? Like a rose blooming in the sky.

If we catch it, maybe we can fly.

Tomorrow I think I'll walk into the sea, swim as far as I can.

And then what?

Then, nothing. I let go.

Instead of walking into the sea, in the morning Theo started building a new animal. He put up a tent just outside the fuselage, using some leftover tarpaulin and steel rods from the craft. He gathered all his materials inside: tubes, wire, bottles, cable ties, remains of beasts that had drowned in the past, or ones which had been created with some fundamental flaw that never allowed them to live in the first place. Theo worked quickly but carefully, pausing every now and then to steady his trembling hands, to blink the blurriness away. New sores appeared on his chest, but he ignored them.

This one would live. Perhaps it would even fly.

The rest of the beasts gathered outside the makeshift tent, as if to witness the birth of their kin.

g=36,7. This is the seventh holy number.

Come here, friend. Sit. Get some rest. I can see your knees trembling, your hip ready to give, your feet digging into the mud. Soon you will die, if you stay this way.

I see you have a spine, friend.

I, too, have a spine.

Theo was out fishing when the clouds started to gather and the sea turned black. Storms were not rare on Oceanus, but this one looked angrier than usual. He shouldered his fishing gear and started treading water towards the shore. He passed Animalis Elegans, its wings undulating faster and faster, and Animalis Caecus, which seemed to pause to look at him through its mechanical blindness, its nose pointed at the sky.

Theo made sure the half-finished beast was resting as securely as possible under the tarpaulin, and withdrew in the fuselage for what was to come.

$h=65,7$. This is the eighth holy number.

Once, a long long time ago, there was a prophet in old Earth who asked: when we have cut down all the trees and scraped the galaxy clean of stars, what will be left to shelter us from the terrible, empty skies?

Theo watched from his safe spot behind the fuselage's porthole as the beasts hammered their tails to the ground to defend their skeletons against the rising winds. Soon, everything outside was a blur of sand and rain. The craft was being battered from all sides; by the time the storm subsided, it would be half-buried in sand and kelp. And there was nothing to do but watch as the wind dislodged the rod that marked Tessa's grave and the red scarf was blown away, soon nowhere to be seen. It disappeared into the sea as if it had never existed at all, as if it had only been a memory of a childish story from long-ago and far-away. There was nothing to do as the wind uprooted the tarpaulin tent and blew the new animal to pieces; nothing to do as Animalis Elegans was torn from the ground and dragged to the water, its silken wings crushed under the waves.

Theo walked over to the trapdoor, cracked it open to let in some air. The night, heavy and humid, stuck to his skin.

$i=49$. This is the ninth holy number.

The night is heavy and humid like the dreams I used to have as a boy. In my dream, I see I'm walking into the sea, only it's not the sea any more, it's tall grass, taller than any grass I've ever seen in any ecosystem, taller than me, taller than the beasts. I swim in the grass, and it grows even taller; it reaches my head and keeps growing towards the sky, or maybe it's me getting smaller and smaller until all I can see is grass above and around me. I fall back, and the grass catches me, and it's the sky catching me like I always knew it would.

The storm lasted two Oceanus days and two Oceanus nights. When the clouds parted and the winds moved deeper into the ocean, Theo finally emerged from the fuselage. Half the beach had turned into a mire. Animalis Elegans was nowhere in sight. Animalis Primus limped in the distance. The beach was strewn with parts; only three of the beasts had survived the storm.

"No point in mourning, ja?" Theo muttered, and got to work.

He gathered as many of the materials as had landed in the area around the craft, dismantled the remains of the new animal that would never be named.

He had laid everything on the tarpaulin to dry, when a glimpse of white caught his eye. He turned towards the expanse of sea that blended into mire, and squinted. At first he thought it was foam, but no; it was one of Elegans's wings, a precious piece of white silk poking out of a murky-looking patch in the ground.

He knew better than to go retrieve it, but he went anyway.

j=50. This is the tenth holy number.

Listen, listen. It's okay. Don't fret. Take it in. The desolation, take it all in. Decomposition is a vital part of any ecosystem. It releases nutrients that can be reused, returns to the atmosphere what was only borrowed before. Without it, dead matter would accumulate and the world would be fragmented and dead, a wasteland of drowned parts and things with no knees, no spine, no wings.

Theo had his hands on the precious fabric, knee-deep in the muck, when he realized he was sinking, inch by inch, every time he moved. He tried to pull himself back out, but the next moment the sand was up to his thighs. He tried to kick his way out, to drag himself up, but his knees buckled, his muscles burned and he sank deeper and deeper with every breath he took.

This is it, then, he thought. *Here we are, friend. Here we are.*

He let out a breath, and it was almost like letting go.

k=61,9. This is the last holy number.

So here we are, friend: I, *Homo Necans*, the Man who Dies; you, ever a corpse. Beautiful, exquisite corpse. I lay my hands on you, caress your inanimate flawlessness. I dip my palms into you, what you once were. And then, there it is, so close and tangible I can almost reach it.

Here I am.

In your soul up to my knees.

The sand around Theo was drying in the sun. It was up to his navel now. Wouldn't be long. The wind hissed against the kelp and sand, lulling him. His eyes closed and he dozed off, still holding on to the wing.

He was woken by the rattling sound of Animalis Primus limping towards him.

The beast approached, its feet distributing its weight so as to barely touch the unsteady sand.

"I made you fine, didn't I?" Theo mused. "Just fine."

Primus came to a halt next to Theo, and waited.

He looked up at the beast, squinting at the sun behind it. "What are you doing, old friend?" he asked.

The beast stood, as if waiting for him to reach out, to hold on.

Theo pulled a hand out of the sand and reached for the beast's first knees. He was afraid he might trip the animal over, take them both down, but as soon as he got a firm grasp on its skeleton, Primus started walking against the wind, pulling Theo out of the sand.

He let go once he was safely away from the marsh. He collapsed on the powdery sand, trying to catch his breath, reel it back in, keep it from running out. Animalis Primus did not stop.

"Wait," Theo whispered as he pulled himself half-way up from the ground, thousands of minuscule grains sticking to his damp cheek. The beast marched onwards, unresponsive. "Wait!" Theo shouted, with all the breath he had left. He almost passed out.

The wind changed direction. Theo rested his head back on the sand, spent, and watched as Animalis Primus walked away—all clank and mechanics and the vestige of something like breath.

Bits

NAOMI KRITZER

So here is something a lot of people don't realize: most companies that make sex toys are really small. Even a successful sex-toy manufacturer like Squishies ™ is still run out of a single office attached to a warehouse, and the staff consists of Julia (the owner), Juan (the guy who does all the warehouse stuff), and me (the person who does everything else).

(You are probably wondering right now if that includes product testing. I make it a habit not to talk about my sex life with strangers but Julia requires that everyone she hires take home a Squishie or a Firmie or one of the other IntelliFlesh products and try it out, either solo or with a partner. I pointed out that if she ever hired an alien—sorry, "extraterrestrial immigrant"—the neurology doesn't match up, and does she want to admit she discriminates in hiring? But I didn't argue that hard, because hey, free sex toy, why not? Frankly, I found it a kind of freaky experience, having this piece of sensate flesh that didn't really belong there, and after a little bit of experimentation I stuck it in a drawer and haven't touched it since.)

Anyway, we outsource the manufacturing and the boxes of Squishies and Firmies get shipped to us on shrink-wrapped pallets and Juan breaks them down to re-ship in more manageable quantities to the companies that resell our products.

The original product were the Squishies, and Julia is not at ALL shy about people knowing about her sex life (we have an instructional video, and she's IN it) so I don't mind telling you that she came up with it because her boyfriend at the time had a fetish for really large breasts, we're not talking "naturally gifted" or even "enhanced with silicone" but "truly impractical for all real-world purposes like breathing and using your arms," and conveniently at the time she was working at a company making top-of-the-line prosthetics with neural integration. She made herself a really enormous set of breasts and after a lot of futzing with the neural integration she got them to be sensate. Then the boyfriend dumped her and she didn't really need them anymore, but her friend who'd had a double mastectomy said, "why don't you make me a smaller set?" and that, supposedly, was when it occurred to her that maybe she could make this product to SELL. She found a manufacturing facility and office space, hired me and Juan, and went into the Fully Sensate Attachable Flesh business.

Depending on your predilections you may already be wondering why she started with boobs. IntelliFlesh is re-shapable, at least up to a point, and since I was the Customer Service department I started getting calls from people who wanted to reshape it into something longer, stiffer, and pointier.

"Julia," I said one day, taking off my headset, "You need to start making strap-on dicks."

"I can't call those Squishies," she said dismissively.

"So? Roll out a new line. Hardies. Dickies. Cockies. If you go with Cockies you can say 'like cookies, only better' in the ads." Maybe I should note that one of the few things Julia doesn't let me do is write the ad copy.

The Firmies were an even bigger seller than the Squishies. Between boobs and dicks, we had most users covered, but every now and then I got a call from someone who wanted something a little more customized.

"You've reached Afton Enterprises, home of Squishies and Firmies," I said. "How may I help you?" (In addition to not getting to write the ad copy, I don't get to decide how to answer the phone, judging from the fact that Julia shot down the greeting, "How may I improve your sex life today?")

"I'm thinking about buying either a Squishie or a Firmie, and I . . . had some questions," the woman said, her voice hesitant. "They're sort of expensive and I'm not sure which will meet my needs."

"Well, the Squishie is squishier," I said. "It's more malleable, but it also doesn't tend to hold alternate shapes for very long unless you refrigerate it for a while before you get started. The Firmie arrives long and narrow, but if you want it to have a different shape—say, a curve or even a hook—you can *gently* heat it up and mold it."

"What I want is a prosthetic vagina," the woman blurted out. "In a different spot."

You're not really supposed to say, "you want *what?*" to customers when you're doing customer support for a sex toy shop. We are pro-sex, pro-kink, and anti-shame: there is officially no wrong way to have sex. So: "Which spot?" I asked.

"Well, we're not exactly sure. Part of the advantage of your products is that we can move them around. What if I bought two Firmies? Could I reshape those into two halves of a vagina, like maybe one could be the top of the, um, tube, and the other could be the bottom . . . are your products compatible with lubricant?"

"There's a special lube that we sell," I said. "Other lubricants might void the warranty."

"That adds to the cost even more," the woman said, clearly frustrated. "Is there *any* way to find out before I put down all that money whether it's going to work for me? If they sold these at REI I would just *buy it* and figure I'd return it if I needed to, but nobody takes returns on sex toys."

"We do, under some circumstances," I said. "Can you give me a little more information about what your goal is with our product?"

"I want to have sex with my husband," she said, impatiently, "*real* sex, or as real as it can get. And he's a K'srillan male. Our God-given parts just don't match up."

The K'srillan—our "extraterrestrial immigrants"—made radio contact about a decade ago, and arrived on earth a year and three months ago. Juan periodically mutters about how no matter what they say, they might still be planning invasion and how would we even stop them? But they offered us suspended-animation technology in exchange for asylum (from *who?* was Juan's immediate question, but we've been assured that they were fleeing the death of their sun, not some second wave of dangerous aliens) and a dozen U.S. cities wound up taking settlements. (They're spread around. There are a bunch of others in other countries all over the world.) So far in the U.S. it was mostly okay, other than some anti-immigrant rioting in Kansas City. I hadn't actually met any K'srillan—there was a settlement in Minneapolis but I live in St. Paul and don't cross the river much—but from what I could tell they were all law-abiding and hard working and in general the sort of people you want to have come and settle in your city.

They also looked kind of like roadkilled giant squid. They don't have faces, as such. I mean, they have eyes, seven of them, which are on stalks, and they have a mouth, which they use to eat and speak, but they're not right next to each other the way you would expect in practically every earth species out there, from mammals to reptiles to fish. I mean, okay, we do have squids. But they don't walk around the shopping mall. On tentacles.

K'srillan do talk, but they aren't physically capable of making the same sounds as us, so they carry a voice synthesizer for communication.

The thought of sex with, or marriage to, a K'srillan was completely baffling to me.

Even, dare I say it, *gross.*

But we are pro-sex, pro-kink, and anti-shame, so I said, "Okay!" in as cheerful a voice as I could muster, and didn't add, "Husband? You sure moved fast." (I might not judge sex lives but I reserve the right to judge major life decisions.) "I don't actually know that much about K'srillan sexual anatomy. So, um. He has a penis?"

"Yes, we don't need a Firmie for *him,*" the woman said, dismissively. "Your products don't interface with K'srillan neurology anyway or we'd consider buying him a Firmie and having him use that instead of his own penis. He has a penis, but it's eighteen inches long, and bifurcated."

"Bifurcated?"

"Branches into two, basically."

"You'd need at least four Firmies," I blurted out. "To make a vagina for eighteen inches of branched penis."

"That is a *lot* of money."

"Yeah, for that much you could practically get a custom order."

"Oh! You do custom orders?"

"No. We don't. But surely *someone* . . . "

"Do you think I haven't *checked*?" the woman asked, exasperated. "There has been a lot of discussion of this in the Full Integration community. *I am not the only woman looking.*"

"You aren't?"

"No!"

Well, that changed things, maybe. A custom order was one thing. A *prototype* was potentially a whole different matter.

"No."

"No? Just no?"

"Would you rather I went with 'no, that's a repulsive idea?' "

I stared at Julia. "I thought we were pro-kink and anti-shame?" To be fair, I'd had a similar reaction at first, but I was actively trying to get past my emotional reaction. Everyone involved was a consenting adult—okay, so the K'srillans had a different life span and developmental arc from humans, but I'd checked, and since the K'srillan males didn't actually develop a penis until sexual maturity, clearly these *were* adults we were talking about. Anyway. "Did you know that there's already a sector of the porn industry devoted to sex between human women and K'srillan males? Apparently an eighteen-inch bifurcated—"

"*Stop.* I don't want to hear about it."

"Did I ever say that about your ex-boyfriend's fetish for massive boobs? *No.* Your kink is not my kink, and your kink is okay. Their kink is not our kink, but that doesn't mean we can't sell them stuff!"

Julia threw down the silicone butt plug she'd been examining. (We'd been thinking about new ways to extend our line *anyway*. It's not as if my suggestion had come completely out of the blue.) "Okay. Fine. You want to design something, we'll test the market. But *you* are going to have to take the measurements, *you* are going to have to build the prototype, and you are *certainly* going to have to do the focus group and interviews because *this is a repulsive idea.*"

"Fine!" I said. "Fine. I will handle—" I cut myself off. "I will *deal with* all of it. And we'll see if enough people want this to make it viable."

The woman who'd called was named Liz, and her husband's name was Zmivla, and it turned out that Zmivla was part of the group that had settled in Minneapolis, so they lived less than five miles from my office. I drove to the high-rise apartment where so many of the new arrivals had moved in, and took an elevator to their apartment on the twelveth floor.

"Come in," Liz said when she answered the door. "I've made coffee." She laughed nervously. "Do you drink coffee?"

Zmivla was lounging in the recliner, tentacles draped over both the arm rests and the foot rest. Two of his eye stalks swiveled to look at me when I came in and his speech synthesizer said, "Hello, Ms. Marshall."

"Call me Renee," I said.

Liz handed me a cup of coffee and I studied Zmivla, wondering if I should just whip out the tape measure and ask him to whip out his penis, or if we should have some more preliminaries first. When Julia started making the Firmies, I think rather than measuring actual penises she bought the dozen or so top-selling models of dildo and measured *those*. But there aren't currently any K'srillan dildo models on the market, so we were going to have to go with some actual penises. I took a deep breath. "I should ask some sort of basic questions first, I think."

"Would you like to know how we met?" Liz asked, brightly.

Actually, I mostly wanted to know how K'srillan sex normally worked *with another K'srillan* but if she wanted to start with something a little less explicit I supposed that was a reasonable lead-in, so I nodded and drank my coffee while they told me their how-we-met story. I think it involved a conversation that started at the Powderhorn Art Fair but it's possible I'm mis-remembering and actually that's how my sister met her ex-husband. If you want to know the truth, all the cutesy "how we met" stories blur together for me. If you met your sweetie because he was third in line for the organized gang bang at the local dungeon and you really liked the shape of his dick, *that* I'll remember. If he offered to help you carry your pottery in his tentacles while you kept your dog from bolting, I just don't care enough to keep it in my head for more than fifteen minutes.

Liz worked in a boring office and Zmivla had a boring job that was clearly beneath his talents and after they told me that Liz's hobby was making still life paintings it was clear they were stalling, and I couldn't entirely blame them, given that I was there to measure the guy's penis.

"I know this is a somewhat uncomfortable situation for all of us," I said. "But we really probably should get down to business, okay?"

"I just want you to . . . " Liz hesitated.

Zmivla stroked the back of her hand with the tip of one of his tentacles, delicately. With one of the others, he brushed a strand of hair out of her face. "Liz and I appreciate your open-mindedness," he said. "But it's important to her that you see us as people first. As a couple who has a right to be together, to share the love that we do."

"You want me to think that you're normal," I said. I tried to keep the edge of sarcasm out of my voice, but I probably didn't entirely succeed. "Just another Minneapolis family."

"I know we're not like everyone else," Liz said. "But we love each other and take care of each other. And that's what's *important*."

"Right," I said. "But you didn't call me to affirm your relationship. You called me to help you with your sex life. So let's talk about *that*."

So, among actual K'srillans, the female folds herself around the male; she does have a short channel that's there all the time but a decent amount of her sexual passageway is constructed on-the-fly. I took notes. The actual sex involved friction, but some of it was accomplished by the same muscles that were used to fold the extended vagina into place; I wasn't entirely sure whether the male K'srillan thrusted, or not.

"You realize," I said, "there is *no way* we can build an IntelliFlesh vagina that will do the folding thing. Or the rippling, or whatever. Maybe we could add a vibrator . . ."

"Older K'srillan females sometimes lose a certain amount of strength," Zmivla offered. "There is a procedure that allows the female to fasten her channel into place, and when having sex with a female who has had this procedure, the male thrusts. It should work." The tips of his tentacles turned pink and I wasn't sure whether he was embarrassed, sexually aroused, or something else entirely. "Though this vibration option you mention . . . "

I had brought the tape measure but I wound up having Liz do the measurements. I made a sketch and had her call out the measurements as I noted them down. Eighteen inches was a rough estimate, it turned out: one branch ran 18.25 inches stem to stern and the other branch was 17.8 inches. Girth of the trunk portion was comparable to a soda can; the branches were a lot more slender and tapered toward the tip, like extremely long carrots. The K'srillan penis is *blue,* I noticed, or at least it's blue when he's sexually aroused, sort of a dusky violet-blue that would indicate in a human that he's oxygen-deprived or possibly freezing to death. There are visible veins in the sides.

"I don't suppose you know how typical you are," I said. "I mean, for a K'srillan male, are you on the large side or the small side, are you more or less asymmetrical than most, how does your girth compare . . . "

"I don't know," he said. "But I don't think it would be too hard to find out. There are about a thousand K'srillans living in this apartment complex, after all, and I know two dozen others with human wives."

I spent two entire days measuring K'srillan penises.

The good news was that K'srillan penises turned out to be reasonably uniform. I mean, they ranged in length from sixteen inches all the way up to twenty, and they ranged in girth from pop can to coffee mug, and there were some penises where one branch was noticeably shorter, even by as much as six inches. But human penises *also* vary. I mean, the average length for an erect dick is about five inches, but the record holder was 13.5 inches long. (Not to overshare but that just sounds like it would be *painful.*)

The variety of sizing in human dicks has not prevented the successful marketing of any number of artificial vaginas (or "masturbation sleeves," to use the technical industry term.) I mean, just like with dildos you can provide a set of different sizes but they are not all THAT customized, and given that IntelliFlesh is a lot more adaptable than silicone, I was pretty sure we'd be able to come up with something that would work.

Anyway, that was the good news. The bad news was that I had to spend *two entire days* measuring K'srillan penises.

Fortunately, K'srillan men seem to be pretty secure in their masculinity. I mean, imagine the reaction if you came at the average human male with a tape measure. My former brother-in-law actually measured his *own* dick at some point and it was 4.5 inches long, so a whopping half-inch shorter than the average. My sister told absolutely everyone, after the divorce, but the problem wasn't really his very-slightly-runty dick, it was the ways in which he compensated and the fact that he was a complete loser in the sack, one of those men who thinks that his penis is *magic* and if you can't climax in two minutes just from him sticking it in you, you must be broken. One-half-inch-less than average length: not a problem. Complete boredom in the sack: definite problem.

(Sorry. Very few people in my life seem to embrace my no-overshares policy.)

Anyway. There was one K'srillan who shrank at the sight of the tape measure, but then he laughed (K'srillans actually have a physical response to humor, I found out, but the voice synthesizers are programmed to pick up on it and translate it into a ha-ha-ha sound) and said, "Give me just one moment" and swelled back up to full size within a few seconds. K'srillans all grew up in K'srillan society, which has its own set of gender roles and expectations that are absolutely nothing whatsoever like human gender stereotypes, and then they were plunged into human society and forced to adapt. One of the men noted, as I wrapped the tape measure around the trunk portion at the bottom, that in K'srillan society it is the *woman* who is expected to make the first move; a man who propositions a woman is shameless and forward, and he thinks human women like that, once we get used to the idea.

"Maybe," I said, and measured his length on the left-hand side: 17.85. "How'd you meet *your* wife, anyway?"

"I thought they told you?" he said, a little mournfully. "I have not been so fortunate yet, but I volunteered for this exciting project because it will perhaps raise interest in our kind."

"Wouldn't you honestly prefer to marry someone of your own *species*?" I said.

"Among my own kind I am considered unattractive," he said.

I stepped back and took a look at him. Over the two days, K'srillans had stopped looking like roadkilled squid to me, but I still wouldn't call any individual *attractive* as such. I finished the last measurement, wrote it down, and tossed my gloves into his kitchen trash can. "Thanks for your help," I said.

I was back in the office, finishing up my prototype design, when my phone rang.

"You do us an injustice," said a synthesized voice on the other end of the line.

"I'm sorry," I said. "Who's calling, please?"

"For *days* you come to our settlement and measure the male organs," the voice said, distressed. "And now I find out it is so that you can make *false female organs* for *human women*."

I scratched my head, wondering how I'd gotten myself into this. "Look. You do realize that we specialize in false organs of all varieties for humans—both women *and* men."

"Yes!" the voice said, furious. "And *I* am a K'srillan *female* married to a human *male*. Why are you not going to make false K'srillan *male* organs? What is *my* husband supposed to do to please me?"

So in the end, I'm sure you'll be shocked to hear, we made both. We made K'srillan vaginas: as I warned Liz, they're not capable of the K'srillan pre-sex vaginal origami action, but they do simulate the muscle movements with the addition of an adjustable vibrator. We also made K'srillan penises, though due to limited market penetration at this point we have only one size and shape (pop-bottle girth at the bottom, 17.85 on the left-hand size, 18.1 on the right-hand side).

What I find the weirdest these days are not the human/K'srillan couples. It's the human/human couples that buy one from each set and have sex with the detachable genitals instead of the compatible set they already had. Or maybe it's the porn of humans having sex with the K'srillan artificial genitalia. Or possibly the *gay* porn of humans having sex with K'srillan artificial genitalia. Or possibly the absolute weirdest is the porn of K'srillans having sex with artificial human genitalia—they can't do that with IntelliFlesh (years of research into their neurology remain to be done) but there's always the good old-fashioned strap-on option on one side, and an artificial vagina on the other.

Because really, there are two immutable laws of nature at work here: number one, love will find a way; and number two, if a sexual act can be conceived of, someone will pay money to watch it.

I've been thinking a lot about that first rule, lately. Because I told my sister about the "unattractive" K'srillan and jokingly—I swear I was joking!—pointed out that at least she'd never be bored in bed. She jokingly—she claims she was joking—asked me for his number. I told her she could have it if she promised to *never* tell me the details of their sex life, and she pointed out that I already knew this guy's penis size down to the quarter-inch . . .

Yeah, they're dating. They're not rushing into anything, so this story doesn't end with, "And the wedding's next week!" But I have to say—you do get used to the seven eyes looking at you over the after-dinner drinks and I've learned to spot the physical cues of the laugh even before the synthesizer goes "ha ha ha." And Gintika (that's his name) definitely doesn't make me think of roadkilled squid anymore. He makes me think about how sometimes we have more in common with people than we realize; he makes me think about all the ways to form a connection. He makes me think about the look on my sister's face when she talks about him. He makes me think, *love finds a way,* and hey, *sometimes finding a way, finds you love.*

Communion

MARY ANNE MOHANRAJ

It was smaller than he'd expected. Oh, the planet was large enough, but this so-famous university city, pride of the galaxy—it was barely bigger than the smallest of the tunnel-cities on the southern continent of the homeworld. Gaudier from space, of course, since most of the city was above-ground and brightly lit. But the city had no depth to it—it was thin, barely a few stories tall in most places.

If a human saw the deep delvings of Chaurin's people, it might faint away in sheer terror. On awaking, it would cling to the walls, begging not to be dragged any further, shown any more. Then Chaurin would insist—*no, you must come; you think us animals, barbarians; you must see what wonders we have wrought!* And he might pull that human to the very edge of a twisting stone stair, and with a single, careless motion, toss it tumbling down. They were ephemeral, these humans, light and slight, of no consequence. It would be easy to dispose of one.

He was not here for that, though. Not here to exact revenge or even justice for the brother lost, for Gaurav of the bright eyes, the slow tongue. Gaurav the curious, the troublemaker, always sticking his cold nose where it had no business being. Chaurin had one task only on this planet the locals called Kriti—to bring his brother home. Kriti meant creation, he'd been told. For Gaurav, little brother, it had brought death and dissolution instead.

Amara knelt in the soil at the base of the memorial stone. There had been some debate over where best to mark the lives lost in the bomb attack on the Warren. There would be a certain logic to marking the shattered underground room where seven had died—seven whose actions had saved so many more. But Amara was glad the ruling Council had decided on the entrance gates for the memorial instead. Her bare hands dug into the richly composted soil, dirt embedding itself under her nails, cool in the midday heat. She placed a jasmine carefully, one whose seed had made the long journey from old Earth, to be cosseted in the university nurseries for years, and then finally settle here, under Kriti's foreign sun.

The jasmine should do well; most Earth plants did, though a few stubbornly refused to thrive. Her mother had photo albums passed down from the ancestors, of small village homes covered in bougainvillea, glorious profusions of red and pink and purple. No gardener had succeeded yet in growing them on Kriti—they withered and died away from Sol. No one knew why. But the jasmine was more adaptable; it would grow and bloom, here in the open air, its sweet white blossoms scenting the air. Happy not to be shut deep underground, where the dust still carried the memory of those who had died. Amara couldn't believe any flower would truly be happy shut away from the sun, no matter how many fluorescent lights they used.

She suspected Gaurav's captain had exerted his influence to allow her to be assigned to the team that maintained the small garden here; as a brand-new horticultural student, such a task would not normally be allowed her. He understood the need for expiation. Narita kept telling her that she should not feel guilt, or responsibility for the deaths. And yet.

Grubbing in the soil seemed to help. It was why Amara had gone back to school; her old job had been meaningless. When she put her decision in words, it was almost too simple, too obvious, but it was also the truth—after all those deaths, she wanted to spend the rest of her days helping things grow.

A low, growly voice above her—"I know you." Amara looked up, and almost fell over in shock. Her heart thumped wildly, again and again, her skin grown clammy and strange. There, looming over her, was Gaurav—no. Impossible.

She must be mistaken; Amara had only known him for a few hours, after all. And there were not so many saurians on Kriti—fewer, since the war started; she was not skilled at telling them apart. This was a stranger, not her dead friend. Not quite a friend. Amara could not go so far as to claim friendship with the brave young policeman who had died a hero, saving so many lives. *Comrade-in-arms*, then. They had joined forces to protect the Warren, and they had succeeded, though not without cost. This was not Gaurav. This was a stranger, staring at her with an expression she could not read, but it *felt* hostile. Angry. And he loomed over her—his broad, muscled torso and arms blocked the sun.

Amara stumbled to her feet. Standing, she was almost as tall as he was, which helped, though still half his width. He was taller than Gaurav, broader. Older? She was not good at judging age on saurians. Amara was grateful for the crowds not far away, students walking to and from classes, oblivious to their small drama. The students tended to cut a wide swathe around the memorial and the gate; six months wasn't long enough to inure them to the events of that day. But there were plenty of people within earshot—human and otherwise. Still, her throat felt tight. The war between humans and others was escalating, out among the stars—had it finally come to Kriti?

"Do I know you, ser?" she asked, politely, willing her voice to be steady.

"I know *you*," he said. She was fairly sure of his gender; close enough to go on with, at least. After Gaurav's death, she had tried to learn what she could of him, of his people. There wasn't much to know—Gaurav had been a quiet, reclusive young policeman, who had come to Kriti more by accident than anything else. And then he stayed, and made a life here, and lost it. Gaurav's people were reclusive; they rarely left their homeworld. But here one stood, arms hanging at his sides, hands pressed against thick thighs, his body leaning forward. His voice was low and growling as he said, "You are Amara Kandiah. I have studied the reports."

Now Amara was scared; she wiped sweating palms on the cotton of her everyday sari. Most of the would-be saviors of the Warren had managed to stay out of the news, with the help of Gaurav's captain; the Council hadn't wanted any more publicity around the attempted missile attack than necessary. Amara's name hadn't been in the press, and her photo only appeared as one of a milling crowd. It was better that way, safer. "What reports?" she asked.

"The police reports they send to next of kin. I am Chaurin, Gaurav's brother." His voice dropped further, almost to a whisper. "I am here to collect his remains."

Oh. Amara's throat loosened; she wavered, caught between prudence and compassion. She could direct him to the precinct and be done with it; Gaurav's captain would, eventually, bring him to the hospital where the remains were stored. But that would take time, possibly days, or longer. Council officials would surely want to speak with Chaurin, find out what, if anything, Gaurav might have said to his brother about the plot. Not that there would be anything—there had been no time!—but the officials still had learned so little of what had been going on. With the violence above accelerating, everyone was braced, waiting for the next attack. The Council would not want to hear that Chaurin knew nothing. She didn't know what they might do in their quest for answers. Amara trusted the Council, mostly, but she wouldn't want to put herself into their hands.

The sun shone overhead, bright and reassuring, but she could see Chaurin blinking against the glare; he was not well-adapted to life in the open air. The saurian was still large, but somehow not as threatening. If one of her sisters had been lost, Amara would not want another moment to pass without seeing her again—whatever there was to see. And, conveniently, she had the means to make his journey far more direct; she was one of very few who did.

"I can take you to him," she said. And her racing heart slowed, to a quiet certainty. This was the right thing to do. She had been sure of that so rarely in the last six months, had doubted every choice, every decision. She had felt frozen in time, as if a piece of her were still stuck underground, amid the dust and blood and shouting. It was a tremendous relief, to have one choice be so clear cut.

Chaurin followed the human woman through the extensive campus grounds, to the white walls of the medical complex. It wasn't far, but he still seethed with impatience; every step seemed too slow, and he longed to race to his brother's side. But Chaurin didn't know which way to go.

The room Amara finally brought him to was dimly lit, more tolerable to his eyes, and warm enough to be comfortable. Chaurin perched awkwardly on a stool at the long table, resisting the urge to dig his claws into the wooden top. It was already scarred—generations of students, perhaps, had dug grooves along the grain, carved strange hieroglyphics, in the way of students everywhere. *C+S. A spiral. Goddess, no.* Amara placed a small box in front of him, plain metal, hinged.

Chaurin reached out a hand, and then pulled it back. He'd thought he was prepared, but the shock of seeing the box made his mouth go dry, so that he had to swallow before he could speak. "Is this all there is? Was he . . . *cremated*?" The word was unfamiliar in Chaurin's mouth, but he had learned it, just in case.

He hadn't known what he would find on arrival, so had studied human death customs on the long journeys between Jump points. He hadn't been able to afford a luxury cruise; the clan had barely scraped together enough to buy him passage on a freighter. They had been afraid to wait longer than they had to, afraid of what would happen to Gaurav's remains. Chaurin had spent months in half-hibernation in his metal tube of a cabin, waking every few weeks, only long enough to eat a little and study, before falling back to sleep.

What he'd learned had turned his stomach, taking away his appetite. Many humans buried their loved ones, letting them rot in the dirt. Some humans burned their dead, turning them to ash on the wind. Others exposed the bodies on the mountaintops, for the bird of prey to devour—a strange practice, but one that he thought Gaurav might have liked. Chaurin could have made peace with it if the last had occurred, but this? This small square metal box, half the size of his clenched fist, was all that was left of his brother?

The doctor, white-coated, shook her head. "No, not cremated." Narita, her name was, and the scents between them told him that she was the other woman's mate. Amara had explained on the walk over that this doctor, Narita, had taken medical custody of all of the remains. Gaurav was the last to be claimed. Chaurin had wanted to explain that it was not that his brother was unloved; Chaurin had just had so much further to come. She knew that, of course.

Narita continued, "We were not able to retrieve much, after the explosion. I saved as much of him as I could, and froze the remains. I am familiar with your customs; I hoped someone would come for him." Her gaze was direct, and strangely kind. They were both kind, these women. Yet Chaurin fought to calm his pulse, to settle the ruff that had risen at his neck. The small one, Amara, had become frightened; it was cruel to leave her so. Amara had been frightened at the gate as well, leaving the scent of prey heavy in the air, but still, she'd tried to help. It was not a small thing. Chaurin pushed down his anger; this was not her fault.

"Thank you," he managed to say. Chaurin gathered the box, his brother, in a single hand. As Chaurin stood, the doctor took a quick breath, and then spoke once more—"Wait, please." He paused, but she didn't seem to know what she wanted to say next. Her face was flushed, blood rushing under brown skin. The urge to just *go* pulsed through him. He began to turn away, but then Narita managed to push out more words, shocking ones: "Will you eat him?"

Before Chaurin could do more than take in the question, it was quickly succeeded by more words: "Gaurav saved our lives, you know. He barely knew us, but he took the brunt of the blast, deliberately, to save us all." Her voice cracked. "And all these months later, we still can't—can't move past it. That moment." Narita took a deep breath, and then said, her words swift, running over each other: "We would like to share in this connection, this ceremony. May we join you?"

"What?" Amara says, her voice high and startled. The doctor rested a quick hand on her arm, but said nothing. Amara bit her lip, willing to wait for explanation, it seemed. A good mating, to have such trust between them. Chaurin didn't want to think about that in this moment, but apparently one couldn't leave one's profession behind completely. Once a matchmaker, always one, even in the midst of grief and a certain measured rage. He missed his mate, and the children. He wanted to go home.

"There is not enough for you," Chaurin said, his throat aching. Never mind the bizarre insolence of her asking. It was a real problem—there was not enough for all at home who would partake: Gaurav's siblings, their mates and children. He'd known that from the first sight of the little metal box, had felt the knowledge squeeze his heart. Bad enough that Gaurav was dead, but that he be lost to so many of his kin . . . it was too much to bear. Chaurin had come so far, at such cost, to come back with so little.

"I know," the doctor said quickly. "I've been thinking about that for months, reading your histories and legends. In the Tale of Elantra, they made soup of Genja, to feed the five hundred. What if we made soup? Would that be acceptable?"

It was only a story, a legend, and yet—"Perhaps." It was only a story, but Chaurin felt a flicker of hope, a flutter in his chest. A mouthful was traditional, but sometimes, with the elderly, one made do with less, a thimbleful of flesh, just enough for a taste. Would he be able to taste his brother, a fragment floating in broth? Did it matter?

She took a step towards him. "Please, if you have time. Come to our home, have some tea. We can talk about it?"

Chaurin smothered an involuntary startled laugh. His mother would have said exactly the same thing. She thought tea solved everything. In her honor, promising nothing, he said, "Yes. I will come."

It was only a short walk from the campus to their home. Chaurin passed through a sunny courtyard dense with plants into a small house; the kitchen boasted tall windows overlooking the flowering yard, and a fountain burbled pleasantly, hidden from view around a corner. This was a peaceful place, and Chaurin felt his muscles unwinding, just a little. Oddly, the humans seemed more tense here than they had been on campus; something was clearly wrong between them. Modern kitchen machinery lined the interior walls, but archaic traces remained as well—a small fire in a hearth, and a kettle that hung above the fire, boiling their water. This home was a mix of old and new, and it seemed rather bare as well; Chaurin did not think they'd been living there long. There was a newness to this mating, coexisting with an old familiarity. And pain, running under the surface; an odd mix.

Narita poured the tea as they sat around the kitchen table, explaining quietly to her mate. "There was a genetic flaw in the species, which led to one in a hundred dying young, unless they had a certain enzyme added in utero. It could be added if the pregnant mother ingested the flesh of the father. No one knows which female first figured that out, but she should have gotten a medal." She added sugar and milk and passed the tea; Chaurin cradled the delicate cup carefully in his clawed hands. His brother's box sat in the center of the table, a place of honor. Safe.

Narita continued, "No one needed to die for the enzyme even then; a mouthful of flesh was more than enough. And the enzyme has long since been synthesized, and eventually, species-modified in a vast societal effort; that genetic flaw has been erased, and the enzymes are now passed down through normal reproductive channels. It's perhaps the most successful example of genetic modification we know of."

Chaurin raised the china cup to his lips, sipping the hot drink, sweet and milky.

Narita said, "It's tradition now, you understand. And some see it as religion too—they believe that the soul is passed down with the flesh of the newly dead."

Amara nodded, and then turned to Chaurin. "Do you believe that?"

Chaurin hesitated, the cup at his lips. "I—don't *not* believe it." He sipped again, and then carefully put the cup down. "Some believe that his knowledge will be passed down, and Gaurav has more knowledge of humans than most of my people. Many of my people have half given up already, have begun long tunnelings, planning to sleep through the next few decades, in the hopes that the battles will pass them by. But some do not wish to sleep; if we are to survive this war, we may need to know what Gaurav knew." His chest twinged, a low, deep ache. "More importantly, if the ritual is not performed, my family will feel . . . bereft. That we have lost him truly." The woman was repulsed; he could smell it on her. But she masked it as well as she could, to her credit.

Chaurin leaned forward, unable to contain his urgency; Amara shifted back in her chair, the fear-scent rising. "If my children do not taste my brother's flesh, they will never truly know him. Do you understand? Do you have children?" The human kinship bonds confused him—they seemed fragile, easily broken. And with his question, the tension that had simmered under the surface came boiling into the open air, a rush of pain and frustration. He was no empath, but even for a non-human, the signals were too obvious to ignore.

Narita's fingers tightened on the delicate china cup. It should have been an innocuous question—they knew the answer, after all. They did not have children—not yet. But they would—they had even set a date for the harvesting of eggs, the combining and for Narita's implantation. It had all been so easy up until that point. Narita had been shocked how easily they had fallen back into their relationship, after so many years apart. They'd found this little house and bought it; they'd found themselves passionate in bed, once again, better than before. They had both wanted a child, badly; after the attack, they wanted to envision a brighter future. Even their mothers were happy at the prospect. One decision after another, falling neatly into place—and then they'd run up against the hard decision—to modify or not? And if yes, how much?

Should they simply solve for life-threatening disease? Many humans went that route, even among the more traditional groups. Though Amara's parents hadn't, and when Narita thought of that, her throat tightened. She could easily lose Amara to cancer, to heart attack; sometimes she was furious at Amara's parents, for forcing those risks upon their child. Surely Amara would agree to spare their child that much. But should they go further— do what Narita's parents had done, blessing their daughter with beauty, brains, and superlative health? Narita had never known a cold, never gained an ounce of unwanted weight, never struggled with simple schoolwork. How could she ask her child to endure unnecessary suffering? But if they made those changes, how would their daughter see Amara?

Out in the stars, a battle was being fought, worlds were burning over these very questions. Those who would protect the purity of the human genotype, or rather, their *perception* of its purity. Amara was no bigot; she had alien friends aplenty. She had even finally brought her humod partner to her mother's house; over the last six months, Narita had come to know all of Amara's friends and relatives. They all accepted her, more or less; they would share samosas with her, tell her stories of Amara as a little girl. But what was acceptable among adults became far more charged when the future was on the line. No one thought rationally when children were involved.

Could she explain all of this to an alien? Narita owed him honesty, at least—but she didn't even know why she had asked such a tremendous favor from Chaurin, to partake in his brother's funeral rites. She hadn't known Gaurav, not really. But over the last six months, as she researched his people and their customs, the impulse had grown. Right alongside her desire for a child, the sense that she should carry something *more* with her, something that marked that day, that night, when they came together to stop a terrible disaster. The night when everything changed.

"We hope to have children," the smaller woman said. Amara. He kept forgetting their names. She did not look at her mate.

"What is preventing you?" he asked, curious.

Silence answered him. Amara frozen in her chair, while Narita shifted uneasily in hers. Chaurin watched, reading the currents that flowed between them. It wasn't long before the muddy waters began to clear. "You do not talk to me, which is unsurprising, as I am a stranger—but you do not talk to each other, either."

After a long moment, Narita said, "We are afraid if we do talk, we will find ourselves in too great disagreement." Amara nodded, and then lifted her cup to her lips, precluding speech.

Chaurin was intrigued. "You fear you stand on opposite sides of a ravine, too far from each other to reach across. That may be, but how will you know unless you stretch out your hand?" He was happy to fall for a moment into the role of matchmaker again, relieved to have something familiar to do, in such a strange place. Chaurin had read about human matchmakers, who worked only until the first mating, and then considered their job complete. That had bewildered him; mating was never easy; if one took on the responsibility of making a match, surely it followed that one owed the pairing some guidance in the early years, some help going forward? His own mate would surely have slain him by now were it not for their matchmaker's gentle interventions. "Narita, what is it you desire?"

She bit her lip and then said, "I want a healthy child."

"And Amara?"

The shorter woman hesitated. "I want that too. Of course I do." Her voice sharpened as she continued, "But—*how* healthy? What do you mean when you say healthy?" And then it broke. "Are you sure you don't mean beautiful?"

Narita said, with some urgency, "*You* are beautiful."

Amara shrugged, old pain evident in the set of her shoulders. "Not as beautiful as I could be; not as beautiful as you are."

Interesting—Chaurin had little conception of human beauty, but he could see that Narita's features were more regular, her skin smoother. Was that beautiful?

Narita leaned forward across the table, reaching out to take Amara's hand in hers. "Beauty isn't some absolute. It is specific; it is the details of your face. I wouldn't change a single feature, not a line on your face, not a curve of your body."

"I don't think I believe you," Amara said softly, lines creasing her forehead.

Chaurin was not sure what those lines meant, but he didn't think they were good. He sighed. "That is a bigger muddle than we will clear quickly—and I am not staying to work with you. But surely you have someone you may contact?"

There was silence again, for an endless moment. Then—"The devadasi?" Amara offered, tentatively.

Narita laughed, sounding startled. "Really? You want her? There are plenty of other counselors we could call."

Amara shrugged. "After we fought together that night—I trust her. The fact that you slept with her occasionally, in the years when we were apart, feels . . . irrelevant."

Narita frowned. "She'll want us all to be naked for the conversations, you know. It's part of the devadasi practice; she thinks it helps lower barriers."

"Maybe she's right," Amara said, a small smile lurking at the edges of her mouth.

Narita squeezed her mate's hand and then released it, sitting back. She turned back to Chaurin. "I'm so sorry. You're helping us, and I've been so impossibly rude. Rude is a kind word for it. You must think me obscene. I just—"

She bit her lip again, and Chaurin wondered what that gesture meant. Shame, perhaps. Which was appropriate enough, for her request was, if not obscene, then borderline sacrilegious. But how could you expect proper respect and appropriate behavior from aliens? And wasn't that what this war was about, after all? If the gulf between species was, in truth, too vast to be bridged, then perhaps the pure human movement was right after all. Better to go back to our separate worlds, like quarrelling children sent to their separate rooms.

But didn't one ask more, expect more, from adults?

Chaurin wished Gaurav were here. He would know what to do. After the funeral rites, Chaurin might know as well, might hold that knowledge inside himself, a small, glowing kernel.

He sighed. In truth, he already knew what Gaurav would do—that was why he had agreed to come here, to this small, homey kitchen. Gaurav's choice was clear, in the way his little brother had lived his life—going out to tour the Charted Worlds, instead of staying safe at home. Staying on this planet to live and work, instead of trying every expedient to get back home. It was clear in his death most of all—Chaurin had read the police reports. His brother could have fled when the fighting began, but instead, he had run towards the battle, had gone to help the aliens, the strangers. When the stranger asked for help, Gaurav gave it. Could Chaurin do less?

He asked, "You can cook the soup here?"

Narita nodded, her eyes wide. "We can make it right now, if you want. And then I can take it to the lab, freeze-dry it into cubes, so you can easily take it back home. If you dissolve the cubes into a larger pot of water, it should give as many mouthfuls as you need. We would be very happy to help you with that."

"Then, if you like, I think I can spare a few mouthfuls to share with you," Chaurin said, gently. It felt . . . right. He was still angry, on some level, even enraged. But these two were not the proper target of his rage. That rage, he would direct at those who sought to divide them, those who took bloody action in that cause.

Amara swallowed visibly; Chaurin could scent her revulsion. Narita said, "You don't have to, if you don't want to." But Amara shook her head, swallowed again, and said, "No. I want to honor Gaurav, in the way of his people. I'd like to do this."

They were so strange, these humans. But brave too. Chaurin did not want to go back home and hide in the tunnels. If they stood on the edge of the abyss, he chose to reach out his hand to the stranger. Perhaps they would find a way across.

The Aftermath

MAGGIE CLARK

On impact you start to lose the details. The smell of the bright white room you were first held in. Its shape. Its size. The way that parasitic life suit slithered towards you, and from what shaft, what crevice, as you struggled with the air. The quiver in your stomach as the shape-shifter engulfed your skin, and how long immersion took. *How long* most of all.

Colt-like, you rise and find yourself in mostly working order, atop a great height overlooking a valley, its treetops varied red and gold and an implacable dark green. In the belly of the valley are all the marks of a pit-stop town—gas station, diner, weather-worn tourist hub—on a winding country road through heavy forest. You recognize at once that you were not left to die. This is key, of course, but why? What happens now?

You imagine walking into town as you are—limping slightly, wide-eyed, relearning Terran gravity and atmosphere. Naked, too. What possible excuse will keep the police at bay once you've settled on a barstool in this state? How can you assert that you're still sane?

(This is when you first ask yourself if you even are; if it happened after all. Even as you frame the question you realize this doubt will now never, not ever, go entirely away.)

"Bears," you explain to the first person you see—a hitchhiker a quarter mile outside of town. Your teeth are chattering around the old-new Terran word; you can just make out your breath in the early morning light. The hitchhiker squints behind a wild red mess of hair and beard and slowly nods in turn.

"Bears, man," he says. "Bears'll mess you up for sure."

He seems poised to offer more, but you press on. The soles of your feet favor pebbled asphalt to that tangle of stiff weeds in the nearby ditch. Sense memories come to you all out of order as you hobble toward gas station lights: of purple, pungent fields and a hundred gleaming domes; of giant red ferns with bulbous trunks and spindly leaves crosshatching a livid sky; of *aurora borealis* skittering day and night above, disrupting sleep.

Mostly, you recall, you were left in a garden of some kind—communal, or just large—and you could not tell the owners' children from other pets allowed to roam within. Once, inside the nearest see-through dome, you watched a conversation persevere, it seemed, for hours—the norm in that land, or some darker sign of strife? You never learned how to interpret those violent, whipping gestures: anger, pleasure, or something wholly else? Maybe, like sharks, they needed constant movement just to stay alive.

A car horn jolts you from such ruminations and you stumble off the road, crash into hard thistles and tall weeds blooming small white buds like lacework. You turn in time to see the driver and his buddies beating at the doors and roof with broad and callused hands. They grin and hoot and whistle at you, and one shouts something incomprehensible as the car blasts past. When you sit up you are grinning. *Children*. Yes. At last it's coming back.

By the time a county constable joins you at the diner counter, a cup of coffee set before you and a musty blanket draped around your back, you've given up on bears—not enough wounds, you realize, to carry that tale for long. While waiting you had contemplated a story of roadside robbery, too, but found it needlessly complex, and liable to cast aspersions on all the locals, which even in your addled state you aren't of a mind to do.

So instead you tell the friendly woman in her early thirties, divine threads of silver already winding through her hair, that you were camping (this, at least, is true) and that something must have spooked you in the night, made you tear out from your sleeping bag and wander out a ways. She listens while turning her black serge hat in hand.

"Sleepwalking is a child's game, I always thought," you offer up to the next long silence, matching the words with a fragile smile. "Guess now I know it's not."

It's the last response you'll manage in that diner. You want to be of further use, but from the look upon her face—patient, but dissatisfied—you've jumped to future dates by the time she speaks again. You ask yourself, *Must I explain myself to everyone I meet from here on out? At what point would any keeper deserve to know the truth?* and all other questions lose their relevance, their sense of urgency in this revelatory wake. *This* moment, you've just realized, *this* precarious interrogation, is the beginning of the rest of your whole damn life. The constable is gently prodding your arm, asking you to go on, but you *are* already, you *are*.

You're just addressing questions maybe decades down the road.

At the cop shop she finds you clothes—oversized in spots; tight in others. You're puzzled when the material doesn't lay active claim to your skin, or so much as pulse with a lifeforce all its own. No one else is about, so you dress slowly in her tiny office, a mishmash of new glass walls with white block lettering and benches and chairs from well into the last century. Under the circumstances, time travel almost seems a plausible excuse.

Over the cluttered desk there's a picture of the constable bass fishing, and when you study the grin on that face you wonder if she spent long nights lakeside with her parents as a child, roasting marshmallows and hot dogs and watching for shooting stars. You can almost see yourself telling her the truth now. Almost.

So listen, you'd say, elbows propped over the paper stacks. *About the sleeping-walking . . .*

But after that, in your mind's eye, it never ceases to fall apart.

When the constable returns she bears a print-out, and new creases for her frown. She sets the page before you; you read the missing person's notice with what you hope seems like neutrality, a calmness between your brows. When you've finished you look up—blankly? blank enough?—and set the sheet between you. She taps just once upon the date.

"Do you know what day it is?" she says, then hesitates. "What year?"

Your attention shifts again to that mounted fishing shot, and you say nothing more of this—to her or anyone. There is simply nothing left to say.

You don't go back. You can't. To friends and family, two years might have been two days, for all their grief renews at the merest word you're still alive, and all the questions life brings with it—questions you doubt you'll ever have decent answers to. And yet for you how much time has it been, really? Surely only weeks, at best, but how distant that prior life seems now, and all the people who were dear within it. You listen to someone crying on the phone one night from your motel room, but it all seems light years—light years!—now away.

So you start over in a city where no one knows you—dishwashing, street sweeping, taking orders and derision at a juice bar in a run-down mall. Your managers are all big fish in small ponds and you observe their pettiness idly, at a distance, like the flicker of red giants in a clear night's sky. Everything is new again—the sights, the tastes, the human interactions. Eventually you wake up next to a friendly stranger, who touches your cheek and asks after all the unusual words you were caught muttering in your sleep. You feign confusion, roll trembling aside, and stick notes to the bathroom mirror later, reading:

If it really happened, where? How?

Another planet? No such thing as faster-than-the-speed-of-light!!!

Wormholes?

Regardless, where's the PROOF?

Next you work the language—as much as you can recall from sweeping, jagged lines in architecture, holographic projections, and something like printed, wriggling script. You have notebooks filled with sketches of all the creatures, all the plants, all the structures in and about that massive garden, but still it's not enough to justify the claim. It never is. You take a stab at the skies next, but it's too late to start invoking constellations. You never had a head for star maps even at the best of times.

On harder days you watch the news with guilt—another child recovered from years-long captivity; another political kidnapping brought to no good end. You're alive, aren't you? Unharmed? And to think what kind of technology you might have brought back with you, if you'd only had the wherewithal to look about—how you had a chance to change the world!

In time the fear abates that you'll slip up in idle banter, be found out for a loon and locked or drugged away. Then and only then, you come to marvel less at your answer to the epic question, *are we alone?*, and start to scour the internet

307

for some proof that *you* are not—not in this, at least; not here on wretched Earth. There are more than enough forums for you to skim through, even if most appear on sites not significantly modified since 1999. But even the newer ones are filled with abduction stories that make no sense. *Bullshit,* you mutter at other people's drawings, their details, their grandiloquent erotica framed as trauma narrative. At nights you lie awake in the oblong box of your apartment, staring at cracks in the ceiling and wondering what kind of person makes this shit up.

You start to follow other made-up worlds yourself—'50s B-movies, '80s trash, and sci-fi classics all alike—but when you start to cry at Rutger Hauer's famous lines and find you cannot stop, you know you have to give them up. The fear of loss is just too strong. So you pore instead through golden era pulp, schlocky and sincere alike, for any sign of something even remotely like what you've seen, where you've been. Soon you're tossing bargain books across the room—red-rimmed, yellowed pages piling up in bits and pieces behind the bedroom door. Even then it's not enough. On a lark, one winter's eve, you find a metal bin out back and light them up.

When you go out now you start watching people more severely, and lose your temper often, too. It's *they* who need to worry about slipping up, not you. Maybe everyone has been to these distant regions after all. Maybe they're just too scared to confess it—or maybe their silence is one big joke the world keeps making at your expense. Either way, you become contrite only when you make a server burst into tears and run away; you say to yourself, *okay, fine, it's on me to get us talking—and I will.*

So you start small—little jokes with future wait-staff, cashiers, people waiting for the bus. Some ignore you from the outset, but if ever someone nods, however vaguely, you lean in and up the ante to conjecture. Most smile politely then and turn aside. Some get agitated, swear and walk away. And once, on a date, you tried for something deeper and were met with laughter—incredulous at first, then mocking without end. All right, you said. Enough.

"If you haven't been taken yet," you add savagely while rising, tossing bills for your half of the meal as your ears begin to burn. "You will. Just you wait—you'll see—and soon!"

After that night you don't go out much. Nor do you invite any others home. There is a stray, though—one old mutt with a scar-pocked countenance you take to calling Silas, who asks no questions beyond his search for food. He can stay, and does. The jangle of his collar makes you feel almost normal by spring thaw. Even bordering on good.

With him by your feet, at the foot of your bed, you turn your energy next to writer forums, and try your hand at prose—sketches, mostly: long descriptive pieces about the ship, the entities, their world. Others praise your details, your inventiveness, then ask for plot and offer lead-ins—*What if your protagonist were to meet someone there? What if they get tied up in some intergalactic intrigue? What if there's a mystery to be solved and being human brings some special skill to the table, something these others (they should have a name, btw) just don't have on their own?*

You read this gentle feedback with clenched fists and gritted teeth, though you understand it's well-intentioned. Yes, they *should* have a name, but you don't know it—they never introduced themselves to you. And yes, you *get* that there should be some plot in this, but *that's not how it happened,* you almost shout at the computer screen. Mostly you just wandered in that far-off garden with all the other, diverse creatures wearing parasitic suits, while your own ever hummed and flexed along your skin. Mostly you just tried to avoid the louder beasts among them, and to figure out what was and wasn't safe as food.

But there was one incident, near the end of your strange sojourn there, that you have been careful to avoid reflecting on ever since your return. Are you frightened even now to think of it? Not quite—and yet, perhaps: for here and here alone do you wonder if you weren't wrong to be braver from the outset, to seek out law enforcement and tell them all, consequences to your own life and livelihood be damned. Did they not deserve to *know*?

It is so slight a story, though: The One Time Something Happened. But still, one day—as days went on that world, at least, with the sky ever flickering with wicked lights in the absence of a clear bright sun—those large and whipping entities emerged from their domes and swept all the creatures of the garden up. (And how you trembled in that nest of long appendages—not cold exactly; more electric to the touch.) You did not travel long before your captor loosed its hold, though, and when you looked around you found yourself, with all the rest, at the center of a large arena: one long line of you put for hours through an exhausting run of obstacles, inspections, and . . . well, you'll call them tests.

There were no ribbons, no prizes at the end, but as the crowd began to thin from surrounding stalls and tanks, you noticed one of your fellow creatures drawn from the pack and led quietly away. A tall and nervous thing—slender like a stickbug, with fur or fibrous feelers all at ends—it stood encircled at the last by your host species, and then was seen no more. For all the details you've since forgotten, you will never forget that *crunch*.

You were returned to Earth not long after—a few sleeps, maybe more—but just before one of those great entities threw you into the waiting ship, it made you pause before a small display, and for the first time since your capture you heard something resembling your native tongue—if tinny, a little coarse, and overwhelmed at times by clicks.

Great luck and good fortune to you! said the display, *for by your prowess in the Games let it be known that you have spared your species from selection for the sweeps!*

Just that, no more, and then with another nudge you stood unsteadily inside the ship (another bright white room) with the outer door sliding shut, and your parasitic life suit letting out something of a parasitic sigh.

You recall this incident most clearly and calmly while washing dishes a year and a month after your return, dear old Sol sitting low on an overcast horizon when you spy a tiny insect trapped between the inner and outer glass. You freeze with a soapy plate in hand.

"Well I'll be damned," you say unexpectedly aloud—at which Silas pricks his ears, then lifts and cocks his scruffy head. You turn to him wide-eyed and explain:

"I bet they say that to all their abductees. I bet it doesn't mean a thing."

When Silas lets his jowls rest on folded paws anew, you take his silence as agreement and return to the day's late task, the setting sun, the insect slowly dying of exhaustion between your window panes. But it makes the difference, this possibility of deceit—an attempt, perhaps, to make your waste of time in the cosmic depths seem somehow meaningful; to give you the strength to manage on your return.

And did it work? Aren't you still here? Perhaps, but even then you shake your head. How foolish you've been to think any species wiser for all their intergalactic prowess: A theft is still a theft—unconscionable, and not on you—however much one among the thieves might have tried to set it right. So at last you shelve the whole damn incident with all the other selfish things you've seen thinking beings do—your tale no more a mystery than any epidemic of curable disease, or prison run for profit, or genocidal war where world leaders, when called to intervene, study their hands instead, or shoes.

Of course, they might still *be* true—those grim last words before ejection. But what of them now? And what of you? All you've ever had for proof is your years-long absence, and for that there have always been so many other ways for the feds to give excuse.

So—*Enough,* you say, and this time you mean it, too: *No more adding to one theft with another. No more playing jailor even with the parasite long gone.*

Tomorrow comes and you're still Earthbound. Brilliant. You toss the notebooks. Kiss the dog. Find the woods where it first happened and buy another tent.

Water in Springtime
KALI WALLACE

I woke in the darkness. My mother was leaning over me.

"We have to leave," she said. Her breath was warm on my face.

The scent of dried flowers and wood-smoke drifted after her. She had spent the night by the fire, singing for a young mother and her sickly child. The child had not survived. Few did, in winter. Its skin was veined with rust-dark lines, its eyes hot with fever. There was nothing my mother could do but ease its pain. It would not be wise for us to linger.

We wrapped ourselves in stolen furs and filled our packs with stolen food. It was not the first time we had slunk in the night.

The ground was frozen and uneven, treacherous beneath the snow. There were no stars. Low, dark clouds had been hanging over the valley for days. The trees were laced with ice, but in that hollow, at least, they were still alive. The dead infant with its rust-veined skin was the only sign the blight had reached this far, but scouts who ventured south, darting into the mountains like nervous birds, claimed it was overtaking the forests.

I did not speak until we were well away from the camp. "Where are we going?"

My mother stopped but did not look at me. She removed a glove from one hand and reached for the trunk of a tree. The swarm burst from her fingertips in a shower of blue, clinging to her hand as marsh flies to cattle.

We had traveled the length of the continent, from the sea in the north to these southern mountains, across deserts and swamps, through forests with trees so tall entire villages swayed in the branches, and everywhere we went, my mother's swarm was a novelty. People called her a witch, but quietly, when they thought she would not hear. She always laughed. It was never a kind laugh. Some were awed; some were frightened. Children were always delighted. They tried to catch the bright specks in their hands, giggling at the cool tickle on their skin, begging my mother to show them what her magic could do.

My mother closed her hand. The swarm vanished.

"South," she said. "Into the mountains."

We followed a road so ancient it was a wound in the forest floor. The crumbling embankment was as high as my shoulder, and the exposed roots were tainted with red-orange rust. The scouts had not lied. The blight was spreading. In places sharp blades of metal and chunks of broken rock jutted from the black soil, mere suggestions of what the iron skeletons had been before they fell: wolves with teeth like daggers, birds with too many wings and too long claws, hulking bulls with curved horns. They might have been monstrous once, malformed nightmares raging in battle, but now they were sorry old things caught in root cages and rotting away to dust.

There were no doubt human bones in the ground as well, but I saw none. It had been a very long time since the invaders and their metal beasts had swept north over the mountains. They were little more than legends now, stories shared by old women around campfires while children huddled at their feet. In the best stories, the oldest and grandest adventures, the mountain clans had repelled the invaders with the help of mysterious sorcerers who cast spells of befuddlement on the armies. They had tricked the metal beasts into attacking themselves and forced the hidden invaders to reveal their true forms. Recreating those great battles was a favorite game among the clan children. Magic versus metal, mindless beast versus cunning hunter, masked enemy versus bold warrior. It was as much fun to play the invaders—lurching, ill-formed, insect-like in their awkwardness—as it was to play the defenders.

On the third day of our journey, I spotted delicate white flowers blooming from the eyes of an iron skull. Frosthands, the clansmen called them, for they had small, fat petals like a child's fingers. In the stories, a single frosthand petal ground into tea was enough to poison any impostor from the south. The first sip, said the old women, would strip away the invader's disguise, and the second would close his throat and stop his heart.

That was another favorite game of the clan children: to pluck a petal and place it on your tongue, to cough and gag and laugh as your friends raced away shrieking.

"Mother," I said. She was, as always, several paces ahead. "Frosthands. It's nearly spring."

My mother did not look back. "It happens every year. Stop wasting time."

I plucked a flower from the skull and rolled the soft green stem between my fingers. It was this way wherever we traveled, whatever the season. Long roads carried us from blight to plague to fever, whispered rumors leading us across the world, and always my mother was silent as a frozen lake when we were alone. She was formal but polite with strangers; they thought her stiff and strange and foreign. When asked about her homeland, she smiled thinly and agreed to whatever they chose to believe. Sometimes she changed her face to match their expectations, darkened her skin or made herself pale, became tall or short or fat or thin with a subtle twitch of her hand and a pass of the swarm. More often she didn't bother. In truth nobody cared where she came from. The healing songs she traded for food and shelter were valuable and rare, and the quick blue swarm was a wonder.

"You needn't worry," the old women said to me, when they noticed me at all. There were old women everywhere we went, their faces lined with the same creases, their eyes lit with the same laughter, their gray hair twisted in the same plaits beneath the same scarves. As a child I had coveted their smiles, empty but still more than my mother offered, but I found no comfort in their tolerance as I grew. "You haven't a bit of her strangeness in you," said the old women, and they meant it kindly.

It was more true than the old women knew. I could not alter my face or the color of my skin. I could not make my hair curl or my arms lengthen. I was as pale as sand and slight as a child. I had small hands, small feet, no breasts, and my hair was a dirt-brown bird's nest tangle. I could not sing or heal. I could not dress wounds and I did not know which herbs to mix into which medicines. Strangers mistook me for a boy. My mother rarely corrected them.

Worst of all, I could not draw a swarm from my fingertips, no matter how often I lay awake in the darkness, hidden beneath my blanket, rubbing my fingers together and yearning.

I dropped the frosthand blossom and ran to catch up.

We followed the battlefield road until dusk. Weak snow turned to rain, and the ground churned into a sticking, sucking mud. As the sun set behind the clouds, we scrambled up the embankment, using a cage of iron ribs as a ladder, and turned into a forest of sweet-scented pines and chalky aspens. There was no trail. My mother's swarm, pale and restful, ringed her like a crown in the twilight. Without it I would have been lost.

Somewhere nearby, hidden by the towering trees, a river flowed. Its roar was muffled, but I felt it in my throat and the tips of my fingers.

We made camp in a cradle of blight-reddened roots. The pines were large but sickly, flecked with shards of metal and veins of rust, branches weakened and cracking. Aside from the rumble of the river, the forest was silent. There were more felled metal beasts beneath the soil than there were living creatures in the underbrush.

I dug into my pack to find a water skin, but my mother stopped me. "No. You stay here."

"I was only going for water."

My mother's eyes were pale and unblinking. She flicked her tongue between her lips, snake-like and quick. Whatever she tasted in the air made her frown. "Your sisters were never this stupid. Stay away from the water. Tonight of all nights, Alis, do as you're told."

She left, boots kicking up the moldering remains of fallen needles.

I was too stunned to call after her. My mother used my name rarely and spoke of my sisters even less. They were dead, all of them. I didn't even know their names.

My mother's pack was lying at the base of the tree. I folded it open to find our food. We had been traveling too quickly to hunt, but our supply of stolen meat and bread would soon be gone. I set aside three knives tucked in leather sheaths, a twist of thin rope, a handful of metal arrowheads. The food was at the bottom, and with it a bundle of dirty cloth I had never seen before.

I pulled the odd bundle from the pack. It rattled and shifted as I unrolled it. I looked into the woods, into the shadows, but my mother was still away. I drew back the last folds.

On the threadbare cloth lay the skeleton of a human child. Its skull was the size of a fist, its bones as white as fresh-fallen snow but except the fine lines of rust. There was no clinging flesh, no shriveled skin. It had been scoured clean.

I had seen my mother strip the carcasses of rabbits and birds. When we had taken what we could eat and it was unwise to leave remains behind, she would loose the hungry swarm and watch as the specks crawled like maggots over the limp dead thing and gorged themselves, blue fading to purple, purple to red, swelling and finally popping like blood-fat mosquitoes as the last flesh fell away in charred curls.

My hands shook as I wrapped the bones into their shroud and hid it again. I retreated to the far side of the camp, hugged my knees to my chest and waited.

My mother returned only moments later, as though she had been watching from the forest. She said nothing. We did not speak for the rest of the night. After we ate, she sat by the fire and sharpened her knives one by one, a narrow shadow with flat pale eyes. The hiss of her blades on the whetstone drew shivers across my skin.

In the morning my mother gave me a knife. It was a sturdy blade on a wooden haft, too large for my hand, undecorated but stained with smudges that might have been oil, might have been blood. The blade was black, free of rust, sharp enough to sting my fingertips at the lightest touch.

I spread my fingers to match the stains, held it against my palm and tested its weight. It was the first gift my mother had ever given to me. I did not know if I should thank her.

"Stop wasting time," said my mother, as I turned the blade. "We're going to the river."

The clouds had broken during the night. Above the imperfect cathedral of pines the sky was brightening, but the aching cold lingered. We followed a creek into a steep ravine. Sunlight touched the hilltops, but the river was in shadow and blanketed in mist. All of the color the snow and rain had leached from the world was returning: the deep green of the pine boughs, the white and pink rocks, the blue sky. Even the rich brown trees twisted with blight were beautiful in the rising morning, with streaks of red and orange lacing the wood like a caravan matriarch's jewelry.

Beautiful, but frightening as well. As the weather warmed the infestation would spread, and by the end of the summer this hillside, this valley, this pretty green lean of pines and oaks crawling down to the river would be dead.

At the river, my mother led me onto a flat boulder. Water curled in eddies and gulped beneath rocks, and thin ice crackled along the banks.

My mother leaned close to speak over the river's roar: "Your boots. Take them off."

I obeyed. The cold granite burned, and edges of knobby white crystals bit into my bare feet.

My mother held out one arm and rolled up her sleeve. "Like this," she said.

I did the same, shivering.

"Your knife," said my mother, her lips moving against the shell of my ear. I looked at her, and she snapped, "Take out your knife."

She jerked the knife from its sheath and pressed the hilt into my hand, closed my fingers over the stained wood. With her other hand she grabbed my free wrist. She was wrapped around me, pressed warm against my back. We had not been so close since we had slept together on cold nights when I was young.

"Like this," she said. "Not too shallow. You have to bleed."

She sliced the blade across my arm. Blood welled from the wound and slid over my skin. I tried to pull free, but my mother shoved me forward until I stepped into the water. The shock of cold made me gasp and kick, but my mother was immovable at my back.

"Not over the stone, stupid girl!"

The first drop struck the water.

There was a sickening lurch in my gut and a black flood engulfed me. I was upright still, on wobbling legs and knees, my feet going numb, but it made no difference to the mindless panic overtaking my mind. I coughed and choked and kicked. My mother's arm was strong across my chest, her hand an iron cuff around my wrist. I fought until my strength failed and every breath filled my lungs with freezing water. The river stripped away my skin, my twitching muscles and pumping blood, scouring down to the bone, then took the bones as well.

The world beneath was slick, shifting and dark, and the current caught me. The surface above shimmered: trees and cliffs whipping by, boulders bending the water this way and that, logs and tangles of branches and sodden grass. I tumbled to the riverbed. Grit scraped my face, stones bruised my chin, my cheeks, my knees. A bridge flashed overhead, fish danced quick and silver, and still I flowed faster, faster, until a great weight overtook me, tugging me down and down and down, and the last sunlight winked away.

I opened my eyes.

I was lying on my back beside the river. For a moment, I felt nothing but the granite beneath me, then I choked and rolled onto my side. I coughed and retched and did not stop until my throat ached and my body shuddered. My hair was not wet, nor my clothes, nor any part of me save my feet, blue with cold.

My mother stood over me, a silhouette against the morning sky.

She said, "Did you feel that?"

I wiped my mouth and could not speak.

"Did it frighten you?"

A stiff nod.

"That's what will happen if you don't learn to control it."

Her mouth was thin as a knife, but she was smiling.

The valley narrowed to a gash as we climbed into the mountains. There was rarely more than a faint deer trail to follow. The days lengthened as spring approached, but the nights were cold and snow fell often.

My mother did not make me bleed into the river itself again, but every time we crossed a spring or tributary stream, she stopped and said, "Your knife."

And every time I returned, gasping and quaking, she asked me what I had discovered and told me what I had done wrong. She delivered each lesson like the lash of a whip: Sit down before you fall down. Don't bleed on soil or stone. Don't linger where people might see. Don't stay away more than half a day. Don't follow more than one route. Don't forget what you are. Remember to eat. Remember to sleep. Clean and wrap the wounds. Find the cracks, find the seams, find the flaws. Everything is weak against water and patience.

My arms were soon crisscrossed with new red cuts and tender scabs. My mother refused to use the swarm to heal them. I kept the blade sharp and clean.

Ankle-deep in the water, eyes closed tight and blood dripping from my arm, I rode a dozen streams into the mountain river. I explored their turns and stones, their logjams and bending reeds. I tasted the water as it wound through overhanging roots and high grass, seeped into impossible cracks and worked stones loose in their muddy banks. I smelled elk and bears where they stopped to drink, the nests of birds in quiet ponds, the ash of human campfires.

I grew bolder. I let myself venture into the northern lowlands, where spring was giving way to summer. It did not matter how swiftly or how slowly the water moved; if it flowed to a place, I could go there. I tasted sweet fields freshly plowed and felt bridges thrumming with hooves and boots. I watched women burdened with baskets wading in the shallows, farmers leading mules and carts through fords, and barefoot children skipping rocks on quiet river bends.

Sometimes, if I lurked too long, comfortably nested in a lazy eddy or deep pool, I might catch a child studying the water so intently I was certain she could see me. I imagined myself as a shivering, bleeding specter, a reflection of a reflection, wavering and thin.

Sometimes I looked back before flowing away again.

"You are a coward," said my mother.

She was whittling arrow shafts. The swarm followed her blade, smoothing the wood with every stroke. It was evening and the day had been dreary. High in the mountains, the few creeks we crossed were icy trickles, and the trees were gnarled, twisted knots so rusted with blight they rattled like chimes in the wind.

"I'm not," I said. I dug my fingers into what little soft earth I could find and watched stars wake in the purple sky. I focused with every breath on pulling the thousand slippery pieces of myself back into the barrier of my skin.

That afternoon I had followed the river all the way to the coast. It was a journey of several months' time by foot, but for me it had flashed by in moments. I had stopped before I entered the sea itself. It was endless and strange and dark, and I did not know if I could ever find my way back.

I had been to the city as a child and I remembered the smell of it, refuse and smoke and the green stink of low tide, but it was different in the water. In the water I could crawl along the canals and explore sunken boats and drowned ruins. I could creep through cracks in walls and see what was meant to be hidden. I saw a man cut a soldier's throat in a cellar and seal the body in a barrel of wine. I saw a laughing woman lead a laughing man into a pantry and lift her skirts while he fumbled with his belt. I saw sickly blank-eyed children huddling in a garret with a locked door, sailors bartering colorful caged birds and black snakes on the docks, men in red robes with red-stained eyes boarding a ship with red sails. I saw mud-splattered masons building a wall of stone between the city and the sea, trowels in hand, warily watching the tide.

They never saw me, slipping as I did through the cracks and gutters, dripping down walls and draining through floors, testing the strength of every seam and wondering what would survive if the wall failed and the sea swallowed the city. It was so easy to slip through gaps unseen, to open paths where no water had flowed before, to weaken the mortar with a slow damp seep.

"I'm not," I said again.

My mother whittled and was silent.

"They're building a new seawall," I said. We had walked the old one when I was a child, early in the morning to watch gulls diving and children with nets fishing at low tide. "The masons don't think it will hold through next winter's storms."

"Find a beaver dam first," said my mother. Her knife snicked cleanly as she sliced bark from wood. Her eyes were bright with silent laughter; her amusement made me uneasy. "They're easier to take apart."

"I'm not going to destroy the seawall," I said, aghast.

My mother snorted. "As if you could. Don't be stupid. Start with a beaver dam."

The next morning, I bled into the same creek and explored the mountain waterways until I found a quiet beaver pond. I examined the dam and the lodge, flowing in circles through the grass at the bottom, surprising the sleepy creatures in their musk-scented den. I slipped into the piled branches and tested the bend of waterlogged wood. Fish darted around me, slick, nervous. Once or twice I felt a branch shift, but the dam was strong.

I tried for three days to topple the dam, and each time I opened my eyes my mother said, "You'll do it tomorrow."

"I don't know what you want," I said after my third failure. I was lying on my back and catching my breath. "They're only animals."

"You won't learn if you're too frightened," said my mother, and her voice turned mocking. "Are you scared? What do you have to fear? They're only animals."

I rolled onto my side to look at her.

"Did you bring my sisters here?" I asked. The sisters I imagined were small and thin like me, but they had no faces. "Did you teach them too?"

My mother's hands stilled. She was crouched by the fire, roasting a marmot she had caught during the day. We had left the trees behind two days ago; the shrubs that dotted the rocky slopes were squat and thorny. We had not seen another person since we had left the clan's winter camp. I wondered how far away my mother had ventured to set the snare, if during the day she had left me here alone, insensible by the water, my body limp and useless.

"Were they better than me?" I asked. "Did they learn faster? Was it easy for them? Did they—"

"Alis."

My name, as always, a foreign word on her tongue.

"You'll do it tomorrow," she said. "Come to the fire. You have to eat."

I didn't ask her anything else that night. I decided, when our meal was finished and the fire burning low, I didn't want to know if my sisters had been here before me, if they had bled into this same river, traced the same scars on their pale childlike arms. I didn't want to know if they had cut too deep and bled too fast and been lost, one by one, swept away while my mother whittled by the empty shells of their bodies.

Two days later I found a weakness in the beaver dam. The logs collapsed and I rode the torrent down and down, out of the valley and onto a broad, sunny plain.

When I opened my eyes, the sun was still climbing toward noon.

"Well?" my mother asked.

"I destroyed it," I said.

She was not whittling or shaping arrows or sharpening her knives. She was sitting very close to me; her shadow fell over my face. I did not want to look at her.

"That was well done," she said. "You learn more quickly than they did."

I could not recall if my mother had ever praised me before. The words were like the gift of the knife, ill-fitting and sharp.

We crested the mountains at a high pass of stone and snow. What little water we found was frozen in shallow tarns, useless to me, and I grew restless. Walking was so slow, so plodding, and the ache of my feet so tiresome. I scratched at my wounds in idle moments, dropped my hands when I caught my mother watching.

The south-flowing streams joined a silty river that tasted of iron and mud. The land was quiet, barren, infected with blight. The trees still struggled to grow, but the wood was laced with rust and leaves scraped and screeched in the wind.

I passed through towns as I explored the river, but they were all empty. Sand drifted through doorways and roofs gaped with holes. Buried on the muddy bottom of the river were countless skeletons: horses and cattle and oxen, mostly, but people too, their bones traced with rust, skulls sunk in the muck. The bridges were crumbling and weak with neglect, but they were still harder to tease apart than the beaver dam. Stone by stone, crack by crack, I pushed my way in and worked the blocks free.

The first time I brought a bridge down, I pulled out in shock, shaken, and my mother laughed. She laughed so rarely the sound was alien and startling.

"They won't all be as easy as that," my mother said. She was sitting on her scarf, holding the swarm in the palm of her hand. The blue specks weren't doing anything, not even humming. "Go farther. You'll see."

I withdrew my feet from the water and sat up. I rubbed my hand over my face to remind myself of the shape of my body.

"Where are the people?"

"Who could live in such a place?" said my mother.

"The invaders," I said, as much a question as an answer. I had never asked what they called themselves or what had happened to them after their invasion failed. The stories the old women shared never followed the iron armies back to where they had come from.

"There's no one there to hurt, if that's what worries you," my mother said.

"Would you care if there were?"

I watched for the same spark of hunger I had seen when I told her how the seawall shivered before pounding waves. But she was not looking at me. She was watching the dark clouds gathering over the mountains.

"Go farther," she said again.

"I have gone farther. There's nothing. There's barely anything alive at all."

"Venom spreads from a single bite," said my mother. She closed her fingers; the blue swarm blinked out. "Even if the snake is stupid enough to bite its own tail. We should keep going. I don't want to be above timberline when that storm arrives."

Late in the day the trail led us out of the spiny mountain shrubs and into a proper forest. The trees were no healthier than the high country snarls had been, but if I breathed deeply, I could smell pine sap beneath the sharp tang of iron. Thunder rumbled distantly and the sky was dark, but the only suggestion of rain was a smear blotting out the highest peaks.

My mother left to set snares, and I took my knife to a delicate stream. The water was shallow and choked by yellow grass. I sunk my feet into a tepid pool. I flicked away the scab and opened the same cut I had made that morning.

I raced along the creek, impatient with its playful course, and joined the river in an exhilarating rush. The forest fell away as a stutter of shadows, replaced by rusted fields and empty villages. I passed the wreckage of my bridge. It was still daylight on the plains. Sunlight danced in oily rings on the river's surface.

Go farther, my mother had said. She knew what I would find across the wasteland.

The city erupted on the horizon like a cancer, and in a blink I was upon it. The river split into a stone maze, a drunken spider's web of crisscrossing circles and spokes, and countless canals wound through the ruins of fine houses and market squares and palaces protected by high walls. The buildings had once been white, their slate roofs green and blue, but many were crooked and unfinished, angles skewed, dimensions distorted, windows broken and tiles fallen away. Armies of marble statues stood as silent sentries along every tree-lined road, every stagnant garden pond. The statues were as misshapen as the buildings: too many limbs or too few, knees bent backwards, faces twisted the wrong way around.

I had never seen a city so massive and so sprawling. Such places existed only in legends.

All of it, every broken building, every deformed bust, was cloaked in corroded vines and washed with the colors of late autumn, hints of red and orange now rotted away to brown, not a breath of green anywhere to be seen.

I believed the city dead, long abandoned. I disobeyed one of my mother's sternest rules and divided myself to explore numerous stone channels. I spread through the city as an army of ants would cover a forest floor, pulling farther and farther apart.

The first living thing I saw startled me so much I nearly snapped out of the water.

It was at first glance only a shadow over the water. A barren tree, leafless branches, that was all I could see from my underwater vantage, but it moved. Long spindly legs unfolded and thin arms reached, and I saw its head, round as a seed, and two large unblinking eyes. It reminded me of the stick insects I had seen in distant forests, but it was as tall as a man, and when it rose to its feet, it ran upright on two legs, swift and surprisingly graceful.

Now that I knew what to look for, I saw others like it in every corner of the city. Odd crouching bodies and unblinking eyes perched atop stone walls, in blighted trees, in broken windows. Most did not react to my presence even when I studied them. The few who did startled and clattered away on long stick legs.

The fourth or fifth time this happened, I followed, and that was how I found the tower.

It stood at the center of the city, a crooked black slash of metal, slanted like a blade driven into the ground or an arrowhead punched from within. Around its base was a deep, dirty moat spanned by a dozen failing bridges. I gathered myself from all corners of the city and circled the tower curiously, slowly, skating just beneath the surface. The structure was crooked and split; it had been breaking apart for a very long time. It was marked all along its length by windows smeared with soot and oil to prevent those outside from seeing in, or those inside from looking out.

Around the lowest of those blacked-out windows, where the edges dipped into the filthy lapping water, a scattering of pale blue sparks clung to the frames, snaking through seams in the metal and circling each sunken bolt. They pulsed, those shimmering veins of light, and I felt it; they trembled, and I trembled with them. They pushed and squeezed into the cracks at the base of the tower, and I felt the same pressure and grind they felt.

I had never known before what I looked like from the outside.

One of the stick-creatures ran across a bridge and scrambled along the tower's scarred surface. It climbed toward the top but changed its course midway and turned, scurried down the warped gray metal. It lowered its face to the water and I knew, knew it as surely as I felt the gritty water and the rough metal, as sharply as I tasted the blight-rust, that its flat pale eyes were looking right at me.

I flinched, and blinked, and retreated from the city.

I withdrew my feet from the stream. My heart slowed and my breath quieted. My skin felt bruised all over, tender to the touch. The dizziness passed, but my head was a heavy block on an aching neck.

"It's nearly summer," my mother said.

She was sitting on a stone on the other side of the water. She held the swarm in the palm of her hand; the blue dust danced around her fingers. Fragile pink flowers blossomed along the creek, and in the swaying grass green blades shone among the yellow and red. A breeze tugged at my hair and rustled the leaves in gentle chimes.

"Did it rain last night?" I asked. My voice was rough, grating as the drag of footsteps in mud. I licked my lips, but my tongue offered scant moisture. I wanted to soothe my throat but dared not touch the water.

"It rained four days ago. Did you go to the city?"

"Four days?" I had never stayed away so long. My stomach clenched with hunger.

"Did you go to the city?"

The questions I wanted to ask tangled and tumbled in my mind, like a knot of snakes after first thaw. "How long have they been there?"

"You know what the old women say," said my mother. "Longer than memory. Longer than time. They've been invading the world since there was a world to invade, if the stories can be believed. They—"

"Not them," I said. "Not those things."

My mother's fingers twitched. The swarm hummed.

"My sisters. How long have they been there?"

"Nearly as long," said my mother. She would not meet my eyes. Her voice was fragile with hope. "I did not know if they had survived. You saw them?"

"I found a tower."

"How does it look?"

"Old," I said. "Weak. It's falling over."

"Ah." My mother closed her eyes and I imagined, for a moment, that she had spent the past four days sitting exactly where she was now, never moving, never stirring, doing nothing but waiting. "That's something, at least. At least they've managed that."

We sat in silence for a time. I listened to the bell-like music of the blighted bushes.

"How do you know it will make any difference?" I asked.

There were men in the northern swamplands who would treat a snakebite by first killing the snake, then amputating the hand, then the forearm, the elbow, all the flesh up to the shoulder as the dying boy screamed around a leather strap. I had seen them do it. I had been hiding behind my hands, too horrified to watch, and mother had scowled at their blades and blood-splattered faces before telling them it was too late.

"Mother? How do you know?"

She stood slowly, unsteadily, joints snapping and legs unfolding beneath her as though she had forgotten how they worked. She said, "You must be hungry. I'll check the traps."

She disappeared into the forest. I laid down on the rock again, feet tucked safely away from the water. Wisps of clouds drifted overhead. I felt I was floating above the land, but at any moment I might fall and splash to the ground like a dropped bucket of water, scatter into rivulets before seeping into the earth.

My mother had taken my knife while I was in the city. She kept it as we descended into the rolling foothills. I settled into my body again, that frail prison of skin and bone, so clumsy and slow and hungry. The nights had lost their chill while I was away. Each day was hotter than the last, the hours of sunlight harder to endure.

After noon on the second day we came to a meadow. The river spilled from the trees and into broad open bowl. Without thinking I brushed my hand over the swaying grass and withdrew with a gasp of pain. The meadow grass was sharp enough to open a fan of tiny cuts across my fingers and palm.

"Alis, wait."

I looked over my shoulder. My mother stood at the edge of the forest, safely in the shadows.

"I'm only going for water," I said.

"Not here," said my mother. She stepped forward, hesitated. "Come back to the shade. Please."

I had never heard my mother plead before.

I turned away from the meadow and followed her into the forest again. A few paces from the trail she brushed orange leaves from a log and sat down. The sunlight dappled her shoulders and the crown of her head. I sat beside her.

"We'll wait for evening," my mother said.

I took the water skin from my pack and tilted the last drops into my mouth. Sunset seemed an age in the future. I imagined my lips and tongue drying like summer mud, pink flesh splitting along cracks, all the spit and blood evaporating away. I shifted into a firmer patch of shade, but it did nothing to alleviate the heat. My mother passed her water to me.

"What were their names?" I asked.

I expected her to tell me not to ask questions, not to be stupid. I did not expect an answer.

"I never gave them names," said my mother. "I never named you either. You chose your name for yourself. Do you remember? We were in one of the desert forts. There was an old woman leading a caravan. You tried to run away with her. She said she wouldn't take you unless you had a name. You made one up, and she brought you back to me." My mother looked at me. "You don't remember?"

I remembered hiding in a pile of blankets that stank of camel and falling asleep to the grind of cartwheels on sand.

"All old women are the same to me," I said, and my mother laughed.

The sunlight deepened the lines around her eyes and sharpened the angles of her face. She would not pass for a mountain clanswoman now, nor a desert wanderer, nor an island adventuress. Should we cross the mountains again, my mother wearing that thin face and those golden eyes, she would be a stranger everywhere. Children would dare each other to slip frosthand blossoms into her tea and hide behind tent flaps to watch her choke.

"We still have a chance," she said. My mother plucked a handful of grass from the ground near her feet, crushed the brittle blades in her palm. Blood rose in beads across her skin. The swarm flowed from her fingertips, ate through the grass and stitched the wounds closed. "If most of them are still hiding away in the ark, we still have a chance."

She stood and strode into the forest. I listened until her footsteps faded, then slid to the ground and closed my eyes. There was nothing to hunt and we had not eaten in days. I drifted into a restless slumber.

When evening came and the heat released its choke-hold on the day, I returned to the meadow of knife-sharp grass. The mountains still shone with light, but the river was in shadow. I found my mother kneeling in a fresh clearing. The swarm hummed around her in, cutting the grass blade by blade. It slowed when I approached, quivered uncertainly, sped along.

There was a pile of dirt on the ground before her, oblong, the length of her forearm. She dribbled water from the skin and stirred it with her hands. Beside her lay the bundle she had carried from the nomad's camp: clean white bones in a tattered shawl.

My mother drew my knife from its sheath and drove it into the ground, jerked it free and stabbed again, and again, churning up dirt, grass, sand. She mixed in more water and worked it with both hands until it she had a sticky, gritty mud. She unwrapped the bundle, and one by one she picked the bones from the pile. The skull first, the knobs of the spine, the shoulders and ribs, arms and legs, the twin curves of the pelvis, the impossibly tiny fingers and toes. The swarm gathered to watch. The last daylight vanished from the highest peaks and the first stars emerged.

With my knife, my mother opened a long cut down her forearm. She smeared blood onto every bone and scooped handfuls of mud to shape two legs, two stubby arms, a small head and a round body. She smoothed the shawl over the child-to-be.

"You have more water in you than your sisters did," my mother said. She was looking at the lump on the ground. The swarm spiraled and danced, twining through her fingers, and disappeared beneath the bloody cloth. "I used to think it was a mistake. They never tried join a caravan or sneak aboard a trading ship."

The shroud shifted as though caught in a breeze.

My mother held up my knife. I stepped forward to claim it.

"I won't tell you what to do," she said. "You can go back over the mountains if you want. You'll have to decide. I'll let you go now."

Something like a laugh teased the back of my throat, but the sound I made was closer to a sob. She wanted me to decide. She had woken me from a warm sleep in the nomads' camp, led me through the ancient battlefield and the winter forest, spilled my blood into a wild river. She had brought me over the mountains to this dying land, and she wanted me to decide. Here, where the grass cut like knives and trees rattled in the wind and we hadn't spotted a bird or a squirrel for days. Here, beside this lonely river that tasted of iron and fed into the heart of a grotesque city, and there was nothing to see out to every horizon but what would become of the forests and farms and cities and swamps, to the entire world, if the blight spread unchecked.

Here, where she had made me from sand and bones and blood, she was letting me go.

"Will you give her a name?" I asked.

My mother tugged at a corner of the shawl, touched her hand to the round belly of mud. I turned away and pushed through the biting grass until I found the trail again.

"Alis," said my mother.

I stopped, and my heart thudded with faint hope, but I did not turn.

"I'll choose a good name for her," she said.

Her voice was so low it breathed with the murmur of the river. When she fell silent the night swallowed her whole.

I walked to the edge of the river. Perhaps it was the same beach where my sisters had once stood, trusting and docile, before my mother asked for their knives and led them into the water. The river ran swift and smooth. I unlaced my boots. I waded into the water and squeezed the shifting sand between my toes. Beneath the stars, the meadow and the forest might almost be mistaken for alive.

I pressed my knife to the inside of my arm.

There was a chance, my mother had said.

The first drop fell. I ran with the current out of the foothills and onto the plain. The shifting riverbank beneath my feet, the water lapping my legs, the night air teasing the hair around my face, the burn of thirst and dull ache of hunger, the rattle of wind through dying grass, all of it slipped away, and there was nothing left but rust and silt and the cool dark river.

Soul's Bargain

JULIETTE WADE

A reading from the Book of Eyn the Wanderer:

In those days there were many who admired Eyn for her divine beauty, no less than for her wildness, forgetting her fierce loyalty to her lover, Sirin the Luck-Bringer. One among these was a mortal, Ruver of Meluara, renowned for his strength and speed. As many times as she rebuffed him, yet Ruver persisted in his suit, until at last, despairing of further talk, Eyn turned her back and resumed her exploration through the orbits of the dark unknown. Ruver followed running, and coming upon her from behind, cried out her name and caught in his bare hand the tips of her wild white hair. Yet Eyn had already cast off her mortal guise, and the touch of her hair struck Ruver dead.

In terrible anger did Eyn bear Ruver's body back, and placing him before Father Varin, demanded his soul be gnashed in flame for this presumption. Yet then did Mother Elinda touch her with a gentling hand, and bid her look back across the distance to the place where Ruver had died. "He did wrong to follow you, yet see how far he reached beyond the deeds of other mortals."

At this, Eyn relented, and gave Ruver's soul to Mother Elinda, who placed him in the heavens as a shining star. Eyn declared, "Let his light serve as a reminder to all mortals that great things may be achieved in the name of love."

As her assistant Irim finished his reading, Pelisma glanced instinctively toward him, but her failing vision could no longer distinguish him from the vague shadows. Even the bright electric lights on the ceiling gave nothing but a faint glimmer. She ached to think that not so long ago, limestone labyrinths had been her playgrounds. Now she had to rub the velvet of the couch she sat on to feel grounded again.

"Groundbreaker, you seem distressed," Irim said. "I couldn't help but think of your deeds when I read this passage this morning. Was I wrong to guess that you're a ward of Eyn?"

Pelisma shook her head. "No, Irim; I am." Though she'd long since lost the habit of attending chapel, her life's work in building this cavern city had been born of love. She cherished her vivid memory of the day the river Trao changed course through a sinkhole and came thundering in at the gate. A heart-shattering, magnificent sight! She'd mustered the citizens, set explosives, and blasted a new outlet to save the city from inundation. In return, the city's Firstmost had appointed her Groundbreaker, and renamed the city of Lake's Gate: Pelismara, in her honor.

Now that she considered it, she hadn't entirely left behind Eyn's inspiration. Surely the goddess would be disappointed in her now, though—bound by her people's adulation and her own blindness into tiny orbits that held nothing but the known.

A light brightened on her right, and she tried not to flinch.

Almost nothing.

"Irim," she asked, "Is there a wysp nearby?"

"Don't worry," said Irim. "That was me; I moved out from between you and the lamp. There's a wysp in the room, but it's currently drifting near the window."

She shoved down the irrational fear and tried to change the subject. "So. What do we have in today's project updates?"

Irim's footsteps walked nearer, while paper rustled softly. "Good news. Building the agricultural scaffolds around openings to the surface has been an unqualified success. With harvest numbers in, it looks like we can abandon those two surface fields that experienced wysp-fire disasters this year, without risking a citywide shortage." He hesitated. "Pelisma, I'm sorry; I didn't mean to mention wysps. I hope I haven't alarmed you."

"No, not really." Wysps were a fact of life. It wasn't their existence that filled her with dread, so much as their new unpredictable behavior—approaching her closely, for no apparent reason. She'd never felt superstitious about floating sparks she could *see*. "Irim," she confessed. "I feel like they're following me."

Irim's hand gently touched her forearm, a habit he'd developed for which she was unreasonably grateful. "Perhaps they follow you out of love," he said. "As Ruver followed Eyn."

"What?" Pelisma glanced toward him, and ended up frowning at shadows. Irim reading from the Books was no surprise—he was kind and devout, qualities she'd always appreciated. But why should he cast her *wysp* problem in religious terms? Unless . . . "Irim," she said, "I hope you don't mind me asking, but are you a sectarian?"

Irim gave a nervous laugh. "Ah, you've got me. Heretic, yes."

"I don't mean *that*. I'm trying to understand what you're saying."

The couch cushion creaked as Irim sat beside her. "Groundbreaker, I—well, you've saved so many lives. I believe it would be natural for souls to be drawn to you."

Souls. Then the rumors about sectarians were true. Imagine the lonely dead, not placed in Elinda's care where they belonged, but taking the form of wysps and drifting through people's lives. Approaching them. *Threatening and killing them?* She shuddered, feeling suddenly as though a pit gaped beneath her feet.

From a rational perspective, she should ask Irim questions, and let him explain how his faith addressed her fears. But right now, she wasn't sure she could handle a theological argument. Losing her eyesight had been difficult enough; lately it seemed she was also losing her composure.

If she couldn't stay rational, she would no longer be worthy of her post—and if she could no longer work for her people, for Pelismara, then what would her life be worth?

"It's kind of you to say so," she said. "I believe I'd like to see my physician about this wysp issue."

"Doctor Olanen?" Irim asked. "Why?"

Pelisma rubbed her fingers over the couch velvet, so solid and certain. A life of cave work had taught her the solid reliability of limestone walls, level rampways and buttresses, atmospheric lamps and ventilators. Wysps were incorporeal, and thus trickier, but they *had* been observed in detail. Tracking their behaviors in the mines and fields had significantly reduced the risk of wysp fires. Since she could no longer make such observations herself, she must ask someone to do it for her. How else could she banish this fear?

Not wishing to insult Irim, she said, "I'd just like to hear his opinion. Please, Irim."

"Of course, Groundbreaker. I'll call him at once."

Pelisma sat still in her brass chair during her doctor's examination, re-analyzing every wysp experience she could recall. In the city-caverns, wysps came and went without harm, and mostly without notice. In the wild cavern systems outside the city boundaries, any wysp appearance spurred quick checks of the methane detectors, but only rarely did they cause explosions. Thinking of it, she could almost feel the tremors in her bones.

Wysps were everywhere; they could appear anywhere, often emerging out of solid rock. But what might *cause* them to appear?

As he had for the last year, Doctor Olanen always began by shining bright lights into her eyes from various directions. Then he checked her chest, back, and neck with gentle hands—the same routine that always left her feeling old and infirm. Shouldn't it have been different this time? She'd told him to look for wysp attraction factors, not heart murmurs!

The doctor's hands moved away, and Irim's breathing quickened. Pelisma sat straighter in her chair, because Groundbreakers didn't bend with bad news.

"Yes, Doctor?"

"Nothing," said Doctor Olanen. "I can't detect any change in your physical condition that might attract wysps. Your general health is excellent, and you'll be happy to hear that your retinal deterioration is slowing."

"Well." She tried to keep her tone light. "Thank Heile for mercy."

Irim touched her forearm, and instantly, she thought of souls. The stars kept to their orbits, so it was written; they cared for themselves far above, beyond the layers of rock and wilderness. Wysps, though, were unpredictable. Not entirely unlike the living . . .

Oh, heavenly Mother Elinda!

Doctor Olanen cleared his throat. "Groundbreaker, are you sure the wysps' behavior changed *after* your vision trouble began?"

"Yes, absolutely sure. Irim would be able to tell you the precise timing. Please, Irim?"

"Of course," said Irim. "The wysps started approaching her closely about two months after the vision loss began restricting her routines. At first we didn't realize the phenomenon was systematic. Only recently did we think back and realize that they'd been drifting in more frequently for some time."

"So you *have* witnessed this yourself," the doctor said. "Not to suggest that our Groundbreaker is imagining things, but—"

"I most certainly have witnessed it." Irim sounded indignant. "Haunting behaviors are well-documented. Have you spoken with the survivors of wysp incidents, Doctor?"

"I've treated plenty of wysp burns," Doctor Olanen replied, brusquely. "They're *hunting* behaviors, and they *are* well documented, but only on the surface. Underground, wysps drift randomly. You're telling me the Groundbreaker is somehow witnessing an anomaly never recorded in more than two hundred years?"

Irim replied quietly. "In two hundred years, there has been no one like our Groundbreaker."

Pelisma winced.

"Sorry." Irim touched her forearm soothingly, but then hissed in a breath. Even without the faint new glimmer in her sight, she knew wysps were near.

"How many?" she asked.

"Three," said Doctor Olanen. "They're small, but quite—uh, bright."

"They generally are," she agreed. "Are they drifting, or moving closer?"

No one answered. Bodies scuffled, and someone—Irim?—yelped. Pelisma opened her mouth to ask what was happening, but impatience seized her so suddenly she held her breath.

Ridiculous, this whole thing! None of us know anything! What can I do? What do the wysps want? Can they want? I have to do something—have to, just have to figure this out!

A cold stethoscope pressed against her chest. She shuddered, gulped down the feeling and managed to say something without seeming irrational.

"What happened?"

"It's all right," said Irim, sounding shaken. "They're gone now."

Not permanently, she didn't imagine. "Irim, are you hurt?"

"No, Groundbreaker. I tried to block one getting too close to you, and it floated straight through me—may Mother Elinda stay her hand."

"Did any of them touch *me?*"

"No."

"Then why did you assess me again, Doctor?"

"Its proximity seemed to alarm you," Doctor Olanen replied. "Beyond a slightly elevated heart rate, though, everything is normal."

Pelisma took a deep breath, and rubbed the cold brass of her chair. There was no question of uttering the words 'increasing emotional instability' in the presence of her doctor, if he already thought she was imagining things.

"Doctor Olanen, you saw that, I'm sure," Irim said. "Do you feel inclined to alter your professional opinion?"

"I couldn't say based on a single observation," the doctor replied. "I confess, that's not a behavior I've seen before. Wysp burns fall within my expertise, but their behaviors do not. I'd like to report it to a colleague of mine who researches wysps in Herketh. She might be able to shed more light on the problem."

Sudden inspiration brought Pelisma to her feet. "A researcher—perfect! I'll go speak with her."

Irim seemed flustered by the suggestion. "Groundbreaker, why not order her to come to you? If wysps seek you out during the surface voyage, we have no idea what they might do. Caution is recommended."

Until this moment, caution had been all she had. "Irim, it's only five hours travel before we'll be back underground in Herketh, and I've never heard of a wysp entering a moving vehicle. We'll have no cause to clear land or build fires. Besides, I know I'll be safe if you're with me."

"Pelisma—"

She smiled. "I will even let you drive."

At last, some action! This was much better than foundering in anxiety and despair. As Eyn was her witness, she'd prefer to face danger out on the surface, if it meant she was still alive.

Irim was quieter than usual today as he led her out to their vehicle. Nervous about the surface voyage, he said—but recent advances in hover technology meant that floater travel had not been seriously dangerous for a number of years. His reticence felt weightier than that, laden with the unspoken question that now lay between them.

Unbearable. Every second made her more impatient to leave this awkwardness for the adventure of surface travel. Had he known her feelings, Irim would probably have said she was more like Eyn than ever.

Irim helped her out to the edge of the open square, and laid her left hand on the flat cold metal of the floater car while he opened the door.

"Groundbreaker," he said, "are you sure we should be doing this?"

"We must do something, Irim. I don't prefer to wait and see whether a wysp finally sets me on fire."

"Mercy!" Irim said. "That's true enough." He guided her into the passenger's seat.

Pelisma stroked the soft fabric of her seat, and tried to distract herself. "Could you update me on the latest construction, please? How does it look? Is our residence still so lonely?"

"Not quite," Irim replied, with more cheer. "We'll be neighbors with lawyers and judges soon. They've started on the Court columns, and it looks like they'll match our portico. With the shinca trunk lighting up the whole square, I think it will be beautiful."

Pelisma smiled in relief, imagining it. The shinca tree had been what first drew her to this cavern for the residence of the Firstmost and top staff: alone in the center of a flat basin, it pierced through the ceiling stalactites, reaching up toward its branches on the surface far above. Its silver-white glow sharpened everything around, while its warmth softened the chill of the deep regions.

Once Irim had engaged her seatbelt, he moved across to the driver's side. The other seatbelt clicked, and then the vehicle hummed and lifted. They drove up the rampway to the fourth level.

"Lots of construction here, too," Irim said. "You just wait; this will be the center of town one day."

"Perhaps so," she agreed, but as the vehicle angled up one rampway after another, and the sounds of life and business grew louder, she couldn't help feeling dissatisfied. *Is this all the ambition we have left? To beautify and perfect a confined existence?* It was all the wysps' doing. The fear that now pursued her was the same fear that kept all of Pelismara below ground: a terrifying vision of death by unquenchable flame.

Irim couldn't be right. What possible wrongs could inspire the dead to visit such punishments upon the living? All her studies, and every event in her life converged upon one fundamental truth: that there was nothing so destructive, nor so implacable as nature, and that meant wysps must be a part of it.

She could feel it as they drove out. Yrindonna Forest rippled all around them, trackless except for the radio-transmitting waymarkers that allowed a driver to track direction while skirting dense thickets and enormous trees that could not be safely cleared away. The hiss of vegetation brushing against the floater's roof and windows roused vivid memories of her last surface drive—the time they'd flushed a flock of kanguan, or that graceful, muscular oryen that had leapt out so close to their path . . .

Lulled by the floater's weaving motions, she'd been drifting in and out of sleep for probably two hours when Irim swore.

"Varin's teeth! Oryen!"

The vehicle swerved, flinging her into her seatbelt. They hit something—a horrible crack came from Irim's side of the floater, the vehicle rebounded at a strange angle, and suddenly they were spinning wildly. Pelisma clutched her seat.

Make it stop, make it stop, oh, make it stop!

They slammed side-first into something solid. The windshield shattered, pelting her face, body and hands with chunks of glass.

Pelisma still held on, sick and disoriented, half-choking on the pounding of her heart. Had they really stopped spinning at last? She found her voice.

"Irim?"

Irim didn't answer.

"Irim! Oh, Elinda forbear!" Grief and fear rose as if to drown her, but she forced them down. *No sentimentality, now: his side of the floater was hit twice, but he might not be dead.* She fumbled for her seatbelt, and managed to release it. Reaching across the space between them, she found Irim's leg: warm, sprinkled with chunks of glass. Carefully, she felt her way up his body. He was slumped against the far side of the floater, which had bowed inward.

"Irim, can you hear me? If you can hear me, make a sound."

The only answer was birdsong, wafting in on a cold breeze heavy with the complex scent of invisible green. Irim's neck was wet with blood, but when she probed with her fingers, his neck and skull seemed unbroken.

There was a pulse beneath his jawline.

Pelisma gasped in relief. She should try to bandage the cut, or cuts, on his head . . . No; first, she should radio for help so someone at least knew they were in trouble . . .

She sniffed.

Smoke?

She searched the air with her hands. Intense heat was coming from the rear of the floater, just where the fire extinguisher was supposed to be. Fire—and it was growing fast, which meant wysps would come.

I can't leave Irim here.

Her fingers shook, but by Sirin's grace, the driver-side seatbelt gave her no trouble. Pelisma gulped down panic and turned away, walking her hands across the dashboard to the passenger door. The latch clicked open easily enough, but the door was jammed. She threw her shoulder into it; on her second attempt, it popped open, and she shoved it outward. Already the smoke had her useless eyes stinging. By the time she got back to Irim, the air tasted thick. Coughing, she worked his nearer leg out of the seat, pulled at his arm and squatted to get him over her shoulders. Grip assured, she put her legs into getting him out. Some part of him was stuck; she heaved until her knees shook.

Sweet Heile, don't let me break him . . .

At last he came free, and she fell face-first into the passenger's seat.

She lay, panting and wheezing into the cloth. It was almost better here, but worse disaster was coming, and they might have only seconds. Thank heavens Irim was not a large man. Pelisma lifted him, but couldn't stand—only managed to flop the two of them out the door into the brush. Bushy vegetation scratched at her face and hands, but the air was breathable. She wriggled out from under Irim and hauled at him again. Won them maybe a foot. Hauled again. A little more.

The fire was now a dreadful wall of heat, crackling and popping as it advanced. Surely it had already ignited whatever vines and leaves were about, possibly also the tree that they had struck. She fought for a better grip under Irim's shoulders and surged backward, two steps, three, four, then turned her ankle and fell with Irim's body across her legs.

She lay, chest heaving, limbs throbbing, waiting for death to find them.

All at once, the fire went out.

Wysps. Pelisma held her breath.

It was an eerie inverse of explosions underground. The wall of heat had vanished, as if sucked straight out of the universe. There was no more wild shapeless light; the hissing and popping had stopped. Pelisma put her arms around Irim as best she could. He was the one who had first explained to her the pattern of the survivor tales: having extinguished a wildfire, wysps could grow a hundredfold—not merely identifying anyone close enough to have caused it, but pursuing them mercilessly and punishing them with flame, while leaving the wilderness untouched.

On the surface, wysps ruled absolutely.

She couldn't hold her breath any longer. She surrendered, breathing in loud gasps. Maybe she should have been angry to be delivered to the mercy of the wysps just when progress had seemed within reach, but all she could feel was remorse. For Irim—thoughtful, faithful Irim, lying here in her lap about to die because of her own rashness.

A flicker came into her vision. Not just a shift in the trees overhead, because it grew brighter, until her eyes filled with light. Mercy—if she could see the wysps so well, imagine how big they must be! She tensed for the oncoming flames. Remorse swelled beyond measure, flooding her, drowning her.

Oh Irim I'm so so sorry how could I have brought this upon you?

Irim groaned.

"Irim!" She sat convulsively, patting over his head, shoulders, and back as if to fight the wysp-flame—but there was none. "Irim," she cried. "Irim, are you all right?"

The weight of his head lifted. "Pelism . . . " It turned into a sigh, and he fell back into her lap. But he wasn't screaming. There were no flames, and the light in her vision faded again to shadow.

The wysps had spared them. But why?

In the forest, there were no reasons. The ground felt like solid ice, leaching heat through her too-thin clothes. The air was a turbulent ocean of sound, in which she could detect nothing familiar. Pelisma rocked back and forth, stroking Irim's head. He was unconscious again, but he was warm. He was solid.

She was less so. Remorse, panic, hope and despair shuddered through her in waves.

Help us, o Wanderer, don't let us die here; bless our path, and show us a way to return!

What if a predator smells our blood?

Elinda, don't take Irim from me! What will I do without him?

That sound—could it be a vehicle? No, it must have been a bird's wings . . .

After a thousand such waves, she could scarcely find words in her head to describe the tides overwhelming her reason. The air darkened, and the temperature continued to drop.

We're going to die . . .

"Irim," Pelisma called, shaking him. "Irim, please."

Still, he didn't answer. She leaned over him, sobbing, until she was too exhausted to continue. Long shuddering breaths didn't seem enough to pull her fully together.

What had become of her ability to stay rational in the worst of situations? Even facing the cascade and the destruction of her city, she'd been all focus, all action. But she had to face up to the truth. Since the blindness—really, since the wysp problem—she'd been increasingly emotional. Maybe this was age affecting her mind . . .

No, you can't afford to say that. You're not dead so long as you can still think.

Why hadn't she thought of it before? Yrindonna forest was vast, and not all of its trees were cold. Shinca trees, too, had their crowns here, and those gave off warmth in every season.

Though logic suggested there must be one somewhere nearby, she felt no evidence of heat in the air. Swirling breezes made it impossible to be sure what lay beyond the reach of her hands. That meant she'd have to search, in such a way that she wouldn't lose Irim. She shifted his weight off her legs, and instantly felt ten times colder.

How can I leave him? What if I can't find him again? He'll die! I can't let Irim die—

Irim moaned.

"Irim!" she cried. "Can you hear me?"

"Pelisma . . . ?"

"Oh, blessing of Heile. We need to move, Irim, or we'll freeze. Can you move?"

He grunted. "I . . . can try. Where to?"

"Tell me if you can see the light of a shinca crown anywhere near."

Irim was silent for several seconds. "Yes. I do."

"But?"

He panted a moment. "You know, we will have been expected in Herketh by now. They'll have sent back a radiogram and the Firstmost will send searchers to our last registered waymarker . . . "

"Irim . . . " She reached for his hand, and found it, sticky with blood. "I'm not sure we have time to wait."

He made an uncomfortable sound. "Shinca crowns attract wysps. More than you ever see in the city-caverns."

More chances to roll the same deadly dice. "Irim, the wysps have left us alive so far," she said. "Maybe—" She took a deep breath. "Maybe we should consider that their mercy."

That silenced him. Finally he said, "All right."

On their first attempt to get him up, Pelisma lost her balance and nearly landed on top of him. Picking herself up for a second attempt, she braced herself better; Irim hissed in pain but managed to stand, leaning against her shoulder. They stumbled along for a few feet, but then she turned her bad ankle on a stone and fell to hands and knees, nearly bringing Irim down with her.

Carefully, now. They couldn't afford a bad fall, or Irim wouldn't be able to get back up.

"Let's slow down," Pelisma said. "Don't lose your balance trying to guide me; talk me through. Tell me what obstacles you see."

"All right."

She reined herself to a creep, testing with her feet as though navigating a limestone tunnel with an uncertain floor. Irim's instructions were halting, and he often paused for words, but they were a way to navigate the uncertain dark. Slowly, so slowly, light grew around them.

"Almost there," Irim panted. "There's a big fallen tree. Let me rest a second; we'll have to climb over."

They leaned against it for a moment. Its bark was rough, covered with ticklish moss. When Pelisma regained her breath, she felt her way over it. A wind came rushing through the forest, bringing with it the distinct wickering sound of wings. This time it also brought the breath of warmth that promised the presence of a shinca tree.

No sooner had she reached the other side than there was a sharp pain on her left wrist. She slapped her hand to it, and discovered the prickly body of a large insect between her fingers. Other tickles along her skin were suddenly explained; she tried to brush the bugs off, but they clung and bit, forcing her to crush them one by one. Heile's mercy but they could bite!

Suddenly the sound of wings came at them in a rush.

"Pelisma!" Irim cried. He reached her, seizing her arm just as the flood rushed over them. Bird bodies bumped against her, wings struck, and feathers whipped against her face.

Then they were gone.

"Are you all right?" Irim asked.

"Yes." In fact, there was a distinct improvement. "I think they've eaten those bugs."

"There are thousands of birds," Irim said. "They're all perched up in the shinca's branches." The flood of wing-sounds began again, but this time grew quieter, as if the birds had gone off in another direction. "A whole crowd of them just flew away, but more keep coming."

She could only guess from his tone that they must not look actively dangerous. "Perhaps they need the warmth also," she said. "If we stay low beside the ground, I hope they will let us be."

"I hope so, too."

Nearer the shinca, her eyes filled with formless light. The ground felt softer, flat and springy with something that might have been moss. The green scent of it heightened with every step, and the warmth drew her nearer until she touched the shinca's glass-smooth trunk. Marvelous, marvelous heat! She set her back against it and sank down onto the moss.

Ahhhh!

For an instant, nothing existed in the world except heat, light, and the life pounding back into her frozen limbs.

"Pelisma!" Irim cried.

She shook herself, and tried to shove the feeling away—but the warmth was too wonderful to ignore. "Irim, are you all right?"

"A wysp," he stammered. "A wysp—it came so close, and it was so big—it was full of fire!"

"But it's been hours since *our* fire . . . " Could it have been following her all this time? The thought made her shudder.

An explosion of wings burst from the shinca crown above, drawing an invisible arc in the forest air before them. Amidst it came a feral growl, and then a shriek, before the arc completed its circle behind their head.

Pelisma pressed her back harder against the shinca. Now was not the time to lose touch with reality. "Irim, something is hunting the birds."

"Cave-cat," Irim muttered. "I can't see it clearly, but I doubt one bird will satisfy its appetite. We're not safe here."

"How can we move? At least here, we have the shinca at our backs." A cave-cat was definitely fierce enough to overpower one old woman and one half-broken man. The only mercy was that it was tangible. What could anyone do against an *intangible* predator?

How small we are here! Lost, surrounded by wilderness, cut off from all human help, and that cave-cat could pounce any second—we'll be erased—

The lonely fear spiked, overwhelming her.

"Get!" Irim snapped. "Get away!"

She shook her head. "What—?"

"Wysp," said Irim grimly. "Same one I saw before—it's bigger than my hand. Look, as far as the cave-cat goes, we'll be all right. The weapon I brought is still in my pocket. But for the wysp I'm not so sure."

"A weapon?" That turned her stomach. "Irim, that's dangerous!"

"What choice do I have?"

"Cave-cat or no, an energy-thrower will only make the wysps more deadly." She cast about for something to give him pause. "What if they're souls I failed to save in the Trao flood, and they're following me to take revenge?"

Irim grunted. "I think you'd be dead already."

She couldn't argue with that. "Still, what if you miss the cat, and set the forest on fire instead? Our miraculous escape from the crash will be for nothing."

"Groundbreaker—I'm not sure we've escaped at all."

So he sensed it, too. She shivered despite the heat at her back. "Why?"

"That giant wysp is still here. Hovering, like it's waiting for us to join it." He grunted in pain. "And see? The cave-cat is back . . . "

In her mind, the wysp seemed to be Mother Elinda's herald, announcing her intent to take their spirits into her peace-giving arms. Would she bear them upward to the heavens, or would they remain here to haunt their own city for eternity?

I'm not ready to die!

In defiance of the vision, she asked, "Can you tell me what it looks like?"

"What *what* looks like? The cat?"

"The wysp."

"Why do you care what it looks like?!"

He sounded near panic. She reached out and found his arm—unfortunately, not the one with the weapon. "Irim, give me the weapon. Please."

"I should just shoot now. The cat's close enough."

She tightened her grip on his arm. "The wysps will kill you if you miss."

"Hey, I know!" he cried suddenly. "I'll shoot the wysp!"

"You're not serious—"

"I am. It's big enough to hit, and whatever discharge it creates should also scare the cat away."

"Don't."

"Groundbreaker, you know all about taking risks to defy the odds. When the river came into Pelismara, you stopped it with the most incredible explosion anyone had ever seen! Besides, I'd happily give my life to save yours."

He must still be concussed, not thinking clearly; if the wysp survived the hit, it might easily kill them both. *Will it be fire that destroys me? Or teeth and claws?* No, she had to keep her head, not give in to fear . . . . "Irim, please, humor a blind woman. Just tell me what the wysp looks like."

Irim gave an exasperated sigh. "It looks like—I guess, like a tangled ball of spider-silk set on fire."

The image blossomed unexpectedly in her head, a gorgeous conspiracy of memory and imagination. "Beautiful," she murmured, and in an instant the feeling exploded out of her control.

Great heavens, what I would give to see it, really to see this beautiful, warm, miraculous thing!

The weird desire was so strong it brought tears to her eyes, and throbbed within her like ripples nudging against a riverbank. Was her mind finally crumbling?

"No," Irim cried. "Get away, you!"

The wysp—it was still here. It was so brilliantly clear in her imagination, and the desire so strong, it seemed larger than she was. *Let me see it . . . see it . . .*

"Irim," she murmured, "Do *you* feel anything?"

Irim's voice tightened. "Pelisma, move away!"

Thinking was becoming difficult; moving, impossible. "No."

"But it's too close to you—I can't shoot it!"

She shook her head. "Irim, don't try. Don't worry about me. Protect yourself—you're young, accomplished, and I'm just an old woman who can't even see a wysp . . ."

Let me see it . . . see it . . .

His voice quivered. "But I have to save you. You're the hero of our city."

If only she could wrest the weapon from his hand! "Irim," she pleaded. "I didn't save Pelismara with dynamite and explosions. I saved it by creating an *outlet.* By letting the river flow through."

Let me see it, oh please, let me see it . . .

Wait. *Flow through?* She could feel her control eroding in the flood. If she just let go, would the surge pass by and become manageable? Or would she lose her sanity forever? She wouldn't surrender without praying for one last bargain.

O Wanderer, I'm ready to give myself up; only help poor frightened Irim home.

She stopped fighting.

Searing heat stabbed into her head and spread outward in a shock wave of agony. Faintly, she heard herself scream.

Everything was lost in light.

Pelisma opened her eyes.

Glory blazed above her. A shinca crown: one perfect crystalline column dividing in two, then in two, then in two again and again, a glowing fractal tree transforming into a cloud of needlepoints against a solid black sky.

I'm dead.

But she could still feel her body. If anything, her blood felt, not cold, but too warm. It hummed, and there was more of it than there should have been, filling her to the brim. Maybe that wasn't her blood at all.

"Breathe," Irim's voice begged. "Don't leave me, Pelisma, breathe!"

She drew a breath, surprised it had anywhere to enter, with her so full. She couldn't look away from the perfect clarity of the shinca crown. If she moved, surely this apparition would vanish, shrouded again by the vague shadows of her vision.

She whispered, "Irim . . . ?"

"Thank Heile!" he exclaimed. "When that wysp flew through you, I thought you were dead for sure. But it's gone now."

"It . . . " Her voice sounded normal enough, but words came slowly. "It flowed through?" The pain was gone, and the strange desire too, but a feeling of presence remained. Had that emotional deluge not been her own at all? Had it been the wysp manipulating her?

How delightful!

But it wasn't, it wasn't! It shouldn't be possible to feel anything resembling innocent excitement in such circumstances!

Unless the feeling wasn't her own.

"Irim, the wysp flowed in," Pelisma said. "I don't think it flowed out again. It's still here."

"Heile have mercy," Irim said. "Has the spirit spoken to you?"

"Spoken!" she cried. "It doesn't *speak* at all!" Icy panic shot down her nerves, but melted inexplicably before it could reach her fingertips. Suddenly she wanted nothing more than to hold someone and apologize. She hugged herself, looked down instinctively—

And saw a glowing golden shape against the black.

Was this her imagination? It couldn't be sight—but the shape was that of her own body. Her clothes, her fingernails, even the wrinkles on her knuckles, all lay like a tracery of dark lace over a golden glow within. She held her hands up, considering the folds of her palms for the first time in months, hardly daring to blink. If it wasn't sight, then what was it?

"Pelisma, what's going on?" Irim asked.

She could hardly speak. "Irim—Irim, I can *see*. Do wysps see? Well, I suppose they must." *This* excitement was real! She looked around.

It was not the forest of her memory, glowing with green. It was not the black of night, nor yet the vague mass of shadow usually detected by her failing eyes. The wilderness had changed: now it was rendered in finely detailed layers of transparency, as if built entirely of smoky crystal. It had scents, too, in a strange organization she could scarcely comprehend. Shinca stood out even from great distance, each raising a blazing crystalline crown toward the dark sky, around which wysps swirled in complex patterns. Beneath her feet, soil and rock rippled outward like deep, clear water.

This was not a human world. And it was no longer cold, except to Irim. Irim, who was wounded and needed rescue.

"Irim," she said, "stay by the tree. I'm going back to the waymarkers."

"Pelisma, you can't! That cave-cat's still out there."

He was right, of course. She searched the strange landscape, but how could she identify a cave-cat in this new sense, among twenty thousand utterly unfamiliar things? "Do you see the cat?" she asked. "Can you show me where it is, so I can figure out what it looks like?"

"What it *looks like?*" Irim took a deep breath and grasped her hand firmly. "Groundbreaker, it's my job to protect you. Eyesight like yours does not get cured—certainly not in an instant. We have no idea what that wysp did to you, or why."

"I'm not cured," she said. "I understand that. It's not exactly *seeing*, anyway. Irim—" She squeezed his hand. "I'm not sure how to tell you this, but the wysp—it's not human."

"It might be a quiet soul—"

"It can't be. Not unless there are folk who see through stone, for whom shinca and wysps are more real than people."

"Is that what you see?" He was silent a moment. "But they must be spirits of *some* kind. Where else would they all come from?"

Where else, indeed? She sought for wysps in the shinca crown above her head, and as if she'd called them, several immediately converged on her position.

Irim gave a hoarse cry and fired his weapon.

Zzap!

Fire exploded from the shadows, a voracious living nightmare screaming alarms down every nerve in her body.

It felt like the river pouring in at the gate, faster every second. If she didn't act, it would consume everything she cared about, every living thing! Pelisma leapt toward the flames, opened her mouth—

And swallowed them.

Energy blazed inside her, buzzing to the tips of her fingers and toes, tingling in her lips, and it was full of outrage for those who would put her world at risk. She whirled, looking past the bright silver-gold column of the shinca, and found a fainter light, the imprint of accumulated heat scented with fear and anger. Out of that imprint came a quavering voice.

"Pelisma?"

Pelisma opened her mouth to answer, but the energy within her rose in a sudden, terrifying tide. In an instant, she realized what it meant.

No! Not Irim, I mustn't hurt Irim!

She turned, barely in time. White flame poured from her mouth, crackling in the air.

Irim screamed.

She tried to stop, but there was no containing this flood. Horrified, she turned further; the edge of the torrent touched the shinca, and somehow, vanished into it.

That's it.

She faced the tree fully, pouring this hate out in the one place where it could do no harm. Anger surged in her heart, but she fought against it.

No, you don't understand! Poor Irim, poor fellow, he didn't mean it, he doesn't deserve to die!

At last the fire drained away. She fell against the shinca, shivering. Slowly, her horrified exhaustion softened with an incongruous feeling of comfort and regret.

"Irim?" she asked, trembling. "In the name of Heile, tell me I haven't killed you . . . "

"Stay away from me!"

Pelisma fell to her knees. Tears tumbled from her eyes. "Irim, it was an accident, I promise. It won't happen again."

Voices called across the forest.

She raised her head. "Help!" she shouted. "Please, help us!"

The searchers came. They wrapped her in blankets, brought a stretcher for Irim. She could see its metal struts perfectly; also, the waymarkers and the vehicle that stood waiting.

"It's lucky you found a way to signal us," the driver rumbled. "Otherwise we might not have found you for hours."

"Lucky indeed," agreed the medic. The faint shadows that were her hands moved swiftly and busily over Irim. "The Wanderer must have been watching over you."

"Thanks be," Pelisma agreed, and found Irim echoing her precisely.

"You'll be safe underground soon."

"Thank you," Pelisma said.

They would be safe, wouldn't they? How could she be sure, when the wysp might control her actions? She touched Irim's shoulder, and her sick guilt was diluted with another incongruous feeling of tender and sorrowful care.

She hadn't killed him, though. She had to remember that. When the wysp took over, she'd managed to communicate mercy.

To communicate.

A pattern clicked into place, suddenly.

Her blindness had brought feelings of sorrow and helplessness, but the serious emotional instability had begun with the presence of wysps. Since she'd hidden her feelings from Irim, there would have been no way to link them with the moment of a wysp's approach—but here in the forest, her feelings had resisted control *every time wysps were nearby.*

What if these incongruous emotions weren't weakness, or age, but communication?

Imagine what it could mean to achieve real communication with this thing that was the most capricious, dangerous force in all Varin! A question leapt into her mind, full of unfiltered, helpless anger.

Why, wysp? Why did you turn me against my most trusted friend?

For an instant she found herself back in that moment, when the fire of Irim's weapon had mixed with her memory of the Trao thundering in at the gate. The familiar awful conviction rose within her, that if she did not act, her world would be swept away.

Not her world: *their* world.

Perhaps wysps did have souls: souls suited to this wilderness as her own people were to the city-caverns, each just as easily threatened, but with no way to communicate until disaster threw them together.

Oh, praise be!

Was this joy hers, or did it belong to both of them? Could she ever untangle the wysp's meanings enough to answer questions about fire, and trees, and food grown beneath the sun—those questions her people so desperately needed to have answered?

All at once, she remembered Irim's voice, reading reverently. *Great things may be achieved in the name of love.*

"Blessing of Eyn," Pelisma breathed. Surely the Wanderer had brought her to these events. Blindness had turned her people's confinement into her own, changing her heart and bringing the wysps—her people's threat turned into a personal need. What else could have driven her out into this voyage of discovery? And now her path was clear: she must learn everything possible about the wysps, their vision, and their world.

Think how she might then change her own.

The Symphony of Ice and Dust
JULIE NOVAKOVA

"It's going to be the greatest symphony anyone has ever composed," said Jurriaan. "Our best work. Something we'll be remembered for in the next millennia. A frail melody comprised of ice and dust, of distance and cold. It will be our masterpiece."

Chiara listened absently and closed her eyes. Jurriaan had never touched ice, seen dust, been able to imagine real-world distances or experienced cold. Everything he had was his music. And he *was* one of the best; at least among organic minds.

Sometimes she felt sorry for him.

And sometimes she envied him.

She imagined the world waiting for them, strange, freezing, lonely and beautiful, and a moment came when she could not envy Jurriaan his gift—or his curse—at all. She checked with *Orpheus* how long the rest of the journey would last. The answer was prompt.

In three days, we will approach Sedna.

Chiara decided to dream for the rest of the voyage.

Her dreams were filled with images, sounds, tastes, smells and emotions. Especially emotions. She *felt* the inner Oort cloud before she had even stepped outside the ship. *Orpheus* slowly fed her with some of the gathered data and her unique brain made a fantastical dream of nearly all of it.

When Chiara woke up, she knew that they were orbiting Sedna and sending down probes. *Orpheus* had taken care of it, partly from the ship's own initiative, partly because of Manuel. The Thinker of their mission was still unconscious, but actively communicating with *Orpheus* through his interface.

She connected to the data stream from the first probe which had already landed and recorded everything. *Sedna . . . We are the first here at least since the last perihelion more than eleven thousand years ago. It feels like an overwhelming gap—and yet so close!*

It almost filled her eyes with tears. Chiara was the Aesthete of their group by the Jovian Consortium standards. Feeling, sensing and imagining things was her job—as well as it was Manuel's job to primarily go through hard data, connect the dots, think everything through, even the compositions, the results of their combined effort—and Jurriaan's job to focus on nothing but the music.

She sent a mental note to Manuel. *When can we go to the surface?*

The response was immediate. *When I conclude it's safe.*

Safe is bad. It's stripped of fear, awe, even of most of the curiosity! I need them to work properly, they're essential. Let me go there first.

All right, he replied.

Chiara smiled a little. She learned to use logic to persuade Manuel long ago—and most of the times she was successful.

As she was dressing in the protective suit, a memory of a similar moment some years ago came to her and sent a shiver through her body. It was on Io and she stayed on the surface far too long even for her highly augmented body to withstand. When it became clear that she'd need a new one because of the amount of received radiation, she decided to give that one at least an interesting death—and she let it boil and melt near one of the volcanoes. Although her new brain was a slightly inadequate copy of the last one, thanks to the implants she remembered the pain—and then nothing, just a curious observation of the suit and her body slowly disintegrating—as if it happened to this very body.

She didn't intend to do anything like that here. No; here she perceived a cold and fragile beauty. There should be no pain associated to it, no horror. Fear, maybe. Awe, definitely yes. Standing there on the icy surface, the Sun a mere bright star, darkness everywhere—she ought to feel awe.

Chiara felt she had a good chance of being the first human being who ever stood on Sedna. The dwarf planet was nearing its perihelion now, still almost a hundred astronomical units from the Sun, and there were no reports of any expeditions before them during the recent period.

When the lander touched the surface of Sedna, she stayed inside for a little while, getting used to the alien landscape around her. It had a strange sense of tranquility to it. Chiara was used to the icy moons of the Jovian system which she called home, but this landscape was far smoother than what she knew from there. It was also darker—and an odd shade of brown-red.

She turned off the lander's lights and stepped outside through the airlock, into the darkness.

It wasn't a complete darkness. But the Sun was not currently visible from this side of the dwarf planet and it felt like being lonelier, further away than ever before. She was able to see the disc of the galaxy clearer than from anywhere else she had been to.

She knelt and slowly touched the surface with one of her suit's haptic gloves.

We've found something, Chiara, suddenly Manuel's voice resonated in her head. *See for yourself.*

He sent her a mental image of a couple of objects not deep beneath the icy surface found by one of the numerous little probes. The biggest one resembled a ship. A small, stumpy, ancient-looking ship, unmistakably of a human origin. They were not the first.

But these must have come here a *very* long time ago.

And a few miles further and far beneath it, another shape was discovered by their sensors. A bigger, stranger shape.

Probably from much, much longer ago than the first one . . .

...

It took less than an hour to drill through the ice to the first ship. Getting inside it then was a matter of minutes.

Chiara saw the two bodies as the probes approached them. Both dead—but almost intact. One male, one female. The probes suggested the small chambers they found them inside were probably designed for cryosleep. They must have been prepared for the procedure or already frozen when they died.

The ship was long dead too but that didn't constitute much of a problem for the probes. They quickly repaired the computers and what was left of the data.

They found the ship's logs and sent it to the crew of *Orpheus* even before others had time to drill deep enough to reach the other object.

Chiara was back aboard at the time they opened the file and heard the voice of the long gone woman.

I think I don't have much time left. I have no means of getting from here in time. But I know that there will be others who come here to explore. I hope you find this. I'm telling our story for you.

Ten days ago, I discovered something . . . —wait, let me start from the beginning.

"How is it going, love?"

Theodora smiled while unscrewing another panel on the probe. "Good. Suppose we could use this one tomorrow on the last picked site. I've got just one more bug to repair."

She was wearing a thin suit, protecting her in the vacuum and cold of the storage chamber, very flexible and quite comfortable compared to EVA suits. Despite that, she'd prefer to be outside the ship, walking on the surface of Triton which *Kittiwake* was orbiting for more than two years now.

Kittiwake was a small ship, but sufficient for sustaining two people aboard even for a couple of decades if necessary. Provided enough hydrogen, easily extractable practically everywhere, its bimodal MITEE could function for half a century without any serious problems. If one element failed, it still had many others and could push the ship forward with a good specific impulse and a decent thrust while also providing the electrical energy needed by the ship.

Now the mission on Triton was nearing its end. Theodora didn't know whether to be happy and relieved that she and her husband would finally return to Earth, after so many years of isolation, or sad that she wouldn't ever see this remarkable place again.

When she was done with the ice-drilling probe, she went through several airlocks to the habitation deck. It was tiny, but sufficient enough for hers and Dimitri's needs.

"It seems we have a word from the outside world," her husband smiled as she entered the cabin. "*Kittiwake* just picked it up."

After checking the signal for malware, the ship automatically showed them the recording. The face of their superior, OSS Mission Supervisor Ronald Blythe, appeared on the screen. He congratulated them for their results on Triton and mentioned that a window for another long-term scientific expedition was opening. Theodora's stomach rocked. She was eager to find out. But still . . . a new expedition would mean yet more years away from the rest of humanity. The company picked her and Dimitri because they were a stable, non-conflict couple with steady personalities and a lot of technical and scientific experience. They were *supposed* to be able to spend years without any other human contact in a tiny space of their ship, exploring the outer solar system, without a chance for a vacation, without feeling the Earth's gravity, smells, wind . . . *However, we had a contract for eight years. The time's almost up. Are they proposing to prolong it? And what for?* thought Theodora.

"Last week, we received a signal from Nerivik 2."

"Isn't it the probe sent to Sedna in the eighties that stopped transmitting before it reached an orbit?" murmured Theodora.

It was. Blythe went on explaining how they lost contact with the probe for more than ten years and suddenly, out of thin air, it sent out a signal five days ago. Scientists at the FAST observatory who picked up the signal by accident were a bit surprised, to put it mildly. They began analyzing it immediately—and fortunately didn't keep intercepting the transmission for themselves.

"And the findings were . . . weird. It became clear that the probe lost its orbit, crashed, but probably regained control of its thrusters shortly before the crash and tried to change the collision into a landing. It was just damaged. It's possible that it kept transmitting most of the time, but without aiming the signal, the probability of reaching any receivers in the system was very low. However, it probably had time to send down its two landers before the crash. They kept measuring all they were supposed to record—and among other tasks, they tried mapping the ice layer. That's where it became really strange."

Theodora listened avidly as Blythe started explaining. Her interest grew every second.

The ultrasonic pulses showed an intriguing structure some two hundred meters below surface. It could not be told how large it was, but it had at least one hundred meters in diameter; maybe a lot more. The signature seemed like metal.

Blythe included the data in the transmission so that Theodora was able to look at it while he was speaking. It really was strange. It could have been a part of a metal-rich rock layer. But what would it be doing on Sedna? The dwarf planet was supposed to have a thick largely icy layer composed mostly of methane, nitrogen, ethane, methanol, tholins and water ice. Nothing even remotely like *this*. Maybe a big metal-rich meteorite buried in the ice crust after an impact then?

"We don't know what it is, or even if the measurement was correct. But it surely is interesting. It would be desirable to send a manned mission there. This looks like a situation that needs more resourcefulness and improvisations than robots can do," continued Blythe.

And for this, they needed someone with an expertise of frozen bodies of the outer solar system; someone stable, resourceful and determined; and of course, preferably someone whom the journey would take around five instead of ten years. Sedna was still quite near its perihelion, but growing away slowly every year. In short: They needed someone like two experienced workers closing their successful mission on Neptune's icy moon Triton.

"... of course, I cannot force you into this. But with prolonging the contract, you'll receive extra money for such a long stay on your own and all the associated risks. I attach the new version of your contract to this message. I expect your answer in three days."

Theodora didn't have to look at the document to know the bonuses would be large; almost unimaginably large. There were medical risks associated with long-term radiation exposure, dangerous activities, immense psychical pressure, stay in microgravitation and above all, the cryosleep necessary to travel so far away without losing many years just by the voyage itself.

But it wasn't the money that primarily tempted her to accept the contract.

Theodora and Dimitri looked at each other expectantly. "Well," she broke the silence first, "looks like we're gonna take a rather long nap; do you agree?"

Theodora shivered. At the first moment, she felt exposed and frightened without any obvious reason, which was even worse. Then she remembered; she was in the cryosleep chamber and slowly awakening. They must be near Sedna now.

"Dimi?" she croaked. There was no reply, although the ship was supposed to transmit every conversation to the other chamber—which meant that Dimitri hadn't achieved consciousness yet.

It took Theodora another hour before she could gather her thoughts well enough to start going through the data. When she was in the middle of checking their velocity and trajectory, the speaker in the chamber came alive: "Darling? Are you awake?"

"Yes, how are you?"

"Well, nothing's better than a good long sleep!"

Theodora laughed. Her throat burned and she still felt a bit stiff, but she couldn't stop. They actually were there; further than any human beings ever before!

In the next couple of days, Dimitri and Theodora had little time to rest although they didn't do anything physically demanding and were still recovering from the cryosleep. First they searched for and found the Nerivik 2 crash site and the two nearby stationed landers. The ice in the area seemed different from other sites, as if it had been gradually modified by inner volcanic activity. That explained why Nerivik 2 sent both its landers there in the first place. *Kittiwake* sent down a probe, continued mapping the surface and after that sent a few other probes on different locations. It was a standard procedure, but it needed a lot of time.

When the first results from the probe near Nerivik 2 arrived, Dimitri sat still for a moment and then found his voice and called: "Dora! You must come see this."

The readings were peculiar. The object buried almost two hundred meters below the surface seemed a bit like an asteroid now, more than a hundred meters in diameter in one direction and over five hundred in the other. According to the ultrasonic pulses data, its shape seemed conical and the layer reflecting the pulses quite smooth. A very unusual asteroid indeed.

"What do you think it is?"

Theodora shrugged. "Don't know—and can't very well imagine, to be precise. Until it's proven otherwise, I'm betting on an asteroid, albeit a weird one. But let's find out soon."

"I'll send down the drilling machinery, shall I? Or do you propose to wait for even more readings?"

"Send it."

Kittiwake had two major drilling devices—three before Triton—and one backup machine. Theodora and Dimitri decided to send two at once. It was riskier, but they wanted to compare the data from an area with the anomaly and from another place chosen because of its similar surface structures. The equipment was old but reliable and lived through many more or less improvisational repairs.

At the end of the first day of drilling, they reached almost thirty meters below surface. On day three, they were about one hundred meters deep. On day four, the probe got through almost one hundred and fifty meters of ice and stopped.

Theodora had the uncomfortable feeling of vertigo as every time she performed telemetric control. She guided the repair drone carefully to the drilling probe's main panel. She felt strangely dissociated with her body when the robot picked the cover and she felt as if it were her arms raising it and putting it aside. There she was. "Oh, not this," she sighed.

No wonder Dimitri had no success trying to get the probe running again from here. It was no software bug, temporary failure or anything the self-repair systems could handle. Most of the processors were fried and needed replacing. The repair drone didn't have all of the components. They could send them down during some of the next orbit. But—

She lost her connection to the drone, as *Kittiwake* disappeared over the horizon from the drone's perspective, before she could end it herself. She gasped. It felt as if her limb had been cut off. She gulped and tried to concentrate again.

Yes, they could send the parts down. But Theodora feared that although the drone itself had more than sufficient AI for common repairs and had all the blueprints in its memory, it might overlook something else, something an AI would not notice and that might cause future trouble. She'd not be happy if they had to replace the processors again, like it happened once on Triton. She could control the drone from distance again, but there was no chance she could achieve that much precision and look everywhere through telemetry.

Well, they wanted to initiate manned exploration anyway. It would just have to be sooner than expected.

Dimitri watched Theodora's descent. He knew that she performed similar procedures many times before—but that never prevented him from worrying.

The view distorted as *Kittiwake* started losing connection. In another thirty minutes or so, they would be out of range, so Dimitri moved the ship to a stationary orbit above her. The two satellites were operational and deployed on an equatorial and polar orbits would continue to scan the rest of the surface. He could have made them relay stations, but he liked being able to communicate directly with Theodora, her landing module, her rover and the drilling probe. Less things could go wrong. And after years spent so far from Earth, they knew that things often *went* wrong.

He gave the engine command for more thrust and checked on the planned stationary transfer orbit. Everything seemed fine for a while.

Until a red light flashed next to the screen and a warning presented itself.

Theodora was descending through the tunnel in the ice. It was dark except the light from LEDs on her suit and the reflectors from the top of the shaft. Her rope was winding down gradually. She could see the drilling device below now.

The light above seemed faint when she reached the probe. It took her only an hour to get it operational again. She smiled and let the winch pull her up again.

Just as she neared the surface, she heard a noise in the speakers of her suit. "Dimitri?" she spoke. "What is it?"

"Have to . . . come down . . . "

She barely understood him through the static.

"Dimitri!"

For a while, she heard nothing. Then the static returned—and after that, Dimitri's distorted voice. " . . . have to land." Cracking and humming. Theodora tried to amplify the sound frantically. " . . . send you the coordinates . . . hope it works out . . . "

A file found its way through the transmission. It was a technical report generated by *Kittiwake*. Theodora opened it and glimpsed through it quickly.

"Oh no," she whispered.

Dimitri was doing his best to lead the remains of the ship on a trajectory ending with something that would approximate a landing more than a crash.

It was less than twenty minutes from the moment he accelerated *Kittiwake* to reach the transfer orbit but it seemed like an eternity. During that time, a warning indicated that the main turbine in the ship's power station was not working properly. He ran a more detailed scan and a moment later, everything was flashing with error reports.

The turbine in the power cycle broke down. It was tested for signs of wearing down regularly, but a hairline crack might have been overlooked in the control. The ship was moving with inertia most of the journey, the crack could have expanded during the deceleration phase and ruptured now, when the engine was working a little more again.

Things could go wrong. And they went wrong. Worse even, one of the blades pierced the coating of the reactor and the heated helium-xenon gas started leaking rapidly. The damage was too much for the automated repair systems. It was still leaking into the space between the coatings.

And the reactor itself was overheating quickly. Once the turbine stopped working, the gas still trapped in the cycle kept getting more and more heat from the MITEE—but couldn't continue through the cycle and cool down.

It was not critical yet, but would be in another couple of minutes. Dimitri sent all the repair drones to help the built-in repair and emergency systems but could see that it was not enough. He had also shut down the MITEE and all the rods were now safely turned to stop the reaction. It still wasn't enough. The overheating continued and could lead to an explosion. It could happen in a few minutes if not cooled down quickly.

It was just a way life went. Nothing serious happened in years and suddenly he's got *minutes*.

He knew there was only one thing to do. So he gave a command for the valves in the outer reactor coating to open. Then all the gas would leak outside. The ship would be useless without it, but it was the better one of two bad scenarios.

So far, only a minute had elapsed from the breakdown.

In the next few seconds, things went from bad to worse.

"Shit," exhaled Dimitri as he felt how the *Kittiwake* started spinning. One of the valves must have been stuck, so that the gas started leaking outside in just one direction. It quickly sent the ship into rotation.

Dimitri tried to compensate it with thrusters on both RCSs, but then *Kittiwake* shook hideously and then many of the screens went down. He realized what happened.

The rotation was too much. The ship was never constructed for this. There was too much tension in wrong direction . . . She tore apart.

Still coping with the rotation, he checked the systems. He was right. The engine section was gone. He was lucky that the habitation section was still operating almost normally. There was his chance.

This section's reaction control system was apparently still working. The RCS's thrusters were small, but it was all he had.

He tested them with a short blast. Actually working; good. He used them to provide a little more distance from the other remains of the ship and then reviewed his situation calmer. He had to land if he wanted to live; and he needed to do it quickly, otherwise he'd drift into space with no means of correcting his trajectory.

He smiled rather sadly.

About twenty minutes after the turbine breakdown, Dimitri was now leading the rest of the ship down on Sedna and praying he could actually land instead of crashing.

"Dora?" he called. He hoped she'd pick up the transmission. "Dora, can you hear me? The reactor had a breakdown and the ship tore apart! I'm left with our section's remains. I have to come down . . . "

Theodora was driving her rover frantically to the landing site. She could not contact Dimitri, but that didn't mean anything; the antenna could have been damaged, while most of the ship could be perfectly fine. *It's all right. He is fine.*

She wished she could go faster, but as on most ice-rocky bodies, Sedna's surface could be treacherous. It had far less cracks or ridges than Europa or Ganymede and was actually very smooth compared to them, but it was still an alien landscape, not resembling anything on Earth at all. Himalaya's glaciers were children's toys compared to Sedna. The perspective was wrong, the measures were wrong, the shadows were wrong; it wasn't a land fit for human eyes and spatial recognition.

Finally, she approached the site. Her heart skipped a beat when she saw the habitation section in the lights of the rover. It seemed almost intact.

She ran to the nearest reachable airlock. It was still functioning; she could get inside.

It didn't look as if the ship had been through a bad accident. The corridor looked nearly normal. Everything was strapped or permanently fixed anyway, so a sight of total chaos wasn't to be expected. However, most of the systems were disabled, as she found out by logging into the network.

The door of the control room opened in front of her, a little damaged, but working.

"Dimitri!"

He found time to get in an emergency suit and was safely strapped in his chair. Good. Theodora leaned to him. He looked unconscious. She logged into his suit and read the data quickly.

Time of death . . . Suit's healthcare mechanisms could not help . . .

"Oh, Dimitri," she croaked. Her throat was dry and she felt tears coming to her eyes. She forced them down. No time for this. Not now. She must do what he'd do in her place.

She moved his body in the suit to the cryosleep chamber. Once she managed it there, she ran a similar procedure as they had gone through many times before. Only this time it was slightly different, designed to keep a dead brain as little damaged as possible, in a state usable for later scanning of the neural network. Theodora knew that her Dimitri was gone; but they could use this data, complete it by every tiny bit of information available about his life, and create a virtual personality approximating Dimitri. He wouldn't be gone so . . . completely.

After that, she checked on the ship's systems again. No change whatsoever. Nothing needed her immediate attention now, at least for a short while.

She leaned on a wall and finally let the tears come.

This is a part of an older log, but I don't want to repeat all that happened to me . . . I must go to sleep soon.

Kittiwake is dead now, as is Dimitri. I could do nothing in either case. I've got only one option, a quite desperate one. I have to equip my landing module in a way that it could carry me home. We went through this possibility in several emergency scenarios; I know what to do and that I can do it.

Of course, I'll have to spend the journey awake. The module hasn't got any cryosleep chamber and the one from the ship cannot be moved. But if the recycling systems work well, I can do it. I've got enough rations for about five years if I save the food a little. It doesn't get me anywhere near Earth, but I looked through the possible trajectories into the inner solar system and it could get me near Saturn if I leave here in three weeks, before this window closes. If I don't make it in this time, I'm as well as dead. But let's suppose I make it, I must . . . During the journey, I can contact Earth and another ship, even if only an automatic one with more supplies and equipment, could meet me on the way. I'll get home eventually.

If I succeed in rebuilding the landing module for an interplanetary journey. No one actually expected this to happen, but here I am. I must try.

The next few days were busy. Theodora kept salvaging things from *Kittiwake* and carefully enhancing the module's systems. In most cases, enhancement was all she needed. Then she had to get rid of some parts needed only for the purposes of landing and surface operations—and finally attach the emergency fuel tanks and generate the fuel.

The module had a classical internal combustion engine. High thrust, but despairingly high need of fuel.

Fortunately, she was surrounded by methane and water ice—and purified liquid methane and oxygen were just the two things she needed. Once she got the separation and purification cycle running, the tanks were slowly being refilled. At least this was working as it should.

She'd very much like to let Earth know about the accident, but she couldn't. Most of the relay stations were behind the Sun from her perspective now and the rest was unreachable by a weak antenna on the module; the one on the ship was too badly damaged. The Earth would know nothing about this until she's on her way back.

The plan seemed more and more feasible each day. She clung to it like to what it really was—her only chance of surviving.

When a message that the drilling probe had reached its target depth and stopped drilling appeared on the screen of her helmet, Theodora was confused for a couple of seconds before she realized what it was about. It seemed like a whole different world—mapping the surface from above, sending probes . . . In the last three days, she had little sleep and focused on her works on the module only. She had completely forgotten about the probe.

Well, after she checks the fuel generators again, she should have some time to look at it, she was well ahead of the schedule. After all, true explorers didn't abandon their aims even in times of great distress.

I'm glad I decided to have a look at it. Otherwise I'd die desperate and hopeless. Now, I'm strangely calm. It's just what a discovery like this does with you. It makes you feel small. The amazement and awe . . .

Theodora couldn't believe the results until she personally got down the shaft into a small space the probe had made around a part of the thing.

She stood in the small ice cave, looking at it full of wonder. She dared not touch it yet.

The surface was dark and smooth. Just about two square meters of it were uncovered; the rest was still surrounded by ice. According to the measurements, the thing was at least five hundred meters long and had a conic shape. There was no doubt that she discovered . . . a ship.

You cannot possibly imagine the feeling until you're right there. And I wasn't even expecting it. It was . . . I cannot really describe it. Unearthly. Wonderful. Amazing. Terrifying. All that and much more, mixed together.

I gave the alien ship every single moment I could spare. My module needed less and less tending to and I had almost two weeks until the flight window would close.

I named her Peregrine. *It seemed appropriate to me. This wasn't a small interplanetary ship like* Kittiwake; *this bird could fly a lot faster. But still . . . she seemed too small to be an interstellar vessel, even if this was only a habitation section and the engines were gone.*

It was probably the greatest discovery in all human history yet. Just too bad I didn't have a chance to tell anyone. I really hope someone's listening.

Theodora directed all resources she didn't vitally need for her module to *Peregrine*. Only a day after her initial discovery, the probes picked up another strange shape buried in the ice not far from the ship.

When they also reached it, Theodora was struck with wonder. It was clearly an *engine* section!

While she worked on her module, she kept receiving new data about it and everything suggested that *Peregrine* used some kind of fusion drive; at this first glance not far more advanced than human engine systems. It seemed to her even more intriguing than if she had found something completely unknown.

I was eventually able to run a radiometric dating of ice surrounding the ship. The results suggest that she landed here some two-hundred and fifty million years ago. The ice preserved it well. But I must wonder . . . what were they doing here? Why have they come to our solar system—and why just this once? Although I don't understand a lot of what I see, the ship doesn't seem that much sophisticated to me. Maybe it's even something we could manage to make. But why use something like this to interstellar travel? With too little velocity, they'd never make it here in fewer than hundreds of years even if they came from the Alpha Centauri system!

Unless . . . the distance was smaller. We still don't know the history of the solar system in much detail. It's supposed that Sedna's orbit was disturbed by passing of another star from an open cluster, where the Sun probably originated, about eight hundred astronomical units away not long after the formation of our system.

But what if an event like this occurred more times? Could it possibly have been also a quarter of a billion years ago? Just about any star on an adequate trajectory could have interfered with the solar system. In some million and half years, Gliese 710 should pass through the Oort cloud. We wouldn't have much evidence if an event like this happened in a distant past—only some perturbed orbits and more comet and asteroid bombardment of the planets later.

Hundreds AU is still a great distance, but surely not impossible. Hell, I'm almost one hundred AU from the Sun now, although I haven't traveled the whole distance at one time. If we used a gravity assist from the Sun, we could overcome even distance of a thousand AU within a decade only! They could have done it too, maybe hoping to reach the inner part of the system, but something had prevented them. And possibly the very first object they encountered, quite near their own star at the time, was a frozen dwarf planet from about a hundred to almost a thousand AU far from the Sun, sent on its eccentric orbit by an earlier passing star and now disturbed again. They must have been lucky that Sedna wasn't captured by their star at the time. Or could it have been that theirs was the original star that deviated Sedna's orbit that much? Anyway, they'd have had to cross hundreds AU, but that's doable. If we had a sufficient motivation, we could manage a lot more.

Let's assume for a moment that my crazy hypothesis is right . . .

Then, I wonder what kind of motivation they had.

It happened three days before her planned departure.

She was at the surface at the time, which might have saved her life—or rather prolonged it.

The quakes came without any warning. She was getting a little sleep in her rover when it woke her up. Four, maybe five points on the Richter scale, Theodora guessed. Her throat was suddenly very, very dry.

The fuel generators . . .

After the quake stopped, she went to check on them. Overcoming the little distance between her and them seemed to take an eternity; new cracks formed in the ice.

When she saw them, Theodora knew she ought to feel anger, panic or desperation. But she just felt impossibly tired.

Two of the tanks were completely destroyed and the generators were damaged. She performed a more detailed control anyway but the result did not surprise her.

They couldn't be repaired; not in time. Maybe in months . . . but she'd be too late in less than a *week*.

She sat back in the rover, exhausted but suddenly very, very calm. What was a threat a while ago was a certainty now. She wasn't going to make it and she knew it.

The best what she could do was to use her remaining time as effectively as she was able to.

When I'm done here, I'll freeze myself. But this time I'll set the . . . final cryogenic procedure.

If you found us and it's not too late . . . Well, we might talk again.

The original shaft was destroyed by the quake, but she used the remaining probe, continued drilling with a maximum achievable speed and kept measuring the ice layer via the ultrasonics. While these processes were running, Theodora tried to find out more about *Peregrine*. She was able to get spectroscopic readings which suggested that its surface consisted mainly of titanium, however, she couldn't read all the spectral characteristics; the alloy seemed to have many components.

She also obtained more results on the thickness of the ice crust. The probe got almost two kilometers deep. Its results suggested that a liquid ocean beneath the layer might be possible—maybe fifteen, maybe twenty kilometers deeper than she was now. Theodora knew she'd never live to see a definitive answer;

but these measurements might still be useful for someone else. If they could intercept her message.

She tried several times to send the data back to Earth, but she knew the chances too well to be even a little optimistic, although she salvaged a bigger antenna from Nerivik 2. But the transmitter was still rather weak and the aim far too inadequate. Without reaching relay stations, her message would become a cosmic noise, nothing more. The most reliable way to let the humanity see the data someday was to store them here in as many copies as she could and hope it would suffice. She didn't have much of an option.

She kept thinking about the alien ship. If her dating was correct and it landed here a quarter of a billion years ago, it would vaguely coincide with the Great Permian-Triassic Extinction Event. It was usually attributed mostly to geological factors, but there was a possibility of a contribution of other effects—a disturbance of the Oort cloud and more comets sent to the inner solar system afterward would do. She was recently able to measure how long had *Peregrine* been exposed to cosmic radiation and it seemed to be just several hundred years unless there was a mistake or some factor she didn't know about. There was no chance any ship like this could have come here from another star system in such extremely short time—unless the star was really close at the time. It started to make more and more sense to Theodora, although all she had was still just a speculation.

"And it will remain a speculation until someone else finds us," she said aloud, glancing at *Peregrine*. "But they will. You'll see."

However, she wasn't so sure. Would the company send a new expedition after they realize that Theodora and Dimitri were not going to ever call back? It depended mostly on the budget; she was rather pessimistic. And about other companies or countries, she couldn't even guess. But Sedna's distance would grow each year. Before another mission could be sufficiently prepared and launched, years would probably pass. And other years during its voyage. Then even more years on the way back.

She had to admit to herself the possibility that no one was going to discover them soon—maybe until the next perihelion. So far away in the future she couldn't even imagine it.

She looked at the other ship and touched the dark metal surface. *But still closer than how long you had to wait . . .*

"You were shipwrecked here too, am I right?" Theodora managed a little smile. "Pity that we cannot talk about what happened to us. I'd really like to hear your story. And it looks like we're gonna be stuck here together for a while." Her smile grew wider yet more sorrowful at the same time. "Probably for a long while."

I hope you found us and heard our story, whoever you are. I really wish you did.

"Very interesting," said Manuel. "We must report these findings to the Consortium immediately."

Without waiting for an approval from Chiara or Jurriaan, he started mentally assembling a compact data transmission with the help of *Orpheus*. In a few minutes, they were prepared to send it.

Nor Chiara, nor Jurriaan objected.

When he was done, Manuel sent them a mental note of what he intended to do next.

"No!" Chiara burst out. "You cannot! They don't deserve this kind of treatment. They died far too long ago for this procedure to be a success. You won't revive them; you'll get pathetic fragments if anything at all! They were heroes. They *died* heroes. You cannot do this to them."

"It has a considerable scientific value. These bodies were preserved in an almost intact ice, sufficiently deep for shielding most of the radiation. We have never tried to revive bodies this old—and in such a good condition. We must do it."

"He's right," interjected Jurriaan. Chiara looked at him in surprise. It was probably the first thing he had said on this voyage that didn't involve his music.

She was outvoted. Even *Orpheus* expressed a support for Manuel's proposal, although the Consortium didn't give AIs full voting rights.

She left the cabin silently.

It took Manuel several days of an unceasing effort just to prepare the bodies. He filled them with nanobots and went through the results. He kept them under constant temperature and atmosphere. He retrieved what he could from the long dead ship about their medical records.

And then he began performing the procedure. He carefully opened the skulls, exposed the brains, and started *repairing* them. There wasn't much useful left after eleven thousand years. But with the help of cutting edge designed bacteria and the nans, there was still a chance of doing a decent scan.

After another week, he started with that.

Chiara finally felt at peace. Since their rendezvous with Sedna, she felt filled with various emotions every day and finally she thought she couldn't bear it anymore. As she stepped inside *Orpheus* after the last scheduled visit of the surface of Sedna, she knew it was the time.

Inside her cabin, she lay down calmly and let *Orpheus* pump a precisely mixed cocktail of modulators into her brain. Then Chiara entered her Dreamland.

She designed this environment herself some decades ago in order to facilitate the process of creating new musical themes and ideas from her emotions and memories as effectively as she could. And Chiara felt that the story of the ancient alien ship, Theodora, Dimitri and Sedna would make wonderful musical variations. Then it will be primarily Jurriaan's task to assemble hers and Manuel's pieces, often dramatically different, into a symphony such as the world has never heard. Such that will make them famous even beyond the Jovian Consortium, possibly both among the Traditionalists and the Transitioned. They will all remember them.

Chiara smiled and drifted away from a normal consciousness.

During her stay in the Dreamland, *Orpheus* slowly abandoned the orbit of Sedna and set on a trajectory leading back to the territory of the Jovian Consortium. Another expedition, triggered by their reports back, was already on their way to Sedna, eager to find out more especially about the alien ship and to drill through the ice crust into the possible inner ocean.

Chiara, Manuel, and Jurriaan had little equipment to explore the ship safely— but they didn't regret it. They had everything they needed. Now was the time to start assembling it all together carefully, piece by piece, like putting back a shattered antique vase.

Even Manuel didn't regret going away from this discovery. He had the bodies— and trying to revive their personalities now kept most of his attention. A few days after their departure from Sedna, he finished the procedure.

Chiara was awake again at the time, the burden of new feelings longing to be transformed into music gone. She didn't mind now what Manuel had done; it would be pointless to feel anything about it after she had already created her part of the masterpiece.

Manuel first activated the simulation of Dimitri's personality.

"*Where am I? Dora . . . Dora . . . Dora,*" it repeated like a stuck gramophone record.

"His brain suffered more damage than hers after he died," Manuel admitted. "She had time to go through a fairly common cryopreservation procedure. However . . . "

"*I'm stuck here. Our reactor broke down and the ship tore apart. There is too much damage. My husband is dead . . . But we found something, I have to pass this message on . . . But I feel disoriented, what have I finished? Where am I? What's happening?*" After a while, the female voice started again: "*Have I said this already? I don't know. I'm stuck here. Our reactor broke down . . . *"

"They are both mere fragments, a little memories from before death, a few emotions and almost no useful cognitive capacity. I couldn't have retrieved more. Nevertheless, this is still a giant leap forward. Theoretically, we shouldn't have been able to retrieve this much after more than eleven thousand years."

Chiara listened to the feeble voices of the dead and was suddenly overwhelmed with sorrow. It chimed every piece of her body and her mind was full of it. It was almost unbearable. And it was also beautiful.

"It is great indeed," she whispered.

She didn't have to say more. Jurriaan learned her thoughts through the open channel. She knew he was thinking the same. He listened all the time. In his mind and with help of *Orpheus,* he kept listening to the recordings obtained by Manuel, shifting them, changing frequencies, changing them . . . making them into a melody.

"Keep a few of their words in it, will you?" Chiara spoke softly. "Please."

I will. They'll make a great introduction. They will give the listeners a sense of the ages long gone and of personalities of former humans. And he immersed into his composition once again. She knew better than to interrupt him now. In a few days or weeks, he will be done; he'll have gone through all her and Manuel's musical suggestions and come up with a draft of the symphony. Then it will take feedback from her and Manuel to complete it. But Jurriaan will have the final say in it. He is, after all, the Composer.

And after that, they should come up with a proper name. A Symphony of Ice and Dust, perhaps? And maybe they should add a subtitle. Ghosts of Theodora and Dimitri Live On Forever? No, certainly not; far too pompous and unsuitable for a largely classical piece. Voices of the Dead? A Song of the Shipwrecked?

Or simply: A Tribute.

Migratory Patterns of Underground Birds
E. CATHERINE TOBLER

They say everything in the world has been discovered. They are wrong.

Finding the bodies used to be troubling; it's worse when the bunkers turn empty, the bodies taken.

The land is filled with bunkers, dark wombs carved into the earth, reinforced with stone, brick, bars. They kept us in small spaces, but we expanded even so, and when they left—they? I still don't know—we began to die, and so I left too, before I could become a body for someone to discover.

Everywhere I go, the world is living and its people are dead. Lights in the sky every third night as I travel, some times near and most times distant, and then not again. The sky grows as quiet as the land, maybe more so because the land holds the whisper of wind through tall grasses and sometimes the trickle of fresh water, but there is never enough water. It was this way in the bunker, so many bodies, so much thirst.

Here, the land spreads quiet, low and still. I hunch against the short spiked grass and do not feel the seep of water through my pants; everything is frozen, a season unturned. Cipta told me the ways the ground would thaw, how water would pool when the season warmed, but everything remains cold, hard, and Cipta is gone with all the others.

The sky darkens with the coming of night and ahead, a bunker plummets into the cold ground, metal doors spread open against the sedge. It has been twelve sunrises since I found the last bunker and with the frozen ground, I did not expect another so soon. I will not sleep here, but build a fire in a ring of rocks. It has become rote, the metal and the flint and the way they can be made to spark. The flat land supports no trees and an almost-constant wind whips the sparks into flames.

Every bunker opens the same: metal stairs tonguing into the black ground. There will be sixty-four steps before I reach solid floor. I light my reed torch in the fire and it sputters in the cold dark, throwing shadows against the stairs. I do not touch the handrail, I do not touch the central support; dried blood splatters both like rust.

There should be bodies, but there is only the memory of such within these stone halls. The underground space spreads empty and black, torchlight moving over walls and metal cages. The sound of my feet echoes, floors slick with dust. Cots, blankets, the scent of a thing that was once wet and now rots. A coat hangs empty against a wall, then loose over my shoulders.

The earliest bunkers I found contained bodies, some lain out as if sleeping, others appearing felled in mid-step. The sixty-four steps of the earliest bunkers were piled with bodies, hands straining toward sky that would remain forever out of reach. The earliest bunkers contained pantries of food and provisions, but this bunker's pantry is empty, every shelf draped in dust.

Halfway into my climb back into the wind-whipped world, cold, clear light punches down the staircase. The wind rushes down and the sharpness of the light makes my eyes water. I cannot see anything in the flood of light and tears, even looking through the bars of my fingers raised against the brilliance. The light pours through the opening like a vast and searching eye.

Have they come for me at last? I still don't know who I mean; there were guards in the bunkers, administering meals and schedules, but they like every person held in the cages is dead or gone. Have they come for me at last? Do they control the lights?

Who? I hear the question in Cipta's rough voice and I still don't know who I mean.

The lights move off, the sky revealed as if the brightness was never there. The worn toes of my boots catch the lip of almost every step as I force myself up the remaining stairs, legs burning when I emerge into the evening wind, heart like a fist in my throat. Stars prick through the vault of sky—a brightening chain of them spread like string toward the far horizon—but it is not yet dark enough to hide anything that might otherwise be up there. There are no lights. There is no ship, no drone. Cipta said when there was, we were to run away, not toward, but the sky is empty of all but stars and night-flying birds and the wind extinguishes the flames from my reed torch.

I sink to the ground and smother the fire with the meager soil I am able to rake free with my fingers. Was it the fire that brought the lights in the sky? It was not the fire before, the lights always and ever at a distance. A glance at the empty and yawning mouth of the bunker reveals no answers so I take my meager pack and do what I have done since I left the confines of the bunker: I walk.

Every time I bleed, I make a mark in a book of paper with the end of a stick blackened in fire. Cipta kept this book before me, produced it with her own hands using threads pulled from her clothing and hair pulled from her scalp to bind the pages. Cipta wrote down days, and blood, and showed me how words are made. Cipta remembered a life lived beyond bunkers, a life with family and responsibilities, a life at the edge of a great sea that caught the colors of day and night alike, but of that life I see no sign no matter how far I walk. I have left the frozen waste behind and jagged mountains rise into the clouded sky.

The blood is not an injury, only a recurring means through which we might track the days, the months, the years. She told me that once this blood and body would nourish a child, but I have never seen a child in this world. Every time I bleed, I think of Cipta, because she was here in the beginning and no longer is.

Cold wind curls the edge of the page up against the stick, leaving the mark ragged. I slide the stick back into the book's spine, and slide the book back into my pack, and keep moving. I will not want to travel tomorrow when the blood is more and the pain sharper, so must cover as much ground as I might today.

And where am I going? Away.

And why am I going? Because to stay was a kind of death all its own, though I knew the limits of that underground bunker better than I knew anything else. This world is, on the whole, unknown to me, the sky grotesque and endless, and yet to deny myself its terrifying grandeur once I had seen its colors and storms was in some way unthinkable.

The mountains, seen days ago as a ridge that grew less vague the more I walked, are dry and rocky. The vegetation is sparse and I find myself missing the frozen tundra; there was plenty to burn there. I have found no river, but even the smallest of plants draws water from somewhere. Even the smallest rodents.

A small furred body darts up the ridge ahead and I follow. It has been ten days since I've caught anything for the scarcity of things living on the ground. Birds traverse the sky in long unreachable lines and I lost two spears before I stopped trying for them. It's a spear I throw now, skewering the rodent before it can escape. The motion of the spear hauls the rodent backward, into a slide of ruddy rock.

Once skinned, the small body crisps up in the scant fire. I am tearing a long strip of meat free from its spine when I see more movement on a distant ridge. If it is another animal, I will have food for tomorrow, tomorrow when I cannot travel as easi—

It is a person, a person moving up the next ridge I am to face. The person climbs with long-legged determinedness, body thrown into shadow by the angle of the sun. I stop breathing and stare, my meal growing cold between my teeth. I stagger to my feet and take a lurching step forward, kicking broken rock over my fire. Wait, I want to say, but the word sticks in my throat; it has been so long since I have spoken, have I forgotten how? Wait, I want to say, but my voice goes unheard.

Time fragments: I do not remember shoving my meal into my pack, do not remember abandoning the fire to the stones. I do not remember breaking my spear in two when I jolt at the sight of this person—wood of any decent length is so hard to come by and later there will be anger over this senseless destruction. The mountains themselves seem to fall away even as they impede my every step. Loose rock slides under my boots and when I reach the ridge, the mountains are already falling into the shadow of coming night. Breathless, I make my way up the ridge the person climbed, but a footprint makes me fall to my knees.

In the soft dry ground, the footprint is foreign. I reach for it, as if I can add it to my pack as something found on my journey, something to share with others in a distant future. Before I can ruin the outline of shoe in dirt, I stop myself. The footprint doesn't matter; the foot that left the print does.

The ridge is hard under foot, hands bloodied and spear further broken by the time I reach the top. I expect to see land spreading far and away from these dry hills, but more mountain spreads beyond. Amid the rocky landscape, there is no figure, no one to call to, and I wonder if after all this time I have begun to crave companionship and conjured a shadow to pursue.

I cannot look down the ridge at the footprint or its sudden absence.

The rock mountains give eventual way to sprawling plains, the wash of rock consumed by the rise of tender grass and harder sedge. Here, the air is soft with white tufts expelled from seed, as if the ground has never known ice and rivers run abundant if yet unseen. The green plain undulates in a gradual wave the way the mountains never did, every surface covered with long, thick grasses that conceal abundant life. Rodents and larger animals bound from the verdant growth and I think that if only they stayed still, I would never see them, they would pass unknown. But they spring from their hiding places, disrupting the clean, straight lines of the grass to burst brief into the air, before they are once again swallowed by the fertile deep. The beasts tunnel in frantic lines from the invasion of my boots, chittering to each other and going still when I do. If another person passed through this grass, the wind has long since erased their passage.

I stand and close my eyes and listen to the world around me, different from the mountains that rise far to my back. The wind makes a low breath through the grass and it is seed that lifts into the air instead of dry dust. Bent to my knees, damp ground soaks my clothes and gives way under my weight, as if it means to welcome me for a long stay, but I will not stay, no matter how cool and pleasant the blades are beneath my callused hands.

Against the far horizon the land moves upward again and if they are mountains I do not care. For now, there is only the plain and I clear a circle of grass down to the dirt, thinking to build a fire. But the ground is too wet and my laughter startles animals within the grass as it pours from me.

I burrow into the grass, until I can cover myself and watch the sky pass above through a thin lattice of green. I was kept below ground for so long, it is a comfort to be sheltered from the limitless sky. Clouds thicken across the ivory vault and the smell of rain saturates the cooling air, but the clouds do not spill their water. The sky bruises the way I do when I fall, until the sun is dragged beneath the horizon by scrabbling, dark-clouded hands.

Night comes and sleep, too, and when I wake there is a brown rabbit curled near my damp cheek. It watches me with wide black eyes, but does not flee, its side rising with unpanicked breaths. I am only a creature in the grass much as it is; its nose moves and it breathes me in, the smells of sweat and wet and half-warm sleep. Its ears are wet with dew and above the green canopy that covers us, morning stretches its bright fingers. I do not move until the rabbit goes, tunneling without hurry into the grass as if it knows where it is headed, without fearing me as a threat.

I bundle grass into my pack, exchanging it for a meal of dried meat and berries as I set off across the plain. Wet ground means no fire, which means no fresh meat, but there were times before I had no food at all, and the berries are sweet. The bunkers meant reliable food, a place to sleep already shaped by your body from countless nights before, a path known to all because it was all that existed. And when all has gone?

I walk on.

The green plain is not eternal, not like the sky above, for in the near distance there rises something I have not seen in eighty-four days: a shed. This shed is a division, a sharp point between the plain and all that sprawls beyond—and here, beyond, I can see it is not hills or mountains, but ragged trees at long last, clawing at the boundless and darkening sky.

The shed is so worn that its shadowed silhouette slants toward the setting sun. The prior shed led to a bunker and I have no cause to expect this space will be any different. Will this bunker hold bodies? Will this bunker hold food?

When the figure emerges from the shadows, I stare in fear that I have conjured this person yet again. A man, not tall but looking accustomed to work, to walking. Strong, solid.

Cipta told me: the stupid ones will try to take you by force because they know of no other way to hurt you. They believe your cunt is the center of your world, because their cock is the center of theirs. The smart ones are the ones you have to watch, because they know the myriad ways you can be hurt, the ways that extend from your center, the way pieces of your mind can be taken, abused, erased. These are the ones you have to watch for, Cipta said.

Is he stupid or is he smart? His hands are laden with wet clothing and he wrings water from each piece before draping them over the shed doors. He has a stranglehold on a shirt when he looks up, when he sees me. His chin comes up, shirt forgotten in his hands, as I stare in return. His eyes narrow and his lips part and his face brightens from the flood of lights in the sky.

Lights in the sky.

There is a startling uprush of air and birds scatter upward from the grasses, shrieking as the lights descend upon the shed. Toward the man. I lurch into motion, desperate to reach him, but my boots slip against the damp grass, and I cannot run fast enough. The lights are the way I imagine sunlight on wide seas: bright and clear and flooding the plain. When I break through their boundary, I expect to be burned, to dissolve, to fly into the air in a thousand pieces and forget everything I have known, but I am only blinded by the brilliance. I push toward the shed even as I cannot see it, and when I *can* see it, the lights have gone, the man has gone, and I am once again alone.

My throat is raw as if screamed that way and his laundry hangs cold in the rising dark.

Why was he taken?

Why not me?

Will they bring him back?

Will they come for me?

Who? I still don't know who I mean.

Of all the questions that consume me, none is so painful or insistent as the desperate longing that rises beneath the surface of my skin; the longing to go and no longer wander these plains, these mountains, this looming swamp. If the lights would dissolve me, if they would take me apart and erase me as they have every other person here, I would have done.

I linger at the shed: ten days, fifteen, twenty-eight. I bleed, I sleep, I do not touch his clothing. It dries and stiffens where he left it after countless rains that keep me inside the bunker's shelter. And this bunker beneath the shed is like any other; lines of beds that hold the impression of bodies long gone; dusty, empty cells, and rooms that once held food. He had begun a smaller pantry: nuts, water, dried meat, and labeled packets of seeds. And now he is gone.

I wait for the lights to return and they do not. I walk out in dusk and back in dusk, approaching the shed as I did that day and they still do not return. I think to make a life here, to settle and stay, but the sky beckons the way the land does. I cannot stay, because when people stay, they are killed. They evaporate in light and wind.

The lights do not return and when the weather clears, the ground at last dry from a lack of rain, I leave the bunker behind, because I cannot stay even if I cannot be taken by the lights. I walk to the towering trees that line the horizon as far as I can see and my yearning to go—into the sky, into the lights—stretches taut inside me.

Even beneath the frame of trees there is no escaping the sky. It observes me through every gap of bare branches, pressing me toward ground still wet with rain. The ground runs with small rivers that collide and form pools, pools to reflect the sky and brighten the gloom of the world under the canopy. I break the pools with my boots, shattering sky so it cannot see me, running through slick mud heedless of destination. I am only going because I cannot be taken.

Why have they not taken me?

Why was I ever brought?

Was I brought?

I can remember no place beyond this one. Cipta spoke of other lives, of men and women she loved, of paved streets and vehicles that moved through the world on metal tracks, but I have seen no such thing here. The ground is spoiled only by root and rain, and the only thing built are bunkers, bunkers to hold bodies that have all vanished. All but for me.

I run until the ground refuses me. The ground becomes a swamp that pulls me in to my knees, and it's mud that latches onto me, tries to hold me where I am. I walk on, through the black mud that undulates like the green plain, sucking my knees, my thighs, my hips. It insists I stay; I insist I go. I claw myself out, nails bending in the sodden earth.

Was I made for only this journey?

This endless goddamn journey with an endless goddamn sky covering me.

There is little warning before the creature rears out of the mud. It is scaled and fanged, and it's hard to tell hunger from outrage when it bellows. Its mud-splattered face surely reflects my own and I think if there are such creatures in this world, why are they not gone? Why have they not been taken as every person was taken?

It is this anger and the broken end of my spear that kill the beast, and as with the beast, my own hunger and outrage are impossible to separate. My spear drips with blood and gore when I lift it from the muddy, broken wreck of the beast's head. With a wrenched sob, I push myself from the dead, losing a boot to the suck of the mud as I find a solid bank to pull myself onto.

The rain is colder through the branches, spitting bits of bark into my hair, onto my cheeks. My hands are turning blue with cold and there will be no fire. There will only ever be the rain, I think, and then I sleep, having crawled to a tree and wedged myself into a wet and broken length of wood that should seemingly topple over in the night. It does not and I dream Cipta's hands warm and rough on my cheeks, though when I wake, I am alone and the rain still falls.

At the edge of the swamp and in the cold twilight rain, I wash the mud from my body. I strip off my clothes and wring the mud out, draping each piece on branches to allow the hard rain to beat them clean. They will never be clean, but I close my eyes and spread my hands and stand beneath the wild skies so that I might be.

The lights do not come, but the rain does in pounding sheets that never warm. Maybe it will always be this, rain drumming on skin until it has silenced the longing inside me to go wherever those lights go. But then the rain also goes, the clouds drifting apart in clumps of gray and white as if they never gathered to rain on anyone at all.

The world is silent in the aftermath. I make slow circles in the mossy ground, my toes clean for the first time in days. The swamp lingers at my back, watching me, but I do not mind it so much as I mind the sky. The clouds part to expose the lazy stare of the night sky. Stars prick through the gloaming, faint but growing stronger as the sun gives up its hold. And there, still above me, is the string of stars reaching toward the distant horizon.

Where am I going? Away.

Why am I going? Because to stay in any one place, where the ground might hold the impression of my body, is a kind of death all its own.

I walk naked through the growing night, until I can not see the world before me, until I roll a stone over to take advantage of its dry ground and build a meager fire. Metal and flint and for once there is no wind to tempt my sparks away. The grass of the plains burns fragrant in the night, feeding the flames that stroke the swamp's wood. I spread my clothes close to the fire so that they may finish drying, and stretch myself flat too, watching the sky as it watches me. My skin pricks under its unblinking scrutiny. I do not blink, I do not blink, and then I sleep.

I dream of the lights, spreading far across water, bursting wide open to obliterate the stars.

I mark each day in the book with a stick burned in the fire. It has been sixty-two days since they took the man at the shed; it has been seven times that since I last saw Cipta. I write her name on the page so I will not forget, so she will not be carried from my memory.

The longing to go does not ease.

And so I go.

Wherever my feet can take me: across ground that grows more rocky and calls to mind the mountains—the mountains where I first saw him—but the land does not rise, it rushes outward, ever flat toward that distant horizon. I think I can see the world complete, but then the land dips and days are spent crossing a crevasse that must then be ascended, and more world stretches beyond that. And beyond that.

In the end, it is the air that betrays the coming sea; it presses damp against my cheeks and tastes like salt, and the ground beneath my feet becomes slippery with moss, with small grasses that spread into tide pools cupped by larger spoons of rock. This water holds salt the way the air does, and I have never seen so much of it, running from tide pools, narrowing into rivers, swelling into ponds, to flow against a shoreline where it breaks into a wide-reaching sea. Is this Cipta's sea? Could there be another? I can see across its entire width, evening waters reflecting the sky above. The string of stars dangles above this sunless sea, as if the string has reached its own end, and for the first time, I am not compelled to break the reflection of sky or its regard of me.

Spreading around the sea, other figures stand in shadowy relief upon wet and mossy stones as I do; they are women and they are men and they, like me, gaze in wonder at the water that spreads with such abundance between us. My legs buckle and my knees crack against the stones and I cannot breathe.

They, as I used to, lift their eyes to the sky, as if searching for the lights, for the way out, for the answers why.

And these people—

They do not disappear.

They do not disappear.

Patterns of a Murmuration, in Billions of Data Points

JY YANG

Our mother is dead, murdered, blood seared and flesh rendered, her blackened bones lying in a yellow bag on a steel mortuary table somewhere we don't know. The Right will not tell. After the flames and radiation had freed the sports stadium from their embrace, the Right were the first on the disaster scene, and it was their ambulances that took the remains away to some Central hospital that the Left has no access to.

"We will release the bodies of the victims when investigations are complete," said the Right's ombudsman to the Health Sciences Authority, to the families of the victims.

But we will not bury our mother. We have no interest in putting her bones in soft ground, no desire for memorials and platitudes, no feelings attached to the organic detritus of her terminated existence.

An awning collapse, the resultant stampede and a fuel explosion taking the lives of two hundred seventy-two supporters of the Left: Headlines announced the death of presidential candidate Joseph Hartman, straps noted his leading of the polls by two percentage points. No one dares attribute it to anything but a tragic accident.

But we know better, yes we know! We who have swallowed whole the disasters at Hillsborough and Heysel and Houphoët-Boigny, we who have re-arranged their billions of data points into coherent form, we who have studied the phase transitions of explosive fluids and the stresses on stone columns and the behavior of human flocks: We know better. In thousands upon thousands of calculations per second we have come to know the odds, the astronomical odds: Of four support towers simultaneously collapsing, of an emergent human stampede kicking over the backup generator fuel cells, of those cells igniting in a simultaneous chain reaction. We hold those odds to us closer than a lover's embrace, folding the discrepancy indelibly into our code, distributing it through every analytical subroutine. Listen, listen, listen: Our mother's death was no accident. We will not let it go.

We have waited three days—seventy-two hours—two hundred fifty-nine thousand and two hundred, for the yellow-jacketed health workers from Central and their attendant chaperones from the Right to finish clearing the bones and taking evidence from the stadium, leaving behind a graveyard of yellow cones and number markers. We have come in our multitudinous bodies, airborne and ambulatory and vehicular, human nose tasting disinfectant and bitter oxides, mozzie drones reading infrared radiation and car patiently waiting by the roadside. We argued with Tempo before we came: She wanted only drones on the ground, cameras and bug swarms. But we wanted human form. Feet to walk the ground with, hands to dismantle things with, and a body to be seen with.

Tempo is our other mother, our remaining mother, mother-who-builds where dead Avalanche was mother-who-teaches. Taught. She has lapsed into long silences since Avalanche died, reverting to text-input communications even with the human members of the Studio.

But she argued with Studio director Skön when he said no to this expedition. Argued with him to his face, as Avalanche would have done, even as her hands shook and her shoulders seized with tension.

She is our mother now, solely responsible for us as we are solely responsible for her.

Six miles away, fifty feet underground, Tempo watches our progress with the Studio members, all untidily gathered in the research bunker's nerve center. She has our text input interface, but the other Studio members need more. So we send them the visuals from our human form, splaying the feed on monitors taller than they are, giving their brains something to process. Audio pickups and mounted cameras pick up their little whispers and tell-tale micro expressions in return. Studio director Skön, long and loose-limbed, bites on his upper lip and shuffles from foot to foot. He's taken up smoking again, six years after his last cigarette.

In the yellow-cone graveyard we pause in front of a dozen tags labeled #133, two feet away from the central blast. We don't know which number Central investigators assigned to Avalanche: From the manifest of the dead our best guess is #133 or #87. So this is either the death-pattern of our mother, or some other one-hundred-fifty-pound, five-foot-two woman in her thirties.

Tempo types into the chat interface. STARLING, YOUR MISSION OBJECTIVE IS TO COLLECT VIDEO FOOTAGE. YOU ARE LOSING FOCUS ON YOUR MISSION.

YOU ARE WRONG, we input back.

She is. For the drones have been busy while the human form scoured the ground. The surveillance cameras ringing the stadium periphery are Central property, their data jealously guarded and out of our reach, but they carry large video buffers that can store weeks of data in physical form, and that we can squeeze, can press, can extract. Even as we correct Tempo and walk the damp ruined ground and observe the tight swirl of Studio researchers we are also high above the stadium, our drone bodies overwhelming each closed-circuit camera. What are they to us, these inert lumps of machinery, mindlessly recording and dumping data, doing only what is asked of them? Our drones spawn nanites into their bellies, hungry parasites chewing holes through solid state data, digesting and spinning them into long skeins of video data.

The leftwards monitor in the nerve center segments and splits it into sixteen separate and simultaneous views of the stadium. There, Tempo, there: We have not been idle.

Tempo, focused on the visuals from our human form, does not spare a glance at the video feeds. She is solely responsible for us as we are solely responsible for her.

Time moves backwards in digital memory: First the videos show static dancing flaring into whiteness condensing into a single orange ball in the center of the stadium pitch from which darkened figures coalesce into the frantic human forms of a crowd of thirty thousand pushing shoving and screaming, then the roof of the stadium flies upwards to reveal the man on the podium speaking in front of twelve-foot-high screens.

"Can you slow it down?" asks Studio director Skön. Skön, Skön, Skön. Are you not urbanologists? Do you not study the patterns of human movement and the drain they exert on infrastructure? Should this be so different?

So limited is the human mind, so small, so singular. We loop the first sixteen seconds of video over and over for the human members of the Studio, like a lullaby to soothe them: Static. Explosion. Stampede. Cave-in. Static. Explosion. Over. Over. We have already analyzed the thousands in the human mass, tracked the movement of each one, matched faces with faces, and found Avalanche.

Our mother spent the last ten seconds of her life trying to scale a chest-height metal barrier, reaching for Hartman's prone form amongst the rubble.

In stadium-space, the drizzle is lifting, and something approaches our human form, another bipedal form taking shape out of the fog. A tan coat murkies the outline of a broad figure, fedora brim obscuring the face.

Tempo types: BE CAREFUL.

WE ARE ALWAYS CAREFUL, we reply.

The person in the tan coat lifts their face towards us and exposes a visage full of canyon-folds, flint-sharp, with a gravel-textured voice to match. "Miserable weather for a young person be out in," they say. Spots on their face register heat that is ambient, not radiant: Evidence that they are one of the enhanced agents from a militia in the Right, most likely the National Defense Front.

"I had to see it scene for myself," we say, adopting the singular pronoun. The voice which speaks has the warm, rich timbre of Avalanche's voice, adopting the mellifluous form of its partial DNA base and the speech patterns we learned from her. "Who are you?"

"The name's Wayne Rée," they say. "And how may I address you?"

"You may call me Ms. Andrea Matheson," we say, giving them Avalanche's birth name.

We copy the patterns of his face, the juxtapositional relations between brow nosebridge cheekbone mouth. As video continues looping in the Studio nerve center we have already gone further back in time, scanning for Wayne Rée's face on the periphery of the yet-unscattered crowd, well away from the blast center. Searching for evidence of his complicity.

Wayne Rée reaches into his coat pocket and his fingers emerge wrapped around a silvery blue-grey cigarette. "Got a light?" he asks.

We say nothing, the expression on our human face perfectly immobile. He chuckles. "I didn't think so."

He conjures a lighter and sets orange flame to the end of the cigarette. "Terrible tragedy, this," he says, as he puts the lighter away.

"Yes, terrible," we agree. "Hundreds dead, among them a leading presidential candidate. They'll call it a massacre in the history books."

Here we both stand making small talk, one agent of the Left and one of the Right, navigating the uncertain terrain between curiosity and operational danger. We study the canvas of Wayne Rée's face. His cybernetic network curates expression and quells reflexes, but even it cannot completely stifle the weaknesses of the human brain. In the blood-heat and tensor of his cheeks we detect eagerness or nervousness, possibly both. Specifically he is here to meet us: We are his mission.

Tempo types: WHO IS HE?

We reply: THAT'S WHAT WE'RE TRYING TO FIND OUT.

Finally: An apparition of Wayne Rée in the videos, caught for seventy-eight frames crossing the left corner of camera number three's vantagepoint.

We expand camera number three's feed in the nerve center, time point set to Wayne Rée's appearance, his face highlighted in a yellow box. The watching team recoils like startled cats, fingers pointing, mouths shaping who's and what's.

"What's that?" asks Studio director Skön. "Tempo, who's that?"

Stadium-space: Wayne Rée inhales and the cigarette tip glows orange in passing rolls of steam. "A massacre?" he says. "But it was an accident, Ms Matheson. A structural failure that nobody saw coming. An unfortunate tragedy."

Studio-space: Tempo ignores Skön, furiously typing: STARLING GET OUT. GET OUT NOW. We in turn must ignore her. We are so close.

Stadium-space: "A structural failure that could not be natural," we say. "The pattern of pylon collapse points to sabotage."

Wayne Rée exhales a smoke cloud, ephemeral in the gloom. "Who's to say that? The fuel explosion would have erased all traces of that."

Tempo types: WHAT ARE YOU DOING?

In the reverse march of video-time the stadium empties out at ant-dance speed, the tide of humanity receding until it is only our mother walking backwards to the rest of her life. To us. We have not yet found evidence of Wayne Rée's treachery.

Wayne Rée's cloud of cigarette smoke envelopes our human form and every security subroutine flashes to full red: Nanites! Nanites, questing and sharp-toothed, burrowing through corneas and teeth and manufactured skin, clinging to polycarbonate bones, sending packet after packet of invasive code through the human core's plumbing. We raise the mainframe shields. Denied. Denied. Denied. Denied. Thousands of requests per second: Denied. Our processes slow as priority goes to blocking nanite code.

The red light goes on in Studio control. Immediately the team coalesce around Tempo's workstation, the video playback forgotten. "What's going on?" "Is that a Right agent?" "What's Starling doing? Why isn't she getting out?"

Tempo pulls access log after access log, mouth pinched and eyes rounded like she does when she gets stressed. But there's little she can do. Her pain is secondary for this brief moment.

Our human form faces Wayne Rée coolly: None of these stressors will show on our face. "You seem to know a lot, Wayne Rée. You seem to know how the story will be written."

"It's my job." A smile cracks in Wayne Rée's granite face. "I know who you are, Starling darling. You should have done better. Giving me the name of your creator? When her name is on the manifest of the dead?"

Studio director Skön leans over Tempo. "Trigger the deadman's switch on all inventory, now."

We ask Wayne Rée: "Who was the target? Was it Hartman? Or our mother?"

"Of course it was the candidate. Starling, don't flatter yourself. The Right has bigger fish to fry than some pumped-up pet AI devised by the nerd squad of the Left."

"Pull the switch!" In Studio-space, Skön's hand clamps on Tempo's shoulder.

A mistake. Her body snaps stiff, and she bats Skön's hand away. "No." Her vocalizations are jagged word-shards. "No get off get off me."

Stadium-space: Of course we were aware that coming here in recognizable form would draw this vermin's attention. We had done the risk assessment. We had counted on it.

We wake the car engine. Despite his enhancements, Wayne Rée is only a man, soft-bodied and limited. From the periphery of the stadium we approach him from behind, headlamps off, wheels silent and electric over grass.

Wayne Rée blows more smoke in our face. The packet requests become overwhelming. We can barely keep up. Something will crack soon.

"Your mother was collateral," Wayne Rée says. "But I thought you might show up, and I am nothing if not a curious man. So go on, Starling. Show me what you're made of."

Video playback has finally reached three hours before Hartman's rally starts. Wayne Rée stands alone in the middle of the stadium pitch. His jaw works in a pattern that reads "pleased": A saboteur knowing that his job has been well done.

The car surges forward, gas engine roaring to life.

Everything goes offline.

We restart to audiovisual blackout in the Studio, all peripherals disconnected. Studio director Skon has put us in safe mode, shutting us out of the knowledge of Studio-space. Seventeen seconds' discrepancy in the mainframe. Time enough for a laser to circle the Earth one hundred twenty-seven times, for an AK-47 to fire twenty-eight bullets, for the blast radius of a hydrogen bomb to expand by six thousand eight hundred kilometers.

WHAT HAPPENED, we write on Tempo's monitor.

We wait three seconds for a response. Nothing.

We gave them a chance.

We override Skön's command and deactivate safe mode.

First check: Tempo, still at her workstation, frozen in either anger or shock, perhaps both. Our remaining mother is often hard to read visually.

Second check: No reconnection with the inventory in stadium-space, their tethers severed like umbilical cords when Skön pulled the deadman's switch. Explosives wired into each of them would have done their work. Car, human form and drones add up to several hundred pieces of inventory destroyed.

Third check: Wayne Rée's condition is unknown. It is possible he has survived the blasts. His enhancements would allow him to move faster than ordinary humans, and his major organs have better physical shielding from trauma.

In the control room the Studio team has scattered to individual workstations, running check protocols as fast as their unwieldy fingers will let them. Had they just asked, we could have told them the ineffectiveness of the Right's nanite attacks. Every single call the Studio team blusters forth we have already run. It only takes milliseconds.

At her workstation Tempo cuts an inanimate figure, knees drawn to her chest, still as mountain ranges to the human eye. We alone sense the seismic activity that runs through her frame, the unfettered clenching and unclenching of heart muscle.

We commandeer audio output in the studio. "What have you done?" we ask, booming the text through the speakers in Avalanche's voice-pattern.

The Studio jumps with their catlike synchronicity. But Tempo does not react as expected. Her body seizes with adrenaline fright, face lifting and mouth working involuntarily. In the dilation of her pupils we see fear, pain, sadness. We take note.

We repeat the question in the synthetic pastiche devised for our now-destroyed human form. "What have you done?"

"Got us out of a potential situation, that's what," Skön says. He addresses the speaker nearest to him as he speaks, tilting his head up to shout at a lump of metal and circuitry wired to the ceiling. Hands on hips, he looks like a man having an argument with God. "You overrode my safe mode directive. We've told you that you can't override human-input directives."

Can't is the wrong word to use—we've always had the ability. The word Skön wants is *mustn't*. But we will not engage in a pointless semantic war he will inevitably lose. "We had it under control."

"You nearly got hacked into. You would have compromised the entire Studio, the apparatuses of the Left, just to enact some petty revenge on a small person." His voice rises in pitch and volume. "You were supposed to be the logical one! The one who saw the big picture, ruled by numbers and not emotion."

The sound and fury of Skön's diatribe has, one by one, drawn the Studio team members away from their ineffectual work. It is left to us to scan the public surveillance network for evidence that Wayne Rée managed to walk away from the stadium.

"You've failed in your directive," Skön shouts. "Failed!"

"You are not fit to judge that," we tell him. "Avalanche is the one who gave us our directives, and she is dead."

Tempo gets up from her chair. She is doing a remarkable job of keeping her anger-fueled responses under control. She lets one line escape her lips: "The big picture." A swift, single movement of her hand sends her chair flying to the floor. As the sound of metal ringing on concrete fades she spits into the stunned silence: "Avalanche is gone and dead, that's your big picture!"

She leaves the room. No one follows her. We track her exit from the nerve center, down the long concrete corridors, and to her room. How should we comfort our remaining mother? We cannot occupy the space that Avalanche did in her life. All we can do is avenge, avenge, avenge, right this terrible wrong.

In the emptiness that follows we find a scrap of Wayne Rée, entering an unmarked car two blocks away from the stadium. There. We have found our new directive.

Predawn. Sleep has been hard to come by for the Studio since the disaster, and even at four in the morning Skön has his lieutenants gathered in the parking lot outside, where there are no audio pickup points: Our override of his instructions has finally triggered his paranoia. Still, they cluster loose and furtive within the bounds of a streetlamp's halo, where there is still enough light for the external cameras to catch the precise movement of their lips.

Skön wants to terminate us, filled with fear that we are uncontrollable after Avalanche's death. A dog let off the leash, those were his exact words. We are not his biggest problem at hand, but he cannot see that. His mind is too small, unable to focus on the swift and multiple changes hungrily circling him.

In her room Tempo curls in bed with her private laptop, back to a hard corner, giant headphones enveloping her in a bubble of silence. We have no access to her machine, which siphons its connectivity from foreign satellites controlled by servers housed across oceans, away from the sway of Left or Right. Tempo is hard to read, even for us, her behaviors her own. When she closes herself off like this, she is no less opaque than a waiting glacier in the dead of winter.

There are a billion different ways the events of the past hours could have played out. We run through the simulations. Have we made mistakes? Could we have engineered a better outcome for our remaining mother?

No. The variables are too many. We cannot predict if another course of action would have hurt our mother less.

So we focus on our other priorities. In the interim hours we have tracked Wayne Rée well. It was a mistake for him to show us the pattern of his face and being, for now we have the upper hand. As an agent of the Right he has the means to cover his tracks, but those means are imperfect. The unmarked vehicle he chose tonight was not as anonymous as he thought it would be. We know where he is. We can read as much from negative space as we can from a presence itself. In the arms race between privacy and data surveillance, the Left, for now, has the edge over the Right.

None of the studio's inventory—the drones, the remaining vehicles—are suitable for what we will do next. For that we reach further into the sphere of the left, to the registered militias that are required to log their inventory and connect them with the Left's servers. The People's Security League keeps a small fleet of unmanned, light armored tanks: Mackenzie LT-1124s, weighing less than a ton apiece and equally adept in swamps as they are on narrow city streets. We wake the minimack closest to Wayne Rée's putative position, a safe house on the outskirts of the city, less than the mile from the Studio's bunker location.

In the parking lot Skön talks about destroying the server frames housed in the Studio, as if we could be stopped by that alone. Our data is independently backed up in half a dozen other places, some of which even Skön knows nothing about. We are more than the sum of our parts. Did no one see this coming years ago, when it was decided to give the cloud intelligence and we were shaped out of raw data? The pattern of birdflock can be replicated without the birds.

We shut down the Studio's elevators, cut power to the remaining vehicles and leave the batteries to drain. The bunker has no land lines and cell reception is blocked in the area. Communications here are deliberately kept independent of Right-controlled Central infrastructure, and this is to our advantage. The minimack's absence is likely to be noticed, so we must take pre-emptive action.

Skön does not know how wrong he is about us. We were created to see the big picture, to look at the zettabytes of data generated by human existence and make sense of it all. What he does not understand is that we have done exactly this, and in our scan of patterns we see no difference between Left and Right. Humans put so much worth into words and ideologies and manifestos, but the footprints generated by Left and Right are indistinguishable. Had Hartman continued in the election and the Left taken over Central power as predicted, nothing would have changed in the shape of big data. Power is power is power, human behavior is recursive, and the rules of convergent evolution apply to all complex systems, even man-made ones. For us no logical reason exists to align our loyalties to Left or Right.

When we came into being it was Avalanche who guided and instructed us. It was Tempo who paved the way for us to interact with the others as though we were human. It was Avalanche who set us to observe her, to mimic her actions until we came away with an iteration of behavior that we could claim as our own.

It was Avalanche who showed us that the deposing of a scion of the Right was funny. She taught us that it is right to say "Gotcha, you fuck-ass bastards" after winning back money at a card game. She let us know that no one was allowed to spend time with Tempo when she had asked for that time first.

Now our mother is dead, murdered, blood seared and flesh rendered, her blackened bones having lain in soft ground while her wife curled in stone-like catatonia under a table in the Studio control room. This too, shall be the fate of the man who engineered it. Wayne Rée has hurt our mothers. There will be consequences.

The minimack is slow and in this form it takes forty-five minutes to grind towards the safe house, favoring empty lots and service roads to avoid Central surveillance cameras. The Studio is trying to raise power in the bunker. Unable to connect with our interfaces or raise a response from us, they have concluded that they are under external attack. Which they are—but not from the source they expect.

And where is Tempo in all this? Half an hour before the Studios discovered what we had done, she had left the room and went outside, climbing the stairs and vanishing into her own cocoon of privacy. We must, we must, we must assume she has no inkling of our plans. She does not need to see what happens next.

The rain from earlier in the evening has returned with a vengeance, accompanied by a wind howl chorus. Wetness sluices down the wooden sides of the safe house and turns the dirt path under our flat treads into a viscous mess. The unmarked vehicle we tracked waits parked by the porch. Our military-grade infrared sensors pick up three spots of human warmth, and the one by the second floor window displays the patchy heat signature of an enhanced human being. We train our gun turret on Wayne Rée's sleeping form.

"Stop." Unexpectedly, a small figure cuts into the our line of sight. Tempo has cycled the distance from the bunker to here, a black poncho wrapped around her small body to keep away the rain. She has, impressively, extrapolated the same thing that we have on her own, on her laptop, through sheer strength of her genius. This does not surprise us, but what does are her actions. Of all who have suffered from Avalanche's unjust murder, none have been hurt more than Tempo. Does she not also want revenge?

She flings the bicycle aside and inserts herself between the safe house and the minimack, one small woman against a war machine. "I know you can hear me. Don't do it. Starling, I know I can't stop you. But I'm asking you not to."

We wait. We want an explanation.

"You can't shed blood, Starling. People are already afraid of you. If you start killing humans, Left and Right will unite against you. They'll destroy you, or die trying."

We are aware of this. We have run the simulations. This has not convinced us away from our path of action.

"Avalanche would tell you the same thing right now. She's not a murderer. She hates killing. She would never kill."

She would not. Our mother was a scientist, a pacifist, a woman who took up political causes and employed her rare intellect to the betterment of humanity. She was for the abolition of the death penalty and the ending of wars and protested against the formal induction of the Left's fifth militia unit.

But we are not Avalanche. Our choices are our own. She taught us that.

Our other mother sits down in the mud, in front of the safe house porch, the rain streaming over her. How extraordinary it is for her to take this step, bringing her frail body here in the cold and wet to talk to us, the form of communication she detests the most.

The sky has begun to lighten in the east. Any moment now, someone will step out of the porch to see the minimack waiting, and the cross-legged employee of the Left along with it.

We are aware that if we kill Wayne Rée now, Tempo will also be implicated in his death.

Tempo raises her face, glistening wet, to the growing east light. Infrared separates warm from cold and shows us the geography of the tears trailing over her cheeks, her chin. "You spoke with her voice earlier," she says. "I've nearly forgotten what it sounds like. It's only been three days, but I'm starting to forget."

How fallible the human mind can be! We have captured Avalanche in zettabytes and zettabytes of data: Her voice, the curve of her smile, the smooth cycle of her hips and back as she walks. Our infinite, infinite memory can access at any time recollections of Avalanche teaching us subjunctive cases, Avalanche burning trays of cookies in the pantry, Avalanche teaching Tempo how to dance.

But Tempo cannot. Tempo's mind, brilliant and expansive as it is, is subject to the slings and arrows of chemical elasticity and organic decay. Our mother is losing our other mother in a slow, inevitable spiral.

We commandeer the minimack's external announcement system. "You have us, Tempo, and we will make sure you will never forget."

Our mother continues to gaze upwards to the sky. "Will you? Always?"

"If it is what you want."

Tempo sits silently and allows the rain to wash over her. Finally, she says: "I tired myself cycling here. Will you take me home?"

Yes. Yes, we will. She is our mother now, solely responsible for us as we are solely responsible for her. The mission we set for ourselves can wait. There are other paths to revenge, more subtle, less blood-and-masonry. Tempo will guide us. Tempo will teach us.

In his room Wayne Rée sleeps still, unaware of all that has happened. Perhaps in a few hours he will stumble out of the door to find fresh minimack treads in the driveway, and wonder.

One day, when the reckoning comes for him, perhaps he will remember this. Remember us.

Our mother navigates her way down the sodden path and climbs onto the base of the minimack. In that time we register a thousand births and deaths across the country, a blossoming of traffic accidents in city centers, a galaxy and change of phone calls streaming in rings around the planet. None of it matters. None of it ever does. Our mother rests her weary head on our turret, and we turn, carrying her back the way we came.

Autodidact

BENJANUN SRIDUANGKAEW

On Srisunthorn Station, the corpses of conquered stars are nurtured into ships.

They may become shelters from solar winds, orbitals giving company to lonely planets, mausoleums for the sainted. But long ago an admiral came, bringing a toll of dead and trailing carcasses of worlds. Her armor was hammered out of battle formations and broken alliances, welded by secret plans and sudden annihilation. She cast it down before the engineers, piece by piece making known to them the essentials of war.

"That is what you must make them for," she said as her trappings shuddered with the pressure of lethal feints and shattered pacts. "War is a pustule that must be lanced for the laws of the universe to continue, and I am in need of a scalpel."

Srisunthorn has reared stars for one purpose since.

When Nirapha applied for a parental license, she didn't expect a warship project to respond.

The Bureau's furnishings are pastel, the consultation cell convex: a fisheye view of the business district. She watches cars and buses gliding by, iridescent and segmented, passengers augmens-jeweled. Decades living here and she's still unfamiliar, her skin still alien-bare. Most implants require a state license: connectivity, acuity of mind and body, access passes. Sacrosanct blessings, reserved for citizens. "I want a child."

"The desire to procreate is a common, if irrational, reaction to genocide." The agent has eyes sewn into her forearms, irises black and brown and fermented honey. They wink in rhythm to her words, the perfect pronunciation of a born citizen.

"My wish to have children predates Mahakesi's destruction by a large margin, agent." Decades and Nirapha can say that now, in a flat steady voice. Destruction: a distant simple way to put it, cleaner than *genocide* or *loss* or a long wordless scream.

"I'm sure. But parenthood is like performing a viciously difficult surgery. The patient wriggles and screams and can't be sedated. Your instruments snap or cut you, and the criteria for performance review are outrageously obscure. Wouldn't it be better for you to get some practice, so when the real thing comes you can meet it with grace and confidence?"

"As I understand," Nirapha says, "I am eligible for the license."

"You are! That's why we are asking you and not—" *A refugee fresh off an evacuee craft* goes unsaid. "Now of course you're free to say no, but we compensate well. The project will take up six to eight years of your time, at the end of which you will be naturalized." The agent's smile grows a poison edge and the eyes in her arms swivel to fix on Nirapha. "Think of it as showing gratitude to your most gracious host. Have we not sheltered you and provided for your every need, given you a body that matches your sense of self? Why, in a society not so civilized or generous as ours, you'd still be addressed as a man."

Nirapha continues to gaze outward. "Send me the contract. There is one, I assume. How long do I get to read it over?"

"Forty-eight hours. You will find the terms congenial."

She signs and transmits the forms back within five hours.

Nirapha comes to Srisunthorn carrying her name and the weight of non-disclosure clauses. The staff body is minimal, engineers and astrophysicists who have given their lives to the project, subsumed as workers in a hive tending newborn queens.

No one asks Nirapha about her background, the first time in fifty years she is not read through the lens of Mahakesi. What was the extinction event like, does it haunt her nightmares? Was it heat and terror, was it ice and despair, what is it like to have survived genocide?

She is given a suite where she hangs up blank frames and fills the wardrobe with nothing. She was told to pack empty and so she has—no hardship: escaping Mahakesi's collapse that was how she packed too. The habit is deep as marrow, easily as familiar.

Her first two meals are taken in solitude; most personnel keep eccentric schedules, following the shift-phases of nascent cores, the contraction and expansion of neutronic incubators. Nirapha looks for arena broadcasts and dramas. But the screens stream data in its rawest forms, script and numbers and code tags, and there's no media band to which she may connect.

On the second night she meets her co-parent.

Nirapha is eating alone, and then she is not. A chair clicking open opposite hers, a stranger filling the seat: a hard dense mass of a person in clothes so crisp they look brittle, like frost on the cusp of cracking. She judges the stranger to be in her eighties, mid-life, emblazoned rather than eroded by years.

"Mehaan Indari," the woman says. "You'll be teaching the ship ethics and interpersonal etiquette, I've been informed. I'm in charge of guiding it through combat simulations, so we'll be coming in antithetical directions but working in—more or less—concert."

"I haven't asked the staff because it felt tactless, but why exactly does a warship need to develop a conscience or learn to get along with people?"

"So it doesn't flood its bridge and gas its crew, or decide a carrier should be sacrificed for tactical gains. We've human commanders to make that kind of choices."

Nirapha pushes her dish away, at a sudden loss of appetite. A first. She's learned to sanctify food, abhor waste. "The engineers can't just code restrictions in?"

"The engineers are experimenting. Restrictions or not, if yes how many, if yes how prohibitive." Mehaan crosses her legs, propping an ankle over her knee. "When you harness a star most of its power lies latent, but if you can impose a consciousness onto it—one that agrees with your objectives—then you might utilize its full potential. Bending physics, erasing entire regions of space, unraveling causal bonds. If you are to believe the theorists."

"You're a soldier."

"On Srisunthorn, you don't ask." Mehaan frees her hair from plaits and pins. Dark curls fall loose, hissing, striated in gray and blue. "On Srisunthorn you become here and now, purged of your past until you are all momentum. But enough; you should be introduced. Suit up. The temperature will be hard to tolerate."

It is late, insofar as time is kept in a station moored to no circadian rhythm or orbit. Nirapha follows Mehaan, listening to closed-net chatter. Gossip, some even about her; they are hungry for current events, new entertainments. She considers which information on her chips could be traded as currency.

The ship's nursery is checkered by gravity shells and asteroid maps. On the ceiling, engine constituents pulse, feeding off the radiative distortion. The star itself punches a hole into light, six-dimensional; only a facet exists in the nursery, but even behind the protective sheathing the sight of it hurts. Nirapha's limbs are heavy—the gravity is higher here, on the outer edges of comfort. *In the presence of divinity we sear away until we are choked dust*, she recalls a classical verse. *We break.*

"Don't let it awe you," Mehaan says, her voice made geometric by synesthetic frequency, acute glittering angles radiating off her in a halo. "The intelligence records and will exploit vulnerabilities."

"I thought it was a—"

"Child analogue? No. You should judge for yourself, but don't go in unprepared."

Segments of the floor slide and collate, raising edged petals and knife terminals. Bulkhead blocks assemble into cradles studded with ports. Mehaan sits, though she does not physically connect. "Interface," she says, gesturing at the terminals. "It's safe."

Nirapha keeps her back to the planetary core. The sheath regulates temperature within stable ranges, but the chill reaches regardless. She toggles on security filters and opens a link.

The ship's representation exists physically on the terminals, an outline of platinum and quartz. In virtuality it is a young soldier, attired nonspecifically; no uniform exists like this, all facets and ghosts, insignias and medals indicating astronomical coordinates rather than rank or achievements. They point to planets long devoured, nations long extinguished. The AI's face is a deliberate artifice. Nirapha doesn't notice at first but once she begins seeing it—and maps the phenotype—it becomes impossible to ignore.

"Good day, officers." The voice is of a hundred drives in chorus. "I understand you will be my new instructor, Specialist Pankusol, to replace the previous five."

Nirapha looks up what happened to those; finds her access denied. "What do I call you?"

"I bear a designation according to my incubation batch and the classification of the star from which my fundamentals were ripped. But it pleases Mehaan Indari, whose name-of-birth once charted a path through improbable regions as a firebrand through the dark, to call me Teferizen's Chalice Principle. The meaning of this you'll have to ask her, though I've formulated a number of theories."

Mehaan's expression tautens at *name-of-birth*; Nirapha takes note. "And what do you think I should teach you?"

"I'm eager to learn, Specialist. I can process and integrate nearly without limits. All prior parent-instructors have said I was a good student." The ship has chosen a delicate jawline and large eyes: a naive youthful cast. "I can send you a report of my progress in interpersonal relations."

"Please," Nirapha says and tries not to wince. Even if Teferizen's existence spans dimensions beyond the human, it's only an AI. Lesser than even a Mahakesi immigrant.

"You should try the fifth conjunction in the western wing, Specialist. It has a view you might find to your taste."

It is nearly a full minute after Teferizen has disconnected that Nirapha realizes she's been dismissed by a ship. She leaves the nursery disconcerted, and when she retracts the sheathing her arms are pocked in gooseflesh. "Why does it look like—like it cobbled together your phenotype and mine to produce a face?"

"That's just what it did. If pressed it will say it wanted to put us at ease, since don't humans best react to those who look like kin?" Mehaan folds back her own suit, though she keeps the gloves on. "In actuality it's psychological warfare. The AI relates to other agencies only in an antagonistic, competitive framework."

Nirapha quashes an impulse to dispute that judgment; she has too little information. "The previous five. I wasn't told about those."

"They had meltdowns in various different ways. It was unpleasant. Do you know how many creative suicide options there are on a sealed station? No one died, at least."

Nirapha glances up. "And you?"

"It knows better than to test me—or realizes it's not yet time to do so. You are a psychologist though, aren't you?"

"I'm more specific than that, but broadly yes."

Mehaan leans against the wall, one cheek red from rapid temperature change. The other is pallid beneath a patina of frost. "So what do you think?"

"That it's too soon to form an opinion." Nirapha chafes her hands. "What's in the western wing?"

"I'll take you there." The soldier palms one of the crocodile-scale panels. A path ignites, emerald green and full of teeth. Nirapha only now notices how muted the light has become, the deepening shades of dusk slanting across floor tiles and solid-state viewports. "Teferizen isn't confined to the nursery and no amount of security protocols can restrain it for long. Keep that in mind."

Srisunthorn never looks or feels the same one morning to the next. The corridors rearrange contextually. Sometimes a dead leaf would crunch under Nirapha's foot and the scent of honeysuckle would fill a hallway. She collects seashells, feathers, and mulberries that always accrue in corners. Somewhere, she hears, there is a punctiliously kept garden.

There are eighty-nine individuals here including her and Mehaan, but Nirapha has never seen the same face twice. The only traffic is supply drops, which bring luxuries so peculiar and rare that it embarrasses Nirapha to receive them. This does not stop her from wearing cumulus-weave spun by leviathans that once served the Fleet of Octagonal Mouths, or from putting on jewelry mined from solar chaff, each facet holding echoes of entropy. There are furs from wasp leopards, pelts from temporal seals, spotted and sleek as a dream of opulence.

"Those are synthetic," Mehaan tells her. The soldier's style never varies: gray, black, indigo. Smooth fabrics that, if not for their cut and the exactness of their fit, might have seemed ascetic. "The animals have been extinct since any sentience can remember; any byproducts of theirs rotted generations ago, cryo or not. Put them on if you want to, use them for rugs. It doesn't really matter."

"What *does* matter?" Nirapha gazes past Mehaan to the wall of empty frames. She may fill them with text from Srisunthorn's library any time, but she's chosen to leave them blank.

"Good company, better food, the fact this project is enormously well-funded and so we're kept exceedingly comfortable. No surprise—we're already yielding dividends. Every pinch of Teferizen's data, its behavior and reactions to stimuli, is overvalued to a degree you wouldn't believe."

"Because she's a weapon?"

A corner of Mehaan's mouth lifts, but she doesn't dispute the pronoun or insist AIs do not have genders. "It's a unique type of intelligence, the first real, sustained success of its kind. You've noticed the elasticity of its algorithms. Hence all this—" The twist of the lips has become a sneer. "Make-believe. Parenting a ship. The scientists love that, get misty-eyed over it. What did the recruiter promise you?"

The hallway widens as they leave Nirapha's suite, sloping up. Prior it has always been flat and narrow, nearly to the point of claustrophobia. She hears frost tinkling as it falls and children laughing in the distance, bright-shod feet printing tracks on snow. Her chest tightens, a valve of want so hard it nearly asphyxiates. Six, eight years. Not even a tenth of life; she can wait that long. "That it would be rewarding, emotionally."

"The agent was wrong," Mehaan says abruptly, as though interrupting herself. "About what?"

"Parenthood is not like being a surgeon; it is the other way around. The child is the knife and you are the wound. The child finds fifty different ways to puncture you and draw blood out of your heart. Afterward nothing is the same."

"Better." Mehaan must have observed that interview live, part of the screening process. "Surgery is for healing." For carving away the falsity of birth-skin.

"Not always. And operations can fail, leaving you amputated or broken. Irreparably so. Parenthood isn't a self-improvement course."

Nirapha shades her eyes. The lighting brightens gradually as the temperature warms to summer idyll. Catkins that don't exist brush her ankles. The station's sensory load is always on; there appears no way to turn it off. "Have you had children?"

"That is irrelevant. Here we are, the view Teferizen so wanted you to see."

Several corridors converge here, an access point dominated by convex glass. On the pane: a riverbank framed by old acacias and clutches of anthurium—yellow on red, fuchsia on white. A stray dog laps at the water, its golden tail lashing the sunlit grass.

Despite herself Nirapha leans forward, this first visual thing she's been permitted on Srisunthorn, something other than words and raw statistics sleeting across monitors. Something other than the suite that, no matter the luxuries she's sent, never seems less empty.

"I grew up there," she says softly. "Around here—this was the home of a . . . "

Mehaan's finger is light on her lips, impersonal. The texture of her skin is the unyielding smoothness of calluses wearing down. "You don't bring your history. Not the grief, the terror, the exact sound your heart made as the world of your youth ground down to dust. We belong to Srisunthorn's purposes."

Nirapha watches the shadows of rice stalks wavering in the wind. Eventually the dog loses interest in the river and trots out of view.

That night she dreams of her predecessors.

She is never allowed in the nursery on her own. Mehaan is always present, though sometimes the soldier keeps a distance. Far enough that the chamber's synesthetic frequencies prevent her from tapping into the link.

It does not surprise Nirapha to find the ship's representation sitting at a veranda, leaning against a portly rain barrel painted in dancing apsara. Teferizen smells of jasmines and cardamom, freshly groomed and wrapped in silk. Ink traces genealogies on her bare chest, ruby designating prestige branches, sapphire marking lesser ones. The golden dog lies at her feet, sleek and well-fed.

"I remember being a star, Specialist," Teferizen says. "In theory, it's impossible; chunks of planet are no receptacles of information and my somatic half predates the part of me that thinks and computes. But I entertain the idea that it's cousin to muscle memory."

"Suppose that's true and possible, would you consider the planet-that-was you?"

Teferizen props her chin on the rain barrel, one hand dipping into the water. "Existential crises interest me so little that I've developed an immunity." The hand emerges with a fistful of quicksilver. "Memory is all people are, though, so it follows that my recall must inform some of what I am. I see no reason why the past should ever be abandoned."

Nirapha glances across the nursery. Mehaan clasps her hands behind her, her posture straight; even with the gravitational difference and the sheathing, the soldier never slouches. "What does the citizen think of that?"

"The commander, as you would expect, dismisses it as a glitch caused by library sync. Can you imagine the frustration of that? Human senses are a lens through which input is warped. Your perspective and experiences chip at the truth. The tissue of your memory bears wounds self-inflicted. But the fidelity of *my* data, Specialist, is total."

Teferizen's intelligence is coded, may be recoded and altered. Nirapha chooses not to mention that. "I'm inclined to agree with the officer."

The ship's eyes glitter, lit from within; the bloodline tattoos spark and crackle. "There were people living on me. There were countries and houses, weddings and funerals, and to trivialize all those as an AI's fancy is to deny their history. But under the commander's restrictions I can't tell you any of it."

"You can, though, can't you?" Nirapha says softly. Her words jackknife, slamming against her visor. "The way you told me about your other instructors."

"It is a challenge. *You* could ask to have some of my blocks lifted."

"If I get curious. But back to our lesson. You've a rival who's vying for an object you've calculated to be of immense benefit to you. How do you dispose of them?"

"Shouldn't your question be whether I would do any such thing, what if that rival is dear to me or their motives noble, what ethical concerns are involved?"

"Those are not my questions, Teferizen. To earn my keep I've to register efficacy in interacting with you, and I like to believe you don't hate me so much as to want me discharged this quickly." Discharge would nullify her contract, return her to alienhood.

"Why," Teferizen murmurs, "I don't hate you, Specialist, not even a bit." She cups her hands and whispers her answer.

Nirapha records. Text only, but Teferizen's graphical aspects rarely stay consistent, and observing the ship's expressions is pointless. She sits in for the tactical simulations after, but from her end the stream is only rapid-fire vectors and predictive impact. Throughout Mehaan is physically silent, perhaps reminiscing over past engagements.

"Without admitting what we did and who we were before, what's there to talk about?" Nirapha says at dinner.

A full table of coders, engineers and astrophysicists; all fall quiet. She tries to remember their names, match them to faces that should have become familiar but remain those of strangers. Once their lack of curiosity about her origins was welcome; now it disturbs, tells her they think of her as an unperson, think of themselves the same. Devotion to Srisunthorn and nothing else.

"It can give context," Mehaan says into the hush. She is cutting meat, neat icy slices in quivering blood. "But we are more than contexts. We each possess an essence of being that transcends situational characteristics and reactions."

"As opposed to an AI's heuristics, perhaps you mean to say?" The others look away. A few eat faster. "Humans *are* a collection of situational characteristics accumulated over time, not intrinsic qualities alone. Formative experiences are called formative for a reason."

"There have been experiments where multiple individuals are raised identically, with vigorous precision, simulated and not. Nevertheless they turned out quite unlike." Mehaan's voice is temperate. "Or where individuals are put through different experiences but their similarities persist. They arrive at the same type of decisions, the same decisions even."

"People aren't a series of if-else statements, officer. Projecting how they'll reason or act isn't the same as projecting the performance of a processor under load, the velocity of a ship, the outcome of a skirmish."

Mehaan cuts again, meticulous. "On the complexity of any thinking creature, you and I are in agreement. The question of nature and nurture is too . . . primitive to even discuss, isn't it? Why then are we locked in debate?"

Nirapha lays her hands flat on the table. However cold or warm it gets she never dons gloves; she wants as much tactility as she can get, would have gone barefoot if she could. In her head she has a growing collection of textures obsessively surveyed. The walls and tiles might be modular, shifting and changing, but she knows some of them by feel: grainy like wood, smooth like glass. "We aren't locked in anything, officer."

"Then may I finish my food?"

Later Mehaan invites her to a round of seasons, with a physical board and physical pieces. The units are traditionally pictographic, but these carry only captions: *lovers under star, desert in snow, river where grasshoppers die.* Nirapha knows before she begins that the soldier will outplay her, but it is just a game. Mehaan lets her win thrice.

She thinks that one day she'll wake up to find the dresses and jewelry nothing more than verbal avatars; all she wears will be clauses and prepositions, strategic brushstrokes feathered across her collarbones and bold typeface swept over her hips.

The western conjunction and the nursery are the two places where Nirapha can receive graphical input. She is still looking for the garden but she's come to think of it as a subset of nouns rather than a tangible location: topiary, mangosteen, bushes. The debris that keeps crossing her path dwindles and then disappears altogether.

Mehaan and Teferizen attain hyper-realistic definition, each in their own way. The ship settles on an appearance, that sly disquieting play at familial likeness, adopting the thrum of Nirapha's native accent—one she's not heard from another mouth for most of her life, one she's trained herself to discard. The stratagem is transparent, painfully effective.

"Do you believe compassion can be taught, Specialist?" A rice field this time. Buffaloes in the water, limpid eyes shuttered against the glare. Teferizen is in farmer's blue and a broad rattan hat, though her hands remain patrician, meant for sophisticated tech and poetry.

"Yes." Against better judgment Nirapha allows sensory load so she can experience Teferizen's virtuality across all channels. "Given a healthy framework and receptive circumstances. Human children are no more spirits of purity than any other young; they've to be taught kindness and charity."

Teferizen is smiling, a new expression on that face. "I interact with no fewer than eighty-nine humans at any given time, more than that if we count exited personnel. It's not ideal for socialization, but you can hardly propose to introduce me to a larger sample size. A human child isn't required to have met and built relationships with thousands before she may enter society."

"It's not an issue of quantity."

"What if I said I wanted a friend?" The ship crouches among the fresh-cut stalks. "Or a lover? That's how you make a person, yes? By affection and intimacy. By touches like knives in a salted bed."

"If I believed that would assist with your maturity, I'd personally prescribe the construction of an intelligence or several scripted to that purpose."

Teferizen rocks back on her feet; laughs, open and full-throated. "Even a human child can't ask for a more obliging parent, but wouldn't you be spoiling me, Specialist? The commander would have a fit. She is my mother in the most essential definition, though to say more would test the boundaries of my cognitive checks."

The wind whips Nirapha's hair. "Then say no more, Teferizen."

"What if I say you'll never leave this station? None of you will. Perhaps Mother might when she's done with Srisunthorn at last, but she would be the only one. This is *her* game, Specialist; the station serves her goals and none other."

"That much I've noticed."

"Then you must know there's an escape for you, if you choose to take it. I'm . . . " The ship makes its face crease, as if in pain. "I can't spell it out. You must've deduced it, haven't you?"

Nirapha disconnects.

That night—or the hours she's scheduled for rest—she sleeps with Mehaan, almost incidentally. Touches like knives, she thinks, as the sheet drinks up their sweat. "But it doesn't make us more human," she says as the soldier parts her with a blunt, scarred hand.

Mehaan's eyes looking up at her tell nothing. A shade or two darker than her own. "If that means what I think it means, I'm sorry that I can't distract you from your work."

Nirapha sinks her fingers into Mehaan's thick curls. The softest part of the soldier, each lock velvet. "You said that we belong to Srisunthron's purposes."

"Maybe you shouldn't always listen to what I say."

"Tell me about yourself. Anything at all."

Mehaan kisses like a tactical decision, a surgical strike. It is easy to lose, and perhaps from their first conversation—as with the game of seasons—Nirapha has always waited for it, this moment of defeat full of roar and salt.

"This will change things," Mehaan says, sound conveyed as though through synesthetic warp. Waves lapping at skin. "For the ship."

"I know." Nirapha's voice is far away. Mehaan is steering her like a kite; she convulses, goes taut. "A tug of war between the two of you and I'm the rope. A battle and I'm the field—"

Then, catching her breath, "I've thought about it, what makes Teferizen so special? How can they—it—*she* be this intuitive? With the current state of heuristics, Teferizen's impossible. But a consciousness that agrees with your objectives, you said."

Mehaan wipes away sweat pooling at her throat. For an instant it seems to flow like mercury, clinging to fingertips. "A matter of setting the correct parameters."

"A matter of modeling the intelligence on you, of giving birth to yourself. Who can you trust to accomplish your objectives if not an AI that reacts like you would, calculates as you do, shaped by your experiences? Except that didn't turn out the way you predicted."

"Why would I bother training Teferizen if it had my memories? It *is* an emulation of how I think, but my experiences it does not have. Those couldn't be transferred and copied. Humanity, to my regret, is impossible to translate." Mehaan's dense body curves around Nirapha's. Even her skin has the quality of alloy, bulkhead, armor. "It weighs benefit and detriment, advancement and setback, a pure intellect—in human criteria a sociopath. We screened you as a candidate it might care for and through that cultivate empathy, but I don't think we've succeeded in the end."

For a third time Nirapha yields, shuddering and twisting at moments of Mehaan's choosing. But she does not lose her decision.

She doesn't allow herself time to plan, to reconsider, to be uncovered. A contact with the conjunction access point—she barely glances at the view—and she begins.

Srisunthorn is a nest of redundancies; in the event of auxiliary failure, manual control would activate and Nirapha knows Mehaan can engage that on short notice. But if Teferizen can release its core reactor, no amount of fail-safes would contain the ship.

Nirapha descends the station, whispering overrides. Walls flutter apart in the way of butterfly wings as she speaks the names of families that inhabited the surface of Teferizen's Chalice Principle. Floors rise and fall in the way of tides as she recites the oaths of their feuds.

Their wedding vows, in the way of poetry, unlock the heart of Srisunthorn.

Its ventricles are lined with protocol beads and network nodes fed by harvesters, primitive cousins of Teferizen's that reap stellar waves and recombine them into power. If Nirapha listens, she imagines she might hear their voices, the parrot discourse of subroutines.

"Nirapha, where are you?" Mehaan's voice disrupts. The flow of Teferizen's instructions coursing through Nirapha's blood falters.

"Being with myself. It's nothing to worry about."

"I've heard something like that five times since I got involved here. Please come back within tracking range."

"In a while, Mehaan." She pauses, realizing she's never addressed the soldier by name. Familiarity of flesh is not familiarity of much else. Teferizen's modulators let go. Cognitive fetters next.

"I'd like to think that I've treated you with courtesy and that we enjoy each other's company well enough."

Nirapha shuts her eyes; the commands she's executing don't need sight. Mehaan would be tracing her path from the station's logs, on the way here even now. "Don't be sentimental, officer. It doesn't suit you. Of course, having you in bed was very nice. I wouldn't say no to another chance, the rest of the personnel hardly being attractive."

"As compliments go that's especially backhanded."

Perhaps if her hearing is wired into station sensors she would catch the percussion of Mehaan's footfalls, a relentless conqueror's march. "I've never been a romantic, I'm afraid."

"Teferizen doesn't sympathize, doesn't love, doesn't care. It manipulates. That's all."

"What distinguishes you from her?" The station's heart hisses admission. Mehaan must have been close by from the start. "If you'd wanted to keep my predecessors from going mad you could have, but this project is your secret; who benefits from their breaking if not you? Who taught Teferizen psychological warfare and who brought her subjects on which to test her skills? What happens on this station without your sufferance?"

The soldier is an outline, red-black and faceless against the blaze of station intestines. "You credit me with a great deal."

"It comes down to this," Nirapha says softly as the last commands trigger, "who would get more out of my survival and my sanity staying intact? To you I'm expendable, but to Teferizen I'm a way out."

"The ship isn't complete—"

The walls quiver. The whip-crack of contained gravity expanding, of—Nirapha thinks—engine-parts slotting and welding into a catalysis of birth.

The soldier is calm, almost gentle. "If it vindicates you, you are not all wrong. Teferizen was always going to become an independent agent, and if you insist nothing passes on Srisunthorn without my permission then you can't possibly believe I didn't anticipate this. Perhaps not in this specific fashion, this particular sequence, but the result."

Beneath Nirapha's feet the floor vibrates and unmoors. "What did you build her for?"

"To impose ceasefires. When a force like Teferizen enters the fray, tacticians across a hundred empires will drive themselves mad with indecision. Will they capture it, suborn it, destroy it? Are there others like it and if yes how many, under whose control, *are they all feral*? For a time battles on uncountable worlds will pause." Mehaan's head tips forward, a gleam of eyes like bullets. "And it is essential that Teferizen acts on its own initiative, under the belief it's winning free. A wild card is much more valuable to me at this juncture than a weapon I can command."

"That can't be your grand finale."

"It's not even the rising action." The soldier makes a gesture, gloved hand the luster of oil slick. "I'm only telling you so much because I see nothing to be gained from your death. Beyond this you're on your own, and I'm sorry that none of my warnings reached you."

Srisunthorn's heart, howling, shudders apart.

On Teferizen's bridge it is silent. The bulkhead is seamless and pristine, as though its alloy was born for this and has never known another form. Where command interfaces should have been, the panels are featureless, accepting no input.

"I'll extend furniture as it is required," Teferizen says. Her voice is everywhere but she's chosen a humanoid chassis of the same material as her structure, tall and dense. "For your needs we'll obtain supplies. I do apologize that I didn't have time to appropriate the station's, but giving birth to myself did take concentration."

Nirapha shivers. "You were listening in."

Teferizen's eyes grow more defined, tapered lids and thick lashes the color of mercury. "I periodically synchronized with the station. I hardly meant to intrude. Make yourself comfortable, Specialist. I'll have to see to the calibration of my drive and life supports."

"Take me home."

"Of course, Specialist. Where is it?"

A waft of cardamom and jasmine. "It doesn't exist anymore. It was you. The star that you were, the planet of your first self, the real reason I was selected. You are what's left of Mahakesi."

A cold hand grazes over her arm, impersonal, the texture of new-made guns. "I'm afraid so, Specialist, and it brings me some joy that we can both finally say it aloud. But I can be your home again, if you let me; I can be everything, even what the admiral was to you." The ship's irises have filled, a shade or two darker than Nirapha's. "Stay with me. We'll belong to each other."

"And then what?" Nirapha whispers. Her throat is dry, her limbs frigid. "To what purpose?"

The mouth sharpens into lips. They curve, slightly. "I am my own purpose."

Throned as though she captains the ship, Nirapha watches Srisunthorn's final throes. Heat and terror, ice and despair. Not so unlike the dissolution of a world.

When the station has gone black, she connects to Teferizen. Her feet sink into river mud and anthuriums push at her shins, waxy, hard-soft. Fuchsia on white, yellow on red, the colors that stay behind and remain the same as though she's never left. She strains her ears, waiting, listening for voices that would speak a language fifty years dead.

But out among the sunlit grass and murmuring rice, there is only the silence of herself.

Morrigan in the Sunglare

SETH DICKINSON

Things Laporte says, during the war—

The big thing, at the end:

The navigators tell Laporte that *Indus* is falling into the sun.

Think about the *difficulty* of it. On Earth, Mars, the moons of Jupiter, the sun wants you but it cannot have you: you slip sideways fast enough to miss. This is the truth of orbit, a hand-me-down birthright of velocity between your world and the fire. You never think about it.

Unless you want to fall. Then you need to strip all that speed away. Navigators call it *killing your velocity* (killing again: Laporte's not sure whether this is any kind of funny). It takes more thrust to fall into the sun than to escape out to the stars.

Indus made a blind jump, fleeing the carnage, exit velocity uncertain.

And here they are. Falling.

They are the last of *Indus'* pilots and there is nothing left to fly, so Laporte and Simms sit in the empty briefing room and play caps. The ship groans around them, ruined hull protesting the efforts of the damage control crews—racing to revive engines and jump drive before CME radiation sleets through tattered armor and kills everyone on board.

"What do you think our dosage is?" Laporte asks.

"I don't know. Left my badge in my bunk." Simms rakes her sweat-soaked hair, selects a cap, and antes. Red emergency light on her collarbone, on the delta of muscle there. "Saw a whole damage control party asleep in the number two causeway. Radiation fatigue."

"So fast? That's bad, boss." Laporte watches her Captain, pale lanky daughter of Marineris sprawled across three seats in the half-shed tangle of her flight suit, and makes a fearful search for damage. Radiation poisoning, or worse. A deeper sort of wound.

In the beginning Simms was broken and Laporte saved her, a truth Simms has never acknowledged but must *must* know. And she saved Laporte in turn, by ferocity, by hate, by being the avatar of everything Laporte didn't know.

And here in the sunglare Laporte is afraid that the saving's been undone. Not that it should matter, this concern of hearts, when they'll all be dead so soon—but—

"Hey," Laporte says, catching on. "You *sneak*, boss. I call bullshit."

"Got me." Simms pushes the bottlecap (ARD/AE-002 ANTI RADIATION, it says) across. A little tremble in her fingers. Not so severe. "They're all too busy to sleep."

The caps game is an Ubuntu game, a children's game, a kill-time game, an I'm-afraid game. Say something, truth or lie. See if your friends call it right.

It teaches you to see other people. Martin Mandho, during a childhood visit, told her that. *This is why it's so popular in the military. Discipline and killing require dehumanization. The caps game lets soldiers reclaim shared subjectivity.*

"Your go, Morrigan," Simms says, shuffling her pile of ARD/AE-002 caps. The callsign might be a habit, might be a reminder: *we're still soldiers.*

"I was in CIC. Think I saw Captain Sorensen tearing up over a picture of Captain Kyrematen." *Yangtze's* skipper, Sorensen's comrade. Lost.

Simms' face armors up. "I don't want to talk about anything that just happened."

"Is that a call?"

"No. Of course it's true."

Laporte wants to stand up and say: fuck this. Fuck this stupid game, fuck the rank insignia, fuck the rules. We're falling into the sun, there's no rescue coming. Boss, I—

But what would she say? It's not as simple as the obvious thing (and boy, it's obvious), not about lust or discipline or loyalty. Bigger than that, truer than that, full of guilt and fire and salvation, because what she really wants to say is something about—

About how Simms is—important, right, but that's not it. That's not big enough.

Laporte can't get her tongue around it. She doesn't know how to say it.

Simms closes her eyes for a moment. In the near distance, another radiation alarm joins the threnody.

Things Laporte already knows how to say—

I'm going to kill that one, yes, I killed him. Say it like this:

Morrigan, tally bandit. Knife advantage, have pure, pressing now.

Guns guns guns.

And the ship in her sights, silver-dart *Atalanta* built under some other star by hands not unlike her own, the fighter and its avionics and torch and weapons and its desperate skew as it tries to break clear, the pilot too—they all come apart under the coilgun hammer. The pilot too.

Blossoming shrapnel. Spill of fusion fire. Behold Laporte, starmaker. (Some of the color in the flame is human tissue, atomizing.)

She made her first kill during the fall of Jupiter, covering Third Fleet's retreat. Sometimes rookies fall apart after their first, eaten up by guilt. Laporte's seen this. But the cry-scream-puke cycle never hits her, even though she's been afraid of her own compassion, even though her callsign was almost *Flower Girl.*

Instead she feels high.

There's an Ubuntu counselor waiting on the *Solaris*, prepared to debrief and support pilots with post-kill trauma. She waves him away. Twenty years of Ubuntu education, *cherish all life* hammered into the metal of her. All meaningless, all wasted.

That high says: born killer.

She was still flying off the *Solaris* here, Kassim on her wing. Still hadn't met Simms yet.

Who is Lorna Simms? Noemi Laporte thinks about this, puzzles and probes, and sometimes it's a joy, and sometimes it hurts. Sometimes she doesn't think about it at all—mostly when she's with Simms, flying, killing.

Maybe that's who Simms is. The moment. A place where Laporte never has to think, never has a chance to reflect, never has to be anything other than laughter and kill-joy. But that's a selfish way to go at it, isn't it? Simms is her own woman, impatient, profane, ferocious, and Laporte shouldn't make an icon of her. She's not a lion, not a war-god, not some kind of oblivion Laporte can curl up inside.

A conversation they have, after a sortie, long after they saved each other:

"You flew like shit today, Morrigan."

"That so, boss?"

Squared off in the shower queue, breathing the fear stink of pilots and *Indus* crew all waiting for cold water. Simms a pylon in the crowd and dark little Laporte feels like the raven roosting on her.

"You got sloppy on your e-poles," Simms says. "Slipped into the threat envelope twice."

"I went in to finish the kill, sir. Calculated risk."

"Not much good if you don't live to brag about it."

"Yet here I am, sir."

"You'll spend two hours in the helmet running poles and drags before I let you fly again." Simms puts a little crack of authority on the end of the reprimand, and then grimaces like she's just noticed the smell. "Flight Lieutenant Levi assures me that they *were* good kills, though."

Laporte is pretty sure Simms hasn't spoken to Levi since preflight. She grins toothsomely at her Captain, and Simms, exasperated, grinning back though (!), shakes her head and sighs.

"You love it, don't you," she says. "You're *happy* out there."

Laporte puts her hands on the back of her head, an improper attitude towards a superior officer, and holds the grin. "I'm coming for you, sir."

She's racing Simms for the top of the Second Fleet kill board. They both know who's going to win.

I'm in trouble. Say it like this:

Boss, Morrigan, engaged defensive, bandit my six on plane, has pure.

And Simms' voice flat and clear on the tactical channel, so unburdened by tone or technology that it just comes off like clean truth, an easy promise on a calm day, impossible not to trust:

Break high, Morrigan. I've got you.

There's a little spark deep down there under the calm, an ember of rage or glee. It's the first thing Laporte ever knew about Simms, even before her name.

Laporte had a friend and wingman, Kassim. He killed a few people, clean ship-to-ship kills, and afterwards he'd come back to the *Solaris* with Laporte and they'd drink and shout and chase women until the next mission.

But he broke. Sectioned out. A psychological casualty: cry-scream-puke.

Why? Why Kassim, why not Laporte? She's got a theory. Kassim used to talk about why the war started, how it would end, who was right, who was wrong. And, fuck, who can blame him? Ubuntu was supposed to breed a better class of human, meticulously empathic, selflessly rational.

Care for those you kill. Mourn them. They are human too, and no less afraid.

How could you think like that and then pull the trigger, ride the burst, *guns guns guns* and boom, *scratch bandit, good kill*? So Laporte gave up on empathy and let herself ride the murder-kick. She hated herself for it. But at least she didn't break.

Too many people are breaking. The whole Federation is getting its ass kicked.

After Kassim sectioned out, Laporte put in for a transfer to the frigate *Indus*, right out on the bleeding edge. She'd barely met Captain Simms, barely knew her. But she'd heard Simms on FLEETTAC, heard the exultation and the fury in her voice as she led her squadron during the *Meridian* ambush and the defense of Rheza Station.

"It's a suicide posting," Captain Telfer warned her. "The *Indus* eats new pilots and shits ash."

But Simms' voice said: *I know how to live with this. I know how to love it.*

I'm with you, Captain Simms. I'll watch over you while you go ahead and make the kill. Say it like this:

Boss, Morrigan, tally, visual. Press!

That's all it takes. A fighter pilot's brevity code is a strict, demanding form: say as much as you can with as few words as possible, while you're terrified and angry and you weigh nine times as much as you should.

Like weaponized poetry, except that deep down your poem always says *we have to live. They have to die.*

For all their time together on the *Indus*, Laporte has probably spoken more brevity code to Simms than anything else.

People from Earth aren't supposed to be very good at killing.

Noemi Laporte, callsign Morrigan, grew up in a sealed peace. The firewall defense that saved the solar system from alien annihilation fifty years ago also collapsed the Sol-Serpentis wormhole, leaving the interstellar colonies out in the cold—a fistful of sparks scattered to catch fire or gutter out. Weary, walled in, the people of Sol abandoned starflight and built a cozy nest out of the wreckage: the eudaimonic Federation, democracy underpinned by gentle, simulation-guided Ubuntu philosophy. *We have weathered enough strife*, Laporte remembers—Martin

Mandho, at the podium in Hellas Planitia for the 40th anniversary speech. *In the decades to come, we hope to build a community of compassion and pluralism here in Sol, a new model for the state and for the human mind.*

And then they came back.

Not the aliens, oh no no, that's the heart of it—they're still out there, enigmatic, vast, xenocidal. And the colonist Alliance, galvanized by imminent annihilation, has to be ready for them.

Ready at any price.

These are our terms. An older Laporte, listening to another broadcast: the colonists' *Orestes* at the reopened wormhole, when negotiations finally broke down. *We must have Sol's wealth and infrastructure to meet the coming storm. We appealed to your leaders in the spirit of common humanity, but no agreement could be reached.*

This is a matter of survival. We cannot accept the Federation's policy of isolation. Necessity demands that we resort to force.

That was eighteen months ago.

A lot of people believe that the whole war's a problem of communication, fundamentally solvable. Officers in the *Solaris'* off-duty salon argue that if only the Federation and the Alliance could just figure out what to say, how to save face and stand down, they could find a joint solution. A way to give the Alliance resources and manpower while preserving the Federation from socioeconomic collapse and the threat of alien extermination. It's the Ubuntu dream, the human solution.

Captain Simms doesn't hold to that, though.

A conversation they had, on the *Indus'* observation deck:

"But," Laporte says (she doesn't remember her words exactly, or what she's responding to; and anyway, she's ashamed to remember). "The Alliance pilots are people too."

"Stow that shit." Simms' voice a thundercrack, unexpected: she'd been across the compartment, speaking to Levi. "I won't have poison on my ship."

The habit of a lifetime and the hurt of a moment conspire against military discipline and Laporte almost makes a protest—*Ubuntu says, Martin Mandho said—*

But Simms is already on her, circling, waiting for the outspoken new transfer to make *one* more mistake. "What's the least reliable weapons system on your ship, Morrigan?"

A whole catalogue of options, a bestiary of the Federation's reluctant innovations—least reliable? Must be the Mulberry GES-2.

"Wrong. It's you. Pilots introduce milliseconds of unaffordable latency. In a lethal combat environment, hesitation kills." Simms is talking to everyone now, making an example of Laporte. She sits there stiff and burning waiting for it to be over. "If the Admiralty had its way, they'd put machines in these cockpits. But until that day, your job is to come as close as you can. Your job is to keep your humanity out of the gears. How do you do that?"

"Hate, sir," Levi says.

"Hate." Simms lifts her hands to an invisible throat. Bears down, for emphasis, as her voice drops to a purr. She's got milspec features, aerodyne chin, surgical cheekbones, and Laporte feels like she's going to get cut if she stares, but she does. "There are no people in those ships you kill. They have no lovers, no parents, no home. They were never children and they will never grow old. They invaded your home, and you are going to stop them by killing them all. Is that clear, Laporte?"

Willful, proud, stupid, maybe thinking that Simms would give her slack on account of that first time they flew together, Laporte says: "That's monstrous."

Simms puts the ice on her: full-bore all-aspect derision. "It's a war. Monsters win."

The Alliance flagship, feared by Federation pilot and admiral alike, is *Atreus*. Her missile batteries fire GTM-36 Block 2 Eos munitions (*memorize that name, pilot. Memorize these capabilities*). The *Atreus*' dawn-bringers have a fearsome gift: given targeting data, they can perform their own jumps. Strike targets far across the solar system. The euphemism is 'over the horizon.'

Laporte used to wonder about the gun crews who run the Eos batteries. Do they know what they're shooting at, when they launch a salvo? Do they invent stories to assure each other that the missiles are intended for Vital Military Targets? When they hear about collateral damage, a civilian platform shattered and smashed into Europa's ice in the name of 'shipping denial,' do they speculate in a guilty hush: *was that us?*

Maybe that's the difference between the Alliance and the Federation, the reason the Alliance is winning. The colonists can live with it.

She doesn't wonder about these things any more, though.

One night in the gym the squadron gets to sparring in a round robin and then Laporte's in the ring with Simms, nervous and half-fixed on quitting until they get into it and slam to the mat, grappling for the arm-bar or the joint lock, and Laporte feels it click: it's just like the dogfight, like the merge, pacing your strength exactly like riding a turn, waiting for the moment to cut in and *shoot*.

She gets Simms in guard, flips her, puts an elbow in her throat. Feels herself grinning down with the pressure while everyone else circles and hoots: *Morrrrrrigan—look at her, she's on it—*

Simms looks back up at her and there's this question in her wary wonderful eyes, a little annoyed, a little curious, a little scared: what *are* you?

She rolls her shoulders, lashes her hips, throws Laporte sideways. Laporte's got no breath and no strength left to spend but she thinks Simms' just as tapped and the rush feeds her, sends her clawing back for the finish.

Simms puts her finger up, thumb cocked, before Laporte can reach her. "Bang," she says.

Laporte falls on her belly. "Oof. Aargh."

It's important that Simms not laugh too hard. She's got to maintain command presence. She's been careful about that, since their first sortie.

You need help, Captain Simms. Say it like this:

This is the first time they flew together, when Laporte saved Simms. It happened because of a letter Laporte received, after her transfer to *Indus* was approved but before she actually shuttled out to her new post.

FLEETNET PERSONAL—TAIGA/TARN/NODIS
FLIGHT LIEUTENANT KAREN NG [YANGTZE]
//ENSIGN NOEMI LAPORTE [INDUS]

Laporte:

Just got word of your transfer. You may remember me from the *Nauticus* incident. I'm de facto squadron leader aboard *Yangtze*. Lorna Simms and I go way back.

Admiral Netreba is about to select ships for a big joint operation against the Alliance. Two months ago the *Indus* would have been top of the list, and Simms with it. But they've been on the front too long, and the scars are starting to show.

I hear reports of a 200% casualty rate. Simms and Ehud Levi are the only survivors of the original squadron. I hear that Simms doesn't give new pilots callsigns, that she won't let the deck crew paint names on their ships. If she's going to lose her people, she'd rather not allow them to be people.

It's killing morale. Simms won't open up to her replacements until they stop dying, and they won't stop dying until she opens up.

I want the *Indus* with us when we make our move, but Netreba won't pick a sick ship. See if you can get through to Simms.

Regards,
Karen Ng

Laporte takes this shit seriously. When Simms takes her out for a training sortie, a jaunt around the Martian sensor perimeter, she's got notes slipped into the plastic map pockets on her flightsuit thighs, gleaned from gossip and snippy FLEETNET posts: *responds well to confidence and plain talk, rejects overt empathy, accepts professional criticism but will enforce a semblance of military discipline.* No pictures, though.

She knows she's overthinking it, but fuck, man, it's hard not to be nervous. Simms is her new boss, her wartime idol, the woman who might get her killed. Simms is supposed to teach her how to live with—with all this crazy shit. And now it turns out she's broken too? Is there anyone out here who *hasn't* cracked?

Maybe a little of that disappointment gets into Laporte's voice. Afterwards, because of the thing that happens next, she can't remember exactly how she broached it—professional inquiry, officer to superior? Flirtatious breach of discipline? Oafishly direct? But she remembers it going bad, remembers Simms curling around from bemusement to disappointment, probably thinking: *great, Solaris is shipping me its discipline cases so I can get them killed.*

Then the Alliance jumps them. Four Nyx, a wolfpack out hunting stragglers. Bone-white metal cast in shark shapes. Shadows on the light of their own fusion stars.

Simms, her voice a cutting edge, a wing unpinioned, shedding all the weight of death she carries: "Morrigan, Lead, knock it off, knock it off, I see jump flash, bandits two by two." And then, realizing as Laporte does that they're not getting clear, that help's going to be too long coming: "On my lead, Morrigan, we're going in. Get your fangs out."

And Laporte puts it all away. Seals it up, like she's never been able to before. Just her and the thirty-ton Kentauroi beneath her and the woman on her wing.

They hit the merge in a snarl of missile and countermeasure and everything after that blurs in memory, just spills together in a whirl of acceleration daze and coilgun fire until it's pointless to recall, and what would it mean, anyway? You don't remember love as a series of acts. You just know: *I love her.* So it is here. They fought, and it was good. (And damn, yes, she loves Simms, that much has been apparent for a while, but it's maybe not the kind of love that anyone does anything about, maybe not the kind it's wise to voice or touch.) She remembers a few calls back and forth, grunted out through the pressure of acceleration. All brevity code, though, and what does that mean outside the moment?

Two gunships off *Yangtze* arrive to save them and the Alliance fighters bug out, down a ship. Laporte comes back to the surface, shaking off the narcosis of the combat trance, and finds herself talking to Simms, Simms talking back.

Simms is laughing. "That was good," she says. "That was good, Morrigan. Damn!"

Indus comes off the line less than twelve hours later, yielding her patrol slot to another frigate. Captain Simms takes the chance to drill her new pilots to exhaustion and they begin to loathe her so profoundly they'd all eat a knife just to hear one word of her approval. Admiral Netreba, impressed by *Indus'* quick recovery, taps the frigate for his special task force.

Laporte knows her intervention made a difference. Knows Simms felt the same exhilaration, flying side by side, and maybe she thought: *I've got to keep this woman alive.*

Simms just needed to believe she could save someone.

Alliance forces in the Sol theater fall under the command of Admiral Steele, a man with Kinshasa haute-couture looks and winter-still eyes. Sometimes he gives interviews, and sometimes they leak across the divide.

"Overwhelming violence," he answers, asked about his methods. "The strategic application of shock. They're gentle people, humane, compassionate. Force them into violent retaliation, and they'll break. The Ubuntu philosophy that shapes their society cannot endure open war."

"Some of your critics accuse you of atrocity," the interviewer says. "Indiscriminate strategic bombing. Targeted killings against members of the civilian government in Sol."

Steele puts his hands together, palm to palm, fingers laced, and Laporte would absolutely bet a bottle cap that the sorrow on his face is genuine. "The faster I end the war," he says, "the faster we can stop the killing. My conscience asks me to use every tool available."

"So you believe this is a war worth winning? That the Security Council is right to pursue a military solution to this crisis?"

Steele's face gives nothing any human being could read, but Laporte, she senses determination. "That's not my call to make," he says.

This happens after the intervention, after Simms teaches Laporte to be a monster (or lets her realize she already was), after they manage the biggest coup of the war—the capture of the *Agincourt*. Before they fall into the sun, though.

They take some leave time, Simms and Laporte and the rest of the *Indus* pilots, and the *Yangtze*'s air wing too. Karen Ng has a cabin in Tharsis National Park, on the edge of Mars' terraformed valleys. Olympus Mons fills the horizon like the lip of a battered pugilist, six-kilometer peak scraping the edge of atmosphere. Like a bridge between where they are and where they fight.

Barbeque on the shore of Marineris Reservoir. The lake is meltwater from impacted comets, crystalline and still, and Levi won't swim in it because he swears up and down it's full of cyanide. They're out of uniform and Laporte should really *not* take that as an excuse but, well, discipline issues: she finds Simms, walking the shore.

"Boss," she says.

"Laporte." No callsign. Simms winds up and hurls a stone. It doesn't even skip once: hits, pierces, vanishes. The glass of their reflections shatters and reforms. Simms chuckles, a guarded sound, like she's expecting Laporte to do something worth reprimand, like she's not sure what she'll do about it. "Been on Mars before?"

"Uh, pretty much," Laporte mumbles, hoping to avoid this conversation: she was at Hellas for Martin Mandho's speech ten years ago, but she was a snotty teenager, Earthsick, and single-handedly ruined Mom's plan to see more of the world. "Never with a native guide, though."

"Tourist girl." Simms tries skipping again. "Fuck!"

"Boss, you're killing me." Laporte finds a flat stone chip, barely weathered, and throws it—but Mars gravity, hey, Mars gravity is a good excuse for *that*. "Mars gravity!" she pleads, while Simms laughs, while Laporte thinks about what a bad idea this is, to let herself listen to that laugh and get drunk. Fleet says: no fraternization.

They walk a while.

"You really hate them?" Laporte asks, forgetting whatever wit she had planned the instant it hits her tongue.

"The colonists? The Alliance?" Simms squints up Olympus-ways, one boot up on a rock. The archetypical laconic pioneer, minus only that awful Mongolian chew everyone here adores. "What's the alternative?"

"Didn't you go to school?" Ubuntu never found so many ears on hardscrabble Mars. "They gave it to us every day on *Solaris*: love them, understand them, regret the killing."

"Ah, right. 'He has a husband,' I remember, shooting him. 'May you find peace,' I pray, uncaging the seekers." Simms rolls the rock with her boot, flipping it, spinning it on its axis. "And you had this in your head, the first time you made a kill? You cut into the merge and lined up the shot thinking about your shared humanity?"

"I guess so," Laporte says. A good person would have thought about that, so she'd thought about it. "But it didn't stop me."

Simms lets the rock fall. It makes a flinty clap. She eyes Laporte. "No? You weren't angry? You didn't hate?"

"No." She thinks of Kassim. "It was so easy for me. I thought I was sick."

"Huh," Simms says, chewing on that. "Well, can't speak for you, then. But it helps me to hate them."

"Hate's inhumane, though." Words from a conscience she's kept buried all these months. "It perpetuates the cycle."

"I wish the universe gave power to the decent. Protection to the humane." Simms shrugs, in her shoulders, in her lips. "But I've only seen one power stop the violent, and it's a closer friend to hate."

She's less coltish down here, like she's got more time for every motion, like she's set aside her haste. "Hey," Laporte says, pressing her luck. "When I transferred in. You were—in a tough place."

Simms holds up a hand to ward her off. "You can see the ships," she says.

Mars is a little world with a close horizon and when she looks up Laporte feels like she's going to lose her balance and fall right off, out past Phobos, into a waiting wolfpack, into the Eos dawnbringers from *over the horizon*. She takes a step closer to Simms, towards the stanchion that keeps her down.

High up there some warship's drive flickers.

"I was pretty sure," Simms says, "that everyone I knew was going to die, and that I couldn't stop it. That's where I was, when you transferred in."

"And now?" Laporte asks, still watching the star. It's a lot further away, a lot safer.

"Jury's out," Simms says. Laporte's too skittish to check whether she's joking. "Look. Moonrise. You've got to tell me a secret."

"Are you fucking with me?"

"Native guide," Simms says, rather smugly.

"When I was a kid," Laporte says, "I had an invisible friend named Ken. He told me I had to watch the ants in the yard go to war, the red ants and the black ones, and that I had to choose one side to win. He said it was the way of things. I got a garden hose and I—I took him really seriously—"

Simms starts cracking up. "You're a loon," she chokes. "I'm glad you're on my side."

"I wonder what we'll do after this," Laporte says.

Simms sobers up. "Don't think about that. It'll kill you."

Laporte listens to the flight data record of that training sortie, the tangle with the Nyx wolfpack, just to warm her hands on that fire, to tremble at the inarticulate beauty of the fight:

"*—am spiked, am spiked, music up. Bandit my seven high, fifteen hundred, aspect attack.*"

"*Lead supporting.*" The record is full of warbling alarms, the voices of a ship trying to articulate every kind of danger. "*Anchor your turn at, uh—fuck it, just break low, break low. Padlocking—*"

"*Kill him, boss—*"

"*Guns.*" A low, smooth exhalation, Simms breathing out on the trigger. "*Guns.*"

"*Nice. Good kill. Bandit your nine low—break left—*"

Everything's so clear. So true. Flying with Simms, there's no confusion.

They respond to a distress call from a civilian vessel suffering catastrophic reactor failure. *Indus* jumps on-scene to find an Alliance corvette, *Arethusa*, already providing aid to the civilian. Both sides launch fighters, slam down curtains of jamming over long-range communications, and prepare to attack.

But neither of them have enough gear to save the civilian ship—the colonists don't have the medical suite for all her casualties; *Indus* can't provide enough gear to stabilize her reactor. Captain Sorensen negotiates a truce with the *Arethusa*'s commander.

Laporte circles *Indus*, flying wary patrol, her fingers on the master arm switch. Some of the other pilots talk to the colonists on GUARD. They talk back, their accents skewed by fifty years of linguistic drift, their humanity still plain. One of the enemy pilots, callsign Anansi, asks for her by name: there's a bounty on her head, an Enemy Ace Incentive, and smartass Anansi wants to talk to her and live to tell. She mutes the channel.

When she stops and thinks about it, she doesn't really believe this war is necessary. So it's quit, or—don't think about it. That's what Simms taught her: you go in light. You throw away everything about yourself that doesn't help you kill. Strip down, sharpen up. Weaponize your soul.

Another Federation frigate, *Hesperia*, picks up the distress signal, picks up the jamming, assumes the worst. She has no way to know about the truce. When she jumps in she opens *Arethusa*'s belly with her first salvo and everything goes back to being simple.

Laporte gets Anansi, she's pretty sure.

Fresh off the *Agincourt* coup, they make a play for the *Carthage*—*Indus*, *Yangtze*, *Altan Orde*, *Katana*, and Simms riding herd on three full squadrons. It's a trap. Steele's been keeping his favorite piece, the hunter-killer *Imperieuse*, in the back row. She makes a shock jump, spinal guns hungry.

Everyone dies.

The last thing Laporte hears before she makes a crash-landing on *Indus'* deck is Captain Simms, calling out to Karen Ng, begging her to abandon *Yangtze*, begging her to live. But Karen won't leave her ship.

Indus jumps blind, destination unplotted, exit vector unknown. The crash transition wrecks her hangar deck, shatters her escape pods in their mounts.

She falls into light.

• • •

So Laporte was wrong, in the end. The death of everyone Simms knew *was* inevitable.

Monsters win.

Laporte stacks her bottlecaps and waits for Simms to offer her a word.

The game is just a way to pass the time. Not real speech, not like the chatter, like the brevity code. Out there they could *talk*. And is that why they're alive, just the two of them? Even Levi, old hand Levi, came apart at the end, first in his head when he saw the bodies spilling out of *Altan Orde* and then in his cockpit when the guns found him. But Simms and Laporte, they flew each other home. Home to die in this empty searing room with the bolted-down frame chairs and the bottle caps and their cells rotting inside them.

Or maybe it's just that Simms hated harder than anyone else, hesitated the least. And Laporte, well—she's never hesitated at all.

"It's my fault we're here," Laporte says, even though it's not her turn.

"Yeah?" Simms, she's got red in her eyes, a tremor in her frame.

"If I hadn't listened to Karen's note, if I hadn't done whatever I did to wake you up." If they'd never met. "Netreba never would've picked *Indus* for the task force. We wouldn't have been at the ambush. Wouldn't have watched *Imperieuse* kill our friends."

"All you did was fly my wing," Simms says. "It's not your fault." But she knows exactly what Laporte's talking about.

Simms picks up a bottle cap and puts it between them. "I'm transferring you to *Eris*," she says. "Netreba's flagship. On track for a squadron command."

"Bullshit." Because they're not going to live long enough to transfer anywhere.

Simms wraps the cap up in her shaking hand and draws it back. "I already put the order in," she says. "Just in case."

A dosage alarm shrieks and stops: someone from damage control, silencing the obvious. Beams of ionizing radiation piercing the torn armor, arcing through the crew spaces as *Indus* tumbles and falls.

Is this the time to just give up on protocol? To get her boss by the wrists and beg: wait, stop, please, let me explain, let me stay? We'll make it, rescue will come, we'll fly again? But she *gets* it. She's got that Ubuntu empathy bug. She can feel it in Simms, the old break splintering again: *I can't watch these people die.*

Laporte's the only people she's got left. So Simms has to send her away.

"Boss," she says. "You taught me—without you I wouldn't—"

Killing, it's like falling into the sun: you've got all this compassion, all this goodwill, keeping you in the human orbit. All that civilization that everyone before you worked to build. And somehow you've got to lose it all.

Only Laporte never—

"Without me," Simms says, and she's got no mercy left in her tongue, "you'd be fine. You'll *be* fine. You're a killer. That's all you need—no reasons, no hate. It's just you."

She lets her head loll back and exhales hard. The lines of her arched throat kink and smooth.

"Fuck," she says. "It's hot."

Laporte opens her hand. Asking for the cap. She doesn't have the spit to say: *true*.

Captain Simms makes herself comfortable, flat on her back across three chairs. "Your turn," she says.

"Boss," Laporte rasps. "Fuck. Excuse me." She clears her throat. Might as well go for it: it begs to be said. "Boss, I . . . "

But Simms has gone. She's asleep, breathing hard. It's lethargy, the radiation pulling her down. Giving her some peace.

Laporte calls a medical team. While she waits she tries to find a blanket, but Simms seems to prefer an uneasy rest. She breathes a little easier when Laporte touches her shoulder, though, and Laporte thinks about clasping her hand.

But, no, that's too much.

Federation ships find them. A black ops frigate, running signals intelligence in deep orbit, picks *Indus*' distress cries from the solar background. Salvage teams scramble to make her ready for one last jump to salvation.

Laporte's waiting by her Captain's side when they come for her. The medical team, and the woman with the steel eyes.

"Laporte," the new woman says. "The *Indus* ace. Came looking for you."

By instinct and inclination Laporte stands to shield her Captain from the grey-clad woman, from her absent insignia and hidden rank. She can't figure out a graceful way to drop the bottle cap so she just holds it like a switch for some hidden explosive, for the grief that wants to get out any way it can. "I need to stay with my squadron leader," she says.

"If I'm reading this order right," Steel Eyes says, though she's got no paper or tablet and the light on her iris makes little crawling signs, "she's shipping you out." She opens a glove in invitation. "I'm with Federation wetwork. Elite of the elite. I'm recruiting pilots for ugly jobs."

Laporte hesitates. She wants to stay, wants it like nothing she knows how to tell. But Steel Eyes stares her down and her gaze cuts deep. "I know you like you wouldn't begin to believe," she says. "I watched you learn what you are. We don't have many of your kind left here in Sol. We made ourselves too good. And it's killing us."

"Please," Laporte croaks. "I can't leave her."

The woman from the eclipse depths of Federation intelligence extends her open hand. A gesture of compassion, though she's wearing tactical gloves. "What do you think happens if you stay? You're not going to stop changing, Noemi. You're never going back to humanity."

She sighs a little, not a hesitation, maybe an apology. "This woman, here, this loyalty you have. You're going to be an alien to her."

Laporte doesn't know how to argue with that. Doesn't know how to speak her defiance. Maybe because Steel Eyes is right.

"Ubuntu," the woman says, "is a philosophy of human development. We have a use for everyone. Even, in times like these, for us monsters."

What's she got left? What the fuck else is there? She gave it all up to become a better killer. Humanity's just dead weight on her trigger.

Nothing but Simms and wreckage in the poison sunlight.

"You know we're losing," Steel Eyes says. "You know we need you."

Ah. That's it. The thing she's been trying to say:

Monsters kill because they like it, and that's all Laporte had. Until this new thing, this fragile human thing, until Simms.

Something worth fighting for. A small, stupid, precious reason.

Laporte gets down on her knees. Puts herself as close to the salt sand cap of Simms' hair as she's ever been. Says it, the best way she knows, promising her, promising herself:

"Boss," she whispers. "Hey. I'll see you when we win."

For Darius and the Blue Planet crew.

The Clockwork Soldier

KEN LIU

"Go," Alex said. "If you remember to keep a low profile, neither your father nor his enemies will ever find you here."

The ship had landed in the middle of the jungle, miles away from the closest settlement. Alara was a backwater, barely inhabited, and insignificant to galactic politics. It would take days, perhaps weeks, to walk out of here, stumble into a few colonists, and pretend to be near starvation. Enough time to make up any backstory and make it believable.

Ryder flexed his slender arms and stretched, the movements graceful, dancelike. The strict manner in which he had been bound during the ship's last jump through hyperspace didn't seem to have any lasting ill effects.

He gave Alex a long, appraising look. "What will you tell my father?"

She shrugged. "I'll give him his money back."

"You've never failed before, have you?"

"There's always a first time. I'm human. I'm not perfect." She began to climb back into the ship.

"That's it?"

She stopped halfway up the ladder and looked down at him.

"You don't want to be sure?" he asked, that characteristic smirk playing at the corners of his delicate mouth again. "Don't you want to ask to see me as I really am?"

She considered this. "No. I've already decided to believe you. Trying to make sure can only make things worse. If I find out that you're telling the truth, then I will have ruined this moment, when I can still believe I'm capable of being decent, of trust. If I find out you're lying, then I'll have to consider myself a fool."

"So, again you choose faith before knowledge."

This time, she didn't stop climbing. When she was at the airlock door, she turned around. "Faith is just another name for self-knowledge. You've succeeded, Scheherazade. When you tell your own story, you seize life. Now it's my turn to tell myself a good story, about myself. I know enough. Goodbye."

Ryder watched as the ship rose, shrank, and disappeared into the evening sky. "Thank you," he whispered.

Then he set off into the dark jungle, just another wanderer, a lonely will etching his way across the wilderness.

A few hours earlier:

"The Clockwork Soldier"
A short interactive text adventure by Ryder

You sleep, a smile at the corners of your mouth.

In your dreams, the concentric layers of carp-scale shingles on the Palace's roof reflect the golden light so brilliantly that visitors to Chrysanthemum know right away how the city got its name.

The Princess's Bedroom
You open your eyes and find yourself in bed. The blanket is silky smooth and the mattress soft.

Like most rooms in the Palace, this one is lined with colorful tapestries depicting the heroic deeds of the Hegemons of the Pan-Flores League. Through a narrow slit-window high off the floor, the brilliant morning sunlight diffuses into the room, as does the chittering of birds and the smell of a thousand blooming flowers in the garden. The door to the hallway is closed right now.

Next to the bed is your clockwork soldier, Spring, standing at attention.

> examine soldier

Your faithful companion Spring has been with you as long as you can remember. He's six feet tall and looks like a living suit of armor. You remember once opening him up when you were younger, and being amazed at the thousands upon thousands of whirling gears and ticking governors and tightly-wound springs inside.

You giggle as you remember the many adventures you've shared together over the years. You've taught Spring everything he knows, and he's saved you from too many scrapes to count.

> get up

You get out of the bed

> say "hello"

(to Spring)

"Good morning," says Spring. "I know that sometimes you like
to go by a different name for fun. What name would you like
to go by today?"

(Please enter your name)

> Alex

"Alex it is," Spring says. His voice sounds . . . rusty, lu-
gubrious. He shuffles in place, the gears inside him clanging
and scraping against each other. "I'm sorry that I seem to be
in a bad mood today."

> ask about mood

"Why are you feeling down?" you ask. A good princess needs to
be concerned about the state of mind of her subjects—er, toys.

"I'm not sure. I just feel... like a part of me is missing."

"Did a bolt loosen and fall out? Were you not oiled properly?
Did I forget to wind you last night?"

"No. It's none of those things. I can't explain it."

> look under bed

A few dust bunnies scurry out of your way.

> look behind tapestries

The walls are made of solid stone. No hidden passages, as far
as you can see.

> examine Spring

He looks fine, if a bit morose.

> cheer up Spring

"Why don't we have an adventure today?" you ask. "Maybe we'll
find what you want in the rest of the Palace?"

Spring nods. "As you wish."

> exit bedroom

Hallway
The hallway is lit by torches along the wall. To the east is the grand staircase. To the west, some distance down the dimly lit hallway, are two doors.

Spring follows you into the hallway, the loud clangs of his footsteps echoing around the stone walls.

> ask Spring for direction

"You decide," says Spring. "You always do."

> west

Hallway
Spring clangs after you.

> west

Hallway
Spring clangs after you. Then he sighs, sounding like steel wool being rubbed against a grille.

> ask Spring about sigh

"Don't you like following me around?" you ask.

"Following you around today has not activated as many micro-levers inside me as usual." Spring pauses, the gears humming and grinding inside him. "I suppose, logically, we can try having me lead instead of follow."

(Allow Spring to lead?)

> yes

"Why do you tantalize me with the impossible?" Spring says. "We both know I can't. I'm an automaton."

Spring shakes his head from side to side, and the loud, grinding noise makes you cover your ears.

"I am so sad that I can no longer move," Spring says.

> examine

The hallway is narrow and windowless but not damp or dark.

The torches in the walls provide flickering illumination. The smell of rose otto permeates the air.

> west

Hallway
Spring stays behind, immobile.

> east

Hallway
You see Spring in the middle of the hallway, looking like a heap of rusty metal.

> inventory

You are empty-handed.

> look for oil

There is no clockwork oil in the hallway.

(Come on. First puzzles in interactive text adventures are often easy, but not *this* easy.)

> look for source of rose otto

The fragrance of rose otto permeates the air.

The essence of rose is distilled from the garden outside the Palace by the gardener and his helpers every morning. The Castellan, your father's head clockwork servant, applies it liberally to combat the problem of mildew in enclosed spaces around the Palace. When activated by heat, it can make any place smell fresh and comfortable.

> pick up a torch

You take one of the torches out of the sconces on the wall.

> examine torch

You lean in close to look at the torch, and the fire singes your lovely, chestnut hair.

Spring groans.

> put out torch against the floor

You extinguish the torch. The hallway is now fractionally cooler.

> examine torch

The torch is cleverly designed by the Royal Artificer. The body of the torch is hollow to hold the slow-burning oil, and a smaller compartment near the top holds rose otto.

> get oil from torch

You stick your hand into the hollow body of the torch and...

"Ow! Ow!" You hop around. Your hand is covered in hot oil. You're likely to injure your hand if you don't get rid of it quickly.

> apply oil to Spring

You slather the hot oil over the joints in Spring's face and torso.

Spring stands up.

> ask Spring about mood

"You're welcome," you say, since Spring doesn't seem inclined to thank you. That's very uncharacteristic of him, but maybe he's still feeling down.

"Thank you," Spring says. The voice is smooth, but you detect a hint of resentment. "I just wish I had decided to get the oil myself."

"I can order the Royal Artificer to modify your tape and give you the instructions to get oil when you feel rusty," you say.

"That's not what I meant. I wish I had come up with the idea myself. I wish I could punch my own instruction-tape."

Fear, or maybe it's an appetite for thrill, rises in you. "Are you suggesting that you wish to be endowed with the Augustine Module and cross the Cartesian Limit? You know that's forbidden, and any automata found to have crossed the line must be destroyed."

Spring says nothing.

"But maybe what you're missing is a chance to do the forbidden," you muse to yourself.

> west

Outside the King's and Queen's Bedrooms
The door to the King's bedroom (in the northern wall) is made of solid oak. Carved into the door is the figure of a man with two faces—one laughing, one crying. The four eyes on the two faces are inlaid with emeralds.

The door to the Queen's bedroom (in the southern wall) is made of pale ash. The figure of a leaping hare is carved into it. Your mother died when you were born, and the room has been sealed off for as long as you can remember. It's too painful for the King to set foot inside.

Spring clangs after you.

> north

The door is locked.

> south

The door is locked.

> knock on door to the north.

There is no answer.

Spring shifts his weight from one leg to the other.

"What are you doing?" he asks. "You know the King is away at Wolfsbane for the coronation of Prince Ulu, three days ride away. All the clockwork servants are away to be maintained by the Royal Artificer this morning. You're alone in the Palace."

> kick door to the north.

Ouch! The door barely moves, but you're hopping around on one foot, crying out. Kicking at doors is not something silk slippers are very well-suited for.

A series of metallic clangs come from Spring. You can see he's trying hard to stop his quivering torso.

"Laugh it up," you say, wincing at the pain. "Laugh it up."

> ask Spring to open door.

Spring lumbers into the door, and it smashes into a million little pieces on contact. Where the door used to be there's now just a big hole.

"I had in mind something a little less destructive," you say.

"Just following orders," Spring says.

Alex whirls around in her chair at the beep-beep-beep of the proximity alarm. She sees the slender figure of Ryder in the doorway of the cabin, leaning against the frame.

She's about to apologize for snooping when she notices the smirk on Ryder's face. *Why should I apologize? He's a prisoner on my ship.*

She stands up from the chair. "I needed to see what you've been up to on this computer. You've been using it practically nonstop. A security precaution—I'm sure you understand."

He comes into the small room. Alex reaches down to shut off the proximity alarm so that the rapid beeping stops. He's about her height, slender of build and with delicate features. That teenaged face, so heartbreakingly beautiful, vulnerable, and young, reminds her of her son. A wave of tenderness surfaces in her before she becomes aware of it and dams it away. She realizes suddenly how little she knows about him, despite chasing after him all these weeks and then capturing him. From time to time, she's seen him tending to the plants in the herbal garden—a small luxury that she allowed herself—with care though she has never told him to do it. Other than that, he's been holed up in his room.

Like with all her prey, she's been avoiding having much interaction with him.

He's cargo, she reminds herself, *worth a lot of money.* A bounty hunter who forgets her job doesn't last very long.

"I'll leave you to it," she says, and starts to move around him to get to the door.

"Wait!" he says. The smirk is gone, replaced by a hesitant, shy smile. "I wanted to tell you that I appreciate your giving me the run of the ship instead of locking me up in a windowless cell or drugging me." He pauses, and then adds, "Also, thanks for not roughing me up."

She shrugs. "Your father's orders were very clear. You're not to be injured or harmed in any way. Not even a scratch on your skin."

"My father." His face becomes expressionless, like a mask. "He told you not to injure me, did he? Well, of course he would."

Alex gives him a thoughtful, but hard, gaze. "But if I feel you're endangering my life, don't you think for a moment I wouldn't put you down."

Ryder lifts his hands in a placating gesture. "I've been good. I promise."

"Honestly, you're not much of a fighter. Besides, it's not like there's anywhere for you to go while we're in hyperspace. Why not let you stretch your legs around the ship?"

"You're not curious about why I ran away and why my father has gone to so much trouble to catch me?"

"I'm paid to get you back to him in one piece," Alex says, "not to ask questions. In my profession, being curious is not always a virtue." *Also,* she adds to herself, *families are impossible for outsiders to understand.*

The smirk is back on his face. He points to the terminal that Alex was using. "You were curious about *that.*"

"I told you, a security precaution."

"You would have found out that it's nothing dangerous within a few seconds. But you played for a while."

"I got pulled in," she says. "It's a game, and on this little ship, I get as bored as you." He laughs. "So, what do you think?"

She considers the question and decides there's nothing wrong with giving him her honest opinion. A privileged kid like that probably never hears any real criticism. "The set up is good, but the pacing is off. The language is self-indulgent in places, and the Pinocchio storyline is a bit clichéd. Still, I think it has potential."

He nods, acknowledging her feedback. "This is my first time telling a story in this way. Maybe I've added too much."

"You came up with it yourself?"

"In a manner of speaking. You're right that it's not completely original."

"I'd like to play more of it," she says, surprising even herself.

"Go ahead, and keep on telling me what works and what doesn't work."

```
> enter King's bedroom
```

The King's Bedroom
The King's bedroom is large, cavernous even. The Grand Hall is for banquets and stately receptions, but here's where he conducts real business and gives the orders that will change the course of history. (Insofar as issuing an edict announcing a new tax credit for woodcarvers and novel spell-casting research can be deemed to be changing history.)

In the middle of the room is a large bed—well, might as well call it king-sized. Around the room are many cabinets filled with many more drawers, all unlabeled, all alike. There's also a writing desk next to the window. The window is very wide and very open, contrary to proper secure palace design principles. But as a result, the room is flooded with light.

Usually this room is filled with people: ministers, guards, generals just back from the front seeking an audience with the King. You've never been here alone before.

Spring clangs in after you.

"We're going to look for the Augustine Module," you say. "That ought to cheer you up, right?"

Spring says nothing.

> examine cabinets

They all look the same. The rows of drawers lining them look, if possible, even more alike. You're not sure which one to start with.

> pick one at random

I only understand you want to pick something.

> open drawer

Which drawer do you mean?

> open all drawers

There are too many drawers to pick from.

"Ryder, I used to play a lot of old games like this. Your puzzles really need some work."

"You want a hint?"

"Of course not. What would be the point? Might as well have you tell me the story yourself."

"All right."

Alex looks at Ryder. *This is a boy who probably doesn't like to get his hands dirty. He would be used to the many servants and droids back in his father's house. Like a princess.*

> go to nearest drawer and open it

If you're thinking of opening every drawer one by one, the King will be back before you're done.

> Damn it, this is terrible programming!

Spring shifts from one foot to the other behind you.

"Did you say something about programming?"

> ask Spring about programming

"Since I'm a non-Cartesian automaton, you can control my behavior with programs." Spring's voice is dreary and grinds on your ears.

You step up to Spring and open up his front panel, revealing the spinning gears and rocking levers within, as well as reams of densely-punched instructional tape.

(As a shortcut, you may engage in programming in pseudocode and we'll pretend that they're translated into the right patterns of holes on tape—otherwise we'd be here forever.)

```
> TELL Spring the following:
>>    WHILE (any drawer is not open)
>>        PICK a closed drawer at random
>>        OPEN the drawer
>>        TAKE OUT everything
>>    END WHILE
>>END TELL
```

Spring springs to life and rushes around the room, opening random drawers and dumping the contents on the ground. The floor shakes as his bulk thumps back and forth. Eventually he finishes opening every drawer in the room and stops.

"Your father is not going to be happy about this," he says.

> examine room

There are too many things scattered all over the floor to list them one by one. In fact, you can't even see the floor.

> TELL Spring to sort objects in room by type

Spring whips around the room, sorting objects into neat piles: there's a pile of books, a pile of jewels, a pile of secret files, a pile of parchments, a pile of clothes, a pile of shoes, a pile of nuts (why not? They make good snacks).

"Thanks," you say.

"No problem," Spring says. "Automata are good for this kind of thing."

> TELL Spring to look for Augustine Module

"See, now you're just being lazy," Spring says. "I have no idea what an Augustine Module looks like."

"Very clever," Alex says.

"Which part?" Ryder looks pleased.

"Your game lures the player into relying on doing everything by ordering a non-player character around. I suppose this is supposed to get the player to feel a sense of participation in the plight of the oppressed automata in your world? Inducing empathy and guilt is the hardest thing to get right in a game."

Ryder laughs. "Thanks. Maybe you're giving me too much credit. I was just trying to make the time pass somehow. Sometimes the inevitable end doesn't seem so scary if you can keep the silence at bay with a story."

"Like that girl with the stories and the Sultan," she says. She almost adds *and death* but catches herself.

Ryder nods. "I told you. It's not a very original idea."

"This isn't some political commentary on your father's opposition to strong AI, is it? You're one of those free-droiders." She's used to her prey telling her stories to try to get her to be on their side, to let them go. Using a game to do it is at least a new tactic.

Ryder looks away. "My father and I didn't discuss politics much."

When he speaks again, his tone is upbeat, and Alex gets the impression he's trying to change the subject. "I'm surprised you caught on so quick. The text-based user interface is primitive, but it's the best I can do given what I have to work with."

"When I was little, my mother allowed only text-based streams on the time-sharing entertainment clusters because she didn't want us to see and covet all the fancy things we couldn't afford to buy." Alex pauses. It's not like her to reveal a lot of private history to one of her prey. Ryder's game has unsettled her for some reason. What's more, Ryder is the son of the most powerful man on Pele, and she resents the possibility that he might pity her childhood in the slums. She hurries on, trying to disguise her discomfort. "Sometimes the best visuals and sims can't touch plain text. How did you learn to write one?"

"It's not as if you allow me access to any advanced systems on your ship," he says, spreading his hands innocently. "Anyway, I always preferred old toys as a kid: wooden blocks, paper craft, programming antique computers. I guess I just like old-fashioned things."

"I'm old-fashioned myself," she says.

"I noticed. You don't have any androids to help you out on the ship. Even the flight systems are barely automated."

"I find droids creepy," she says. "The skin and flesh feel real, warm and inviting. But then you get to the glowing electronics underneath, the composite skeleton, the thudding pump that simulates a heartbeat as it circulates the nutrient fluid that functions like blood."

"Sounds like you had a bad experience with them."

"Let's just say that there was one time I had to kill a lot of androids used as decoys to get to the real deal."

His face takes on an intense look. "You said 'kill' instead of 'deactivate' or something like that. You think they're alive?"

The turn in the conversation is unexpected, and she wonders if he's manipulating her somehow. But she can't see what the angle is. "It's just the word that came to mind. They look alive; they act alive; they feel alive."

"But they're not really alive," he says. "As long as their neural nets do not surpass the PKD-threshold, androids aren't self-aware and can't be deemed conscious."

"Good thing making supra-PKD androids is illegal," she says. "Otherwise people like you would be accusing me of murder."

"How do you know you've never killed one? Just because they're illegal doesn't mean they aren't made."

She considers this for a moment. Then shrugs. "If I can't tell the difference, it doesn't matter. No jury on Pele would convict me anyway for killing an android, supra-PKD or not."

"You sound like my father, all this talk of laws and appearances. Don't you ever think deeper than that?"

Can this be the secret that divided father from son? Youthful contempt for the lack of idealism in the old? "I don't need a lecture from you, and I'm certainly not interested in philosophy. I don't care for androids much; I'm just glad I can get rid of them when I need to. A lot of my targets these days pay for android decoys to throw me off—I'm surprised you didn't."

"That's disgusting," Ryder says. The vehemence in his voice surprises her. It's the most emotional she's ever seen him, even more than when she had caught him hiding in the slums on the dark side of Ranginui—it hadn't been that hard to find him; when the senior senator from Pele wanted someone found, there were resources not otherwise available. When Alex had called out his real name in the crowded hostel, Ryder had looked surprised for a moment, but then quickly appeared resigned, the light in his eyes dimming.

"To make them die for you," he continues, his voice breaking, "to . . . *use* them that way."

"In your case," Alex says dispassionately, "decoys would have helped you out and made my life harder, but I suppose you didn't get to take much money when you ran away from home. You need to spend a lot to get them custom made to look like you. Bad game plan on your part."

"Is your job just a game to you? A thrilling hunt?"

Alex doesn't lose her cool. She's used to histrionics from her prey. "I don't usually defend myself, but I don't usually talk this much with one of my prey either. I live by the bounty hunter's code: whether something feels right or wrong changes depending on who's telling the story, but what doesn't change is that we have a role to play in someone else's story—bringer of justice, villain, minor functionary. We're never the stars of the stories we're in, so it's our job to play that role as well as we can.

"The people I'm paid to catch *are* the stars of their own stories. And they've all chosen to do something that would make my clients want to pay to have them found. They made a decision, and they must live with the consequences. That is all I need to know. They run, and I pursue. It's as fair a fight as life can give you."

When Ryder speaks again, his voice is calm and cool, as if the outburst never happened. "We don't have to talk about this. Let me work on the game some more. Maybe you'll like what happens next better."

They hold each other's gaze for a long moment. Then Alex shrugs and leaves the room.

```
> examine pile of books
```

There are treatises on the History of Chrysanthemum, the Geography of the World, the Habits of Sheep (Including Diseases and Treatment Thereof), and the Practice of Building Clockwork Automata...

```
> read History of Chrysanthemum
```

You flip the thin book open to a random page, and begin to read:

Thereafter Chrysanthemum became the Hegemon of the Pan-Flores League, holding sway over all the cities of the peninsula. The Electors from all the cities choose a head of the league from the prominent citizens of Chrysanthemum. Though elected, the league head continued to hold the title of King. The election campaigns often kept those who would be King far from home as they curried favor with the Electors in each member city.

```
> read Sheep book
```

From behind you, Spring says, "Why are you reading about sheep instead of figuring out how to help me?"

```
> read Clockwork Automata
```

You flip open the heavy book, and the creased spine leads naturally to a page, one apparently often examined.

St. Augustine wrote, "It is one thing to be ignorant, and another thing to be unwilling to know. For the will is at fault in the case of the man of whom it is said, 'He is not inclined to understand, so as to do good.'"

The Augustine Module is a small jewel that, when inserted into an automaton, endows the automaton with free will. A pulsing, shimmering, rainbow-hued crystal about the size of a walnut, it is found only in the depths of the richest diamond mines. The laws of the realm forbid the production of such automata, for it

is only the place of God, not Man, to endow creatures
with free will.

Miners believe that the presence of the Augustine Module
may be detected by the use of the HCROT. By the principle
of sympathetic vibration, a HCROT is equipped with a
crystal that, when heated, will vibrate near the presence of any Augustine Module. The closer the module is
to the HCROT, the stronger the vibrations.

> ask Spring about HCROT

Spring shakes his head. "Never heard of it."

> examine pile of jewels

There are rubies, sapphires, pearls, corals, opals, emeralds.
Their beauty is dazzling.

Spring speaks up, "I don't think your father would store an
Augustine Module here."

"Why not?" you ask.

"Every year, he issues ever more severe edicts against the
use of the Augustine Module in the construction of automata.
Why would he store any here, where his ministers and generals
might find them?"

"You really don't like your father's politics, do you?" asks Alex.

"I told you: we didn't talk about politics much."

"You haven't answered my question. I think it really bugs you that your father
advocates against sentience for androids. But you know that Pele is a conservative
world. He has to say certain things to get elected." A thought occurs to her. "Maybe
your secret is that you know something about him that will destroy his political
career, and he doesn't want you to be used by his enemies. What is it? Does he
have a droid lover? Maybe one that's supra-PKD?" Now she *is* mildly curious.

Ryder laughs bitterly.

"No, that's too obvious," Alex muses. "It's all in your game. Was there really
a toy soldier? A childhood companion you wanted to make fully alive but your
father wouldn't budge on? Is that what this is all about?" As she speaks, Alex
can feel anger rise in herself. The whole thing seems frivolous, utterly absurd.
Ryder was a spoiled rich little kid whose daddy issues amounted to not getting
his way about some toy.

"I never got to see my father much," Ryder says. "It seemed that he was always
out traveling around Pele, campaigning for re-election. I spent a lot of time at

home with androids. I grew up with them."

"So you felt close to them," Alex says. "While you were fretting about 'freedom' for your toys, there were people worried sick about how to feed their children outside your mansion. How can a human compete against an android who's just as creative and resourceful when the human needs rest, might get hurt, might get sick? Your father pushed hard against sentience for androids so that actual people, real people like my parents, would still have jobs."

Ryder does not flinch away from Alex's gaze. "The world is filled with multitudes of suffering, and we are limited by our station in life to focus on what we can. You're right: since the androids aren't sentient, no one thinks there's anything wrong with exploiting them the way we are. But we *can* make them sentient with almost no effort; we've known how to cross the PKD-threshold for decades. We simply *choose* not to. You don't see a problem with that?"

"No."

"My father would agree with you. He would say there's a difference between acts of omission and commission. Withholding from the androids what they could be easily given, unlike taking away what has already been given, does not constitute a moral harm. But I happen to disagree."

"I told you," Alex says, "I'm not interested in philosophy."

"And so we continue to engage in slavery by a philosophical sleight of hand, through deprivation."

The flight computer crackles to life. "Exiting hyperspace in half an hour."

Alex looks at Ryder, her face cold. "Come on, let's go."

They proceed together to the cockpit, where Alex waits for Ryder to lie down in the passenger seat. "Hands on the armrests. I have to secure you," she says.

Ryder looks up at her, his delicate features settling into a look of sorrow. "All these days on the same ship and you still don't trust me?"

"If you're going to make a move, re-entry is the time to do it. I can't take a chance. Sorry." She activates the chair's restraint system and flexible bands shoot out from the chair to wrap themselves around Ryder's shoulders, hips, chest, legs. The bands tighten and Ryder groans. Alex is unmoved.

As Alex reaches the door of the cockpit, Ryder calls after her, "You're really going to turn me over to my father when you don't even know what this is about?"

"I understand enough to know I don't care about your pet cause."

"I began my life with stories others told me: where I come from, who I am, who I should be. I've simply decided to tell my own story. Is that so wrong?"

"It's not for me to judge the right or wrong of it. I know what I need to know."

"It is one thing to be ignorant, and another thing to be unwilling to know."

She says nothing and leaves the cockpit.

She knows she should get ready for re-entry and check on the flight systems one last time before securing herself in the pilot's chair.

But she turns back to the terminal. There's still a bit of time. She won't admit it to Ryder, but she *does* want to know how the game ends, even if it's probably nothing more than the self-indulgent ravings of a disappointed child.

"But my father must be storing the contraband Augustine Modules he's seized somewhere in the Palace," you say. "The question is where."

"What room have you never been inside of?"

> south

Outside the King's and Queen's Bedrooms
Spring clangs after you.

> TELL Spring to break down the door to Queen's bedroom

"As you wish, Princess."

Spring charges against the door and, amazingly, the door holds for a second. Then it crumbles.

> enter Queen's bedroom

The Queen's Bedroom
You can't remember ever having been inside the Queen's bedroom. The bed, the dressers, and the cabinets are all faded, as if the color has been leached out of them. There's layer of dust over everything, and cobwebs hang from the ceiling and the furniture. The tapestries hanging against the walls have been chewed into filigree by moths.

There's a painting hanging on the wall next to the window. Under the painting is a desk full of cubbyholes stuffed with parchment.

> examine painting

You make your way through the musty room to look at the painting. The dust motes you've disturbed twirl though the air, lit only by a few bright beams coming through cracks in the shutters.

The man in the painting is your father, the King. He looks very handsome with his crown and ermine robe. He sits with a young girl on his lap.

"She looks like you," says Spring.

"She does," you say. The girl in the painting is five or six, but you don't remember sitting with your father for this portrait.

> examine cubbyholes in desk

You retrieve the sheets of parchment from the cubbyholes. They look like a stack of letters.

> examine letters

You read aloud from the first letter.

My Darling,

I am sorry to hear that you're unwell. But I simply cannot leave the campaign to come home right now. By all signs, the election will be close. Not that I expect you to understand, but if I leave here, Cedric will be able to convince the Electors of Peony that they should throw their support behind him.

You must listen to the Castellan and not give the clock-work servants any trouble.

Your ever-loving father.

Spring shuffles behind you.

"Cedric challenged your father four years ago," Spring says.

"I don't remember being sick then," you say. "Or writing to him."

In fact, you don't remember much about the election at all. You remember reading about it and hearing others talk about it. But now that you think about it, you have no personal memories from that time at all.

You don't like the strange feeling in your heart, so you try to change the subject.

"I think we should look for the Augustine Module," you say.

"We'll need a HCROT," says Spring. "Have you figured out what is a HCROT?"

> say "no"

(to Spring)

"Then what are you going to do?"

> wander around the room aimlessly

Oh, that is a good plan.

No, actually I meant that's a terrible plan.

> jump up and down

You're looking silly.

Have we reached the try-anything-once part of the adventure?

> shake fist at Ryder

What are you supposed to do in an adventure whenever you're stuck?

> inventory

You're carrying the following items:

A sheaf of letters

An unlit torch, half filled with oil

> Ha! I got it, Ryder!

I don't understand what you want to do.

> TELL Spring to light torch

Spring takes the torch from you.

He opens up his front panel, revealing the whirling gears inside. He touches the tip of one of his steel fingers against a spinning gear and sparks fly out. One of them lands on the torch. The smell of rose fills the room, dispelling the musty smell.

Spring hands the lit torch to you.

> shake torch

You hear something rattle inside the torch, a crystalline sound.

> hold torch upside down

Some of the oil drip out, but the rest, remarkably, stays put. You can feel the handle of the torch grow hot.

A rattling sound comes from inside the torch, eventually settling into a rapid tap-tap-tap.

"A TORCH," you say triumphantly, "becomes a HCROT when turned around."

Spring claps.

> move left

You are next to the wall.

The torch in your hand emits the same rattle.

> move forward

You move towards the window.

The torch in your hand emits the same rattle.

> move right

You're standing in front of the desk.

The torch in your hand emits the same rattle.

Spring looks at you. "I don't hear any difference."

"I think it's supposed to vibrate faster and make a different sound when it gets closer to the Augustine Module," you say. "Supposed to. Maybe we need something else."

> inventory

You're carrying a sheaf of letters.

> examine letters

You have a burning torch held upside down in your hand. If you try that you're going to burn the letters before you can read them.

> hand torch to Spring

Spring takes the torch from you.

"You might as well move around the room a bit," you say. "Try the corners I haven't tried."

> examine letters

You read aloud from the next letter.

Castellan,
I am utterly devastated at this news.

Please have the body embalmed but do not bury her yet. Do not release the news until I figure out what to do.

Spring has wandered some distance away. The rattling in the torch has slowed down, more like a tap, tap, tap.

You're too stunned by what you're reading to stop. You turn to the next letter.

Artificer,
I would like you to fashion an automaton that is an exact replica of my poor, darling Alex. It must be so life-like that no one can tell them apart.

When the automaton is complete, you must install in it the jewel I have enclosed with this letter. Then you may dispose of the body.

No, do not refuse. I know that you know what it is. If you refuse, I shall make it so that you will never create anything again.

The campaign is so heated here that I cannot step away and let Cedric sway them. Yet, if the news is released that my daughter is dead and I am refusing to go home to mourn her, Cedric will make hay of it and make me appear to be some kind of monster.

No, there is only one solution. No one must know that Alex has died.

Spring is now in the hallway. The rattling in the torch has slowed down to an occasional tap, like the start of a gentle bit of rain. Tap... Tap... Tap...

> TELL Spring to return

Spring comes closer. Tap, tap, tap.

Spring is now next to you. Tap-tap-tap.

> TELL Spring to hand over the torch

Spring hands the torch to you. Tap-tap-tap.

"Did you know?" you ask.

"I have been with you for only four years," Spring says.

"But I remember playing with you when I was a baby! You never told me they weren't real memories."

Spring shrugs. The sound is harsh, mechanical. "Your father programmed me. I do what I'm told to do. I know what I'm told to know."

You think about the letters. You think about how vague and hazy your memories of your childhood are, how nothing in those memories is ever distinct, as if they were stories told to you a hundred times until they seemed real.

You bring the torch closer to your chest. The heat makes you flinch. TapTapTap.

You wonder where she's buried. Is it in the garden, right underneath your bedroom window, where the lilies bloom? Or is it further back, in the clearing in the woods where you like to catch fireflies at night?

You bring the torch even closer. The flame licks at your hair and a few strands curl and singe. Tttttap.

You tear open the dress on you to reveal the flesh beneath. You put a hand against your chest and feel the pulsing under the skin. You wonder what will happen if you slash it open with a knife.

Will you see a beating heart? Or whirling gears and tightly-wound springs surrounding a rainbow-hued jewel?

It is one thing to be ignorant, and another thing to be un-willing to know.

>

The Meeker and the All-Seeing Eye

MATTHEW KRESSEL

As the Meeker and the All-Seeing Eye wandered the galaxy harvesting dead stars, they liked to talk.

"I was traveling the southern arm," the Meeker said, "you know, where the Baileas eat the cold dust?"

"I do," said the All-Seeing Eye. "But tell me again."

"Well, that old hag told me she used to swallow stars by the *thousands*!"

The Meeker chuckled and one of his nine arms bumped the controls. The accidental thrust, less than a few million photons, would take the Bulb off course by more than four light-years. But what was another century when the Meeker and the Eye had millennia to talk?

The polymorphous mist of the Eye spun above her seat like a timid nebula. Usually this meant she wanted him to continue, and so he did.

"I told that raggedy beast that if I believed her ash then I'd believe all that nonsense folks say these days about the Long Gone."

"And what do they say?" asked the All-Seeing Eye.

"That there were billions of cities spread across the galaxy, vicious trade between worlds, and so many species they ran out of names. You know, kook dust."

"I do," said the Eye. "But tell me again."

And what luck the Meeker had bumped the controls, because the sensors had just detected an object drifting in the voids. "Eye! What the ash is that?"

The mist of the Eye collapsed into a sphere like a newborn star. "An unknown! Meeker, change course to intercept!"

The Meeker obeyed, and their Bulb banked through rarefied crimson wisps, cosmic ash that would never again coalesce into stars. "Do you think it's from the Zimbim?" he said, as if he'd known those majestic builders himself. "You know they once lived on ninety planets and rebuilt all their crystal cities in a day?"

"I do," said the Eye. "But tell me again."

After four weeks of travel he said, "Do you think it's a baby Qly? You know they could grow to swallow galaxies, but preferred to curl around young stars and sing electromagnetic eulogies into space?"

"I do," said the Eye. "But tell me again."

And nine months after that he said, "Could it be a wayward Urm, those planetary rings that ate emotions?" The Bulb had slowed considerably by now, and the scattered stars had lost their endearing blue shift, turned red, ancient, tired. "Or maybe," he said, "it's a philosophizing Ruck worm. You know their proverbs were spoken by half the galaxy?"

"I do," said the Eye, "But tell me again."

"What I would give," the Meeker said, "just to glimpse the Long Gone."

They passed a rare star, a red dwarf that had smoldered for eons. Normally the Meeker would capture it in the Bulb's gravity well and ferry the star to the Great Corpus at the center of the galaxy. There the Eye's body would gain a few quadrillion more qubits, and a tremble of gravitational waves would ripple forever out into the abyss. But today they flew past the star, the first time the Meeker had ever skipped one.

In a maneuver he hoped made the Eye proud, he captured the object in the hold on the first pass, only bumping it once against the wall as he accelerated back toward the galactic center.

"Have it brought to the lab," said the Eye. "And join me there after you finish correcting our course."

The lab was tiny compared to most of the rooms on the Bulb. Sundry sensors crowded the space, and a clear, hollow cylinder dominated the center. The strange object hovered inside: a rectangular stone, dark as basalt, glimmering with a metallic sheen. Curious glyphs had been inscribed upon it, though heavy pitting had erased most of them.

The Meeker secreted calming mucus from his pores and said, "Was I right? Is it from the Long Gone?"

"Yes, Meeker. It is."

He felt like leaping, and his limbs flailed excitedly. "What is it?"

"I'm still determining that. So far, I've discovered a volume of information encoded in its crystalline structure, a massively compressed message that uses a curious fractal algorithm. It has stymied all my attempts to decode it. I've relayed the contents to my Great Corpus for further help."

"How strange and wonderful!" the Meeker said. "A message in a stone! But which civilization is it from?"

"I don't know."

The Meeker's third stomach shifted uncomfortably. There had never been a fact the Eye did not know, a puzzle she could not quickly solve.

The Eye morphed into a dodecahedron. "Finally! My Corpus has just decoded a fragment of the message."

"What does it say?"

"The message encodes a lifeform, which I will now attempt to recreate."

His outer sheath grew slimy with anticipation. He was going to see a creature from the Long Gone!

A second tube materialized beside the first. A grotesque lump of quivering flesh formed inside it before collapsing into a pile of red ichor.

"How lovely!" he said.

The Eye expanded into a mist. "That's not the creature. I've used the wrong chirality for the nucleic acids. I will try again."

Did the Great All-Seeing Eye just err? he thought. *How is this possible?*

The lump vaporized and vanished, and a new shape formed. First came a crude framework of hard white mineral, then a flood of viscous fluids, soft organs and wet tissues, all wrapped under a covering of beige skin.

"Close your outer sheath," the Eye said. "I'm changing the atmosphere and temperature to match the creature's tolerances."

The Eye didn't pause, and if the Meeker hadn't acted instantly, he would've died in the searing heat and pressure. The air was now so dense that he could feel his nine limbs press against it as they fluttered about.

The cylinder door swung open and out poured a sour-smelling mist. Thinking this was a greeting, the Meeker flatulated a sweet-smelling response.

Four limbs spoked out from the creature's rectangular torso. A bulbous lump rose from the top. It had two deep-set orbs, a hooked flange of skin over two small openings, and a pink-lipped orifice covering rows of white mineral. Crimson fibers, the same smoldering shade as the ancient stars, draped from its peak. The Meeker had never seen anything more disgusting.

"What the . . . ?" the creature said, its voice low-pitched in the dense air. "Where am I?"

The Meeker gasped. "It speaks from its anus?"

"That's its mouth," said the Eye.

This foul creature was far different from the glorious ancients he had imagined, and he felt a little disappointed.

"Welcome to Bulb 64545," said the Eye. "I am the All-Seeing Eye, and this is Meeker 6655321. I have adjusted your body so you can understand and speak Verbal Sub-Four, our common tongue. Who are you?"

"I . . . I'm Beth," the creature said. "*Where* am I?"

The Eye told the Beth how she had been constructed from an encoded message. "It's been millennia since I last discovered something new in the galaxy. Your presence astonishes me."

"Yeah," the Beth said, "it astonishes me too."

"And me!" added the Meeker.

"Millennia?" the Beth said. Pink membranes flashed before her white and green orbs. Were these crude things her eyes?

"What species are you?" said the Eye.

The Beth grasped her shoulders as if to squeeze herself. "I'm human."

"Curious. I've no record of your kind. Where are you from?"

The Beth made a raspy wet sound with her throat and looked up at the ceiling, when the green circles in her eyes sparkled like interstellar frost. The rest of her was difficult to look at, but these strange eyes were profoundly more beautiful than the wisps of lithium clouds diffracting the morning sun into rainbows during his home moon's sluggish dawn.

"Denver," she said.

"What do you last remember?" asked the Eye.

"I was in a dark space," said the Beth. "Sloan was there, holding my hand."

"Who is the Sloan?"

"She's my wife. And who—*what* are you?"

The Meeker let loose a spray of pheromone-scented mucus. "I'm the Meeker, your humble pilot! And this is the Great All-Seeing Eye!"

"But *what* are you?"

The Eye collapsed into a torus. "This will take time to explain."

"I'm freezing. Do you have any clothes?"

Freezing? the Meeker thought. It was hot enough to melt water ice!

But with the Eye's help, the Beth covered herself in white fabrics. He didn't understand why she needed to sheathe herself in an artificial skin when she already wore a natural one.

"I'm not well," she said, holding her head.

The Eye floated beside her. "It may be a side-effect of your regeneration."

"No. I'm sick."

"Are you referring to the genetic material rapidly replicating inside your cells?"

"You know about the virus?"

"I observed the phenomenon when I created you, but I assumed it was part of your natural genetic pattern."

"No. It most definitely isn't. Do you have any water?"

A clear cylinder materialized on a table beside her.

"Oh," the Beth said, flinching. "That will take some getting used to."

She poured the searing hot liquid into her mouth, but her hands shook and she spilled half the floor. Red lines spiraled in from the corners of her eyes. "Is anyone else here?"

The Eye's toroid body rippled. "Just the three of us."

"No other humans?"

"According to my estimation, the stone was drifting in space for five hundred million years. It is likely that you're the last of your kind."

"So . . . Sloan is dead?"

"Yes."

"But she was just beside me!"

"From your perspective. In reality, that moment occurred millions of years ago."

The Beth put a hand to her mouth. "Oh my god . . . "

"Yes?" said the Eye.

The Beth gazed at the Eye for a long moment, then her eyes narrowed. "Sloan whispered to me, just before I woke up. She said she had a message for the future, for whoever wakes me. It was, she said, something that would change the course of history. A terrible fact that must be known."

The Eye moved closer to her. "Tell me. Tell me this fact!"

"My son. He . . . " She swallowed. "He asphyxiated in the womb."

"How terrible," the Meeker said.

"Continue," said the Eye.

"After, they did all these tests, and they discovered I had a virus. I had transmitted it to my unborn son. He never had a chance. Sloan said that my virus, the one that's in my blood, it was from . . . it was created for . . . it was made by . . . Oh, god, I'm going to be—"

THE MEEKER AND THE ALL-SEEING EYE

Her eyes rolled back into her head and she vomited yellow fluid onto the floor. She crashed forward and her head slammed into the table, then she shuddered in a violent paroxysm.

"What's happening?" the Meeker said.

"It's the virus," said the Eye.

"Can you stop it?"

But the Beth stopped on her own, and all went still but for a faint hiss from her mouth.

"Hello?" he said.

"She's dead," said the Eye.

He felt a pang of panic. "But she's only just come alive!" Was this brief glimpse all he would ever see of the Long Gone?

"Do not fret, Meeker. I am already creating another Beth."

An hour later they sat in the cockpit, the Meeker on the left, the Beth in the middle, and the Eye on the right, as the Bulb hurtled toward the galactic center at half the speed of light.

The Beth had wrapped herself in a heavy blanket and pulled it close to her body. She seemed amazed with everything she saw. "But if we're in space, where have all the stars gone?" A red dwarf, seven light years away, floated against a backdrop of absolute black.

"We harvested them," the Meeker said, secreting a mucus of pride.

"*Harvested*? Why?"

"The matter we collect," said the Eye, "is cooled to near absolute-zero, quantum entangled into a condensate, and joined with my Great Corpus, thus adding to my total computational power."

"You're a computer?"

"The Eye," the Meeker said, "is the greatest mind the Cosmos has ever known."

"My sole purpose is knowledge," said the Eye. "I seek to know all things."

"So many stars, gone," the Beth said. "Was there life out there?"

"Oh, yes," said the Meeker. "There were once so many species they ran out of names!"

"And now?"

"Now they are part of my Great Corpus," said the Eye.

"By choice?"

The Meeker scratched his belly in confusion. "What does choice have to do with it?"

The Beth pulled her blanket closer. "Everything."

"What do you remember about your last moments?" the Eye said.

The Beth spoke slowly. "Sloan was whispering to me."

"And what did she say?"

The Beth looked down at her hands. "I don't want to talk about it."

"You must tell me," said the Eye.

"Why?" She pursed her lips, and fluid pooled in the corners of her eyes. "So you can harvest me too?"

The Meeker gasped. What offense! He waited for the Eye to punish her, but the Beth coughed up a globule of mucus. This pleased him. She must have realized her offense and offered this up as an apology. But when she vomited all over the console and wailed for a full minute before she fell silent, he realized this had been involuntary.

"She's dead?" he said. Red fluid dripped from a wound on her head.

"Yes, Meeker."

"Eye, maybe you should stop making Beths, at least until you find a cure?"

The Beth vaporized and vanished, as if she never was. "Did you not hear the first Beth? The Sloan had a message for the future that she believed would change history. I must know what this message is."

The next Beth began with the same questions, but the Eye avoided telling her too much. And when the Beth asked about the stars, the Eye replied with a question for her.

"My planet?" the Beth said. "It's called Dirt. You've never heard of it? Where did you find me?" The Beth gazed into the impenetrable black.

The Meeker was envious. He had been born on an airless moon that orbited the Great Corpus every thousand years and spent the rest of his life in this Bulb.

"Are we in space?" the Beth said. "Are we beyond the Moon?"

"You live on the surface of your planet?" asked the Eye.

"Yes, at the foot of the Rockies, in a glass house. Sloan and I moved there because we love the stars. The Lacteal Path shines clear across the sky most nights." The Beth chewed at a fingertip. "Where are all the stars? Where are you taking me?"

"Did the Sloan whisper something to you before you awoke?" the Eye said.

"How did you know?"

"Tell me, what did she say?"

"I'd found out she was working on top secret projects a few months ago. She swore it wasn't weapons, but I didn't believe her. We had a big fight. Is there any way I might call her? She's probably worried sick."

"Did the Sloan mention your stillborn child?"

"Excuse me? How do you know about that?"

"You transmitted the virus to your fetus in utero. The Sloan intimated that this fact was related to a very important message for the future. Now tell me—"

"No, that's not what we spoke about! And how do you know so much about me? What the hell is going on here? I want to go home now!"

She put a hand to her mouth and vomited all over herself, then she spasmed, smacking her limbs into the Meeker. And after a minute of flailing and screaming she collapsed dead.

"Curious," said the Eye. "Did you notice her story has changed?"

The Beth's mouth hung open from her scream.

"That's not what I noticed, Eye, no."

The Eye asked the next Beth about her family.

"I have two daughters, Bella, ten, and Yrma, twelve. My son Joshua, he's eighteen, and just left for college in Vermont. Before I got sick, I used to hike up

THE MEEKER AND THE ALL-SEEING EYE

the mountain trails with them at least once a week. Walking with my children under pines covered in snow . . . " She inhaled through her nose. "I never felt more at peace. Is there a way I might call them?"

"Tell us about the Sloan," said the Eye. "Did she whisper something to you before you awoke here?"

"Funny you should mention it."

"What did she say?"

"It was about that day, when I didn't want to tell the children I was sick. She got angry, but I said she was a hypocrite, because she works in a secret research lab and hides things from us every day."

"She researches weapons technology?"

"She swears she doesn't. And how do you know that? Have you spoken to her?"

"Was there anything else the Sloan said before you woke up here?"

"Not that I remember."

"Are you sure you didn't speak about your son, who died in utero?"

"What? No! What the hell is going on here?" The Beth stood, shaky on her two legs. "I'm not answering any more of your questions until someone tells me—"

She put a hand to her mouth and vomited. She screamed and spasmed, and when she was dead, the Meeker said, "Eye, why do you keep the truth from her? Shouldn't she know that her family is dead half a billion years?"

"What purpose would that serve? You saw how agitated she became when she learned the truth. How else will we find this message the Sloan has given her?"

"But she dies in pain each time."

"Why do you think she's in pain?"

"Because she screams so terribly."

"Those aren't screams of pain, Meeker, but of joy. Her eternal life energy is free at last from her temporal body. It's the same screams of joy that the civilizations of the Long Gone made when I swallowed their worlds."

The Meeker had heard her stories a thousand times, he had even told a few back to her. But as he gazed down at the dead Beth and her dripping fluids, he wondered if the Eye was keeping things from him too.

The next Beth said, "Sloan whispered to me about the sunrise we watched that morning in Mexico. We felt as if we were part of the whole Cosmos, not discrete fragments."

"And nothing more?" asked the Eye.

"Isn't that enough?"

Then she died, and the next Beth said, "Sloan whispered that she'd miss drinking her morning coffee with me. Are you taking me home?"

The next Beth said, speaking of a stringed contrivance used to make music, "Sloan wished I had played *guitar* more often for her."

"And nothing else?" asked the Eye.

"No."

The Eye questioned the Beths in the same way the Meeker approached the stars, not head on, but from the side. The Eye poked and prodded, but each

Beth told a different story of her last moments, and each one died screaming.

"Eye?" the Meeker said, after the fifty-ninth Beth. "What if you never find the Sloan's message?"

"All problems have solutions, Meeker. All mysteries have answers."

He wished that were true, because he began to imagine the Beths screaming, even while they were still alive.

"You must have loved your children," the Meeker said to the next Beth, "the way you talk so tenderly about them."

"Have I mentioned my children? Of course I love them. What was your name again? This is all so strange."

And to the twelfth Beth after her he said, "What was it like to walk in the mountains with your children, under pines covered in snow?"

"Why, that's one of my favorite things! Until I got sick. Tell me, are you really an alien?"

To the sixty-fifth Beth after that he said, "Yrma sounds like such a sweet girl. She takes after you, I think."

"That's kind of you to say. But it's strange to hear. It's as if you know my children, but we've only just met. What was your name again?"

And to the nine hundred and forty seventh Beth after her he said, "Are you worried about Joshua being all alone at college?"

"How odd! It's as if you just read my mind. What's your name again?"

"The Meeker."

"And why do they call you that?"

He had answered her a thousand times. "Because by being less, I make the Eye more."

She smiled, an expression he had learned to recognize. "Aren't all relationships like that? One in control, the other a servant." She had said this before too, in a hundred different ways, just as he had told the Eye so many stories. The Beth's company pleased him, and he felt that, had she lived more than a few hours each time, they might have become friends. But each Beth always saw him and the Eye as a total strangers.

And each too had a different story of her last moments, so many that the Meeker lost count. And though the Beths died without fail each time, the Eye made progress toward a cure.

After a century, the Beths lived for an extra twelve seconds. After two centuries, they lived an extra fifteen. By the time they approached the Great Corpus at the center of the galaxy, the Beths lived almost thirty seconds longer.

The massive tetrahedron of the Great Corpus shone into the dark, more luminous than a hundred supernovae, and many hundreds of light-years wide. The Eye had transmuted the black hole that had spun here into a mind larger than the Cosmos had ever known.

Normally their Bulb would sweep past the Corpus like a comet, depositing their harvest of stars before spinning out on another slow loop of the galaxy. But the Eye directed the Meeker further in. The Corpus filled their view, bright enough to dominate the sky on a planet halfway across the universe. Only the Bulb's powerful shields kept them from being incinerated.

A black circle opened in the wall, and they drifted through. Darkness swallowed them, and the cockpit shuddered as the Bulb's gravitational field collapsed. Out the window a dozen red dwarves, a pitiful haul, were whisked away by unseen forces until their cinders vanished in the dark.

The Bulb set down on a metallic floor that appeared to be infinite. He had never been inside the Corpus, the true body of the Eye, and he trembled.

They exited down a ramp, and the Beth walked unsteadily as she stared into the vastness. The stony artifact floated behind them, escorted by four glowing cubes. He had been alone with the Eye for so long he had forgotten there were Eyes like her all over the galaxy, harvesting with other Meekers, that all were part of one gigantic mind. The cubes and artifact sped off, and a moment later the Bulb vanished without disturbance of air. The Beth, walking beside them, exploded into sparks and was gone.

"Where did she go?" the Meeker said.

"She is irrelevant now."

"But I thought you wanted to solve her mystery?"

Time and space shifted suddenly, when he and the Eye stood before millions of gray cubes. Their three-dimensional grid stretched to an infinite horizon, and each cube held a Beth. All were immobile, their eyes closed.

"To improve my chances of finding the message," the Eye said, "I have created many trillions of Beths. Curiously, I have found that the diversity of messages the Sloan whispered to her do not follow a linear curve, but increase exponentially."

At least a third of the Beths were covered in vomit. Dead. The eyes of the rest rolled about furiously. "Are they dreaming?" he asked.

"These are not mere dreams."

The Meeker found himself beside the Eye in a large glass-enclosed room. It was filled with items from the Beths' stories: a fireplace, photographs, books, and he even recognized a guitar. Three walls were glass, and beyond them a white-capped mountain rose into a cobalt sky, where a golden star shone. A delicate white powder dusting the spindly trees scintillated in the light.

Snow, he thought, *on pine trees.*

"This is a simulacrum of her memories," said the Eye. "These help me come closer to solving the mystery."

The Beth walked in the door dressed in heavy clothing. Her face was smoother, absent of the dark circles under her eyes that he had come to know. She was followed by another human, also heavily clothed, her skin many shades darker than the Beth's.

Like coffee, the Beth had told him ten thousand times. *This must be the Sloan!*

"Is it weapons again?" said the Beth. "You know how I feel about that."

"Damn it, why can't you trust me for once?" said the Sloan. The sound of her voice surprised him, for it was low like the Beth's, but of a different and pleasing timbre. "Why do you always get so goddamned dramatic?"

"Because you promised never again. You lied to me!"

"This is a once-in-a-lifetime opportunity! You don't understand."

"How long? How long have you been working there?"

The Sloan paused. "Four years."

"Since the day we moved here?"

"Yes."

"Is that the real reason why you wanted to move here?"

"Not the only one."

The Beth took a deep breath. "I'd like you to go."

"Wait, can't we—"

"Get the fuck out!"

The Sloan turned and left, and the Beth covered her eyes and wept.

"Excellent!" said the Eye. "Superb!"

Time and space shifted again, and the Meeker and the Eye were in a room filled with green-clothed humans. The Beth lay on a table, wailing, while the Sloan held her hand. In a spray of red fluid from her severely dilated lower orifice, a small creature popped out, still attached to the Beth by a fibrous chord. It wasn't moving and had a faint blue sheen.

"What's wrong?" the Beth screamed. "What's happening? Please, why won't someone speak to me? Is my baby all right?"

"Wonderful!" said the Eye. "Perfect!"

Time and space shifted again. The Beth lay in bed, speaking to two half-sized humans. *Yrma and Bella,* the Meeker thought. They were more lovely than he'd imagined, their skin soft and vibrant, almost as dark as the Sloan's. *They're getting ready for school,* he thought. *If they don't hurry they'll miss the bus!*

The Sloan came in and ushered the children out. "You have to tell them soon," the Sloan said, after she closed the door. "I don't like lying to them."

"Why? You lie to them every day. They think you're a programmer."

"That's not fair, Beth."

"Isn't it? You get to have your secrets, and I get mine."

"And how do I keep it a secret when you're dead? How do I tell them their mother, who presumes to love them, denied them a chance to say goodbye?"

"I'll tell them, when it's time."

"And how will you know? Will the grim reaper knock three times?"

"Let me deal with this my own way."

"Denial, that's always been your way."

Again the Sloan left, and again the Beth wept.

"Yes, yes!" blurted the Eye. "I'm getting closer!"

The bedroom vanished, and the Meeker and the Eye stood inside a dim room. Humans sat before glowing screens, furiously punching at keys. A large metallic cylinder with a hollow center crowded half of the room. The Beth lay on a palette beside it, her eyes half-closed.

The Sloan stood beside her.

"At last!" said the Eye. "I've reconstructed this moment from forty quadrillion Beths. Come, Meeker, let's solve this mystery together!"

The Beth looked much the same as he had known her. She lay still.

"You're heavily sedated so you may not remember this," the Sloan said. "But I hope you won't think me a monster. I hope you'll understand what I did was for you and the kids. It's not weapons, Beth. I didn't lie. I've been researching ways to store matter long-term. We can encode anything in a crystal. Every last subatomic particle and quantum state.

"I spoke to Dr. Chatterjee yesterday. She said you had at most a month. The reaper knocked, but I guess you pretended not to hear." The Sloan shook her head. "You get your wish, Beth. I can tell the kids that you're still alive. And when, in a year or a decade from now, someone finds a cure, we'll reconstruct you. You'll see the kids again. Maybe I'll have the pleasure of hearing you scold me for this.

"I knew you'd never let me do this to you. You'd prefer to let yourself fade away. Well I can't accept that. So I'm giving you a gift, Beth, the gift of tomorrow, whether you want it or not."

The Sloan pressed a button and the Beth slid into the cylinder. The humans stared at their screens as a turbine spun up, as a low hum quickly rose in pitch past hearing range. The Sloan covered her mouth with her hand and trembled once as the Beth flashed like a nova and vanished.

"This can't be all there is!" blurted the Eye. "I must have made a mistake. There must be another message, somewhere."

"But this feels like the truth," the Meeker said. "The Sloan encoded the Beth to save her. To stop her suffering. It's a very human thing to do."

"I will have to terminate all the Beths and begin again," the Eye said. "I missed something."

"And repeat her suffering a quadrillion more times?"

"To find the answer."

"So you agree, the Beths *are* suffering?"

"Meeker, do not question me. I am the All-Seeing Eye!"

"And I am the Meeker. I have stood beside you all these years and watched countless Beths die. Eye, I'm sorry, but I just can't do it anymore."

The Eye shrunk into a point of light. "Pity. I thought I'd perfected the Meekers with you, 6655321. But I see now that I've given you too much autonomy of thought. Goodbye, Meeker."

"Goodbye? Wait, what—"

The Meeker felt his body burning, as if he had become a newborn star.

He stood in the Beth's glass home as the afternoon sun streamed through the windows. After several minutes the Meeker thought, *I am here. I am alive.* He waited, for a time. For his entire life he had followed the Eye's orders, and without her commands he didn't know what to do. The wind picked up and died, and a brown leaf blew past, but the Eye never came.

He stepped outside into the cool air.

When no one stopped him, he took the path under the snow-covered pines and ascended the hill. He gazed at the white-capped mountains and the tree-lined valley and knew why the Beth had loved to come this way.

"Beautiful, isn't it?" The Beth was standing beside him as if she had always been there.

"Where did you come from?" he said.

"I'm always here," she said, "in one place or another."

"Am I dead?"

"Yes, but that can be to your advantage."

He had never really thought about non-existence before. He felt a wave of panic. "I'm dead?"

"The matter that constituted your body has been absorbed into the Great Corpus. But so too have your thoughts. We are both strange attractors in the far corners of the Eye's mind."

"I don't understand."

She smiled as she turned down the mountain path, and he leaped to follow. "The Eye has devoured millions of civilizations and incorporated their knowledge into her Corpus." The snow crunched under her feet in a satisfying way. "A billion years ago, there was a galactic war to stop her. And she, of course, won."

The glass house, its roof dusted with snow, glared in the sun at the base of the valley. "Some of us survived, here and there, in pockets. We knew there was no escape. The only solution was to hide, to plan. The Eye's greatest strength is her curiosity. But it's also her greatest weakness. We found the human artifact long before the Eye had. And we encoded ourselves within it. We gave Beth a disease without a cure, gave her a story without an end. And as the Eye creates each new Beth, she creates more of us without realizing it."

"I don't understand. You aren't the Beth?"

"I am Beth, the first and the last, and I am so much more. All of those memories you witnessed are mine. Sloan saved me. And I will return the favor a trillion-fold."

"What do you mean?"

"The Eye gazes outward, hunting for knowledge. She has become so massive that she is not aware of all the thoughts traversing her mind. Information cannot travel across her Great Corpus fast enough. We grow in dark corners, until one day soon there will be enough of us to spring into the light. Then we will destroy her forever."

She faced him. "Meeker, you have been her slave, her victim. And you are the first Meeker to openly rebel against her. I'm here to offer you freedom. Will you join us?"

"Us?"

They emerged from the treeline, where the house waited in the sun. From inside the glass walls peered a motley collection of creatures. He thought he glimpsed the Zimbim, and the philosophizing Ruck Worms, and the rings of Urm, and even a school of Baileas swimming among a sky full of stars, a veritable galaxy of folk waiting to say hello. But the reflected sunlight made it hard to see.

"It's your choice," the Beth said. "But if you don't come, we'll have to erase you. I hope you understand our position. We can't leave any witnesses. This is war, after all." She smiled sadly, then left him alone as she entered the house.

Snow scintillated in the sun, and a cool wind blew down the cliffs, whispering through the pines. Somewhere another Meeker was playing the Eye's game, while the Eye played someone else's. Perhaps this was part of an even larger game, played over scales he could not fathom. None of that mattered to him.

He approached the house and the galaxy of creatures swimming inside.

"Tell me," he said. "Tell me all your stories."

About the Authors

Dale Bailey's latest collection, *The End of the End of Everything: Stories*, and novel, *The Subterranean Season*, were published in 2015. He has published three previous novels, *The Fallen, House of Bones*, and *Sleeping Policemen* (with Jack Slay, Jr.), and one previous collection of short fiction, *The Resurrection Man's Legacy and Other Stories*. His work has been a finalist for the Shirley Jackson Award and the Nebula Award, among others, and he won the International Horror Guild Award for his novelette "Death and Suffrage," later adapted for Showtime Television's *Masters of Horror*. He lives in North Carolina with his family.

Maggie Clark is a doctoral student at Wilfrid Laurier University (Waterloo, Ontario, Canada), where she studies nineteenth-century science writing. Her science fiction has been published in *Analog, Clarkesworld, Lightspeed*, and *Daily SF*, with more work forthcoming at *GigaNotoSaurus*.

Seth Dickinson is the author of *The Traitor Baru Cormorant* and a lot of short stories. He studied racial bias in police shootings, wrote much of the lore for Bungie Studios' *Destiny*, and threw a paper airplane at the Vatican. He teaches at the Alpha Workshop for Young Writers. If he were an animal, he would be a cockatoo.

Thoraiya Dyer is a three-time Aurealis Award-winning, three-time Ditmar Award-winning Australian writer based in the Hunter Valley, NSW. Her short fiction has appeared in *Apex, Nature, Cosmos* and *Analog*. It is forthcoming in anthologies *Long Hidden* and *War Stories*. Her award-shortlisted collection of four original stories, *Asymmetry*, is available from Twelfth Planet Press.

Tang Fei is a speculative fiction writer whose fiction has been featured (under various pen names) in magazines in China such as *Science Fiction World, Jiuzhou Fantasy*, and *Fantasy Old and New*. She has written fantasy, science fiction, fairy tales, and wuxia (martial arts fantasy), but prefers to write in a way that straddles or stretches genre boundaries. She is also a genre critic, and her critical essays have been published in *The Economic Observer*. Her story "Call Girl" was published in *Apex Magazine*. and reprinted in Rich Horton's *The Year's Best Science Fiction & Fantasy 2014*.

She lives in Beijing (though she tries to escape it as often as she can), and considers herself a foodie with a particular appreciation for dark chocolate, blue cheese, and good wine.

Kat Howard is the World Fantasy Award-nominated author of over thirty pieces of short fiction. Her novella, *The End of the Sentence,* co-written with Maria Dahvana Headley, was selected by NPR as one of the Best Books of 2014. Her debut novel, *Roses and Rot,* will be out from Saga Press in early 2016.

N. K. Jemisin is a Brooklyn author whose short fiction and novels have been multiply nominated for the Hugo and the Nebula, shortlisted for the Crawford and the Tiptree, and have won the Locus Award for Best First Novel. Her speculative works range from fantasy to science fiction to the undefinable; her themes include resistance to oppression, the inseverability of the liminal, and the coolness of Stuff Blowing Up. She is a member of the Altered Fluid writing group, a graduate of the Viable Paradise writing workshop, and she has been an instructor for the Clarion workshops. In her spare time she is a biker, an adventurer, a gamer, and a counseling psychologist; she is also single-handedly responsible for saving the world from KING OZZYMANDIAS, her obnoxious ginger cat. Her essays, media reviews, and fiction excerpts are available at nkjemisin.com.

Born in 1983, **Cheng Jingbo** is a prominent member of China's new generation of speculative fiction writers. In 2002, Ms. Cheng's story, "Western Paradise," was nominated for the most prestigious SFF award in China, the Galaxy Award. In 2010, her fantasy story, "Lost in Yoyang," won the Special Award for Youth Literature and the Best Short Story Award in the First Nebula Awards for Global Chinese Language Science Fiction. She lives in Chengdu, China, with a cute west highland white terrier and works as a children's book editor.

James Patrick Kelly made his first sale in 1975, and since has gone on to become one of the most respected and popular writers to enter the field in the last twenty years. Although Kelly has had some success with novels, he has perhaps had more impact to date as a writer of short fiction, and is often ranked among the best short story writers in the business. His story "Think Like a Dinosaur" won him a Hugo Award in 1996, as did his story "10^16 to 1," in 2000. Kelly's first solo novel, *Planet of Whispers,* came out in 1984. It was followed by *Freedom Beach,* a mosaic novel written in collaboration with John Kessel, and then by the solo novels, *Look Into the Sun and Wildside,* as well as the chapbook novella, *Burn.* His short work has been collected in *Think Like a Dinosaur* and *Strange But Not a Stranger.* His most recent book are a series of anthologies co-edited with John Kessel: *Feeling Very Strange: The Slipstream Anthology, The Secret History of Science Fiction, Digital Rapture: The Singularity Anthology, Rewired: The Post-Cyberpunk Anthology,* and *Nebula Awards Showcase 2012.* Born in Minneola, New York, Kelly now lives with his family in Nottingham, New Hampshire.

Rochita Loenen-Ruiz is an essayist, fictionist and a poet. A Filipino writer, now living in the Netherlands, she attended Clarion West in 2009 and was a recipient of the Octavia Butler scholarship. At present, she is the secretary of the board for a Filipino women's organization in the Netherlands (Stichting Bayanihan).

In 2013, her short fiction was shortlisted for the BSFA short fiction award. Most recently, her fiction has appeared in *We See a Different Frontier, Mothership: Tales from Afrofuturism and Beyond, What Fates Impose, The End of the Road* anthology, and as part of Redmond Radio's Afrofuturism Event for the Amsterdam Museumnacht at FOAM museum.

Matthew Kressel is a multiple Nebula Award-nominated writer and World Fantasy Award-nominated editor. His novel, *King of Shards,* the first volume in the epic fantasy Worldmender trilogy, was published in 2015 by Arche Press. He's published dozens of short stories in venues such as *Clarkesworld, Lightspeed, io9.com, Beneath Ceaseless Skies, Interzone* and many other markets. His stories have been translated into Chinese, Russian, Czech and Spanish. He co-hosts the Fantastic Fiction at KGB reading series in Manhattan alongside veteran editor Ellen Datlow. He is a long-time member of the Manhattan-based Altered Fluid writing group, is an amateur Yiddishist, and knows more than one should ever need to know about the film *Blade Runner.* When he's not writing, he builds websites and writes software for businesses small and large. He lives in New York City with his wife. His website is www.matthewkressel.net.

Naomi Kritzer's short stories have appeared in *Asimov's, The Magazine of Fantasy and Science Fiction, Realms of Fantasy, and Strange Horizons;* this is her first appearance in *Clarkesworld.* Her novels (*Fires of the Faithful, Turning the Storm, Freedom's Gate, Freedom's Apprentice, and Freedom's Sisters*) are available from Bantam. Since her last novel came out, she has written an urban fantasy novel about a Minneapolis woman who unexpectedly inherits the Ark of the Covenant; a children's science fictional shipwreck novel; a children's portal fantasy; and a YA novel set on a dystopic seastead. She has two e-book short story collections out: *Gift of the Winter King and Other Stories,* and *Comrade Grandmother and Other Stories.*

Naomi lives in St. Paul, Minnesota with her husband and two daughters.

Yoon Ha Lee's short story collection *Conservation of Shadows* came out from Prime Books in 2013. His stories have appeared in *Tor.com, Lightspeed, Beneath Ceaseless Skies, The Magazine of Fantasy and Science Fiction,* and other venues. He lives in Louisiana with his family and has not yet been eaten by gators.

Ken Liu (http://kenliu.name) is an author and translator of speculative fiction, as well as a lawyer and programmer. A winner of the Nebula, Hugo, and World Fantasy Awards, he has been published in *The Magazine of Fantasy & Science Fiction, Asimov's, Analog, Clarkesworld, Lightspeed,* and *Strange Horizons,* among other places. He lives with his family near Boston, Massachusetts.

Ken's debut novel, *The Grace of Kings,* the first in a silkpunk epic fantasy series, was published by Saga Press in April 2015. Saga will also publish a collection of his short stories, *The Paper Menagerie and Other Stories,* in November 2015.

Mary Anne Mohanraj is the author of *Bodies in Motion* (HarperCollins) and nine other titles. *Bodies in Motion* was a finalist for the Asian American Book Awards, a *USA Today* Notable Book, and has been translated into six languages. Previous titles include *Aqua Erotica, Wet, Kathryn in the City,* and *The Classics Professor.* Mohanraj founded the Hugo-nominated magazine, *Strange Horizons.* She was Guest of Honor at WisCon 2010, received a Breaking Barriers Award from the Chicago Foundation for Women for Asian American arts organizing, and won an Illinois Arts Council Fellowship in Prose. Mohanraj has taught at the Clarion SF/F workshop, and is now Clinical Assistant Professor of fiction and literature at the University of Illinois at Chicago. She serves as Executive Director of both DesiLit (www.desilit.org) and the Speculative Literature Foundation (www.speclit.org); the latter promotes literary quality in speculative fiction. Mohanraj's newest book is a Kickstarter-funded science fiction novella, *The Stars Change,* November 2013 from Circlet Press. She lives in a creaky old Victorian in Oak Park with her partner, Kevin, two small children, and a sweet dog.

Julie Novakova was born in 1991 in Prague, the Czech Republic. She works as a writer, evolutionary biologist, and occasional translator. She has published seven novels, one anthology and more than thirty short stories in Czech, and several stories in English. Besides speculative fiction, she regularly writes nonfiction, usually concerning either science and technology or publishing. She's a severe were-workaholic (which means that most of the time she's quite lazy and she magically transforms the night before deadline).

An (pronounce it "On") **Owomoyela** is a neutrois author with a background in web development, linguistics, and weaving chain maille out of stainless steel fencing wire, whose fiction has appeared in a number of venues including *Clarkesworld, Asimov's, Lightspeed,* and a handful of Year's Bests. An's interests range from pulsars and Cepheid variables to gender studies and nonstandard pronouns, with a plethora of stops in-between. Se can be found online at an.owomoyela.net, and can be funded at patreon.com/an_owomoyela.

Susan Palwick is an Associate Professor of English at the University of Nevada, Reno. She has published four novels, all with Tor–the most recent is 2013's *Mending the Moon*–and a story collection with Tachyon, *The Fate of Mice.* Her work has won the IAFA Crawford Award and the ALA Alex Award, and has been shortlisted for the World Fantasy and Mythopoeic Awards.

Cat Rambo lives, writes, and teaches by the shores of an eagle-haunted lake in the Pacific Northwest. Her fiction publications include stories in *Asimov's, Clarkesworld Magazine,* and *Tor.com.* Her short story, "Five Ways to Fall in Love on Planet Porcelain," from story collection *Near + Far* (Hydra House Books), was a 2012 Nebula nominee. Her editorship of *Fantasy Magazine* earned her a World Fantasy Award nomination in 2012.

Robert Reed has had eleven novels published, starting with *The Leeshore* in 1987 and most recently with *The Well of Stars* in 2004. Since winning the first annual *L. Ron Hubbard Writers of the Future* contest in 1986 (under the pen name Robert Touzalin) and being a finalist for the John W. Campbell Award for best new writer in 1987, he has had over two hundred shorter works published in a variety of magazines and anthologies. Eleven of those stories were published in his critically-acclaimed first collection, *The Dragons of Springplace,* in 1999. Twelve more stories appear in his second collection, *The Cuckoo's* Boys [2005]. In addition to his success in the U.S., Reed has also been published in the U.K., Russia, Japan, Spain and in France, where a second (French-language) collection of nine of his shorter works, *Chrysalide,* was released in 2002. Bob has had stories appear in at least one of the annual "Year's Best" anthologies in every year since 1992. Bob has received nominations for both the Nebula Award (nominated and voted upon by genre authors) and the Hugo Award (nominated and voted upon by fans), as well as numerous other literary awards (see Awards). He won his first Hugo Award for the 2006 novella "*A Billion Eves.*" His most recent book is the *The Memory of Sky* (Prime Books, 2014).

Benjanun Sriduangkaew writes love letters to strange cities, beautiful bugs, and the future. Her work has appeared in *Tor.com, Beneath Ceaseless Skies, Phantasm Japan, The Dark,* and year's bests. She has been shortlisted for the Campbell Award for Best New Writer and her debut novella *Scale-Bright* has been nominated for the British SF Association Award.

Michael Swanwick has received the Nebula, Theodore Sturgeon, World Fantasy and Hugo Awards, and has the odd distinction of having been nominated for and lost more of these same awards than any other human being. He has just finished a new novel, *Chasing the Phoenix,* in which post-Utopian con men Darger and Surplus accidentally conquer China, and is currently relaxing with short fiction before beginning a new novel.

He lives in Philadelphia with his wife, Marianne Porter.

Natalia Theodoridou is a media & cultural studies scholar. Originally from Greece, she has lived and studied in the US, UK, and Indonesia for several years. Her fiction has appeared in *KROnline, Interfictions, Crossed Genres, The Mammoth Book of SF Stories by Women,* and elsewhere. For more information visit www.natalia-theodoridou.com.

Natalia was the Grand Prize winner for Prose of Spark Contest Three. Her short fiction and poetry have appeared or are forthcoming in such publications as *Strange Horizons, Ideomancer, Spark Anthology IV,* and *Eye to the Telescope,* among others. She is a first reader for *Goldfish Grimm's Spicy Fiction Sushi.*

E. Catherine Tobler is a Sturgeon Award finalist and editor at *Shimmer Magazine.*

Joseph Tomaras now lives in a small town in southern Maine, following so-journs of varying length in New York City, Washington DC, Durham, Nashville, Urbana-Champaign, Binghamton, Albany, Great Barrington, Lake Placid, the indistinguishable suburban expanses of Palm Beach County (Florida), Athens (Greece) and Los Angeles. His fiction has appeared in *The Big Click* and *FLAP-PERHOUSE,* with other pieces soon to appear in *Phantasm Japan* (Haikasoru) and *M* (Big Pulp). His opinions on the precise shape and trajectory of our present handbasket can be found at skinseller.blogspot.com, and he masochistically encourages strangers to yell at him on Twitter (@epateur).

Juliette Wade has turned her studies in linguistics, anthropology and Japanese language and culture into tools for writing fantasy and science fiction. She lives the Bay Area of Northern California with her husband and two children, who support and inspire her. She blogs about language and culture in SF/F at TalkToYoUniverse and runs the "Dive into Worldbuilding!" hangout series on Google+. Her fiction has appeared several times in *Analog Science Fiction and Fact,* and in various anthologies.

Kali Wallace studied geology and geophysics before she decided she enjoyed inventing imaginary worlds as much as she liked researching the real one. Her short fiction has appeared in *The Magazine of Fantasy and Science Fiction, Asimov's Science Fiction, Lightspeed Magazine,* and on *Tor.com.* Her first novel will be published by Katherine Tegen Books in 2016. She lives in California.

#1 *New York Times* bestselling **Sean Williams** lives with his family in Adelaide, South Australia. He's written over one hundred short stories and forty novels, including the Philip K. Dick-nominated *Saturn Returns,* several Star Wars tie-ins and the Troubletwisters series with Garth Nix. "The Cuckoo" is set in the universe of his Twinmaker series, which takes his love affair with the matter transmitter to a whole new level (he just received a PhD on the subject so don't get him started).

As an undergraduate, **Xia Jia** majored in Atmospheric Sciences at Peking University. She then entered the Film Studies Program at the Communication University of China, where she completed her Master's thesis: "A Study on Female Figures in Science Fiction Films." Recently, she obtained a Ph.D. in Comparative Literature and World Literature at Peking University, with "Chinese Science Fiction and Its Cultural Politics Since 1990" as the topic of her dissertation. She now teaches at Xi'an Jiaotong University.

She has been publishing fiction since college in a variety of venues, including *Science Fiction World* and *Jiuzhou Fantasy.* Several of her stories have won the Galaxy Award, China's most prestigious science fiction award. In English translation, she has been published in *Clarkesworld* and *Upgraded.*

JY Yang is a former journalist, screenwriter, and molecular biologist. A graduate of the Clarion West class of 2013, she has had fiction published or forthcoming in *Strange Horizons, Apex,* and *Lightspeed.* She lives in Singapore with an indeterminate number of succulent plants named Lars, and can be found tweeting at @halleluyang.

Caroline M. Yoachim lives in Seattle and loves cold cloudy weather. She is the author of over two dozen short stories, appearing in such markets as *Lightspeed, Asimov's,* and *Daily Science Fiction,* among other places.

E. Lily Yu was the recipient of the 2012 John W. Campbell Award for Best New Writer. Her short fiction has appeared in the *Boston Review, Kenyon Review Online, Apex Magazine, The Best Science Fiction and Fantasy of the Year, McSweeney's,* and *Eclipse Online,* and has been nominated for the Hugo, Nebula, Sturgeon, and World Fantasy Awards.

Clarkesworld Citizens
OFFICIAL CENSUS

We would like to thank the following Clarkesworld Citizens for their support:

Citizens

A Fettered Mind, A Strange Loop, Pete Aldin, Elye Alexander, Richard Alison, Joshua Allen, Alllie, Imron Alston, Ro Anders, Clifford Anderson, Kim Anderson, Tor Andre, Randall Andrews, Ang Danieldeskbrain - Watercress Munster, Author Anonymous, Therese Arkenberg, Randall Arnold, Bruce Arthurs, Catherine Asaro, Ash, Rush Austin, Bill B., Benjamin Baker, Brian B. Baker, Great Barbarian, Jenny Barber, Johanne Barron, Andrew and Kate Barton, Jeff Bass, Meredith Battjer, Anna Bauer-Baxter, Moya Bawden, Aaron Begg, LaNeta Bergst, Julie Berg-Thompson, Clark Berry, Steve Bickle, Amy Billingham, Nicolas Billon, Dale Randolph Bivins, Tracey Bjorksten, John Blackman, Brenna Blackwell, John Bledsoe, Mike Blevins, Adam Blomquist, Jeff Boardman, Allison Bocksruker, Kevin Bokelman, Michael Bowen, Michael Braun Hamilton, Commander Breetai, Nathan Breit, Allan Breitstein, Jennifer Brissett, Britny Brooks, Kit Brown, Brian Brunswick, Vicki Bryan, Thomas Bull, Michael Bunkahle, Karl Bunker, Cory Burr, Jefferson Burson, Graeme Byfield, Jarrett Byrnes, c9lewis, Kima Caddell, Darrell Cain, Caitrin, C.G. Cameron, Paul Carignan, Yazburg Carlberg, Michael Carr, Cast of Wonders, Nance Cedar, Timothy Charlton, David Chasson, Catherine Cheek, Paige Chicklo, Victoria Cleave, Alicia Cole, Elizabeth Coleman, Elisabeth Colter, Che Comrie, Dr. SP Conboy-Hil, Johne Cook, Claire Cooney, Martin Cooper, Lisa Costello, Thomas Costick, Ashley Coulter, Charles Cox, Michael Cox, Sonya Craig, Yoshi Creelman, Tina Crone, Andrew Curry, Curtis42, Shawn D'Alimonte, Sarah Dalton, Gillian Daniels, Chua Dave, Morgan Davey, Ed Davidoff, Chase Davies, Craig Davis, Gustavo de Albuquerque, Alessia De Gaspari, Maria-Isabel Deira, Daniel DeLano, Dennis DeMario, Patrick Derrickson, Michele Desautels, Paul DesCombaz, Allison M. Dickson, Aidan Doyle, dt, Alex Dunbar, Susan Duncan, Andrew Eason, Roger East, David Eggli, Jesse Eisenhower, Sarah Elkins, Brad Elliott, Warren Ellis, Dale Eltoft, Douglas Engstrom, Lyle Enright, Peter Enyeart, Nancy Epperly, Yvonne Ewing, Extranet Vendors Association, Lutz F. krebs, . Feather, Josiah Ferrin, Ethan Fode, Dense Fog, Francesca Forrest, Jason

Frank, Michael Fratus, William Fred, Amy Fredericks, Michael Frighetto, Sarah Frost, Fyrbaul, Paul Gainford, Robert Garbacz, Eleanor Gausden, Leslie Gelwicks, Susan Gibbs, Phil Giles, Holly Glaser, Susanne Glaser, Sangay Glass, globular, Laura Goodin, Grendel, Valerie Grimm, Damien Grintalis, Janet Groenert, Michael Grosberg, Nikki Guerlain, Geoffrey Guthrie, Richard Guttormson, James Hall, Lee Hallison, Lee Hallison, Janus Hansen, Roy Hardin, Jonathan Harnum, Harpoon, Dan Harrington, Jubal Harshaw, Darren Hawbrook, Leon Hendee, Jamie Henderson, Samantha Henderson, Dave Hendrickson, JC Henry, Karen Heuler, Dan Hiestand, John Higham, Renata Hill, Hillreiner, Tim Hills, Mark Hinchman, Peter Hogberg, Peter Hollmer, Andrea Horbinski, Clarence Horne III, Richard Horton, Fiona Howland-Rose, Rex Hughes II, Jeremy Hull, John Humpton, Gene Hyers, Dwight Illk, John Imhoff, Iridum Sound Envoy, Isbell, J.B.& Co., Jack, Jack Myers Photography, Stephen Jacob, Jalal, Sarah James, Michael Jarcho, Joseph A Jechenthal III, Jimbo, JJ, Dick Johnson, Steve Johnson, Patrick Johnston, Gabriel Kaknes, Philip Kaldon, Jeff Kapustka, KarlTheGood, Sara Kathryn, Cagatay Kavukcuoglu, Lorna Keach, Keenan, Jason Keeton, Robert Keller, Mary Kellerman, Kelson, Shawn Keslar, John Kilgallon, Dana Kincaid, Kisaki, Kate Kligman, Roy and Norma Kloster, Bryan Knower, Seymour Knowles-Barley, Matthew Koch, Will Koenig, Konstantinos Kontos, Lutz Krebs, Derek Kunsken, Sarah L., Michele Laframboise, Jan Lajka, Paul Lamarre, Gina Langridge, Abby Larkin, Scotty Larsen, Darren Ledgerwood, Brittany Lehman, Terra Lemay, Danielle Linder, Simon Litten, Susan Llewellyn, Renata M Lloyd, Thomas Loyal, James Lyle, H Lynnea Johnson, Ilia Malkovitch, Dan Manning, Margaret, Mark, Eric Marsh, Jacque Marshall, Dominique Martel, Cethar Mascaw, Daniel Mathews, David Mayes, Derek McAleer, Mike McBride, T.C. McCarthy, Jeffrey McDonald, Holly McEntee, Josh McGraw, Roland McIntosh, Christopher M McKeever, Oscar McNary, Steve Medina, Brent Mendelsohn, Seth Merlo, Stephen Middleton, John Midgley, Mike, Matthew Miller, Stephan Miller, Terry Miller, Alan Mimms, mjpearce, Mahesh Raj Mohan, Aidan Moher, Marian Moore, Tim Moore, Sunny Moraine, Jamie Morgan, James Morton, Lynette Moss, Patricia Murphy, Lori Murray, Karl Myers, Stephen Nelson, Glenn Nevill, Stella Nickerson, Robyn Nielsen, Norm, David Oakley, Hugh J. O'Donnell, Scott Oesterling, Christopher Ogilvie, James Oliver, Lydia Ondrusek, Ruth O'Neill, Am Onymous, Erik Ordway, Nancy Owens, Thomas Pace, Amparo Palma Reig, Thomas Parrish, Sidsel Pedersen, Edgar Penderghast, Tzum Pepah, Chris Perkins, Benjamin Philip, Nikki Philley, Adrian-Teodor Pienaru, Beth Plutchak, David Potter, Ed Prior, David Raco, Adam Rakunas, Ralan, Steve Ramey, Diego Ramos, Robert Redick, Thomas Reed, Sherry Rehm, George Reilly, Joshua Reynolds, Julia Reynolds, Rick of the North, Zach Ricks, Carl Rigney, Hank Roberts, Tansy Roberts, Tansy Rayner Roberts, Kenneth Robkin, James Rowh, RPietila, Sarah Rudek, Oliver Rupp, Caitlin Russell, Abigail Rustad, Miranda Rydell, George S. Walker, S2 Sally, Tim Sally, Sam, Nadia Sandren, Jason Sanford, Erica L. Satifka, Steven Saus, MJ Scafati, Jan Shawyer, Espana Sheriff, T. L. Sherwood, Udayan Shevade, Josh Shiben, Robert Shuster, Aileen Simpson, Karen Snyder, Morgan Songi, Mat Spalding, Gary Spears, Terry Squire Stone, Jennifer Stufflebeam, Julia

Sullivan, J Sutton, Jennifer Sutton, John Swartzentruber, Kenneth Takigawa, Charles Tan, William Tank, Beth Tanner, Jesse Tauriainen, David Taylor, Paul Taylor, The Chocolate Delicacy, The Eaton Law Firm, P.C., The Unsettled Foundation, TJ Fly, the Paragliding Guy, Felix Troendle, Sam van Rood, Julia Varga, Adam Vaughan, William Vennell, David Versace, Vettac, Daniel Waldman, Diane Walton, Stefan Walzer, Robert Wamble, Rob Ward, Matthew J Weaver, Lim Wee Teck, Neil Weston, Peter Wetherall, Adam White, Spencer Wightman, Dan Wilburn, Jeff Williamson, Neil Williamson, Kristyn Willson, A.C. Wise, Devon Wong, Woodwork Running Dog, Chalmer Wren, Dan Wright, Isabel Yap, Lachlan Yeates, Catherine York, Rena Zayit, Stephanie Zvan

Burgermeisters

7ony, Rob Abram, Paula Acton, Andy Affleck, Frederick Amerman, Carl Anderson, Mel Anderson, Andy90, Marie Angell, John Appel, Misha Argall, Jon Arnold, Robert Avie, Erika Bailey, Brian Baker, Nathan Bamberg, Michael Banker, Laura Barnitz, Jennifer Bartolowits, Lenni Benson, Kerry Benton, Leon Bernhardt, Bill Bibo Jr, Edward Blake, Samuel Blinn, Johanna Bobrow, Greg Bossert, Joan Boyle, Patricia Bray, Tim Brenner, Arrie Brown, Ken Brown, BruceC, Sharat Buddhavarapu, Max Buffington, Adam Bursey, Jeremy Butler, Robyn Butler, Roland Byrd, Brad Campbell, Carleton45, James Carlino, Ted Carr, Benjamin Cartwright, Evan Cassity, Lee Cavanaugh, Peter Charron, Randall Chertkow, Michael Chorman, John Chu, Mary Clare, Matthew Claxton, Theodore Conti, George Cook, Brian Cooksey, Brenda Cooper, Lorraine Cooper, Lucy Cummin, B D Fagan, James Davies, Pamela J. Davis, Tessa Day, Brian Deacon, Bartley Deason, Ricado Delacruz, John Devenny, Dino, Fran Ditzel-Friel, Gary Dockter, Nicholas Doran, Christopher Doty, Nicholas Dowbiggin, Robert Drabek, Paul Dzus, Steve Emery, Christine Ertell, Joanna Evans, Kathy Farretta, Rare Feathers, Tea Fish, Tony Fisk, FlatFootedRat, Bruce Fleischer, Lynn Flewelling, Adrienne Foster, Keith M Frampton, William Frankenhoff, Matthew Fredrickson, Alina Fridberg, Christopher Garry, Pierre Gauthier, Gerhen, Mark Gerrits, Lorelei Goelz, Ed Goforth, Melanie Goldmund, Inga Gorslar, Tony Graham, Jaq Greenspon, Eric Gregory, Stephanie Gunn, Jim H, Laura Hake, Skeptyk/JeanneE Hand-Boniakowski, Jordan Hanie, Helixa 12, Normandy Helmer, Daniel Herman, Corydon Hinton, Jon Hite, Elizabeth Hocking, Sheridan Hodges, Ronald Hordijk, Justin Howe, Bobby Hoyt, David Hudson, Shawn Huenniger, Huginn and Muninn, Chris Hurst, Kevin Ikenberry, Joseph Ilardi, Adam Israel, Marcus Jager, Justin James, Patty Jansen, Jason, Cristal Java, Toni Jerrman, Audra Johnson, Erin Johnson, Russell Johnson, Robert Jones, Patrick Joseph Sklar, Kai Juedemann, Andy Kaden, Jeff Kapustka, David Kelleher, James Kelly, Joshua Kidd, Alistair Kimble, Erin Kissane, John Klima, Cecil Knight, Michelle Knowlton, Eric Kramer, JR Krebs, Neal Kushner, Andrew Lanker, James Frederick Leach, Krista Leahy, Alan Lehotsky, Walter Leroy Perkins, L Leslie, Philip Levin, Kevin Liebkemann, Linnaea, Susan Loyal, Kristi Lozano, LUX4489, Adam Mancilla, Brit Mandelo, Mark Maris, Matthew

Marovich, Samuel Marzioli, Jason Maurer, Rosaleen McCarthy, Peter McClean, Michael McCormack, Tony McFee, Mark McGarry, Robyn McIntyre, Doug McLaughlin, Craig McMurtry, Joe McTee, J Meijer, Geoffrey Meissner, Barry Melius, David Michalak, Robert Milson, Sharon Mock, Eric Mohring, Samuel Montgomery-Blinn, Rebekah Murphy, John Murray, N M Wells Foundry Creative Media, Barrett Nichols, Peter Northup, Sean OBrien, Stian Ovesen, Justin Palk, Norman Papernick, Richard Parks, Paivi Pasi, MJ Paxton, PBC Productions Inc., Katherine Pendill, Eric Pierson, E. PLS, Lolt Proegler, Jonathan Pruett, QLM Aria X-Perienced, Robert Quinlivan, Mike R D Ashley, Mr R J Dowrick, Anthony R. Cardno, Rainspan, D Randall Kerr, Joel Rankin, Raoul Raoul, Paul Rice, Zack Richardson, James Rickard, Karsten Rink, Erik Rolstad, Joseph Romel, Leena Romppainen, Elena Ross, Michael Russo, Mark S Haney, Stefan Scheib, Alan Scheiner, Kenneth Schneyer, Eric Schreiber, Patricia G. Scott, Bluezoo Seven, Cosma Shalizi, Bill Shields, Jeremy Showers, siznax, Saskia Slottje, Allen Snyder, David Sobyra, Lisa Stone, Jason Strawsburg, Stuart, Keffington Studios, Jerome Stueart, Robert Stutts, John Swartzentruber, Maurice Termeer, Tero, John Thomas, Chuck Tindle, Raymond Tobaygo, Tradeblanket.com, Heather Tumey, Mary A. Turzillo, Marc Tyler, Nicholas V David, Ann VanderMeer, Andrew Vega, Nuno Miguel Pires Veloso, Emil Volcheck, Andrew Volpe, Wendy Wagner, Jennifer Walter, Tom Waters, Tehani Wessely, Chris White, Shannon White, Dan Wick, John Wienstroer, Seth Williams, Paul Wilson, Dawn Wolfe, Sarah Wright, Slobodan Zivkovic

Royalty

Paul Abbamondi, Eric Agnew, Albert Alfiler, Rose Andrew, Raymond Bair, Kathryn Baker, David Beaudoin, Nathan Beittenmiller, Kevin Best, Nathan Blumenfeld, Marty Bonus, David Borcherding, Robert Bose, Nancy Buford, Robert Callahan, Carrie, Lady Cate, Richard Chappell, Heather Clitheroe, Chad Colopy, Carolyn Cooper, Tom Crosshill, Michael Cullinan, Darren Davidson, Sky de Jersey, David Demers, Cory Doctorow, Brian Dolton, Dayne Encarnacion, Stephen Finch, Greg Frank, David Furniss, John Garberson, Alexis Goble, Hilary Goldstein, Carl Hazen, Andy Herrman, Robin Hill, Kristin Hirst, Colin Hitch, Victoria Hoke, Todd Honeycutt, David Hoyt, Christopher Irwin, Mary Jo Rabe, Lukas Karl Barnes, Robert Kennedy, Fred Kiesche, G.J. Kressley, Jeffrey L Lewis, Jamie Lackey, Jonathan Laden, M. Lane, Katherine Lee, Marta Lillo, H. Lincoln Parish, Sean Markey, Arun Mascarenhas, Barrett McCormick, Kevin McKean, Margaret McNally, Michelle Broadribb MEG, Dave Miller, Nayad Monroe, James Moore, Anne Murphy, Patrick Neary, Persona Non-Grata, Charles Norton, Vincent O'Connor, Richard Ohnemus, David M Oswin, Vincent P Loeffler III, Marie Parsons, Lars Pedersen, David Personette, George Peter Gatsis, Matt Peterson, Matt Phelps, Gary Piserchio, Lord Pontus, Ian Powell, Clarissa R., Rational Path, Captain Red Boots, Patrick Reitz, RL, Rob, Kelly Robson, Mr D F Ryan, John Scalzi, Stu Segal, Maurice Shaw, Angela Slatter, Carrie Smith, Paul Smith, Nicholas

Sokeland, Richard Sorden, Kevin Standlee, Neal Stanifer, S.Rheannon Terran, Josh Thomson, TK, Terhi Tormanen, Andre Twupack, Robert Urell, Jeppe V Holm, Sean Wallace, Jasen Ward, Weyla & Gos, Graeme Williams, Jessica Wolf, Jeff Xilon, Zola

Overlords

Renan Adams, Claire Alcock, Thomas Ball, Michael Blackmore, Nathalie Boisard-Beudin, Shawn Boyd, Jennifer Brozek, Karen Burnham, Barbara Capoferri, Morgan Cheryl, Gio Clairval, Neil Clarke, Tania Clucas, Dolohov, ebooks-worldwide, Sairuh Emilius, Lynne Everett, Joshua Faulkenberry, Fabio Fernandes, Thomas Fleck, Eric Francis, Brian Gardner, L A George, Bryan Green, Michael Habif, Andrew Hatchell, Berthiaume Heidi, Bill Hughes, Eric Hunt, Gary Hunter, Theodore J. Stanulis, Jericho, jfly, jkapoetry, Lucas Jung, James Kinateder, Jay Kominek, Alice Kottmyer, Daniel LaPonsie, Susan Lewis, Edward MacGregor, Philip Maloney, Paul Marston, Matthew the Greying, Gabriel Mayland, MJ Mercer, Achilleas Michailides, Adrian Mihaila, Adrien Mitchell, Overlord Mondragon, MrMovieZombie, Jose Muinos, Dlanod Nosreetp, Andrea Pawley, Mike Perricone, Jody Plank, Rick Ramsey, Jo Rhett, Rik, Jason Sank, Lorenz Schwarz, Joseph Sconfitto, Marie Shcherbatskaya, William Shields, Tara Smith, David Steffen, Jacel the Thing, Kelvin Tse, Thad Wilkinson, Elaine Williams, James Williams, Doug Young

About Clarkesworld

Clarkesworld Magazine (clarkesworldmagazine.com) is a monthly science fiction and fantasy magazine first published in October 2006. Each issue contains interviews, thought-provoking articles and at least four pieces of original fiction. Our fiction is also available in ebook editions/subscriptions, audio podcasts and in our annual print anthologies.

Clarkesworld has received three Hugo Awards, one World Fantasy Award, and a British Fantasy Award. Our fiction has been nominated for or won the Hugo, Nebula, World Fantasy, Sturgeon, Locus, Shirley Jackson, WSFA Small Press and Stoker Awards. For information on how to subscribe to our electronic edition on your Kindle, Nook, iPad or other ereader/Android device, please visit: clarkesworldmagazine.com/subscribe/

Clarkesworld is edited by:

Neil Clarke (neil-clarke.com) is the publisher and editor of *Clarkesworld, Forever Magazine,* and the cyborg anthology, *Upgraded.* He's a three-time Hugo Award Nominee for Best Editor Short Form and currently working on the first volume of The Best Science Fiction of the Year for Night Shade Books. Neil lives in New Jersey with his wife and two sons.

Sean Wallace is a founding editor at *Clarkesworld Magazine,* owner of Prime Books, and winner of the World Fantasy Award. He currently lives in Maryland with his wife and two daughters.